Angela Huth has written three collections of short stories, and several novels, including *Nowhere Girl, Virginia Fly is Drowning, Sun Child, South of the Lights, Wanting, Invitation to the Married Life* and *Easy Silence*. She also writes for radio, television and stage, and is a well-known freelance journalist, critic and broadcaster. She is married to a don, lives in Oxford and has two daughters.

Land Girls was released as a major feature film in 1998.

ANGELA HUTH OMNIBUS

Land Girls
Wives of the Fishermen

ANGELA HUTH

An *Abacus* Book

This omnibus edition first published in Great Britain by Abacus in 2001

Angela Huth Omnibus copyright © Angela Huth 2001

Previously published separately:

Land Girls
First published in Great Britain by Sinclair-Stevenson in 1994
This edition published by Abacus in 1995
Reprinted in 1995 (eight times), 1996, 1997 (twice), 1998 (twice),
1999 (twice), 2000 (twice)

Copyright © Angela Huth 1994

The author and publishers are grateful for permission to reproduce
words from songs as follows:

'They Can't Black Out the Moon' (Strauss, Miller & Dale) reproduced by permission
of EMI Music Publishing Ltd, London WC2H 0EA

'We'll Meet Again' (Parker & Charles) reproduced by permission
of Dash Music Co Ltd, 8/9 Frith Street, London W1V 5TZ

Every effort has been made to trace holders of copyrights. Any inadvertent omissions
of acknowledgement or permission can be rectified in future editions.

Wives of the Fishermen
First published in Great Britain by Little, Brown and Company in 1998
This edition published by Abacus in 1999
Reprinted in 1999 (twice)

Copyright © Angela Huth 1998

The moral right of the author has been asserted.

A CIP catalogue record for this book is available from the British Library.

ISBN 0 349 11458 7

Typeset by M Rules
Printed and bound in Great Britain by Clays Ltd, St Ives plc

Abacus
A Division of
Little, Brown and Company (UK)
Brettenham House
Lancaster Place
London WC2E 7EN

www.littlebrown.co.uk

Land Girls

For
Candida and Rupert

'If a man will begin with certainties,
he shall end in doubts;
but if he will be content to begin with doubts,
he shall end in certainties.'

Francis Bacon, 1605

Prologue

Agatha saw Prue creep along the crossbeam of the barn, arms stiffly outstretched, awkward, determined, brave. Her thin white legs were lit by a torch held far below. Her thick regulation socks and heavy brown shoes were cast somewhere into the hay.

Agatha saw Prue pause, flutter, not daring to look down. Her left foot wavered, suddenly unsure where to land. The toes panicked. She was nearly at the end, where a ladder waited. But she could not make it.

Agatha saw Prue fall into the darkness, heard her scream. No one in the house could have heard, because at that moment a siren began to wail. Its mournful voice and the ragged shriek coiled into a terrible sound that, even now, some fifty years later, Agatha still heard.

With an effort she withdrew from the picture of that night, and returned to her place at a prim restaurant table in a London hotel.

Agatha was the first to arrive, as always. Stella could never be on time. Prue was unpredictable.

She pulled off a slither of black kid glove and let her finger run over the whiteness of tablecloth that radiated before her. She hoped the nearby waiter, officiously observant, would not present her with the enormous menu poised in his hand nor make enquiries as to her desire for a drink. She did not want anything, except a few moments

1

to gather herself before the others arrived. It had been a long journey from Tiverton, and her grandson Joshua had driven through the London traffic too fast for her liking. She felt a little ungrounded. Cities always filled her with unease. She was glad she had refused her daughter's invitation to stay the night, and had decided to return on the five o'clock train. Her husband would be at the station to drive her home. He would have lit the fire and put the pie in the oven as instructed. In old age, she relished the safety of their quiet evenings together. There were few occasions for which she would sacrifice one of them for a night in London. She came up rarely, now, though nothing but real disaster would keep her from the annual meetings with her oldest friends.

When she looked up she saw that the waiter had turned his back. He had probably decided an old lady, peacefully waiting, was not worth approaching. Quite right. Agatha knew the usefulness of her stern look, and she was glad she had employed it. The professor had married her, he always said, because she was so alarming. He had wanted to know whether, over the years, he would grow less alarmed by her. Had he? She didn't know. It was not a question she could ever ask.

Outside the window, the trees of Hyde Park were more thickly gold than the trees in Devon. Their own beech had only just begun to turn. She remembered that frivolous park trees were always far ahead in their maturing. This she had observed so many times while waiting for the others. It was a wonder the amazement remained. And the trees, of course, were the reason they had chosen this place originally. As ex-land girls, all of them, they wanted to be able to see the sky while they were eating. They had had their first reunion lunch in this very dining-room just after the war, a few months before Prue's wedding. Terrible food – corned beef and boiled potatoes – but none of them had minded. Some years later they had experienced their first avocado together – a table in the corner, if Agatha remembered rightly. It had been exciting, that first slipping of silver spoons into the creamy green flesh of an unknown fruit. That was the year, Agatha recalled, when the lunch had started more easily than usual – all laughing over their reactions to the avocado. They had felt none of the initial awkwardness that overcame them on re-meeting after a gap of a year or more. They lived so far apart, their lives had taken such different directions – it was difficult, sometimes, to know where to begin.

Agatha's fingers, calmer now, slid up the thin silver flute of the flower vase. It held a single pallid rose and a wisp of fern. She tried to work out how many times the three of them had contemplated each other's metamorphosis over similar, scant little flower arrangements. But what did it matter, how many times? It was a tradition that would go on till one of them died. Then, would the remaining two . . .? When one of them died, would the remaining two consider it loyal or disloyal to continue the lunches?

Agatha looked up. She saw Prue in double image – young and high on the beam but, more sharply, a tiny figure dwarfed by the great door of the dining-room, alert little head pecking round the tables in search of her friend. Agatha waved her glove. Prue smiled, pursed her bow lips. She hurried over with such speed that waiters, poised to offer their assistance, saw any help would be redundant and stepped back with secret smiles. They were used, Agatha supposed, to eccentric old ladies.

When Prue reached the table, Agatha stood up. They bent towards each other, making a triangle over the rose. They kissed. Prue smelt of the exotic, musky scent she had always worn: Stella and Agatha had never been able to approve. She was dressed in green, as usual, to match her eyes. A velvet beret slumped fashionably over one side of her forehead, half hiding the white fringe. In the past the fringe had been very long – a cause of constant

3

complaint – and blonde. From under it she would flutter those down-turned eyes at any man who came into the farmyard, in imitation of the glamorous film stars whose lives she found so fascinating. The eyes were still an extraordinary green. It was hard to imagine that Prue, the youngest of them, must be nearly seventy. Whereas she, Ag . . .

'You look just the same, Ag. How are you?'

'In pretty good spirits.'

They sat down, both fiddled with their stiff napkins, veered their eyes from each other lest further scrutiny reveal changes they had no wish to see.

'Sorry I've kept you waiting. Manchester train's not usually late. Still, I've beaten Stella.'

'I had a postcard from her only last week saying she'd be catching the eight fifteen from York.'

'So did I.'

'Did she mention her health?'

'Only to say there'd been another attack of bronchitis.'

'She wrote the same to both of us, then.'

'She always does.'

'She always had such an innate sense of fairness, dear Stella.'

'So fair, yes.'

'That time – that harvest time.'

'That harvest! I often think of that.'

They paused. Agatha was fingering the damask cloth again, while Prue ran a pink nail up the stem of her wineglass. A nearby waiter, seeing his chance, was upon them in a trice.

'And would the ladies care for an aperitif?'

Agatha put on her fiercest face. She didn't care for the way waiters addressed people these days.

'You'll be having your usual White Lady, Prue?'

'Why not?' Prue twinkled.

'And I'll have a Kir Royale.' Then, in a voice so low the

4

waiter was denied the private information, she added: 'Something Joshua introduced me to last Christmas.'

'Joshua!' Prue, who had no grandchildren, clapped her hands. Agatha had always admired her enthusiastic interest in other people's relations. 'He must be thirty?'

'Almost,' said Agatha.

But she was not thinking about Joshua. She was thinking about her husband: at this moment he would be sitting with his cheese sandwich by the Aga, preoccupied by the future of his Friesians. Alone, without her there to deflect his thoughts, he would be worrying once more about whether they would have to sell up the farm. Agatha dreaded his decision. They did not want to move, after forty years.

'*So?*' said Prue, when the waiter had gone off with the order.

'So,' said Agatha.

The very thought of having to distil her news made her curiously tired. The friends had not met for eighteen months, though they had kept in touch with occasional letters and cards. In that time nothing exciting had happened to Agatha: probably nothing very much exciting had happened to the other two, either. But having made the effort to travel so far to see one another, each felt it incumbent upon her to do her best to entertain. What usually happened was that they found themselves racing through contemporary news with perfunctory speed. However much they intended to convey to the others the nature of their present lives, what really fired them was their past. To reminisce was so much easier – the jokes that never dulled, the intriguing speculation about what might have happened, the realisation of what the hard years of the war had taught them. Prue and Stella and Agatha never ceased to marvel at the powerful warmth that still emanated from a shared experience of so many years ago. They would leave their meetings reinvigorated:

newly grateful that something that had bound them in the past could remain so benevolently alive, untouched by the vicissitudes of the intervening years.

Agatha and Prue glanced at each other with a feathery shyness that would soon be dissipated by their cocktails. They had a mutual need of their friend to enliven this reunion. Stella, who was always the best one at breaking the ice. Stella, who used to say she could not imagine living without being in love – it would be a wasted day, a day not loving someone, she used to say. Stella, who, as Agatha had recognised the moment she met her, was blessed with the kind of exuberance for daily life that could accommodate other people's awkwardness. Agatha had learned so much from Stella.

'She'll be here any minute, I expect,' she said, a little desperate, longing for her drink, and longing even more for the train journey home when she could dwell on all that was about to be said.

'Of course she will. Dear Stella,' said Prue, also a little desperate, and flashing her green eyes in what Agatha recognised as a familiar, hopeful fashion towards the door.

One

On an evening in early October, 1941, John Lawrence drove the three land girls home from the station.

It was unusually cold for the time of year. There had been a hard frost that morning which had not melted all day. Frozen puddles spat at the wheels of his cumbersome old Wolseley. He could hear the angry hiss and crackle as the ice splintered. The noise reminded him of those small fireworks that he had waved round in his hand, on bonfire night, to please Joe when he was a child. He kept his eyes on the road.

There were two girls in the back, one by his side. Faith had told him their names several times, but he remembered none of them. At the station, he hadn't liked to ask. He had shaken hands, introduced himself, and picked up their suitcases before they could protest. They looked a nice enough lot, far as he could tell. The district commissioner had guaranteed she would send some good ones.

But good or not, Mr Lawrence was unhappy about the arrangement. He knew nothing about girls, didn't much like what he'd heard. He and Faith had married at eighteen, two months before the 1914 war was declared. Faith had managed on her own, somehow, for the four years he was away. She had never complained, in her wonderful letters, about the cold and meagre cottage, the poverty, the giving birth to Joe alone by a small fire. When Mr

7

Lawrence came back alive, unwounded, she said they must never part again. They never had: they never would. She was the only woman in his life. He could not imagine another one. He was glad they had no daughters.

It had taken him some time to be persuaded about this land girl business. But his two farmhands had been called up within weeks of the outbreak of the new war, and it was clear he and Joe could not physically cope with the farm on their own. They worked a sixteen-hour day and still things were left undone. Why not try this Land Army plan, Faith had said, as one who read every word of the newspaper on the days someone brought one to the house, and knew all about the scheme. If it didn't work, she said, they could think again. With an acute shortage of men in the whole neighbourhood, Mr Lawrence was forced to agree there was no alternative. He had conceded with reluctance.

Now, here they were, the three of them, in his car. Very quiet, not a word between them. Mr Lawrence sniffed. The pungent smell of wet collie, which had eaten its way into the fabric of the car years ago, was pierced by a new, high-pitched feminine smell, the kind of thing Faith would call exotic. Disgusting, in his opinion. Already an invasion into his car, where he liked to be alone with his dogs and their rightful smell. He rubbed his nose in protest. The girl beside him stiffened. He could see from the corner of his eye that she had turned her head to look out of the side window. Slowing down, he took this opportunity to glance at other parts of her: prim little gloved hands folded on her lap, skirt made of a pinkish fuzzy stuff. Her legs were crossed, just one knee visible. The small, square plane of knee bone strained against the bronzish fibre of a stocking. As Mr Lawrence looked, fascinated, a streak of light broke through the grey cloud, flared through the windscreen. For an infinitesimal moment the knee bone dazzled like a jewel. Mr Lawrence withdrew his eyes. Rayon stockings! That was it. Faith only had one pair, for church. Well, this young lady would soon learn there was little time or place for rayon stockings on the farm. Already he could not like her. She'd be all over the house with her blessed stockings, hanging them up in the bathroom to dry if he wasn't careful – he could see it all. Total invasion.

'And what's your name?' he asked.

'Stella.'

Stella! Christ. He might have known she'd have a fancy name. He determined not to ask the others. The names would come to him in time. If he gave them time, that was.

He adjusted the mirror, glanced at the passengers in the back seat. Two blurred little faces, spotted and clouded by the imperfections of the glass. One of them had a long pale fringe that covered most of her strange-looking cat's eyes, greenish as far as Mr Lawrence could tell. She wore more lipstick than Clara Bow. Obviously saw herself as a film star: he'd enjoy seeing her scrape the shit off a cow's backside, he would. The thought made him smile. The other one struck him as more schoolmistressy, prim. Dark bobbed hair, pale skin, nothing on her lips. What a trio, he thought. With them in the house . . . still, he'd give them a chance. He was a fair man. He could be wrong.

'Just half a mile to go, now,' he said. He felt a general shifting in the car. 'This is where my land starts, on the left. You'll be working the fields up here.'

A turning of heads. A swing of blonde curls reflected in the freckled mirror. Curious widening of green eyes. He wondered how they saw his neatly trimmed hedges – a master hedger himself, they would never believe how many man hours the job took him, and what satisfaction it gave him. He wondered how they saw his nicely harvested fields, the yellowing woods on the rising distant land. Did it seem wild to them? Alarming? Faith had said none of them was a country girl. Somewhere as remote as Hallows Farm would seem very strange.

He swung the huge steering wheel. The Wolseley

lurched through an open gate, throwing the dark girl up against the fair one. Slight nervous giggles. Apologies. He slowed down through the farmyard, came to a halt near the house. When he had switched off the engine, he returned his hands to the steering wheel. It crossed his mind that he should attempt a smile and say, *Well, here we are, girls,* in a voice of welcome. But he decided against it. He was not a man accustomed to stating the obvious, and lack of histrionic talent meant he could not disguise the foreboding he felt. On the other hand, he had no wish to be unfriendly, and the girls must be puzzled by his long silence.

'This is it,' he said at last. 'I'll hand you over to my wife, Faith.'

God, how he longed to hand them over.

The girls clambered out of the car. Mr Lawrence saw them scanning the ground, each one silently planning her route through seams of mud that had spilt through the frost. While he unloaded their cases from the boot, he watched them skitter from patch to patch of hard, silvered gravel, protecting their fine little shoes from the spewing mud. The tallest one, the dark one, seemed to be the most skilful on her feet. The pink skirt was hesitant, delicate; the film star teetered and giggled and almost fell. They looked like an unrehearsed chorus line, Mr Lawrence thought: bright banners of colour – pink, green, pale blue, so odd against the dour stone façade of the house. They reminded him of flowers.

One of Faith's neurotic birds came squawking round the corner.

'Look! Have you ever seen such a small chicken?' squealed the film star in a broad northern accent.

The tall dark girl bent down over the bird, as if to stroke its frantic head. 'I think you'll find it's a bantam,' she said.

Faith appeared in the doorway of the porch. Her eyes met her husband's, then sped from pink to green to blue, uncritical.

10

'I'm so glad you're here,' she said. 'You must be ravenous and tired. Come in, come in.'

Mr Lawrence watched the coloured banners march through the dark doorway to begin their invasion.

The girls followed Mrs Lawrence into the kitchen. Prue was last in the line, silently smarting at the snub by the snooty dark girl. How was she supposed to know a bloody bantam from a hen? There had been no instruction on the subject of poultry at the training course, and the only birds she saw in Manchester were hanging upside down and naked at the butcher's.

The kitchen was large, dim, steamy, billowing with a warm mushy smell of cooking, a smell Prue could not quite place. The pale flagstone floor was worn into dimples in front of the enamel sink. On the huge spaces of the dun-coloured walls, scarred with flaking paint, the only decoration was a calendar, dated 1914. Its faded picture was of a young soldier kissing a girl in front of a pretty cottage. *Farewell* was the caption, in copperplate of ghostly sepia. Prue felt her eyes scorch with tears. She longed for the small box of a kitchen at home, the shining white walls and smell of Jeyes Fluid, and the shelf of brightly coloured biscuit tins her mother had collected from seaside towns. This place was so horribly old-fashioned, gloomy, dingy. And the two collies lying on a rag rug in front of the stove looked dangerous. Prue hated dogs. She turned to look out of the window so that the others should not see her tears. But the view was smeared with condensation. All she could see was the indistinct hulk of a barn or outbuilding, and the slash of darkening sky.

The characteristics of a hard-working farm kitchen that so distressed Prue left Stella unmoved. In her dreamy state, having left Philip only twenty-four hours ago (Philip whom she loved with her whole being, Philip for whom she trembled and sighed and longed with a pain like hot wire that

11

strangled her gizzards – the simile had come to her in the train), she was indifferent to all external things. She knew that in automatic response to her disciplined childhood, and the four weeks' training course she had enjoyed, a sense of duty would ensure she worked efficiently. She would not let her mother down, and would willingly do whatever was required. On the other hand, she would not be *there*. Her soul would be with Philip as he boarded ship at Plymouth, so *meltingly beautiful* in his uniform that the very thought of that stiff collar cutting into his neck filled her with glorious weakness. And in the impatient weeks waiting for his first letter her mind would feed on the memories she had of him, rerunning the pictures over and over again. She would never tire of them. The best, of course, was Philip at her birthday party, removing his jacket, despite her father's disapproving look. It was too hot to waltz in comfort, he had said. That waltz! Their skill at dancing had been hampered by their mutual need to be joined at the hip bones. Exactly the same height, they had found the need increased – breast bones, chins, a scraping of cheeks, a clash of racing hearts becoming clamped together. By the time the music had slowed they weren't dancing at all, merely rocking gently, oblivious to everything but their extraordinary desire.

'Jellies are now served in the dining-room,' her mother had shrieked, 'and there's plenty more fruit cup.'

Stella and Philip had not wanted jellies: they'd wanted each other. They'd slid from the room and raced upstairs towards the old nursery. It housed a large and comfortable sofa, useful to Stella on several passionate occasions in the past. She had shut the door behind them. Blackout was nailed to the window frames, the darkness unchipped by any glimmer of light. Stella had taken Philip's hand and guided him past the rocking horse, giving it a wide berth: one of her suitors had bruised his leg so badly that kisses had been interrupted by howls of passion-quelling pain.

12

They reached the sofa. Blindness added to the excitement. She had felt him sit next to her and wondered impatiently why he was fiddling with his sleeve.

'What are you doing?'

'Taking out my cufflinks.'

'Why are you taking out your cufflinks?'

'I want to roll up my sleeves.'

'Why do you want to roll up your sleeves?'

'I always roll up my sleeves, that's why.'

'Rather as if you were getting down to *gardening*, or something?' Stella giggled.

'That sort of thing.' It didn't sound as if he was smiling.

Philip had pushed her back on to the sofa. As his mouth splodged down on to hers (in the blackness she suddenly forgot what it looked like, but tasted sausage roll and beer) she felt him expertly flick up the skirt of the sophisticated dress that old Mrs Martin had made from a *Vogue* pattern. As Philip's finger had run up the back of her leg, following the line of her stocking seam till he reached the stocking top, Stella realised Mrs Martin was the only person she actually *knew* who had been killed by a bomb. The finger continued its journey over the small bumps of suspender – not to object to a man's acquaintance with her suspenders was surely a sign of real love, she thought – and by the time he had reached the leg of her knickers, all sympathy for Mrs Martin had fled. Stella had heard herself moaning, and felt herself squirming in a way which could have been embarrassing had she been visible, but in such utter darkness anything seemed permissible. Then, as Philip employed a second efficient finger to part the way, the warning siren had wailed through the room. They disentangled themselves, made their way back through the blackness, whispers lost in the siren's moan. The music had stopped. Shouts of instruction came from downstairs. Stella remembered feeling very cold.

If it hadn't been for the siren, what might they have done?

Crowded into the wine cellar with the other guests, Stella had watched Philip roll down his shirtsleeves and put back his cufflinks. He'd whispered to her that it had been a damn shame, the interruption.

'But my first shore leave, I promise . . .'

'Promise what?'

'You know what. We must be patient.'

Stella had felt the tremor of his impatient sigh. They'd held hot hands.

'How can we be patient?'

'We can't. But I love you. What a place to have to tell a girl.' He looked terribly sad. Stella took his other hand.

'Say it again and again and again so I believe it.'

'I love you.'

'Well, I love you too. Listen: that's the all clear.'

'That was quick. Thank God no bombs.'

The guests had shuffled back upstairs, but the party was clearly over. Philip had kissed Stella goodbye at the front door. Then he'd left her in such a deliquescent state of love that today's journey had brushed past her like ribbons. She'd had the sensation of not moving, though finding herself in trains, in cars, landscape flowing by her.

But she was standing still at last. Things had stopped rocking and swaying. Reality imposed itself more sharply. She could focus again, focus on the large expanse of scratched but clean blue oilcloth that covered the kitchen table, the four white mugs fit for a giant's kitchen, a mahogany-coloured teapot big enough to house several Mad Hatters, the matching jug filled with creamy milk that frothed like cow parsley.

Stella raised her eyes to her new employer's wife and wondered if Mrs Lawrence could see the state of her tangible love. Mrs Lawrence gave the slightest nod, and bent to wipe the immaculate oilcloth with a clump of grey rag. This small acknowledgement was enough for Stella. She was instantly drawn to the gaunt, bony woman with her cross-over apron,

14

sinewy forearms, ugly hands, and grey hair rolled so high round the back of her neck the vulnerable hollows between the tendons were cruelly revealed. Stella liked her flint-head face, its slightly protruding jaw, sharp nose, wrinkled lids over dark brown eyes. She admired the beige flesh scored by years of hard physical labour. She looked down at her own unsullied hands, nails buffed to a luminescence that was apparent even in the dusk-grained light of the room. She felt a sense of guilt at her own easy life.

Mrs Lawrence was pouring thick noisy tea into the first mug.

'I must get you straight,' she was saying. 'Which of you is . . . ?' She glanced at Stella, who felt the honour of being chosen first to reveal herself.

'I'm Stella Sherwood.' The breathiness of her voice was a private message to Mrs Lawrence.

'And you?'

'Prue Lumley.'

'Prue. So you must be Agatha?'

'Yes, but please call me Ag. Everybody does. Nobody calls me Agatha.'

'I wouldn't think they would, would they?' said Prue, still smarting from the incident of the bantam.

Mrs Lawrence handed the girls the mugs of dark tea, told them to help themselves to bread and butter: she had arranged thick slices on a plate. Prue, suffering withdrawal symptoms on her first day for years without a chocolate biscuit, scanned the dresser. All she could see was a rusty old bread bin. She thought Mrs Lawrence was pretty odd, not offering them biscuits after their long journeys.

'When we eat this evening my husband will explain the plan of duties,' Mrs Lawrence said. 'We eat at six thirty. I'll take you upstairs, let you unpack, settle in.' She paused, gathered herself to break difficult news. 'I hope you don't mind all sharing a room. We only have two small spare rooms, so one of you would have had to board in the

15

village. I thought you'd rather be together . . . so I set to work on our attic, a lot of unused space. It's nothing very luxurious, but it's clean and comfortable. In the evening you're at liberty to sit in the front room with us, of course. We have the wireless on, and the wood fire. It can get quite snug in there.' She paused again, braced herself for another difficult announcement. 'All I would ask is that you don't try to engage my husband in conversation in the evening. He's exhausted after his day. He likes to listen to the news with his eyes shut . . . You could always bring down your darning, the light's better than in the attic.'

Darning? Stella and Ag looked from Prue's appalled face to one another.

Their mugs of tea finished – in Stella's case only half finished – the girls followed Mrs Lawrence. The stairs were covered in antique linoleum, and led to a single passage with walls of stained wood. Its old floorboards, spongy beneath their feet, hollowed as if they had been carved, were covered by a strip of carpet worn to its ribs of fibre. The passage led to a bathroom similar to Prue's in Manchester only in its small size. As she gazed at cracked tiles, the tail of rust from taps to plug in the bath, the scant mat on the linoleum floor, Prue was overwhelmed by the memory of fluffy pink bath towels and the crocheted hat which covered the lavatory paper at home. She felt tears rising again.

'We all have to share this,' said Mrs Lawrence, 'but it can be done. Two baths a week, evening if you don't mind, and easy on the water. Three inches, my husband says. Four if you cut it down to one a week. And please remember to clean the bath before you leave, and keep your towels upstairs. We'll be through by four forty-five, so you can fight to wash your faces after that.'

Four forty-five *a.m.*? In her astonishment, the comforting thought of the pinks of home faded from Prue's mind. Mrs Lawrence, sinewy arms folded under a flat chest, led

16

them up a steeper, narrower staircase to the low door of the attic room.

It stretched the length of the house, a sloping roof on one side, with three dormer windows. The exposed beams had recently been limewashed: there were spots of white on the scrubbed floorboards and the few old rugs. Ag, with her observing eye, immediately appreciated how hard Mrs Lawrence must have worked to achieve such sparkling cleanness. As one who had spent five years in spartan boarding schools, it was all wonderfully familiar to her: the narrow iron bedsteads with their concave mattresses and cotton bedspreads – these, Ag guessed, must have begun their days as dustsheets. She took in the marble-topped washstand with its severe white china bowl and jug, the two battered chests of drawers, the lights with their pleated paper shades. Each bed had a wooden chair at its side – at school there was an inspection of these bedside chairs every night. If clothes were not folded neatly upon them, there would be a black mark. Ag wondered how neat her companions would be. The room did not dispirit her. She liked it already. By the time each one of them had arranged her things, stamped her own corner with ornaments and books, and arranged photographs, it would be very agreeable as dormitories go.

What Ag would miss, she knew, was privacy. In her three years at Cambridge, her greatest delight had been in retreating into the solitude of her small, bare, cold room. Here, there would be nowhere to be alone. That, for her, would mean great deprivation. Somehow she would have to find an hour a day on her own – a walk, perhaps. She did not know the West Country but she had read her Hardy and was eager to discover it. The east coast was home. The house in which she had been brought up was almost unprotected in a plain of flat fields. She liked it best when the fields were planted with cabbages: she liked the way they clicked and chinked as you walked through the sharp frills of their stiff, silver-purple leaves. She had never understood

17

why painters did not find cabbages as beautiful as flowers. Ag glanced out of one of the small windows. She would miss the Norfolk skies, too, and the nearness of the sea. All the same, she saw the job as an adventure, a chance she had eagerly accepted. One day, should she survive the war, she would enjoy telling her grandchildren what it was like to be part of the Women's Land Army. 'That first evening I wished there had been a bookshelf,' she said to herself, as she took a pile of Penguins from her bag. Ag often found herself dictating her memoirs even as she led her life.

When Mrs Lawrence left the room, Prue picked up her case and dumped it on one of the two beds that stood side by side. The third bed was at the far end of the room, by a window.

'If you don't mind, you two, I'd rather be next to someone,' she said.

'I don't mind where I am,' said Stella. Wherever she was, she would be alone with Philip, so to her it didn't matter. In her state of all-consuming love there was no such thing as physical hardship, only the pain of waiting.

'Then I'll go over there, if that's all right.' Ag sounded relieved. The extra distance from the other two would be some small measure of privacy.

Prue was pleased by this decision, too: she was not a one to bear a grudge, but it would be some time before she would get over the bantam incident. Instinctively, she didn't fancy Agatha. Making a fool of her in public so soon: it was a mean thing to have done. She found herself sniffing again – stupid tears.

'This your first time away from home?' Stella asked.

Prue nodded. 'What about you?'

'Oh, I was sent away to a convent at twelve,' said Stella.

At her far end of the room, Ag, piling up her Penguin copies of Hardy, gave a small acknowledging smile.

'I never been ten miles from Manchester, myself, except for the training course.'

18

'You get used to it.'

'Hope so.'

Prue sat in the hammock-like dip of her bed, child's legs swinging above the ground, a photograph clutched to her chest. She was extraordinarily pretty – the beguiling looks that come from a timeless mould, recognised in any age. Nothing original, but the kind of simple juxtaposition of features that makes prettiness look so easy when it's before you – heart-shaped face, curling lips that are halfway to pouting in profile, slanting eyes, tousled ash hair. Yellow-green tears glittered in her eyes. One of them spilt on to her cheek and instantly lost its colour.

Stella put a hand on the girl's shoulder. 'Show me your photograph,' she said.

Prue held up a picture of the façade of a small shop. *Elsie's Bond Street Salon.*

'My mum's hairdressing shop,' she said. 'If it hadn't been for this bloody war I'd be almost under-manageress by now. I'd done eighteen months of my apprenticeship, shampooing and perming and that. I was just about to get on to tinting.' She giggled. 'Perhaps I can keep my hand in here. Be of service.' She smiled up at Stella. 'You've got nice hair. I've brought my scissors, my peroxide, my kirby grips.' She nodded towards Ag. 'I could give you a new style any time, too – you only have to ask.'

'Thanks,' said Ag.

'Blimey: who's the handsome fellow?' Prue indicated the photograph Stella was holding. She handed it over: a large Polyfoto portrait of Philip. It had been taken in a studio in Guildford only a week ago – Philip the sub-lieutenant, stern in his uniform, defiant hair cowed by Brylcreem, mouth a thin line of serious intent, though Stella herself could perceive the tiniest upturn at one corner which privately indicated the other side of him.

'Cor,' said Prue, after a moment's awed silence. 'He's quite something. You in love?'

19

'Totally, hopelessly, absolutely.' Stella laughed, pure happiness. 'I can't sleep for thinking of Philip, I can't eat for thinking of him, I've lost half a stone.'

'That's going quite far,' said Prue. 'I've never felt like that. Have you, Ag?'

'No,' said Ag. She was wondering if the others would mind if she arranged her books on the top of one of the chests.

'You're right lucky, then,' said Prue.

'I am.' Stella took the photograph back. 'But then what's the point of life if you're not in love? I always have to be in love. I can't imagine not being in love.'

'Has it always been Philip?'

'Good heavens, no!' Stella laughed again, a delighted cooing laugh that Prue envied. 'There've been lots of others, but Philip is the *real thing*.'

'Marriage, you mean? Wedding bells?'

Stella touched the outline of Philip's face. 'We haven't known each other long,' she said. 'But I think you know, somehow, when it's . . . I mean, I wouldn't be surprised, when the war's over . . .'

'Anyone mind if I put my photo on the chest of drawers?' asked Prue, standing up.

'Course not,' said Stella. 'I'll have Philip on my chair.'

'What about you, Ag?' Prue thought that if she tried hard enough she might eventually get the tall, snooty dark girl to loosen up.

'I'll put mine beside yours.' Ag took a small double leather frame over to the chest. On one side was a photograph of her mother, who had died when Ag was two, taken in the 1920s. On the other side was a recent snapshot she had taken with her own Box Brownie: Colonel Marlowe, her father, gentle solicitor, outside his office in King's Lynn.

'Now *she's* what I call a beauty,' said Prue, snatching up the frame as soon as Ag had put it down. 'Smashing, isn't she? Just like Vivien Leigh. Your mother, is it?' Ag nodded.

Prue returned the photograph to its place. 'Can't say you're much like her.'

Now their score was even, and Prue was full of regret. She wished she hadn't said that. It was worse than the bantam, more hurtful. She hoped she would be forgiven. But she could not tell what Ag, so dignified, was feeling. Ag quickly returned to her bed. She searched for something in her handbag.

Prue felt in urgent need of a cigarette. 'Anyone mind if I have a fag?' She took a packet of Woodbines and a box of matches from her pocket.

'Not at all,' said Ag, so lightly it seemed she had not noticed Prue's jibe.

'I don't mind anything,' said Stella.

Prue went over to Ag. 'Sorry I said that,' she said. 'I didn't mean it. You can't tell nothing from a photo. Don't know what got into me.'

'That's all right,' said Ag.

'But your mum *is* beautiful,' said Prue.

'Was,' said Ag. 'Hadn't we better be going down for high tea?' She looked at her watch. 'It's almost time.'

Prue moved over to the single armchair, sat on an arm, inhaled deeply. 'Just a quick drag,' she said. 'D'you suppose we're going to have to eat whatever that terrible smell was in the kitchen?'

'Rabbit and turnip,' said Ag. 'I'll take a very large bet.'

'Rabbit and turnip? Crikey, I'll never get that lot down my throat. And do you think Mr Lawrence'll find his tongue?'

'He was very nervous in the car,' said Ag.

'Huh! What did he think we were?'

'I wasn't nervous,' said Stella, 'I was just thinking of Philip.'

''Course you were.' Prue pecked fast at her cigarette. 'You were just thinking of Philip. As for Mrs Lawrence, she's a real old battleaxe.'

21

'I like her,' said Stella.

'So do I,' said Ag.

'That makes two of you, then,' said Prue. She swung her legs faster. 'It don't feel much like there's a war, here, do it?'

The dining-room had a patina of gloom. It smelt of darkly polished furniture. The central light, whose shade was fretted with the abstract wings of dead moths, feebly illuminated a bleakly laid table: fork, knife, pudding spoon, and napkin in a bakelite coloured ring at each place, glasses and a jug of water. In the centre of the table, island in a brackish lake, was a stand of lacy silver which held cut-glass pots of salt and pepper. A gleaming silver spine rose between the pots, its apex twisted into a small handle. This fragile object, the single shining thing in the sombre room, made Stella smile. She wondered when Mrs Lawrence had time to polish it. She imagined it was important to Mrs Lawrence to make the time.

Ag, standing by the table – none of them was sure what to do, whether they should sit down – straightened a table mat, a gravy-spotted scene of rustic Dorset a century ago. In the awkward silence that had netted them all, the grandfather clock ticked – muted, insistent, its fine brass hands stroking their imperceptible way round the brass sun of its face.

'Give me the creeps, grandfather clocks do,' said Prue. She moved over to the sideboard to study a photograph in a cheap leather frame. It was of a stern-looking young girl, her flat hair rolled up in the same way as Mrs Lawrence's. '*She* don't look like much of a laugher, do she?'

Mrs Lawrence came in with a pot of stew. It was rabbit. She was followed by her husband who carried a dish of mashed potatoes and roast turnips. The girls exchanged private looks. Prue, behind the Lawrences' backs, imitated someone being sick. But she took the piled plate Mrs Lawrence handed her.

'Where's Joe?' Mr Lawrence asked his wife, an

22

enormous plate of food in front of him. Mrs Lawrence, the last one to sit, had taken a tiny helping herself.

'Went to deliver that feedstuff to Robert. Said they might have something to eat at The Bells.'

Mr Lawrence sniffed.

There was a long silence, but for the subdued chink of knives and forks in thick gravy. Prue, despite herself, was eating hungrily. The ticking of the clock bored through her. She turned to Mr Lawrence, sitting next to her.

'Is that your daughter?' she asked, nodding towards the photograph.

'No,' he said.

Prue gave him fifteen ticks of the clock to tell her more. He kept his silence. She turned to his wife.

'Who is it, then?'

Mrs Lawrence wiped her mouth on her napkin. Already she had finished her food.

'That's Janet,' she said. 'Joe's fiancée.' She waited till Ag and Stella had both turned to look at the photograph with new interest, and returned to their food. 'They're to be married when the war is over. In the spring, we hope.'

'Depending on Mr Churchill,' said her husband.

'They know they may have a long wait. They seem quite resigned.'

Mrs Lawrence spoke tightly. Stella and Ag both hoped Prue would ask no more questions. Prue felt no such reticence. She turned again to the farmer.

'So Joe, your son, he's not been called up, then?'

'No, he hasn't, and he won't be. Asthmatic. Not a hope. Suffered all his life.'

'He's been very unfortunate, Joe,' said Mrs Lawrence.

'He would have liked to have joined the navy,' added her husband.

'He would have liked to have gone to Cambridge. He got a place, they thought very highly of him. But then the war . . . we couldn't spare him from the farm.'

23

'My – I have a friend in the navy,' said Stella.

'I went to Cambridge,' said Ag. 'He shouldn't miss it if possible. He could go once the war's over.'

'Perhaps,' said Mrs Lawrence.

They fell back into silence. The ticking clock dominated again. It wasn't until Mrs Lawrence had helped them all to large plates of apple pie and custard that her husband got down to business.

'You'll have heard about the place from the district commissioner, I dare say,' he began. 'Bit of this, bit of that, mixed farming. Up to now, we've done what we like best, though I hear there'll be orders any minute to turn the place mostly over to arable land. For the time being we've got a small herd of Friesians and a hundred or so sheep, though we're thinking of giving them up after the next lambing. Duties are pretty obvious. Faith, here, manages everything to do with the house – shopping, cooking, cleaning, laundry and so on. Land girls aren't supposed to help with domestic chores, but I dare say she wouldn't say no to the odd helping hand.' He watched his wife shake her head, cast down her tired eyes. 'She takes care of all the fruit – just a small orchard, we have, damsons, plums and apples. She does all the pruning, picking, boxing up, everything, don't you, Faith? Besides the jam and chutney – you'll not be short of good jam, here, will they, Faith?'

'They won't,' said Faith.

'Apart from all that, in a real emergency the wife helps us out with the milking, the lambing – she can turn her hand to anything, can Faith.'

He stopped for a moment, glanced at Prue. Once again glassy green tears danced in her eyes.

'I've never heard anything like it,' she said. 'Poor Mrs Lawrence.'

Mr Lawrence ignored her. His instinct had been right. He could see this film star bit of fluff wasn't going to be much use, women's tears at the very thought of an honest day's work.

'Everything else's up to Joe and me and you lot. You can all have a go at different things, see what you're best at. Five twenty a.m. there's tea on the kitchen table, five thirty it's down to milking. I'll sort you out, your various duties, in the morning. Anyone have any preferences?'

Prue volunteered at once. 'Well, I found on the course I loved tractors, Mr Lawrence. Don't suppose you'd ever believe it, but I could plough a pretty straight furrow, they said.'

'I'd find that hard, I must admit,' he replied, unable to resist a slight smile.

'I loved working with cows,' said Ag. She would be the one, perhaps, he would introduce to hedging. He could imagine her, slasher in hand – kind, studious face, thoughts hidden behind hooded eyes. He couldn't picture her, somehow, serious head bent into the muddy side of a cow.

'I'll remember that, then. And you?' He turned to Stella. The picture of her knee still flickered in his mind.

'I'm afraid I got to the course late because my father was ill, so I missed learning to milk. I'm just a general sort of all-rounder . . . I'll do anything.'

'That's good. Well, then, you start at dawn tomorrow. I warn you now, I'm a fairly easy man' – Ag saw his wife's mouth twitch almost imperceptibly – 'but one thing I can't stand is anyone late for anything, see? And another thing: there's to be no shirking. It's tough work, long hours, but it's the satisfaction of a job well done you'll get. The satisfaction of knowing you're doing your bit for your country in this damn war. Now –' he pushed back his chair, flushed from the exertion of so much speaking. 'I thought we should . . . celebrate your first night with a sip of the wife's home-made ginger wine. You'll never have tasted anything like it, I can tell you that.'

He strode over to the sideboard, opened a cupboard,

25

took out five wineglasses and put them on the table. Their glass, so pale a pink as to be almost an illusion, was engraved with butterflies that flew through swirling ribbons. It was a wonder their fine stems did not snap in Mr Lawrence's huge clumsy hands, thought Ag. They were the first beautiful objects she had seen in the house. She could not contain her response of pleasure.

'They're so pretty,' she said.

Mrs Lawrence blushed. She was confused by the least of compliments. 'My mother's,' she said. 'My mother liked to collect pretty things. We've not many left. We had to sell off gradually. Bad years.' She put her hand to her mouth, as if she had said too much. The merest gathering of shadows beneath her eyes – which almost smiled – indicated a feeling of modest pride as she watched her husband pour the thick golden wine. Filled, the blush of the glass deepened against the wine.

By now it was almost dark outside. No one put on the light. The room was warmer, furred with the merged smells of food and polish, and the faint note of musky scent that came from Prue. Mr Lawrence, his dutiful speeches over, was suddenly looser in his movements, sitting heavily back in his chair – the only one with arms – swinging a frail glass to his lips.

'A toast,' he said. 'To Mr Churchill.'

'To Mr Churchill,' the girls muttered, holding up their glasses.

The smoky light through the window joined the pink of glass and gold of wine. So now the glasses were the colour of misted plums, thought Ag, spurred by her usual private wonder at the antics of colour.

'And, of course, to you girls.'

'Thank you, Mr Lawrence,' giggled Prue. 'That's nice of you.'

Again the farmer could not resist a smile as he watched three white little hands tipping the glasses to their pretty

26

little mouths: tomorrow they'd be piling the dung heap, sweeping the yard, slapping grease on sore udders.

They all drank, Mrs Lawrence with tiny sips. The fiery wine burned their throats, their chests, their stomachs. It warmed their hands, and their heads spun with new ease and expectation.

The glasses were emptied, the cork put back with no invitations for more, the bottle returned to its cupboard. The girls helped Mrs Lawrence take the dishes through to the kitchen. Her husband stayed for a while in the empty room, made unfamiliar to him by the new presence of strangers. The wine still burned his lips, the ticking of the clock soothed. Perhaps he would get used to it, the full house. Might not be so bad after all. Even the film star looked as if she might shape up. In a moment, he would summon the energy to go out again. With Joe still not back, there was plenty to do before nightfall. He allowed himself a moment with his eyes shut, head thrown back. Behind the heartbeat of the clock he could hear laughter across the passage.

The kitchen was blurry from the steam of hot water from the sink. Mrs Lawrence's arms were deep in murky bubbles, from which she produced shining white plates. The girls fluttered round her, competing to snatch each plate from her first. They had tied dishcloths round their coloured skirts. In the near dark they fumbled through strange cupboards guessing where to put things. They bumped into each other. The ginger wine surprised them with its strength. It made them laugh.

As they were all tired, and eager to be alert on their first morning, they agreed on early bed. Mrs Lawrence warned them not to put on the light unless they pinned the black-out stuff across each window. None of them had the energy to do this: they undressed beside their beds, turning their backs to one another as they slipped nightdresses over their heads. Prue, the only one to have been denied these

27

lessons at boarding school, copied the modest gestures of the other two. She had difficulty in seeing her face clearly in her hand mirror: it took her some time to wipe the mascara from her eyes and the lipstick from her mouth.

She watched, fascinated, as the other two brushed their hair with short, strong, dutiful strokes as if it was a ritual they had performed for many years. Ag's hair was dull and heavy. It needed thinning, shaping. Stella's could do with a restyle, too. When Prue knew them better, she would introduce them to her scissors, persuade them to allow her to make improvements. The plans in her mind diffused the small feelings of homesickness.

'Funny, me a hairdresser's daughter and never brushed my hair at night,' she said.

'Very odd, that,' agreed Stella.

Ag sat on the edge of her bed rolling up her stockings. She wore a flannel nightdress with a bodice of lace frills, and carpet slippers. So *grandmotherly*, thought Prue, slipping off her own pink velvet mules with their puffs of matching swansdown. And now the grandmother figure had laid the small neat bundle of stockings on her chair, beside a pile of books, and had turned to face Stella and Prue.

'I think I must tell you something,' she said quietly, folding her hands like a nun. There was a long pause. 'That is, my name isn't really Agatha.'

'Oh?' Prue was prepared to be surprised by any announcement this prim girl liked to make.

'No. It's much worse than that. It's Agapanthus.'

'*What*? Aga – what?' Prue doubled up with giggles. 'There's no such name.'

'Well, there is,' said Ag. 'It's both the name of a flower and the name of my grandfather's . . . boat.'

Prue studied her own incredulous face, with its mascara-streaked cheeks, in her hand mirror.

'Fishing boat, or what?'

Ag hesitated. 'More of a yacht, really,' she said at last.

'Just a small one. My father insisted I should be christened Agapanthus. He's a strange man in some ways. But he also agreed I'd have a bad time at school with a name like that. So we settled for Agatha – which isn't actually that much better, is it? Anyhow, in the end everyone called me Ag, so I never had to explain.'

She bowed her head. The warm confusion of the ginger wine was draining away. The compulsion to confess the matter of her name had come so powerfully upon her: now, having done it, she wondered why.

'I think that's *wonderful*,' said Stella. 'Agapanthus! You could be famous with a name like that.'

'Wouldn't be bad for a salon, to my mind,' said Prue. 'Have you ever told anyone before?'

'Just one friend at Cambridge. Desmond.'

'And here you are telling us the first night we meet? I'd say we're flattered, aren't we, Stella? Any trouble, and I'll be shouting it from the haystacks. "Agapanthus!" I'll shout!'

They all laughed.

Ag got into bed, sat with arms round raised knees. The feeling of the first night at a new school was overwhelming: on the one hand it was all so familiar, on the other there was the strangeness of being grown up in what felt like a child's world.

'I don't know what came over me. I just felt I had to tell you. Good night.'

At school, they always bade each other good night, no matter how sleepy. She lay down and in a practised way shuffled about until she found comfort in the unyielding mattress. In a moment she was asleep.

Prue, in her bed, tossed about in search of softness: she doubted she'd ever get used to a mattress like this. Still, the ginger wine had cheered her, and she had to admit there was something intriguing about Ag's confession. The tears her mother had warned her she would probably shed on

29

her first night did not come. She, too, was quickly asleep.

Stella reached for Philip's photograph on her chair, as soon as she judged the others would not hear. Terribly awake, she kissed his face in the dark. She replaced it, but could not sleep. After a while – it was too dark to see her watch, and Ag's clock was too far away – she slipped out of bed and crept to the nearest window. There was a full moon. It shone hazily through dark clouds, fraying their edges. She looked down into the farmyard: looming black sides of barns and sheds, a huge pile of dung whose acrid smell just reached her. The night was so ominously quiet she feared bombs. Fighter planes often zoomed out of the deepest silence. What would they do in a raid? Mrs Lawrence had said nothing about a shelter . . .

Stella saw a man ride into the yard on a bicycle. He braked with a rather dashing little turn; had anyone been watching, she'd have thought he was showing off. He dismounted, pushed the bike into the barn. She could see he was tall, large. When he came out of the barn he paused, looked up at the moon, scratched his head. Now Stella could see he wore enormous muddy boots. Instead of moving towards the house, he turned back to the barn, leaned heavily against it, face to its wall. He protected his forehead with a bent arm, shoulders hunched. For a long while he did not move – two or three minutes, Stella thought it must have been.

She could be imagining it – he was a long way off – but his position struck her as one of despair. Eventually he moved, drew himself upright and took long mournful strides back the way he had come, towards the gate. Cold now, Stella returned to her bed. She picked up the photograph of Philip again, and clasped it in her arms. Under the bedclothes she kissed his icy glass face, and swore to love him till she died.

Two

W hen the wind was in the right direction, the church bells at Hinton Half Moon could be heard at Hallows Farm. The hamlet was no more than a straggle of stone cottages, one of which had been converted into a small sub-post office. It offered little in the way of provisions: Bird's custard, Horlicks, Bovril, a few pads of Basildon Bond, soggy from their long shelf-life. These basic provisions were sometimes enhanced by a few luxuries which appeared according to the mood of Mrs Tyler, who ran the shop. On a good day, she would be up early, baking, and set a few brown loaves on a sheet of greaseproof paper in the cloudy front window. The smell of baking would hail the neighbours at dawn. A queue of some half-dozen buyers would hurry to the door at eight thirty, official opening time. Mrs Tyler, a law unto herself, as she was so fond of saying, would wave a plump hand urging patience. Not until eight thirty-five, or even eight forty, would she at last turn the rusty key very slowly, and let the eager buyers in. There were never enough loaves. There was always an argument, disappointed voices. It was known that Mrs Tyler enjoyed these small dramas played out in her shop once or twice a week: it was her measure of power in an uneventful life.

From time to time, Mrs Tyler's annoying ways so incensed the other members of the community that they vowed to boycott her wares. But this plan never worked for more than a day or two. They needed stamps, their pensions, they needed to add a few shillings to their savings accounts. And once in the shop they would be tempted by a surprising cauliflower or cabbage, a punnet of tomatoes or Russet apples from the Tyler garden. These were put out, they knew, by way of a bait. The ploy succeeded. Despite their good intentions, the inhabitants of all the eleven cottages that made up Hinton Half Moon found themselves sneaking back into the post office, greed overcoming principle quite easily, to purchase Mrs Tyler's trap of the day.

Ratty Tyler, married to the post mistress for fifty-one years, was party to his wife's small triumphs, because she described them to him with untiring glee every evening. His reaction was neither to encourage nor to discourage. A dignified neutrality, he had discovered over the years, was the wisest attitude to adopt in matters concerning Edith. In the past, in the heat of youthful loyalty, he had found himself in many a scrape through lending her support. It was due to an unwise act on Edith's part that he had been forced to give up his thriving butcher's shop in Dorchester just before the last war. A question of slander, though the exact circumstances had long since evaporated in his mind. Total boycott of customers. Confusion. Shame. Ratty hated ever to remember it, though sometimes the whole horrible business came back to him when Edith was in a particularly tricky mood. He warned her that if she went too far they would be driven from Hinton Half Moon just as they had been from Dorchester. But Edith seemed not to understand the danger. She continued taking her risks.

When the Great War was over, the Tylers had found the cottage they still lived in today. Their first Sunday, Ratty signed up as a bell ringer, and it was in the cold vestry of the church that he met the young and energetic John Lawrence. In those days, the Lawrences, too, lived in a cottage in Hinton, but they owned a few acres of land on which they kept a small flock of sheep. The two men had a brief conversation in the churchyard. Ratty sensed Mr Lawrence's ambition: already he had his eye on Hallows Farm, occupied at the time by a senile old woman.

'And your line of country?' Mr Lawrence had asked.

'We've just moved here, sir. Casual labour's what I'm after. Any farming work, I'd be pleased.'

'We're beginners ourselves, but I could offer you a few hours a week.'

'Righto, sir.' The two men shook hands.

'John Lawrence.'

'Ratty Tyler.'

'Ratty?'

'Term of affection, sir, should you suppose otherwise. Adopted at the time of our engagement by my now wife.'

Ratty allowed himself the lie. The truth was that Edith had chosen the name for him as soon as they had been introduced. Reginald, his real name, she said at once, she could not abide. Ratty had been rather taken by her busy little head of blonde curls and her pretty ankles, and he feared his objection might have blasted the plan that was beginning to form in his mind. So Ratty he was from that day forth, though in the secrecy of his soul he often thought the name was more appropriate to Edith than to him.

It was plain from the start that he and Mr Lawrence understood one another. He began with three hours' labour a week, two shillings an hour. When the sheep did well and the flock increased, this was increased to a day and a half. By the time Mr Lawrence acquired Hallows Farm, Ratty was working every day, all hours. Within a few years, things became too much for the two of them: it was Ratty who suggested they should hire more hands. He found the two keen young lads himself – one from Hinton, one from a couple of miles west – and thereby earned himself the title of Farm Manager.

These days, although Ratty still thought of himself as Farm Manager, and Mr Lawrence would never do anything so inconsiderate as to suggest there was any change in the position, both men understood the title was now more honorary than practical. What with his arthritic hip and the bad pains that sometimes struck his eyes now, Ratty would only come up to the farm a couple of days a week. When the boys had been called up, he had reluctantly agreed that Mrs Lawrence's idea of land girls might be the solution.

Every working day of his life Ratty rose at four o'clock in the morning. He liked the silence of the dawn, the silence of the kitchen as he boiled water in the huge black kettle for tea, and ate a chunk of Edith's rich brown bread. Just before leaving he would take a mug up to the bedroom under the eaves, leave it on the table beside her. Sometimes he would pause for a moment to study the now white curls of his wife, and the creased face, cross even in sleep. Years ago, without disentangling herself from drowsiness, she would ask him for a kiss. He would oblige, and be rewarded with a sleepy smile. She had not smiled for years now, properly, Edith. Not with happiness. The only thing that brought a shine to her eyes was *triumph*. Scoring over the neighbours, her customers. Scoring over anyone she could find, not least Ratty himself. What was it, he sometimes wondered, that caused a carefree young girl to turn so quickly into a crusty old woman? Nothing Ratty could put his finger on: he did his best to please her. But marriage was a rum business, he had learned. At the time – foolish young lad – he had no idea what he was letting himself in for. But it had never occurred to him to desert his barren ship. He had made his promises to the Lord, and they would not be broken. Besides, if he tried hard enough, he sometimes thought, everything might miraculously change, and Mr and Mrs Ratty Tyler might become as happily married as Mr and Mrs John Lawrence.

Fortunately for Ratty, he was blessed with a compartmentalised mind. He was able to abandon the tribulations of his marriage as he shut the front door behind him. At four thirty precisely he hobbled into the lane that led to Hallows Farm, limping slightly, hands scrunched into the familiar caverns of his pockets, ears stinging cold beneath his cap.

For twenty years Ratty had been walking this lane, witnessing thousands of early mornings, each one so infinitesimally different that only a habitual observer could feel the daily shiftings that formed the master plan of each season. Since he had been forced by health and age into semi-retirement, and now only made the journey twice a week, the privacy of dawn was more precious than ever before to Ratty. He listened to his own footsteps on the road – no longer firm and brisk – and the scattered choir of birds. Sometimes a blackbird would soar into a solo, his song only to be muddied by a gang of jealous hedge sparrows. Sometimes an anxious mistlethrush would call to its mate, and be answered by a cheeky robin. There were few unseen birds Ratty could not identify by their song, and their sense of dawn competition made him smile.

He slashed the long grass of the verges with his stick and noted, as always, the neatness of Mr Lawrence's hedges. In the sky, a transparent moon was posed on a belly of night cloud. But the dark mass was beginning to break up where it touched the low hills. Streaks of yellow, pale as torchlight, illuminated the line of fine elms that protected Hallows Farm from northern winds. Over the gate that led into the meadow Ratty could see the Friesians, legless in a rising ground mist, intent on their last grass before milking. By the time he had walked the last half-mile the mist had all but evaporated, and the familiar outline of the old barn was black against the sky. A strand of smoke rose from the farmhouse chimney. In the old days, Ratty always arrived before Mrs Lawrence lit the kitchen fire. His current lateness troubled him. Although he knew Mr Lawrence would have understood, and urged him not to hurry, he took the precaution of disguising the precise time of his arrival. This morning, for instance, he would go straight to the barn to sort out some stacks of foodstuff. When Mr Lawrence dropped by some time between five thirty and six, he would have no idea when Ratty had started, and could be counted on not to ask.

This morning, too, Ratty had another reason for wanting to start off in the barn. The girls would be here this morning, and he wanted to get a look at them before they saw him. See what he was up against, as it were. Get their measure. He had never worked with women on the land, and could not imagine how it would be. But as a man who could be stimulated by very small changes, he was not against the idea – not as against it, in fact, as Mr Lawrence. Chances were they wouldn't be up to much – he couldn't see a girl on a tractor, himself. But in all fairness, he must give them the opportunity to prove their worth. And if they weren't up to the job, they'd be out. As he had agreed with Mr Lawrence, there'd be no mucking about with second chances. There was no time for mucking about with a war on.

Full of benevolent intent, Ratty reached the barn. His enthusiasm to tidy a pile of heavy sacks had waned. He could deal with them later. For the moment, he felt like a rest.

Ratty leaned up against the high bumper of the red Fordson tractor. Once a handsome scarlet, its paint was now chipped and dull. He fished for his pipe from an inner pocket, spent a long time lighting it. Its sour smoke joined the smells of the few remaining piles of last year's hay, rotting mangolds, tar, rope, rust. Up in the dusky beams, the dratted pigeons carried on with their incessant silly cooing. (Ratty's love of birds did not extend to indolent pigeons.) A cow screamed in Long Marsh: Betty, by the sound of her. He kept his eyes on the empty yard, looking forward to the entertainment of one of the girls getting down to sweeping. Confident his position would not be observed, he took a long draw on his pipe, began his patient wait. After a while he was conscious of a slight agitation in his heart. The feeling reminded him of something. Ratty struggled to remember. That was it: the long-ago event of his wedding. Standing at the altar, waiting for his bride, he had experienced exactly the same thunder of anticipation, excitement. And look where that had landed him . . .

At five fifteen, Stella, Ag and Prue presented themselves at the kitchen table. They stood stiffly in their new uniforms. Ag folded back the sleeves of her green pullover: its wool scratched her wrists. Stella was having trouble with the collar of her fawn shirt. Prue stamped her feet in their sturdy regulation shoes.

'Each one feels heavy as a bloody brick,' she complained. 'It's *these* I became a land girl for . . .' She stroked her corduroy breeches, gave a small wiggle of her narrow hips.

Prue was the only one who had taken the liberty of adding to the uniform – not against the rules unless deemed inappropriate. She had tied a pink chiffon scarf into a bow on top of her head. Although she wore no lipstick today, the mascara was thick as ever.

Mrs Lawrence poured mugs of her dark, hot tea, and passed a plate of thickly cut bread and butter. Her look at Prue made her silent opinion quite clear. Then her husband came in and spoke her thoughts for her.

'That thing on your head,' he said, 'won't stand much chance up against the side of a cow.'

Prue fluttered her eyes at him, defiant. 'I'll take that risk,' she said.

'Very well.'

Mr Lawrence found himself curiously moved by the sight of the three girls, eager to work for him, lined up in his kitchen so early in the morning.

'Besides,' said Prue, helping herself to a second slice of bread, 'I thought it was agreed I'd have a go on the tractor. I told you I was good at that.'

'This isn't a fairground, I'll have you know. You don't

37

"have a go" on things. You do a job of hard work. What's your name?'

'Prue. *Prudence.*' She raised her chin.

Mr Lawrence sniffed in distaste. 'And what's that *smell,* for Lord's sake?'

Prue, her cheeks two pink aureoles that matched the chiffon bow, was delighted he had noticed. '*Nuits de Paris,*' she smiled.

Her employer was silenced by the prettiness of Prue's cocky young face. 'This is a farm,' he said at last, his voice less rough than he had intended. 'I don't want my cowsheds smelling of the Moulin Rouge, thank you. You're a land girl, you understand, not a film star.'

Mrs Lawrence kept her eyes on her tea.

Prue smiled on, pleased Mr Lawrence should find something of a film star in her. 'Perhaps *Roman Days*'d be more up your street?'

'I want none of your fancy scents, just your mind on the milking, thank you, Prudence.'

Mr Lawrence was brusque now. He nodded towards Ag, not wanting to ask another one her name. 'You'll get going with the yard broom, and muck out the pigsty, young lady, and you, Stella –' he remembered her name all too well – 'will have to learn to milk before we can let you loose among the cows. Headquarters provided us with the wherewithal, didn't they, Faith?' His mouth twitched in a limited smile. He allowed himself a glance at Stella's knee. The jewel was now disguised by corduroy breeches, though its sharp edges were just visible. Again Mr Lawrence nodded towards Ag. 'You – you'll find Ratty Tyler out there somewhere. He'll show you the brooms, get you going. As for you, Lady Prudence, you'll take yourself over to the milking shed where my son Joe will sort you out in no time. Stella can come with me.'

Stella saw Mrs Lawrence's eyes raised to her husband's flushed face.

He went with the girls out into the cold early air of the yard. Stella followed him to the shed where she would receive her 'training', as he called it.

As she walked beside him, the squelch of their gumboots in step, the farmer felt an acute sense of betrayal.

He kept his eyes from Stella, and cursed the war.

Ag stood alone in the yard, hands in her pockets, wondering what to do. She could see no one who might be Ratty Tyler, and did not feel like shouting his name. Ratty? Mr Tyler? What was she supposed to call him? And who was he? Ag listened to the sharp clash of farmyard noises. She dreaded Mr Lawrence returning from the shed, to which he had gone with Stella, and finding her not at work.

A tall, large-boned man, hooded lids over very dark eyes, appeared from behind the barn. He carried a heavy spade, a pitchfork and a broom. Unsmiling, he approached Ag.

'Thought you might be wanting these,' he said.

'Thanks. I was looking for Mr Tyler.'

'Ratty appears when he appears. I'm Joe.'

'I'm Ag.'

Joe handed her the broom. He had had a hard five minutes in the barn trying to persuade Ratty to come out and show the girl what to do. But Ratty, in one of his most stubborn moods, insisted on staying hidden. He wanted to sum up the strangers unseen, he said. Take his time to get used to them. Joe was sympathetic. But in the end he took pity on the tall girl in the yard and agreed with Ratty to set her on her way.

'You want to sweep the yard absolutely clean, sluice down the drains with Dettol – buckets and water over there. Dung heap's round the corner. Pigsty's past the cowshed: only the one sow. Not good-tempered. Shouldn't get in her way. Plenty of clean straw in the barn. I'll be milking if you want anything.'

He strode away. Their eyes had never met.

Ag tested the weight of the broom, surprised at its heaviness. She must devise her own method, she thought, and began sweeping the corner farthest from the barn.

As there was no sign of Joe Lawrence in the milking shed, Prue took her chance to become acquainted with the cows. They were a herd of twenty Friesians. Each one, chained to her manger, had a name over the stall: Betty, Emma, Daisy, Floss, Rosie, Nancy – Prue wondered if she would ever be able to distinguish between them. She observed their muddy legs, but clean flanks and spotless udders. Looked as if someone else had done the washing down, thank goodness. That was the part of this job she could never fancy.

Prue came to an almost entirely black cow, Felicity. She had particularly intelligent and gentle eyes, surrounded by long blueish eyelashes. Prue wondered what they would look like with mascara, and smiled to herself. She glanced down at the swollen pink udder, with its obscene marbling of raised veins. She ran a finger the whole length of Felicity's spine, the wrong way, so that the cow's black hair was forced up over the bone.

'I like you,' she said aloud.

She raised her eyes above the animal's spine and found herself looking into the hooded eyes of the man she assumed was Joe. Cor! *He* was quite something . . . Her mind flicked through the handsome film stars she had dreamed of, but could come up with no one comparable. Anyway, she quickly decided, she'd be happy to sacrifice ploughing, and milk the whole herd morning and night if this Joe was to be her supervisor. His eyes shifted, expressionless, a bit *spooky*, to her hair, the bow. Funny how she'd been impervious to everybody else's opinion, but there was something about Joe's look that made her feel a bit foolish. The one thing she did not want was instant disapproval. That would start them off on the wrong foot.

'Why's she called Felicity, this one?' she asked at last,

head on one side, coquettish – a gesture she had learned from Veronica Lake.

'She was a happy calf. She's a happy cow.' Joe slapped Felicity on the rump. He seemed to have forgotten about the bow.

'Can I start on her?'

'No. We start at the other end with Jemima.'

Prue pouted. 'I'm Prue, by the way. Your father calls me *Prudence.*'

'I know. How's your milking?'

'Just the few weeks on the training course. I'm not bad.'

'Gather you're keen to get on the tractor.'

'I *said* that, just in case Mr Lawrence had any ideas about women not liking ploughing. I'm quite happy to milk.'

'Rather enjoy it myself. A lot of farms have gone over to machines. Isn't really worth it for a herd of our size, though Dad was talking about it before this bloody interruption.' They both listened to the noise of a small aircraft squealing overhead. Joe pointed to the far end of the shed. 'There are a couple I haven't washed down – Sylvia and Rose. Mop, bucket and towels through there. Rule here is that we change the water every two cows. Stool and milking bucket in the dairy. I'll show you how to put on the cooling machine when we've finished.'

'Don't worry. I *understand* about cooling machines,' said Prue. She managed to sound as if her understanding went far beyond mere technicalities.

'We should get going. I'm running late this morning, seeing to your friend.'

'I'll make a start.'

Prue blushed with annoyance: to think that Ag, asked merely to sweep the yard, had been the first to engage Joe's attention. She moved slowly down the concrete avenue that divided the two rows of cows' backsides, swinging her hips. Joe's eyes, she knew, were still on her. She picked up the mop and bucket with the calculated flourish of a star performer, and began to swab Sylvia's bulging udder as if the job was a movement in a dance. When she had finished washing both cows, she sauntered back to where Joe was milking a restless creature called Mary.

'And where,' she asked, hand on one hip, provocative as she could manage in her given surroundings, 'might I find a cup for the fore milk?'

Joe released Mary's teats. He looked up at Prue, impassive. 'I don't believe we have one,' he said.

'Don't have one?' Prue's voice was mock amazed. 'We were taught it was *essential* –'

'Dare say you were. We don't do everything by the book, here. We just draw off the first few threads before starting with the bucket.' He turned back to his milking.

'On to the *floor*? Do you suppose,' said Prue, after a few moments of listening to the rhythmic swish of Mary's milk hitting the bucket, 'this is a matter I should bring up with your father? Or the district commissioner? Or –?'

'Bring it up with who you bloody like,' said Joe. Although his face was half-obscured by Mary's flank, Prue could see he was smiling.

In the dairy, she washed her hands with carbolic soap in the basin. She was aware of a small triumph, a feeling that some mutual challenge had been recognised. If nothing else, a teasing game could be played with Joe. That would give an edge to the boring old farm jobs – and who knows? One game leads to another . . .

Astride the small milking stool, head buried in Jemima's side, hands working expertly on the hard cold teats, Prue allowed herself the thrill of daydreams. Surprisingly, she was enjoying herself. She liked the peaceful noises – muted stamp of hooves, and chink of neck chains – that accompanied the treble notes as jets of milk sizzled against metal bucket. She was aware that the sweet, hay smell of cow breath obliterated her own *Nuits de Paris* – she would tell Mr Lawrence, at the right moment, he need have no fears.

The thought of the hugeness of Joe's boots made her feel at home, somehow – which was an odd thought considering this chilly milking parlour was as far away from her mother's front parlour as you could get. She found herself praying that milking would be her regular job, if Joe was to be her milking partner. But her mind was diverted from imagining the many possibilities of this partnership by the distant sound of rattling marbles. She stiffened.

'Miles away,' shouted Joe. 'Just practice, by the sound of it.'

Prue waited tensely for a few moments, fingers slack on the teats. She had forgotten the war. She stood up, easily lifted the bucket of foamy milk. It smelt faintly of cowslips. Beaten Joe to it, she saw with pleasure. It was tempting to point out to him what a quick milker she was. But Prue decided against this. She went to the dairy, sloshed the milk into the cooling machine and chose a bucket from the sterilising tank for the next cow. She had had her one small victory this morning. That was enough to begin with.

Stella, when she saw her 'cow', laughed out loud. It was a crude, ingenious device: a frame made of four legs, inward sloping, like the legs of a trestle table. From its top was slung a canvas bag roughly shaped like an udder and from which dangled four rubber teats the pink of gladioli. It reminded Stella of a pantomime cow.

'Oh Mr Lawrence,' she said, 'is this to be my apprenticeship?'

'Won't take long. You'll soon get used to it.'

Mr Lawrence gave her one of his curt smiles. He picked up a bucket of yesterday's milk and poured it into the bag. Then he squatted down on the stool drawn up to the ersatz udder, placed the bucket beneath the empty bag, and took a teat in the fingers of both hands.

He was no expert, and was aware of the ridiculous

picture he made. His fingers were curiously shaky. A feeble string of milk trickled from the teat.

'Easier on a real cow,' he said. 'Here, you have a go.'

Stella took his place, held the smooth pink teat.

'It's a rhythm you want to aim for,' he explained, when he had watched her for a while. 'Once you've got the rhythm, you're there, and the cow's happy. That's it, that's a girl.' The farmer moved proudly back from his pupil. She was bright, this one, as well as attractive. 'Fill the bucket a couple of times, and you can be on to the real thing tomorrow. All right?'

'Fine.'

Mr Lawrence allowed himself a few moments in silent appraisal. Funny girl. So formal in her speech, and yet so quick. He let his eyes rest on her back, the pretty hair tumbling forwards. Where it parted he could see a small patch of her neck, no bigger than a man's thumbprint. With all his being he wanted to touch it, just touch it for an infinitesimal moment, feel its warmth. As he stood there, fighting his appalling desire, his hands and knees began to shake. Dizziness confused his head. Stella's voice came from a long way off.

'Am I doing all right, d'you think?'

It was several moments – silence rasped by the silly sound of the squirting milk – before he dared answer.

'You're doing fine.'

He took a step towards her, watched his hand leave his side, stretch out to her innocent back: hover, quiver, withdraw.

Stella turned, smiling. She saw what she thought was a look of deep misgiving in Mr Lawrence's eyes. The shyness of the man! It must be dreadful, she thought, to find the peace of Hallows Farm suddenly disrupted by unskilled girls from other worlds. Sympathy engulfed her, but she could think of no appropriate words with which to convey her feelings.

'I'll be back in a while,' Mr Lawrence said. He waited till Stella returned to concentrate on the rubber teats, and quickly left the shed.

Alone, Stella sniffed the sour milk and manure smell of the shed. It was cold, damp. Her fingers on the teats were turning mauve. She determined to get her peculiar training over as fast as possible, and concentrated on the rhythmic massage of the ludicrous teats. At the same time she began to compose the funny letter she would write to Philip tonight: *my first day a land girl – with a rubber cow.* This prompted the thought of the post. Philip had promised to write immediately. She ached to hear from him. The two hours till breakfast, when she could ask about the delivery of letters, seemed an eternity. In some desolation, Stella looked down at the thin covering of milk on the bottom of the bucket.

Two hours later, shoulders and legs stiff from the awkward position (it would be much more comfortable with a real cow to lean against), Stella rose and stretched, her apprenticeship, she hoped, over. She had filled the bucket twice and felt like a qualified milker. Once she had got the hang of it – the rhythm, as Mr Lawrence had said – it had been quite easy. Behind the gentle splish-splash of the milk she had dreamed of Philip, going over in her mind every detail of the few occasions on which they had met. And when she swooped back to the present, she saw the humour of her situation – the adrenalin of being in love making bearable the milking of an imitation cow.

Now, she leaned over the bottom half of the shed door, looked out on to the yard. The Friesians were ambling towards the gate. They took turns to enjoy the distractions of familiar sights. Sometimes one would pause to give a bellow, puffing silver bells of breath into the sharp sunny air. Stella understood their lack of concentration, and smiled at the sight of Prue and Ag urging them on, with the occasional tentative whack of a stick. Prue's pink bow had lost some of its former buoyancy but still fluttered among her blonde curls like a small demented bird. She bounced and jiggled and enjoyed shouting bossily to the cows. In contrast, Ag walked with large dignified strides, never raising her voice. There was something both peaceful and wistful in her face. Stella felt drawn to this girl, wondered about her.

The last cow left the yard. At that moment two men came out of the barn. Stella assumed the tall one to be Joe, and recognised at once the shape of the man she had seen last night. His hand was on the shoulder of the much older man who wore thickly corrugated breeches and highly polished lace-up boots, the uniform of grooms before the last war. Joe seemed to be trying to persuade the old man of something, and was meeting resistance. On their way across the yard, Joe looked up and spotted Stella.

'Breakfast,' he shouted, but did not wait for her.

The idea of breakfast reminded Stella of her hunger. But reluctant to go into the kitchen alone, she made her way down the lane to meet the others returning from the meadow. They, too, declared their hunger. All three compared stiff joints and cold fingers, and hurried back to the farmhouse.

By the time they reached the kitchen the three men were already half-way through huge plates of bread, bacon, eggs, tomatoes and black pudding. Mrs Lawrence was shifting half a dozen more eggs in a pan at the stove. She wore the same faded cross-over pinafore as yesterday, which hid all but the matted brown wool of the sleeves of her jersey. There was something extraordinarily detached, but reassuring, in her back view, thought Ag. It was as if the outer woman was performing her chores, while an independent imagination also existed to power her through the mundane matters of daily life.

Mr Lawrence introduced Ratty to the girls, remembering all their names, having checked with his wife. Ratty, a

46

man of economy in his acknowledgements, made his single nod in their direction extend to all three of them. In that brief moment of looking up, Ag observed his extraordinary eyes, grained with all the colours of a guinea fowl's breast. Here was a man who would provide much material for her diary, she felt, as she sat beside him, unafraid of his distinctive silence. Prue took her chance to sit next to Joe. Mr Lawrence observed her choice with a hard, flat look.

'Well, we got through that all right, I'd say, didn't we, Joe?' Prue turned to the others. 'I did twelve cows, Joe did the other eight. Just think, only a few more hours to go and we start all over again, don't we, Joe?'

Joe shook his head. 'Not me. Dad's on the afternoon milk.'

Prue's face fell. She accepted the plate of fried things from Mrs Lawrence and concentrated on eating.

Mr Lawrence, finishing first, seemed eager to be away. He outlined the chores for the rest of the morning. Ag was to help Mrs Lawrence with the henhouse, and try to patch up the tarpaulin roof. Prue was to sluice down the cowshed, sterilise the buckets, scour the dairy, and put the milk churns into the yard. 'Ready,' he added, 'for the cart. Think you'll manage to get them on to the cart, Prudence?'

Prue looked up from her eggs, alarmed, knowing what a churn full of milk must weigh. But she had no intention of looking feeble in Joe's eyes. 'Of course,' she said.

'I mean, you're at least a foot taller than a churn, aren't you?' Mr Lawrence's fragment of a smile indicated he was enjoying his joke.

Now he turned to his left, where Stella swabbed up egg yolk with a fat slice of bread. 'Know anything about horses?'

'A little.'

'Then you can come with me. We'll walk down to Long Meadow, give you an idea of the lie of the land.'

The three men rose, leaving their empty plates and mugs on the table. Mrs Lawrence sat down at last, with a boiled egg. Her cheeks were threadbare in the brightness, caverns of brown fatigue under both eyes. She cracked the egg briskly, looked round at the girls.

'You'll get used to it,' was all she said.

By the end of their first day, the land girls were exhausted. After four o'clock mugs of tea, they lay on their beds, trying to recover their energy for supper.

'If we're this fagged, what must poor Mrs Lawrence be?' asked Ag. 'Up before us, never a moment off her feet. And now cooking. Perhaps we should go down and help.'

'*Couldn't*,' sighed Prue. 'Twenty-four cows milked dry first day – ninety-six teats non-stop, you realise? That's me for day one. Finished.'

None of them moved, despite the guilty thought.

'We should be less stiff in a week or so,' said Ag, rubbing a painful shoulder, 'able to do more.'

'*More?*' giggled Prue. 'We're land girls, not slaves, I'll have you know.'

'I *liked* the day,' said Stella, sleepy. 'I liked the walk to get Noble, and then getting into a terrible muddle with the harness.'

'Mr Lawrence can't keep his eyes off you,' said Prue, after a while.

'What?'

'Haven't you noticed?'

'Don't be daft.'

Ag laughed. 'Your imagination, Prue,' she said, from her end of the room. 'I think Mr Lawrence is so giddied by our presence he doesn't know where to look. He's not used to women on the farm, or anywhere. But you can tell about him and Mrs Lawrence: soldered for life, I'd say. They don't have to speak, or even look. They're bound by the kind of wordless understanding that comes from years

48

of happy marriage. My parents were like that, apparently.'

Prue sat up. She pulled the pink bow from her hair. 'Don't know about all that,' she said. 'My mum and dad love each other no end, but they don't half scream at each other night and day. Do you think we stay in these things for supper? I bloody *stink*. Cow, manure, Dettol – you name it, I reek of it. As for my nails . . .' She looked down at her hands. 'What are we going to do about our nails?'

'Give up,' said Stella, smiling.

'Not bloody likely. Land girl or not, I'm going to keep my nails, any road. Anyhow, what did you two think of him?'

'Who?' asked Ag.

'Joe, of course.'

'Seems nice enough. Shy.'

'*Nice enough*? Are you blind? Don't you recognise a real smasher when you see one? He's something, Joe, don't you realise, *quite out of the ordinary*? No easy fish, I reckon, but I'll take a bet. Joe Lawrence and I won't be too long before we make it.'

She looked from Stella to Ag, trying to read their reactions.

'There's Janet,' Ag said at last, 'isn't there?'

Prue giggled. 'Janet? Did you take a look at her photo? She's not what I'd call opposition.'

'But they're engaged,' said Stella.

'Long time till the spring.' Prue continued to study her nails. 'Anyhow, I'll keep you in touch with progress, if you're interested.'

'Immoral,' said Ag, half-smiling.

'Are you shocked?'

'Rather.'

'All's fair in love and war's my motto. And this *is* a war, remember? Don't know about you two, but I'm getting out of these stinking breeches. Green skirt, pink jersey, lashings of *Nuits de Paris*, whatever Mr Lawrence says, and Joe'll be beside himself, you'll see.'

While the other two laughed, Prue took a shocking-pink lipstick from a drawstring bag and concentrated on a seductive outline of her mouth. 'I've never gone for anyone so huge. What do you bet me?' She challenged Stella, the most likely to take on the bet. But Stella's mind had wandered far from Joe.

'The only bet I'm interested in,' she said, 'is whether or not I get a letter from Philip tomorrow. But *probably* he won't have time to write for ages.'

She wanted to begin the letter she had composed that morning. But tiredness overcame her good intentions.

By the time Prue had chosen the right pink from a row of nail polishes, and delivered her opinion about the hopelessness of men when it came to letter-writing, Stella was asleep. Ag, too, lay with her eyes shut and made no response. Pretty queer bunch, the three of them made, Prue couldn't help thinking, as she dabbed each nail with the brush of flamingo polish and wondered if her shell earrings, for supper, would be going too far.

Contrary to her predictions, the object of Prue's desire was far from beside himself at supper. He sat between his mother and Ag, silently eating chicken stew and mashed potatoes. He seemed not to notice the trouble Prue had taken with her appearance: spotted green bow in her hair, dazzling lipstick to match a crochet jersey, and smelling extravagantly of her Parisian scent. Mrs Lawrence, who as usual sat down at the table last, was the only one to react to all Prue's efforts. She sniffed, grimacing.

'Janet's coming, Sunday lunch, Joe,' she said. 'She rang while you were out.'

'Oh yes?'

'Janet,' Mrs Lawrence explained to the girls in general, 'manages to get here about once a month. It's a long journey. She's stationed in Surrey.'

'That's nice, her being able to get over at all,' said Prue.

'Nice for you, Joe.' A thousand calculations buzzed in her head. She gave Joe a smile he arranged not to see.

Mrs Lawrence's news failed to open a lively conversation. The aching girls became sleepier as they ate, only half listened to talk between Joe and Mr Lawrence about problems with the tractor. Supper over, they were invited into the sitting-room to listen to the news, but all volunteered to go to bed.

As the girls went upstairs – Mrs Lawrence insisted she needed no help with the washing-up – Prue observed Joe slip out of the front door. Where was he going? If her plan was to work, she must find out about his movements. The idea excited her enough to dispel her sleepiness. When the other two were in bed, their lights quickly out, she went to the window, stared moodily down at the farmyard. She saw Joe mount his bicycle by the barn and ride out through the gate. If his beloved Janet was three counties away, who was it he was going to see? Prue remained at the window, intrigued, until eventually she heard a distant church clock strike nine. Cold by now, she went to her bed, but could not sleep for the dancing of her plans.

On the stroke of nine from the same church clock, Ratty Tyler, sitting by the range in his small kitchen, knocked out his pipe and rose to make his wife a cup of tea. Edith was ensconced at the kitchen table, a dish of newly iced buns beside her, all ready to cause distress among early customers next morning. The dim light, over-protected by a dark tin shade, was pulled down as far as its iron pulley would go. Edith's hands, parsnip coloured in its murky beam, concentrated on the darning of a sock.

'So?' she said.

'So what?'

Ratty had been waiting for this all evening. He had observed the difficulty Edith had had, holding herself in, all through their soup and bread and cheese.

'What're they like?'

'What're who like?'

'You know what I'm saying, Ratty Tyler.'

'That I don't.'

Edith sighed, bit off a new length of grey wool with her dun teeth.

'The girls.'

'The land girls?'

'Of course the land girls. What other girls would I be asking about?'

Ratty gave her question some thought. 'Just girls, far as I could see,' he offered eventually. He put a cup of tea on the table. There were more questions to come, he could see that. He must play for time. Anything for time.

'Where's the sugar?'

'Same place it's always been for the last thirty years. Your mind must be elsewhere.'

It was elsewhere, all right. It was always elsewhere when he came home.

'I was thinking about Mrs L., so happens,' he said. 'Taking on the girls eases some problems, but makes a lot more work for her.'

'Pah!' spat Edith, disbelieving. 'Never known you trouble yourself about Mrs L. before. It's the girls you were thinking of, I've no doubt.' Her needle, newly charged with wool, dived swift as a kingfisher towards its prey of a hole in a brownish heel. 'You may as well tell me.'

Ratty placed the sugar bowl by the cup, returned to his chair. For peace, he thought, he may as well.

'There's the small one,' he said.

'Name?'

'Prudence, they call her.' He judged it not worth referring to her as Prue, as the others did. The implications of a nickname would be bound to set Edith's fears alight.

'Huh!' She was easily offended by mere names. Her indignation came as no surprise. 'What's she like?'

What was she like? Ratty asked himself. Prudence was the one with a face like the girls photographed in newspapers on the first day of spring. Small, but frightening. He wouldn't fancy time alone with her.

'As I said, not large. Nothing to write home about.'

Ratty had intended to say something more definite about her, to assure his wife that the girl, young enough to be their granddaughter, was no threat of any kind. But he feared that silent cogitation, striving for the right description, might itself inspire further suspicion. He need not have worried. For some reason Edith was not interested in the idea of Prue.

'And the others?'

'There's the medium one, the one I took to Hinton in the cart with the milk. Not much experience in harnessing up.'

No point in saying she'd been mighty quick to learn, that one. He'd shown her what to do his side of Noble: she copied quick as a flash on her side. And lovely manners. All polite remarks about the countryside, on their way to the village, and doing more than her fair share of unloading the churns. Nice face, too. He liked her.

'Name?'

'Stella.'

'Nothing like Cousin Stella?'

Ratty shook his head. Edith's Cousin Stella was the nearest to a witch he knew. No comparison with this girl. He smiled at the thought, knowing his wife, in her quick glance, would misunderstand his expression.

'You lay your hands on a Stella and it would be *incest*,' snapped Edith in the furious voice she used for her most illogical remarks.

'No fear of that.'

'And the last one?'

She was suspicious, here, Ratty could tell. *How* could she be suspicious? He cursed her instincts.

53

'The tall one. Agatha. Ag, they call her.'

'Much taller than you?'

'Good foot,' he said, permitting himself the exaggeration of an inch or so.

Edith contained a sigh of relief. 'You've never liked a tall girl.'

'No.'

Foxed her! Ag was the one he liked even more than Stella. He'd studied her for a long time from his unseen position in the barn. There was something about her kind, private face that had struck him. He had been intrigued by the way her short hair had blown apart while she was sweeping, so he had had glimpses of white scalp. Reminded him of watching a blackbird in a wind, feathers parting to show white skin of breast. If he'd met someone like Ag when he was a lad, Lord knows, he'd have done something about it.

'Blonde?'

'Dark.'

'You've never liked dark hair, neither.' Edith briefly touched her own white fuzz of thinning curls.

'I haven't, neither.'

He saw the tension in Edith's body slacken. She held the darned sock away from her, admiring the woven patch she had accomplished with such speed and skill. It would go unacknowledged by Ratty, like all the darns she had held up over the years. It wasn't that he lacked appreciation, but words to express it froze before he could utter them. Hence the constant disappointment he caused her.

'And what did they make of you?'

Ratty sucked on his empty pipe. Although he had anticipated this one, no firm answer had come to mind.

'We chattered nineteen to the dozen, all very friendly,' he heard himself say. Reflecting on this lie, he considered it permissible, after so much partial truth.

Edith sniffed. 'You be careful what you say.'

'You can trust me.'

'You were all sweet words when you were young.'

Ratty shifted. This was the nearest to a compliment Edith had paid him in three decades. It made him uneasy. He could never confront her with the truth: how she had killed the sweet words very early in their marriage by her laughter, her scoffing. It was she who caused his prison of silence when it came to women. The banners, with all the things he wanted to say written on them, still danced in his mind, sometimes, but their benefits went unknown, locked into wordless silence. No problems with Mr Lawrence, with Joe. On occasions he could even mutter a word or two to Mrs L. But three strange new girls all up at the farm in one day . . . to have spoken was quite beyond him.

'Time to turn on the news,' said Edith, picking another sock from the basket with the curious gentleness that she employed for inanimate things.

'So it is. I'll do it.'

Ratty felt his bones soften with relief as he got up – land girl conversation over for tonight. He hoped it wouldn't come up again for a while: give him time to gather his thoughts. Edith gave a small nod of her head, which was the nearest, these days, she ever got to a smile. She could never get the hang of the wireless, understand the tuning. Ratty twiddled the knob. His skill in finding the Home Service was one of the small ways in which he could oblige his wife with very little effort. Had she known the paucity of this effort, her appreciation might have been less keen. As it was, admiration for her husband's technical ability was conveyed in a small but regular sigh that Ratty had learned to recognise. The fierceness went out of her needle.

Three

L and girls were entitled to one and a half free days a week. Mrs Lawrence suggested that this first week they took Sunday off, even though they had only been working for two days. Unused to the physical activity, they would be needing the rest, she said. The girls conceded gratefully. They offered to make sandwiches and go off somewhere for a picnic lunch, keep out of the way. But Mrs Lawrence responded by asking them to stay to lunch with the family: Janet would be coming. She'd like them to meet Janet.

At five a.m. Prue, waking suddenly, remembered she had no need to get up. About to return luxuriously to sleep, a picture came to her mind of Joe alone in the cowshed. He would have to do all the milking himself today. When did *he* have any time off?

In a moment, Prue was out of bed, all sleepiness gone. She dressed quickly and quietly so as not to disturb the others, and chose a yellow satin bow for her hair. What a surprise she would give him. How pleased he would be – someone to share the work on a Sunday.

Creeping downstairs, Prue heard voices in the kitchen: Joe and his mother talking. She had no wish to dull the impact of her good deed by joining them for a mug of tea, so she crept towards the front door.

As she put out her hand to turn the key, she heard a sound like the slap of a hand on the kitchen table. And, distinctly, the shouting of angry words.

'You just take care, Joe!'

'Mind your own business, Ma.'

Prue's heartbeat quickened. Silly old interfering thing, Mrs Lawrence. His age, Joe could do what he bloody well liked. Quickly she opened the door.

In the cowshed the animals were chained in their stalls, restless as always before milking (how quickly she had come to learn their ways!), heads tossing, tails lashing, muted stamps of impatience. Prue fetched bucket and pail, began work on the first cow.

Joe arrived by the time the bucket was half full – she was an even faster milker by now. He must surely be aware of how quickly she'd learned. Prue felt his gaze upon her, from the doorway, but did not look up. She heard the slish and thud of his footsteps as he strode towards her. Still she made no acknowledgement of his presence, kept her head dug into Pauline's bony side. She knew her yellow bow was badly flattened, but resisted releasing one hand to puff it into life.

'What're you doing here? It's Sunday. It's meant to be your day off.'

Joe's voice was far from grateful. For a full minute Prue listened to the rhythmic hiss of the milk she was drawing from the cow's abundant udder, calculating her answer.

'I woke as usual. Thought you'd be glad of the help.'

'You did, did you?'

She could hear Joe moving away with surly tread. Why had her kind act so annoyed him? She felt the sickness of having made a bad decision. There was nothing she could do but carry on: she managed to avoid him each time she finished a cow and had to collect an empty bucket. The two hours went by in a frenzy of speculation. What had she done wrong? How could she put matters right? Usually, she could rely on the soundness of her instincts. This morning no answer came.

When Prue finished milking the last cow she stood up

and saw that Joe was no longer in the shed. Well, bugger him, she thought: he hasn't half taken advantage of my kind offer. Leaves me most of the work, then buggers off early to breakfast.

She stomped crossly up the aisle, swinging her last full bucket. Milk splashed on to the floor, mixing with streaks of chocolate-coloured water, paling it to a horrible khaki, that warlike colour Prue so hated. Bugger everything, she thought. I'm off back to bed.

Joe was standing by the cooling machine, arms folded, blank-faced, impervious to its insinuating whine. Steam, escaping from the sterilising machine, blurred the handsome vision. Prue, nose furiously in the air, inwardly quaked. She sensed there was to be some kind of showdown, and dreaded it.

Then through the steam she saw – she was almost positive she saw – a tremor of a smile break his lips, though his eyes were hard upon her.

'Little minx,' he said.

In her surprise, Prue lowered her bucket to the ground too hard. Wings of milk flew over its edges, curdling on the concrete: she didn't care. Nothing mattered now except that she should conceal her sense of triumph.

'And *careful*, for Pete's sake,' she heard him say.

He bent and picked up the bucket, threw the milk into the cooling machine with something of her own carelessness. He could blooming well deal with the sterilising, Prue thought, heart a mad scattering of beats as she hurried out without speaking, pretending to ignore all messages.

In the short march from the cowshed to the kitchen – smell of frying bacon quickening the early air of the yard – Prue reflected on her good fortune. She thanked her lucky stars she had made the right decision. Joe's earlier behaviour, she had somehow failed to understand, was merely a form of teasing. He was no longer a problem. Her path was clear, Janet or no Janet. It was now just a matter of *when*

58

and *how*, and at what point she should tell the others how right she had been.

While Stella and Ag helped Mrs Lawrence in the kitchen, Prue spent an hour of luxurious contemplation in the empty attic room as she re-did her nails, chose combs for her hair instead of a ribbon, and finally decided to wear her red crêpe dress with its saucy sweetheart neckline.

Coming downstairs – heavy skirt of the dress flicking from side to side, not without impact – she found Joe and his father in the hall, both dressed in tweed suits. Mr Lawrence carried a prayer book. Christ, one Sunday it would probably be to her advantage to go to *church* with them, she thought – though she hoped it would not have to come to that. She'd never exactly seen eye to eye with the church, all those boring hymns. But she didn't half fancy Joe in his posh suit, despite the egg on his tie. She smiled. Mr Lawrence, with a look of faint distaste, hurried towards the kitchen. That left her and Joe alone in the hall. She carried on smiling.

'Been *praying*?' she asked eventually.

'None of your sauce,' said Joe. He swung past her up the stairs, banged the door of his room.

None of your sauce . . . Prue went over the words carefully. He'd said them with such lightness of tone, in a voice so mock serious as to be transparent in its meaning, that for the second time that morning Prue found herself triumphant. How she enjoyed the careful analysis of that short remark! What he meant was, he wouldn't mind a *lot* of sauce, but he would be grateful if she was careful. Well, she'd never been one to enjoy upsetting any apple carts. She'd play the game by his rules, if that's what he wanted. But there was no reason not to enjoy herself until the time came.

Prue slipped into the kitchen where Mr Lawrence was polishing his shoes. The three women were all hard at

59

work, stirring, tasting, moving in and out of clouds of steam that billowed over the stove.

'Can I do the gravy or anything?' Prue asked.

'It's all done.' Mrs Lawrence sniffed, distaste less well disguised than her husband's. She seemed to have some sixth sense, aware no doubt of everything that went on under her roof. Her disapproval would be terrifying to behold.

Prue left the room.

She found herself in the yard, leaping over patches of mud on to small islands of dry ground, trying not to ruin her scarlet Sunday shoes. On reaching the barn – she had grown to like the barn – she crossed her arms under her breasts, shivering. It was a cold, sunless morning. She leaned against the icy metal mudguard of the tractor, making sure she was hidden from the house. There was no time to ask herself why she was there, the tractor her only companion, because almost at once a small navy Austin Seven, beautifully polished, drew up to the front door. Rigid with curiosity, Prue watched a girl – probably about her own age – get out of the car, lock the door with a fussy gloved hand. She wore a grey coat. Her hair was rolled into a bun. She stood looking about, as if disappointed there was no sign of Joe to greet her. Then she moved to the door and rang the bell. Prue decided the girl's prim little step, in highly polished lace-up shoes, was proprietorial.

Joe opened the door. They exchanged a few words, moved back to stand by the car. Joe seemed to be admiring it. He put a hand on the gleaming bonnet. Janet patted his arm, tipped back her head. She seemed to be asking for a share of his admiration. Joe bent down and gave her forehead the merest brush of his lips. Janet took his arm. Together, they went into the house.

That's all I need to know, Prue said to herself. She skipped back across the yard so fast she splashed both the red shoes and her thinnest pair of silk stockings, but she didn't care.

*

Janet sat on the edge of an armchair at one side of the fire-place in the sitting-room. Joe sat in the chair opposite, while the hard little sofa was occupied by Stella and Ag. Ag looked about the olive and green furnishings, the cracked parchment of the standard lamp, the faded prints of York Minster. Joe fiddled with a minute glass of sherry, cast in silence. Janet, who had refused a drink of any kind, feet crossed on the floor, hands asleep on her lap, registered in her pose something between demure good manners and disapproval. She had a long face and a down-turned mouth set awkwardly in a protruding chin, giving her a look of stubborn melancholy. The surprising thing was that, when she ventured a smile, her down-turned eyes turned up, and the plainness of her face became almost appealing.

Stella, sensing the awkwardness, felt she should make some effort at conversation.

'What is your actual job in the WAAF?' she asked.

'Sparking plug tester.' Janet thought for a while, decided to go on, seeing the genuine interest in Stella's face. 'What I want to be, eventually, is a radiographer. But I don't suppose I'll ever make it.' She shrugged, looked at Joe. The thought of disputing this did not seem to occur to him.

'I'm sure you will,' said Stella, surprised by Joe's meanness. 'I can't imagine what it must be like, the job of testing sparking plugs.'

'No, well, it's not that interesting. And the working conditions aren't very nice. All day in a cold and draughty warehouse, oil everywhere . . .' She trailed off, eyes on the door.

Prue flounced in, a dishcloth tied over her skirt.

'You must be Janet,' she said. 'I'm Prue. 'Scuse my apron.'

She smiled wickedly, shook hands with Janet whose incredulous pale face bleached further. Prue unknotted the dishcloth and shook herself free as seductively as a striptease artist. Joe drank his few drops of sherry in one gulp, not looking at her.

'I've come to tell you dinner's ready.'

Janet stood up, straightened her grey flannel skirt.

'Where've you come from?' asked Prue. 'In that wonderful car!'

'It belongs to my parents. From Surrey, near Guildford.'

The sharpness of her reply brought Prue's bobbing about to a stop. She looked at Janet with a new curiosity.

'Never been to Surrey, myself,' she said. 'Isn't that rather a long way to come for Sunday dinner?'

'It is, but if it's my only chance to see Joe, then I don't mind the miles.'

Janet tipped her head back again, giving Prue a defiant little smile which she then dragged round to reach Joe. Ag, from her corner of the room, admired the girl's show of spirit. Janet took Joe's arm, indicated they should be the first to leave the room.

Possessive little Surrey madam we have here, thought Prue, and winked at Stella and Ag.

'Have you ever been to *Surrey*?' she asked them.

'Shut up, Prue,' said Ag.

Janet sat between Joe and Mr Lawrence. Prue, taking Ag's advice, resisted sitting on Joe's other side and chose a place opposite him. Mrs Lawrence helped everyone to large plates of roast pork and vegetables.

'You'd never know there was a war on here,' said Stella, desperately trying to ease the silence.

'You would if you had to eat in my canteen,' said Janet. 'Last week they ran out of custard powder. We had to have cornflour sauce with the jam roll. As for the chocolate shape . . .'

'I love chocolate shape,' offered Prue, solemnly. 'Anything chocolate, for that matter.'

'I've never made a chocolate shape. And now I can't get

chocolate,' said Mrs Lawrence, to fill another silence. She glanced at Prue. 'So I doubt I ever shall.'

'And your mother, Janet, how's she getting on?' Mr Lawrence, struggling to do his bit, cast a glance at his son.

'She's doing fine, Mr Lawrence. A lot on her plate, what with the WVS and the knitting group she's organised.'

'You said, Joe, you'd bring down those piles of magazines from the attic for Janet's mother.' Mrs Lawrence looked sharply at her son.

'I did,' said Joe. 'I'll put them in the car for you.'

This was his first direct remark to his beloved fiancée, Prue noticed. Perhaps they made up in private for their public reserve.

'Mother will be pleased. Thank you, Mrs Lawrence.' Janet turned to Joe. 'Will we have time for a stroll before I have to start back? Father said he'd rather I was home before dark.'

Joe looked at his watch. 'Depends,' he said, 'on how quickly I can get through the milking.'

He didn't look at the girls, but Mrs Lawrence's eyes travelled from Stella, to Ag, to Prue.

'I'll do the milking!' Prue turned to Joe. 'You and Janet go for your walk.'

'We'll help,' offered Ag quickly.

' 'Course we will,' said Stella.

'Well,' said Joe. 'If you insist.'

'We do.' Prue giggled.

'That's very, very kind,' said Janet. 'Joe and I are very, very grateful. We get so little time.'

Prue giggled again. 'Shall I bring in the apple pie, Mrs Lawrence?'

This gave her the chance to rise slowly from her seat with a small flick of her skirt. Janet's eyes, she was pleased to observe, were riveted by her narrow hips, small waist and the rise of bosom above the sweetheart neckline.

Praise for the pudding did little to brighten the dismal

63

lunch. When it was finally over, Mr Lawrence was the first to get up, with the air of one about to make an announcement. He addressed the land girls.

'Faith and I make it our business to be off duty till tea-time on Sundays,' he said quietly. 'It's the only time we get for a rest.'

Stella, glancing at Mrs Lawrence, saw that her face had turned a thunderous colour.

Joe, also embarrassed, patted Janet on the shoulder. 'Come along, then, Jan. Hope you've brought your boots.'

'We'll bring the cows in,' said Stella, urging the other two to hurry.

'Race you,' called Prue, brushing past Janet and Joe.

Ag was the last to leave the room. As soon as she was out of the door she heard a wail from Mrs Lawrence.

'John! How dare you!'

'Sorry, love. Sorry. I wanted them out of the way, didn't know how –'

Ag hurried after the others, wanting to hear no more.

Back in their breeches, the three girls strode down the lane towards Lower Pasture to fetch in the cows. Prue's previous high spirits had subsided.

'Lucky Janet,' she said.

'Oh, I don't know. She doesn't seem to be getting much response,' said Stella.

Ag swung her stick through the long grass of the verge. She turned to Prue.

'You were rotten,' she said.

'Rotten? Why rotten?'

'All that flirting. Crucifying Janet.'

Prue laughed.

'For Christ's sake, if she can't take another girl smiling at her man, she'll be in for a bad time. Where I come from, all's fair in love and – besides, Joe needs cheering up, any road. He's made a sodding great mistake. He needs a bit of fun.'

'Whatever he needs, it's not your business,' said Ag.

'Lay off, posh face.' Prue struck the grass with her own stick, harder than Ag.

'Come off it, you two.' Stella moved between them.

Prue ignored her, turned an angry face to Ag.

'What you're saying, *Agapanthus*, is you fancy Joe yourself.'

The absurd accusation, so insulting, whipped the colour from Ag's face. Their eyes met in mutual hostility, but Ag kept her control.

'I'm not saying that, no. You can have no idea how wrong you are.'

Prue thrashed once more, but less viciously, at the grass. The silence that followed was broken by the pooping of a small horn.

They turned to see the Austin Seven coming up behind them. Joe was driving. Janet, smiling, sat beside him. As they went by, everyone waved. With the passing of the car the tension eased.

'He looks quite happy, actually,' said Ag.

'He likes cars, I dare say,' said Prue. 'New cars like that.'

'Well, good luck to them.' Stella's thoughts were more concerned with Philip and herself. She had had no word from him.

Prue looked at Ag, suddenly contrite.

'Sorry. Once I fancy a man, some devil gets into me.'

'You take care,' said Ag. 'Think of Janet.'

'I'm not one to upset apple carts, believe me.' Prue ruffled her curls, smiling again.

At the gate to the field all three girls paused for a moment, arms resting on the top bar, eyes on the herd of impatient cows. Ag thought that with any luck she could return to *Jude the Obscure* in just over two hours: so far, there had been little chance to read. Stella began to compose her next letter to Philip. Prue sighed.

'Wonder what they're up to,' she said. 'I can't imagine Joe would get very far with that grey skirt, can you?'

Mr Lawrence made sure that he was downstairs before the girls came in from the cowsheds. There were disadvantages, having your house full of strangers. But on the whole, judging by this week, the advantages outweighed them. Faith had been right about the land girls: they were shaping up pretty well. Faith was right about most things.

He cut thick slices of her home-made bread, hungry. But calm. The nervous energy, the buzz of anxiety that had been hounding him since the girls' arrival, had been dissipated by the hour of making love to his wife. As on all Sunday afternoons, he felt powerful. He alone was able to chase the rigidity from Faith's bones, soothe the tension, make her smile. The fascination of this regular unwinding of his wife never wore off, and the tea that followed, prepared by him, was the occasion he most looked forward to in the week. Newly bound together in a way that never became stale or mundane, Sunday afternoons revived John Lawrence's scattered energies, strengthened him for the days ahead.

Slowly, gravely, the farmer spread the bread with butter, put fruit cake on a plate, a spoon beside a jar of Faith's gooseberry jam. He wished the present silence could go on for hours, the girls never return, the war be over. But in a few moments they would be back, hungry. Nice of them to have done the milking, give Joe an hour or so with Janet. The girls, the girls . . . that Stella girl. As John stirred the tea, he found himself facing the truth – something that usually, in his busy days, he had no time to afford himself. But here it was confronting him, in all its starkness: he no longer felt unnerved by Stella. The curious, unwanted sensations she had aroused in him so unexpectedly, almost as soon as he met her, had abated. Further probing of the devil that had taunted him – and here the flow of milk from jug to cup wavered – found the exact nature of those

66

feelings put into words: old man's lust. Disgusting, shaming, horrible. He was fifty-three, married a long time, never looked at anyone but Faith, had never had the opportunity to be tempted. Then an entrancing creature young enough to be his daughter arrives, and the unsettled feeling she causes him is like an illness he's unable to shake off.

Until now. Now, normal again, he could trust himself. What he would do to prove this would be to test himself. The test would be a simple one – nothing dangerous. On Monday, he would switch the girls' jobs around (good idea to make sure they could all do anything) and take Stella hedging with him. He'd enjoy teaching her the skill. At the end of the day he'd invite the others to help with a bonfire. By that means the ghost would be laid: he could never have cause for shame again.

Faith came in quietly, dark skin burnished in the deep afternoon light. She tied an apron over her Sunday skirt, stood straight and noble as she poured tea, the merest smile on her lips as she glanced at the thickness of butter on bread.

'Rationing, remember.'

'It's our own.'

'All the same.' Mrs Lawrence sat. 'I hid the last pot of damson jam. Do you want some before the girls come?'

Her small, innocent conspiracies were always a delight to her husband. He shook his head.

'Not today. They're good girls.'

'Not at all bad.'

Mrs Lawrence blushed for the second time that afternoon. Her husband read her thoughts.

'I've said I'm sorry. I'll say it again.'

'No need to go on.'

'What we could do is walk up to The Bells for a drink and a sandwich. Ratty'll be there.'

'Escaping Edith.' Faith laughed. 'He'd be so surprised to see us it might unnerve him altogether. It's been an alarming enough week for him anyway with the girls.'

'We wouldn't have to face them if we went to The Bells.'

'I don't mind facing them. Don't suppose Joe'd be very happy alone with the three of them, Prudence fluttering her eyelashes. Besides, you'd miss a rice pudding. And it's *Postscript*, remember. Can't see you missing Mr Priestley. We'll stay where we are.'

They heard the slam of a door, voices.

The girls burst in, socks and breeches muddy, bringing cold air with them. They had been for a long walk, got lost on the way back, had problems helping Prue over a stile. As they ate hungrily, laughing, easy, Mr Lawrence reckoned their minds had been far from Faith and himself, and felt relieved. This was the first meal, he observed, at which polite conversation had given way to real banter, merriment. Joe, who had slipped in just as the last of the bread and butter had been taken, seemed surprised by the laughter, the unusual liveliness. He sat by his mother, who cut him a vast slice of cake. He ignored Prue's surreptitious looks. Maybe he genuinely was not aware of them, but they did not go unobserved by Mr Lawrence, who for once was pleased to see his son's face as inscrutable as ever. He was a hard one to fathom, Joe. Always had been. Bit of fluff like Prudence would never get the measure of him, of that Mr Lawrence was sure. All the same, Janet's flat grey skirt and flat grey voice came to mind, and he felt uncomfortable. It didn't do to think too much about Janet. He slid his eyes to Stella: beautiful – despite mud on her cheeks, hair blown into tangles, total lack of make-up. She smiled at him, innocent. It did nothing to him. His resolve remained firm. Tomorrow he would teach her to lay a hedge.

That night, the girls joined the Lawrences by the wood fire in the sitting-room. Mrs Lawrence darned, Prudence repainted her nails, Ag half-concentrated on a crossword puzzle. Stella just sat, her mind on Philip. While they all listened to J. B. Priestley decrying the government's policy against ordering potatoes to be sold for a penny a pound,

68

Mr Lawrence gave Stella several glances, wondering at her preoccupation. Still he felt nothing but safety.

But at breakfast next morning the resolve wavered, then fled. The stirrings of disloyalty, an uncontrollable physical thing, assaulted him as he watched her sip her tea. He wondered at her distraction. She kept glancing at the window. When the postman arrived, she leapt up before Faith and took the bundle of letters from him through the window. Quickly she shuffled through them and snatched for one for herself. She slipped it into her back pocket with a look of such vivid joy Mr Lawrence knew he would have to change his plans. He could not hedge all day beside a girl in such rapture, and not be moved, tempted, agonised. She was all smiles again, now: pink cheeks, a portrait of high expectation. Happy the man who is loved by her, thought Mr Lawrence, and realised his wife's eyes were heavy upon him.

'I need someone to help with the last of the damsons,' she said.

'I'd be willing,' volunteered Stella at once.

'In that case, I'll take Agatha hedging with me,' said Mr Lawrence, 'and as for you, young Prudence, you can have your way at last. When the sheds are sluiced down, there's Upper Meadow to be ploughed. Joe'll explain the Fordson to you – she's a temperamental old thing, some days. He'll take you up there. Then you're on your own.'

'*Mr* Lawrence! I'll not let you down. You'll not see a straighter furrow,' Prue squealed. She put down her tea, flung excited arms round his neck. 'Thank you, thank you!'

Mr Lawrence awkwardly disentangled himself from her embrace, to laughter from the others. Even Joe was smiling.

'Calm down, child,' he said, 'and don't be surprised if the novelty wears thin after a couple of hours in the metal seat.'

'You wait,' she said. 'My *dedication* to the plough will

surprise the lot of you. Down in half a tick, Joe. Just do my lipstick. Never know who you might meet in a furrow . . .'

Faith explained that, as the last of the damsons were to be made into chutney and jam, there was no need to take great care in the picking. Picking plums for sale, the day before, Stella had chosen only perfect fruit.

She carried a large basket and a stepladder to the orchard, and made for the last unpicked tree, its branches weighed down by a heavy crop.

It was a fine, warm morning. The freak frosts of last week had not returned: Mr Lawrence said it had been the finest summer for many years. Its warmth overflowed into autumn, tempered with an almost imperceptible breeze.

Stella made firm the stepladder and climbed up, buried to the waist in branches and leaves. She liked fruit picking, had enjoyed stripping several trees of apples and plums, though she was still not half as fast or skilled as Mrs Lawrence, who had worked beside her the first few days.

In her last letter to Philip, Stella had tried to describe how she enjoyed the privacy of leaves, their green flickering with sun and shadow all about her, the whispery silence snapped by the breaking of a twig or the rhythmic thud of the new fruit dropping into the basket. Even as she wrote such things, she had been aware of her mistake. In their short acquaintance, Philip had never shown much interest in nature: most probably all he wanted to hear were declarations of undying devotion. She had included those, of course, at the end, but had wanted to convey what it felt like, this strange land girl life – one moment so funny, milking the rubber cow, another so hidden, among the fruit. She had written him three letters. By now, although her impatience for a reply was almost unbearable, she decided to prolong the agony. The reading of the letter would be a reward for filling the basket.

Stella picked faster than ever before, with agitated

fingers. Yellow freckles were beginning to splatter the leaves. Some of the fruit had burst upon the stem. From the gashes in the flesh, a kind of transparent gelatinous stuff had bubbled up and hardened, and sparkled fiercely as crystal. Stella threw these wounded fruit into the long grass under the tree. Sometimes she tried to polish a damson before eating it, but could not brush the blue haze from its skin. Damsons could not be made to shine like plums. Each fruit has its reasons, she supposed: fruits had as many different habits as roses. But she was too excited to dwell further on the nature of damsons, and as she was alone in the orchard she sang 'The Rose of Tralee' out loud in her clear voice. The letter burned in her pocket.

The basket was full. Stella wedged it between two branches. She could see no more damsons within reach. Her brown arms were warm, her job well done. She settled herself on the platform of the stepladder in an archway of branches, tore at the envelope of cheap paper that was standard issue for officers on HMS *Apollo*. There was a single sheet within. As Stella began reading, the leaf shadow jigged among the words, at first confusing.

My dear Stella,

    Thanks very much for your letters. Glad to hear you are enjoying life as a land girl so far, and get on with the other two.

    Here, it's the usual routine. We've been escorting Channel convoys all week, not very interesting, no trouble. I shall be glad when we go up to Liverpool, not that there's much change of scenery at sea.

    Last night I gave Number One a game of draughts in the Wardroom. His bark is worse than his bite. He's quite friendly, really.

    You keep asking me about leave and when we can meet. I go for a gunnery course at Portsmouth in a couple of weeks and will probably get a night off after that. Perhaps I could make a detour on my way back to Plymouth,

*though with no car getting cross country would be difficult.
We'll probably have to wait for a boiler clean, when I'll get
five days. Then, if you could make it, we could manage
something. Forgive short note, I'm due for the mid-watch.
Somehow, I've managed never to be late so far. Miracle!
    Careful of those cows. Will try to write again, soon.
    Love, Philip.*

Stella read the letter twice, incredulous. She crumpled up
the horrible paper, then quickly straightened it out again,
returned it to the envelope and put it back in her pocket.
There was nothing between those lines: nothing, nothing.
She lifted down the basket of damsons – oh, the stupid
hope that had speeded her picking! – struggled back down
the ladder, and set it on the ground. Then she sat in the
grass beside it, leaned back against the trunk of the tree.
She found tears of furious disappointment plundering her
cheeks. She bit her knuckles to silence her sobs. How could
he? How could a man who so recently had declared himself so passionately in love write such a hopeless, useless
letter, giving her no indication of how life was at sea, how
he felt, how he loved and missed her? Whereas she had
done so much describing, so much declaring.

When the worst of her sobs were over, a new thought
came. Perhaps it was merely that Philip didn't like writing
letters. There were, amazingly, such people. A dynamic
communicator of the flesh, perhaps he suffered from gross
disability when it came to expressing himself on paper.
Perhaps he had no notion of the pleasure of winging
thoughts to someone else, or indeed the pleasure such a
letter would give. That must be it, surely. No man was perfect, and the man she loved had just one small
imperfection: rotten at letters. There could be many worse
faults: she must consider herself lucky. Besides, once the
war was over, there would be no need to correspond. They
would be married almost at once.

Consoled by such thoughts, although they scarcely added up to a satisfactory solution, Stella got up at last, lifted the heavy basket of damsons. She dried her tears with the coarse wool of her sleeve, and turned to make her way back to the farm. Joe was coming towards her, not ten yards away. There was no escaping him.

With just a yard between them, he stopped. 'Anything wrong?'

Stella sniffed, managed a smile. 'Not really, thanks. Just overcome by my first letter from Philip.'

'Ah. He's, what . . .?'

'Sub-lieutenant. HMS *Apollo*. Escorting convoys across the Channel, that sort of thing. Nothing exciting. Hasn't seen any fighting yet.'

'Lucky.'

'Anyway . . .' Stella shrugged, prepared to move.

'It must be worrying. I mean, all the time.'

Stella nodded. 'The missing,' she said. 'The waiting for leave. The not knowing. Still, after the war we'll get married straight away. At least, I suppose we will.'

'Might not be too long a wait.'

'Hope not. *You* must know what it's like: you and Janet. Waiting.'

'I was on my way to see how Prue was getting on,' said Joe, as if he had not heard her. 'If there's a single wavy furrow, there'll be trouble.'

Stella found herself laughing.

Leaning against the gate, Joe watched Prue for some time before she saw him. The tractor was at the far end of the field, its snorting reduced to a distant stutter. The tiny figure of its driver, very upright, was bobbing up and down on the seat, so light she was bounced by every jolt. There was a speck of colour just visible on her head – a scarlet bow. In the air just behind her, a flotilla of gulls dipped and soared, while on the ground the dark earth was dragged into a sluggish wave by the teeth of the ploughshare.

The tractor disappeared down a dip in the land, the noise of its engine now even fainter. A hundred yards to the hedge, Joe calculated, then it would have to turn. He waited to see it reappear over the slope.

But there was sudden, complete silence. After a few moments, Joe shifted his position. He made no move to enter the field. For some minutes, weight on the gate, he let his eyes follow a collection of clouds that chased, crashed, snapped off and went their newly ragged ways. At last a couple of snorts puckered the silence, then the rhythmic stutter began again, and the gulls reappeared.

Joe's eyes never left the tractor as it chuntered towards him across the long field: he saw the precise moment Prue noticed him, clutched harder at the steering wheel, deciding not to wave. She had managed almost a quarter of the field – not fast, but reasonably straight. When Prue was almost at the gate she stopped the tractor, but did not turn off the engine.

'How'm I doing?' she shouted.

Joe touched his forelock with a seriousness to match hers.

'Not bad. Not bad at all.'

'I've had trouble stalling.'

'Remembered to put in the paraffin?'

' 'Course.'

'And the sewing-machine oil?'

'What d'you take me for?'

'How about the plugs?'

'I checked them, idiot.'

'I'll look at her when you come in.' He made to open the gate.

'I'm not coming.' Prue began to pull at the heavy steering wheel, a dimpling of sweat on her nose and scarlet cheeks. 'So don't bother.'

'It's lunch-time, near as dammit.'

'I'm not eating a thing till I've finished this bloody field.'

Their eyes met.

'Very well,' shouted Joe. 'I'll tell Ma . . .'

The tractor was turning. She managed it with skill. For several moments longer, deep in thought, Joe watched the bobbing and leaping of her small bottom and the bow on her bouncing hair, then made his way to the barn.

'Trouble with hedges is they don't stand still,' Mr Lawrence explained to Ag as they walked the lane carrying their hooks, bill-hooks and slashers. 'They get in the hell of a mess if they're not cared for, sprawling out into the fields either side, clogging the ditches. Some people think hedging's a boring business, but I'm not one of them. In fact, there's no job on the farm I like better. You've got something to show for your work very quickly, besides a pile of firewood. There's a lot of satisfaction.'

Ag nodded in silence, wondering how skilled she would be at wielding the heavy tools.

They arrived at the destined thorn hedge, which divided a recently cut cornfield from a strip of mangolds. There were ditches, invisible under a mess of bramble and wayward shoots, both sides. Ag let her eyes trail the length of the hedge, which ended at the entrance to a small copse. She doubted her enthusiasm for trimming it into shape would match that of her employer, but gave a gallant smile.

'Don't despair,' said Mr Lawrence. 'You'll soon get the hang of it.'

He started to hack dead wood from the bottom, singling out new young shoots to judge their worthiness of being left to flower. The hedge, he explained, was a windbreak, so it should be left at a good height.

'I've been neglecting it, though, what with all the extra work,' he said. 'It takes time and a certain skill, that I will say, to lay a hedge decently, but it's a pleasing sort of task, to my mind. What you want to do is get a flexible stem, like this, weave it through other wood across a hole – something like darning – and make sure it's secure, won't pull out in a wind. Next spring, shoots will start to appear from every joint.' He turned to Ag for a moment, judged from her expression she understood. 'Best thing to do is you watch a while, then get into the ditch behind me and gather any stuff I throw down for a bonfire. When you're not dealing with my stuff you can start hacking away at the sides of the ditch: neaten it all up.'

Once Mr Lawrence had given his instructions he no longer seemed aware of Ag's presence, concentrating fully on the complicated geography of the thorn hedge. For a long time, Ag watched his deft gloved hands foraging in the leaves, weaving shoots, snapping off dead wood, hacking at stubborn joints with his slasher. She was glad he had not asked her to begin in front of him, and after a while began her own task of clearing the ditch. She stood on its muddy floor, a stream of brown water lying slackly around her boots. Slashing at the long grass and brambles was not hard and when, after twenty minutes, she paused to look back on the neat bank of her own making, she began to understand her employer's pleasure in the job.

After an hour, they paused for a few minutes' rest. The sun was high by now and they were hot. Mr Lawrence rolled up his sleeves. Ag, with aching back, sat a few feet from him on the ground. Mr Lawrence took a packet of Craven A from his pocket, offered her one, which she refused, and lit his own. They sat in easy silence, their eyes following the smoke.

'Finding it hard, this land girl business?' Mr Lawrence asked eventually.

'I ache a bit. We all do. But we're enjoying it.'

'Good, good. It's healthy work, anyway. As for the war . . . Terrible in London last night, they said on the radio this morning. Poor devils.'

'We're lucky here. Hardly aware of it.'

'Only danger is those German buggers dropping off their bombs on the way home. That happened not twenty miles from here just before you came. Flattened half a village, killed two.'

Ag's burning face was beginning to cool. The sweat on her back was drying. Mr Lawrence drew deeply on his cigarette. The smoke smelt pungent, good. A churring and a flapping of wings behind them broke the silence. A speckled bird flew into the sky, swerving towards the copse.

'Bugger me if it's not a mistlethrush, a storm cock. Haven't seen one for a week or so,' said Mr Lawrence. He gave a small smile. 'I used to know the Latin name.'

Ag paused. Then she said: '*turdus viscivorus*, isn't it?'

'That's right. That's it! Stone the crows – are you a scholar?'

Ag laughed. 'Far from it. But my father used to teach me about birds.'

'Know some of its other names?'

'I know shrite, and skite.'

'How about gawthrush?'

'Gawthrush, yes. And garthrush?'

'Then there's the more common jercock: Ratty talks of jercocks.'

'How about syecock?'

'I'd forgotten syecock.' Mr Lawrence stubbed out his cigarette. 'So you know your birds,' he said quietly. 'That's good. That's quite unusual, these days.' He smiled. 'Here's a bit of rum information for you: did you know there's a saying that a mistletoe berry won't germinate till it's passed through the body of a mistlethrush?'

'I've heard of that, yes. I think the idea came from the Roman writer Pliny.'

The expression on Mr Lawrence's face made Ag bite her lip.

'Did it, now? There's university education for you.' He stood up brusquely, took up his bill-hook. Ag feared she

77

had offended him in some way. Perhaps the airing of such arcane knowledge sounded boastful. 'Joe got into Cambridge, you know,' Mr Lawrence said, back to her, surveying the hedge again. 'Rotten luck he wasn't able to go.'

Two hours later Ag had cleared several yards of ditch, and had made a large pile of undergrowth for burning. Her back ached horribly. Despite thick socks, her feet were cold in her Wellingtons from standing in the stream, and a blister seared her heel. Reluctant to say she had had enough for one morning, she remembered a promise to Mrs Lawrence.

'I said I'd bring in the eggs before lunch. Would it be all right –?'

'Off you go,' shouted Mr Lawrence, no pause in his slashing at a root. 'Thanks for the help. You've done pretty well.'

Ag hobbled back down the lane, coarse wool chafing her blister. She was hot, sweating, tired, hungry. The thought of a whole afternoon's hedging was daunting, though perhaps lunch would recharge her. Hedging and ditching were hard work, she thought, but she had enjoyed it. She had enjoyed her bird conversation with Mr Lawrence: funny man – sudden spurts of talk, then back to long, concentrated silences.

As soon as Ag reached the barn she sat on a pile of straw and began to pull at her boot. As she struggled, she wondered if there was any valid excuse for sending a postcard to Desmond. She knew instinctively, from the few brief conversations they had had, he would enjoy hearing about her life as a land girl. But what excuse would she have to write to him in the first place? He might not even remember her – despite her explanation about her odd name. He might have no recollection of their occasional meetings, which he believed were by chance. To write would perhaps embarrass, confuse, or, worse, warn him off an unwanted affection on Ag's part. So the answer to the question she asked herself was *no*: she should not write to him. Wait till it was time for a Christmas card.

Depressed by the solution she had known for days she would come to, Ag looked up to see Joe watching her.

'Can I help?' he asked. 'Looks as if you're having a bit of trouble.'

'Thanks.'

Ag lifted her leg. Joe pulled at the boot with both hands. It came off easily.

'You should put fresh chalk inside,' he said. 'We've got some in the house. Makes them much easier to get off and on.'

'Right. I will.'

'How did the hedging go?'

'I enjoyed it. I liked watching your father. His skill and speed are amazing. And I liked looking back to see the job I'd done on the few yards of ditch. Certain feeling of job satisfaction. I can agree with him there.'

'Looks as though Prue's experiencing some of that, too. She's managed a third of the field but refuses to stop till she's finished the lot. As a matter of fact, she's done rather well.'

They both smiled. Joe sat down opposite Ag. He watched her as she rolled off her thick wool sock, and the thin one beneath it. He watched her bending the leg so that she could look closely at the blister on her heel.

'It must be a funny contrast, this life, with Cambridge,' he said eventually.

Ag shrugged. She touched the soft swelling with a gentle finger.

'Well, that had come to an end anyway. I only half wanted to do a graduate course. I wasn't really sure what I wanted to do, in fact. Farm work gives me plenty of time to think.'

'I was due to go to Trinity,' said Joe.

'You still could, couldn't you? When all this is over.'

'Suppose I still could. Though I don't much fancy being a mature undergraduate.'

'Lots of others will be in the same position.'

'True. Meantime, the brain's rotting.'

'No!' Ag smiled.

'It is. When do I have time to read? It's a sixteen-hour day here. I listen to music on my gramophone when I'm in bed – five minutes later I'm asleep, book in hand.'

'I know what you mean.'

'So I might have to ask your help for some mental limbering up.'

'Fine! Sunday afternoons I could tutor you in the *Iliad*.' They both laughed. 'That is, if Janet wouldn't mind.'

'Janet's not here many Sundays.'

Joe got up and moved closer to Ag. He bent down, took her heel from her hand, gazed at the blister intently as a doctor preparing his opinion.

'Nasty. Ask Ma for something. Best cover it up.' He handed back her foot. 'You must have the smallest ankles in the world,' he said.

Ag laughed again, and put the socks back on.

'Sticks, my legs,' she said. 'I was dreadfully teased at school.' She made to get up. Joe put a hand under her elbow to help. 'Thanks. I promised your mother I'd collect the eggs from the barn . . .'

'I'll do that. You go on in, see to the blister.'

'Sure?'

'Sure.' Joe moved away. 'I'll be quicker than you. I know all their favourite places.'

'Thanks very much.'

'It'll cost you something.'

'My reflections on the *Iliad*? Really? Any time you like.'

Joe nodded. He cradled two brown eggs in his hand, that he had plucked from a hiding place. 'To begin with,' he said.

For the space of her hobbled journey back across the

farmyard, Ag thought about Joe. Was it disappointment about Cambridge that made him so gruff? Was it the punishment of asthma upon his youth and regret at his inability to join the war? Or was he by nature an unforthcoming and gloomy figure? And why – perhaps an unnecessary question – did Janet's presence on Sunday do nothing to cheer his spirits? For her own part, Ag would be delighted to find a kindred spirit with whom she could share ideas. She rather fancied herself bringing succour to the starved soul of Joe Lawrence. It was the sort of thing that would appeal to Desmond's humour. In fact, Desmond would hardly fail to be interested in the whole curious Lawrence family of Hallows Farm . . . If he responded to her Christmas card, she would write to him in the New Year. It would be an excitement she instantly imagined herself looking forward to.

Ag began to compose a description of the very gradual unbending of father and son, and of the strong and dignified figure of the woman who gently tended her blister, for whom, already, Ag felt considerable affection.

That afternoon, after milking with Stella, Joe walked down to the field where his father and Ag were still working on the hedge. He helped Ag drag the heavier stuff to the large pile of wood and bramble that would be burned before nightfall. None of them spoke. The quietness of the autumn afternoon was broken by the soft-edged sound of Mr Lawrence's slasher among thorn leaves: the snapping of small twigs, the drag of leafy branches over hard ground. Ag, proud of the length of her cleared ditch, could smell the pungency of her own sweat. She found herself working harder and faster than she had in the morning. Her blister no longer stung, her back no longer ached. The nearness of the earth affected her, as it did at home: the cloud of distant war was dissipated in the low light of the late sun, the long shadows thrown by the hedge, field, copse and men. *Oh, Desmond,* she thought.

At five, Mr Lawrence laid down his tools. 'Time for burning,' he said.

Joe took a box of matches from his pocket, bent down to light the base of the bonfire. In seconds it had caught, flames leaping high among the dry crackling stuff, their yellow matching a few high clouds in the sky.

They stood watching, Joe close to Ag, soon feeling the warmth. Ag had no idea how long the three of them remained there, unmoving: but suddenly she was aware of Mrs Lawrence and Stella at the gate. They carried a basket full of tin mugs, and a large thermos.

'Tea,' called Mrs Lawrence. 'We thought it might be welcome.'

Indeed, by now a thin sharp prickle of chill, intimation of a cold autumn ahead, had crept round Ag's body like a frame, while the centre of her being was still warm and sweating from her labours. She was glad of the hot, sweet tea, and of the flames on her face.

By the time Prue arrived the sun was low. Violet clouds were adrift among the yellow – gathering, consolidating, putting up an impenetrable defence against the last of the light.

Prue's entrance on the scene, catching the last webs of light, was impeccably timed. She prettily climbed the gate, scarlet bow bobbing on curls whose blonde rallied with a last shimmer.

'*Field's finished*, all! How about that?' She did not try to conceal her pride.

Mrs Lawrence handed her a mug of tea. 'Well done,' she said.

But Prue was looking for other praise. She cocked her head at Joe.

'You didn't think I could do it, did you?'

'I didn't have any opinion, as far as I remember.'

'Like to come and see my furrows? Straight as a die.'

'I will later.'

'It'll be dark in a minute. If you don't come now, it'll be too late.'

Joe slashed the fire. The confetti of ash made by his stick briefly arched before falling to the ground. The tiny red eyes went out as they touched the earth.

'Then I'll come in the morning,' he said.

'You mean beast, Joe Lawrence.' Prue stamped her foot. Ag saw she was near to tears.

'Will my opinion do, child?' Mr Lawrence asked with a smile.

'Suppose so. God, I'm hungry as a dog, aching all over, juddering from that bloody seat. My whole body's juddering still – do you realise?' Prue's petulance made everyone uneasy.

Again she looked at Joe. He concentrated on more bashing of the flames.

'Calm down,' said Mr Lawrence. 'We'll all come and see your handiwork. Joe can take back the tools.'

As Joe went to pick them up, Ag turned to tell him she had left hers some way along the ditch. As she did so, she saw Ratty leaning over the gate, his face flame-pale under a dark hat. She felt a moment's fear: the unexpected sight of him, the anguish in his face.

'Ratty!' she called. 'Come and have some tea.'

Mrs Lawrence, too, turned to the gate. But Ratty had already gone.

'He can smell a bonfire five miles off,' Mrs Lawrence said. 'He never misses one.'

'Come on, you lot. Please. My ploughing –'

Prue impatiently opened the gate. Mrs Lawrence gathered empty mugs into her basket. All but Joe followed Prue into the lane. He remained behind to quell the fire, knock out the last remaining flames, and to spread the embers to die in the cool of the evening that was now falling fast.

Four

Edith Tyler was the first to congratulate herself on
making her war effort. In Hinton Half Moon she
led the way, when the rallying call came, to hand in
aluminium saucepans to make Spitfires. She left herself
just a kettle, a frying pan and one small saucepan, and
thrived on the difficulties that this heroic parsimony
caused.

Generous, noble and honourable though Ratty was
often forced to agree she had been, the culinary inconvenience they now had to put up with fired him with an
irritation that often he could not control. Lack of kitchen
implements became the most frequent reason for their
quarrels. In Edith's relish of these rows Ratty was able to
discern a malicious pleasure in taunting him that, he
feared, might not cease even when the war was over. He
increasingly suspected that victory would not be celebrated
by Edith re-stocking with saucepans, and she would make
some new excuse to keep the kitchen under-supplied.

On the evening of the bonfire, Ratty walked home with
slow, reluctant step. He had set out, lured by the sweet
smell of thorn smoke, to enjoy himself: he always enjoyed
a bonfire. But he had arrived too late. By the time he
reached the gate a tableau was in place round the flames.
He felt that to enter would be to interrupt, to intrude.
Nothing unusual about the sight of the boss and Mrs L., of
course: it was the girls who had cast their spell. Unseen,

Ratty had gazed for a few moments on their fresh young faces, eyes full of the sort of wonder that never dulls when confronted by flames, and a million unspeakable regrets had gathered in his breast mysteriously as the swifts overhead were gathering in the sky. What were those regrets? Ratty had not liked to question himself too deeply: something to do with missed chances, unfulfilled love, wasted youth. The tall one with the short, dark hair – Ag – she was the one who had nearly been his undoing . . . the way she called to him asking him to join them – thoughtful, kind, such sweetness in her unformed face, lighted by the flames. He would almost call it holy.

Ratty had been tempted to hurry to her side, accept a mug of tea from Mrs L., join the magic circle. But even as he put a hand on the latch to open the gate, he knew he could go no further: he would be committing himself to too much enjoyment, a sensation Ratty had guarded himself against for years. He had learned from experience: on the occasions he had allowed himself unexpected moments of deep happiness, the return to reality, the barrenness of his life, had been too cruel.

So now he walked the lane, through a rising ground mist, with mixed feelings. On the one hand, he would have liked so much to have been part of the brief group, the fire a symbol of triumph at the end of a hard day's work. On the other, he knew that had he allowed himself to do this, the inevitable homecoming, and Edith's sneering, would have added further pain to his corroded heart.

Edith! Ratty saw her face in the evening sky, jaws working furiously in response to some imagined insult, unfairness or domestic difficulty. Was it his fault that she had turned so swiftly into one of life's enemies? When Ratty reached the cottage he paused for a moment on the front path, looking into the lighted window of the kitchen. Why hadn't the bloody woman put up the blackout? He had to tell her every day. They'd already been reprimanded by

the warden a couple of times. Why couldn't she understand the necessity of any war effort, or cooperation,
beyond saucepans for Spitfires? The selfish cow . . . Ratty
could see her at the sink, peeling potatoes with the same
defensive hunch as she darned, making the knife, like the
needle, seem fierce as a dagger. And why weren't the
bloody potatoes *on*, cooking? Ratty's hunger was a twisting
fist in his stomach. He went in.

'No, your tea's not ready yet so there's no use looking
like that,' was Edith's greeting. The smell of frying bacon
increased Ratty's hunger. 'Potatoes not boiled yet,' she
added triumphantly, 'then there's the carrots to do. I don't
know how you expect me to get it all up together, just the
single saucepan . . .'

'If we had just one more . . .' Ratty trailed off. He knew
any such suggestion was a waste of breath.

'The command from the government was: give up your
saucepans for Spitfires.'

'It wasn't a command,' Ratty sighed.

'Good as. Besides, if I bought another one I'd have to
give *that* up, wouldn't I? Logic. Bare necessities are what
we've got to put up with. Hardships of war. No point grumbling.'

'Is there a cup of tea while we're waiting?'

'*Tea*, Ratty Tyler? Don't you listen to a word I say? I told
you last night: I said now there's rationing we've got to cut
down to three cups a day. There's a war on.' She began to
scrape carrots. 'We've got to do our bit. There'll be
rewards. A week or so ago, when that Spitfire flew over, I
left the shop to watch it. Noisy thing. Still, I thought,
Spitfires are defending our country, and if it hadn't been
for my own very small effort – just the six saucepans and
cooking pots – that very Spitfire might not be there now. It
might have been held up in the factory, waiting for a bit
more aluminium to make the tip of the wing. For all I
knew, my saucepans were a small part of the undercarriage

of the plane that was going over our house. That gave me a good feeling, I can tell you. That made me more determined than ever it's not our business to grumble if the carrots have to take their turn with the potatoes. Trouble is, you've got no vision. You can't see things like that.'

'I'll go and deal with the blackout,' said Ratty. '*My* war effort,' he muttered under his breath.

Later, sensing the vegetables were still far from ready, Ratty went to sit in the chilly front room to listen to ITMA on the wireless. But, distracted, he turned the sound down low, hardly listening. Instead, his eyes fell on the framed photograph of Edward – Edward Tyler, their only son, killed in action in the last war.

Stored in boxes in the attic were bundles of letters from Edward, written from the trenches, many of their envelopes mud-splattered. Strangely, neither mud nor ink had faded. Ratty knew most of these letters by heart. The descriptions of a soldier's life were so extraordinarily vivid that Ratty felt he had shared the experience of every sensation with his son: sometimes he used to think Edward would be a writer when the war was over. He had the talent, surely. Ratty never mentioned this to Edith: she would have scoffed at so unmanly a suggestion. She probably had no idea the letters still existed. Unsentimental woman. Ratty had found her screwing up Edward's letters as she read them. If it hadn't been for Ratty's secret hoarding, there would be no voice, no words from Edward left. Edith even threw away the official letter that came to announce Edward had been mentioned in despatches. Ratty would never forgive her for that. Her lack of pride in her own son's courage was proof of her paucity of imagination: she was unable to understand or picture the horror, the fear, the bravery of a life unknown to her. She had never been able to read a face, a heart, a soul.

And what a funny old war, this one, compared with the last one, thought Ratty. So much of it, to date, had been spent in suspense and anticipation since the Polish invasion. The Battle of Britain had meant a little excitement and anxiety for six weeks: the Blitz in London, for all its horrors, had little effect on the rest of the country. Raids on the south coast were rare. In rural areas what you were left with were the frustrations of wartime regulations: rationing and blackouts, shortages of farm workers and clock menders – Ratty's broken alarm clock caused him great sadness when he discovered every clock mender for twenty miles had been called up. Indeed, here in Dorset you could be forgiven for thinking the war did not exist. The only thing that never faded, through every waking hour of the day, and troubled the dreams at night, was the tension, the constant anticipation of unknown possibilities. If Edward had lived, Ratty would have enjoyed discussing the two wars, the philosophical aspects of the loathsome thrill of danger, the peculiar pulling together of people by a common cause.

Ah! Ratty would have enjoyed discussing that and a thousand other subjects that held no interest for his wife. If Edward had lived – wife and family nearby, maybe, grandchildren coming to their grandfather to learn the ways of the land – life might have been very different. As it was, all Ratty could do was to try to carry out his son's last wish. In a letter that Edward had not known would be his last, in which he had been full of his usual humour, optimism and hope, he had ended with the binding words *Take care of Mum till I come back, Dad* . . . Which meant, when Edward was blown up a week later, take care of Edith for ever.

'So there you are,' she scoffed, standing at the door, interrupting his reflections. 'One moment you're grumbling because the food's not ready, then when it's on the table you've vanished.'

Ratty got up. He was no longer hungry.

'What've the girls been up to?' Edith sniffed.

'The tall one was hedging with Mr L. That's all I know. There was a bonfire this evening.'

'Huh! Trust you not to miss a bonfire.'

'I didn't stay.'

'I should hope not. Standing round bonfires when there's work to be done.'

Ratty, tired, tried to deflect her mind from the girls. By now he had learned to his cost that they were a lethal subject.

'It's been uncannily quiet for a week or so, hasn't it?' he offered. 'I've got a feeling in my bones there's going to be a raid, soon. Something's going to happen.'

'If your bones are as full of silly feelings as your head, then there's nothing to fear,' said Edith. 'All gloom and doom as normal. I don't know what you're talking about.'

She handed him a plate of bacon rashers, boiled potatoes and carrots. She watched eagerly as he pushed his knife into the underdone vegetables, testing. Just as eagerly she waited for him to complain, her answer about Spitfires all ready to shout him down. But Ratty, no fight left in him this evening, had his own, small revenge.

'Very good,' he said.

At supper that night at Hallows Farm, Stella thought she detected a smell of thorn smoke that clung to them all, more powerful than the smell of rabbit stew and mashed swede. By now she was used to the dining-room, with its clumsy dark furniture and ugly light, and, during the day, often found herself looking forward to the suppers there, Mrs Lawrence's huge plates of food filling their hungry stomachs. There were still silences at meals, but they were easier. Sometimes a proper discussion flowered, and there was laughter. Mrs Lawrence would reminisce about her childhood on a farm in Devon; her husband would sometimes mention his concern for his brother Robert, who farmed in Yorkshire, and was suffering from terminal cancer; Prue would spend time between courses examining her hands, which she claimed were a dreadful red from the Lavalord that went into the bottle-washing water.

'Blow me down if I don't end up a *fright*, all this manual labour,' she would complain. 'Raw hands, filthy nails, weather-beaten skin, stinking of cow muck . . . Will there be a man in the world left to want me?'

This last question, with a slight cock of the head in Joe's direction, observed by Stella and Ag, was ignored by Joe who always made the minimum contribution to the meal.

Tonight, Mr Lawrence, after a day at his favourite occupation, and filled with the agreeable thought of further hedging tomorrow, was in rare good humour.

'Tomorrow,' he said, 'it's time to be rewarded for your first week's good work with an entirely new sort of job – the kind of job every land girl in the country most probably dreams of. Can you imagine what that might be, Prue?'

Prue, in a pink crochet jersey with tiny crystal beads sewn to its collar, blushed.

'Why you should pick on me for an idea, I can't think,' she smiled back. 'Still, if I had to say . . . I'd say a day on a tractor with a nice little shelter to protect me from the wind and rain, and a velvet padded seat.'

Mr Lawrence laughed. 'Out of luck, I'm afraid. No: tomorrow it's dagging, and checking for foot rot. Sheep.'

'It's *what*? And what?' Prue's expression of horror was comical.

The Lawrence family exchanged glances. Joe tried to suppress a smile.

'It's not one of the pleasantest jobs, and it doesn't have to happen that often, but everyone should know how to do it,' explained the farmer. 'You have to keep a check on the sheep's feet, pare the hoof if necessary. Don't worry: I'm an experienced instructor. Got young Joe down to the job at twelve or thirteen, didn't I, son?'

'And what's the other thing?' asked Prue.

'Dagging,' said Joe. 'I was doing that not long out of my cradle, wasn't I, Mother? Dad found me some special small shears.'

Joe, Stella could see, was beginning to enjoy himself.

'I think,' said Mrs Lawrence, handing round plates of steamed ginger pudding, 'you could explain that, John, when the time comes. I don't want people put off their food.'

There was a moment's silence, then Joe cast his eyes towards Prue. She met his glance at once.

'I can see you're dying to know,' he said. 'So here goes. Dagging, in a word, is cutting the dried shit off a sheep's backside.'

The shocked silence was quickly broken by the laying down of astonished spoons. Ag laughed, but was at once cut off by a whiplash look from Mrs Lawrence.

'Joe!'

'Sorry, Mother.'

Prue was smothering a giggle in her hands. 'Well, I tell you what, Joe, Mr Lawrence,' she said. 'Count me out. A girl has to draw a line somewhere, and if you think I'm going to cut shit off a sheep's bum you can think again. I'd rather . . .' she tried to think of some slightly less horrendous task – 'I'd rather *clean out the pig*.'

'You do what you're told, my girl,' snapped Mr Lawrence, his good humour suddenly gone. 'If you're so keen on cleaning out the pig, you can take that job over from Faith once you've finished the dagging.'

The girls had never known him so stern and darkly flushed. He picked up his spoon and plunged it into his pudding again. The others, all but Prue, followed his example. She looked down at her uneaten sponge, suddenly pale, and gasped.

'Oh my God! I've forgotten something.' She stood, addressed Joe. 'I've forgotten to put the sacking over the tractor engine.'

91

'Did you remember to drain the radiator?'

' 'Course I remembered to drain the radiator.'

'Then it's not that serious,' Joe said.

'Sit down, it can wait till we've finished eating.' Mr Lawrence's anger still simmered.

'I'll give you a hand.' Joe was less brusque than his father.

'I don't want a hand, thanks.'

Prue left the room at a run.

'Stupid girl,' said Mr Lawrence, and shouted through the door that there was a torch on the dresser.

The night was cool and hazy. A diluted moon cast greenish light over sauntering clouds, too feeble to light the farmyard. Prue hurried across to the barn, the beam of the torch paddling like a single oar over the muddy ground and piles of dung.

Even in the darkness the security of the barn touched her: the smells of hay, chaff, sacking; the scurrying of mice in the straw, the purring of sleepy pigeons in the rafters. The tractor, in silhouette, was an enormous queenly hunk in this softly shining kingdom, old mudguards spread like proud but ailing skirts. Prue put a hand on the engine. The metal was icy cold, but not frozen. She found two or three sacks and covered it. She'd remembered everything else: how could she have forgotten this last, essential act?

Prue switched off her torch, moved towards a dim bank of stacked straw. She climbed until she was higher than the tractor, could look down on it and the farmyard beyond. In her hurry she had forgotten her coat. Although she had changed out of her working shirt and jersey for supper, she had kept on her breeches, thick socks and shoes. So only her arms were cold. But she didn't want to go back. Not just yet.

She clutched her arms under her breasts, rested her head on her corduroy knees. The feeling that prevailed was anger – anger with herself. The last thing she had wanted to do was make Mr Lawrence angry: her reaction to the dagging had been half in jest – surely he could have seen that? Of course she would have cleaned the blinking sheep's bum without a murmur when the time came – but a girl is entitled to make a protest, even if there is a war on. She wanted very hard to prove herself, guessing what farmers must think of hairdressers. But it wasn't easy. She'd spent ten hours ploughing that field, no stop for lunch or tea, furrows straight as a die – and what praise did she get? None. Not a word. Great reluctance on the part of the Lawrences even to come and look at her handiwork. Mr Lawrence had just stood by the gate, muttered 'Looks all right to me,' and had moved away when his wife had nodded, supposedly in agreement. They were cross with her, of course. Cross about Joe. And Janet. But if it hadn't been for Stella and Ag, almost too extravagant in their praise and amazement, Prue would have burst into tears. Just the tiniest bit of appreciation from the Lawrences was all she had wanted: the understanding of what it took for a girl used to doing permanent waves, in a warm and cosy salon full of chattering customers, suddenly to spend a whole day carving up acres of bitter earth, alone. At the thought of the salon, Prue began to cry.

She realised, in this first moment really to think since she had arrived, that she was homesick. She missed her mum: that funny, warm, bleached-haired, spoiling lady, buoyed by eternal optimism and nightly gin, never quite sunk by disillusion. She missed the local gossip, the northern jokes, the laughter, the intricate schemes for making do – her mum was a genius in that respect. Just before leaving home, Prue had been asked to a charity tea-dance in aid of the Home Guard: in a trice Mum had run up a beautiful dress made from left-over blackout stuff. She had stuck it with sequins and Christmas tree tinsel, swore it would look almost like ostrich feathers under the electric light. The next morning, when Prue presented the blackout dress ripped of its decorations (an impatient pair of RAF hands had quickly seen to that) – well, they'd had a laugh.

They had agreed, Prue and her mother, not to say in their stilted, badly spelled letters how much they missed each other: it would be too painful. But they both knew. God, how Prue longed to hear her voice, to be back in the *smallness* of things at home: the salon, the small terraced house, the back row of the picture palace just down the road. Here, there were such houseless miles, such silence – except for the tractor, whose grunting Prue found a comfort. And indoors, for all Mrs Lawrence's hard work, there were no . . . what Prue would call *nice touches*: no aspidistra in a copper bowl, no crochet antimacassars, no wooden clock carved to look like a setting sun, no Victorian tins with their Christmas pictures of ruddy children with toboggans and holly, or coaches and horses. For some reason, Prue missed the sterile little kitchen with her mother's collection of biscuit tins more than anything.

She raised her hand, sniffing, to be dazzled by the beam of a powerful torch. It quickly moved to one side. Prue could make out the figure of Joe standing by the tractor.

'So there you are,' he said. 'Tractor covered, I see. Coming down?'

'Soon.'

Joe banged one of his jacket pockets. 'I've got a Mars bar.'

Prue giggled. Her tears dried. Biscuit tins fled.

'Where did you find that? There aren't any in the village.'

'I have my sources. I'm stocking up against sweet rationing. Come on down and I'll give you a bit.'

'You come up here. Why not? It's warmer.'

'If you insist.'

In a few huge, climbing steps, Joe was beside her. It was almost completely dark: she could only just make out the blunt edges of his profile. There was a strong smell of animal on his boots. Vaguely, she could see him take the Mars from his pocket, strip off its paper wrapping which crackled thinly as finest taffeta, and hold it out to her. She felt almost faint with desire for a taste of the chocolate.

'Got a knife?' she asked.

'No. Can't you just bite a bit off?'

He pushed it at her. Duskily, their hands met. She took it from him. Unable to see how far she was biting, she aimed for a modest length. The sweetness of the toffee, malt and chocolate was more delicious than any taste of Mars she had ever known.

'Thanks,' she said, smudgily, mouth full. 'That's absolute heaven on earth, that is. That'll have me working, resting, playing, *dagging*, like nothing you've ever seen.'

For the third time, Joe laughed, firing Prue's confidence. Somewhere in the dark she recognised the outline of her chance.

'Aren't you cold?' he asked, after a while.

'Not really.' Prue shivered, not entirely from the cold. 'Where do you go most evenings? We've all been trying to guess.'

There was a long pause before Joe answered.

'Walk up to The Bells, have a couple of pints with my friend Robert. We talk. Nothing very exciting.'

'That all? I imagined something very different.'

'I bet you did. Robert owns a farm nearby. Like me, he can't be called up for medical reasons. Like me, he's stuck on the farm all day, no one to talk to.'

'There's us, now,' said Prue, after a while.

'I suppose there is. But I'm not used to that idea, yet.'

'You're not easy to talk to, actually, are you? Pretty surly, on the whole.' Prue turned on him with a sweet smile, hoping his eyes had grown accustomed to the darkness and it would not be wasted.

'Surly? Me? Strange idea. Reflective, more, I would have said. More Mars?'

Again their hands briefly touched as she took the half bar, bit off another modest share.

'Thanks. Well, you're not at all surly tonight. First time.'

'I expect you find it all a bit strange, don't you? There's so much to do, I dare say we're all rather preoccupied. It must be very different from your normal life.'

'It is, of course. But I rather like it.'

'It's tough work.'

'I don't mind that.'

'Some pretty disagreeable. Wait till it's your turn to do the pig.'

Prue was colder, now. She clutched her arms more tightly about her.

'What I wanted, you know, was to be in a circus. That was my childhood dream. I used to practise little bits of acrobatic stuff from about five onwards. I used to put a plank between two chairs and call it my tightrope. I could do a backwards somersault from standing, when I was eight. I'd go to every circus I could – not many, mind – and long to be one of those acrobats in sequins. But my dad put his foot down, said no daughter of his was going into a circus. I went on practising whenever I had a chance, but then the enthusiasm sort of went.'

She sensed Joe turning towards her, interested.

'I walked a plank about twelve feet high, once. Never a real tightrope.'

'Could you have gone higher?'

'Easy. Just never had the chance.' She gave a small sigh.

'Here's your chance, then.' Joe stirred. He switched on his torch, lighting a crossbeam high above their heads. 'Bet you couldn't walk that.'

Prue studied the huge beam of blackened wood. It was wide enough, but many times the height of anything she had ever tried before. Disturbed by the torchlight, pigeons in the rafters broke into murmurous complaints.

'Ooh, Joe. How'd I get up?'

'There's a ladder. If you fell you wouldn't come to much harm – all this hay and straw. Besides, I'd catch you . . .' He swung the beam of the torch so that half Prue's face was lighted. 'Don't do it if you don't want to. I just thought it might be a lark.'

Prue looked into the deep, complicated shadows of his face.

'What would you think if I said yes, if I had a go?' she asked.

'Well, I don't know. I suppose I'd think you were rather brave.'

'Switch off the torch, then.'

'Why? I'll have to light your way very carefully.'

'Just for the moment. I want to take my shoes and socks off. I don't want you watching that.'

Joe turned off the torch. The darkness, renewed, seemed deeper. While Prue fumbled with her laces and pulled off her woollen socks, she heard Joe finish the Mars.

'Right?'

'I'm ready.'

'I'll help you down, put up the ladder. Sure you want to do this?'

' 'Course.' Prue's voice was light.

Joe jumped down to the ground, put out a steadying hand to help Prue scramble after him. They landed close together by the tractor. Prue touched its mudguard, steadying herself. Her heart was battering. She was no longer cold.

'Pity there's no fanfare of trumpets,' Joe said. 'Really, you need trumpets.'

Prue cocked her head, again hoping the wan light of the moon would be just strong enough to illuminate her devil-may-care expression.

'That's the nicest thing you've ever said to me,' she said. '*You need trumpets*. I shall always remember that: *you need trumpets*.' She was surprised by the shakiness of her voice.

'Come on, silly.' Joe touched her shoulder. 'I'll get the ladder.'

Here on the floor of the barn she was better able to see the large dark figure of Joe as he collected the ladder and propped it up against one end of the beam. Then he lit his torch again, flashed it up the rungs.

'All right?'

'Fine.'

Prue moved to join him, straw and rubble of the floor troubling the soles of her feet. She trembled with excitement, with fear.

'Don't worry about the ladder. I'll hold it firm. Then I'll keep the beam of the torch just ahead of you.'

'Okay.'

Prue took hold of the ladder's sides, put a foot on the first rung.

'Imagine the trumpets,' said Joe quietly.

Prue began to climb.

For the first time since she had been at Hallows Farm, Ag felt restless. Neither the news nor her book could fully engage her attention. In the sitting-room, where Mrs Lawrence made progress with a pair of socks for the troops, and Mr Lawrence sat with head tipped back, eyes shut, Ag studied the mauve-blue of the flames as they hissed up through a pile of damp logs. It was too early to go up to the bedroom. Besides, she did not want to disturb Stella in her letter-writing. Ag believed in protecting people's need to be alone: she was always at pains not to intrude. She could not be sure of what she wanted to do, where she wanted to go. Some vague anxiety about Prue assailed her, and then a larger worry seared: she had shut up the chickens, but not the bantams. Dear God, how could she have forgotten? Just like Prue, she had failed over a vital matter. Dreadful pictures flashed into her mind: the corpses of fox-chewed bantams littering the yard in the morning: Mr Lawrence's anger, Mrs Lawrence's sadness, disappointment . . . they would be unbearable. She would never forgive herself, such stupidity . . . *Never disappoint* had been her father's unofficial motto, branded deep into her since childhood. Here she was, just one week into her job, about to disappoint deeply.

Ag put down her book and swiftly left the room, whispering goodnight to Mrs Lawrence.

Outside, she found the denseness of the night confusing. No stars were visible. The moon, elusive in wandering clouds, would give ghostly light for a moment, then disappear again, leaving total blackness. Ag had a torch in her pocket, but determined not to use it till she reached the bantam house. You had to be so careful about light after dark, Mr Lawrence had warned them. She made her way cautiously through the garden. Unseen branches brushed at her face and snagged her arms. Despite the firmness of the ground, there was a sense of drowning. The sudden hoot of an owl made her heart race: she dreaded what would surely be a long hunt under hedges for the bantams.

Far sooner than she expected a familiar smell of creosoted wood came to her out of the darkness and she ran to the henhouse. She switched on her torch, slid the door of the peephole to one side. Inside were all ten roosting hens, heads drawn down into raised neck feathers, giving them a look of unconscious indignation. A couple of them, disturbed by the torchlight, began a minor, sleepy clucking. Ten pairs of wrinkled eyelids quivered, but none of them quite opened.

Ag moved away to the bantam house. She switched off her torch at the sudden return of the moon. In its brief light the wire netting, nailed to the wooden frame of the run, looked fragile as cobwebs. There were no birds in the run. The door was ajar, just as she had left it when she had let them out this morning. Ag closed it, shone her torch through the peephole of the house. To her amazement, there were birds inside, huddled more closely than the chickens, their feathers a grainy sheen. Five of them had returned to the fold on their own: just one was missing.

Ag's feelings of relief at the safety of the five were clouded with anxiety about the missing one. She hurried back through the garden, torch beam discreetly sweeping the ground, but with little hope of finding the bird here. The barn, she thought, would be the most obvious place. The bantams always congregated in the barn by day. It often took a while to flush them all from their hiding places when it was time to shut them up at night.

According to the restless rhythms of tonight's sky, it was the turn of darkness again when Ag reached the farmyard. She made swiftly for the barn. From halfway across the yard she saw a slash of torchlight inside. She stopped, straining to hear muted voices. *Have you seen a bantam in there?* she wanted to shout: but then her concern for the bantam was overwhelmed by curiosity, fear, dread. What was happening? She slowed her steps.

By the time she gained the barn's entrance, Ag could hear exchanged words clearly.

'Sure you're all right?'

Long pause. 'I'm fine. It's fun up here.'

It was *Prue*, for heaven's sake, with Joe.

'You're doing well. Not much further.'

Ag flattened herself against the outside wall of the barn, peered round. She saw Joe, back to her, looking up, torch trained to somewhere high above him. As her eyes grew accustomed to the dim scene she could see shadows huge as sails flapping at the walls of the barn, their shapes cut into by the expanding beam of torchlight that showed Prue – dear God, the fool, the fool – engaged on some flight of madness in the rafters . . .

Ag turned away, clasping her hand to her mouth.

'Well done, you're over half way,' she heard Joe say.

Ag turned to look again. She saw Prue more clearly now, creeping along the crossbeam, arms stiffly outstretched, awkward, determined, brave. Her thin white legs were lit by the torch. Far below, Ag caught sight of thick regulation socks and heavy brown shoes cast into the hay.

She saw Prue pause, flutter, not daring to look down. Her left foot wavered, suddenly unsure where to land. The toes panicked. She was nearly at the end, where a ladder waited. But she could not make it.

She saw Prue fall into the darkness, heard her scream.

No one in the house could have heard because at the same moment a distant siren began to wail. Its mournful voice and the ragged shriek coiled together, then were split by a sound even closer to Ag as a terrified bantam ran squawking from the barn across the yard. To save? Or to protect? Ag found herself running towards the house before she had time to make a decision. She saw the door open, the figure of Mrs Lawrence holding a candle.

'I was looking for a bantam,' she cried.

'Never mind the bantam: straight down into the cellar.' Mrs Lawrence slammed the door behind Ag. 'You didn't see Joe?'

'No.'

'He must be at The Bells. Either there or on his way back.'

The siren was fading. Ag followed Mrs Lawrence down the cellar steps. Stella was already there, sitting on the floor beside a small rack of ginger wine, a pad of writing paper and a pen on her knee – scarcely interrupted, it seemed.

'You didn't see Prue?' Mrs Lawrence was brusque in her anxiety.

'She might have gone to The Bells, too. She was upset about that tractor business,' said Ag.

Mrs Lawrence gave a sharp sigh. 'Little fool,' she said.

Ag sat on the cold stone floor beside Stella.

'You all right?' Stella asked, smiling, still half-entangled by the thought of her letter.

Ag nodded. She wrapped her arms round her bent knees,

pressing them against her body, trying to extract the various feelings: the fear of bombs, the guilt at lying, the worry of the Lawrences' scorn at her inefficiency about the bantams. But far more disquieting than these was the horribly familiar feeling, experienced all too often in Cambridge when she had caught sight of Desmond in the distance – on the Backs, or passing through a quad – with another girl. *That*, at least, was understandable, loving him as she did.

But with Desmond miles away, unaware of her love, hope of anything ever bringing them together almost dead . . . why had jealousy followed her to Hallows Farm? And what, when the horror of the night was over, would it mean?

To Prue, falling into darkness, the siren was part of her own scream. How could such a huge and terrifying sound emerge from her own small throat? In the immeasurable moments as she plummeted down into the hay, that was her only thought.

Part of her thumped against another body. There were arms supporting her, though her legs seemed to be far away, detached from her body, one knee spinning in agony. Then the arms encased her more firmly. She was lying on her back. Hay spiked through the fragile crochet of her jersey. The knee had become a gold disc in her mind, spitting fire. The scream petered out, a horrible sound skulking into the distance. So it was a *siren*, not her . . .

'I caught you. I've got you.' A man's voice from somewhere, alarmed.

Who caught her? Ah, that was it! Bloody hell: *Joe* caught her. She'd wanted to be caught by Joe for a whole week, hadn't she? Hadn't imagined it would happen this way. But here he was, waterproof crackling against her bare arm. Not exactly on top of her, but she could feel his heaviness at her side.

'Thanks.'

Her head was full of sparks from an invisible anvil. They danced confusingly in front of an accumulation of shadows that was Joe's face, low over her own. One of his eyeballs was ignited with a small shard of white, then the flash of moonlight outside was gone and all was dark again.

'You all right?'

'Think so. Bit dizzy. My knee . . .' Prue tried to shift. Joe ran a hand along a corduroy thigh, stopped at the knee. 'Think I may have twisted it. But it's my heart I'm worried about, banging away overtime.' She gave a faint giggle.

Joe's hand slipped back up the thigh, over the stomach, ribs, found its place on her heart.

'It'll calm down,' he said. 'I'm sorry. I'm really sorry. It was a stupid challenge. You could have –'

'I could've said no. Don't worry. It was fun.' Prue let his hand continue to cover her breast, calming the flurry of heartbeats. It was huge, warm, heavy as a flat-iron. 'What about the siren?' she asked.

'Raid somewhere. Or could be a false alarm.'

'Hadn't we better . . .?'

'No. They'll be in the cellar. They'll think I'm at The Bells.'

'Won't they wonder where I am?'

'Let them wonder. We'll think of some explanation.'

At this nefarious suggestion, all Prue's anxiety about the raid and her own disappearance fled. She wanted to lie in the hay with Joe for ever, not caring about anything. She put a hand on top of his, feeling the enormous rough fingers.

'Anyway, I couldn't possibly walk across the yard with this knee, could I?'

In truth it was no more than a small stab of pain now, nothing that a brisk rub and a measure of determination could not deal with – though none but a fool would assure Joe of the unserious nature of her injury just at this moment.

'I don't suppose you could, you little minx.'

The word fired her, just as it had in the cowshed. No one had ever called her a minx before. It meant pert, a flirt, a hussy – she'd looked it up, once. It was a compliment, in her book. The mass of Joe's head seemed nearer. She could feel his breath on her face. He smelt of melted chocolate.

'Are you really all right?'

'I'm really all right. Did I fall far?'

'Twenty feet or so. You'll see when I find the torch. I dropped it, struggling to catch you.'

'So much for my circus act.'

Joe withdrew slightly, moved his hand. Prue quickly retrieved it, returned it to its place.

'Don't go,' she said.

'I won't go.'

They listened to the black silence. After a while it was stirred by the churring of a rafter pigeon. They heard the distant squealing of a small plane.

'Bombs?' asked Prue. 'It'll be my first raid. Crikey: I'm terrified, Joe.' She kneaded his hand.

Then his mouth was on hers, plundering the worry. He whipped up the cobweb wool of her jersey, tugged at the stout cotton stuff of her brassiere, pulled forth a wild breast. Acting like a man in a hurry, he grabbed at the waist of her breeches. Prue wriggled to help, wires of hay burning her back with each impatient movement.

'I thought . . . you'd never get around to this.' Prue's legs, now bare, were scratched by the hay, too.

'Had to give it a week, didn't I? Little temptress, you . . .' Joe smudged the words with kisses. 'Batting your pretty green eyes at me over the udders your very first morning . . .'

'With a war on, there's no time to be lost. That's what I think.'

Prue was in a state of total deliquescence now, pliant, quivering, flaming cheeks, icy impatient limbs.

'I knew the moment you arrived exactly what you thought . . .'

Joe's mouth clamped on to Prue's again. He made a pillow under her head with one arm. His free hand worked miracles wherever it brushed, spinning her skin into whirlpools of such intense pleasure she found herself cooing in tune with the pigeons. The wondrous hand, firm as a piece of farm machinery, parted her legs. The cooing turned to whimpering as the vastness and the weight of Joe crushed the breath out of her and he, too, began to chortle and pant like a powerful engine on a cold morning. In some small independent corner of her mind, despite the state of desire to which Joe had brought her, Prue thought of the tractor and wanted to laugh.

Had bombs fallen, the lovers in the barn would have been too preoccupied to be concerned. As it was, the all clear merged with their own cries, joined the dying fall that faded into eventual silence.

'Crikey!' said Prue, at last, shifting under Joe's full dead weight.

'Your first raid. Plenty more to come.'

'Should hope so. There's a war on, isn't there? Where've you put my breeches?'

'Lost in the dark.'

'Come on, Joe. We'll be in trouble. I'll be sent away. Not having it off with the farmer's son is the land girl's number one unspoken rule.'

'If you don't tell the others, no one'll ever know.'

'Promise.'

'Tomorrow night, when they're asleep, you can creep back out here again.'

'And how'll I ever get up at five, night after night at it in the barn with you, tell me that?'

'You'll get used to it,' said Joe, stroking her hair, kissing her eyes. 'Keep still. I'm not letting you go just yet. We've only just begun.'

Some hours later, when the first light scratchings of dawn

105

appeared in the sky, they gathered up their clothes, dressed, and crept through the mists in the yard. Only Ratty saw them. Disturbed by the sirens, he had risen earlier than usual, and was making his way to the barn for an early pipe before breakfast.

Ratty managed to avoid direct confrontation by mere seconds. When he saw the couple emerge blurrily from the barn, he ducked down behind the dung heap. He could hear voices, but no words. Once they disappeared through the farmhouse door, he completed his journey to the barn. The first thing he saw, poised like a pale, windless flag in the gloom, was a white handkerchief hanging from a pile of hay. Ratty removed it, put it in his pocket. *Idiots*, he thought.

Then, settled on one of the lower stacks, pipe lit, he turned to musing about Joe. Joe had always been quite a lad – something he, Ratty, regretfully, had never been. No land girl would be safe from Joe: Ratty had known that from the start, soon as the idea of employing girls had come up. But of course it would not have been his place to have warned the boss and Mrs L. Funny they didn't think for themselves. Maybe they reckoned that Janet girl would keep Joe on the straight and narrow. Huh! some hope. Then when the girls arrived – well, Ratty guessed straight away it would only be a matter of time, Joe and the flirty flighty one. And good luck to them . . . They should fit in all they can, the young, before they're bombed to bits, was Ratty's opinion. So long as Joe stuck to that one . . . What Ratty wouldn't fancy, come to think of it, would be if he laid his hands on the tall one, Ag, the one with the holy face. If Joe had the cheek to touch *her*, and Ratty got to know about it, there'd be no accounting for his reactions. He could imagine doing something terrible to Joe: something he hadn't thought of yet, but it would come to him. It would definitely come to him . . . He clicked his pipe against his teeth, watched the paling of the sky over the farmhouse roof – going to be a fine day. Going to be a fine clear day for thinking. Why, already a plan was beginning to form in Ratty's mind.

The girls caught the two o'clock bus from Hinton Half Moon to Blandford. It was the first half-day. Each had fourteen shillings in her purse – half of their first week's pay: the other half went to Mrs Lawrence for board and lodging.

The ancient bus bumped along yellow-leafed lanes, jostling the girls in their various moods. Prue's lack of sleep was well disguised: in honour of the shopping trip she wore an emerald skirt and matching bow, and flamingo lipstick – on the grounds, she had explained to the others while they were changing, that you should be prepared for any eventuality. The eventuality she had in mind in Blandford was a chance encounter with an off-duty soldier or airman from a nearby camp.

'And what would you *do*, exactly, if this mythical man ran into us in the street?' Stella asked, intrigued.

'Get to know him before the bus back, of course,' giggled Prue, jabbing her eyelashes with thick mascara.

Ag was in unaccountably low spirits. As they chuntered through showers of falling leaves (*Yellow and black and pale and hectic red, Pestilence-stricken multitudes* came automatically to mind) she could not extinguish the picture of Prue falling from the crossbeam into the darkness, her terrified scream curdling with the siren. She could not understand why she had lied to Mrs Lawrence before there had been time to think. Nor could she understand why she had lain awake hours after the all clear, and then found the sight of Prue creeping in at dawn, dishevelled, ravished, scintillating, so disturbing. Perhaps it was envy of Prue's ability to make the whole business of men seem so easy: if a man is your target, go for him, get him. Ag could never behave like that. On further reflection, she put her melancholy

107

down to disillusion. How could Joe, a man whom she was coming to respect, be so easily misled by a shameless young hussy like Prue? It was not as if he was a *free* man, after all: he was engaged to Janet. Did Janet not come into his considerations as he gave vent to his lust in the barn?

Ag smiled to herself, knowing her weakness for the schoolmistressy phraseology that came to her in moments of disapproval: *gave vent to his lust*, indeed. They probably had a wonderful time. And was that, perhaps, the trouble? The thought of Joe and Prue achieving something she and Desmond would never have? Or was it – and here surfaced the question Ag hated to contemplate even as she saw it coming – was it because, despite her love for Desmond, she would like to know she had at least the *power* to attract Joe: to feel they were soulmates, intellectual equals, friends? Somehow his skirmish with Prue managed to scatter the normal calm of her mind. It both repelled and excited her. It also alarmed her on Janet's behalf. What would happen to Janet? Ag's mind was a whirl of questions and unsatisfactory answers. Thus preoccupied, she kept her silence, barely nodding when Prue squealed about some new item she remembered for her shopping list.

Stella, too, was quiet. The ragged autumn landscape, bronzed golds and flame yellows against mole-dark earth, was lost upon her. She was concentrating on God.

'Please make HMS *Apollo* need a boiler clean soon,' she prayed, 'because if I don't see Philip soon I don't know what I'll do . . .'

They straggled round the streets of Blandford, disappointed. The old film *Rome Express* was on at the pictures, but there was no time to see it before the bus back. Prue insisted on visiting the chemist immediately, only to be greeted by a notice on the door saying *Sorry, no lipsticks or rouges.*

'How *can* a war affect lipsticks and rouges?' she wailed,

suddenly feeling her sleepless night, and almost in tears.

Her anticipation of Revlon's new colours shattered, she trailed dismally after the other two, uninterested in their quests. Ag could not find the book she was hoping for in the library, but bought a bunch of shaggy-headed chrysanthemums for Mrs Lawrence instead. Stella gloomily stocked up on writing materials. They all felt cold: the sun's brightness concealed the raw edge of a rising wind. By four they were sitting in a tea-room of dark wooden tables and checked cloths, the windows running with condensation, passers-by outside flattened into pearly ghost shadows. Ag and Stella chose savoury mince with greens, and stewed apples and custard, for sixpence. Prue scorned their economy.

'I'm going to lash out,' she announced with a flutter of her incredible eyelashes. 'I need energy.' She ordered toad-in-the-hole, butter beans in white sauce, prunes and junket for sixpence halfpenny. They all drank orangeade. 'What I wouldn't give for a gin and lime,' sighed Prue.

The fuggy warmth of the tea-room and the steaming food revived their spirits. They threw off their cardigans, lolled back in their wheelback chairs as if, on their day off from the land, they could resume a sophisticated nonchalance. After the main course Prue offered round her Woodbines and the others, usually non-smokers, accepted. They pecked inexpertly at the wizened little cigarettes, coughing and spewing smoke in all directions. Prue, with her superior habit, was laughing by now, sipping her orangeade as reverently as if it were the dreamed-of gin and lime.

'I've got news for you, anyway,' she said, when the cigarettes were at last finished, their lipstick-printed butts squashed into the ashtray, and the stewed fruits, junkets and custards trembling in bowls before them. 'Can you guess?'

Ag concentrated on polishing her spoon with a clean handkerchief. Stella shook her head.

'I made it! *Joe*. In the barn, last night. Told you I would.' She giggled. The emerald bow bobbed in the brownish light.

'Goodness,' said Stella, in some awe.

'Should you be telling us?' asked Ag, unsurprised.

'Blimey! You're right there.' Prue clamped her hand over her mouth. 'Don't suppose I should. Though he couldn't expect me *not* to tell you.'

'He could,' said Ag. 'What about Janet? I told you you should think about Janet.'

'Enough of your lectures, Ag. *He* didn't mention Janet.'

'What did you feel about her?' Ag heard the disapproval in her voice, sharp as it had been on the Sunday walk.

'Can't say I gave her a thought. None of my business. Think that's very wicked, do you?' Prue turned to Stella.

'I think,' Stella said, thinking fast, 'you should stick very carefully to your philosophy of not upsetting apple carts. You don't want to be thrown out by the Lawrences, and cause difficulties between Janet and Joe.'

Prue shrugged. 'It's not as if they're *very* engaged, is my way of seeing it. Besides, all's fair in love and war, like I *keep* saying. What Janet doesn't know won't hurt.'

'That's not entirely the point,' said Ag. 'What if you got pregnant?'

'Don't be daft. I know how to take care of all that. Haven't been caught out yet, have I?' Prue hailed the waitress, asked for another round of orangeades. 'Anyway, now we're over the serious bit, d'you want to know what it was like?' She looked from Ag, who blushed deeply, to Stella, who could not quite disguise a look of interest. 'It all happened easy as pie. According to plan. My plan. His too, if I know anything about randy farmers' sons. And I have to tell you –' she drew herself up, squashed the bow with an emphatic hand – 'Joe Lawrence is quite a man. If you're ever feeling like it, he'd be a good start. Set a high standard to go by in the future, know what I mean?'

'Prue! You're dreadful!' Ag felt sweat on her forehead.

'You're wicked!' added Stella, laughing. 'Go on.'

'Well, he's no miniature, that's for sure. More like a bloody great stallion.'

Prue put out her hands, measuring a width to match the side of the table. Her huge, green, mascara-spiked eyes opened wide, her tiny, manicured hands were held up in angels-bending-near-to-God position. For a second she looked more like something by Fra Angelico than an over-sexed land girl, and Ag, despite herself, began to laugh. Stella joined in. Prue, looking from one to the other, see-ing they were not mocking but enjoying her account, was fired to further revelations.

'Mind you, he sounded like a bloody tractor, and cor blimey am I *crushed* this morning! But it was all good fun. Wouldn't mind a bit more any time . . .'

'You're completely incorrigible,' said Ag, still laughing.

For some reason Ag's heart had lightened: must be something to do with the fact that, whatever had gone on between Joe and Prue, she couldn't believe it was serious.

Prue was about to ask what incorrigible meant, but her attention was snatched by a young man in RAF uniform who came through the door. He had very short, gleaming fair hair and a shaven neck, features that were enhanced by the severity of his cap. Assaulted by Prue's admiring stare, he hesitated, but then made his way to a table in the win-dow – as far as possible from the girls – and ordered a cup of tea and a scone.

'How about that?' asked Prue. 'Quite promising, I'd say.'

'Stop staring,' whispered Stella.

'Your manners, Prue!' Ag heard herself being prissy again, even in laughter. She also felt reckless. In a strange way she wanted to urge Prue on, see if she would live up to her boasting. 'So what are you going to *do*?'

'Look friendly, that's all,' said Prue. She turned her head in the airman's direction, fluttered her huge lashes.

'You're shocking,' said Stella, smiling, aware of a certain admiration in her admonishment. 'Last night you seduce Joe; how could you even contemplate someone else not twenty-four hours later?'

'It pays to notch them up.' Prue slowed down the fanning of her lashes, gave a dimpled smile at the airman. 'Specially in a war.' She picked up her bag, searched for her purse. Ag, alarmed at the thought of Prue taking the next logical step, and moving to his table, asked for the bill.

'We ought to be getting back,' she said. 'We don't want to miss the last bus.'

'I wouldn't mind.' Prue dreamily counted her share of coins. 'By the way, did either of you see Joe this morning? I did the milking with Mr Lawrence. Didn't like to ask him where Joe was.'

'Mrs Lawrence said he had an asthma attack,' said Ag. 'He was in his room.'

The thought seemed to amuse Prue. 'Must have been the hay,' she said. 'We'll have to find somewhere he's not allergic to. His bed, perhaps.'

'Are you completely off your head?' Stella stood. She took Prue's arm. 'Come on, we're going. Fast.'

Dragged by the firm Stella, Prue, unable to linger at the door, cast the airman a final, signalling glance.

'Spoilsports!' she complained once they were outside.

But the complaint had no depth and once more the three of them were joined in laughter. They hurried along the streets through the sharp evening air, arms linked, drunk on orangeade and an afternoon's freedom from toiling on the land. Stella and Ag refused to let Prue pause by unlit shop windows awaiting their blackout.

'I'll come on my own next time,' she protested, 'buy some new ribbon, find my way to the RAF camp . . . Why do you think, after all Mr Lawrence's threats, there was no dagging this morning after all?'

'He was probably too busy, with Joe off,' said Stella. 'Probably be tomorrow.'

'I'm going to be the best bloody dagger in Dorset,' sang Prue. 'You'll see.'

And then all thoughts of dagging were blasted from her mind: in the bus shelter was a poster announcing a dance at a nearby RAF camp, in aid of the Merchant Navy Fund.

'Stone the crows, girls, do you see this?' she gasped. 'We're in luck! Here's something to look forward to, isn't it? Here's a chance for the diamanté, or would diamonds in Dorset be too much?'

The others bundled her up the steps of the bus and into a seat on her own. But there was no escaping her bubbling anticipation. She twisted round, lay her chin on the back of the seat that divided them, restless hand running through her curls, plucking at the wilting bow.

'What's the betting we run into Romeo of the tea-room, eh? Come on, you two fuddy duddies . . . Imagine . . .'

The bus started with a reluctant growl, moved out of the town and into dark lanes. Over the hedges and shaven fields a gun-metal sky glowed behind a grid of green-black clouds. The first evening star – the 'slippered Hesper' in Ag's mind – was bright. A dance in an RAF camp was the last thing she wanted to imagine: nothing would persuade her to go. She would have liked to have been alone in the bus, watching the darkness gather, then walking silently back from Hinton to the farmhouse. She was suddenly tired. For the first time since she had left home, she ached for the silent privacy of her own room, a quiet evening with her father. Until now, she had been too busy to think of him often. Now, imagining his domestic struggle without her, a disquieting anxiety caused her a private tear beneath closed eyes.

Stella, too, sat with head tilted back, only half listening to Prue's daft expectations. Fragments of Prue's description of Joe came back to her: *stallion*, indeed. Such a crude word for a man. Stella gave a small shiver, knowing it to be inappropriate for Philip. Philip was no stallion, thank God, was he? What *was* Philip, in fact? Did she know? And where was he this very minute, and why, again, hadn't he written?

'I'll lay a sixpenny bet with the two of you,' Prue was saying, head still bobbing over the seat, 'that at the RAF dance I'll have tracked him down in the first half-hour, and we'll have made it by midnight.'

'Do pipe down, Prue.' Stella wanted to be at peace with her own fantasies: Philip on boiler-cleaning leave, weekend in a hotel, a double bed, a bottle of wine . . .

'I mean the funny thing is,' Prue went on, 'this war does at least offer a lot of opportunities, especially for a girl like me who can't resist a uniform. I mean we have to do our bit for our country: plough the land, entertain the troops, make them feel wanted, so we're entitled to some fun in between – don't you agree, Stella? Oh crikey: you're not asleep, too? What a couple . . . Old before your time.'

Five

When Prue returned from her second visit to the barn, at three in the morning, she bumped into a piece of furniture while stumbling to find her bed.

Her yelp of pain woke Ag, who said nothing. The next sound to be heard was the unscrewing of a jar. Even in complete darkness, it seemed, Prue was determined to take off her mascara.

Rigid in her bed, Ag lay fighting against pictures of Prue's night. Details were blurred in her mind. She was too shy – too prissy, she thought with scorn – to ask even herself how they did it in the hay. But the general imagining of their flailing joy, combined with feelings of shameful envy, sickened. She hated Prue for so easily achieving what she herself might never have with Desmond. She despised Prue's silliness, her vanity, her preoccupation with material things. More confusingly, she admired her, too: the rough wit, outspokenness, warmth, energy, sense of fun. Ag would willingly sacrifice all her literary knowledge for an ounce or two of Prue's sex appeal, she thought. Silent tears, for her own inadequacy, dampened the pillow.

Unable to go back to sleep, she got up at four and dressed in the dark. There were lights on downstairs. Ag was surprised. She crept along the passage to the kitchen door. It was slightly ajar. Peering through, she saw Mrs Lawrence at the stove pouring boiling water into a teapot.

Ag went in. Then she saw Joe sitting at the table, which was bare of everything but the jug of flowers. There was a muddied silence – the kind of silence in which angry words had been spoken and had run out, or remained unspoken between them. Joe was pale, unshaven. He wheezed slightly with every breath.

'You're early,' said Mrs Lawrence.

'I'm sorry. Shall I –?'

'Get yourself a mug.'

Ag put three mugs, milk, sugar and spoons on the checked oilcloth. Thus furnished, it seemed more familiar. But the customary warm ease of the kitchen was missing. With the blackout still in place, there was a night-time feel to the room. Ag had no idea whether her presence was a relief, or made matters between Joe and his mother more difficult.

The three of them sat at one end of the table. They listened to the rhythmic hiss of Joe's breath. They stirred their tea quietly.

'Are you better today?' Ag turned, after a while, to Joe.

'Thanks.' Joe nodded. 'Dagging this morning,' he added.

It was no time to smile. Ag concentrated on her tea. She saw that Mrs Lawrence stirred hers with a hand that slightly trembled – round and round, far longer than was necessary, eyes cast down at the small milky whirlpool she made with her spoon.

'I doubt Prudence will be up to dagging,' she said. There was more silence. Joe did not respond to the challenge of her look.

'I'll take down the blackout, Ma,' Joe said then.

'You do that, son.'

Joe got up from the table and pulled the stuff down from the window. There was a flat grey sky outside, and a transparent sliver of moon. The two collies, half alert on the rag rug, tapped their tails as Joe passed. He left the room.

'It's his asthma,' said Mrs Lawrence, when he had gone. She looked hard at Ag with her tired eyes. 'Sometimes he

116

goes for weeks on end all right, then he has two bad nights.' Her voice defied Ag not to believe this.

There is justification in lying if it's to protect those you love, thought Ag. She was moved by Mrs Lawrence's fierce dignity, what sounded like the truth of her conviction. Conviction? Perhaps she really did think Joe's two sleepless nights had been caused by asthma. Was it maligning Mrs Lawrence to suppose that she knew what Joe had been up to? Or was it granting the strength of her instinct?

'Rotten for him,' said Ag, quietly.

'Still, he's better today than yesterday.'

Mr Lawrence, Stella and Prue arrived. There were black smudges under Prue's eyes. Despite her rouge, she looked pale. It was the first morning she had not bothered with her make-up though perhaps, thought Ag, this was from carelessness rather than lack of spirit.

'So it's dagging, this morning, is it?' Prue asked Mr Lawrence, helping herself to a thick slice of home-made bread.

'That's it.' Mr Lawrence gave a small smile. 'Your time's come.'

Mrs Lawrence brought a new pot of tea to the table. The sky was paling beyond the barn. A few yellow leaves blew across the window.

'You're going to be as surprised by my dagging as you were by my ploughing,' grinned Prue.

'We're not, actually,' said Mrs Lawrence. She stood at the end of the table, fingers of both hands stiffly digging into the oilcloth, denting its surface. 'Because you, Prue, are going to do the pig this morning.'

The grin left Prue's face. A whiplash glance was exchanged between the Lawrences. It was evident Mrs Lawrence's decision had been made on the spur of the moment, and her husband knew better than to query it. In the long silence, Prue decided to conceal her disappointment.

'Very well,' she said. 'I don't mind.'

'And then you can do some muck-spreading,' Mrs Lawrence added, 'and this afternoon, the cowsheds need a good scrub down and a limewash.'

Prue looked at Mr Lawrence: his nod meant he concurred with his wife's plan.

'Anything you say.' She gave a small shrug. Her back and legs were aching. The inside of her lips were swollen. She could taste tiny specks of salt blood.

'Ag and Stella will do the morning milk, then Joe'll supervise the dagging,' Mrs Lawrence went on. 'John will show you what to do with the pig, Prue: I'll be busy all morning with the laundry.'

This was the first morning Mrs Lawrence had been the one to initiate plans and she listed them with unusual ferocity.

Prue pushed away an unfinished slice of bread on her plate.

'I'm sure the pig and I will get on very well, any road,' she said, plumping up the yellow bow in her hair.

No one responded.

When the three girls and two men had hurried away from the uneasy gathering, Mrs Lawrence remained at the table, still stirring her tea, jaw muscles working. She watched the gathering light seep across the oilcloth, ignite the sides of the old mugs and teapot with small pale flames. After the last door had banged, and there was complete silence except for the dogs' faint snoring, she pressed her head into the darkness of her hands and said a quick prayer. Then she rose to begin her morning's work.

'Hello, Pig,' said Prue. 'Hello, Sly.'

She leaned against the wall of the sty, wondering what first move she should make. Mr Lawrence had left her with a pitchfork and yard broom, and instructions which, the moment he left, ran amok in her mind. The pig lay in its

118

sleeping quarters under a corrugated iron roof, on a bed of straw that gleamed a sodden gold. It appeared to be dozing. Eyes shut. The occasional soft grunt made the whole jelly-bristle fabric of its body quiver.

Apart from disliking roast pork, Prue had never before given any thought to pigs. She had scarcely seen one alive. Now, postponing the dreadful moment when she had to try to move the animal, she fell to wondering about its life.

In her tired state, small blisters and pricks of blood still troubling the inside of her mouth, she found herself full of pity for its boring captivity, and less repelled than she had expected by its ugliness. There was something rather dignified, she thought, about Sly's swollen pregnant belly of mauve-pink skin, the stubby sprawling legs, the ridiculous tail and huge alert ears. Animals, she was learning from her week of closeness to the cows, are without vanity, and she admired that. Although – she smiled to herself – Sly's appearance would be much improved with a touch of mascara. The white lashes stubbing round the tiny eyes gave the sow a pathetic, spinsterish look. In fact, Sly was far from a spinster. She'd been mother to dozens of piglets in her time, Mr Lawrence said. Did she enjoy being pregnant again? Prue wondered. Was she lying down out of boredom, fatigue, happiness or misery? Men would do well to concentrate harder on the subject of whether animals had thoughts, rather than how to make bombs and endanger the whole world, reflected Prue, to whom procrastination brought multitudes of thoughts.

She opened the gate and squelched along the muddy floor of the concrete run. A powerful smell came from the straw. The lattice of mud that spurted over her boots was slimy, disagreeable, unlike the dark fresh earth of the fields. The pig opened her eyes, looked without interest at Prue, shut them.

'Hello,' she said again. 'Sorry, but you've got to move.'

To give herself further time, Prue thought about what

119

Mr Lawrence had told her concerning the severe shortage of pig food. Many pigs were being slaughtered, he said. For the time being, Sly was in no danger: the Lawrences had a good supply of Silcock's Pig Feed No. 1, which was supplemented with leftovers from the house and semi-rotted fruit. But what of the future of the unborn litter? Tears came briefly to Prue's eyes at the thought of killing innocent piglets. She moved nearer to the sow, tapped her with the broom.

The pig heaved herself up so fast, with such a loud and hideous squeal, that Prue leapt back in surprised fright.

Sly gave an ungainly jump off the dented bed of steaming ammonia straw. She skidded towards Prue, who cowered in the corner of the run, planting broom and pitchfork in front of her in pathetic defence. The sow was grunting loudly, intent on something terrible, Prue could see. More than anything in the whole world, Prue wanted to be in the salon at this moment, warm and steamy, cosily surrounded with all the ingredients of a permanent wave.

Don't annoy her, whatever you do, Mr Lawrence had said. But he hadn't told her how to avoid this. Plainly, she'd done something wrong. Sly was definitely annoyed. She stuck her great head between the two handles, looked up at Prue, and furiously wiggled her obscene great snout.

'Go away!' screamed Prue, jabbing Sly's head with the handle of the broom. Then, more quietly, 'Just let me by, please . . .'

The pig's scrubby ears flapped back and forth. One of them brushed Prue's bare hand. The skin was pumice-hard, cloudily transparent, matted with purple veins.

'Bugger off!' Prue shouted again, as the snout now jutted into Prue's thigh. 'I'm not a bloody truffle.'

Suddenly bored, the pig turned away. Prue stayed where she was for a moment, contemplating the purple backside, the indecent meeting of bulbous thighs, the swing of dugs already swelling in anticipation of the forthcoming litter.

With extraordinary speed, adrenalin racing, Prue tossed the old bedding over the wall of the sty. Later, should God grant her the strength, she would have to load it into the barrow and put it on the dung heap. Later still – today, of all days – she would then have to spread it in some field, Mrs Lawrence had said. Now the danger was over, her thoughts no longer fled for comfort to the salon, but to the plough. She would like, this afternoon, to go back to ploughing. But no chance of that. What she would like best of all, of course, was the entire afternoon on one of the highest stacks in the barn with Joe.

The sty cleared and swept, Prue spread a pile of sweet-smelling wheat straw. Sly immediately returned to her newly made bed and slumped down on her side, ungrateful as a cantankerous patient. At least the way was clear for Prue to tackle the mud in the outside pen, and sluice down the drain with a bucket of Jeyes Fluid.

'Doing all right?'

Prue looked up to see Joe.

'You know she bites if she's annoyed.'

Prue shrugged. Her shoulders, arms and back were aching. The thought of transferring the muck from where she had thrown it to the dung heap depressed her so much she was unable to answer. She wanted Joe to lift her over the wall, carry her off somewhere – anywhere – and soothe her aches, kiss her, crush her, blast her with his extraordinary explosive force from the reality of pigs and dung and farm life.

'You look a bit weary,' he said. 'I think we should give tonight a miss. Get some sleep. The hay doesn't do my asthma any good. We're going to have to change locations.'

'All right.'

Prue gave a weak smile. She was aware of smelling as pungently as the pigsty. *Nuits de Paris* stood no chance in such circumstances.

*

121

An hour later, Prue realised to her relief and astonishment, the first part of her job was finished. Sly's dirty straw was piled high on the dung heap. There wasn't a stray straw in the entire yard: Prue had taken the precaution of sweeping it – Mr Lawrence was obsessive about the neatness of his yard. Now, with squelching triumph, she climbed to the top of the dung heap, leaned on the pitchfork for support. There was no one about, no one to condemn her for a few moments' rest. The words of a song she'd learned on the training course came back to her. She began to sing.

She volunteered,
She volunteered to be a land girl
Ten bob a week – 'not true'
Nothing much to eat – 'not true'
Great big boots
And blisters on her feet,
If it wasn't for the war
She'd be where she was before –
Land girl, you're barmy.

'Too bloody true, that bit,' she added, as she began to sink into the dung. She could feel its heat coming through her boots, and the ammonia smell rose powerful as incense. Prue leaned more heavily on the pitchfork. She felt quite faint.

After the milking was finished, Stella took the cows back to the pasture by herself. Ag went to let out the hens. On her way back to the house she passed the laundry room – a minimally converted old cowshed close to the kitchen – and happened to glance through the open window. There, clouded in steam, she saw Mrs Lawrence at work. The place was littered with sheets and shirts, some soaking, some hanging. There were pools of water on the stone floor. On a slate shelf, two old-fashioned irons were reared up on their backs, their steel underbellies a pinkish bronze in the smeary light. Mrs Lawrence stooped to pick a sheet from an enamel bowl of water. She wrung it out fiercely, the sinews in her thin strong arms pulled taut as cords. Then she manoeuvred the sheet into position in the mangle, and began to turn the handle furiously. Water poured into a bucket below. When there were no more than a few drips left, Mrs Lawrence slung the sheet on to a pile of others. She paused to wipe sweat from her forehead, push back a wisp of grey hair from her eyes. Her apron, faded to a pot-pourri of indeterminate flowers, was damp. She contemplated another bowl containing another coil of cotton to be wrung, but seemed to decide against it. Perhaps her hands needed a rest from the cold water. Instead, she pulled a huge, rough man's shirt from the pile and threw it over the ironing board. She picked up one of the irons – its custard-coloured back, Ag could see, was so chipped it reminded her of a monster ladybird – and thundered it down the length of the sleeve. Her mouth was a single hard line.

Ag took a step back. She had wondered whether she should offer to help, but decided Mrs Lawrence would not have wished anyone to see her working out her private rage. It was then Ag felt sure that there had been no words concerning Prue between Mrs Lawrence and Joe at dawn. Mrs Lawrence was in lone battle with her instincts, her suspicions. She was in a turmoil, no doubt, about what, if anything, she should do. Ag longed to help. But she knew all she could do was to remain alert to any indication that Mrs Lawrence might want to discuss the troubles on her mind, which was unlikely. She was a strong, proud woman who would judge the sharing of private matters a deplorable weakness. Without a sound, Ag went on her way. She had to find Mr Lawrence, put from her mind the pictures of his wife's battle in the laundry, and concentrate on rounding up the sheep.

*

Stella, returning from the field in which she had put the cows, heard singing. She paused, listened. Prue? A harsh, tuneless voice, but some passion behind the words. Stella walked round the side of the barn into the beautifully swept yard. By now the singing had stopped. Prue, on top of the dung heap, rested hands and chin on the handle of the pitchfork.

'Prue!'

'I'm resting between jobs. Pausing between *mucking* out –' she gave a chorus-line twist of her hips – 'and muck-*spreading*.' The blobs of rouge, bright as sealing wax, emphasised the whey colour of her cheeks.

'You all right?'

'Fine, all the muck-raking considered. I came over a bit dizzy a moment ago. Must be the bending.'

'You're not going to join us with the sheep?'

'Seems not. Instructions to spread this stuff over about a hundred acres.' She gave a grim smile, digging her pitchfork into the wet straw. 'To think that once I thought two perms and a colour rinse was a hard day's work. Well, in a war you learn, I suppose.' She sighed. Stella, looking up at her, smiled too. 'You know what I dream of, Stella? Up here – everywhere? I dream that when it's over I finish my apprenticeship and this man comes along. This *final* man. I tell you: I'll recognise him soon as he puts his head round the door. He'll be a great big hulk, something like Joe, except he'll have pots and pots of money. We'll get married and live in a huge big house on the outskirts of somewhere posh like York – no more Manchester, thanks very much. We'll have a marble bath with gold taps and lots of marble shelves where I can line up all my powders and lotions – many as I like. We'll have wall-to-wall carpeting *all through*, a wireless in every room and one of those big new radiogram things in maple wood that looks like a cupboard, and the maid will bring us *cocktails*, Stella, I'm telling you, on a silver tray every evening, and we'll be happy. In the

124

day' – she prodded the dung again – 'I'll lie on a sofa like a film star, reading romances and eating chocolates, and all this muck will be a far distant thing, almost forgotten, and every night my husband will come back from his factory – or wherever it is he's made his money – in a Rolls-Royce. That's my dream.'

Stella laughed quietly. 'Children?' she asked.

'Kids? Three or four. That'd be nice. But only with a nanny.'

'What a dream. You'd be bored out of your mind.'

'No, I wouldn't. Not for a while, any road. Do you imagine anything like that for yourself?'

'No, my dream is more modest,' said Stella.

'Might as well aim for the big time.'

'What's going on?' Mr Lawrence strode into the yard just then, surprised to see a figure more like a cabaret singer than a land girl on top of his dung heap. 'Pig done?'

'Pig done, Mr Lawrence. And yard swept, Mr Lawrence, as you can see.'

'I don't want any of your cheek this morning. You'd better get this dung on the trailer and take it down to High Field. Sharp.' His look swerved to Stella, softening. 'Come and help me get the stuff, Stella, then we'll give Ag a hand with bringing in the sheep.'

Prue ostentatiously loaded a heavy lump of dung on to her pitchfork. 'Do you ever have time to dream, Mr Lawrence?' she asked.

'I'm warning you, young lady . . .'

Stella, following him to the shed to collect shears, knives and clippers, saw a dark flush spread up through his neck and wash over his weathered cheeks.

'Cocky little film star'll get her come-uppance one day,' he said. 'Though it's not her work I'm complaining about.'

An hour later Stella and Ag were grappling with their first sheep. The ewe lay on her back on a bench designed to make control of the animal easy. When Mr Lawrence had been there to demonstrate, it had looked simple enough. Left to themselves, the girls were struggling.

Ag had volunteered to hold the animal still while Stella, armed with her paring knife, examined its feet. Hands plunged deep into its greasy wool, Ag sympathetically contemplated the ewe's unease. The delicate black neck, jutting out of the great rug of its body, spun about, twisting the bony head with its roman nose and indignant yellow eyes. It cried out pitifully, lips drawn back to show long dun teeth scored with green, spittle thick as marshmallow spurted from its gums, flecking Ag's overall.

'Steady, old girl,' she soothed, feeling the frantic shoulder muscles writhe queasily in her hands. 'It's all for your own good . . .'

She remembered drawings of a sheep in a childhood book: anthropomorphised into a stern teacher, it was, with glasses on the end of its nose and a cane in its hoof. She thought of her father's love of boiled mutton and caper sauce, rainbow bubbles of fat in the gravy. Sunday after Sunday they would lunch alone together, the bowl of wax fruit between them, using their spoons to gather up the last grains of pearl barley swollen with the mutton juices.

'I think this one's okay,' said Stella. 'No rot, far as I can see. Just needs a trim.'

She clutched a waving leg, flushed with the effort. The horn of the hoof was splayed at the edges. There were two small splits. Biting her lip, Stella dug in the sharp knife and started to peel off a strip of hoof just as she would peel a potato. The ewe struggled harder, but in a moment a black half-circle of stuff like hard Plasticine fell to the ground.

'There – triumph!'

Stella let go of the frantic leg and was promptly kicked in the stomach. Ag laughed so hard she released her hold on the ewe's shoulders. If Stella had not then thrown herself, sack-like, over its belly, the animal would have escaped.

'You're a natural hoof trimmer,' was Ag's praise to Stella when the long job of manicuring all four hooves was completed. It was time for the dreaded dagging.

By now the sheep was weary, easier to handle. Stella bent over its head, hands plunged into the sticky matted chunks of its wool. She watched with some amusement as Ag picked up the clippers and assessed, with a look of mock wisdom, the dung-knotted expanse of the animal's hindquarters.

'Here goes.'

She took up a length of wool, rigid with dried mud and dung. Carefully, she snipped. It hit the ground with a small thud, like the shell of an empty nut. She chose another lump, snipped with more confidence. It was like cutting through pebbles, she thought, not half as revolting as she had expected. She worked faster. The animal scarcely twitched by now. Soon its hindquarters were shorn and clean. Ag felt pleased with herself. She and Stella gently helped it back to the ground. It went bleating away to join its companions in the pen Mr Lawrence had rigged up in the yard. Its head pecked the air like a great black beak, the spittled lips flung into a grimace of relief.

'Philip wouldn't believe it,' sighed Stella, rubbing her back. 'Only fourteen more to go.'

'We must try to get them finished by dark.'

'Easy,' said Stella. 'We're experts, now.'

At the end of the afternoon Joe drove the tractor to the field where Prue was muck-spreading. He had to pick up the empty trailer and tow it back to the yard.

He found Prue standing in a sea of tawny dung, the limp straw just lighted by dwindling sky. Her pitchfork moved feebly, twitching at the stuff she had already scattered. She heaved a clump from the small pile that was left, and threw it carelessly. When she saw Joe she stopped and gave up all pretence of effort.

He jumped down from the tractor, climbed the gate and strode towards her. She put out her arms. He held her, lightly kissed her hair. The satin bow had slumped over sideways, lying among the curls like a dead canary.

'You've done well,' he said.

'But Joe,' she said, 'I'm all in. Never, ever been so exhausted.'

His chest, where she lay her head, was saturated with sour farmyard smells. She found them more comforting than any bottled scent. The stuff of his waterproof crackled beneath her cheeks when she stirred.

'You go to bed very early tonight,' Joe said, 'and you'll be fine in the morning. Tomorrow, when the others are asleep, come down to my room.'

'But surely that's mad? I don't want to be sent away.'

'We'll take care.'

'There was something up, today – your mum and dad. All the rotten jobs they gave me. They were being tough: sort of testing me.'

'They have their ways. Best not to question them. Shall I run you back in the trailer?'

'I haven't quite finished – that small pile.'

'Leave it till tomorrow.'

'I'd like to get it finished.'

'I'll do it for you.'

'No.'

Joe lifted Prue's face, gave a wry smile. 'You're a determined one, I'll say that for you.'

'Might as well do my bit for my country well as I can.' She giggled, energy returning. 'God, I smell awful. I stink.'

'Not so awful that I couldn't take you right here on this sodding bed of straw, if we had the time,' said Joe. 'Kiss me.'

Their mouths clashed. Behind Prue's closed eyes she saw that their heads had merged into one huge flower of inter-locking petals that spurted with light, like sparklers. She felt herself sway. She felt Joe hold her more tightly, to stop her falling. She dropped her pitchfork. It fell to the ground.

Mr Lawrence saw them as he passed the field on his way back from looking at a sickly cow. A mist had begun to rise, making them legless. They looked like the top half of a statue on a fragile plinth, swaying slightly, loosely soldered.

Mr Lawrence felt the burning of his face. He walked on, quickening his stride.

Ag and Stella failed. It was too dark to see clearly, and there were still five sheep left.

'We can't go on, we could hurt one of them,' said Ag. Both girls' backs ached badly. It was chilly, dank. Their last sheep skittered away to join the small flock. 'Still, we haven't done badly.'

They gathered up the tools, then each took an end of the heavy bench and moved it back to its place in the shed.

'What I'd love more than anything in the world is a long, hot bath,' said Stella.

'Me, too. Followed by some sort of silly cocktail in front of an open fire.'

When they returned to the yard, they found Mr Lawrence, flanked by the two collies, had already let the sheep out of the pen. The creatures pivoted about in the dusk, followed first one of their number then another, bleating with articulate monotony.

'Silly animals, really,' said Stella.

'Best as part of a landscape,' said Ag.

Mr Lawrence whistled to the dogs. In a trice they lowered their backs, nosed swiftly off towards the scattered flock, and formed it into an orderly bunch.

'We didn't quite finish, I'm afraid,' said Stella. 'Five to go.'

'Never mind. Tomorrow. We'll leave the pen up overnight.' Mr Lawrence seemed unconcerned, moved off to the gate.

'Can we help?' called Ag.

'I can manage.'

A few yards down the lane Joe, on the tractor, met the flock. He switched off the engine, watched them divide in confusion each side of the machine. The dogs skilfully kept them from running into the ditches – barking, pausing and sprinting with a subtle bossiness. Mr Lawrence, crook in hand, followed a little behind them. When he drew level with the tractor, Joe called to him.

'How did it go, the dagging?'

'Fine.'

Mr Lawrence strode past, not able to look at his son. Joe started the engine, drove into the yard. Ag and Stella were still there, leaning against the sheep pen – laughing, he thought. One of them waved: hard to tell which one. He drove into the barn, jumped down. The thump of gumboots warned him the girls had come to join him.

'It wasn't at all bad,' said one, with a happy voice.

'We became quite expert,' said the other. 'We managed almost all of them.'

'Good.'

One of them helped him unlock the trailer. The other threw a piece of sacking over the Fordson's engine. Then they found themselves looking towards the black hump of the house.

'One of the things I most miss in this war,' said Joe, 'is lighted windows. Imagine how it would be if we could walk towards a lighted kitchen window.'

'Never mind,' said Stella – he thought it was Stella. 'We're getting pretty good at finding our way in the dark.'

Joe put a heavy arm across each of their shoulders. 'I'll guide you all the same,' he said.

Prue, her muck-raking finally finished, tottered towards the gate. She decided to sit on it for a while, summon the energy to walk back up the lane. She would have done anything to accept Joe's invitation of a lift in the trailer, but some sense of pride insisted she finish the job completely before leaving the field.

She sat on the top bar of the gate watching the last light fade from the sky, trees change into black hoods, the ground mist stretch higher. She put out a foot, dipped it into the silvery skeins as if trying the water of a ghostly sea.

Prue didn't much like the dark. A shiver went down her spine. She feared an owl might hoot (something she had never heard, always wanted to hear, but not *now*). If a bat brushed past her, she'd scream bloody murder.

There was silence. Then, the distant shuffle and thud of sheep, anxious bleats, dogs barking. Prue swivelled herself precariously round, using the pitchfork for support, to face the lane. She could just make out a rumbling wave of fat woollen bodies, spectral cushions lumbering past, the occasional glint of an eye. Bloody hell, she said to herself, this is what I'd call *spooky*. What's more, they came with a phantom shepherd and his crook. Not till the shepherd reached the gate could Prue see it was Mr Lawrence.

'Finished,' she called. 'I done the lot, Mr Lawrence.'

Perhaps he did not hear, for he gave no answer. He strode past her, legs lost in the mist, whistling to the dogs.

'Old mean face,' she said out loud, jumping down.

With the last of her energy she hurried up the lane. She was very cold by now. She craved a hot bath in a bathroom like the one in shampoo advertisements – soaking in asses' milk or pine essence, gin and lime to hand. And what would she get? Three inches of tepid water, if she was lucky, in the Lawrences' mean and icy bathroom, followed by a glass of water and rabbit pie.

'*Land girl, you're barmy,*' she sang.

Her eyes had grown accustomed to the dark. When she reached the yard she could make out, quite easily, three figures walking towards the house. Joe seemed to be in the middle, arms slung across Ag's and Stella's shoulders. Prue stopped for a moment, to make sure.

Blimey, she thought, a week ago he was hardly speaking to any of us, and now he seems to *like* land girls. Very peculiar, men, as her mum always said.

Mr Lawrence strode into the kitchen without stopping to wipe his boots.

His wife, heeding the warning, glanced up from the pudding she was making at the table.

'Little hussy,' he said.

'What's she done now?'

Mr Lawrence frowned. He had meant to keep his silence. Calculations circled swiftly in his mind.

'Nothing you could put your finger on,' he said eventually. 'I told you. I always said land girls wouldn't work.'

'I don't know what we'd do without them,' she said. 'I'd begun to think you were getting used to them.'

'That Prudence girl. She's a menace.'

Mrs Lawrence put the dish in the oven, took her time to answer.

'I thought she might have been a threat – Joe. But I've come to the conclusion she's harmless. And she's a worker. It's Stella I worry about.'

'Stella?'

Mr Lawrence, on his way to the doormat, looked back so sharply the movement could have been taken for guilt. 'What's the matter with Stella?'

His wife coolly met his eye. 'Pining for the lover at sea. She seems so troubled by his lack of letters.'

'Is that all?' Mr Lawrence kicked off his boots with some relief. 'She'll get used to it. Pining'll get her nowhere. Hankering for what is not – stupid waste of time.'

'Quite,' said Mrs Lawrence.

Was it a smirched conscience, the farmer wondered, that caused him to think Faith knew he was addressing himself?

He felt a sudden desire to be far from the house – a house so full and changed by its new occupants. He wanted no part of the bustle, the chatter, the evening ahead. He wanted to get away, collect his thoughts in peace.

'I'll be out tonight,' he said. 'There's something on Ratty's mind and I've had no time to listen to him this past week. He needs an hour or two to unwind. Said I'd meet him for a pint in The Bells.'

'You'll need a shave, then. There's a clean shirt in the drawer.'

'Thanks.'

Mr Lawrence was convinced he saw a shadow of incredulity in his wife's tired eyes as she looked up at him. He left the kitchen too perturbed to drink the mug of tea waiting on the stove. It was the first time in their married life he had ever lied to her.

The others, at supper, were subdued by fatigue, but not uneasy. Joe got up after the cottage pie, saying he was going to his room to read. Before leaving he kissed his mother lightly on the top of her head – something none of them had ever seen him do before, and patted her shoulder. She did not respond.

Some moments later, Prue, with schoolgirl politeness, asked to leave the table: she didn't fancy any pudding and feared she would fall asleep in her chair. Mrs Lawrence nodded her assent, mouth reduced again to a thin line of disapproval.

Stella and Ag, on their way upstairs when the washing-up was finished, heard the thin sad sound of the Brahms cello concerto coming from Joe's room.

'Good heavens,' said Stella, pausing on the stairs. '*That*. I didn't know Joe liked music.'

'Do you? Do you play?'

'I play a little. I sing a bit, dance a bit. I'd like to teach one day, but at this rate I'll be far too rusty.'

They found Prue on her bed, the cover crumpled beneath her, fully dressed. She had fallen asleep even before taking off her shoes. She wore the crochet jersey again: the crystal beads on the collar sparkled like two inanimate smiles round her neck. Her bow-mouth was slightly open, two child-like front teeth resting on the bottom lip. Even in sleep she looked tired.

Ag struggled to pull off the regulation shoes. Lumps of dried mud fell to the floor. Stella began to tug at the breeches.

'What about the bow? The make-up?'

'Nothing we can do.'

'She'll be horrified in the morning. Panda eyes for milking.'

'She'll cope.'

When they had relieved Prue of her breeches, shoes and socks, they managed to bundle her under the bedclothes.

'More important, I hope she'll cope with Joe,' said Ag. 'The whole thing seems to be fraught with danger.'

'With any luck it'll burn itself out very quickly. No one will come to any harm.'

'Hope you're right. Apart from anything else, what land girl could find the time and energy for sex *and* farm work? They're not physically compatible, I'd say. Though maybe Prue will prove us wrong.'

'She's so pretty.' Stella studied the blonde head nestled in the pillows. 'You can see why Joe, alone here for so long, finds her irresistible.'

'He's an odd one, Joe.' Ag went to her own end of the room, turned down the bed. 'I didn't take to him at first. Now, I rather like him.'

Stella, as she did every night, picked up her framed photograph of Philip. 'As long as we all keep on liking him,' she said, 'we'll be all right. We'll be fine. We'll have a good friend.'

*

In The Bells Mr Lawrence found Ratty, as he guessed he would. The sight of the old man by the fire, tankard in hand, released some of his guilt. He had lied about a planned meeting, but at least Ratty's presence meant there *was* a meeting. The full weight of the lie was thus eased.

Mr Lawrence ordered himself a pint of bitter and joined Ratty by the fire. They nodded at each other, felt the warmth of the flames on their hands and shins.

'Poison day coming up soon,' said Mr Lawrence at last.

'This ruddy war.' Ratty shook his head. His eyes, the colour of tea, rolled about. 'Messes up everything. Girls ratting! Changes the nature of things.'

'Girls dagging, hedging, ploughing . . . odd, I agree. But something we'll have to come to think of as normal.'

Ratty's thin brown mouth stretched into an approximate smile. 'You've come round pretty quickly, then? Not two weeks back you were full of doubts, you said.'

'There's only one causes a bit of trouble.'

A growl of a laugh came from Ratty's throat. 'They're nice enough girls. The tall one puts me in mind of my mother.' Brightening, Ratty finished his drink. 'Then there's the floozie – you want to mind her. Then there's the – other one.'

'Stella.' The pleasure of saying her name, Mr Lawrence noticed, registered like a tiny graph moving upwards in his heart.

'That's right.'

'Another drink?'

'Thanks, no. Must be going.' Back to the furious darning Edith, thought Ratty. She'd managed to burn the single saucepan this evening. Potatoes abandoned, he had had to quell his hunger with drink.

'Couple of weeks, then, the ratting. I'll leave you in charge. You can explain to them, can't you?'

'Dare say I could if I put my mind that way.'

Ratty stood up, reluctant to think about it. He arched his

back, stiff. He didn't fancy the idea at all. Women screamed when they saw a mouse, in his experience. Lord knows what they'd do at the sight of a rat. As for explaining: words weren't easy on that sort of occasion. Still, he could *show* – like the day he'd shown the Stella girl to harness Noble. She'd learned surprisingly quickly.

'Night, Ratty,' said Mr Lawrence.

'Night, guv.'

Ratty touched his head with a kind of smudged salute. However close they had grown over the years, Ratty would not consider abandoning this deferential gesture. They were boss and hired hand, and nothing would persuade Ratty to alter his ways: he knew his place, and had no intention of changing the behaviour that was customary in his job.

'There's two things we must talk about, Joe, you and me,' said Prue. 'Two things we must talk about *first.*'

She stood just inside the door, dressing-gown clutched about her. It was the following night. After a long day lime-washing the cowsheds, she had had some difficulty waiting for the others to fall asleep before she crept downstairs to Joe's room. But she had promised to keep this date. He had reminded her several times during the day, assured her there was no danger providing she did not put on her torch. His room, luckily, was at the bottom of the attic stairs, the far side of the house from his parents.

It was lit by a dim lamp on the bedside table, knights in armour cut out from a scrapbook stuck on its shade. Even in the poor light, Prue could see it was still a schoolboy's room: pictures of trains and aeroplanes on the wall, a stack of board games in old boxes under a table. The bed was narrow, covered with threadbare candlewick. Pallid wool slippers stood neatly on the mat, a wooden chair was heaped with untidy clothes. Records in paper sleeves were stacked everywhere on the floor. Wedged in among them were piles of books that overflowed from the many shelves. There was a smell of toothpaste and dung, and it was cold.

Joe sat in the only comfortable chair, in an open-necked shirt and no shoes. 'Have this chair,' he said, rising after a long silence.

'I'd rather sit on the bed.'

'Sure?'

'Sure.'

Prue climbed on to the bruise-coloured cover. The springs whined. She curled her legs beneath her, hoping to warm her feet. She would have given anything for a Woodbine, but knew that was not possible – smoke brought on Joe's asthma.

'So what is it you have to say – first?' Joe gave a small smile.

Prue shivered: combination of cold and constraint.

'First: there's a party at the RAF camp in a couple of weeks' time. We all want to go. I mean, we must have a bit of fun.'

'So?'

'How do we get there?'

Joe rubbed his jaw, mock-serious. 'There's the Wolseley, I suppose.'

'Exactly. But it needs a driver. Would you – might you . . . be able?'

'I could see what I can do. There's a pretty tight rein on petrol, but we haven't used much lately. Dare say I could swing it.'

'Joe! You're a bloody angel!' Prue hugged herself.

'Of course, it would mean my having to *stay* at the party to bring you back. Dad would never agree to a lot of to-ing and fro-ing.'

'You wouldn't mind that, would you?'

'I'm not much of a party man. But no, I wouldn't mind for once.'

'We could *dance*.'

'It would take a lot to get me on a dance floor. A very large reward.'

'Promise you that!' Prue fluttered her eyelashes.

'And what was the other thing?' Joe began to take off his socks.

'The other thing was Janet. I think we should talk about her.'

'No need for that, is there?'

'I think there is.'

Joe undid the two top buttons of his shirt. 'You're at liberty to go back upstairs. I won't lay a finger on you again if it troubles your conscience.'

'It's *your* conscience I'm thinking of.'

'For various reasons that I won't bother you with, my conscience is having no troubles at all. But thanks for thinking about it. And come here.'

He put out a hand. Prue took it and slid herself off the bed. Joe guided her on to the floor between his legs. She put a hand on each corduroy knee. Her cheeks were scarlet. She wanted to laugh, but knew she must contain herself.

'Would you be terribly cold if you took off your dressing-gown?'

'Probably.' Prue giggled. She untied the cord, slipped it from her shoulders. Joe shifted forward in his chair.

'You realise,' he said, 'I could never see you properly in the barn. I could only imagine.'

'Well, here you are,' said Prue, giving a small wiggle so that her breasts shimmered. 'All right, are they?'

'All right? My God, come here.'

Joe took Prue's head in his enormous hands. She opened her shining pink mouth in readiness, the fluttering eyes not quite innocent. Suddenly fierce, he pulled her down.

Some time later Prue slipped out of the small, awkward bed. She felt exhausted by constraint. They had had to stop themselves from shouting. They had had to curb the instinctive wildness of their movements because of the singing bed springs. Prue longed to be back in the barn. Now, Joe put a warning hand on her arm.

'Listen,' he whispered.

Prue could hear footsteps in the passage. They hesitated. She quickly slipped into the small space between the wardrobe and the window, dressing-gown slung over her shoulders, heart battering. Joe struggled into his pyjamas. There was a small tap on the door.

'Joe?'

'Yes?'

'I thought I heard you coughing.'

Joe went to the door, opened it a few inches. His mother stood in the passage clasping a candle in a tin holder of cobalt blue. She wore a long cream nightdress of frayed wool: she had worn such nightdresses for as long as Joe could remember.

'Would you like me to put on the kettle? Do you a bowl of Friar's Balsam?'

Her sad beige mouth was drawn down, a tail of long dark hair hung over one shoulder. The slight trembling of her hand made the candle's flame to sway, and shadows to tremble on the walls.

'No thanks, I'm all right.'

'Very well, then.'

'Night, Ma.'

'Good night, Joe.'

Joe shut the door. Prue came out of her hiding place.

'Cor blimey,' she said. 'That was a near one.'

'Ma's always on the alert,' said Joe. 'Always worrying about my health. But she didn't have a clue – honestly.'

'I'll be going,' said Prue. She put up her cheek to be kissed, then on tense bare feet felt her silent way up the stairs. Night three: and complications, she thought. Trouble with Mrs Lawrence was the last thing she wanted.

Perhaps Joe wasn't such a good idea after all. Perhaps things would be easier all round with the RAF man in the teashop. At the thought of his severe blue cap tipped so neatly over his shaven head, Prue gave a small shiver as she climbed into her cold, dark bed.

Six

Stella's prediction that Prue's infatuation for Joe would burn itself out very quickly was proved right: just a fortnight after the affair began, it came to an end. Prue was exhausted by nights of scant sleep and dangerous journeys to Joe's room. She was fed up with the constraint, by day, of having to conceal her feelings. The impracticalities of illicit passion were too daunting, she found: she had had enough. For her, as always, the pleasure had been in the snaring. Once in the bag, the familiar melancholy feeling of having won too easily came upon her. Excitement waned. For some, affairs are flamed by enforced secrecy. For others, like Prue, it's a corrosive element that quells magic in a very short time.

'That's it, Joe,' she said, after an encounter in his unconducive room that had lasted till dawn. 'I can't be doing with any more of this. I'll collapse.'

She stood by the door in her dressing-gown, shivering. Joe scarcely shifted in his mean little schoolboy bed.

'Anything you say.'

'You're not bothered?'

'No.'

Prue hesitated before she smiled. His take-it-or-leave-it attitude was both a relief and something of an insult – mostly a relief, she quickly decided. There was nothing she would fancy less than Joe pouncing on her in the milkshed once she had said *enough*. In fact, his behaviour was so decent she felt she owed him something of an explanation.

'I can't take all the worry of creeping back upstairs expecting to run into blooming Lady Macbeth with her candle, night after night,' she said. 'It's a strain on the nerves.'

'I can understand that.'

'Besides, they've been giving me a hard time, your parents. Why should I be the only one who does the muck-spreading? It's not fair. Still, it's been fun – you and me, I mean.' She paused. 'I only hope all this won't change your mind about driving us to the dance . . .'

'It won't, no.' Joe turned away from her, pulling up the bedclothes. 'You have my word about that.'

Upstairs, careless in her strange sense of release, Prue made more noise than usual. The others stirred. Prue kept on her dressing-gown as she climbed into her cold bed. She sat with her arms round her knees. There was no point in trying to sleep for the half-hour before it was time to get up. Stella's voice came out of the dark.

'What's going on?'

'We've packed it in, me and Joe.'

'What?'

From the other end of the room, the squeaking of Ag's bed indicated she had sat up with some interest.

'Well, it couldn't go on, could it?'

'No,' said Ag.

'I think you've done the right thing,' said Stella.

'Pointless,' said Prue. Their voices, small chimes of agreement in the dark, were followed by a long silence. 'So what I've got to concentrate on now,' said Prue at last, 'is collecting jugs of rainwater. What I need is *rain*.'

'Whatever for?'

'The dance, of course, stupid. We're going to have Drene shampoos and rainwater rinses. I've got it all planned. You won't know yourselves by the time I've finished with you. The RAF boys'll think we're Rank starlets.'

Stella laughed. Ag lay down again, cold. In the darkness she touched her short, unremarkable hair. She wondered if, had she known about Drene and rainwater at Cambridge, it might have made all the difference.

There was no rain, that day, but the autumn weather had turned dank and misty. Ag, deputed to move the sheep from one pasture to another, strode through the long, grey grass, each blade tinselled with dew. She had no fears about the job: it was simply a matter, Mr Lawrence had assured her, of opening the gate between the two fields. The dogs would do the rest.

The collies swished along beside her, crouched with intent, tails low. Their bodies made dark paths through the grass. Overhead the sky was a dense grey, distinct from the earth only in its lack of sparkle. Earth and sky were divided by indistinct hedgerows, neither green nor brown nor grey, but a colourless density of bare wood. The only points of sharpness in the landscape were the few trees whose branches were raised like charred fans, brittle against the sky, awaiting a breeze to make them flutter.

As she made her way through this patch of land, silent and enveloping as a cloud, she should have felt at peace, thought Ag. It was the sort of surprising moment in nature that she loved, when a shift of weather transforms a familiar landscape so completely that the wonder of it fills the viewer with profound awe.

In fact, she was full of dread. Mr Lawrence had announced at breakfast that later this morning there was to be a rat hunt. Ag suffered an old fear of all scurrying creatures. She remembered the nights she had lain in fear listening to the sound of obscene little claws scraping against the wooden boards in the attics above her bedroom, terrified they would find a chink in the floor, hasten through it like lemmings and fall upon her. She had imagined them tearing at her with their eager paws, baring their teeth to shred her eyelids to morsels. Their overhead clatterings were at times so noisy she was positive they were rats and squirrels, though her father had assured her they were only harmless mice. She hadn't been able to tell him of her fears. After dinner, he would sit in his leather armchair fiddling with his pipe, listening to a concert on the Third Programme. He would not have welcomed a child disturbing his habitual evening peace. Kind, he would have been reassuring, patient. But secretly scornful. Afraid of mice? What nonsense, child, he would have said. Back to bed with you, go to sleep. So Ag had never gone down, but had remained rigid in her bed. She would long for the comfort of a mother she could not remember. On many such nights she prayed tearfully to God to show her just one picture of that mother's face. She willed her subconscious to pluck a single image from her babyhood. But none came. She would block her ears against the attic noises, and long for morning.

Ag opened the gate, its wood soft and wet under her hand. The dogs sped off to the distant huddle of sheep. She strained her eyes to observe their skills through the mist. The flock began to move. She could make out black heads jerked backwards, sensed their feeling of mass indignation at the disturbance the dogs were causing. An occasional bleat shredded the damp silence. Then they were close: a glint of yellow eye, the smell of acrid wool. The dogs crouched, swayed their tails across the dew, barked. On such a morning the sheep had no heart to resist the old routine. They spurted through the gate, muffs of dun wool puffed over skinny legs, their bleats turned to what now seemed to be pleasure at the small change of scene. Ag noted with some satisfaction the still-pristine condition of their hindquarters.

When the last sheep had skittered through, she pulled shut the gate. The dogs returned to her side, panting. Their breath rose in pale bulbs, lingered, vanished. Ag stayed where she was for a few moments, watching the sheep's indeterminate decision to make for the west corner of the field. Soon they became again as she had first seen them, an indistinct, distant skein. Her job done, dread of the next part of the morning returned with greater force. She could feel the beating of her heart.

'Desmond!' she said out loud, and the dogs looked curiously up at her.

When at breakfast that morning Mr Lawrence suggested Prue help Stella load the trailer with mangolds, Prue wondered whether her new innocence was as visible as her previous guilt.

'Bloody marvellous – no mention of muck-raking. Miracle,' she said later to Stella.

Side by side in the murky yard, they bent, picked up a mangold from the pile, swung it into the trailer. There was a huge pile to be loaded in the hour before they were to be handed over to Ratty for instruction. They worked fast, bending and throwing with easy rhythm. Their backs and shoulders soon ached with the grainy pain that had become a familiar, everyday occurrence. Prue paused, fingers exploring the knobbled muddy skin of one of the vegetables.

'Can't imagine fancying one of these even if I was a hungry cow,' she said. 'Do you think they know, or something? The Lawrences? I mean, why am I suddenly not muck-raking this morning?'

'Conscience,' said Stella, 'plays all sorts of funny tricks on the imagination. I expect there was just no more muck-raking to be done.'

'I didn't have a conscience.' Prue flung a mangold with some force. 'Well, not much of one, any road. I gave Joe some fun. He doesn't get much of that with Janet. He'll have something to look back on. Years and years of boredom with Janet, and he'll have me to look back on – the land girl who rogered him to a standstill in the barn.' She giggled, pushed damp curls out of her eyes. Stella laughed. 'What about you and Philip?' Prue asked, then, still resting, arms folded.

'What d'you mean, what about me and Philip?'

'Done it yet?'

Stella felt herself blush. 'Get on, Prue. I'm five mangolds ahead.'

'Go on, tell me.'

'I'll tell you if you do ten while I take a rest.'

'Done!' Prue bent at once.

'One, two, three . . . very good. You're doing well.'

Hands on hips, Stella watched Prue's small figure bending, straightening, throwing. In the grey air, her blonde curls were alive with light from an invisible source.

'Now come *on*, or I'll stop,' chided Prue. 'I want to *know*.'

Stella bit her lip. 'We haven't yet, no. No opportunity.'

'Poor old you, rotten luck,' said Prue. 'Still, only a matter of time. Once you get down to it you'll not want to stop, I'm telling you.'

'We'll only have a night or two, when his ship gets a boiler clean.'

'When's that?'

'Wish I knew.'

Stella returned to work. She hoped her voice conveyed a lightness she did not feel. The strain of waiting for a second letter was sometimes deflected by hard manual labour but, increasingly, even that antidote was often ineffective. The job of transporting cold heavy mangolds from yard to trailer on a damp and gloomy morning did nothing to raise her spirits. She wondered, as she so often did, how *so much love*, transported on air waves towards its object, was not felt and instantly returned.

'Don't envy *him* his job on a morning like this,' Prue was saying.

146

Stella followed her look to the yard gate. The postman pushed his dulled red bike through the mud, heavy canvas bag slouched over the handlebars.

'Silly to hope,' said Stella.

'You might as well,' said Prue.

To avert his mind from the dreadful prospect ahead – the instruction of the land girls in the art of ratting – Ratty allowed himself to daydream as he applied an extra polish to his boots and gaiters. He had been listening to a discussion on the wireless about the employment crisis in munition factories. Last September it had been announced that an extra 1,750,000 men and 84,000 women would be needed for the three Services and the Civil Defence by the end of this year. Therein the problem: if half a million men were withdrawn from the munitions industries to fight, and the industries had to expand by one and a half million, who would work in the factories to equip the newly swollen forces? Answer: women. A million and a half of them would have to leave their children, their kitchens, their darning, jobs such as running a local post office, and go into the factories. It was here that Ratty's dream brightened: he polished the toe of the second shoe with renewed vigour. For it might just be possible, it had occurred to him, to persuade Edith to go to work in a factory. He let a small scene, planned for the near future, run through his mind.

'You ought to consider it, Edith. You're a fine worker. It would be an honourable way to do your bit for your country.' (She'd be bound to like the idea of honour.)

'And how would I do that? Where's the factories near here? Besides, my age . . .'

'You're a fine strong woman upon whom the years have left no trace, my dear.' (If he really spoke to her like that she'd clout him about the ears in disbelief. In his dream she smiled pinkly with modest pride.) *'You could lodge with your*

147

sister Nancy: plenty of work in Southampton. You might have something of a social life. Forces' dances, that sort of thing. It would be a much livelier war than staying here with me . . .'

'*Ratty*!' Her face lighted just as it had, once or twice, as a girl. '*I do believe you've hit on a good idea . . .*'

After that, the daydream swerved into other areas of pleasure: the cottage to himself, freedom from her tyranny, the luxury of being able to think uninterrupted. Best of all, the possibility that she might never come back.

Ratty put his brushes, dusters and polish neatly back in their tin. He straightened up to see Edith in the flesh at the door. In a nasty mood, this morning, she was – sort of mood where she'd rather give her loaves to the hens than let her customers buy them.

'What's all this polishing for?'

She was sharp, though. Had to say that for her. Nothing escaped her.

'Nothing special.'

'Huh.'

The meeting of dream and reality had come a little too quickly. Ratty knew that to say anything now would be foolish. Dregs of his fantasy would blur his powers of persuasion. On the other hand, he was impatient to try. If it worked, he could be rid of her within the week.

'They're saying on the wireless they're still wanting more women in the factories. Urgent,' he added, seeing the suspicion that instantly clouded her face.

'What's that got to do with me, pray?'

'It occurred to me you'd be a good woman on a factory line, all your energy, Edith. Wonderful sort of war effort. Greater sacrifice than any amount of saucepans . . .' He trailed off. His eyes lumbered over the whole rigid edifice of his wife's body, only avoiding her eyes. 'Plenty of work near Nancy. Livelier life for you than here. I could manage fine on my own.'

Edith began to laugh, a nasty cackling sound. Ratty was

148

filled with regret for his decision – such mistiming. Judgement distorted by disappointment, he wondered for a moment if she really was amused. He smiled in uneasy complicity. Would she stop that dreadful noise in a moment and say she agreed to the idea? Confused, Ratty put the tin of shoe-cleaning things on the table. Edith uttered a piercing scream.

'You can't get rid of me as easily as that, you can't! Have to try something better than that. And take that tin off my table! How many times have I told you . . . ?'

Over the years, Ratty had learned the advantages of appearing calm in the face of her hysteria. He let himself out of the room without a word, screams of abuse following him down the garden path. Once through the small gate, he turned to secure the latch. He was aware of Edith's contorted face at the kitchen window. As he moved away with a polite wave, the window opened. You wouldn't credit so small a woman with such strength of insult, such powerful lungs, thought Ratty. And then he saw an object flying through the grey air.

Ratty paused for less than a second to confirm the object, landed on the grass, was what he most feared it might be – their last saucepan. He hurried down the lane, determined not to think what kind of an evening this would mean. His knees were shaken by the scene: they always reacted first to Edith's outbursts. But then, rounding the corner, he saw in the distance the tall figure of the one with the holy face. She waved, friendly. As they drew closer Ratty saw her hair hung lank in the damp air. There was something hesitant, unwilling, in her step.

What then occurred was the kind of thing Ratty would rate as a small miracle. She smiled at him, the girl, and it was as if all the troubles of his life with Edith ceased to exist. Instead, the only thing that engaged his mind, indeed his whole shaky body, was a deep longing to convey to this gentle creature the skills, the joys, of hunting rats.

'Morning,' he said, weak with a gratitude she would never know she had caused. They walked together into the yard.

'You may sit,' said Ratty. He stood before his audience of three in the barn. The girls sank on to piles of hay. Ratty observed Ag's kindly look, her half-smile.

She was thinking of this time last year: the undergraduates in the lecture hall would stand as the Professor in Elizabethan Literature shuffled in, never less than ten minutes late, dropping his many notes on metaphysical poetry as he climbed the platform. He would survey them all for a very long time in silence, nodding his head as he silently counted how many had bothered to turn up. Small pieces of coloured papers covered with illegible writing sprouted from his pockets and the books he carried. It often seemed that he was so preoccupied with some erudite problem that he had forgotten his job was actually to speak. Sometimes he would leave his students standing for as much as three minutes before murmuring *You may sit*. Then, shaking himself free of all the notes, he would begin, and hold his audience spellbound for the next hour.

Now the girls were sitting down, Ratty felt more at ease. He could see over their heads to the tractor and the sacks, cast his eyes up to the familiar rafters and the mysterious darkness beyond, stirred now and then by the pale fluttering of a pigeon. It had been his idea to speak to the girls in the barn. Mr Lawrence had suggested that round the kitchen table would be most convenient – but no, Ratty had thought. That would be too close. He would like to stand while they sat. The barn was the place he had retreated to, for shelter and private thought, for so many years. It was the fit location for his first attempt at formal instruction.

He leaned on his stick, more for moral support than physical, kneaded its smooth wooden knob in his hand.

150

One knee still shook slightly, but he doubted any of the girls would notice. With his free hand he patted his jacket pocket, checking the huge ball of his handkerchief was there: these days drips from his nose and water from his eyes would appear without warning. The pert little film star shifted, impatient. The bow in her hair was the nastiest colour he had ever seen.

'Come on, Ratty,' she said.

Bugger you, you little floozie, he thought. Then he lifted his chin, as he did in church before the first hymn, and began.

'You may have been expecting a whole team of pest exterminators here today, girls – handsome men, real professionals: tour the country, they do, enjoy themselves. But what's the point of employing them, Mr Lawrence says to me, when we've got you here, Ratty? Truth is, I've been ratting all my life, though matter of fact that's not the reason for my nickname.' He paused. The girls all seemed to be listening. 'It could be said, what I don't know about ratting isn't worth knowing. Now, what you have to be to become a good rat hunter is something between a murderer and a detective. Like a detective, you have to be good at looking for clues. Like a murderer, you have to face a nasty job at the end – gassing and poisoning are the most effective. And I may say you don't get used to that, not really.' He paused, fumbled for his handkerchief, to deal with a rush of dampness irritating his nose.

Prue watched the distant figure of Joe, carrying two buckets, cross the yard. She wondered at the fickleness of her own nature. Just a week ago, a single glance from Joe in the milking shed or on the tractor turned her guts to flame – it was all she could do not to assault him on the spot. Now the sight of him left her cold. She felt nothing. She didn't ever want to touch him again. He was too big, too gruff, too unobservant, somehow – never seemed to notice what she wanted once the love-making was over.

That wasn't to say he was not a nice enough bloke: rather sad, what with the prospect of Janet, the fact he could not go either to the war or to university, and being stuck here with his parents working as a farm hand. Poor old thing, Joe. With any luck he'd meet some girl more suited to him and get rid of Janet.

Prue turned to look at Ag. Ag's hair was in a bad way: lifeless in the damp. Thin and dreary as old curtains. Still, come the day of the dance, Prue would do her best. She'd bought the curling tongs and a whole bag of kirby grips. She had good supplies of setting lotion and enough Drene to last six months – her mother had warned her that Dorset was most probably not rich in Drene shampoo. So all Prue had to do was to secure Ag's trust. Ag only had to give the go-ahead and Prue would transform her – waves, a little fringe perhaps to soften the wide expanse of her fore- head. By the time Prue had finished, Ag wouldn't know herself. She might even look rather beautiful, in a quiet sort of way: she had good bones, a friendly smile, what could be lovely eyes if Prue could persuade her to try a lit- tle spit and mascara, and a dab of True Blue eye shadow . . .

'What you must never underrate,' Ratty was saying, 'is the *intelligence* of the rat. In my opinion, there are many more intelligent rats than there are human beings. But that's only my opinion, you understand.' His small joke was rewarded by another smile from the holy one. The floozie was fiddling with her hair ribbon. The other one, hands in her pockets as if she was cold, looked interested. 'So what you have to do is outwit them. It's a slow process. It could be said it's not a fast process. But it's interesting and it's a challenge. That's what it is. It's an interesting challenge. The rat has skills we don't have. For instance, he can camouflage himself by hiding behind his own shadow. The glint in his eye is the only thing that betrays him. You have to look for that glint, that tiny speck of light. You have to look for clues: tail trails running over heaps of grain, empty husks on the ground, tunnels through ricks or piles of loose hay or straw – that sort of thing.'

In her right pocket Stella's hand lay flat against the new, unopened letter from Philip. There was a picture in her mind that had been building in detail for the last few days: a grand Edwardian hotel by the harbour in Plymouth, crimson carpets of soft deep pile, chandeliers. The bed-room would be so large they could dance. They could order up a gramophone, put on some Glenn Miller, draw the curtains, turn out most of the lights. They would recapture the way they had danced at the party. But there would be no siren to interrupt them, this time. God willing, they could dance until they fell exhausted on to the huge bed, carry on where they left off . . . to the end. In the morning there would be the cry of gulls outside their window. No reason to get up until they felt like a soak in the deep marble bath, tons of hot water – breaking all rules of economy just for once – and back to bed, smelling of pre-war lavender soap from the small collection Stella had brought to Hallows Farm and husbanded so carefully . . . Ratty caught her eye. She struggled to put aside her thoughts of Plymouth.

'First day, we lay the bait. We lay bits of bait all over the place – here in the barn, the sheds, the yard. But don't expect a rush of rats. They'll take their time. They'll have their suspicions. They won't go near it the first day. Second day, much the same. Note where it is, they will, but leave it. Third day, we lay fresh bait. Temptation becomes stronger than caution, now. The word goes round. There's definite interest. But still some instinct holds them back. As I said, a rat hunter must be patient.'

Ratty stopped to shift his weight on to the leg that had been shaking. It now felt surprisingly firm. He tapped his stick on the ground a few times, no longer feeling the need to lean on it for support. In explaining the nature of a rat-hunt he had almost forgotten the girls were listening.

When he saw their eyes intent upon him, the warmth of encouragement flowed through him. He would have been quite happy to carry on a long time, now he'd got going – he had a hundred theories about the ways of the rat. But it would be foolish to presume upon the depth of their interest. He must come to an end in a moment or so.

He would have made an excellent Professor of Ratting, thought Ag, entranced by his lecture as she had been by the Professor at Cambridge. She alone of the girls admired his timing, the rhythms of his West Country voice – above all, his ability to convey enthusiasm for the subject he had studied most of his life. So few are blessed with that gift. She wondered if she had it herself. Could she inspire others with her own love of literature? Could she ever convey it to Joe? There he was, crossing the yard again . . . Or is a love of poetry as impossible to describe as a love of music? One day, she would like to try. It would take courage. It would take Ratty's kind of courage. Here he was, by nature a taciturn man, talking to three almost strange girls about a subject in which he was an expert, a subject he loved. His own enthusiasm was contagious. Stella hadn't moved, Prue had stopped fiddling with her hair. Ag herself would have liked him to go on and on.

But she could see he was bracing himself for the end. He straightened his bent shoulders, wiped his moustache with a huge handkerchief. On his fine, battered old face, pebbled with small shadows beneath jutting cheekbones and deep-set eyes, there was a look of confidence, enjoyment. He may never have fought a war, been in command. But something of a natural soldier in him seemed to be taking over. Rallying his troops for the fight, or hunt, came to him with almost Churchillian inspiration.

'On the fifth day,' he said, the whole length of his handkerchief having been stuffed back into his pocket, 'we put down fresh bait again. But this time it's *poisoned* fresh bait.' He paused, while the seriousness of the fact resounded. 'By this time, the little devils are impatient. Out they come, eager.' He broke off again, glanced up at a pigeon side-stepping along a rafter, cooing in time to its own movements. 'And here it wouldn't be honest, girls, if I didn't tell you the next part is not very agreeable. The poor buggers come snucking out of tunnels half dead, gasping for air. The effects are horrible, but no one can afford a farm overrun by rats. They have to be finished off . . .' He noticed a jerk of the holy one's head. She'd gone very pale. 'But don't worry. We won't ask you to take care of that. That's a man's job. Joe and Mr Lawrence and me will deal with that side of things. Now, no more talking. Sorry if I've kept you too long. I'm not much used to this sort of thing, explaining. Would one of you care to help Mr Lawrence lay the bait? The others can collect the orchestration, I call it, from the kitchen. A good percussion is what we want – banging saucepan lids together, spoons in pans, anything to frighten the buggers out of their hiding places. I wish you good luck.'

When the girls had gone, Ratty lowered himself on to the place vacated by Ag. The hay was warm through his breeches. He clasped his stick with both hands, leaned his chin on his knuckles. He was exhausted, drained, astounded, elated. He had done it. It was over. It seemed to have gone down with the girls better than he could ever have expected. They hadn't laughed or sneered or shown lack of interest. It was extraordinary . . . Edith would never believe it, not that there was any point in telling her. Matter of fact, he could scarcely believe it himself.

'You all right, Ratty?' Joe was beside him, smiling.

'Never strung together so many words in my life. I'm all right, just need a few moments to recover.'

'Ag said you were terrific.'

'Did she, now?'

'Do you want to come in for a cup of tea?'

'That I don't. Soon as my knees have brightened up I'll

155

be out to show them some of the clues. There's a good tail mark in the grain in the stable.'

When Joe had gone, Ratty felt tears in his eyes. He reached for his handkerchief again. What was such snivelling all about, he wondered. Perhaps something to do with a private victory. But no matter. It was time he returned to his duties – marshal the troops, alert the rats, get on with the day.

Out of sight of the others, Ag banged her saucepan lids with little enthusiasm. Despite her enjoyment of Ratty's talk, the last thing she wanted to do was to encounter a rat, especially on her own. To keep out of the way – Stella and Prue were enjoying themselves making a terrible din in the milking shed and yard – Ag went to an old stable, now used as a grain store. She opened the door, let herself in. If anyone found her taking a rest from clashing these cymbals, she would say she was looking for clues. Ratty had said nothing about having to make a noise while you were looking for clues.

She stood quite still, eyes travelling up and down the piles of grain. On one of them, she saw, there was a curved indentation that ran from the floor halfway up, then stopped in an untidy swirl of grain, as if the rat had changed its mind about going to the top, and jumped down. Was that what Ratty had meant by the trail of a tail? Had she found the first clue?

Heart beating fast, she backed her way quickly to the stable door, put a hand on its lower half for support. Then, on the ground between two piles of grain, she saw it – the glint of an eye Ratty had described. A moment later another speck of light joined the first one: Ag could now clearly see two red eyes, pink-rimmed. The ears lay flat back on the head, making the animal's face seem longer and meaner. Whiskers twitched. The whole body – large and oddly flabby – was poised to flee, or to attack. Ag held her breath, too scared to move. The rat, lifting its head, took a few steps to one side. In the silence Ag could hear the high-pitched scraping of its claws on the floor. With horror she watched the obscene way in which the small toes parted, revealing the slithers of pink flesh lining between them, as the claws gripped. The terror of her childhood nights returned. She screamed. Black moments later, she opened her eyes. The rat had gone. Ag edged herself from the door to the limewashed wall so that she could lean her whole body against it: she feared she might faint. Then she heard the thud of hurrying boots, and turned to see Joe leaning over the door.

'You must have seen a rat!' He was in cheerful mood.

'I did! I did!'

'First one?'

Ag nodded. Her head was beginning to clear. She could see Joe was smiling.

'Everyone screams when they see their first rat,' he said, and came in.

Ag turned to face him. 'So silly of me,' she said, unable to control the quaver in her voice.

'Ratty should've told you not to come in here. It's one of their favourite places.'

'He couldn't have known I didn't want to see one.'

'Are you all right? You look a bit shaken.'

'I'm . . . fine. It's just that I've always had this silly sort of thing, this phobia, about scurrying things. Rats, mice – hamsters, even.'

Joe nodded.

'When I was a child they used to make a terrible noise in the attic above my room at night. Even now, when I go home, I don't like it. Funny how long it takes to overcome such silly fears. I thought it might have gone for my throat.'

'That's an old belief, I know. Can't say I've heard of a single case where it's actually happened. Tell you what, I've just said to Dad I need some help unloading the mangolds for the cows if he wants me to see to the tractor before this afternoon. He said I could ask one of you. Not much of an offer, but perhaps better than ratting. How about it?'

Their eyes met: his anxious, hers relieved.

'Do you think anyone else heard me scream?' Ag asked.

'No one, I'm sure.'

Joe took the saucepan lids from her and put them under his arm. His gentle concern was not lost upon her.

On the Saturday afternoon of the dance, Mrs Lawrence sat at the kitchen table polishing the silver handle of the salt and pepper holder. It did not need a polish: she had rubbed it up not long ago. But for once, free time on her hands, she was at a loss what to do. From upstairs came the squeals and giggles of the girls preparing themselves. The sound of their high spirits did nothing to ease her own feelings of melancholy.

She had agreed to their taking their half-day today, to give themselves time for all the beautifying Prue had been planning for the last few days. At first, Ag had said she had no wish to go to the dance. For a moment, Mrs Lawrence had envisaged a quiet evening in conversation with this calm, agreeable girl. But Prue had been persuasive. Ag gave in, albeit reluctantly. She even agreed to let Prue do something to her hair. Stella, too, had shown no particular enthusiasm to go, but had agreed to for Prue's sake. But then Stella was so in love with her absent sailor that she never minded what she did. The intensity of her love protected her completely from the ups and downs of reality, that was clear. Mrs Lawrence could remember such feelings herself.

Polishing finished, she stood up, restless. No task appealed to her. What she would like was to see the girls, join in a little of their fun. She might be needed, she thought: a placket to be done up, a necklace fastened. Surely they wouldn't mind her asking if they wanted any help . . .

Climbing the stairs, she heard music coming from Joe's room. The song, on his old gramophone, was scratchy, shaky. But it did something to her limbs, her head.

> *Gee, it's great*
> *After sitting up late*
> *To be walking my baby back home . . .*

Mrs Lawrence caught herself half smiling. Joe's door was ajar. She could see him grimacing into the small mirror on the wall, struggling with a tie.

'You look smart, son,' she said.

'Mustn't let them down,' he said.

He had not complained at all about his job as chauffeur. Mrs Lawrence privately thought he was rather looking forward to the evening. Well, he didn't get out much, deserved the occasional break. And this dance caused no worries. Joe may have been quite the ladies' man in his time, but with three girls to chaperone him there was no danger. Prue, the wicked little flirt, had done nothing but talk about some RAF lad she had seen in the tea-shop – her sights were clearly not on Joe tonight. It was only a pity Janet wasn't here.

She stood in the shadow of the girls' doorway, unnoticed for a while. The attic room was hilariously untidy, unrecognisable from the neat and spotless place it had become after days of scrubbing and painting before the girls had arrived. Now, it was like a communal dressing-room in a theatre, ravaged by a series of quick changes. Clothes were flung everywhere – signs of several dresses being tried on and rejected, Mrs Lawrence guessed. Coloured shoes and shiny stockings were strewn over the floor. Lipsticks clustered on the top of the chest of drawers, and every surface was sprinkled with a fine dust shaken from a box of Pond's powder decorated with its comforting design of floating puffs. The war seemed to have made no difference to the extravagance of youth, thought Mrs

Lawrence. She remembered the meagreness of her own wardrobe even when she was young.

Ag sat on a chair under the central light, feet together, hands folded primly on her lap. Prue twittered round her, dabbing and pulling at Ag's transformed hair – a mass of scatty curls and waves that twinkled in the light from the low-watt bulb.

'We're getting somewhere at last,' assured Prue, tottering on her high-heeled black suede sandals, their ankle straps fastened with ruby buckles. 'You won't know yourself. No, you can't look till I've finished.' Ag gave a trusting smile. She touched a thin gold chain round her neck, from which hung a small gold heart. 'That doesn't do much for you,' said Prue. 'Haven't you anything *sparklier*?'

'No,' said Ag. 'I like this. It was my mother's.'

'Very well.' Prue gave the small sigh of one who knows best but is forced to agree to less sure taste for tactical reasons. 'Tell you what, then: I'll lend you my chiffon leopard scarf – cheer your shoulders up a bit.' She tweaked the dark green stuff of Ag's quiet dress.

'Thanks,' said Ag. Prue passed her a hand mirror. Ag studied herself in silence before handing it back. 'Good heavens, what *have* you done to me?'

'One more thing,' said Prue, 'and the transformation'll be complete.' She moved to the chest of drawers, picked up an open lipstick. '*Fire and Ice*,' she threatened, holding it dagger-like towards Ag's mouth.

'*No*.'

'*Cherries in the Snow*, then?'

'No! Prue, please. I'm not going to wear lipstick. I never do.'

'*Spoilsport*! It's yourself you'll be letting down. No hope of wowing the RAF without a bit of lipstick.' Prue pouted. Her own mouth was a squealing pink, designed to seduce an entire squadron, thought Mrs Lawrence, smiling. 'How about a touch of Vaseline, then?'

160

'Just for you,' agreed Ag.

Prue giggled, rummaged through a tangle of scarves in an open drawer. Ag stood, saw Mrs Lawrence at the door. She was immediately embarrassed.

'Mrs Lawrence! Goodness knows what I look like . . .'

Mrs Lawrence came further into the room. Prue leapt at her.

'What d'you think of my handiwork, Mrs Lawrence? God, do I need a fag. *Shine on, shine on harvest moon,*' she shrilled a tuneless snatch of song. 'There.' She knotted a wisp of chiffon round Ag's neck, searched her dressing-gown pocket for a packet of cigarettes. 'And what about Stella, here?'

Stella, sitting on the edge of her bed, concentrated on putting on her own lipstick. A red spotted skirt was drawn up over a pair of sharp little knees, pressed together as if for comfort. Her legs splayed out like two sides of a triangle: the feet, in pink slippers, turned in, ankles bent. There was something childlike in the pose, thought Mrs Lawrence, as if Stella had no interest in trying for sophistication when Philip was away at sea. Stella looked up, blotted her lips, smiled.

'You all look very nice,' said Mrs Lawrence. In this scene of frivolity she felt herself a symbol of dourness, awkward. She did not know where to put her hands, wished she had taken off her apron. 'I wondered if there was anything I could do to help . . .'

'*Please*, Mrs Lawrence.'

Prue flung off her dressing-gown, which sank into a foam of blue on the floor behind her. With a shimmy of her wiry little body, she defied them all not to observe the breasts that swelled above the peach petticoat, the lean hips to which the bias cut of the satin skirt clung. She stepped out of the foam, ankles jigging in their straps, waved a thin arm above her head.

'Who would believe this very arm has spread ten acres of

muck, milked five hundred cows, fought a pig, frightened a rat? *Land girl, you're barmy*,' she sang.

The others laughed. Encouraged, Prue stubbed out her half-smoked Woodbine, and stepped into her dress with a single fluid movement whose natural grace Mrs Lawrence could not but admire.

'Please, Mrs Lawrence.' She presented her back. Faced with a plummet line of small gold buttons, Mrs Lawrence raised her hands, wondering at the sudden clumsiness of her fingers.

'All this just for the RAF,' said Stella. She looked admiringly at Prue. 'Now, if it had been the Navy . . .'

'I'm not fussy,' said Prue, bending about, impatient.

'Keep still,' said Mrs Lawrence.

'Army, Navy, Air Force, Home Guard, anything. Ag, give me that bottle and I'll treat you all to a spray.'

Ag handed Prue a cut-glass bottle of scent. 'Not for me, thanks,' she said.

'Don't be daft, Ag. You don't want to smell of sheep.'

Prue pressed the small bulb in its filigree cover of golden thread. A spray of vapour hit Ag's chest. She laughed, backed away, clutching at herself. Prue swerved round to Stella, sprayed her, too.

'I said, keep *still*.' Mrs Lawrence found herself smiling.

'And last of all, me. Ears, throat, cleavage, wrists. There.' With each steamy puff the smell of tuberose thickened the air. 'No: not quite last – here, Mrs Lawrence!' Prue snapped round on her heels, aimed a squirt of scent at Mrs Lawrence's apron.

'No! Not for me – please, Prue.'

Mrs Lawrence, to her own surprise, joined in the others' laughter. She tugged Prue round again to finish the last of the buttons. A picture came to her mind of dancing in a summer barn, years ago: a harvest supper, perhaps. John coming up behind her, putting his arm round her waist. Streamers looped from the rafters, a small band that made her feet tap long before they reached the dance floor.

'It's magic, I'm telling you,' giggled Prue. 'It'll *do* something for you, Mrs Lawrence.'

There was a shout from downstairs to hurry. With one accord, the girls swerved about the room gathering up scarves, bags, coats. Mrs Lawrence moved about trying to keep out of their way. The sugar smell of powder, combined with the sickliness of Prue's favourite scent, could not quite disguise a sharp, sour smell of sweat.

'Excitement!' shouted Prue, the first to run to the door.

Mr Lawrence and Joe stood side by side in the hall, waiting. They heard the patter of feet on the stairs, saw three pairs of silky legs make a brief moving trellis among the stair bannisters, followed by flashes of coloured skirts. Then they were there, swirling about in the dim milky light of the hall, filling the air with the overwhelming sweetness of cheap scent. Stella's hand clutched a dark oak bannister as she paused for a moment, laughing, catching her breath. Mr Lawrence, staring at her, met her eyes, more visible than ever before now her hair had been caught back each side in combs. He quickly looked away. The curve of a pearly lid, the curl of thick lashes, seared in his mind. Ag – he vaguely noticed something different about her – was struggling into an old grey coat. Joe was helping her.

'I've brought the Wolseley to the door,' he said.

'Joe, you're wonderful.' Prue spun over to him, kissed him quickly on the cheek. 'What would we do without you? Can I sit next to the driver?'

Mr Lawrence undid the bolts on the front door. He meant to wish them all a good evening, but could not manage it. As they crowded past him to the car, Stella saw the sudden paleness of his cheeks.

'Good night, Mr Lawrence,' she said. 'Thanks for the use of the car. Have a peaceful evening without us.' She put a hand on his arm, brief as a bird touches water, sees nothing there, and soars away again.

' 'Night, Stella,' he said.

When they had gone, Mr Lawrence shut the door. Mrs Lawrence came downstairs quietly in her slippered feet. Fearful she would recognise his infidelity in the murky place full of horrible scents that the hall had become, he hurried into the kitchen. His wife followed him.

'Just eggs and bacon, tonight,' she said.

Mr Lawrence took a bottle of ale and a glass from the dresser. He sat down at the table. Mrs Lawrence leaned up against the range, the dogs at her feet. She undid her apron, took it off, folded it, hung it over the back of a chair. Such a pale, worn thing, the binding coming unsewn round the edges.

'Did we have anything like that, in our youth?' she asked.

'Not exactly, no.' Mr Lawrence stood up. 'Can smell that filthy stuff even in here. Don't say you . . . ?'

Mrs Lawrence smiled. 'Prue squirted it over all of us: very generous . . .'

'God forbid. You'll have to have a bath.' He moved over to his wife, lowered his head to sniff at the brown wool of her shoulders. 'It reeks.'

Mrs Lawrence half raised her arms, as if to encircle her husband's neck, then thought better of it. It wasn't Sunday, after all. Instead, she undid the top button of her cardigan. Mr Lawrence watched her, puzzled. Their eyes remained locked for several moments, the disparity of their thoughts almost tangible.

'Reach me down a frying pan, will you,' said Mrs Lawrence at last.

'You're a good woman,' her husband said. 'You're a good woman, you are.'

A plane squawked overhead, shredding the sound of the RAF band. They did not miss a beat, but a few of the dancing couples gripped each other more tightly. Stella, at a small table with the other girls and Joe, clasped her glass of ginger beer.

'It feels more as if there's a war on, here, somehow,' she said.

She looked round the large, rather cold hall. The organisers had tried to disguise its dreary walls with paper chains and clumps of tinsel. Flakes of cottonwool snow had been stuck to the blackout stuff over the windows. At the far end of the hall, next to the bar, someone had struggled to make the buffet look tempting. Coming in, Stella had noticed piles of bridge rolls filled with fish paste, and plates of sliced Spam lay with an exhausted air on lettuce leaves. There were several bottles of salad cream and what must have been a pre-war jar of French mustard. A second table was reserved for a small townscape of castellated jellies. Bright primary colours, some flecked with tinned fruits; they rose out of dazzling white imitation cream skilfully piped to look like shells.

Prue had no interest in the surroundings: her eye was busy on the crowd of uniformed pilots at the bar with their soft, young faces, red necks and noisy laughs. The cheering thing was there were at least three men to every one girl in the room. Prue tossed her curls, tapped a foot under the table – quite Glenn Miller, really, she thought – impatient. She would have to make a break soon, waste no more time. Finish this first gin and lime, kindly bought by Joe, then she'd be off. But there was no time to finish the drink – *for there he was*, the tea-room flight lieutenant, even more handsome without his cap. Prue jumped to her feet.

'Sorry, folks,' she said, 'but I have to go. Don't want to miss my chance. See you.'

The others watched her spraunce off towards the crowd at the bar, hips waggling, hair bouncing, hands on hips. Many heads, they noticed, joined in observing her progress.

'Same performance as in the milking shed the first

morning,' said Joe. Stella and Ag laughed, then they fell into the awkwardness engendered by a trio. Ag, conscious that Stella was looking extraordinarily attractive in a very different way from Prue, folded her hands. tried to assume a settled sort of look.

'If you two want to dance,' she said, 'I'm quite happy sitting here just looking.'

'I don't want to dance,' said Stella, without conviction.

At that moment, a short, heavily built wing commander approached their table, gave a little bow in Stella's direction.

'Might I have the honour,' he said, with a teasing smile, 'of the next one?'

Stella hesitated.

'Go on,' said Joe. 'You can't rely on me.'

'Very well, thanks. I'd love to.'

'My name's Stephen,' said the wing commander.

'My name's Stella.'

'You look to me like a girl who *can* dance.'

'Oh, I don't know.'

He put out his hand, led Stella towards the floor. They were quickly lost in the crowd.

Ag felt all the humiliation of failure. There was no one, she noticed, on the way to ask her to dance. The agony of teenage parties, when the same sort of thing had happened so often, returned. She felt a fool in Prue's silly chiffon scarf and the ridiculous curls: she wished she hadn't come, she wished Joe didn't look so bored.

'Your curls seem to be falling out,' he said.

'The damp.' Ag managed a smile.

'Much better your usual way.'

'Prue enjoyed doing it.'

'I bet she did.'

A small, irrational pain skewered Ag's heart. She watched Joe looking into the distance – remembering Prue, she supposed.

'Who are the other girls here, do you think?' she asked.

Joe stirred himself. 'Some from the Services. Probably quite a few other land girls.' Then he smiled at her kindly. 'Can't say any of them look as if they've made the same effort as all of you.'

'It's a pity Janet can't be here,' said Ag.

'She wouldn't like this sort of thing. She doesn't like dancing.'

'Then you have that in common.'

'I suppose we do have that, yes. Shall I get you another drink?'

'It's my turn. I'll come with you.'

'I can't let you buy me a drink . . .'

'You can in a war. Besides, how can I spend my vast wages? My fourteen shillings a week?' Ag jumped up, suddenly carefree. She would enjoy the sensation of walking across the hall with Joe behind her.

When they reached the dance floor, he said:

'Shall I surprise you?'

Without waiting for an answer, he took her loosely in his arms. Neither was a skilled dancer: they shuffled awkwardly, others twirling past them. 'Are you as much in love as Stella, with someone far away?' asked Joe.

Ag felt herself blush. She spoke the truth. 'I dream about someone who scarcely knows of my existence,' she said. 'He was a graduate student, medicine. We did once have tea, with some other friends. For some reason, I found myself telling him my name was really Agapanthus and he didn't laugh. But I don't suppose he'd remember.'

'Agapanthus? Well, it's hard not to laugh.' Joe suppressed a smile. 'You are an odd lot, you three. Not at all as I imagined land girls.'

By now they had reached the bar and gave up all pretence at dancing. Ag bought Joe a pint of beer and an orange squash for herself. They made their way back to the table.

'I like your *deportment*,' teased Joe. 'You walk so straight, ramrod back like a gym mistress.' He pulled out her chair.

'I went to a very strict convent,' said Ag. 'We had to train with books on our head.'

Joe smiled. A jitterbug number had started. 'Lucky we missed this one,' he said.

Their eyes were drawn to the dancing. It was an exuberant crowd on the floor, some skilled at the steps, others merely jumping about, not caring. Then it became apparent there was unanimous recognition of a couple of stars among them, and they were being given space. Lesser dancers had drawn back, still moving, but their concentration was on the stars: Stella and her partner.

The wing commander's short, bulky figure, lightened by the music, was transformed. His jitterbugging had all the vitality of a younger man's actions, but also a precision that was astonishing to watch. He flung Stella hither and thither and she followed, sure as Ginger Rogers, adding her own inventive little flurries – a flick of the head or skirt, a sharp circling movement of her hands. The band, aware they were playing for experts at last, stepped up the tempo: the rest of the dancers fell away, leaving Stella and her unlikely Astaire on their own till the end of the number. Stella kicked off her shoes. The combs fell out of her hair. Her cheeks were scarlet as she spun faster and faster.

When the music stopped, the wing commander lifted her easily above his head, like a ballet dancer. There was cheering all round the hall, applause. Stella dizzily returned to earth. She hurried back to the table, followed by her smiling partner. Her hands rushed through her now wild hair. She was panting.

'You can *dance*,' said Joe. He stood up in acknowledgement. His clear admiration spurred Ag to rise, too, and turn to the wing commander.

'*You* must have been jitterbugging all your life,' she said.

'I like to dance,' he conceded. 'Your turn. Shall we?'

'I can't do anything like that,' said Ag.

'It's a nice slow number. Come on.'

I'm in the mood for love was rising and falling through the hall. Ag followed the wing commander to the floor. He clasped her with such expertise, his lead making the slow steps so easy to follow, that she began not to mind the fact she was a good head taller than him. She looked down, studied the intricate waves of his Brylcreemed black hair, then averted her eyes. All round them, other couples, on just an hour or so's acquaintance, clung to each other as if to make the most of the last moments of life on earth: eyes shut, whispering things inspired by the rarity of such occasions. One of these couples was Prue and her tea-shop flight lieutenant. His chin nuzzled into the bow in her hair, her arms were clasped round his back. Again, Ag felt a pang of a sensation she despised. How did Prue manage it, every time?

At the table, Stella finished her ginger beer in one gulp. Her face shone, excited.

'You were amazing,' said Joe.

Stella shrugged. 'I've always loved dancing, singing.'

'Is that what you're going to do, eventually, be a dancer?'

'Heavens, no. I'm nothing like good enough for that. I'd like to teach the piano – though I'm so out of practice I may never get it back. Where's the nearest piano to Hallows Farm?'

'There's always The Bells,' said Joe. 'There's an old one there, very out of tune.'

'Anything'd do me.' Stella leaned back in her chair, eyes shut. 'That was fun,' she said. 'You don't find many men as good as that. I'd have done anything tonight. Celebration.' She opened her eyes, smiling.

'Might I guess? Something to do with the sailor?'

Stella nodded. 'I heard at last. Two weekends from now he's got several days' shore leave. He wants me to join him for forty-eight hours. Do you think your Ma . . .? Mr Lawrence?'

169

Joe rubbed a huge hand across his face, straightening out a frown. 'Dare say that could be arranged. It seems very unfair, land girls only entitled to a week's holiday a year. Ma appreciates that.'

'I'd make up for it.'

'I'll put in a word for you.'

They sat listening to the music, watching the dancing. Prue and her partner had by now ceased to move at all. Ag and the wing commander were nipping expertly through the more statuesque dancers, Ag with a tight little smile.

'Do you know what Prue wants in the end?' asked Stella. 'She wants a rich Yorkshireman, gold taps, cocktails on silver trays. She told me her dream, standing on the dung hill.'

Joe smiled. 'What Prue wants, Prue'll get. She's a determined little thing if ever there was one.'

Their eyes met. They laughed.

'Jesus, I was rash,' said Joe, 'but it didn't seem worth resisting, offered like that on a plate. Couldn't have lasted long – too dangerous, under my own roof. I like her spirit, though. And I don't know any girl better at ploughing a straight furrow.'

Stella smiled, honoured to have been taken into Joe's confidence.

She watched his eyes, suddenly dulled, trail round the hall.

'Times like this,' he said, 'it hits you. Being one of the very few not in uniform. You feel such a rotten shirker.'

'Well you certainly shouldn't,' said Stella. 'Everyone knows if a man doesn't join up it's for good reason.'

'Not much comfort in that sort of logic, I'm afraid. The day I failed my medical was the worst day of my life. Never forget it: this icy room with that poster on the wall – you know the one, *Your Country Needs You*. This cocky little doctor. Afraid your country doesn't need *you*, my lad, he said. You can't expect to fight the enemy if you're fighting for

170

your own breath. Stands to reason. I told him – I told him I was much better than I had been as a child – growing out of the asthma fast. But nothing would change his stubborn little mind. Same thing happened to my friend Robert – his lungs are seriously rotten. They laughed at him wasting their time, turning up for a medical. But Robert's a pacifist at heart. He didn't give a damn that he was ordered to stay at home. My ambition was to join the HAC.'

'I'm sorry,' said Stella. She paused, knowing the inadequacy of any sympathy. 'But think about what you are doing. Someone's got to organise the massive job of feeding the country. Hallows Farm is making the sort of contribution you shouldn't undervalue.'

Joe shrugged, looked Stella in the eye.

'I don't,' he said. 'You're wise and you're right. But I can't help the guilt, the shame. I'd rather be fighting.'

Ag and her partner returned to the table. The four of them sat talking over more drinks. The wing commander was a married man, his wife at home in Edinburgh. In civilian life, they had won prizes for dancing. He missed regular dancing, he said.

As midnight drew near, the evening sloped into a minor key. The music slowed. Couples disappeared. Prue and her flight lieutenant were nowhere to be seen.

They reappeared just in time for the national anthem. Intent on reaching the table, Prue's progress across the hall was uncertain. She leaned heavily on the flight lieutenant, his scant baby hair a pinkish gold under the harsh lights. Her ankles gave way several times, but he supported her nobly, rewarded with a constant, lipstick-smudged smile.

'Rather overdone the gin and limes, I have,' she said. 'This is Barry.'

Barry had just time to shake hands all round before his body was flicked to attention by command of a thunderous chord from the band. *God Save Our Gracious King* boomed out. All the uniformed men, moments ago so slack and soft on the dance floor, now adopted unblinking rigidity. Prue, through the gin-induced silvering of her mind, somehow appreciated that to cling to Barry at this solemn moment might be unwise. Instead, she leaned against Joe with the lack of inhibition of an old friend who dares to impose. She then found herself firmly guided to the door between Ag and Stella.

They supported her in the doorway of the hall while Joe went to the Camp car park to fetch the Wolseley. Cold night air ripped through their bones. Barry, still in his upright national anthem position, boldly stayed close enough to the trio of girls to plant a kiss on top of the sagging head of the one in the middle.

'See you, Prue,' he said. Saluted. Left.

'What did I tell you?' Prue giggled. 'Mind out – your feet! I think I'm going to be sick.'

After supper at Hallows Farm, Mr Lawrence went out to check a sick cow. Mrs Lawrence settled to a pile of darning by the wood fire, listening to a concert on the wireless. When her husband returned, he slumped in his usual chair, tipped back his head and shut his eyes.

'Strange, having the place to ourselves again for an evening,' ventured Mrs Lawrence.

Mr Lawrence nodded, but did not answer. He slept for a while, then roused himself to go to bed. Mrs Lawrence knew that if she followed him she would not sleep. She stayed where she was, put more logs on the fire as the night grew colder.

Sometime after midnight, she heard the car. Quickly she switched off lights and went to the window. She pulled back a little of the blackout stuff, peered through a chink. The girls and Joe were getting out of the car: there seemed to be some confusion. By the light of a full moon Mrs Lawrence could see a discussion between Joe, Stella, and

Ag. Then Joe bent down to the front passenger seat. He emerged with Prue in his arms, awkwardly propped her up against the open car door. Mrs Lawrence had a brief glimpse of a floppy blonde head, smudged lips. Then she saw Joe pick up the girl, sling her over his shoulder like a sack. The thin legs and silly shoes twitched against him but Prue made no protest.

Mrs Lawrence stood in the darkness of the room watching the last flames. She heard Joe and the girls make their way upstairs.

There was laughter, urgent whispers as they urged each other to be quiet. Mrs Lawrence waited till she heard Joe return from the attic to his own room, shut the door. She wondered if there was any chance of waking John. Her own wakefulness, alone, was almost unbearable.

After the house had been silent for some time, she made her way to the sitting-room door, crept upstairs through the darkness to the bedroom. Would any of them tell her how the evening had been? She wondered, too, at her own curiosity, and the impatience she felt for the morning.

Seven

In the wake of his success as a lecturer, Ratty found himself newly impervious to Edith's unreasonable behaviour. When she claimed it had been his fault the saucepan had flown through the window, and his fault it was lost, he did not offer to go and look for it (knowing quite well in which patch of long grass it lay) or attempt to extract himself from the blame. In silence, he ate fried vegetables and bacon, gleefully aware of Edith's own distaste for fried food. Give her a few days, he thought, and the saucepan would be back, no explanation.

The girls, he was bound to admit, had grasped the nature of the sport better than he had supposed they would. The floozie swore she had seen a right great bugger of a rat hiding in its own shadow. Here, Ratty felt, was an element of exaggeration – it wasn't something he often saw himself. He had a feeling she was trying to please, worm her way into his good books. The holy one, he must confess, had not come up to scratch. She reported one tail trail in the grain store – right enough – but tapped a wooden spoon on the side of a pan with such feebleness Ratty could tell her heart was not in it: the pathetic noise wouldn't have scared a mouse. In a word, though Ratty hated even privately to recognise this, when it came to ratting the holy one was a disappointment.

The Monday after the RAF dance was the fifth day of the hunt. Ratty took it upon himself to lay the lethal bait before dawn: he had no wish to be responsible for the girls doing something silly with the poison. He crept about, torchless in the freckled dark, slipping scraps of food, well marinated in ensearic zinc phosphide, under bales of hay, by piles of grain and hen food, the dung heap – all their favourite places. Now, it was just a matter of waiting. Ratty was a satisfied man: the buggers would come sneaking out today, not knowing what had hit them, begging to be clobbered on the head. He could never relish that part, as he had told the girls. But it had to be done.

At breakfast, Mr Lawrence warned the girls to be on the look-out. Should they come upon a dying rat, he said, they were to call Ratty, Joe or himself to deal with it.

Ag hoped her job for the morning would be spraying the fruit trees, a place far from the rats. But her luck was out: Faith wanted the eggs gathered early so that a collection could be taken into Dorchester, where the WVS distributed them to the old. The other two were assigned to a morning's hoeing.

Armed with her basket, Ag went first to the barn. She calculated that, as Ratty had laid the bait only a few hours ago, chances were the rats were exercising their habitual caution, and had not yet been tempted. She put a gloved hand nervously into the small holes between piles of loose straw that she had come to know were the bantams' favourite places for laying. Then, in one of the secret nests, she came across a gristly piece of lamb, just recognisable from a stew some days before. Ag quickly backed away, revolted, to battle with her conscience. Should she continue in her egg hunt in the normal way until she had gathered a dozen or so eggs? Or should she call it a day? The poisoned bait had unnerved her.

Tense and self-despising, she left the barn, walked towards the harness room. It housed an old horse rug that had been left folded on the floor for countless years. Stiff and mildewy underneath, its top had been moulded into a nesting place by some long-ago duck, whose descendants still took the opportunity to lay in this ancestral nesting place. Eggs were to be found there most days.

A few yards from the tack-room, Ag saw Ratty come out, a pleased look on his face. He held up a large dead rat that swung from a hairless tail. In the split second before a blurring of vision came to her rescue, Ag observed a glimmer of obscene tooth and claw. She shouted to Ratty not to bring it near her, then clamped a hand over her mouth to stifle a scream.

Ratty, in his own pleasure, was confused. He had imagined she would share his triumph, gloat with him over the monster. He could not understand her incomprehensible cries, nor why she turned away from him and fell into the arms of Joe.

'Take it away, Ratty,' said Joe, over Ag's shoulder. 'She doesn't like them.'

Ratty at once turned away and shuffled off fast, reduced from his few moments of uprightness to his old stoop.

When he had gone, Joe gently unclasped his arms and stepped back from Ag.

'All right?' he asked her.

Ag pushed back her hair, tossed her head. She was pale, ashamed. 'Fine, thanks. I didn't think I'd mind a dead one so much, but the revulsion is just the same.'

'They're obscene, dead or alive. Like me to make you a cup of tea?'

'What, and earn your father's medal for utter feebleness?' Ag managed a laugh. 'No, thanks. I'll go down to the orchard, help with the fruit spraying.'

'Right.'

'And thank you for rescuing me. I felt dizzy for a moment. Where were you? You appeared from nowhere.'

Joe looked at her for some time without answering, his brows drawn into a frown.

'I was about,' he said. Then he patted her on the shoulder, and strode off to the barn, own shoulders hunched, preoccupied by some private thought.

He had offended and alarmed the holy one, and regret swung within him heavy as a cast-iron bell. Desolate, Ratty had fallen from the heights of the morning to the murkiest of depths. Pride came before a fall, he muttered to himself. Oh, to have undone the morning: to be given the chance to start again, act with more sensitivity. All the signs of Ag's aversion to rats had been there to read, and he had ignored them. Ratty spat on the hard ground, cursing himself. Would she ever forgive him? What could he say to her? How could he ever explain his regret for causing her such a fearful moment?

Once he had disposed of the dead rat – and no rat had he ever loathed so much for causing all this trouble – Ratty had little heart to continue his search for others. The joys of rat hunting had vanished. He wandered down to Lower Pasture, leaned over the gate to watch the cows. So often he found their indifference a comfort. But another horrible thought assailed him: Joe and Ag. The holy one in Joe's arms – Joe, who'd turned up like some bloody magician on cue – sure way to a girl's heart, being there at the right moment.

Exactly what Ratty did not want to happen between Joe and Ag was not clear in his mind. But the old unease he had felt some days ago, which had died down, now returned. He had not liked seeing the girl fall back spontaneously against the great hulking figure of Joe, and the swift comfort of Joe's arms. He did not want to see any such thing again. He did not like the ease between them. Besides, the holy one should be protected, be warned: Joe was no bloody good. Not to be trusted, relied upon. Ratty had witnessed many wild couplings in the lad's youth, seen many a girl with a broken heart whom he had left without reason. The holy one was as innocent and vulnerable-looking a creature as Ratty had ever met, inspiring him with protective feelings that were new, in this his eighth decade, and troubling. His old plan of revenge returned. Any hint of Joe's selfish intentions towards the girl, and he, Ratty, would step in and rescue her from a far graver situation than the event of the dead rat this morning. He was not sure, yet, what measures he would take, but a pitchfork would probably come in useful. Joe should have learned by now the cruelty of dallying with an innocent girl's feelings. Besides, there was Janet. Ratty had no great respect for Janet, but she was Joe's fiancée, and had done nothing to deserve this deceit. So Joe had better mind his Ps and Qs, thought Ratty, and with his new resolve strength returned. He saw on his watch almost an hour had passed in contemplation. He must return to the farm, keep searching for dying rats, before the light faded and he would be forced to go home.

'I don't know what a girl's supposed to do, this clothes rationing,' grumbled Prue. 'Sixty coupons a year! *One* complete outfit. What makes those idiots in the government think we can get by on that? They're barmy.'

'You've got more clothes than anyone I know,' said Stella.

'Luckily, I stocked up before June. I'm all right for *now*, but what if Barry and me take off? You have to keep a man surprised. Something new for each time you see him. Keep up the interest.'

The girls hoed side by side. Deserted in the weeks the farm had been short of labour, before their arrival, the field was waist-high in thistles, mutton dock and charnock. As usual, they suffered aching backs. They found the long handles of the hoes difficult to manoeuvre. Their work was slow and clumsy. After a couple of hours they had cleared a disappointingly small amount of ground.

'Don't know why they don't just let me plough this all

in,' sighed Prue, straightening up for a pause. 'God, what I'd do for a fag. Look at my hands. Scratched, purple, fingers swollen. Lucky if anyone ever looks at me again.'

'You should wear gloves.'

'Hate gloves. Bloody hoeing. I'm exhausted. How come Ag always gets the orchard?'

'Spraying the fruit trees isn't that much fun. The stuff blows back into your face in the slightest breeze.'

'I'd rather do the *pig* than hoe. I've grown quite fond of Sly, matter of fact. But ploughing's my best thing. Wouldn't mind ploughing every day. Joe did finally admit, you know, he was impressed by the straightness of my furrows. Joe, I said, my apprenticeship in hairdressing wasn't for nothing. I been well practised in giving clients straight partings, haven't I? Course I can plough a straight furrow.'

Stella laughed. She, too, straightened up, leaned on her hoe.

'This time tomorrow,' she said.

'Where'll you be?'

'On the train to Plymouth, any luck.'

'That's good.' Prue took a packet of Woodbines from her pocket, lit one in the cup of her hand. 'Mrs Lawrence easy about letting you go?'

'Very understanding. It's only two nights. I said I'd stay here over Christmas to make up.'

'I'm going home, Christmas, whatever.' Prue inhaled deeply. Then she puffed a ribbon of lilac smoke into the cold, clear air. 'Don't suppose I'll ever get used to this silence,' she said after a while. 'Ag and you – you seem to find it all less surprising than me – the mud, the dogs, the cold house and everything.' She wiped a gleam of sweat away from her face, leaving muddied cheeks. 'Suppose it's been less of a leap from Surrey than from Manchester.'

'Oh, I don't know. It's just that with Philip on my mind I don't care what I do, where I go. When I'm not with him I seem to be indifferent to everything. In fact, I'm enjoying

179

it all more than I expected, despite the hard physical work. But perhaps that's just because Philip *exists*.'

'You really *are* in love,' said Prue, in some awe, inhaling again.

'I am,' said Stella dreamily.

The sour, pinkish smell of Prue's cigarette spumed above the deeper smells of earth and weed.

'Well,' said Prue, after a while, 'I just might be on the way to join you. There was something very nice about Barry. Not just a handsome face, I'd say.' She flung down the butt of her cigarette, stamped it fiercely with her boot. 'I'll be ready, Barry, I said, any time you want me.' Giggling, she angled her hoe towards the root of a large thistle, tapped at it with little effect. 'I suppose you're thinking I'm promiscuous.'

'More, just your way of trying to find the right man,' said Stella. 'I do the same. The only difference is I don't sleep with them. I'm too scared. Instead, I fall in love. Not very deep love. I'm such a hopeless romantic, the very idea of love is almost enough for me, though I know in my heart most of it's make-believe and I'll be disillusioned. I nearly always am. Though this time, with Philip, I think it's different.'

'I'll keep my fingers crossed,' said Prue. 'I don't go for all that soppy romance stuff myself. Especially with a war on – no time. Get your knickers off as fast as you can is my belief, before the poor buggers are shot down. Bit of quick fun, then off to the next one. End of the war, when we're all a bit older and wiser – that'll be the time to look for a husband. That's when some unsuspecting millionaire's going to come in handy. Meantime, I get my fun where I can find it. Not as easy stuck out here as it was at home, of course. But I'm not off to a bad start. Joe's a good bloke, bit of a dark horse, pretty good lover by my standards. But what was he? Just a challenge. Seduce the farmer's son was my number one priority, then start searching out the local talent. I think he quite enjoyed it, mind: holding out for all of a week, then shagging me stupid. One morning I actually fell asleep propped up against Marybelle, teat between my fingers . . . Not practical, me and Joe, really. Besides, Mrs Lawrence was beginning to have her suspicions. I didn't want to be sent anywhere else, one of those land girl hostels or anything. It's a good place, here. I wrote to my mum only last night. I said: Mum, we're lucky. Then I said, I've got my hopes pinned to this Barry. I wouldn't half mind if he came looking for me, I said.'

They returned to their hoeing, their silence. The only sounds for a while were the chinking of tools against stony earth, the distant crunking of rooks and crows restless in the bare trees of the copse. Then, a piercing whistle startled them: the whistle of an experienced shepherd commanding his sheep. Both turned towards the gate, some fifty yards away, expecting to see Ratty or Joe. Instead they saw a young airman on an old bicycle, smiling.

'*Blimey*!' hissed Prue. 'It's Barry. *Talk* of the . . . Mind if I go? Wonder how much time he's got. Don't go back to the yard without me, *please*. I'll come and get my hoe.'

She flung it to the ground, automatically ruffled a hand through her hair, muddy fingers checking the state of the blue satin bow. Then she began to run through the weeds, waving, shouting Barry's name. Barry dismounted his bike, opened his arms, smiling, blushing – even from so far away Stella could see the sudden ruddiness of his cheeks. When Prue reached him, they kissed frantically, oblivious to the gate between them.

Stella turned away. She wondered if Philip's welcome tomorrow would be as ecstatic. The nervous anticipation, which she had been trying so hard to conceal, returned. Its force made her feeble. With a great struggle, she returned to her hoeing, knowing that with Prue gone she must do double the work.

*

When Prue and Barry's first embrace, and its encores, finally came to an end, Prue climbed over the gate and took the flight lieutenant's arm. They quickly reached the entry to the copse, some yards along the lane, and found themselves a comfortable place in the densest part of the wood. Barry sat on the trunk of a fallen tree, having assured himself its fuzzy yellowish moss would not stain his trousers. Prue placed herself in an alluring curve on the ground ivy, positioned so accurately that when the time came she could rest her head on his knee without having to move.

Barry's scarlet face was smeared with the deeper red imprints of Prue's lipstick. His shorn gold hair, released from the forage cap folded in his pocket, stood straight up as if in alarm. Prue herself, purring in the knowledge of her own allure, was the epitome of a rural pin-up: a blending of mud and rouge on her cheeks, blonde curls a chaotic nest on which her satin bow clung like a wounded bird. They both trembled. Prue reached for her cigarettes. Barry found a match. He lit her cigarette with great finesse, as if it was a skill he had been practising all his life: cupping his hands round the flame, touching Prue's wavering fingers for no more than a second. Then he took a cigarette himself, lit it with equal precision. They blew smoke in each other's faces, then scattered it with floppy hands, laughing. Barry looked at his watch.

'I wasted a lot of time,' he said, 'biking from field to field, looking. Didn't like to ask up at the farmhouse. An old boy with gaiters eventually said I'd find you down here.'

'Ratty,' said Prue.

She wondered if Barry appreciated the faint traces of her own scent beneath the sweet smell of the mingling smoke. Barry looked at his watch.

'So I can only stay ten minutes,' he said. 'Then I'll have to ride like blazes to get back in time. It's a good seven miles.'

Prue exhaled very slowly. Stupid, it would be, to reveal any show of disappointment.

'Pity,' she said.

'It's a pity, all right. You're so gorgeous.'

Prue had never liked the word gorgeous, but it wasn't Barry's adjectives she was after. She looked up at him from under her lashes.

'Moment I saw you,' she said, 'in the tea-room, I thought pretty much the same. I thought: he's the one.'

'I knew you thought that. It made me quite nervous.' Barry laughed.

'Couldn't let a man like you get away,' said Prue. 'That's why I made them all come to the dance.'

'I saw through your planning, of course, and I was lost.' He gave a small, contrite smile, like a schoolboy. 'I thought: I'm a pushover. I'm going to say yes to whatever she suggests.'

Prue smiled. She put a hand on her battering heart. Barry stretched down and put his hand over hers.

'My loins are on fire,' he said, solemnly.

Prue giggled. 'Oh, Barry,' she said, 'you're the sweetest thing. Well: I'm here for the asking, aren't I? I'm here for you to take, to do what you like with.'

'We've only got eight minutes now,' said Barry.

Prue pouted. 'We could just make a start,' she said. 'We'd have longer next time.'

'But there's so much I'd like to do to you. It's been haunting me, all the things . . . Shall I tell you? I'd like to start kissing you at the top, go round and about, everywhere, very slowly . . .' The blush had by now suffused his neck. He grasped the heavy wool of Prue's jersey, that strained across her breasts, with a hand that was as red as his face. 'I don't know if I can wait, sweetheart.'

Prue saw his desperate state. She removed his hand from her jersey.

'You might have to wait, old cock,' she said nicely. 'Six

minutes being really too much of a rush, trying to fit in everything you have in mind, as it were. You'd have to exceed the speed limit. We might not get the full benefit, such pressure of time.'

Barry gave an agonised sigh. 'You're probably right.'

They both stubbed out their half-finished cigarettes, threw them into a thorn bush.

'What's your actual job?' asked Prue. Take his mind off the matter that was obviously causing him a lot of pressure would be the kindest thing, the best way to calm him down, she thought: though God knows that was some sacrifice, considering the wicked way she fancied him.

'Mostly night flying.'

'That's terribly brave.'

'I'm not brave. I'm terrified every time we take off. Every time, I think this is it. My number's up. I could come again Friday,' he added. 'Two o'clock, free afternoon. Could you make it?' Prue nodded. 'It's nice here in the woods.' He looked at her, trying for calm. 'That land girl uniform does something wicked to me. Christ, those breeches. Come here, sweetheart. I must kiss you again, at least.'

Prue knelt up, startling a nearby blackbird which flew away with a thin hollow sound of wings. Barry's face, against hers, was hot and damp. This time, kissing, she felt none of the excitement she had felt at the gate. Barry's urgency was almost apologetic, as if life itself might be running out, chance must be taken. But in their very few moments together this afternoon Prue had worked out that, for all his sweetness, Barry was not to be her Philip. He was too young in his ways for her: he reminded her of a choir boy, the angelic blushing face and golden baby hair. In her post-Joe afternoon in the tea-shop, and in her gin-fired dreams at the dance, enthusiasm had caused her to miscalculate. Still, he'd do nicely for a while.

She could sense him raising his watch above his head, glancing at it through her hair.

'Just under three minutes left,' he said.

Prue felt a kind of sadness.

'No time for the *actual*,' she told Stella and Ag later that night, 'but a good beginning. He's a real charmer, Barry, in his way – brave as anything. He'll be my fourth pilot.'

On the train next morning, cold in her third-class carriage, Stella thought about Prue. She pondered her gather-ye-rosebuds-while-ye-may approach to men, and wondered at its benefits. She could not imagine herself flitting from one state of intense carnality to another, in Prue's light-hearted way; she could not imagine the swift cutting off from one man, apparently no untidy trails left, followed so quickly by a new and untarnished keenness for another. Prue suffered no disillusions because she had no illusions in the first place. Her short-term goals were sex and fun. Conquering was the stimulus. Endings were of no consequence. She acted with the confidence of one who knows the ruling power of her own heart. Her heart would not be touched until it was convenient – until, when the war was over, it was the right time for the millionaire to provide marriage and security.

Stella could not but admire Prue's philosophy, even though the thought of quite so many casual men disturbed the depths of her puritanical psyche in a way she would never admit. She wondered if Prue ever missed the vicissitudes of other ways: the highs and lows of constantly being in love, the anticipation, the excitement of waiting for letters, for declarations, the general shimmering of daily life that love of a man can bring about. In her brief experience, if she had to be honest with herself – a difficult process Stella rather enjoyed – most of her own 'loves' were figments of an optimistic imagination. Her feelings, so eager to bestow themselves upon someone, were often – for lack of choice – bestowed randomly. She would stamp upon the love object the required attributes so clear in her mind. The reality behind the resulting picture, when it burst through, caused many a downward spiral in her heart. But she was not one to succumb to melancholy for long. She would never blame a man for letting her down. Rather, she would admit her choice had been mistaken. There would be others, she felt. And somehow there always were. To those who believe there is little point in being alive without being in love – Stella's creed – there is no shortage of objects upon whom the cloak of fantasy can be flung.

In her short acquaintance with Philip, Stella had had more rewards than usual. His heart-breaking handsomeness combined with a lack of vanity, his sense of fun balanced by a serious side of his nature, his prowess at dancing, his way of making her believe his declarations of love – all these things were new and wondrous to Stella, a spur to the idea that life ever after, with him, was a strong possibility. And perhaps his letters would improve. Their love was crystallised by the uncertainties of an insecure world: fear of an unknown future, an unknown amount of time, possible death that would snatch away their chances – such things were common to so many wartime lovers, Stella knew. All the same, she was convinced this was very different from the majority of desperate, unstudied wartime affairs. This had a lasting quality . . . didn't it?

Stella turned to look out of the window. Through the strands of rain, looped and pearled across the glass, she saw small hills of reddish earth. Devon, she thought it must be: names of stations were no longer displayed, just as signposts had been taken down. England had become a mystery place in which you had to find clues, guess where you were. But apart from that, here, as in Dorset, the only evidence of war was the sight of women working in the fields. She caught a glimpse of a row of land girls bent over hoes in a mangold field, and smiled.

The guard who came to check her ticket said they were half an hour from Plymouth. Stella's heart constricted. She thought for the thousandth time of Philip waiting for her on the platform, of his dear face breaking into a smile as she ran towards him. Except the face in her imagination was suddenly a blank. It had gone.

In her panic, another picture came to mind, horribly clear – Mr Lawrence's. *His* face, as he turned in the Wolseley to say goodbye to her, she would remember for ever. His look had been a mixture of anguish, sympathy, regret. He had briefly patted her knee, wished her well, assured her he would be there to pick her up on her return. He had opened the passenger door, handed her the suitcase and said goodbye at the ticket office, his face so stricken Stella had been tempted to ask what troubled him. He was an odd one, Mr Lawrence, she thought, but she liked him. She then remembered that he had mentioned at breakfast his brother, terminally ill in Yorkshire, was worse. No wonder he had looked so unhappy, and the power of his unhappiness had touched her own high spirits.

Stella took out her wallet, searched for the small Polyfoto of Philip. At the sight of the familiar features, her moment of amnesia was forgotten. Relief and rising excitement made her heart beat crisply, as if it was a razor-edged organ thumping with peculiar precision in her chest, hurting the parts nearby. She took out her silver compact – a legacy from her grandmother – and dabbed at her nose with a piece of swansdown fluff. No point in lipstick, she judged, and smiled to herself at the thought of the cosmetic preparations Prue would have been making in the circumstances.

The rhythmic grunting of the train began to slow. Stella closed her bag, folded her hands on her knees. She studied the sepia photograph of St Ives, Cornwall, framed above the opposite seat. Maybe she and Philip would go there for a holiday one day. It looked an unspoiled place. Maybe she and Philip would travel the world. Then come back to a suburban house (they shared a love of suburbia) with spotted laurels, two cats, room for a piano so that she could give lessons . . . three, no, four, children.

The train bucked, throwing her forward. There was a screech of steam. Through the rain-blurred window, a misted view of the large station, dozens of troops crowding the platform.

Plymouth. Philip.

Stella, trembling, stood up.

Meeting can be like drowning. In the moments leading up to the encounter, a whole life can flash by. As Stella jostled her way through the army greatcoats, the stamping boots, the cloudy breaths gathered like small parachutes in the air, she realised she had only ever seen Philip at night. This would be her first view of him in *daylight*. Their three previous meetings (was it really only three?) had all been at parties: low lights, drink, dancing, the pitch dark of the old nursery. Any moment now she would see him in the cruelty of this grey light.

His head was suddenly there in the distance, the familiar photograph coming alive, cracking into a semi-smile, the dark blue of his uniform handsome against the crush of khaki. They pushed towards each other, fell into each other's arms like dozens of couples in wartime movies. Stella could taste rain on his cold lips, smell the damp of his hair, and the brown musky wood scent of his skin, peculiar to him, that she had forgotten.

Outside the timeless cavern of their kiss, she heard the train pulling out and hundreds of cheers and calls of encouragement – envious laughter. Extracting herself from Philip to see what was happening, she realised that they were the objects of derision. Philip took a moment longer to realise this. His reaction was to laugh. But Stella saw his rain-smudged face had turned a raw red, and knew her own cheeks were the same colour.

188

'Jealous bastards,' he said, and waved back at the troops leaning from the train windows, a merry-faced lot who had latched on to an unknown couple's moment of joy to hide whatever they themselves were feeling.

Suddenly, the train gone, the station was quiet. Philip picked up Stella's case from the damp platform.

'Come on,' he said. 'Food. You must be famished.'

He took her hand. The high tap of Stella's shoes made small unsynchronised chords with the deeper sound of Philip's boots. They made their way to the ticket barrier, and the city beyond.

They sat in a small café, a place with none of the refinements of the tea-shop in Blandford. There was cracked oilcloth on the tables, covers of *Picture Post* stuck randomly on the walls to disguise a web of dirty marks. The place was empty, but for a slack-mouthed, greasy-haired waitress whose weariness, almost tangible, seemed to be smeared thickly over her like lard, hindering her movements. Philip ate scrambled dried eggs, so gritty and gristly-looking Stella wondered how he could swallow them. She herself, not hungry, toyed with two slices of bread and marge. They both drank strong cups of tea, which they sipped with great concentration, each waiting for the other one to choose a beginning.

'We're booked into quite a decent room,' said Philip, at last.

Stella smiled. She saw the hotel lobby of her dreams: chandelier, the ruby carpets soughing up the swirling staircase leading to their suite. And, somehow, a gramophone.

'We're asked to check in at five,' he added.

This was puzzling. But Stella imagined there were wartime rules in hotels. Regulations about which she knew nothing.

'That's fine. I'd like to look round Plymouth.'

'We'll go down to the harbour, take a look at the ship. Journey all right?'

189

Stella nodded. The days of waiting for this moment, the agony of anticipation, had turned, like all past pain, to dust. She wondered if Philip had been through any of the same agonising moods of impatience, and wondered whether she dared to ask.

'It's so good to see you,' she ventured at last. 'I thought I'd go mad, waiting, sometimes.'

'It's good to see you, too,' said Philip, after some thought. 'Very good.' But he went no further, gave no clues as to how the wait had been for him.

They ordered another pot of tea. Philip decided to try the jam roll. The single nicety of the café was a small china jug, patterned with morning glory, for the custard. While Philip struggled to hold back the skin with a fork, and encourage the thick flow of custard beneath with a spoon, he asked Stella to marry him.

Stella stared hard at the jug, the delicate pattern of flowers engraving itself on her memory for the rest of her life. Such havoc of thought skittered through her mind she wondered if she had heard right, if she was imagining the question. This was so far from the picture of where and how the proposal would take place, she found herself in a silent, desperate struggle to appear composed.

'I thought,' said Philip, eventually alerted to Stella's confusion, 'if we made it clear marriage was on the books, things would be easier tonight . . .'

'How do you mean?' Tears skinned Stella's eyes.

'I didn't want you to feel any guilt, any apprehension . . . any nervousness that I might be one of those chaps who makes love to a girl then leaves her.'

'Nothing like that had entered my mind.'

'No, well. We don't know each other terribly well, do we? I wanted you to feel sure. Anyhow, what's the answer to be?' He sounded almost impatient.

Stella put down her cup, blinked back the tears. She had only a few seconds in which to straighten out the surge of feeling that had rendered her physically useless. She looked down at her own shocked hands lying dead on the oilcloth, the nails painted a pale pink by the insistent Prue last night. She tried to sort out the muddle in her brain. The main factor was one of relief, an out-of-focus sort of joy that what she had been planning, hoping for, had happened so fast, so easily. But clambering about this main sensation were small, worrying shoots: the profound sense of bathos, the disappointment that Philip had not engineered so important a moment with more skill.

'You look surprised,' he said. 'Surely it's no surprise. I thought . . .'

Stella braced herself, managed a small laugh. 'I'm only surprised by the time, the place,' she said. 'Being a hopeless romantic I somehow thought the proposal was bound to happen with champagne and music.'

'On bended knees, I dare say. You've seen too many films. I'm sorry, I don't work like that.'

Philip took one of Stella's hands. The electric shock between them revived her. The familiar love that had so consumed her while hoeing fields, milking cows, spreading dung, returned. Ashamed at her sense of disappointment, she gripped Philip's hands tightly, leaned towards him. The moment of her humility was accompanied by the sickly smell of suet and hot jam sauce.

'Am I to be turned down?' Suddenly anxious, Philip's voice.

'Of course not. Of course I'll marry you. I love you.'

'I love you too. That's all right, then.'

Philip extracted his hand from Stella's, pushed away the plate of unfinished pudding. He signalled to the waitress for the bill, pulled a handful of change from his pocket with which he made three small towers of sixpences.

'When I'm back at sea it'll be good to know there's a future wife waiting at home. Sometimes, on the night watch, especially, staring out at those miles of sea, you begin to think nothing else in the world exists. You think you're the only ship on the only sea. Your mind plays all sorts of funny tricks.'

'Hope the idea of a wife will make that better.'

'I think it will. Let's go.'

Down at the harbour a thin sun was breaking through a taut, colourless sky. Gulls shrilled overhead, their indignant cries dying away into low, tattered, affronted notes. Small groups of sailors trailed back and forth with no apparent purpose. There was a smell of salt and tar, a suspicion of fishy depths to the wind.

Stella and her sub-lieutenant stood looking up at the massive sides of HMS *Apollo*, a powerful ship built with the sharp sleek lines of an attacker. For some reason she reminded Stella of a pointer she had once seen at work when her father was out shooting – nose to the ground, cutting through a field of long grass. She could imagine the *Apollo* scything through the endless waves with the same sleek determination as a hunting dog – but that was a silly thought, not worth putting to Philip. She linked her arm through his, looked up at him, so handsome in his cap, the gold braid gently fired by the sun. His head was back, eyes on the White Ensign fluttering at the mainmast.

'So lucky I got a destroyer,' he said. 'A lot of my friends were appointed to drifters and trawlers. I wouldn't have wanted that.'

'You'll be a captain one day,' said Stella. 'Perhaps even a rear-admiral.'

Philip transferred his look of devotion from the White Ensign to Stella. He gave her the friendliest smile since she had arrived.

'The future wife of the sub-lieutenant speaks,' he said. 'Look at those.' He pointed up to a row of wickedly snouted guns – menace in waiting.

Stella shivered. 'I can't really imagine a battle at sea,' she said. 'A destroyer of this size snapped in two like a toy, burning, sinking. What I'd like' – a sudden boldness gripped her – 'is to know *exactly* what your life is like . . . I want to know your daily routine, all the details, so that when I'm back at the farm I can imagine you accurately. Up to now, I've just been guessing.'

'I wouldn't be very good at describing all that,' Philip said.

They moved away from the shadow of the *Apollo*, walked hand in hand further down the harbour. Several ships were at anchor, unmoving on the flat water.

'Awesome things, they seem, to someone not in the navy,' said Stella. She thought that by making any observation, quickly enough, she would not have time to reflect on Philip's lack of cooperation. 'Whole, strange worlds.'

'By the time we get to Hamilton Road,' said Philip, looking at his watch, 'it'll be five o'clock.'

Mrs Elliot, the widow who ran The Guest House in Hamilton Road, was a woman of such deep suspicions that she was not ideal material for a landlady. Her pessimistic imaginings were fired at the very sight of strangers walking up the concrete path, and lingered long after they had gone. Her mind, filled with the possible activities of past guests, was thus always ready to come up with some point of reference. When Philip had come round to book the room, Mrs Elliot was able to inform him that not only had she had many lads from the forces staying under her roof but also, of particular coincidence, a sub-lieutenant from the *Apollo* had once stayed two nights. Her veneer of friendliness was calculated to make the new incumbent forthcoming with the sort of information she could pass on to the guests of the future.

As Stella and Philip walked in uneasy silence up the street of identical semidetached houses, Stella struggled to put aside her picture of a uniformed doorman ushering her through huge glass portals into a hotel lobby of rococo magnificence. Approaching Mrs Elliot's establishment up the sterile little path, she had her misgivings – but then put them quickly to one side, because nothing, she told herself, now mattered except that she was here *with* Philip at last. While they waited for the door to open, Stella studied the grey stucco walls of the house, the windows veiled with thick net curtains, the highly polished brass knocker on the nasty green paint of the front door. She was aware that a kaleidoscope of material images was collecting in her mind where they would retain a significance for the rest of her life, simply because they were part of the weekend when, as Prue would say, she finally Did It.

The door opened. Mrs Elliot, from her superior position in the hall, was able to look down on Philip and Stella on the path. Her glance told them she was well appraised in all tricks of human nature – there was no point in any pretence. Stella was curious to know how Philip would deal with her censoriousness: silly old bat, she thought – what we are has nothing to do with her. The woman's silent, instant disapprobation was intrusion into a privacy that meant much to Stella. She felt sudden anger, but said nothing.

Inside, they were greeted by smells that had never escaped the tightly closed windows: years of soup, cabbage, gravy, tea, had combined to thicken the airless atmosphere like invisible cornflour. The place was spotless, immaculate: the front room was crowded with a three-piece suite covered in rust rep, a material Stella's mother had always sworn she would never resort to, no matter how long the war lasted. Starched white lace antimacassars hung over the back of the chairs and sofas indicating their owner was a connoisseur of such refinements, and woe betide any brazen member of the forces who dared lean his head against them. Despite the warm, claustrophobic air, Stella shivered. What on earth would they do, all evening, she and Philip, in this dead room?

Mrs Elliot was studying an appointments diary. 'Sub-Lieutenant Wharton, that's right, isn't it? The two nights.'

'That's right.'

'And . . .?'

Stella saw Philip turn pale. She saw his hands shake.

'I'll soon be Mrs Wharton,' said Stella.

'Soon as the war's over,' added Philip.

'That's what they all say.' Mrs Elliot snapped shut the diary, waved a grey-skinned hand towards the window ledge. 'You may be interested in my collection of corn dollies,' she offered; 'most of my guests are. You'll have the opportunity to study them before the evening meal.' She took them upstairs and delivered a little speech concerning house rules – blackout, locking-up time, essential economy of bath water, and absolutely no alcohol on the premises. Finally, in consideration of others, she would ask that they refrain from undue *noise*. This last rule, calculated further to inhibit young seamen bent on nefarious activities with a future 'wife', was accompanied by a bang on the bedroom wall: the dull echo of plasterboard proved its thinness. Perhaps to counter-act such fierce warnings, Mrs Elliot pointed out that their window, thickly clouded with netting, overlooked the 'front'.

When she had gone, leaving them with a knowing smile, Stella went over to the window, pulled back the net curtain. The view was of houses on the other side of Hamilton Road, identical to Mrs Elliot's.

'So where's the promised front?' she asked.

'I think she meant the front of the house rather than the sea.'

Stella turned back to Philip who was sitting on the bed. She began to undo her coat. Smiled.

'Nothing matters,' she said. 'Absolutely nothing matters except that we're here at last.'

'I suppose not,' said Philip. He rose and came over to Stella, helped her off with her coat. 'We'll eat here tonight, but tomorrow night we'll go to some big hotel.'

'That would be lovely.' Chandeliers began to retwinkle on some faint horizon: the possibility of champagne. Philip looked at his watch.

'We've exactly an hour till Mrs Elliot's gourmet feast at eighteen hundred hours. And what we've got to remember is no noise . . .'

They both laughed. Philip tipped Stella's head back into the gathering of net curtains so that it rested against the window pane. He began to kiss her with an eagerness which Stella would have shared had she not been anxious about cracking the glass behind her.

Exactly an hour later they sat at a table in a back room eating corned beef salad and – speciality of the house, Mrs Elliot had assured them – baked potatoes.

The silence was stifling. Fatigue, readjustment and a sudden dread of things to come had deprived Stella of all ideas to entertain the blank-looking Philip. Joined only in mutual hunger, they ate their etiolated salads fast, and spread extravagant amounts of salad cream on their potatoes to counteract the tiny wafers of marge Mrs Elliot had laid on a small saucer. In the quietness, Stella contemplated for a long time the inspiration behind the salt and pepper pots – crude china mushrooms painted with identical spots. Whose idea had it been to create such objects? What pottery had agreed they would catch the discerning landlady's eye, and set about their manufacture? Stella always enjoyed asking herself such unanswerable questions, and added the mushrooms to her list of memorable things in this unforgettable weekend. She smiled.

'What are you thinking?'

'I was thinking about the salt and pepper pots.'

Philip showed no flicker of understanding her train of thought.

'*I* was thinking we ought to get out of this place for a

drink somewhere. We can't just sit in that room waiting to go to bed.'

'No.' Stella finished her glass of water.

'There's a pub just down the road.'

'There is,' said Mrs Elliot, coming in from the kitchen, 'but locking-up time is nine thirty and I'll not tolerate any incidents of drunken behaviour. They've been known to happen in the past, especially able seamen.' She knew how to fling an insult: watched Philip stiffen. 'There's butterscotch shape to follow. They've quite a reputation, my shapes. I've not had a guest yet who's not complimented me, that I can tell you.'

Philip and Stella, still hungry, could only accept her challenge. Mrs Elliot fastened the blackout across the small window, and switched on a dim central light. Scene set for triumphant entry of pudding, she brought in a beige mound on a cut-glass plate.

'You'll like that,' she said, 'or I'll be blowed.'

When Mrs Elliot left the room, Stella gently moved the plate. The shape wobbled very slightly. They both laughed.

'Come on,' said Philip, 'out of here as soon as possible.'

They smeared a little of the butterscotch stuff on the bottom of their pudding plates, spooned the rest into the two unused paper napkins, and stuffed the squashy package into Stella's handbag.

Ten minutes later they were back at the harbour. In the winter dusk they threw the pudding ceremoniously into the black water, joined in laughter, relief, sudden new excitement. From now on, Stella knew all would be well. She took her future husband's arm, rested her head against his shoulder as they walked. A full moon lighted their way to the pub.

It was warm, light, crowded with seamen and their girls. Too noisy for conversation, Philip and Stella had their drinks at the bar. They leaned against each other, the thrill of proximity piercing through their coats. Stella, on Prue's advice, drank gin and lime. Unused to alcohol, she felt delightfully out of focus after two glasses. Philip chose neat whisky. But even in their alcoholic state of careless rapture, Mrs Elliot's threats hung over them with a penetrating chill. They left at nine fifteen.

Stella's steps were a little unsure. Philip supported her with a firm arm the short distance along the street. Back in the house, they braced themselves for a silent passage up the narrow stairs, determined Mrs Elliot – surely awake and listening out for the slightest sign of trouble – would be thwarted. In their stark little room they found the blackout had been drawn, and the vicious lilac walls were muted by the low-watt light.

Stella was grateful for Prue's advice. The gin had done much to improve the setting for her seduction. She sat on the bed and longed for music, candles, dancing. But, thanks to the gin, the hideous carpet and curtains and the designed meanness of the room could not really touch her. These were merely another cause for laughter, should they dare laugh . . .

Philip left the room carrying a sponge bag and dressing-gown. Stella took advantage of his absence to undress quickly and put on her dressing-gown. In her slightly inebriated state the regular nightly duties of brushing teeth and hair did not occur to her. She climbed into the small hard bed with its scant blankets and firm pillows, and waited.

After what seemed a very long time, Philip returned. He slapped his jowls, a watery sound in the quiet.

'Thought I'd better shave,' he said. He hung his uniform neatly in the upturned coffin of a cupboard, and placed his shoes by the door in a strict to-attention pose, as if his feet were in them for the national anthem. Then he flung himself on the bed, smelling of toothpaste, aftershave and whisky. They drew quickly towards each other, wool dressing-gowns pulled open by the roughness of the blankets.

'Remember,' said Philip, 'no noise, no cries, no laughing. We'll have to save all that for the rest of our lives.'

Stella, in her eagerness to get on with the event in hand, would have sworn eternal silence.

'Think we'd better put out the light,' she whispered smudgily. 'If I see you, I might cry out in wonder.'

In the absolute dark, they giggled nervously. As their hands hesitated over each other's bodies, and their lips met and parted, met and parted, Stella was aware that the quality of their desire had shifted since the night in her old nursery. It was as if a premature familiarity, an unwanted sign of how it would be for untold future years, had emerged unbidden. A little afraid, but wanting more (more what? she kept asking herself), she lay wide-legged in the blackness, waiting for the moment in her life she had been taught was so important and must not be given lightly. She was glad Philip could not see her, glad she could not see him. The confusion in her mind was between the imaginings of how it might have been and how it actually was. *This.*

Here he was, very sudden, unexpectedly heavy. There was a moment's pain. A burning in the depths of her. Then there was nothing. Just the emptiness of darkness.

It was over. She knew this because Philip rolled off her, panting. Now, not even their hands touched.

'The first time, always . . .' Philip murmured eventually.

'I know.'

'I didn't hurt you?'

'No.'

'She won't have heard a thing, bloody woman.'

Stella, puzzled by the extent of Philip's concern about their landlady, heard him turn away, shift himself comfortably. He slept very quickly. She herself remained on her back. There was much she would have to ask Prue, she thought. There was also much she would have to keep from Prue, for fear of her laughter.

*

199

They were woken by a tapping at their door next morning: Mrs Elliot called out that breakfast was on the table.

'Silly old cow,' murmured Philip. 'Her only pleasure in life must be spoiling others' fun.'

Stella studied his sleepy face, less familiar than the photograph she looked at every morning. He drew her towards him, kissed her on the forehead.

'Don't let's give her any satisfaction,' he said. 'Let's get up.' Ten minutes later they faced a scant breakfast. Philip seemed in much better spirits than the day before. He dabbed a knife in the minuscule ration of marmalade.

'There are some economies not worth making,' he said, 'and this place is one of them. I've decided: we're *moving*. We're going to book in to your glamorous hotel. My godmother sent me ten pounds for my birthday. We're going to spend every penny . . .'

'The two nights we agreed, they'll have to be paid for.' Mrs Elliot, who had been listening behind the door, strode over to the table and picked up the empty metal toast rack with a vicious flick of her wrist. 'I'll not be replenishing the toast,' she said, 'neither.'

Philip produced a crumpled ten-shilling note from his pocket and slammed it on the table.

'Keep the change,' he said.

Mrs Elliot could not help gasping. 'I dare say I could do another slice if you want one,' she said.

Her offer was firmly declined.

They sat in the sun lounge of the Grand Hotel in wicker chairs, a tray with coffee laid on a wicker table between them. Outside, destroyers lay motionless on a sun-petalled sea: the cry of gulls was dulled by the domed glass roof, the palm trees in pots, the condensed warmth of the place. No one else was there. The hotel was so short of visitors that when Philip had asked for a double room and bath, the receptionist offered a suite for the same price.

In the lobby, Stella had found her chandeliers, her ruby carpet and swirling staircase. There was a wireless in their sitting-room, a vase of dried honesty, comfortable chairs, and a view of the harbour. Stella took so long to examine every detail of her dream that Philip had to urge her to hurry if she wanted coffee before lunch.

In the sun lounge, he asked her to marry him again.

'But I said yes yesterday. Did you doubt me? What makes you think I might have changed my mind?'

'I just want to be absolutely sure.'

'You can be.'

Philip frowned, but still seemed to be in high spirits. 'Then I have a confession to make.' He was silent for a while. Stella waited, curious. 'Those girls I mentioned when we first met – those girls in the past . . .'

'Not that many of them, as far as I remember.'

'Two. Two especially. The thing being . . . I may have exaggerated. Whatever I may have indicated, I was boasting. I didn't actually . . . with either of them.'

'Well?'

'So . . . last night was the first time for me, too.' He looked down.

'Does that matter?'

'I thought it might. I hadn't the courage to tell you. I rather fancied the idea of your thinking of me as an experienced hand . . . I was ashamed of being such an amateur. I mean, I'm twenty-three. Most men, by then . . .'

Stella's love, which had waned a little in the darkness of her lonely night, returned – a small poignant gust in her chest. She reached for his hand.

'You don't mind?' Philip asked.

'Of course not. I'm rather pleased.'

'Rather?'

'Very.'

'It'll get better. It probably wasn't any good for you. It'll get better and better, I promise. And also, I love you. I love

201

the way you don't mind about that awful cafe yesterday, the dreadful guest house. I don't know why we didn't come straight here. Mustn't give into her dream too soon, I thought. Silly confused thoughts, something to do with showing who's boss.'

Stella smiled. 'I wouldn't have minded where we'd gone, what we'd done. Though I confess this place is . . . the sort of thing I was rather hoping for.'

'Good. Let's give that bored waiter something to do. Let's have sandwiches in our room for lunch. Let's turn on that wireless –'

'– and dance,' said Stella.

'Don't imagine there'll be much time for dancing.' Philip grinned.

They spent the afternoon in the large double bed, a bright winter sun lighting their bodies, hours flying in the concentration of each other. They bathed together in the deep cast-iron bath, revelling in six inches of very hot water and Stella's lavender soap. They dined, along with only two other couples, in the silent cavernous dining-room crowded with ghost tables of white napery. The underemployed waiters made much of trundling the meat trolleys to their table, pulling back the silver-domed lids with a grand flourish, and serving two minuscule cutlets with the kind of solemnity that must have applied to vast joints of pre-war beef. With a pudding of jelly, given status by a frill of imitation cream, they drank half a bottle of champagne. Stella made Philip laugh with stories of Hallows Farm.

Aware of the shortness of time left to them, they climbed back up the red stairs at nine thirty. Blackout in their rooms was concealed behind thick curtains: pink lamps had been lit, the bed turned down. They heard on the news that the Allied Armies had invaded French North Africa. But their concern was the few hours left: their last chance for God knows how many months. They hurried back into the bed, leaving on the lights. They spent the kind of night that would have shaken Mrs Elliot and her prim Guest House to their foundations.

'I knew very early on,' said Philip the following afternoon, at the station, 'that I loved you – or at least that I *thought* I loved you: you were the sort of girl I'd always had in mind. But – I don't know how to put this: I don't think I *felt* the kind of love you're meant to feel when you ask a girl to marry you. I think what I felt was the urgency of war, the need for firm plans.'

'I expect a lot of couples feel the same: such an unreal, unsure time.'

They sat on a bench on an empty platform. The train was due in two minutes.

'I have to admit I'm not really sure I loved you properly even when I first proposed, the day before yesterday.' Philip spoke rapidly, wanting to say so much before the departure. 'But now I *do*. I do. Believe me?'

Stella nodded.

'Since the nights, I suppose. That's why I proposed twice: once, semi-sure, once absolutely sure.'

Stella smiled. Philip glanced at his watch.

'Hope I've not spoiled anything, confessing. It was just terribly important you should know the truth. Will you tell me just once more? Will you tell me you'll marry me as convincingly as you can?'

'I will, yes.'

'Whatever happens?'

'Whatever happens.'

'Thank God for that. That means the weeks apart, however long, don't matter so much. I mean, being sure.'

'No.'

'I love you, I love you.'

'I love you, too.'

They kissed. They hugged, tears in their eyes. Then the

train, horribly punctual, came roaring up to stop their shorthand promises, and remind them it was now time to brace themselves, as Churchill had urged, to their duties.

Stella slept on the journey. She had never known such tiredness. She wondered how she would manage to stay awake through supper, fend off Prue's curiosity. She dreaded the dawn rising tomorrow, milking the cows in the freezing darkness. Sleepily, it occurred to her that, for all her stories of Hallows Farm, she had not told Philip the place was beginning to feel like a second home.

At the station she found light snow. A few flakes were falling from the dark sky, but they quickly melted on the windscreen of the Wolseley.

It was very cold in the car. Mr Lawrence had brought a scarf and thick jacket for Stella to put over her coat. She was touched by his thoughtfulness.

'All went well, I hope,' he said, after a few miles of silence.

'Philip asked me to marry him. I said yes.'

She could hear Mr Lawrence grinding his teeth.

'Good,' he said eventually. 'If he's the right one, you won't regret it.'

Eight

A few weeks after Stella had returned from Plymouth, Mrs Lawrence fell ill. She struggled for a couple of days with a bad cough and a temperature. Then Mr Lawrence announced one morning at breakfast he had insisted she spend the day in bed.

'It'll be the first time for twenty years she's done any such thing,' he said, 'but I told her if she didn't I'd call the doctor – an even worse threat, in her eyes. One of you will have to take over from her today. Which shall it be?'

Prue's reluctance was instant. She had an assignation with Barry. She busied herself spreading plum jam on a second piece of bread to avoid meeting her employer's eye.

Stella, since her official commitment to Philip, had discovered that she had become less indifferent to any duty that was required of her on the farm. Being engaged, it seemed, had altered the frizzy nature of love. Now, knowing she was secure, her thoughts were not, curiously, permanently with Philip. There was no longer a glazing of indifference between herself and whatever the matter in hand. She found herself better able to concentrate on the animals, the fields, and actively enjoy them. Secretly, she was missing Philip less than she imagined possible. Instead, what she now craved was music – a piano, a concert on the wireless. She wondered if there was a need for some kind of craving, at all times, in human nature, and spent many hours contemplating the subject of solace. If the thing you most want is missing, where do you turn for comfort? A line from Keats, vaguely remembered from school, came to her in answer. 'Glut thy heart on a morning rose . . .' Well, she thought, in her job as a land girl she was brutally exposed to Nature: she would try. She began to observe more accurately, find strange pleasures in the smell of earth newly turned by the hoe, the gilt-edged clouds of winter skies, the feeling of awe within a wood. She confessed these new sentiments to Ag, who had understood at once.

'I'll have to get you reading Wordsworth,' Ag said. 'No one better on the partnership between Man and Nature. He's pretty well convinced me of the compensations of the earth. Hope he's right, because if Desmond doesn't come about it'll be all I'm left with.'

She had sounded so solemn, envisaging a spinster life with Nature her only lover, Stella wanted to laugh.

'I'd be happy to do whatever's needed, Mr Lawrence,' Stella now offered, 'though I'm not much of a cook.'

She had been looking forward to a day freeing a gate from a tangle of brambles. Yesterday, she had begun the job armed with thick gloves and powerful secateurs. Surprised by her own skill in disentangling the thorny mass, she was eager to finish. Also, it was a solitary task – one of the occasions on which, without inhibition, she could sing as she worked.

'I'd positively *like* a day indoors,' volunteered Ag. 'I've been watching Mrs Lawrence making bread day after day – I'd like to have a go.'

'Ag it is, then,' said Mr Lawrence. 'Up you go for instructions from Faith, and we'll be expecting lunch at the usual time, two courses.' He smiled at her nicely.

'*At least* two courses,' giggled Prue. 'Canary pudding and syrup, if you can manage it.'

Prue found she needed especially large lunches the days of Barry's visits, to keep out the cold, and to give her strength for the acrobatics in their bed of leaves under the trees.

*

206

When they had all gone, and Ag had cleared and washed up after breakfast, she allowed herself a few moments by the stove, hands resting on the dogs' heads, to accustom herself to the strangeness of staying indoors. She was by now so used to spending most of each day outside, it seemed very curious, tame, to be left to the world of the housework. But this is what it must be like every day for Mrs Lawrence, she thought: sudden silence, the looming of domestic plans, lists of tasks to be accomplished by nightfall. There was no freedom from the discipline of deadlines: food must be on the table by midday, no matter how much ironing. The pile of socks to be darned must be kept under control; the grading of eggs, in the stone-chill of the scullery, was necessary before sending them off twice a week. For the first time, Ag began to reflect on the life of a housewife, doubly hard if you were married to a farmer. She wondered how it would be, how she would like it, when her time came – if, that was, she was not left entirely to Nature.

Stirring herself with a sigh, Ag went up the dark stairs to the Lawrences' bedroom – a side of the house she had never visited before. Mrs Lawrence called to her to come in.

Ag took a moment or so to adjust to the duskiness of the light in the bedroom, with its beamed ceiling and small windows. Then a few objects, touched by the grey sky outside, began like just-lit lamps to burn into view – a set of silver-backed brushes on the dressing-table, a framed sepia photograph of a girls' lacrosse team, a jug of dried thistles. Mrs Lawrence lay propped up on pillows in a high bed made of dark wood. Her hair was bound in a plait that lay over one shoulder; her face was flushed the colour of a bruise. She wore a long-sleeved calico nightdress, folded hands emerging from frilled cuffs and lying on the bedspread, stony as the hands of an effigy. The sight of her was a reminder of mortality: death from illness and old age, not just death from slaughter in the war.

There was a faint smell of cough sweets and honey. Despite a one-bar electric fire, it was very cold. Mrs Lawrence stirred.

'Do you mind, Ag? So silly, this. But John insisted . . .' Her voice was painfully hoarse. Shadows under her eyes scoured the drawn cheeks. Ag wondered whether she was seriously ill, or suffering from exhaustion, or both. What age was she? Probably early fifties, but she looked sixty. Affection for this contained woman, with her silent strengths, swept over Ag with renewed force.

'Don't worry,' she said. 'Just tell me what there is to do, then I'll bring you a cup of tea.'

'Sausages and mash for lunch, stewed apples and custard. Corned beef hash tonight, perhaps – whatever's there. I'm not thinking very clearly.'

She gave a small, self-despising smile, shut her eyes. *Tired eyelids upon tired eyes* . . . Pith-white skin stretched over the deep eyeballs. Open, the lids were crinkled as aged tissue paper. Closed, an illusion of youth clung to Mrs Lawrence's strong features.

'I'll have a go at making some bread,' said Ag.

'There's enough left from yesterday.'

'I'd like to try.'

'Very well. Don't overdo the salt. John doesn't like much salt.'

Their quiet voices chimed, church-like, in the soft brownness of the room. Then Ag crept away, leaving her employer to sleep.

It was the strangest morning since she had been at Hallows Farm, Ag later told the others. Working in the cold and silent house, her main anxiety was that she would not have done all the normal morning tasks, besides cooking the lunch, by twelve o'clock. Where was the Hoover, the dusters? What should be polished? Was it the day to scrub the stone flags of the kitchen floor? What rewards were there in doing such things *every day*? Guiltily she realised, as she buffed up the bannister rails in the icy hall, rewards did not come into it: Mrs Lawrence would never think in terms of rewards. Keeping house was merely a job to be done.

In the sitting-room, a forlorn place in the daylight, Ag turned on the wireless. The jaunty tunes on *Music While You Work* spurred her to polish the brass fender in time to the music, trying to keep herself warm. Then she listened to the news. It was announced that the Japanese had attacked Pearl Harbor.

Ag sat back on her knees, twisting a duster – slash of yellow in the dull light – in her hands. She tried to imagine the distant carnage, the destruction, the horror, the terrible suffering and pointless loss of life. She felt impotent anger, fear. This was followed by feelings of equally impotent guilt at her own lot, which was comparatively safe. There was never a day she could take for granted her luck in being here, a place where the war scarcely touched them, but there was also never a day when she did not wonder if she should not volunteer for some less protected field of action. Should she not join the Red Cross, or drive ambulances in the Blitz, rather than milk cows and feed off Mrs Lawrence's secure stews? Should her courage not be tested? And yet, while the men were fighting, girls to work on the land were vital: she had chosen the job, she loved it. But when news came of disasters, Ag was racked by the thought she should be helping the wounded rather than sweeping a safe yard or tending to the sheep.

She turned off the news, returned to work. Dully she set about preparing the lunch – at least the kitchen was warm. She was haunted by imaginings. Never having seen a photograph of Pearl Harbor, she had no idea of its scale. Visions came to her of gentle harbours on the East Anglian coast, crowded with pretty sailing boats. She tried to swap the familiar scenes for a more massive place, with destroyers at anchor. The paucity of mental pictures caused tears in her eyes.

When the others came in to eat they found her kneading a large lump of dough at the kitchen table. They wondered at the fierceness of her thumping, but made no comment. Ag's first loaf, which later rose magnificently in the oven, was filled with the stupidity of mankind, the futility of war, the helplessness of one individual such as herself to enable the world to come to its senses.

Ratty, too, heard the news on the wireless. It was one of his days off from the farm – never a good time, the hours would stick to him like mud, nothing would shake them off – petty chores in the house or woodshed were useless at accelerating the long minutes. What Ratty missed, in this state of semi-retirement, was the discipline of long hours at work in the open air. Alone in the front room, tapping his pipe against the grate, the news increased his restless state.

'Poor buggers,' he muttered. 'More trouble to come.'

He needed to be with someone. Anyone. Even Edith.

The kitchen was unusually welcoming: warm from baking, and filled with the sweet smell of dough. Edith, at the table, was regimenting troops of scones into neat lines on wire racks. Ratty was suddenly, piercingly, hungry.

'Will you spare me one?'

'That I won't.'

Ratty shuffled a little nearer the table, watched his wife's floury hand whisk among the crinkled edges of the beautiful scones, moving them into pure lines.

'Japanese buggers have bombed Pearl Harbor,' he said.

'Ah.'

Edith, devoid of all imaginings beyond the confines of her own life, was immune to most of the horrors of the war. She could only believe in what she read in the papers – her faith in the printed word had always puzzled Ratty – and then only if there was a photograph to prove the story. Thus it was a picture of Beaverbrook waving an armful of saucepans that had fired her own wartime effort, and she conceded the Blitz took its toll because the photographs 'said so'. Any wider understanding of the war, particularly 'abroad', was beyond her. Of late, Ratty had begun to wonder whether her lack of interest in the state of the world, affecting millions of lives, was some kind of disease. But then it occurred to him that solution was merely a figment of his own vivid imagination, and the real answer was that Edith's professed ignorance was a defence against intense, private fear.

'One thing after another. They're for tea, then, are they?' Again Ratty looked longingly at the scones.

'They're not for tea. They're for the shop. Got to keep the customers happy. Got to make a living.'

A new tack to deny Ratty the odd luxury, he thought. Usually, her concern was to cause unhappiness among the customers in their fight for her few loaves. Ratty looked at his wife carefully. Sighed.

'What's for dinner, then?'

'Thought I'd boil up a couple of parsnips.'

On such a grey day, so full of bad news, Ratty did not feel like boiled parsnips.

'Don't think I want any,' he said, knowing his rejection would cause a disproportionate measure of offence.

'Get yourself a sandwich, then. It's not the Ritz here, you know. I'm not bothered.'

Ratty had expected worse. But Edith's concentration on her scones, he noticed, was out of the ordinary.

He cut two slices from the loaf of hard, dark bread, and spread it thinly with shrimp paste scraped from a small ribbed jar. He knew better than to ask for butter: Edith had obviously availed herself of his carefully hoarded ration for her scones, and was in no mood to be confronted with her thieving. *Yes*, said Ratty savagely to himself, he would definitely call it *thieving*. If the point came he would, in all honesty, have to call his wife a thief.

'Think I'll take my dinner out,' he said. 'Sky's clearing.'

211

'Up to you if you catch your death,' said Edith.

Ratty pottered about making himself strong tea which he poured into a thermos. Edith, so preoccupied, failed to notice his stirring in two forbidden spoonfuls of sugar: that was at least one triumph. He wrapped the leaden sandwich in greaseproof paper.

'Mind you fold it up carefully, bring it back; it can be used again,' Edith snapped. She had been listening to the crackling of the paper, though she had not bothered to raise her eyes to check how much Ratty had taken.

'It's only a scrap, for Lord's sake.'

'Every scrap counts in a war.' When it came to the petty necessities of war, her perverse mind worked well enough. She raised her eyes. 'I suppose you're going off to join those girls.'

'That I'm not.'

'One of them, anyway.'

'No.'

'That's not what I've heard.'

'What d'you mean, Edith? Whatever are you talking about?'

'I keep my ear to the ground.'

Guilt seized Ratty's heart. Despite his innocence, and knowing he had never uttered a word to anyone, or made any kind of untoward gesture, he wondered how his wife could have guessed at the admiration, the secret *esteem* in which he held the holy one. In a moment of panic, he thought that maybe he had confessed this to Edith, and amnesia had blotted out the occasion. But no, that was mad. Surely . . . the mere sense of wistfulness – for that is what it was – he felt about Ag, was an absolute secret between Ratty and his God, and would always remain so.

'You're being ridiculous, woman,' he said. 'You know you are. You know those girls mean nothing to me. We're just fellow workers.'

'Huh. And since they've come, your working hours are

almost back to full time, aren't they? That's what everyone's noticed. That's what they're all saying to me.'

There was a long, incredulous silence. Then Edith began to brush flour from the bosom of her apron. It fell in a light dust on the cracked linoleum floor. If her snappish movements indicated a nefarious imagination could be called upon by his wife when necessary, Ratty did not notice.

'You're a wicked woman, Edith, that's what you are,' he said at last. He picked up his stick from the corner and thrust the thermos into his free pocket. Then he left the kitchen before she could answer, moving faster than he had for several years.

The heavy lunch and a strong cup of tea left Ag feeling calmer. She longed to do the afternoon milk, clean out the pig, anything rather than face the huge pile of ironing, but praise for her cooking had given her heart to face the domestic afternoon, and as soon as the lunch was cleared she went to the laundry room and set up the cumbersome ironing board.

Ag was an unpractised, unskilled ironer. It took her a long time to negotiate the difficult points of collars and spaces between buttons: compared with them, the stretches of sheets and tablecloths were easy, though the ancient iron was heavy. Within an hour her arm ached and her feet were icy on the stone floor. She began to recite to herself every long narrative poem she could remember, and was pleased to find there were few blanks. By the end of *Lycidas*, there was a pile of neatly folded clothes on the table – very professional-looking, she thought, and could not decide which gave her more satisfaction: remembering the long poem, or finishing the first basket of laundry.

The window of the laundry room was misted with condensation, but she could see the vague figures of Prue and Stella in the yard, driving the cows back to the field. She could hear the beasts' lowing – a different, deeper sound of relief, once they had been milked – and the squelching of dozens of hoofs in mud. Ag looked at her watch. Amazingly, two hours had passed. She finished the last of Mr Lawrence's shirts, allowed herself a brief image of ironing shirts for Desmond in some eternal future, then decided to pause for a while. Here she was, mind on *ironing*, when Pearl Harbor had been bombed . . .

She put a tray of tea beside Mrs Lawrence, who was sleeping, then went downstairs to sit at the kitchen table. Clasping cold hands round a mug of tea on the bare stretch of oilcloth, she listened to the muggy silence of mid-afternoon. Suddenly the quietness was split by the screech of a plane overhead. Within seconds the alarming sound had withered back to nothing, and Ag could hear the dripping of a tap again, and the beating of her own heart. She looked up to see Joe, in gumboots – not allowed in the kitchen when his mother was there – standing at the door.

'Hasn't been one like that for a long time,' he said.

'Come to shake us out of our complacency, perhaps. Pearl Harbor –'

'I know, I heard. How's Ma?'

'Asleep. I took her some tea.'

'How are you managing?'

'Fine I think.'

'I've got to walk down to River Meadow, look at a sheep. Like to come?'

Joe poured himself a mug of tea from the pot. Ag took her time, weighing things up.

'There's the bread to come out, the rest of the ironing.'

'I said would you *like* to come.'

'Yes.'

Ag smiled. She carried the tea things to the sink, moving with the kind of languor that assails those who have been indoors for many hours and now face the prospect of a walk in the cold.

'I'll get my boots,' she said.

The fronds of a plan, so indeterminate she could not be sure of its meaning, began to pulse in her mind. She felt suddenly courageous. Or was it reckless? As she followed Joe through the back door, Ag could not be sure: nor did she care.

'The wicked, wicked woman,' Ratty muttered to himself. He stomped down the lane, slashing at the verges with his stick. Sometimes he spat ahead of himself, a hard ball of sputum that sizzled out and died by the time he strode past it. His anguish was twofold: Pearl Harbor, poor buggers, and himself: deprived of a single scone by a wife who also – with no scrap of evidence – accused him . . . of what? And how was it she managed to undermine his innocence? What made her suspect there was more respect in his heart for the land girls – yes, even the floozie, a gallant little worker for all her silliness – than there had ever been for her?

The winter sky was heavy on Ratty's head. His temples throbbed, his arthritic hip ached. He needed shade, shelter from the cruel glare of the heavens. He turned into Long Wood that ran half a mile beside fields, then straggled on up the hill. In the path between the trees he found some relief. The purplish light that clings to winter branches, and the myriad shadows scattered finely as broken glass, confused his eyes in an agreeable way. He was in no mood to see things clearly. The muffling of his own footsteps was a blessing, too. Here, the only sound was an occasional soft snapping of twigs, mushy from rain, breaking underfoot. No birds sang.

Then the aeroplane, from nowhere. Ripped from the bowels of silence, it screamed invisibly overhead. Interrupted in their winter husbandry, birds rattled out of the undergrowth calling in alarm, and fled to high branches that trembled in the wake of the monster. Ratty peered up. Was it ours? Theirs? It had gone too fast for him to see. Knees trembling, he moved off again more slowly. After a while the wood returned to its old quiet and he came to a clearing, a junction of paths.

Ratty had intended to walk to the top of the hill – thus keep safely out of the house for a couple of hours. But, shaken by the plane and the mess of anxieties in his head, he took the wrong path. He progressed some fifty yards before realising this, but decided to carry on. Then, rounding a bend, he saw the distant figures of Joe and Ag coming towards him. A thumping and boiling of blood in his temples told him this was the last straw . . . Joe and the holy one . . . Such anger scorched his being he came to a halt, stood helpless in the path. They waved, *waved*: the cheek of it, thinking they could deceive him, no doubt. They smiled, *smiled*: how dare they! Ratty stood glowering back at them, his look signalling their time had come. By the time they were just a few yards from him, Ratty had made up his mind. Pity he hadn't got his pitchfork, but his stick was solid enough. He would thrash the life out of Joe: teach him to stop mucking about with the feelings of innocent girls.

With a gesture that might have been less fierce than he intended, Ratty raised his stick in the air, shook it threateningly. Even as he did so, he felt his free hand automatically touch his cap.

'Ratty!' The bugger Joe was smiling. The girl, too, happy as a lark. 'About to show Ag a nice bit of foot rot,' Joe said. 'We must keep on before the light goes.'

' 'Bye, Ratty,' said the holy one.

They passed each side of him like a tide that divides effortlessly round a rock in its path. If only he'd been quicker, silly old fool. Now he'd missed his chance – and Joe would have his way with the holy one, like he had with all the rest. Though in truth, and here Ratty began to potter on, even more slowly, Joe did *seem* bent on his mission with a sheep. Didn't look as if he was up to any funny busi-

216

ness, but you never could tell. The art of deceiving, as Ratty well knew, is to wear a look of innocence with such ease that suspicion is never ignited, never has reason to flame.

The sheep were gathered together in the far corner of the field – probably suffering from shock of the plane, Joe said. Sheep panicked more easily than cows, he explained: nervous, silly creatures – but, all the same, he would be sorry to see them go, next spring, after lambing.

'But, like everyone else, we have to turn most of our acreage over to plough,' he said to Ag. 'Price of living in a country that produces a third of its food. Come a war and animals must be sacrificed. We'll probably have to reduce the cows, too: just keep one or two for house milk.' His eyes travelled over distant fields. 'It's odd to think that in 1939 there were eighteen million acres of grassland, twelve million of plough. The rate things are going, in a couple of years that'll be reversed. But I don't suppose we'll be here to see the complete changeover at Hallows. We may have to move to Yorkshire.'

'Yorkshire?'

In the fast-fading light, they walked slowly towards the flock.

'My uncle, Dad's brother, isn't going to recover. His farm's the Lawrence family home. My aunt and cousin can't manage it on their own. They're struggling, even with the help of two land girls. When Jack dies, Dad'll have to take over. He'd rather be here than there, but he hasn't much choice. He feels he can't sell a place that's belonged to the family for a couple of hundred years. Rotten time to try to sell Hallows, middle of a war. And after all he's put into this place. But it can't be helped.'

'I didn't know any of that,' said Ag quietly.

'I'd be grateful if you didn't tell the others. I probably shouldn't have said anything.'

'Of course.'

'There's the one I'm after.'

Joe pointed to a dejected-looking ewe. When the rest of the flock swerved away and began to run, she hobbled so badly she was soon left behind.

Ag held the animal's shoulders while Joe examined the rotten hoof. The great black head worried about, bleating pathetically. Ag spoke soothing words, trying to calm her, but not succeeding.

'Treatment first thing in the morning,' said Joe at last, lowering the painful hoof to the ground. 'Off you go, old girl.'

They watched the ewe limp to join the rest of the sheep, who showed no recognition of her plight.

'You can become fond of them, somehow,' said Joe, eyes anxiously following the animal's progress, 'especially if you've known them from birth. I never forget the circumstances of a single birth, don't know why. Maybe you'll see what I mean, come the spring. We'd better hurry back, or you'll not have tea on the table in time.' He smiled.

'I don't much want to hurry,' said Ag.

For twenty-four years Ratty had been walking the woods on Mr Lawrence's land. He could find his way about them on the darkest night, learned – folly of a distant youth – by snaring the odd rabbit or pheasant, when he and Edith had found it hard to make ends meet. But today, in the gathering dusk, at the end of so disagreeable a day, he was confused. He turned down a small path that he thought would eventually lead back to the lane. He then realised he was again mistaken, and knew it would take him deeper into the wood. Ah well, he thought, he'd keep ambling aimlessly about: anything better than going home.

By now it was almost dark. It was hard to see where grass and brambles met roots of trees. The millions of individual bare branches had turned into solid, dense shapes. A tawny owl cried. Then there was the sound of a human cry, followed by laughter.

Ratty paused, listening intently. The laughter came again, from behind a holly bush. Ratty knew the holly well. Years ago, there had been a badger sett beneath it. He had taken Joe there, one night, to see the badgers play. Joe, at seven or eight, was a real one for wildlife. Ratty had often thought he might become a naturalist . . .

There it was again – the human cry clashing with the lugubrious note of the owl. Ratty took small side steps closer to the bush. He peered round. He saw a pile of something on the ground – a collapsed tent, perhaps. Trespassers? Poachers? Maybe, worst of all, *picnickers*?

He narrowed his eyes, forcing them to focus through the gloom, and saw that it was no tent but a pile of clothes. He could just make out the bluish jacket of an RAF uniform, forage cap tucked neatly into the pocket. Then he saw, slightly to one side of the general pile, a pair of corduroy breeches. He caught his breath, edged closer still to the place from which wild shouts and laughter were now coming.

What Ratty focused upon then caused him for a moment to think that he was hallucinating: two spectral melons rising and falling with beautiful rhythm in the darkness. As he watched, entranced, the ghostly fruits turned into the human flesh of buttocks. These buttocks, pale as moonstone, flew up and down so fast that Ratty, following them with incredulous eyes, soon found himself dizzy. He dug his stick deeper into the ground for support. A small hand had slithered up on to the buttocks, and was frenzying about in excited patterns, the fingers fluttering, fast. The air was suddenly filled with cries of abandon that, like the plane, frightened hidden birds. They flew up into the darkness, wings stirring the air near Ratty's face.

He could bear no more. He stepped backwards. Blindly, he moved down the path, tapping the roots of trees. The noises grew fainter behind him. An early moon, he saw through a gap in the trees, had just slit the sky, forcing a strand of light down through the branches that enabled Ratty to see he had arrived back at the main clearing.

There, he sat down on an old tree stump, a place where for many years he had paused in his walks. He could hear no more sound from the lovers . . . *lovers doing it on the earth, rutting like rabbits under the trees* – a dream so deeply secreted away that only the sight could have brought it back. The floozie and her airman: God forbid, the floozie and her airman were experiencing something he, through decades in the marital bed, had never known, would now never know. Oh Lord, he envied them.

For their pleasure, and for so many things he himself had never known, Ratty wept in the darkness.

'Can we go round the long way?' asked Ag. 'It'll be dark in the woods.'

With matching long strides, they moved across the field to the path by the hedge that divided the grassland from the wood. They walked in easy silence for fifty yards, then Joe came to a halt.

'Listen,' he said.

From somewhere distant in the trees came a thin trill of laughter, familiar in its running cadences.

Ag smiled. 'Wood spirits,' she said. 'They must be terribly cold.'

'Hope one of the spirits remembered to sterilise the bottles this time,' said Joe, with good humour. 'On Monday she was in such a hurry she forgot. I had my work cut out trying to cover for her.'

They began to walk again.

'If Ratty comes upon them,' said Ag, 'he'll have a seizure.'

'Poor old Ratty. He's ageing fast. Gets pretty confused these days – waving his stick at us like that, as if we were poachers.'

'Prue says he unnerves her, his silence. Stella and I are

his fans.'

'How was Stella's weekend in Plymouth?' asked Joe after a while. 'I never heard.'

Ag took some time before answering. 'I suspect something happened,' she said at last, 'but I'm not sure what. She said it was all wonderful and she's pleased to be actually engaged. But I don't know. I privately think there was some kind of . . . disappointment.'

'She's not quite her old exuberant self. She seems to have come down from the clouds.'

'She does. That's just it. She concentrates more on the matter in hand now. Her dreamy look is gone. She talks in practical terms about marriage, houses, children, life after the war. It's almost as if spurred by just three meetings with Philip, before she came here, her imagination superseded the reality. She's always saying she has to be in love, Stella. She can't live without being in love. So there she was, in love with this almost imaginary figure, goes off to meet him and, well . . . But I'm only guessing.'

They had reached the gate that led to the lane. Joe leaned on its top bar. He seemed in no hurry to open it, or climb it. Ag imitated him, fingers of one hand drumming the damp wood. By now a dew was falling. The darkness, characteristic of a late winter afternoon, seemed to cascade inefficiently over what was left of the daylight, so that the struggle between impending night and departing day was visible. In an hour or so, the transparent quality of the ensuing gloom would have thickened, become dense. A skeletal moon was stamped on the sky, the most fragile of seals, which gave no light.

Joe turned to Ag. 'And you, Ag,' he said, 'do you have a secret, imaginary love, too?'

'As I think I told you, there was this research graduate at Cambridge.'

'Was?'

'Never *was*, really. Still *is*, in a way. I still cling to the idea

221

of him, though I knew him even less well than Stella knew Philip. Just saw him in the distance a few times. Had one tea in a café with him and a few friends. Listened to him. You'll think this mad, but if, that evening, he'd asked me to go anywhere in the world with him, I would have gone without further thought.'

'Highly romantic. Good thing he didn't give you the chance to be so unwise.'

Ag smiled. 'I wouldn't expect anyone to understand,' she said, 'but I felt a kind of *certainty*. I felt such certainty, such conviction, that here was my other half, or whatever the silly phrase is, that in some strange way my life changed absolutely from that day on. From June the sixth, 1941, I've been borne along by the indescribable sensation that . . . everything I do is significant only in that it's a step nearer to the inevitable outcome . . .' She sounded solemn, shy.

'And what's that outcome?' There was a trace of sceptical laughter in Joe's voice.

'Him and me. Together in some form.'

'Ah.'

'I suppose you think all that's ridiculous?'

'No. Most people need their fantasies. I rather envy you such a dream. What happens if it doesn't work out?'

'It will,' said Ag, 'but if it doesn't I'll be all right – just lesser, somehow.'

She glanced sideways at Joe, could just see a smile twitching the corners of his mouth. Suddenly she felt the warm rush of an unfamiliar feeling: skittishness, she thought it was. Confidence, ease. And the vague shapes of the plan that had come to her earlier in the afternoon returned, beating faster.

'But if it's all a disaster, doesn't happen, I never see him again, then I'm quite prepared to live a solitary life.'

'For a clever graduate with a face which won't go unnoticed, you're talking a lot of nonsense,' Joe laughed. 'Aren't you cold? Shouldn't we be getting back?'

'Not very. In a moment.'

Scarcely aware of what she was doing, Ag, inspired by some peculiar boldness, stepped on to the gate and sat on the top bar. She faced Joe.

'Here's some more nonsense,' she said. 'If it *does* go right, and we meet again one day, I want to go to him *experienced* . . .' Her face blazed in the darkness. Wondering at her own recklessness, she went on. 'I don't want him to think I'd been pathetically keeping myself for him.' She paused. 'I'm quite keen to be shot of my virginity . . . There: I've said it.'

In the silence that followed, Ag realised the extent of her impropriety. But, still fired by her inchoate aims, she went further in her madness, and rested her arms on Joe's shoulders. He did not protest, or move, but kept his silence.

'I knew I'd go too far eventually,' Ag murmured at last. 'I've made a complete fool of myself. Please don't tell the others.'

She removed her arms, climbed back off the gate to the other side. Joe followed her.

'I think I could probably oblige,' he said.

'*What?* I didn't really mean you, Joe . . .' His reaction caused her such confusion she turned from him, began to walk.

'I think you did.'

'I've been in a terrible muddle. Waiting, waiting: it's a sort of canker. It does things to you.'

Joe caught up with her. He took her hand.

'I can imagine that,' he said.

They walked in silence up the dark lane, so fast that the cold that had bitten into them was replaced by an almost feverish heat beneath their thick clothes. As they turned the corner to the farmyard gate, Joe released Ag's hand. She felt briefly deprived of warmth, comfort, understanding. The expectation that his offer had provided was a calm, sweet thing: no desire attached, just curiosity.

'When?' she said.

'Soon,' said Joe.

Two days later, Mrs Lawrence, recovered but weak, was up and resuming her usual duties. The first evening of her return to normal life, she stirred the Christmas pudding in a huge bowl.

'It'll be a thinnish pudding, this year,' she said to Stella, who was chopping vegetables at the other end of the kitchen table. 'Rich only in sixpences. I've been saving as much dried fruit as I can, and John's let me have a bottle of brandy from the cellar. But it won't be like the old days.'

Stella smiled. In her pocket was an unopened letter from Philip – the first since Plymouth. Curiously, her impatience to read it was manageable. The idea of keeping it till she was in bed throbbed no more fervently than the idea of a minor luxury. Her chief feeling was one of a childlike excitement about Christmas. Earlier in the day Mr Lawrence had brought in a Christmas tree, and set it in the sitting- room. Mrs Lawrence had brought down a box of decorations from the attic, and given them to Prue. As the experienced window-dresser of a leading Manchester hairdresser, Prue had said, she was the most qualified to dress the tree. No one had quarrelled with this. She burst into the kitchen now, twigs in her hair – there were twigs in her hair most days, Stella quietly observed – starfish lashes blinking wildly.

'It's done, it's beautiful! No one's allowed to go in and see it till after supper. Only thing that's missing, Mrs Lawrence, are small candles. I'll get some in Blandford tomorrow. You coming, Stella? It'll be good fun. We could get Christmas cards and presents and things, and go back to the tea-room. Then we could see what's on at the picture house, have a drink somewhere, catch the last bus . . . couldn't we, Mrs Lawrence?'

Mrs Lawrence nodded. She passed the spoon to Prue. Prue stirred the uncooked pudding.

224

'Shouldn't I be making a wish?' she asked. She shut her eyes for a moment. 'I know what I'm wishing.'

Stella thought she had a pretty good idea of Prue's wish, too: she wondered what her own should be. For a return of the old impetus, perhaps.

'I always wish the same, every year,' said Mrs Lawrence, taking back the spoon. What could *that* be? Stella wondered.

'You just keep on,' giggled Prue. 'You just need enough faith, and anything'll come true.'

'I hope so,' said Mrs Lawrence. 'Come on, Stella, your turn. Where's Ag?'

Ag, her three days of intense domestic duties over, had returned with some relief to her tasks outside. She was pleased to be reunited with the bantams and hens. Collecting eggs, feeding and cleaning their houses, had become one of her regular jobs. She had come to learn the birds' various moods, their stubborn ways, their flights of stupidity, their sense of detachment. While the others stirred the pudding in the kitchen, Ag searched the barn for two missing bantams: the rest were shut up in their houses for the night.

She held a hand over her torch, released a few bars of almost useless light. But she knew her way about well by now: knew their favourite corners, far from the tractor – they had separate places for sleeping and laying. As Ag felt among the sacks she could hear the familiar churring of pigeons high in the rafters. Then, from a place near her, the higher, tremulous clucking of bantams. She uncovered the face of the torch, swept its dim beam over a cluster of nesting places. In a comfortable dip in the hay, croodled the two lost birds.

'Come *on*,' she chivvied. 'You're late.'

In an obedient mood, the bantams flopped to the ground, squawking and flapping. They ran towards the farmyard, heads jabbing furiously. Ag switched off her torch. Turning to follow them, she saw the dark silhouette of Joe. Her heart quickened. The arranged seduction, whenever that was to be, was not going to take place here in the barn, copy of Prue's experience. Of that, Ag was determined.

'I need some books, Ag,' said Joe. 'I've finished everything. If I take you all in to Blandford tomorrow afternoon, would you help me choose some?'

Ag was glad of the darkness. Glad he could not see her blush. Glad it was only books he wanted.

'Of course.'

'Then,' said Joe, 'we could go out to tea.'

'Fine. Anything. I must make sure the bantams have gone back, shut them up.' She hurried past him.

'Hurry in and stir the pudding,' Joe shouted after her, 'and wish us luck.'

Five minutes later, it was Ag's turn with the spoon. Screwing up her eyes, she saw a picture of Desmond's face, and wished to do the right thing. When she opened them, she found Joe looking at her. This unnerved her. She had been strangely calm since their conversation two days ago at the gate. Now, her usual composure left her.

'I think we all need a drink,' said Mrs Lawrence. 'Joe, there's a bottle of whisky in the cupboard.'

Joe fetched glasses and the bottle. Stella and Ag exchanged looks. Apart from the ginger wine on the first night, it was the first time an alcoholic drink had appeared since they had arrived. Ag drank hers, neat, in one gulp. It would steady her, she thought. She needed something to dissipate troubling thoughts of Janet. Her own conscience was not loud enough to halt the planned deed, but planned betrayal, she was finding, is full of noisy rebuke.

'Joe,' Mrs Lawrence was saying, 'Janet rang earlier. She says she can get off midday on Christmas Eve, be here by supper time.'

Ag took a quick look at Joe's face. The neat whisky had

had its impact already: his features spun like a Catherine wheel. Indeed the whole room, all faces, trembled with uncertainty. Joe had no time to answer his mother before Prue dashed in singing *I'm dreaming of a white Christmas*. She wore garlands of tinsel round her neck. Silver balls hung from her ears and gold paper stars were wedged in her hair. Everyone laughed: Joe poured her a drink. Ag, to her own amazement, found herself moving right up to Prue and putting her hands on her shoulders – the same gesture she had so curiously made to Joe by the gate.

'Prue,' she said, 'you look *marvellous*. You should be on top of the tree.' The words, like the glittering vision before her, were a little unsteady.

'Good heavens, Ag,' said Prue, 'whatever's got into you?' There was more laughter.

Joe answered for Ag. 'The Christmas spirit,' he said.

My dearest darling Stella, Stella read in bed later that night. Well, at least he's upped the tempo a little, she thought. A good start.

> *That was a lovely weekend. I keep thinking of so many bits of it, and it's a good feeling knowing you're as sure as I am about getting married. It's frustrating not being able to make any plans because of the war. We must just hope it's over soon and then we can make arrangements very quickly. We're escorting a convoy to Liverpool tomorrow which will make a slight change. Hope you're happy back with the others and the animals. Forgive brief note.*
>
> *In great haste.*
> *With all my love, Philip.*
> *PS My friend Michael and I are planning a day trip to London in the New Year. Perhaps you might be able to come and join us?*

Stella folded the letter, returned it to its envelope, put the envelope by the photograph, still in its same place. She sighed, turned out the light.

'Letter from Philip?' Prue's whisper came out of the darkness. She never missed a thing, Prue.

'Yes.'

'Anything the matter?'

'No. I'd just hoped it would be a bit longer. A bit –'

'Don't worry. Practically nobody in the world can write a good letter.'

'True,' Ag joined in, from her end of the room. She had been wondering, now the spinning of her head had calmed down, whether or not she should buy a Christmas card for Desmond in Blandford tomorrow. She turned this way and that, making the bed creak. Yes, she decided. She would.

'Stella?' It was Prue again.

'Yes?'

'Are you coming, tomorrow?'

'If you like . . .'

'Ag? How about you? Do our shopping, have some fun?'

'As a matter of fact,' said Ag, 'Joe mentioned that on condition I helped him choose his books he'd give us all a lift.'

Prue giggled. 'Blimey! You mind out. Choosing books is as good a way as any.' There was a brief silence. 'Shall I tell you something? Barry says he's not sure how much longer he can keep up all this cycling.' Prue giggled again. 'So, obviously, I've got to be on the lookout for a replacement, for when he's finally exhausted. We could go to the pictures, Stella, couldn't we? Always a chance, there. Will you come, too, Ag?'

'Think I'll come back earlier, if Joe will give me a lift,' Ag answered carefully. 'I've got letters to write, Christmas cards.'

'Anything you say.' Prue gave a final giggle. 'Tell you what, I recommend the barn. One of those stacks up on the right – very comfortable.'

'Don't be *silly*, Prue,' said Ag. 'You know there's Desmond.'

'Well, there *isn't*, exactly. Desmond, I mean. Is there?'

There was another long silence. Ag thought the other two had gone to sleep. Then Prue had the last word.

'Ag, you awake? Because let me tell you something. What you're going to be shocked by, this time, is *yourself*. I bet you.'

Ag put her head beneath the bedclothes. She had no wish to hear any more truths from Prue. She had no wish to think further about the extraordinary resolve to behave badly that seemed to have overwhelmed her.

While the others went off for their Christmas shopping, tea, and the hunt in the cinema for a Barry replacement, Joe and Ag spent a long time searching the shelves of a small bookshop. Joe was keen to buy the entire works of Gissing. Ag persuaded him that to start Balzac would be more rewarding: the compromise was *Eugénie Grandet* and *Born in Exile*. Joe began to enjoy himself. He randomly chose a disparate selection of Penguins: *Can You Forgive Her?*, Chekhov short stories, Hardy's poems (Ag's strongest recommendation), various books that had slipped through the net of his reading, as he put it. It took over an hour to fill the large shopping basket Ag had brought.

They then went to a grocer, where Joe bought a bag of ginger biscuits, two anaemic iced buns and half a bottle of red wine. Ag, curious, but determined to ask no questions, helped him carry the purchases to the car.

It was three o'clock when they drove out of the town. The light had not yet begun to fade.

'Poor Stella,' said Ag, 'I bet she would have liked a lift home with us.'

'Probably,' said Joe, 'but Stella wasn't part of my plan.'

His plan, he explained eventually, as they drove into deep country of small wintry hills, was for tea in Robert's cottage. Robert was his oldest friend, unable, like Joe, to be called up, because of weak lungs.

'Before you all arrived,' Joe said, 'we used to meet most nights in The Bells. Have a drink or two, talk about anything except the war and farming. It was something to look forward to at the end of the day. But since you've all been here . . . I don't know. I've grown used to Prue's mindless chatter, your serious little head bent over a book, Stella's dreamy look while she keeps up polite conversation. There's more to the evenings, now, somehow.' He smiled. 'When I rang him last night, he reminded me we hadn't spoken for a week. Some friend, he said. What Robert needs is a woman, a girl. He's lonely. I was rather thinking –'

'I know exactly what you're thinking.' Ag laughed.

'Think she'd do? Save her a lot of scouring the streets and cinemas of Blandford.'

'I don't know Robert. How can I judge?'

'He's a good man. Funny. He'll make an uxorious husband one day.'

'Rich?'

'Far from it.'

'Temporary measure only, then. Prue's set on her gold taps. But you could try.'

They turned off the lane into a muddy, uneven track between high hedges, and reached a grey stone cottage. Its moss-clad thatched roof, in danger of slipping off, was only held in place by the frailest netting. Paintwork was peeling. Windows were thick with cobwebs and grime.

Joe took an old iron key from the lintel above the front door. He led the way into a dark, damp room. It smelt of past cats and rotten fruit. There was little furniture, but for an old sofa in front of an empty grate. Dozens of books were piled on the floor, some of their covers smeared with mildew.

'He doesn't have much chance to be domestic,' Joe said. 'You go and boil a kettle while I organise a fire.'

Ag took some time to find her way round the unpleasant kitchen. She had to wash dirty tin mugs under the single cold tap, and she could only find one plate. By the time she returned to the sitting-room with tea things on a rusty tray, Joe's fire had brightened the place a little.

'So when's he arriving, Robert?' Ag asked.

'Don't be silly. He's not.'

'I see.'

'Biscuit? Bun?'

'I'm suddenly not hungry.' Ag sat at the far end of the sofa.

'We needn't go through with this if you've changed your mind,' said Joe, gently.

'Last night I was awake for hours, thinking I was mad, immoral, wicked, a ridiculous fool. I was going to say I had changed my mind. But now I'm here . . .'

Joe took two cloudy glasses from a shelf and a corkscrew from his pocket. His pre-planning was exemplary, Ag thought. He opened the bottle of red wine. 'This'll take the edge off things for you.' He handed her a glass.

'Thanks.'

Ag took a sip. It was cold, bitter. She forced herself to keep drinking, treating it as medicine. A flicker of warmth came from the fire. She began to feel better. The outrageousness of her behaviour seemed slightly less outrageous. By the time she had finished the wine, there was only one real worry left.

'I fear you may not find me very attractive,' she said. It came out sounding prim as a governess. To obliterate the taste of the wine, she tried the nasty tea. She could not meet Joe's eyes. 'So if . . . it doesn't work, I'll quite understand.'

Joe touched her hot cheek. 'In a few years' time, when this roundness has fined down a little, you'll be more striking, more original-looking, more *arresting* than either Prue or Stella.'

'Do you really mean that?'

'I do. Prue's prettiness, her kitten looks, won't last. Stella can look beautiful – that night at the dance she was stunning – but she doesn't take enough trouble. But you've got the bones. Somewhere. Waiting to emerge.' They both laughed. 'I said to Robert how lucky we were. Imagine the three land girls we might have been sent, I said.'

'We're the ones who've been lucky. We might have been landed in one of those hostels – not much fun, I hear. Or with some tyrannical farmer. Hallows Farm, the kindness of your parents – no land girl could ask for more.'

'It was Ma's idea.'

They finished the wine. The second glass Ag found less difficult. It had, as Joe predicted, taken the edge off things. The bleakness of the room, the apprehension of the act they were about to commit, lay more gently on her spirits. Joe stood up, took Ag's hand.

'I think we should go up.'

Ag stood, too. She was as tall as Joe. Their eyes met on the level. He kissed her on the forehead.

'Just one more thing,' she said.

'What's that?'

'Janet.'

'What about her?'

'Isn't all this very immoral? What about your conscience – and mine, for that matter?'

Joe sighed, impatient. 'It's not the time to discuss Janet, is it? You should have said something about her before if she troubled you. I can't tell you why, but for some reason she's not on my conscience. I've given her my word: I'm going to marry her. Until that time I feel free to do what I like. All right?'

Ag nodded.

Joe led her out of the door and up the narrow wooden stairs. Ag wondered how many other times he had made use of his friend's house: how many other girls had followed him up those stairs, and into the little cold bedroom with its sloping black wood floor and crooked window. Joe drew the scant cotton curtains. Dead moths fluttered to the ground. Then he pulled down the bed cover. Two blankets lay folded on an ancient mattress. Stained pillows were slumped, caseless. He switched on an exiguous bedroom light. The low-watt bulb smeared the walls with a dun light, increasing the gloom. Ag stood by the window, taking in the scene of her impending seduction.

'Not exactly a honeymoon suite, I'm afraid,' said Joe, 'but I don't think we should use Robert's room, which isn't much more cheerful anyway.' He sat heavily on the bed. The springs yelped. 'Why don't you get undressed?' He bent down to untie his own laces.

Ag wanted to say that she had imagined a lover would help with this process. But then she remembered Joe wasn't a proper lover, just a friend about to oblige her in her irrational request. So, in silence, she slipped off jersey, skirt, shoes, let them slide to a heap on the floor. She paused before raising her petticoat above her head. There would be something either comic or distasteful, she felt, in the sight of her knickers, suspenders and brassière. But Joe must be used to such things. The glance he gave her did not indicate surprise.

'You've the body of a ballet dancer,' he said. 'Degas would have liked to have painted you – the blue lights on your skin.'

Ag smiled politely, rolled off her stockings. A moment later she was completely naked. This time Joe's look was appraising. She stood to attention, knees touching, a blade of light between her thighs. Her cold fingers curled about in small whirls over her thumbs. She told herself this would probably be the only time in her life any man would sit looking at her body, taking in the thinness of her legs, the smallness of her breasts.

But even as Ag enjoyed Joe's silent approbation, a worrying thought came to her. What if she became pregnant? It would be a dreadful irony, that – to conceive a child in a single sexual experience designed (in a fit of madness, she now thought) to impress the stranger of her fantasies, Desmond, with her past 'experience'. In some alarm, still not moving, she tried to remember what Prue had said. One night, just before Stella had gone to Plymouth, Prue had volunteered to advise them on the matter of birth control. Something about making quite sure the man either used a french letter or – a bit riskier – 'unplugged', as Prue called it, before the vital moment. But what was the vital moment? Ag hadn't liked to ask Prue, and she certainly wasn't going to ask Joe, displaying even further her pathetic naïvety. She remembered, too, Prue declaring that sometimes, at safe times of the month, she couldn't be bothered with any of the whole boring palaver, and, touch wood, she'd been lucky so far.

Ag put a hand on the chest of drawers. When was the safe time? Anxiety clouded her swift calculations. She wished she had listened to Prue – whose advice was chiefly aimed at Stella – more carefully. But she'd fallen asleep, probably missing important details. There was nothing for it, now, but to take a risk. If this was to be her one and only sexual encounter, possibly *ever*, then it should not be complicated with technicalities. It should be as uninhibited and enjoyable as possible in the peculiar circumstances. Screw your courage to the sticking place, Ag told herself, privately relishing the aptness of the self-advice, and get through the whole business with as much dignity as possible. She gave the faintest smile of encouragement.

Joe rose from the bed, came towards her. The fact that he had taken off only his shoes seemed to Ag unfair. She was curious to see his body, too. The nearest she had come to the study of a naked man's body was her study of Michelangelo's David. She had judged that Joe, with his height, his broad shoulders, narrow hips and firm thighs, would be something like that. She wanted to see the private parts. She was curious to learn what happened when stone turned to flesh. But this she was to be denied.

Joe picked her up. In a concave position, slung over his arms, she knew he was studying the flatness of her stomach, the hands modestly placed over the Mons Venus. He laid her on the bed. It smelt of cat, like the sofa downstairs.

'I'm going to put out the light,' he said, 'and we can pretend we're somewhere better.'

A murky dusk clogged the room. Joe, his face a clutch of indistinct shadows, bent over Ag. He rested on stiff arms placed each side of her shoulders.

'Are you sure . . .?'

Ag nodded. Joe moved to lean on a bent elbow. With one hand he began to unbutton his shirt. With the other he traced a gentle path from her neck to breast, to stomach, to thigh. Ag closed her eyes.

Later, lying stiff and cold in his arms, the experience reminded Ag of a visit to the doctor. It had been efficient, clinical, easy, swift. It had not hurt. Neither pleasure nor displeasure had been present: all Ag could think about, feeling the bulk of Joe upon her, was *this is happening*. It did not differ from the imaginings, because she had never been able to imagine exactly what it would be like. How it felt, in the end, was not very exciting. Perhaps, with someone you loved, it would be different. The only really curious thing about it all, she thought, was her lack of concern about what she called her wickedness. Thoughts of betraying Janet – for which she had berated Prue – existed no longer. Perhaps, it occurred to her, such callousness is a sign of maturity.

In a matter of moments Joe was swinging his legs off the bed, sitting up. He switched on the lamp, glanced at his watch.

'We'll be back in time for supper, complete innocence. You all right?'

'Fine. Thank you.'

Joe patted her leg with an uninterested hand. 'There,' he said. *There,* she had heard him say, so many times, at the end of a task: milking, muck-spreading, parking the tractor. *There,* he would say, meaning *a good job done, and now it's time to eat.*

He stood up and reached for his clothes, his back to Ag. Gone was her last chance to view the sight she had craved for so many years.

'Hope it wasn't too disappointing.'

'No. Thank you.' Ag shook her head. It wasn't disappointing: it wasn't anything. So she could not bring herself to say the deflowering had been either satisfactory or happy. It had been merely interesting. He had efficiently performed a function she wanted, needed, for her own esteem. And the best thing about it was that it was now over. The small web of deliquescence that had netted Ag as she lay in his arms, due more to fatigue than fulfilment, now broke. She leapt up and scurried to her pile of clothes, dressing with her back to Joe.

Ten minutes later they were in the Wolseley, on the way home.

'Now that's over,' said Joe, 'we can spend our time with more important things, like books.'

Ag smiled. Really, he had been – was being – very kind about the whole thing. Her only concern now was that her new status would not be observed.

Joe carried the basket of books into the kitchen. Mrs Lawrence was pouring soup into bowls, inspiring Ag with unusual hunger.

'Very literary afternoon,' Joe said, 'advised by my tutor, here.'

He gave Ag an open smile.

*

236

Ratty spent the evening in the front room, smoking his pipe by an unlit fire. He wanted to listen to the news, imagine the war. Edith did not. She darned peacefully – it had been a strangely peaceful evening, not a single argument – at the kitchen table.

At ten o'clock, she opened the door, stood looking at Ratty slumped in his chair. She always liked to keep bad news till late, to ensure Ratty would have something to trouble him in bed.

'There's a stomach upset going round the village,' she said. 'Seven or eight down with it.'

'Ah. Hope it won't clobber us.'

'Don't suppose it will.' Edith sounded oddly definite.

She went on standing there, not moving, arms folded defiantly under the bolster of her bosom.

'I forgot to tell you,' she said at last, 'my batch of scones went like greased lightning, everyone wanted more. Fighting over them like cats and dogs, they were.'

They returned to silence. Ratty could think of no appropriate answer. He could hear the tick of the grandfather clock in the hall. Its rhythm set something off in his brain: a thought so vile he must quickly speak – say anything – to block its progress.

'How many customers did you have, in the end, then?' He tried to give the question lightness.

'Seven or eight in all,' said Edith, without hesitation. She moved away.

Fear spread over Ratty like a cold dew. From now on, for survival, he knew he must keep a close watch on Edith. Driven by some cankerous demon, there was no knowing how far she would go in her bitter hatred of mankind.

Ag went up to bed early. She was almost asleep when Stella and Prue returned from the late bus, string bags full of Christmas presents. Prue, flinging herself on her bed, chattered excitedly about the outing. She hadn't a penny left, she said, but had bought all the presents she needed. No: they hadn't found a Barry replacement in the tea-shop or in the pub, but a friendly old farmer had bought them two gin and limes and told them there was to be a New Year's Eve party in the town hall to raise money for the Red Cross.

'So there's hope *there*.' She giggled. 'Barry'll do till then.'

She lay on her back on the bed, lifted her legs, admiring the rayon stockings and dove-grey suede shoes, with their neat little pattern of holes, and thick platform soles.

'So let's hear about your news, then, Ag. What were you and Joe up to?'

'We bought a lot of books, we had tea,' said Ag.

'Come on. You don't expect Stella and me to believe that, do you? Not with two hours on your hands, Joe plainly keen for you.'

'It's the truth.'

Prue sighed, mock impatient. 'We don't want details, do we, Stella? We just want to know how it was. What it was like.'

Ag imitated the mock sigh. 'Don't go *on*, Prue. I'm almost asleep. I tell you, it was shopping and books. If you don't believe me, I can't help it.'

Prue screeched with laughter, squirming on the bed, clutching her knees to her chest. 'I can see by the look on your face. Okay, you go to sleep. But we'll get it out of you one day, see if we don't.' She winked at Stella.

It wasn't till 1947, their second lunch after the war, that Ag confessed. By then the activities of the afternoon had turned to such fine dust in her memory that secrecy was no longer of any importance.

Nine

Stella had never intended to go home for Christmas. She had had her two nights away and her mother, who drove ambulances for the Red Cross, was to be on duty in London. Ag had planned long and complicated train journeys to King's Lynn. She would arrive home, after many hours waiting on cold platforms, late on Christmas Eve, and have two days with her father. She, like Prue, would return the day after Boxing Day. Both promised to undertake unpaid overtime when they came back.

On the night before their departure, Prue lighted the candles on the tree. She had devoted an entire half-day off to finding them. After several long bus journeys, and a ride in a farmer's cart, she had returned triumphant with two dozen small red candles, and tin holders shaped like daisies. General appreciation made her declare her terrible afternoon had all been worth it. Mr Lawrence produced a new bottle of ginger wine, which they drank, from the pink glasses, round the fire. Small presents were exchanged. Ag came in with a tray of white hyacinths – a single flower for everyone, in a pot tied with a red bow. Mrs Lawrence gave Ag a parcel to take home with her. To Prue she gave a flat white envelope.

'I know I shouldn't, now,' Prue said, 'but I'm that intrigued I can't wait.'

She sat down and split open the envelope. Dizzy blonde curls jumped excitedly round the tinsel star, left over from the decorations, on her head. She pulled out a Christmas card. A page of clothing coupons fell to the floor. She leapt up, incredulous, scarlet with pleasure.

'Oh, Mrs Lawrence – I don't believe it! Better than *diamonds*, better than anything you could possibly have thought of. Thank you ever so much.'

Prue hugged her employer, who stood stiffly by the tree. Small shadows from the candles flickered over Mrs Lawrence's brown dress, softening the rigidity of her thin body. Unused to such celebration – for years Christmas had been just the three members of the family – she smiled at Prue's delight.

'When I get back,' Prue gabbled on, 'I'll be off to some great town, kit myself out with a whole new wardrobe – you wait!' The others laughed. 'Can you really spare them?'

'What would I do with them?' asked Mrs Lawrence, glancing at her husband.

Joe refilled glasses. There was the sound of a hand-bell ringing outside. Then, singing.

> *It came upon a midnight clear*
> *That glorious song of old . . .*

'That'll be Ratty and his carol singers,' said Mr Lawrence, going to the door.

Ratty trudged in, thickly coated and scarfed, carrying a church candle.

'No lantern again this year, blackout rules, blasted war,' he said, 'and only these members of the choir willing to come with me.'

He was followed by two young boys, also holding candles. Each cupped a hand round the flame, so that their palms shone pinkly as shells, and a visible incense of cold blew off all three of them.

'What'll it be, then?' asked Ratty. 'Come all this way up the lane, we got to give you your pie's worth.'

'"In the bleak mid-winter",' suggested Ag.

This time last year she had heard it sung at King's College. She had spent every minute of the carol service looking round for Desmond. She did not see him.

'*In the bleak mid-winter,*' the small choir began. Ratty's deep growl made an unharmonious base to the boys' pure voices. After a line or so, the others joined in. They stood in a semicircle, eyes filtering from flames of the fire to the miniature flames on the tree. They stood very upright, as if for 'God Save the King', private thoughts hidden behind the familiar words. A particularly sweet female voice stood out from the rest. Mr Lawrence let his eyes glide towards Stella. Tonight, as on the night of the dance, she was so beautiful in her unadorned way that he felt his heart contract, and a pricking behind his eyes. He quickly dashed his look from her face, left the room to fetch more glasses.

The evening passed with more carols, and hot mince pies sprinkled with sugar that Mrs Lawrence had been saving all autumn. Two bottles of ginger wine were drunk. The room had never been so warm. The candles on the tree burned down to their stubs. Prue extinguished them with an expert pinch of her fingers dampened with spit. Brief wisps of smoke replaced the flames. Ratty, confused by several drinks, observed to no one in particular: 'Look at that! The floozie's gone and filled the tree with smoke!'

He swayed slightly, pleased to find laughter at his comment. Had he said anything so foolish at home, Edith would have struck him. Joe took his arm.

'And leave me be, thanks, Joe. The boys here'll see me home. Sober up in the midnight clear, I will.'

He smiled for the first time since his lecture on ratting all those weeks ago. And, heaven forbid, bless her lovely heart, the holy one smiled the sweetest smile back. That made his Christmas, that did.

Not till after midnight did Ratty and the boys leave. Mrs Lawrence pulled back a corner of the blackout to watch

241

their departure. The girls crowded round her. They could just make out the trio – dark figures against dark – moving across the yard, the boys each holding one of Ratty's arms. With their free hands, they held up their candles, which made firefly lights to guide their way under a sky devoid of stars.

Prue and Ag left early next morning. Janet arrived in the evening.

She came in the Austin Seven, carrying a utility suitcase and a string bag of presents wrapped in Christmas paper. Mrs Lawrence was shutting up the hens, Joe was out some-where, Mr Lawrence was affording himself the rare treat of an evening bath. Stella found herself the one to welcome Janet, who looked cold, pale and tired. She led her upstairs to the attic, where Janet was to sleep in Prue's bed.

'Goodness me . . . Aren't you frozen up here? And no privacy. I wouldn't like that.'

'We've grown used to it,' said Stella. 'In fact I think we'd miss each other if we had separate rooms.'

'Well, well. Better than a hostel, I suppose.'

Janet took off her grey coat, to reveal a grey skirt and matching jersey – clothes no more alive on her dull body than they would be on a coat hanger. She sat on Prue's bed.

'At least it's comfortable,' she said, with a grateful smile.

'Why don't you unpack your things? Prue's cleared two top drawers. I'll go down and make a pot of tea.'

'I haven't brought much. I'll come with you. I'm not here to be waited on.'

'Don't be silly. You must be tired after the journey.'

'Well, my goodness, I did get a little lost once it was dark, I must say. No signs make it so confusing. Don't tell Joe: he'd think me so stupid. He'd never get lost.'

She pulled some hairpins from the roll of hair that coiled round the back of her neck. Shaking her head, she stirred her hair with cautious hands. Lustreless locks fell on to her shoulders, altering her face: the pale eyes seemed to retreat, while the nose gained prominence.

'After I was here last time,' she said, 'seeing all of you . . . I thought maybe Joe would like me to let it loose over Christmas.'

Stella nodded kindly, unable to find an answer.

In the kitchen Mr and Mrs Lawrence were stuffing the turkey. Mr Lawrence held the bird's thighs while his wife spooned in a coarse mixture of chestnut and onions. They greeted Janet without pausing in their task, leaving Stella to fetch the girl bread and tea.

'What a lovely sight, very Christmassy,' said Janet shyly. Stella observed a small shiver under the grey wool.

Then Joe came in, the dogs behind him. He did a swift double-take, for a second confused about the creature with forlorn locks. To mask his hesitation he hurried over to her, gave her a peck on the cheek.

'Good journey? I've put the car in the barn.'

'Oh, Joe. Thank you. Four and a half hours. Sorry I was a bit late.'

Joe was already far from her, washing his hands in the sink. He returned to the table, picked up the bread knife.

'I'm famished,' he said.

'Let me,' said Janet.

'You never cut it thick enough.' Thin smile.

'Then let me get you a mug of tea.'

Janet stood up, awkwardly bustled between stove and table. Her desire to please was so blatant Stella found it painful to watch.

'I mean, goodness me, I'm here to help, you know.'

'That's very kind, Janet,' said Mrs Lawrence, after a silence which no one else attempted to fill, 'but I should think you could do with a couple of days' rest.'

She pulled a flap of skin across the stuffing-filled cavity. Mr Lawrence let go of the bird's legs, wiped his hands on his corduroy trousers. His eyes drifted over the grey figure of his future daughter-in-law before swerving to Stella, healthy-cheeked under the kitchen light, messy hair lit with reddish gold. She gave him so faint a smile he understood it was private. In acknowledgement, Mr Lawrence returned her sign with so slight a movement of his mouth that it, too, went unobserved by the others.

None of the gaiety of the previous evening prevailed. The hours were long until it was time to go to church. They sat by the fire listening to carols on the Third Programme: Mrs Lawrence with her usual darning, her husband stretched out in his customary position, eyes closed. Janet placed herself close to Joe on the sofa. He concentrated on a crossword puzzle, only half listening to her news about life as a sparking-plug tester.

'It's getting so cold, the work, now, we freeze to the bone,' she was saying. 'We take turns in getting the sniffles, although none of us ever takes a day off. I'm still hoping to become a radiographer, but the path doesn't seem clear. I talked to Andy Barrett – he's our boss – about it the other day: he said he'd bear it in mind but didn't hold out much hope.'

Janet's prominent ankle bones just touched each other: she always sat with her feet together, as if for security, Stella noticed. Her hands were in their habitual position, too – tense on her lap, fingers of the right one rubbing knuckles of the left.

'Actually,' Janet went on, with a coy look at Joe, 'Andy called me aside last week.'

She paused, waiting for the impact of this information. Joe carried on with his puzzle. The small attempt to arouse jealousy, or at least interest, was pathetic. Stella felt acutely for her.

'But don't worry, Joe – it was nothing, really.' Janet, suddenly bold, nuzzled one of her fiancé's knees with a screwed-up fist. 'It was just that apparently his wife was having trouble setting up their Anderson shelter. Would I take a few hours off and help her, he said. Of course, I could tell he didn't approve of the whole idea, anyhow. "I said to Marion," he said, "what do you want with an Anderson shelter out here? We're not London. It's not the Blitz, here." But she's apparently the nervous type, Marion, and insisted. So, anyway, off I go. At least it made a change, an afternoon digging up earth in their back garden, trying to stop it sliding off the roof of the shelter. We did quite a good job of it together, Marion and me. But was Andy grateful? Huh! We'd made a b-awful mess of his Brussels sprouts was all he said.' Janet returned her hand to its place on her own knee. '"People like Marion go to pieces in a war," he said, which I thought was rather unkind, don't you?'

Stella nodded, to make up for lack of agreement from anyone else. From the hall came the unusual sound of the telephone. It had not rung more than a dozen times since the girls' arrival. The older Lawrences regarded it with misgiving. For them it was an instrument that conveyed either bad news from John's brother in Yorkshire, or dull information. None of them stirred. Puzzled by their peculiar reluctance to answer it, Stella – to whom the telephone had been a wondrous link with the love objects in the past – offered to do so herself.

In the cold of the hall she picked up the receiver, heavy as a hammer, and held it curiously to her ear. Philip's voice. Her heart gave the merest flutter.

'Stella?'

'Philip!' She was pleased, of course. But wondered why she wasn't more pleased.

'Sorry it's so late. I've been waiting in a queue for ages. Everyone wants to ring home.'

'Of course.'

'Everything all right?'

'Fine –'

'Got my card?'

'I did.'

'They're laying on quite a show on board, Boxing Day. Vera Lynn herself, the rumour goes.'

'How wonderful.'

'I'm looking forward to that, I must say.'

'I can imagine.'

'This time next year, perhaps it'll all be over.'

'Quite. Now America's joined –'

'This time next year, you'll be Mrs Wharton, any luck.'

'I hope so.'

'Must go, now. Chaps behind me getting impatient. I think about our weekend a lot. Gosh, I do. The nights.'

'So do I.'

'Love you, Stella. Love you, darling.'

'Love you, too.'

Conversation over, Stella remained sitting on the stairs in the dim hall. The mean thought entered her mind that Philip was no better on the telephone than he was at letters. Perhaps talking across distances was an art not yet much practised, and future generations would take to it with complete ease, laughing at those who still regarded the telephone with dread and awe: a machine which had the power to make articulate men stumble, and those less talented with words cause endless disappointment.

She was aroused by footsteps, and the appearance of Joe.

'Boyfriend?'

Stella nodded.

'All well, I hope.'

'Fine. They're expecting a Vera Lynn concert on Boxing Day.'

'Lucky old them. It's time to go to church.'

As Stella watched Joe rummaging about through the mess of scarves and gas masks hanging from a row of pegs, she heard herself making a spontaneous declaration. It was one of those peculiar moments, she thought later, when an unpremeditated thought surprises its owner as much as it does the receiver. The sudden idea was not part of the plan she had put to Mrs Lawrence.

'Joe,' she said, 'I couldn't find anything I thought you'd want in Blandford. So I thought my Christmas present could be a lie-in tomorrow morning. I'll do the entire milk, scrubbing down, sterilising, everything. You sleep.'

Joe turned to her, winding a scarf round his neck. She could see the struggle on his face as he grappled to try to decide how to react.

He smiled.

'Heavens! That's the most imaginative Christmas present I've ever been offered,' he said at last. 'It'd be very churlish of me to turn it down. I can't sleep late, ever. But an extra hour or so in bed, reading . . . what a luxury. Thank you.'

'I'd do the same in the afternoon,' Stella went on, 'so that you and Janet can have an hour or so to yourselves. A walk, whatever.' Joe's eyes avoided hers. 'Well, yes, perhaps, thanks.' He pulled on a jacket. 'But it can't be all one-sided, this present giving, can it? I've done hopelessly by you – hideous little scarf. So my real present can be identical to yours to me – but on Boxing Day. All right?'

'Lovely.'

They both laughed.

Outside, the cold was bitter, dry. Snow in the air, Mr Lawrence thought. The sky was clear, full of stars. A bright moon lighted their way up the lane.

Stella walked between Mr and Mrs Lawrence. Some yards behind, the engaged couple followed – Janet with an arm tucked firmly through Joe's. She was prattling on, though Stella could not hear what she was saying. As they neared the church a quiet bell began to chime.

247

'Ratty'll be strung up if anyone in charge gets to hear about this,' smiled Mr Lawrence. 'Breaking rules again.'

But as they walked through the porch and saw Ratty at the back of the church pulling on his bell rope, Stella could see Mr Lawrence's look was one of admiration. Ratty waved. Pulling on the rope lent his old limbs a balletic quality: if he had suddenly alighted from the ground, swung up to the sixteenth-century rafters, clinging monkey-like to the rope, it would have been no surprise.

'Christmas Eve, bugger the war,' grinned Ratty. 'Christmas isn't Christmas without church bells.'

The echo of his single bell sounded with unusual urgency, thought Stella: a warning of mortality. Just two weeks ago today, HMS *The Prince of Wales* and HMS *Repulse* were sunk. Since then, pictures of a flaming *Apollo*, disappearing between mammoth waves, had been haunting her. They came to mind now as the bell insisted. She had always feared the ability of bells to stir unwanted imaginings. But then a woman at the organ – who wore a badge saying *Dig for Victory* among the speckled feathers of her hat – launched into 'Jesu Joy of Man's Desiring', her plump fingers chomping at the notes with surprising skill, and the flames faded.

The Lawrences, Stella, Joe and Janet filed into a pew near the front: there were only six others in the congregation. Stella knelt on a tapestry stool made, it said in cross-stitch, in 1916: by someone's mother or wife waiting for a son or husband to return from that war, no doubt. Stella prayed for peace, for those who were fighting for their country, dying for their country, the wounded and the grieving. She prayed for the safety of her mother, and for Philip, the prayers slipping mechanically through her mind. She glanced at Joe, hands jabbed right over his face, fingers running into his hair, and Janet, mouth pursed, fingers a gloved temple beneath her chin. One last mechanical prayer that they should be happily married, though God knows . . .

The vicar, wounded in the last war, came limping up the aisle. The congregation stood. Stella looked at the red-berried holly on the altar, the mistletoe that dangled from the pulpit, the jug of white chrysanthemums squat and defiant on the chancel steps. Someone had gone to the same effort as Prue to find candles: they stood lighted on every ledge, their flames making leaf-shadows across the old stone. The thought of all the time that villagers had invested to ensure the church would be the same as ever at Christmas, despite the war, Stella found deeply moving. She sometimes wondered at people's lack of appreciation of invisible effort: effort that, in the context of the larger world, is of small importance, but whose ultimate results – a decorated church, an embroidered fabric – give so much pleasure. To Stella, such effort, made by what her mother called 'the unsung saints of England', could be as disturbing as music.

O come all ye faithful . . .

The party from the farm joined in.

At some point Stella felt Mr Lawrence's eyes upon her, and saw they sparkled with the kind of embarrassed tears that strong men fight at a funeral but cannot completely control.

'I'm not sure he noticed,' said Janet. She dabbed a sad hand at the slabs of loose hair. 'What do you think? Should I put it back to normal tomorrow, what Joe's used to? I'll feel easier like that.'

It was almost one in the morning. Janet sat once more on the edge of Prue's bed. She made no effort to undress. Stella, in her dressing-gown, put her working clothes into some order on a chair ready for the morning.

'Do you know something?' Janet said. 'Joe's never kissed me. I mean, not properly. Not what I call a full-blown kiss like you see at the pictures.'

'He will,' said Stella. 'You haven't had much chance.'

'We've had the odd chance – he's just never taken it. What worries me sometimes is I think his mind hasn't been on that sort of thing at all. Not with me.' She gave a small sigh. 'I suppose it'll all be different when we're married. I expect he's just holding back, not wanting to alarm me. He knows I . . . Well, I wouldn't want that to change, of course, till we're married. But I wouldn't mind just a bit of, you know. All the girls at work go quite far with their boyfriends. They all tell each other what they do. I have to pretend Joe and me do much the same.' She pulled the grey jersey up over her head, revealing small breasts encased in a stiff pink brassière, its surface a complicated pattern of white stitching. 'Sometimes I think I just don't understand men at all.'

'None of us does, really,' said Stella, getting into bed. She looked at her watch. 'The thing is, I have to be up in about four hours . . .'

'Goodness me, I'm sorry.' Janet stood up, attempted to complete the rest of her undressing, but was distracted by the photograph of Philip.

'Your fiancé?'

Stella nodded.

'My, he's handsome. Do you really love him?'

'I do, I think, yes. It's difficult ever to be quite sure.'

'I don't agree with that at all,' said Janet. 'I'm quite sure of my love for Joe. Always have been since the moment we met, years ago, not much more than children. Any little bothers in my mind are all due to this b-war. They'll all be sorted out when we're married, that's what I believe.'

'I'm sure they will,' said Stella, almost asleep. 'Do you mind if I turn out the light?'

'Oh, I am sorry, chattering on – you go ahead, go to sleep.'

In the darkness, Stella heard Janet get into bed, churn about, making the springs squeak.

'Just one more thing, Stella: it's lovely being here. You're all being so kind. Christmas Day! My goodness, it's Christmas Day at last. I think what I'll do is give Joe the surprise of his life. I'll put on some lipstick, make him *want* to kiss me . . . What d'you think? Would you lend me some of yours?'

'Of course.'

'D'you think it's a good idea?'

No answer to this question told Janet that Stella had fallen asleep. Still, it didn't matter: she was quite confident so sympathetic and beautiful a girl would agree with her. Yes: Janet liked Stella.

A few hours later, in a clear, cold dawn, Stella let herself out into the empty yard. She tried to determine whether this morning held the childlike excitement she still felt every year on Christmas Day, whether it was different from normal days. It was, in a way, she decided, on account of the silence. There was no Mr Lawrence trumpeting into his handkerchief, as he did first thing outside every morning. There was no Joe clumping about the place with his long strides and preoccupied face. Besides, the extra exhilaration of having decided to do everything herself added to the especial feeling of the day. Joe had been pleased by her idea just as she had been delighted by his. Tomorrow, her turn for a few extra hours in bed, would be bliss.

She was about to turn into the lane, make for the cows' field, when she heard a bellow from the shed. Puzzled, she turned and hurried back, wondering if Joe had changed his mind and come to help her after all. In the shed, she found the animals in their stalls, chains clanking with their familiar heavy sound. Steam was rising from muddied hindquarters, strained wide by bulging udders. And hobbling down the aisle came Ratty, in his bell-ringing clothes, looking very pleased with himself.

'Thought I'd get them in for you, at least,' he grinned.

'Knew you were planning to do them on your own. Takes a very long time, no help at all.'

'Ratty! Thank you. But your best clothes . . .'

Ratty's smile disappeared. 'Didn't bother to go to bed, as a matter of fact, after the service.' He paused, wondering whether to confess further. 'Edith, she doesn't – well, she doesn't hold with Christmas. We had words.' He gave a rattling cough. 'Better be on my way. Get a bit of sleep before *Christmas dinner*, if you can call it that. Edith's got in a tin of Spam and a Mrs Peek's Pudding . . .'

'I'll make sure you have some of ours.'

'They're all ready to go.' Ratty's cloudy eyes dragged along the rows of black and white rumps. 'A happy Christmas to you.'

Stella knew that to wish him the same would only encourage further thoughts of his own bleak day, so said nothing.

It was mid-morning by the time she had finished the sluicing down and the sterilising. Pale sun, colourless as a Christmas rose, slanted through the open door, gilding a patch of watery concrete floor. Stella couldn't deny feeling a certain satisfaction. She had completed the long job all alone, efficiently, and was undaunted by the thought of repeating the whole process this afternoon.

Mr Lawrence appeared. 'Happy Christmas, marvellous job, Stella, thanks. But I think you'd be appreciated indoors now. I'll take them back to the pasture.'

In the kitchen, Mrs Lawrence was stirring a pan of gravy on the stove. Janet, her back to Stella, was at the sink washing the pink glasses very slowly. Stella sat at the table, where she began to prepare the sprouts. Janet turned, dishcloth in hand, back-lit by the winter sun. Her hair had returned to its usual tight roll and she had, as threatened, put on a red lipstick (it must have been Prue's: Stella did not own such a colour). In the whey colour of Janet's face it resembled a crude line drawn by a child. When she smiled it emphasised the primrose tint of her long teeth.

'What do you think, Stella?' she asked, licking at the gash of red with a nervous tongue. 'Improvement?'

'Definitely,' said Stella.

'Christmassy, I thought.' She held up the pink glass, blinked at its crisp shine, gave it another fussy polish.

No wonder more hands were needed indoors, thought Stella, who had been looking forward to the walk down the lane with the cows.

Joe came in, then, his face blurred by unaccustomed sleep. Janet, in her excitement, almost dropped the glass.

'The best Christmas present ever, Stella,' he said. 'Christ, I only woke up ten minutes ago. Unbelievable.'

Janet's red mouth fell for an instant, then winched itself into a terrifyingly bright smile.

'Happy *Christmas*, Joe.'

She moved towards him, dishcloth and glass still in hand, head positioned for a kiss. Stella observed the varying emotions that crossed Joe's face. First, blankness, as if he had forgotten Janet's existence. Then, surprise at her being present. Finally, horror at her appearance. Janet seemed not to notice any of these reactions. By the time she had reached Joe, he had organised an expression of greeting, and obliged with the required kiss on the cheek. This brief affair over, Janet kept her head tilted back, this time awaiting an opinion.

'So – what d'you think?'

'What about?' Joe looked puzzled. The ruby bar brooch, which Janet had pinned to the neck of her beige cardigan, in celebration of Christmas, or some more private reason, caught his eye. He touched it. 'Very pretty,' he said.

'No – not the brooch, silly.' Janet smiled. She found the smallest measure of attention from Joe intoxicating. It made her daring. 'The lipstick.'

'It'll take some getting used to,' he said. 'You know what

I am: man of habit. Slow to change.'

This, in Janet's eyes, was approbation enough. Suffused with pleasure, she nuzzled her head against his shoulder, a dreamy smile slipping this way and that.

'I thought you'd like it.'

'Come along with those glasses, Janet,' snapped Mrs Lawrence. 'They're needed on the dining-room table.' She gave an impatient stir to the gravy. Spots flew over the side of the pan and landed with an angry sizzle on the top of the stove.

'Sorry, Mrs Lawrence,' Janet murmured, still impervious to the sharp voice of her future mother-in-law. 'I'm all of a dither, this lipstick.'

After Christmas lunch – which, due to Mrs Lawrence's careful husbandry turned out to be a pre-war affair – Stella excused herself as soon as possible to start on the afternoon milk. She could not bear to watch Joe undoing the parcel Janet had brought him – a pair of Fair Isle socks she had taken months to knit in between working on socks for the Forces. She had no wish to watch Janet's reaction to the box of four handkerchiefs Joe had bought her, nor witness the struggle over plans for the afternoon. She knew having a few hours alone with Joe was Janet's intention, and sensed the reluctance to comply with any such thing on Joe's part.

Stella devoted most of her Christmas afternoon to hard work with the cows. By early evening she was exhausted. She went upstairs to lie down for an hour before changing out of her working clothes for supper. Janet was sitting in her now customary position, ankles just touching, on Prue's bed. She was near to tears.

'Oh, Stella. I'm glad you're back.'

'What's the matter?'

'We went out in the car. Joe likes driving the Austin. After a while I said, why don't we stop, Joe, study the view?

He looked at me, honestly, as if I was mad. He said when he had a chance to drive a nice car, he wanted to drive, not look at a view. I think he must have guessed what I was hinting at . . . Well, eventually we did stop, in a gateway, not at all private, no view. I gave him the box of chocolates I'd brought – I wanted it to be a small, private present, and my goodness, it went down much better than the socks. He seemed really pleased. You're a good girl, Janet, he said, and patted my knee. *There*, he said. He began on the chocolates. I refused to have one. I wanted to take my chance.'

Here, a single tear ran down Janet's cheek. She quickly wiped it away with one of the childish handkerchiefs that had been Joe's present to her, and gave a brave little grin.

'Anyhow, I said, things don't seem to be going too well, Joe. We never seem to have the chance to talk, and you hardly ever write. I'm not complaining, I said, but I always supposed when people were engaged they wanted to be in touch. And then, when they met, they were pleased to see each other. Joe was on to his fourth chocolate, by now, a rose cream. You must give me time, he said. I'm *sorry*, he said. But somehow it didn't sound very convincing. After that, he concentrated on that little map – you know, saying what's inside the chocolates. Then he said, the thing was he had a lot on his mind, or words to that effect, that he didn't want to talk about. Not even to me, Joe? I said. Not even to you, he said.' Another tear appeared. 'But I do understand, I said. Of course I understand. I know how fed up you were not being able to go and fight. I know how disappointed you were not to be able to go to Cambridge. They're big things to cope with. But you could always go to Cambridge at the end of the war: we could *live* in Cambridge, I said, and he just looked out of the side window so I couldn't see his face.'

Janet paused, made sure of the sympathy still in Stella's eyes.

'Then – and please don't tell the others – I made my mistakes. I said, Joe, have things changed because of the land girls? I'd quite understand if you'd fallen in love with the Prudence girl. She's so pretty and bright . . . He looked at me again, as if I was off my head: quite comforting, I suppose that was. Don't be ridiculous, he said. I like them all in their different ways and I don't know what we'd have done without them. But I'm not in love with Prue – the idea has never crossed my mind. He gave a kind of a smile at such a ridiculous thought, which sort of cheered me up. But I could see that I'd also annoyed him. So then I said, trying to sound bright and light-hearted: and how did you like my lipstick? You couldn't really say, earlier, in front of the others. Silly of me to have asked then. This time he turned to me quite fiercely, his mouth full of chocolate. There's no point in trying to ape the others, he said. You're not that kind of girl. I like you best as you always are, unadorned. A scarlet mouth doesn't suit you, if you want the truth. I just thought, I said, it might make you want to kiss me . . . It did just the reverse, as a matter of fact, he said, so cruelly – I know he didn't mean to be cruel – I had to hold myself in not to cry. So I took out this handkerchief' – she held up the damp, pinkish screwed-up ball – 'still fresh from its box, and wiped all the lipstick off in one go. There, I said, is that better?'

There was a long silence. Stella could see Janet no longer fought to ward off tears. Her struggle, rather, seemed to be to find the right words.

'So he did kiss me. No words. Just a kiss on the mouth, his arm awkwardly round me. All the time, though, I felt there was something not quite right. I mean, I'm not experienced like I expect you and the others are. I don't know about kissing. But I'd always imagined it would sort of be . . . warmer, somehow. I began to open my lips, like I've seen them do at the pictures, and he backed away. I didn't let him see I was disappointed, of course: after all, it was the longest kiss we've ever had. I was very grateful. So I told him I loved him and he said, again, that I was a good girl, and started up the engine. On the way home I said that I thought it would be all right once we were married; waiting gets everybody down. And he said yes, once we were married everything would fall into place.'

'So you must be happier,' said Stella, after another long pause.

'Well, I am and I'm not. I have faith in Joe, I don't think he'll let me down. Just be patient, I keep on telling myself, and we'll end up married. But it's hard not to suspect he doesn't love me half as much as I love him, and never will. He doesn't ever say how he feels, he just says he won't let me down. Perhaps that's all I should ask. I mean, goodness, I know how lucky I am – not exactly Veronica Lake and far from brilliant, and still a rare man like him, who could have anyone, chooses me. So all I can do is go on being sure, chasing away doubts while waiting for the war to end – there must be so many couples feeling just the same. I'm ashamed of feeling sorry for myself.' She gave a dim smile. 'And once we *are* married, not a day will go by when I don't prove to him how much I love him. I think he'll come to feel the same. I pray he will.'

'It's time,' said Stella, 'to go down to supper.'

Janet jumped up, smoothed out her skirt. 'Do I look as if I've been crying?'

'Let me put a touch of powder . . .' Stella dabbed a powder puff under Janet's eyes, and rouge on the pale cheeks. 'If only Prue was here. She's much better at this sort of thing. There, you look fine.'

Janet took a nervous glance in the hand mirror. 'You've been so kind. I told Joe how kind you've been.'

'I haven't at all.'

'You've listened. Hardly anyone listens. I wish I didn't have to be off so early in the morning. It's gone so fast, my stay. And there won't be another moment to be with Joe alone. Mrs Lawrence says there's a tradition of gin rummy on Christmas night, so I'll have to put a brave face on for that.'

'No cards for me,' said Stella. 'I'm going to bed straight after supper. I want to make the best of my luxurious Christmas present from Joe.'

'You mean the long lie-in while he does the milking? He can be very imaginative, sometimes, Joe.' Janet looked so melancholy Stella feared more tears.

'Come *on*,' she said. 'Devilled turkey and mince pies.'

'At least Joe'll be pleased,' said Janet following Stella downstairs, 'that I'm back to no lipstick again. That, at least, should make his Christmas. Funny old Joe.'

On Boxing Day morning, Stella slept till midday, unaware of Janet quietly packing her bag and leaving. She came down in time for lunch to find a lightness in the air: it could well have been her imagination, but the tension of the last two days, while the sad grey figure of Janet hovered about trying to help, doing her best to fit in, had lifted. The Lawrences chattered more easily. Joe, who had gone to visit Robert when he had finished with the cows, returned with the news that he had invited his friend to supper on New Year's Eve.

'I told him about the Red Cross party,' he said. 'With any luck, he'll suggest to Prue they give it a try.'

His mother gave him a look.

In the afternoon, Stella helped Joe with the milking, and the delivery of the churns to the village. Mr and Mrs Lawrence went for a long walk with the dogs – another of their Christmas traditions. Joe invited Stella to his room to listen to some music but she said she must write a letter to Philip. The break in routine and the strangeness of a few hours' rest during the daytime had begun to wane. She looked forward to the return of the others tomorrow, and the return to normal, disciplined days.

After supper Mrs Lawrence suggested that Joe went for a drink at The Bells, taking Stella.

'It's often quite cheerful up there, Boxing Night,' she said, 'and you haven't had much fun.'

A couple of hours in the cold air had ruddied her wan cheeks. Stella guessed she would like an evening alone with her husband.

'It's been a lovely Christmas, but I'm all for a drink, if that's what Joe would like,' Stella replied.

They walked quickly up the lane. It was much colder than Christmas Eve, deep shadows sharp-edged under a full moon.

The bar at The Bells was warm and crowded. Paper chains and silver bells swooped between the low beams, and the landlord wore a paper hat.

'Almost everyone from the village here,' said Joe, looking round, 'except Ratty and Edith. That augurs badly.'

He carried two glasses of mulled wine – seasonal speciality at The Bells – to a table near the fire, where a child, the landlord's son, was roasting chestnuts. Joe helped Stella off with her coat. She sat back in the old oak chair, looking about, smiling. She felt no need to talk, as she had done in the pub in Plymouth, with Philip. Joe was not a man to be provoked by others' silence. He remained unspeaking himself, eye on the door, hoping Ratty would appear. After a while he leaned towards Stella.

'This bloody war,' he said.

She knew, for him, all the things that meant, but judged it best to make some neutral reply.

'You know,' she said, 'I've only had one real sighting of it. My mother – she works for the WVS as well as the Red Cross – was on duty at Victoria Station when the soldiers were returning from Dunkirk. She said I should come and help on her tea stall, it would be something I would never forget. At the station, there was chaos. Hundreds and hundreds of soldiers wandering about so shocked and exhausted they seemed almost to be sleepwalking. Many of them were bandaged up, wounded – the strong helping the weak. I handed a cup to one man, and he gave me twopence. No need, I said, it's free. *Free?* he said, and tears poured down his stubbly cheeks. It was the first time I'd ever seen a man cry, the tears spilling down his greatcoat, running into the buttons . . . that was my only glimpse of the war. Otherwise, the nearest I've got to it was listening to my mother's stories of the Blitz. At home we only had to go down into the cellar a couple of times during a raid. Here, at the farm, there's such extraordinary peace it's hard to believe the horrors of London, the big cities, the remote world.'

'There's always the tension, the uncertainty.'

'There's always that, yes. You remember it first thing every morning; you're reminded by the odd screaming plane.'

'Has its effects – the feeling nowhere is absolutely safe.'

'Of course.'

'Though, here, I think I'd be right in saying the arrival of you girls has been something of an antidote. It was a bad time before you came.' Joe broke off at the sight of Ratty coming through the door. 'Thank God for that,' he said quietly, signalling to Ratty to come and join them.

The old man pushed his way through the crowd, Adam's apple working furiously above his scarf, troubled eyes blinking. He drew up a chair. Joe went to fetch a pint of beer, and two more glasses of wine.

'I'm later than I should be,' said Ratty. 'Edith's on about something or other.'

'You couldn't persuade her out, then?' asked Joe, on return, with a teasing smile.

'You can say that again. She's in one of her festive moods, all right. Thanks.'

The three of them sat quietly drinking. Their silence was broken by a sudden commotion in the crowd. There were shouts of encouragement. Stella saw an elderly man being hustled towards an even more ancient piano.

'Told you.' Joe smiled at Stella. 'There's music at The Bells. Hugh Wadley, there, is the keenest pianist for miles. He used to teach at a school in Dorchester.'

The sprightly old man settled himself at the piano, laid his hands on the keys. The notes were bruised, out of tune. At the sound of the imperfect chord, a frisson zipped down Stella's spine. It was a long time since there had been any possibility of a musical evening. She was enjoying herself.

It's a long way to Tipperary, the drinkers round the piano began to sing. Stella, Joe and Ratty joined in. There was applause at the end of the song: much slapping on the back and cries of *Down with bloody Hitler*. Mr Wadley took a sip of beer, and looked towards the fire.

'Is there anyone here with a real voice?' he asked.

General laughter.

'Stella?' whispered Joe.

Stella shook her head.

'If there was, I'd be much obliged,' said Mr Wadley. 'All this shouting you lot call singing can damage a man's ears.'

'Go on,' urged Joe.

Stella hesitated, tempted. Her cheeks were warm from the wine. Happy in the crowd of strangers, she was filled with an unexpected longing to sing.

'You know what I'd like to hear?' Ratty bent towards her. 'I'd like to hear "They Can't Black Out the Moon".'

'All right, Ratty, just for you.'

Stella was on her feet, elated by her spontaneous decision. She moved towards the piano. The drinkers – mostly men – made way for her, eyes curious. Regulars at The Bells were not used to such a sight. They disguised their stares with cheers of encouragement.

Bending over Mr Wadley, Stella hummed the first line of Ratty's song. Mr Wadley, overcome by the response to his request, was bowed over the stained keys in a position of great reverence for the instrument, as if his concentration would magically clean their ivory.

'Anything you like, dear. G major do you?'

Stella nodded. The noise died away. A moment's silence was chipped only by the soft shuffling of logs among flames. Stella clasped her hands, let them hang against the skirt of her red dress. She looked up at the smoke-grained ceiling, felt twenty pairs of eyes upon her.

She began. Quietly, for a few lines. Then, encouraged by smiles, she increased the melancholy power.

> *I see you smiling in the cig'rette glow,*
> *Though the picture fades too soon*
> *But I see all I want to know*
> *They can't black out the moon . . .*

When the song came to an end, there was another moment's silence before rough applause and shouts for more. Stella, blushing and bowing her head, could see that the only two people who sat unsmiling, and not clapping, were Joe and Ratty. Confusion: what had she done wrong? They had been the ones to encourage her – how had she let them down? Anxiety flooded her enjoyment. She moved to the piano, leaned on the cracked maplewood of its top.

'You know what that pose reminds me of?' Mr Wadley laughed. He played a few notes. More shouting as Stella smiled. It was the introduction to one of her favourite songs. She would sing it, she thought, then go. Find out what she had done to cause Joe's thunderous look. She glanced over at him, caught his eyes.

'*Falling in love again,*' she began. Her pure, husky, sweet voice curled through the smoke, the warmth, the nostalgic faces of men and women reminded of their own love stories that had begun before the war.

While she sang, Joe stared.

Ratty, watching Joe, saw before him a man transfixed: a man within whom some life-shattering process was taking place. With his keen eye for a rat's trail, Ratty could not fail to observe what was happening to Joe: something he thought Joe could never mention, a secret he, Ratty, would take to his grave. Whatever the nameless experience was, Ratty felt he understood it long before Joe himself. It was not often a spectator had the privilege of witnessing any such private rite of passage: it was as rare as coming across the mating of a wild animal, the hatching of a bird's egg, the closing of a daisy's petals at dusk. Ratty wiped an eye, moved, suddenly very tired.

Stella was coming back to the table, cocooned in more applause. She was smiling, sparkling, one hand on the white skin visible above the low white Peter Pan collar of her red dress.

Dear God, Joe said to himself, *here she was*: how could it have happened that she'd been under his nose all this time and he'd never thought twice about her? From time to time he had reflected on the flirtatiousness of Prue, the gentle melancholy of Ag, the kindness of Stella – but it had not occurred to him that any of them was destined for him. Unlike Robert, he had never tried to envisage the perfect girl. He didn't believe she existed, he used to say. Or if she did, well – he'd recognise her when she appeared.

He recognised her now.

He stood up.

'Was I all right? You didn't mind, Joe, did you?'

'You were very good. They loved you.'

He sat down again, not daring to put out a hand, not daring to touch her. He did not even dare to smile, lest he should give himself away.

Someone handed Stella a glass of wine with the land-lord's compliments. As Joe sat watching her modestly accepting congratulations, revelling in her success, he tried to fathom what it was that gripped him with such physical force it was all he could do to breathe normally. Time, that night, was a smashed globe too complicated to reconstruct. But at some point an explanation of his feelings came to him, blindingly: *certainty*. Ag's words, he remembered. *I felt such certainty, such conviction, that here was my other half; or whatever the silly phrase is, that in some strange way my life changed absolutely from that day on* . . . She was a wise old thing, Ag. He hadn't understood at the time. He did now. This was *certainty*, all right. This was certainty as he had never known it. This was iron conviction, this was light from heaven, this was something so utterly devastating that, on return to the real world, it would take all his strength to hide.

'Is there anything the matter, Joe?' The sweetness of Stella's voice . . . why had it not reached him before? He cursed the lack of poetry in his soul, longing for words he knew did not exist. Like a man bemused, he kept on looking at her, unable to answer.

'I'm just a farmer,' he said at last.

Stella laughed. 'Farmer Joe! You've had several glasses of wine, Farmer Joe. I think it's time we were going home.'

He could not blame her for thinking him intoxicated. On the walk home, under the arc of freezing stars, he kept his distance. Had not the extraordinary thing happened to him in The Bells, and had he still felt about Stella as he had only an hour ago, he would have taken her arm in polite, friendly fashion. Now, fear of the slightest physical contact was too great. In the silent night he tried to deflect his thoughts by imagining a ghostly gas balloon in their path: their entering it and soaring up to the heavens to the music of its flames . . . Christ, Stella was right about the wine. Perhaps he *was* suffering merely an alcoholic fantasy. All the same, having opened the back door, he moved quickly away for Stella to pass, making sure even their coats should not brush.

'That was such fun,' she said in the hall. 'I haven't sung for months. Thank you for taking me.'

So young, so careless, she sounded. Sometimes, at the end of a long day's work, Joe now remembered, Stella was subdued as well as dreamy. She ran up the stairs. In the wake of her smile he thought she looked happier than she had for some weeks. But then, completely sober, he remembered that a mind diseased – whether by good or evil – plays tricks. And the possessed lover – what he now felt himself to be – sees what he most desires to see, and foolishly sets store upon it.

Joe gave up all hope of sleep that night. He sat in his room, cold, battered, perplexed, entranced. He put his favourite Brahms clarinet quintet on the gramophone to calm himself. But when the first side of the record was finished, he found himself too preoccupied to turn it over and wind the machine. So he sat in his chair in silence, cogitating upon unconsciously stored pictures of the girl who had blasted his senses: Stella the dreamy one, Stella crying in the orchard over her boyfriend's letter, Stella surprising them all with her extraordinary dancing, Stella the modest, helpful, quietly cheering one, so kind to Janet . . . then Stella this evening, casting a spell over a crowd of strangers with those two wistful songs. Why had her perfection not come to him before? The Lord is devious in his revelations, he thought. He keeps a man in the darkness of no expectation, then sends light blindingly. Joe had never expected what he had always regarded as impossible – the force of certain love so great that it changes all perceptions. If he had believed such a thing existed, beyond the poets' imaginations, he would never have committed the treacherous deed of proposing to the wretched Janet. That was the most unaccountable act of his life, he now reflected, lethargically committed in a moment of misplaced desire to please his parents. And now what could he do?

Nothing. There was nothing to be done. Go ahead and marry the unlovable Janet. Carry on as if nothing had happened. Keep his word. And yet, knowing what he now knew, would that be humanly possible?

Joe pulled back the blackout to watch the first silvery snail-tracks of light trail across the sky. He'd read his Byron: he knew the necessity of keeping a hopeless love secret. His priority must be not to burden Stella with the knowledge of his feelings. She was in love with Philip . . . wasn't she? Her feelings for Joe were of friendship, nothing more. To make any indication of the chaotic sentiments within him would be unfair, unwanted. All he could do would be to try to come to terms with the agony caused by such mistiming, to attempt to quell fears and desires. After the war, or whenever Stella and the others left the farm, he would have to try to forget. *Forget* . . .? He fumbled among a pile of clothes for his working things. How could it be possible to forget an event as important in its mystery as birth, as death? Joe began to hurry. He wanted to get the cows in before Stella came down. He wanted her to find them all in the shed when she arrived, to surprise. He wanted his first act for her in his new state to be as soon as possible. He smiled grimly to himself, thinking it was hardly a romantic notion, herding the cows. But there was no alternative. Surely she would be as pleased with waiting cows as with red roses . . .

Soon after four o'clock Joe crept downstairs.

The magic of change in ordinary things, brought about by the existence of another human being, acted with a power, that day, that Joe found as moving as it was remarkable. As the extraordinary hours shifted in their new form he realised, in wonder, what he had been missing until now, and was humbled. The change, he observed, touched everything. It was a heightening of the world that the poets and writers of loves songs are inspired to convey – whether through genius or trite skills – in coded words only understandable to those in a state of love. Nowhere was too lowly for its reach. The kitchen – the kitchen he had known all his life – was almost unrecognisable because at any moment Stella was about to appear. He had found the cowshed, the fields, the farmyard, all equally unfamiliar. He sensed a kind of static in the air, a trembling of solid things, a feeling of glorious hallucination. And the exhilaration of the new feelings, he quickly realised, was an illness both of body and mind. He trembled as he planned how to cross Stella's path many times during the day without arousing her suspicions.

Suddenly, he could not bear to continue his wait in the kitchen. He was not yet ready to deal with the proximity its size would force upon them. He hurried out to the cowshed, forced himself to concentrate on work. He had already started to milk Nancy, the oldest of the herd, when Stella came in.

'Joe! You beat me to it. You shouldn't have – my treat was yesterday.'

Joe kept his head against Nancy's flanks, not looking at her. He felt her hand, for an infinitesimal moment, on his shoulder.

'I woke early. Thought I might as well get going.'

'Well, thanks. I'll start the other end.'

Joe allowed himself a glance at her retreating boots. His fingers shook against Nancy's teats. *I'm a crazed man . . .* It was far from an unpleasant feeling.

As he listened to the whine of milk shooting into the bucket, and struggled once more for calm, he became aware of a certain sense of objectivity. By the time he rose, the bucket full of warm froth, and glanced down the cowshed for a glimpse of Stella's head leaning against the infinitely fortunate Belinda, he realised there were now two look-out posts within him: one with which to observe Stella at every possible moment; the other to study his own peculiar behaviour.

*

That evening Prue and Ag returned. For different reasons they were both in high spirits. After supper there was a merry reunion in the attic, a chance for private news.

'Nice, quiet Christmas with my father,' said Ag, '*but* . . . this. Waiting for me.'

She held out a Christmas card for the others to examine. It was an ink drawing of Trinity College under snow. Inside, under the printed wishes, was the signature *Desmond*.

'I couldn't believe it,' smiled Ag. 'I still can't. In the train I kept taking it out of my bag and looking at it. It must mean, surely, he hasn't quite forgotten me, don't you think? It must mean something.'

'Well,' said Prue, her attention not entirely on Ag, 'look what *I* got!' She rustled among tissue paper in her case, pulled out a dress of ruby velvet with a white fur collar.

'My mum found this old curtain material in a market, ran it up for me. Isn't it just heavenly? She swears the fur is rabbit: I say it's ermine. It's the most beautiful dress I ever saw . . .' She held it up in front of herself, danced about the room glancing in various small looking-glasses as she passed. 'When can I wear it? That's the only problem.'

'New Year's Eve,' said Stella. 'Joe's asked his friend Robert to supper. There's the Red Cross dance you could go to.'

Prue's face relighted. 'Gosh! How about that? I've been thinking . . . Barry's time is up. Maybe this Robert . . . What about you, Stella? How was it having the beautiful Janet in my bed?'

'We had a quiet time. Nothing much happened. I enjoyed it. I sang in The Bells one night.'

'You didn't!' Prue laughed. She curled up on her bed, hugging her dress, rubbing the fur against her cheek, childlike. 'It was so strange going home, you know. Did you find that, Ag? So small. Noisy, our street, too: funny how I'd never noticed that before. Lovely being with Mum, of course. She said, Prue, what on earth's happened to your hands? I said, you try mucking out Sly and keeping your hands in good shape, Mum. I rather missed Sly, actually, though I didn't tell her that. Anyway, she gave me a shampoo and set. Very odd, with a proper basin and dryer and everything again. Took some getting used to. Funny thing is, I'm quite glad to be back. What about you, Ag?'

Ag murmured agreement. She was concentrating on arranging her Christmas card on the chair by the bed. She found a position which allowed her, from her pillow, to see Desmond's signature. When the lights were out she secretly kissed the card, just as Stella used to kiss her photograph of Philip. That, Ag noticed, had been moved to the chest of drawers.

On New Year's Eve, Robert arrived promptly at seven for supper. Just a year older than Joe, he looked like a man of thirty who had suffered illness all his life. He was small, thin, cowered over a concave chest. There were bluish shadows under deep eyes, and his skin had a pale, skimmed look that made it hard to believe he spent most of his life in the open.

The girls, curious about Joe's friend, arrived in sparkling line to shake his bony hand in turn. Prue had insisted on being the last. She wore her new dress, had curled her eyelashes into spikes of unbelievable length.

'I'll give you a kiss, too, Robert,' she said, 'seeing as it's New Year's Eve,' and his arms went round her in automatic response.

Later, she told the others, she fell for Robert as soon as her mouth touched his deathly cheek. The attraction was mutual. Prue concentrated her full attention on him during supper, fluttering the absurd lashes, her dimples and pouts working overtime. Too preoccupied to offer any help, she smiled, duchess-like, as Stella and Ag acted as waitresses. Supper over, she and Robert left at once for the Red Cross dance.

'So that's worked,' said Joe, smiling at Ag. 'I thought it might. No more Barry. Hope Robert enjoys himself.'

'*Really*, Joe,' said Mrs Lawrence, a note of wistfulness beneath her stern look. 'It's a very unlikely match. What could a girl like Prue give Robert?'

'Fun,' said Joe. 'Nothing wrong in that, for a time.' He felt the strength of one to whom the emptiness of mere fun, nothing else, is a thing long past.

Stella and Ag sat with the Lawrences listening to the wireless, waiting for Big Ben to strike twelve. They raised their glasses to each other, conveyed polite formal wishes – but were not the sort of people to seal those wishes with random kisses. This was a relief to Joe. The proximity of Stella this evening – beautiful, a little subdued – was both an ecstasy and a torment. His own, private wish for the New Year, as he raised his glass briefly in the direction of the girl who had ungrounded his life, was for strength.

Ten

P rue, alone in the cowshed, no one around to complain, was taking her chance to sing.

> *If you want to go to heaven when you die*
> *Wear a pair of khaki breeches and a tie.*
> *Wear an old felt bonnet with WLA on it*
> *If you want to go to heaven when you die . . .*

She was doing her best to whitewash the battered walls. Bloody awful job, but at least better than carting loads of mangolds down to the cows, like Ag. Or harnessing the stubborn Noble, like Stella. *They* would have rain gushing down their necks, sodden hair, soaking wool gloves. It had been raining hard for the first week of the New Year – Prue had collected enough buckets of rainwater for a month's hair-washing. Also, it was freezing. Bloody freezing. Prue was the only one of the girls still awaiting a greatcoat. Shortage of cloth for land girls' coats had still not been overcome: there was no saying when hers would arrive. Mrs Lawrence had made several enquiries to the district commissioner, who held out no hope of a coat in the near future. So Prue had to make do with three jerseys under one of Joe's old macs, and still the cold cut through her bones.

But Prue had learned as a child that hardship is a challenge. She remembered her mother's advice: when the going gets tough, remember Winston Churchill.

271

Remember everything you can that he says. He's an inspiring man. Prue's mother was given to muttering *Now is our finest hour* as she strove to overcome the shortage of solution for permanent waves. Now *is* my finest hour, said Prue to herself, sloshing whitewash over a daunting new area of dirty brick wall. Her arm ached so badly she wanted to cry. But there was no use in crying, or stopping. Mr Lawrence expected the wall to be finished by midday.

Besides, there were thoughts to dwell on that made up for everything: Robert. She and Robert had made a swift start on New Year's Eve. Half an hour at the Red Cross dance was enough to convince them that his cottage would be a better place in which to celebrate the New Year. Robert had lit the fire and shaken out the rag rug in front of it. He had heated up a tin of soup, and found half a bottle of wine. Thus the setting for her third seduction as a land girl, while not perfect, was both slightly warmer and more comfortable than either the barn or the woods.

Prue found herself much taken by Robert's shyness. She liked the way he averted his huge, moth-like eyes when, halfway through the revolting soup, she considered it time to stop dilly-dallying, and remove the velvet dress. She laid it on top of the rug, pushing the fur neck into a kind of fairy bolster. For some moments Robert looked so charmingly embarrassed Prue felt herself inclining towards him in a way that immediately alerted her to its inconvenience. Just in time, she remembered that to go falling in love with an anaemic young farmer, penniless to boot, would not fit in with her ultimate calculations. She quickly placed his chilly hand (in all her experience she had never known such icy flesh) on the silken thigh beneath her slip, and was rewarded by an electric reaction.

'It's the bombs urge a girl on,' she said, fluttering lashes winged by three layers of mascara. 'I'm not forward by nature, but when it comes to a race against the bloody bombs I want to win.'

'Quite,' said Robert.

He hastened out of his own clothes while Prue languorously released her stockings from their suspenders, an art she had learned from close study of many film stars. She smiled at the sight of her new lover-to-be's feet – the smallest, most delicate men's feet she had ever had the pleasure of observing. Blue-white skin stretched over fine bleached bones. The miniature toes wriggled in the folds of red velvet – *crustacean* (a word she had recently learned from Ag), somehow, and making Prue giggle. She looked up to see Robert naked but for his watch.

'Five to twelve,' he said.

'And Big Ben ready to strike, I see.'

Prue collapsed into further giggles as Robert lowered himself beside her. As on many previous occasions, she was oblivious of the precise moment of the passing of the old year, but was able to rejoice, very early in the new one, at the presence of a new lover.

Now – the tiresome thought returned to her in the cold of the cowshed – the only thing that had to be *tidied up* was Barry. She thought of their last meeting – December the tenth. Quite a day for loss, as a matter of fact: Singapore, according to Mr Lawrence, who was a keen listener to the news, and her interest in Barry. She said nothing at the time, just promised she'd be in touch. This new turn of events meant she'd failed to keep her word. Perhaps she would write to him tonight. It wasn't fair to keep a man mooning about in hope. Hard to know what to say, though.

Dear Barry

I can't ask you to keep up all the bicycling any more and it wouldn't be much fun in the woods this wintry weather, we'd catch our deaths, and anyway it's difficult me slipping off so much even though Stella and Ag are kind and cover for me. So I think we shall have to call it a

*day. It was good fun. When it comes to telling
grandchildren about wartime romances I shall say, well
there was Barry . . .*

Nah! Soppy, that last bit. She wouldn't put that. *Love and
good wishes* at the end, though: she didn't want him to think
he'd been nothing more than a bloody good shag.

In the past week, there had been much meal-time talk
about the end of the war. Now that America had joined the
fighting, Mr Lawrence seemed to think there was some
hope it wouldn't drag on too long. Prue herself thought
such speculation pointless. She agreed with Ratty, who
declared much worse was to come before victory. She had
no wish to think about the future. She was happy – despite
the cheerless rain and cold – with each day as it came:
tough work, long hours, plenty of good hot food, and odd
moments of reward in Robert's dingy bed. He was something of a mystery, Robert, Prue had often thought in the
past week: no matter how passionately they made love his
skin never warmed up. Quite a challenge, that. One day
she'd like to be responsible for replacing his corpse-like
temperature with a warm pink glow (Prue giggled to herself at the thought). She liked his company, too: dry little
phrases, their academic references usually way over her
head, shy little compliments, quaint little jokes. And the
way he stroked the bridge of her nose when he was being
very serious about the war or something. He said the
bridge of the nose was an erogenous zone. Perhaps it was
among academics, she had replied, but she could think of
more erogenous places in the opinion of ordinary folk.
All the same, she didn't try to stop him – tickle tickle tickle
with his cold little finger.

'You've done well, Prue,' said Mr Lawrence.

Prue turned to see him at the door of the cowshed,
appraising her work. Rain ran thickly down the raw-
coloured runnels of his face. Swift as balls of mercury they

slid down the creases of his neck. 'Not *exactly* my finest hour, Mr Lawrence,' she said, pleased, 'but I'm getting on.'

At times like this, it occurred to her, there was a darn sight more reward in being a land girl than there was in hairdressing. In fact – it had crossed her mind several times – when the war was over it might be worth trying to find her millionaire somewhere in the country, rather than in Manchester.

'You're not half as daffy as you look,' said the soaked Mr Lawrence, smiling.

Joe was avoiding her. This Stella noticed within a few days of their evening at the pub. At first she thought it was her imagination, and he was avoiding everyone. Certainly he seemed less forthcoming – the others had observed and remarked on that, too. Perhaps two days of the beautiful Janet's company had caused his despair, suggested Prue. Ag's view was that no end to the war in sight depressed everyone. But Stella knew it was neither of those things. It was something to do with her. She had inadvertently acted in some way to offend or annoy him, but could not imagine what it was she had done.

In the cold and gloomy days of early January, Stella puzzled over Joe's behaviour. It was definitely her he singled out for the cold shoulder (she noticed a hundred small occasions) and the worry of her unknown misdemeanour was beginning to blight the days. She would have liked to confront Joe: ask him what had happened, clear the air. But he was not an easy man to confront. He had become more and more elusive, always the one willing to undertake jobs far from the farm that could be done alone. Stella watched for her chance. But, as the dreary days dragged by, it did not come.

On the afternoon that Prue was assigned the unenviable but dry task of whitewashing the cowshed, Mr Lawrence asked Stella to take the milk churns to the village. Usually, this was a task he undertook himself. But the persistent heavy rain had taken its toll on the old roofs. There was a leak in the laundry room: water had poured down on to a basket of Faith's ironing. Repairing the tiles was urgent. Mr Lawrence apologised to Stella, said if he caught sight of Joe he would ask him to give a hand.

Stella, setting off for the field to catch Noble, leaned against the heavy slant of the rain. A dour mass of dark cloud was low in the sky, releasing no chinks of light to play among reflections. And yet the puddles in the lane dappled with inky blues and muddy pinks as Stella splashed through them. In the leafless hedges dishevelled sparrows cowered, unsinging. The thrumming of the rain would sometimes switch into an *adagio* passage, giving hope it would soon be stopping altogether. Then, like a tease who knows not when to stop, it would fall *prestissimo* again, defying all such silly hopes. The persistence of such weather had affected Stella's spirits.

Noble sheltered under a tree, darkened by the rain. He came at once when Stella called. She removed her sodden glove and gave him half a carrot, snorts of warm breath agreeable on her cold hand. In the next field she could see the drenched figure of Ag, sou'-wester falling over her eyes, throwing mangolds from the trailer behind the tractor on to the ground. The cows were hustled round her in a selfish crowd, a black and white puzzle whose individual pieces, at this distance, were indistinguishable.

Ag waved. Stella waved back. Ag had been much more cheerful since Desmond's Christmas card. Strange how thin a hope the human soul can survive on, Stella thought, gripping the soaking rope of Noble's halter. She and the horse sloshed their way through the long grass back to the gate. If Ag ever did secure this almost non-existent love, surely the stuff of fantasy, Stella would remind her of this rainy afternoon, January 1942, when she, Stella, had been quite convinced nothing would ever happen with Desmond. And with Philip? In his last letter, he had said that when he went to London he was going to buy her a ring. Then they would be engaged. Then they would be married. Then they would live together ever after. Wartime bride and groom. Romantic stuff. But happily? Stella supposed so, in some ways.

She tethered Noble to a post in the barn, made several journeys to and from the tack-room lugging the heavy harness. Her hands, wet and cold, worked inefficiently. She struggled to do up the hard old straps. She tugged at the stubborn leather, determined not to be beaten and have to call for help. As finally she led Noble towards the shafts, a thought came blindingly to her. It came with such terrible clarity that for a moment she was forced to lean against Noble's damp withers, bury her head in her arms so that she could be submerged in blackness. The suspicion that had been nudging her for some weeks, that she had kept at bay, had suddenly stormed her fragile defences. It was Philip, not the weather, that caused her dejection. The sprightly love she had felt for him when she came to the farm, which had protected her in the many bleak moments that manual labour produces in all those who would rather be engaged in some more intellectually creative activity, was gone. Absolutely gone. She was fond of him, respected him . . . she would marry him: *but she was not in love with him.* And, as she had so often said to Prue and Ag, what is the point of life if you are not in love?

Stella moved back at last from the warmth of the horse's body. She looked again at the swathes of rain that billowed across the yard. There was only one thing to do. The only antidote to any kind of unhappiness, her father used to say, was work. She must apply all her energies, all her concentration, on work: do her bit for her country to the best of her ability. She must remember that, while thousands of girls were suffering the premature death of their loved

277

ones, her fortune was to be loved by a good man who, thank God, was still alive. The thought of Philip being *killed* sent a spasm of guilty horror down her spine . . . Should he be spared, she would make a good wife. Learn to come to terms with the kind of love, based on friendship and affection, that, buffed by marriage, lasts. She realised, as she tried to persuade Noble to reverse himself between the shafts of the milk cart, how young and silly she had been, hoping that the froth of love she felt so quickly for Philip, and others before him, was the stuff of permanence.

There was a helping hand, suddenly, on the bridle. Joe muttered a few magic words to Noble who instantly obeyed. The inexplicable discord with Joe was the other reason for her unusual depression, though minor by comparison. She looked up at his grim face, veiled by water that poured off the brim of his waterproof hat. Perhaps there would be a chance to confront him, discover what had caused his hurtful behaviour.

'Thanks,' she said.

'I'll give you a hand with the churns.'

When they had secured the shafts, Joe led Noble over to the milking shed, where the streaming silvery churns stood in a line. He swung each one easily into the cart, signalling to Stella not to help. She climbed into the driving seat, sat waiting. Joe, to her surprise, when all the churns were loaded, joined her. He looked at his watch.

'I'll come with you. Give you a hand the other end. They're buggers when they're wet.'

Stella relinquished the driver's seat.

They clattered out into the lane. The rattling of the churns, Noble's hoofs, and the drumming rain, made an orchestra of sweet sound. Branches of vapour drifted from the hedgerows, ghostly extensions of the hedges themselves. For all the discomforts of the wet and cold, Stella found herself enjoying exposure to such weather. She was awed by the mercilessness of the rain. She was fascinated to

278

find so familiar a journey made unrecognisable by the gauzes of mist that filtered through it.

In no time, Joe unloaded the churns on to the wooden platform from which they were daily collected. The rain fell harder.

'Think we should shelter for a moment or two,' he said. 'This'll pass.'

He urged a reluctant Noble on a few yards, halted under the oak tree beside the gate to the church. There, they were protected from the main force of the rain, although it still managed to fall between the intricacies of bare branches. Joe, hunched on the seat, let the reins fall slack on Noble's back. He stared ahead at the cascade of water battering the dark stone of the cottages opposite, oblivious, it seemed, to Stella's presence.

'Joe? Joe, what have I done?' Stella broke a long silence between them. 'You've been so distant, since that night at The Bells. Did you mind my singing?'

She watched his profile carefully. Even in the poor light under the tree his skin gleamed with running rain. Drips trickled from his eyebrows to join drips falling from the brim of his hat in a squiggling journey down his cheeks. He frowned, causing a rush of more drips to scurry down the bridge of his nose. His dark waterproof, silvered with rain, creaked as he turned towards her.

'No,' he said, 'you haven't done anything. I liked your singing. You've a lovely voice.' He paused, sighed. The slight hunching of his shoulders caused another flurry of water to scuttle down his arms. 'I suppose it's just the thought of the long year ahead. Dark. Getting ill with asthma. The not knowing. The suspense. The waiting. The waste, for everyone. The utter waste.'

Stella, half appeased, half believing him, gave no time to the weighing of her next words.

'But you're just the same to Prue and Ag. It's only to me, I feel . . . I've felt you've changed. Unfriendly, somehow.'

279

'Really?' He shifted further round so that Stella could see both his eyes. The irises were the same colour as the rain, flecked with light. He gave her a curious look that quickly wafted away, light as a flake of ash in a breeze. 'Am I?' Then he turned away.

'You must know,' said Stella. 'It's not my imagination. There must be a reason, beyond the doom of war we all feel.'

'Maybe.' He went on staring at the rain ahead, falling so hard it bounced back off the road only to fall again. 'If that's so, and I dare say it is, then I'm sorry. I don't mean to be unfriendly.'

Stella was aware of the effort he made, then, to remedy things. He turned to her again with a teasing half smile.

'I could, I suppose, come back at you. Where've all your spirits gone? You're neither so dreamy nor so happy, seems to me. But I could be wrong. People's shifting moods, in a war, are almost impossible to keep up with. Hopes chasing fears: strain of broken rhythms, traumas, upheavals from the norm . . . What's happened to you?'

Stella shrugged. Now, dozens of tiny streams ran down her own sleeves.

'Perhaps a case of mistaken identity of a feeling. Perhaps I've been in love with an idea, instead of a reality . . .'

'Ah. That.' Joe looked as if he was attempting to concentrate very hard on the weather. 'Doesn't look as if this is going to ease up. I think we'd better brave it. I should be helping Dad with the roof.'

But as he picked up the reins, a cyclist came into sight. Head down, miserably hunched over the handlebars, his waterproof glinted dully as the feathers of a wet crow. 'That's Barry, isn't it?' said Joe.

The airman rode towards them, stopped at Noble's head. He raised his sodden forage cap, looked at them enquiringly. It wasn't Barry, but a man of similar physique: shaven head and ruddy countenance.

'Could you tell me where I could find Prue? Prudence? Hallows Farm?'

'Half a mile down the lane,' said Joe, pointing. 'We're going there. Can we give her a message?'

The young man bit his lip. He squeezed and released the handlebars of the bicycle several times, as if to some private rhythm. Tapped the ground with his heavy black boot.

'She was a friend of my friend Barry. I came to tell her he was . . . was shot down night before last. I thought . . . I thought she'd want to know. . .' He replaced his soaking cap. Stella thought she could distinguish tears among the raindrops on his cheeks. 'If you're going back there, if you know her . . . I'd be grateful. My name's Jamie Morton, should she want to get in touch. At the Camp.'

'I'm so sorry,' said Stella.

'Buggeration!' screamed Prue, when Joe told her Barry was dead.

She picked up a tin of whitewash and slung it at her newly painted wall. 'That's what I think of this bloody war. It's come here, now. It's hit *here*!' She dropped on to a milking stool, thrashing her heart. Began to sob. 'Poor Barry! He was so brave. He told me he hated night flying. I think he knew he was going to die. Oh God, he's the only person I've ever known to *die* . . .'

As she buried her head in her hands, the yellow satin bow slumped in her sad curls. The toes of her white-streaked rubber boots were turned inwards: so often there was a childlike innocent look about Prue, thought Stella, for all her superior experience. She put a hand on the shaking girl's shoulder.

'You just cry,' she said. 'That's the best thing.'

'I just hope the same thing doesn't happen to your Philip . . .'

Joe quickly picked up the tin of whitewash. 'Marvellous job you've done in here,' he said. 'Finished on time, too.

Why don't we all go in and have some tea?'

Any approval from her employers affected Prue deeply. Her wails stopped for a moment. She looked up, her stricken face a grid of running mascara.

'Heavens, you two – drowned rats! Whatever have you been doing?' She sniffed, brightening. 'Well, at least there's one good thing. I hadn't sent my farewell letter. I was planning it only an hour ago. So he died not knowing it was all over between us. I'm glad of that. Because he was a funny boy, Barry: I think he loved me.'

She stood, gave the faintest smile. The three of them made a dash through the rain to the house. When they had changed into dry clothes, and Prue had repaired her face, they gathered round the kitchen table with mugs of tea.

'I can't quite believe it,' sniffed Prue, who had exchanged her wet yellow bow for a new black one. '*Barry*. One moment you're with someone. The next moment they're dead – and for what? This bloody, bloody war . . .'

A couple of silent tears fell from her naked eyes, dampening the long soft lashes which, devoid of mascara, glistened. She wiped them away with an impatient hand, cocked her head towards Joe.

'This friend of Barry's, Joe, who broke the news – what did you say his name was?'

'Jamie Morton. He said you should get in touch, if there's anything you want to know.'

'What was he like?'

'Sad, and soaked to the skin,' said Stella.

'I must write to him. I'd like to know . . . where it happened. I'd like to thank him for his trouble.'

She gave such a minor smile that her dimples were only just stirred into action. As Stella and Joe both recognised, and acknowledged with a private look, even in the darkness of Barry's death Prue, with her resistant spirit, saw the light of some possibility in his friend, Jamie Morton.

*

That same afternoon of unforgettable rain, Ratty was at home making an attempt to celebrate his wife's birthday. He had given her a card in the morning; at tea-time he produced a present made bulky with many layers of newspaper beneath the final wrapping – a sheet of paper decorated with holly, left over from Christmas.

Edith, never a gracious receiver of presents, tore impatiently at the string.

'What's this, then? Who said I wanted my birthday remembered? I'm past all that sort of thing.'

Nonetheless, she scrabbled through the paper like an excited child. Eventually she found the present, a small porcelain robin perched on a porcelain tree stump. Edith had always had a fondness for robins, though no interest in other birds. Ratty had made several difficult journeys to local towns in search of the robin in his mind. He had been pleased to find it at last, dusty in a junk shop – lifelike little fellow with a bright eye, especially attractive for its bargain price of sixpence. He anticipated Edith's pleasure – stupidly, as he later reflected. He should have remembered there was nothing in the world he could give her that would please.

Except, curiously, the paper.

Edith picked up the robin with a sniff of disdain, put it on an empty shelf (previous home of saucepans) and said not a word.

Then she returned to the bundle of newspaper and wrapping paper, and began to flatten out the creases of each sheet with a trembling hand.

'Where'd you get all this? This'll be a help.'

Ratty was mystified. 'Here and there. Got a store of old newspaper in the back shed.'

'*What*? Storing up paper in the back shed without so much as a word? What for? Lighting bonfires? Don't you know the Government's asked us to save our paper? One envelope makes fifty cartridge shells, they say. They want every scrap. You bring me those papers, Ratty Tyler, or there'll be trouble.'

By now she had folded one of the sheets of newspaper into small, neat squares. She took a pair of kitchen scissors and began to cut the squares reverently as if they were finest silk, mouth pursed in concentration.

'What are you cutting them up for?' Ratty ventured. 'What's the use of that?'

Edith snorted at his stupidity. 'It's a lot more use than not cutting them up,' she said. 'I must have cut up thousands of squares this week,' she added, with some pride. 'They're all stacked away in boxes waiting to be collected. But I don't suppose you've noticed.'

'I haven't, no,' admitted Ratty. He wondered what sort of a man would instinctively know his wife wished him to hunt about the house for boxes of cut-up paper, and then to praise her for such husbandry.

'Trust you,' said Edith. 'But then you've never been like me when it comes to doing your bit for the country. All you do is hang about the farm mooning after those useless land girls. First you complain about the saucepans, now you make a fuss over collecting paper.'

'I'm not making a fuss,' said Ratty. He watched her cut up the second lot of squares, carefully balance them on top of the first. Some devil within him urged him to express his puzzlement once more. 'I still don't see the use of all this cutting up,' he said. 'Paper is paper, just as good not cut up.'

'That's what you think. That's what you would say, after I've spent all these hours doing my best.'

Ratty watched his wife's tense shoulders as she hunched over the piece of holly paper, smoothing it again and again with swift little strokes. 'The war's got to you, Edith,' he said gently.

'Some of us have to take it seriously,' she said. 'Now you just go and get those papers from the shed. I'd like to make a start on them.'

'What, in this rain?'

'Are you a man?'

Ratty stood, tapping out his pipe. 'Did you like the robin?' he asked, playing for time, dreading the downpour in his already soaked mackintosh.

'The robin?' Edith looked wildly round, eyes veering over the shelf where the ornament perched, but seemed not to see it. Then she returned to stroking the holly paper.

In the New Year, evening habits shifted at Hallows Farm. After supper, instead of the family and girls gathering in the sitting-room, they went their various ways. Stella, on Ag's recommendation, was reading the *Iliad*. As Homer needed a greater measure of concentration than she applied to her own choice of novels, and even the Third Programme was a distraction, she had taken to going up to the attic early and reading peacefully on her bed till the others came up. Prue went out with Robert several times a week. Joe had reverted to his old habit of disappearing. (Stella could see light under his door and hear faint music as she crept upstairs.) Only Ag stayed downstairs with Mr Lawrence dozing in and out of the news, and his wife upright on a chair beneath the standard lamp that cast a pale disc of light on to her darning. Ag herself, speeding through a pile of old *Telegraph* crosswords, reserved a small corner of her mind for further Desmond detective work: *why* had he sent a Christmas card? What could it mean? The answers never came. As is often the case when there is no evidence to the contrary, optimistic possibilities gathered strength.

On the evening of the news about Barry, with unspoken consent – perhaps to show support for Prue – they reverted to their old pattern and converged round the fire after supper. Prue, pale but calm, played Solitaire in a corner. She wore an unusually dark lipstick which, she had earlier told Stella, she thought appropriate to the occasion. When, on the wireless, there was news of a bombing raid on London, Mr Lawrence quickly changed to a symphony concert. Behind the music they could hear the single, persistent note of rain shredding against the windows.

The telephone rang. Mrs Lawrence, to whom it could only ever mean bad news, physically started. She put down her darning and ran from the room. A moment later she returned, flustered by relief that it wasn't the call she dreaded from Yorkshire, but confused by another concern.

'Prue, it's for you. Robert. He wants to know if you'd like to go out for a drink.'

Prue's back still ached, her eyes stung, an appearance of small appetite at supper had left her hungry. She would have done anything for a drink with Robert: the smoky warmth of The Bells, his cold fingers on her neck, his awkward comforting ways. But there were rules that had to be observed when your ex-boyfriend had been killed. She was aware of disguised glances towards her. Her answer was awaited with curiosity.

'Not tonight, Mrs Lawrence,' she said at last. 'If you could explain . . .'

Further relief softened Mrs Lawrence's face. She went off with her message. Prue returned to her game.

Joe, who had been restless all evening, stood up.

'Ag,' he said, 'it was weeks ago you promised me some tutoring. I don't know where to begin on all those books. Could I ask you . . . could we mark a start?'

Ag's surprise was evident. Pleased to think that here was a sign at last that Joe was emerging from his gloomy mood, she jumped up, eager to help. The memory of their one strange afternoon was skeletal in her mind. She knew nothing like that would ever happen again. Joe had merely been obliging. She had no fear of going alone to his room and looked forward to their evening.

They left the room, causing Prue a private smile. She

liked the thought that she had been the *first* of the girls invited to Joe's room, albeit for different reasons.

Later, alone in the attic waiting for the others to come up, Stella was conscious of the kind of restlessness that physically chafes. She hurried into bed without kissing Philip's photograph, lay listening to the slurry sound of rain against the windows, the whining of the wind. Why this feeling of discomfort? She put it down to the events of the day: the puzzle of Joe's behaviour was not resolved – if it hadn't been for the appearance of Barry's friend, Stella would have probed further. The news that Barry had been killed. Prue's distress. The endless rain. And now Joe's invitation to Ag. Stella supposed, of all the disparate characters under this roof, Joe and Ag probably had the most in common. And maybe a little communing with books would cheer Joe up. All the same, for some reason she felt quite cross. She would like to talk to him – about music. Well, Prue and Ag had gratified him in their different ways. She would not like to be the only one who did not contribute to his life. Since she had been freed of the mists of romantic love of Philip, she had noticed Joe more often, and discovered she liked him.

His literary evening must have been a success because Ag came to bed unusually late. Stella pretended to be asleep.

It was long after midnight and still Edith had not come upstairs. Ratty, unable to sleep in a half-empty bed, stumbled to the kitchen. He found his wife standing at the table, as she had been most of the day, regarding a landscape of dozens of paper towers, made of hundreds of small squares of cut-up paper. The room was lighted by a single candle on the table. Shadows stretched darkly across the walls. The table of towers, each with its matching, paler shadow, was a picture of mad geometry, thought Ratty:

something he couldn't understand. Any more than he could understand the look on Edith's face. Bent over the candle, her turnip skin pocked and scored in the halo of the flame, she seemed to be going through some kind of private mystic experience.

'You'll have us burnt to the ground,' said Ratty at last.

'That I'll not,' Edith replied, her voice quite normal.

'Come to bed, Edith. It's nearly one in the morning.'

'Our country needs our paper,' she said. 'I'll come by and by.'

With extraordinary calm – Ratty had feared his interruption would mean one of her funny outbursts – she began to knock over the paper towers. She flicked each one with a finger, watched it tumble. He regarded her for a while. Soon the table was covered with a thick layer of paper squares. Still Edith went on standing there, running her hands through them. Ratty could bear the scene no longer. Afraid, he turned and went back up to bed.

None of the land girls could remember a time when, if they came upon Mrs Lawrence by chance, she would not be engaged in some form of work. She never grumbled about her endless duties. In fact, the disparate jobs that occupied her, both indoors and out, from early morning till late at night, seemed to give her pleasure. She was an example of a married woman totally preoccupied by the narrow confines of her life, and happy within them. This gave all the girls food for thought. Prue, whose respect for Mrs Lawrence was infinite, was not for one moment deflected by her example: to swap such a life for her own dream of servants and cocktails did not occur to her. Ag had been romantically tempted by the thought of ironing Desmond's future shirts (all that white linen, so Lawrentian). But of late she had begun to think about becoming a barrister: she would be willing to undertake household duties, but they would have to be arranged around a post-war life at the

Bar. Stella, too, was inspired by the loving energy Mrs Lawrence put into every loaf and pot of home-made jam: something her own mother, a useless cook, had never instilled into her. But, like Ag, she was determined to go out to work when she and Philip married. Life would certainly not consist entirely of looking after his needs. Perhaps, she thought, when the war was over, a new and enlightened breed of women would feel much the same.

On a cold February morning – rain had given way to bitter frosts – Ag came into the kitchen to fetch a carrot for Noble. She had spent half an hour trying to catch him – Stella was the only one to whom he came at a call. Mrs Lawrence was sitting at the table, unoccupied. This was so unusual a sight Ag felt a sense of shock, as well as surprise. On the table was one of the small churns in which milk for the house came straight from the dairy. Also, two opened letters.

Mrs Lawrence looked at Ag, unsmiling. There was a tidemark of milk on her top lip, a comic moustache quite out of keeping with her grave demeanour.

'Oh Ag,' she said, 'good news and bad.' She patted the letters. 'John will have to go to Yorkshire tomorrow. He's been putting it off for ages. But they can't cope much longer. Things have to be sorted out.'

Ag sat down.

'What it means, of course, is deciding *when* . . . when we have to leave here and take over up there. John's brother will stay to the end. He won't go into hospital. But then we'll have to go. It's much bigger than here, several hundred acres, mostly arable. God knows how we'll manage.'

'Perhaps we could be transferred with you,' said Ag, touched by Mrs Lawrence's despair.

'Perhaps, perhaps.' Mrs Lawrence looked out of the window. 'We've been here all our married life.'

'It won't be easy, going.'

'No. Some people don't mind about houses, places. I

289

wish I could be like that. Rootless. A happy mover, a wanderer, with a desire to see new places. But I'm not. I love our small world. I love this place. John loves this place. Joe, I think, too.'

'Understandably.'

'Still, there's time left. Till the end of the year, I should think. We must warn you all. Give you plenty of notice so that you can make up your minds about what you want to do next. The immediate problem, John having to go tomorrow, is the lambing. We need all the hands we can get.'

'Don't worry, we'll help all we can,' said Ag. 'I expect Ratty wouldn't mind –'

'Ratty?' Mrs Lawrence smiled at last. 'Ratty wouldn't miss lambing for anything in the world. He more or less camps in the shed. We'll manage. Now: the good news.' She picked up the second letter. 'I've been in correspondence with the district commissioner. Believe it or not, you've been here six months: reward time, if the authorities think rewards are in order. Anyhow, there's to be a little ceremony next week. Nothing very much: tea and badges. I was asked for a private report of your progress, naturally. Apparently there have been quite a few problems with land girls round the country. One Agricultural Executive Committee had to take disciplinary action against fourteen girls who refused to thresh in twenty-five degrees of frost. I said, nothing like that here.' She paused to smile again. 'My girls will do anything, I said . . . I don't know what we'd do without them . . . But what am I up to? Sitting here chattering, the lunch not on. Go and tell the others, Ag. Best bibs and tuckers, four o'clock on Wednesday. Lardy cake, would you like? Egg sandwiches? Glass of ginger wine? We'll try to make it a small celebration, if I have a moment.'

She hurried to the stove, her old self again.

*

Mr Lawrence left for Yorkshire early the next morning. As his wife waved goodbye, Ag noticed a small pulse began to beat in her neck. In twenty-four years of marriage, the Lawrences had never been apart for more than a couple of nights.

Joe drove his father to the station. Mr Lawrence had planned a complicated and slow journey by train. He hoped to return in a week.

There was too much extra work to allow time for much reflection on his absence. Lambing had begun. The night frosts were so hard that Joe worked to divide the lambing shed into many small folds. As the entire flock of ewes and lambs was to be sold in the spring, it was essential to make sure as many lambs as possible survived. Other years, only problem ewes or sickly lambs were given shelter. This year, Mr Lawrence believed, cosseting was the best policy.

Ratty and Joe set up the folds. Prue tossed wheat straw on the ground, filled troughs with water. She had already seen a lamb born, an experience which had inspired a long letter to her mother concerning Nature's miracles: by comparison, she had said, even the most beautiful permanent wave was no great shakes. (*By that I don't mean I won't always admire your talent and skill, Mum*, she had added in brackets.) Her greatest excitement was for the forthcoming birth of Sly's last litter. Although Joe assured her they were not due for at least another week, Prue kept running to the sty to judge for herself the pre-natal state of the sow with whom she had come to have a very good understanding. She was determined to be present at the birth.

For all their fitness and strength, the girls found themselves tired by the extra work and went to bed earlier than usual. Joe, having completed the night check straight after supper, did likewise. Frequently he was called out by the indomitable Ratty in the middle of the night to help with a ewe. A few hours' early sleep was essential to the maintenance of his efficiency and temper.

*

At three o'clock one morning, Stella, eyes on her clock, happened to be awake. There was a bang on the attic door.

'Could one of you come and help? There's a lot going on. Sorry.'

Stella sat up in the dark. Silence from the other two meant they were deeply asleep. She fumbled as quickly as she could into her clothes. Crept out. What help did Joe need? She had no experience of lambing . . . She put on her coat and scarf, hurried across the freezing yard.

In the shed, she found biblical light from a few lanterns that hung from the walls, and were secured to the pens. There was a smell of hay, earth, blood. A discordant chorus of bleating filled her ears: tremulous notes from the ewes in labour, piteous high squeaks from one or two newborn lambs. In one pen Ratty was huddled over a ewe who lay on her side, mumbling comforting words to her as he dug a syringe into her hindquarters. He was watched by a tiny black lamb, its wool skin glistening like broken cobwebs. In another fold Joe was kneeling on the straw, one arm deep in a ewe's backside. Stella made her way towards him. He looked up for a moment.

'Oh, it's you. Ewe in the far corner over there: turning on her lamb. See what you can do. I've got a nasty mess here.'

Stella hurried away, wondering what she was supposed to do.

The lamb needing her help lay on wet straw, its head tipped back, alarmed eyes a milky blue. It was still covered with a translucent skin, silvery over the dun-coloured wool, that its unmaternal mother had felt disinclined to lick clean. Stella stroked its neck, watched the flaring of the small black nostril. She felt helpless, useless. But the lamb, encouraged by her presence, struggled to rise. On tottering legs it made a precarious journey to its mother who stood sulking in a corner. She sighed deeply, twitched her ears.

The lamb gently butted its mother's stomach in search of milk. With extraordinary speed the ewe lashed out with a hind leg, making the lamb jump back in fright. Then she turned and lowered her head towards her offspring with all the aggression of a ram. The lamb fell back on the straw from the fierce butt of its mother's head. Stella saw a flash of dun-coloured teeth: the ewe was going to attack further. She quickly bent and picked up the squealing lamb. The slime of its skin slobbered down her greatcoat. The lamb felt cold and tense. It struggled. Stella, keeping a tight grip, swung herself back over the side of the pen and returned to Joe.

He was standing now, fiddling with a syringe. His bare right arm and hand were skeined with blood, as was the straw on which the ewe lay panting on her side. Beside her stretched the unmoving body of a lamb, obviously dead.

'First one we've lost,' said Joe. He glanced at Stella holding the rejected lamb, which had grown quieter.

'Case of post-natal depression over there,' said Stella. 'Had to rescue this one. The mother was about to butt it.'

'Good timing, at least.' Joe put the empty syringe into his pocket. The upper half of his body was in shadow: she could scarcely see his face, but knew it was grave. Shadows flickered in the pen. Only a small stretch of straw bedding was illuminated by a nearby lantern. 'Hang on to it, for a moment,' Joe said, 'while I deal with this.'

Stella leaned up against the pen to watch the process of adoption. Joe knelt down, patted the tired ewe, then picked up her dead lamb. He took a knife lying beside him in the straw, tilted back the rigid little head with its unlit eyes. Carefully he dug the tip of the blade into the skin, began to pull down towards the chest. Then, very fast, the knife travelled this way and that, its blood-laced blade giving an occasional muted flash in the dim light. With a surgeon's skill, Joe began to ease the skin from the body and limbs. It came away all of a piece in his hands, a dishevelled old jersey, leaving a naked lamb behind. The small body, Stella could see, was an extraordinary blue – the blue of wild flowers, bluebells, forget-me-nots: the flesh iridescent between patterns of tiny veins. She burrowed her own icy hands into the warmth of the living lamb in her arms.

Joe picked up the corpse, slung it into a sack.

'Now, give me yours.'

He took the animal from Stella. Again, fascinated, she watched as he struggled to fit the dead lamb's skin over the orphan lamb. In a few moments he had succeeded. The creature stood beside its foster mother, bemused and shaky in its new ill-fitting clothes. The ewe, nostrils twitching, heaved herself up on spindly legs. She began to sniff the lamb, who stood patient, curious, wobbly. Then, with sudden confidence, it pushed and nuzzled towards the udder. Moments later it was sucking, a whispery, rubbery sound. Its tail wavered from side to side. The ewe, ears back, eyes half shut, did not move.

'Worked,' said Joe. 'Usually does. Thank God for that.' He threw the sack containing the dead lamb towards the door, glanced round the shed. Ratty had gone. The bleating had died down. 'All calm for the moment. I'd better hang on, though. There should be a couple of others by the morning. Thanks very much for your help.' From his side of the pen he patted Stella's shoulder. 'You'll have to clean up your coat,' he said, swinging a leg over the fold. 'And you should go back to bed. But let's sit down just for a moment.'

They sat on a pile of hay between two pens. Joe picked up a clump of straw from the ground, began to wipe the mess from his arm. Then he pulled down his sleeve, fastened the cuff, dragged a thick jersey over his head.

'I suppose it's freezing,' he said, 'but I stopped feeling the cold some time ago. *You* must be . . .'

He turned to Stella, whose hands lay flat on her corduroy knees. Like his, they were smeared with blood. Joe put a hand on top of one of Stella's, covering it. Then he snatched it away. The touch was as transitory as a V in water after a bird has passed. The coldness of its imprint, on Stella's own chilled skin, she could not feel.

'There. I knew it.'

'I'm all right.'

'It's a hard time, lambing.' Joe now ran both hands randomly round his face. Stella could hear the squeak of flesh as he rubbed his eyes. She felt him shudder.

'Stella?' he said, after a while.

'Yes?'

They listened to the stirrings of the animals in the dark straw. The weak mewing of the lambs indicated they were well-fed, sleepy. Outside, an owl hooted. Candles in the lanterns were low. The small patches of light they made were murky as cloud. Stella wanted to go on sitting there, sitting there.

'I think it's time you went back to bed,' said Joe, at last.

'I could stay and help,' said Stella.

'No,' said Joe.

The unexpected appearance of Stella, followed by the cold night hours in the shed while lambs were born, dead and alive, very nearly blasted Joe's resolve. After the brief, foolish touch of her hand, he felt he could keep his silence no longer. In the few minutes that they sat – tired, bloodied, cold – listening to the sounds of new life among the sheep, a thousand good reasons for telling her how he felt dazzled his weary senses. She would never know the effort he summoned to say, instead, in a normal voice, that it was time for her to go. She further confused him with her offer to stay and help. Almost more than he could bear. He prayed that she would go quickly – which she did – before weakness overcame him.

Left alone, he remained sitting staring at the moonless

295

sky outside the shed. The darkness had that peculiar density, known to those who are up before dawn, before the first cracks of light, subtle as the camouflage of tiger skin, indicate the new day. Recent pictures of Stella shuffled across his mind: the anxiety on her face when he told her to deal with a ewe, the maternal relief as she stood by the pen holding the lamb. As he skinned the dead lamb her eyes, he knew, never left his knife's journey. Then, as he fitted the skin on to her orphan lamb, he saw a look of – wonder, was it? Admiration? Or, in the poor light, was he merely seeing what he hoped to see? In a state of acute love, misinterpretation is so easy. Most probably all that had been in her eyes was the normal fascination anyone would have on witnessing an operation they had not seen before.

Since Stella's accusation of unfriendliness, Joe had been doing his best to act as he had before his revelation and yet, for his own preservation, to avoid her as much as possible. For some reason, in the urgency of the moment, it had not crossed his mind she might be the one to answer his night call for help. And for all his concentration on the sheep, Stella's very presence in the shed, followed by the terrible proximity on the hay, had caused him new agitation. Wearied by a week of broken nights with the sheep, he had little energy to fight the feeling. He found himself succumbing to an idea that raced suddenly from nowhere. He knew, however unwise, there was no holding back from his next plan.

Long hours later, he walked into the attic bedroom without knocking, holding a mug of tea. He allowed himself a moment to look down on the sleeping figure of Stella, hair awash on the pillow, one shoulder showing above the sheet. He called her.

Stella woke quickly, struggling through shards of dream to focus on reality. There was still a knife in the air, skinning a lamb: there was a silvery-blue corpse on bloody straw, there was Joe's cold and bloody hand on hers. When the remnants of the dream dissolved and she saw the real Joe, tired eyes, small smile, mug of tea stretched out, Stella gave a cry.

'Joe? Whatever . . . ? What time is it?'

'Seven.' He passed the mug, stretching his arm rather than moving nearer.

'Oh my God. I'm *sorry*. I've never overslept before.'

'Don't worry.'

'Where are the others?'

'Milking.'

'They should've woken me.'

The sheet slipped down her shoulder as two hands cupped the mug. There was a glimpse of low-necked white nightdress. The slight humping of one breast as the arm she leaned on squeezed her side.

'I told them not to.'

'I'm sorry, I really am.' She shook her head. Hair surged about in natural waves.

'I've said. It doesn't matter a bit.'

'What about you?'

'There were two more lambs. Both fine.'

'So you've not been to bed all night?'

Joe shook his head. 'I'll get a couple of hours now. Would you mind doing Sly?'

' 'Course not. Where's Mrs Lawrence?'

'Gone to the village with the eggs.'

In the cold air of the room Stella and her bed were an island that smelt of warm sleep. Joe wanted to kneel on the floor beside her, tell her of his certainty. He held on to the doorpost.

'I won't be long. Down in time for lunch.'

'And what about all this luxury?' Stella lifted the mug. 'I don't deserve this.' She smiled at him. 'Thanks. I won't be a moment.'

297

She sipped her tea. Hair parted over shoulder. Eyelids, cast down, the colour of iris petals, blue-veined. Joe would have liked to watch her drinking tea for ever.

Stella quickly pulled on her breeches and thick jumpers. She ran across the yard to fetch a pitchfork from the lambing shed. Her special lamb, still wearing its adopted coat, was asleep beside its foster mother. Late, guilty, she did not linger to see the rest of the newborn lambs, but hurried to the pigsty. There she found Sly, in the last stages of her last pregnancy, in an irritable mood. First she refused to move from the bedding that had to be discarded, then she butted Stella's side with a complaining snout. Stella's usual patience was frayed. She wished she could swap jobs with Prue. Sly and Prue had a special relationship the others would never acquire. She did her best, flinging sodden straw into a barrow in the yard, to be moved later. While she tossed down the sweet-smelling new stuff, a wayward thought came to her: simply, she looked forward to lunchtime. She looked forward to Joe's being there.

Engaged in this small reflection, it was some moments before she realised Prue was leaning over the sty wall, a critical eye on her work.

'What's going on?' Prue asked.

'Joe said would I –'

'Sly's my special job.'

'None of us has special jobs, really, do we?' Stella paused in her work, leaned on the pitchfork. Prue, she saw, looked unaccountably put out. 'I'm sorry. I overslept.'

'We have special things we're good at,' Prue snapped back. 'Hedging and hens and the fruit for Ag. You're good at milking and Noble and the cows. I'm the plougher and the pig lady.'

Stella had never seen Prue so petulant. 'That's probably so. But we all swap about without making a fuss, don't we?'

'Don't you understand? Sly's about to give birth and *I*

wanted to look after her till it's all over,' Prue suddenly shouted. 'I don't want *you* interfering, taking my job, thanks very much.'

'Calm *down*, Prue –'

'I'm not calm, I'm furious.'

'I can see that. Here.' Stella handed over the pitchfork. 'You take over. I'll finish off the cows with Ag.'

Prue's outburst was quickly demolished by Stella's gesture. She entered the sty as Stella left it, ostentatiously rearranged the already well-tossed straw, gave Sly a proprietorial scratch behind one ear. Then she turned to Stella with an apologetic smile.

'If you think about it, there's not many hairdressers who fall in love with pigs.' They both laughed. 'Sorry. I didn't mean to shout. Everything's got on top of me. Nightmares about Barry. A letter this morning from his friend Jamie with details of how he died . . . Too many late nights with Robert. My nerves seem to have gone all to pieces.'

'You could do with a good night's sleep,' said Stella.

'You sound like my mum,' said Prue.

It was the first squabble Stella could remember in their six months at Hallows Farm. That, she reflected on her way to the cowshed, was an amazing fact that perhaps the war could account for. Civilians, horrified by the fighting, instinctively wanted to live in extra peace at home. And, in any case, they were too busy to indulge in petty quarrels.

At four o'clock that afternoon the girls, in clean jerseys and breeches, sat round the kitchen table with Mrs Lawrence and the district commissioner, a Mrs Poodle. There was an air of a children's tea party. The girls had brushed their hair: Prue, for the first time, for Mrs Lawrence's sake, had left off a bow. They had washed every trace of mud from their hands and nails, laid a cloth on the table, and arranged a lardy cake and two sorts of sandwiches. Beside each of the girls' plates lay three red

299

half-diamonds, rewards for six months' satisfactory service, which they were now allowed to sew on to the sleeves of their jerseys and coats.

'The badges are usually just sent through the post,' explained Mrs Poodle, 'but I wanted to come and see how you're getting on in this remote spot.' She smiled round merrily.

'We wouldn't want to be anywhere else, would we?' said Prue. 'Stella and Ag and me.' Overcome by her badge, the first prize of any kind she had ever received in her life, Prue was close to speech-day tears. She fingered the half diamonds in disbelief, shuffling them together to make whole ones. 'My mum'll not believe this.'

'It's curious that the Land Army is the only one of the services in which there's no promotion,' Mrs Poodle went on. 'Seems very unfair to me. But at least the badges are some recognition of your loyal service. If you keep up the good work you'll be entitled to a special armlet in eighteen months' time, and a special *scarlet* one after four years. Think of that!'

'Good God,' said Prue, tear-bright eyes flicking to the ceiling, 'surely we're not going to be needed that long. Surely the bloody war's not going on for another bloody –'

'*Prue*,' said Mrs Lawrence.

'Sorry.'

'No one can say how long you'll be needed.' Mrs Poodle, unused to such feasts, was enjoying her third piece of lardy cake. She had cut it up into tiny morsels to prolong the treat. In return for such hospitality, she felt, her knowledge of how the WLA fared beyond Hallows Farm would be bound to interest. 'But enrolment is galloping ahead,' she said. 'In Dorset alone, by the end of last year, three hundred and nineteen land girls had signed up. I reckon there'll be twice that many by the end of this year.'

Mrs Poodle shook hands with each one of them, before she left, and wished them well in their long and hard service to their country that lay ahead. She, like Prue's mother, found the famous words of Winston Churchill invaluable when it came, as it often did in her job, to encouragement on formal occasions. '*We are moving through a period of great hope*, as our great leader put it, *when every virtue of our race will be tested and all that we have and honour will be at stake*.' Her eyes dimmed at the poignancy of her own rendering of the great man's words. She pulled on a pair of black kid gloves, adjusted her hat. '*It is no time for doubt* . . . Good luck, girls. And congratulations.'

'Bugger everything,' shouted Prue, as soon as she had gone. 'I'm going to sew on all my diamonds *now*.' But as she was about to turn back indoors, they all heard Joe's urgent shout from the pigsty.

'Prue! You'd better hurry. Sly's begun.'

Prue gave a shriek. Her half-diamonds dropped to the ground. Stella bent to retrieve them for her. Again, she felt a brief sense of annoyance. It was unreasonable. Unaccountable. But a fact.

That evening Robert came to supper and suggested that they should all go to The Bells to celebrate. Ag and Mrs Lawrence declined in favour of an early night. Joe said he could not leave the sheep. Stella volunteered to help him.

'Just you and me, then,' Prue giggled to Robert, the only one to accept a second apple dumpling and more Bird's custard – love never affected her appetite. 'But before we go you'll have to be introduced to every single one of Sly's litter. Help me give them names.'

The sow's late-afternoon lying-in had inspired Prue with unexpected maternal feelings.

'Never seen such a performance,' she had kept on saying to Joe. 'Look! There's another one! How does she do it? Good old Sly . . .'

She had stood for a long time watching the fourteen tiny piglets writhing and squeaking, snouting among their mother's dugs, their gristly bodies slipping over her panting belly – contemplating the miracle of birth. It was something to which she had given no previous thought: now, beguiled by Sly's piglets, the attraction of having babies seemed suddenly understandable. She'd like four, she decided, and looked forward to telling Robert this new decision. So she was relieved to find the others would not be coming to The Bells. The announcement that she wished to make should be private. There was much to tell Robert: it had been a memorable day, what with prizes and piglets and decisions about children. The kind of celebration she fancied was several stiff gin and limes, followed by wild activity in the hard and noisy bed, and bugger Stella's prissy suggestion about an early night.

As soon as the washing-up was finished, Mrs Lawrence and Ag went upstairs. Joe followed Stella into the sitting-room.

'Cold?' he asked, and put another log on the small fire before she could answer. Stella switched on the wireless. Rubinstein was playing a Chopin prelude. 'I'm not much of a Chopin fan,' said Joe. 'I've got things to do.' He left the room.

Stella curled up on the hard sofa, disappointed. She had spent the last half-hour looking forward to a short time alone with him. Why she wanted this, she found impossible to explain to herself. But somehow, she had discovered since Christmas, his presence was a luxury, a comfort, a warm pleasure. Watching him skin the dead lamb last night, and skilfully introduce the orphan lamb to its foster mother, had inspired her admiration. This morning, tea in bed, he had surprised her. Now, he had sort of . . . insulted, rejected her. The curious thing was, however he acted seemed to affect her. This was confusing. Stella, not wanting to understand for fear of discovering the truth, allowed herself to believe that the distortions of the war were more devious than she had supposed. They accounted for Prue's sudden temper, Ag's unflagging hope of a non-existent relationship, and her own jumpy reactions to one who had become a friend.

The warmth of the fire, combined with Chopin's sad and plashy chords, made her drowsy. She would make herself a cup of Ovaltine, go to sleep hoping Joe might call upon her again to help with more lambing.

Stella imagined he was already out in the shed, so was surprised to find him in the kitchen. He had spread paper over the table and was cleaning his shoes, chipping mud off a heel with a blunt knife.

'Job I most hate,' he said.

'I was going to get myself some Ovaltine before bed. Like some?'

Joe nodded. Stella poured milk into a saucepan, prepared the drinks.

'Good about the half-diamonds,' said Joe.

Stella smiled, brought the drinks to the table, sat down. She held her mug to her nose, sniffing the hot, beige-smelling froth, enjoying the warmth of the steam. Joe kept his eyes on brushes, polish, dull leather that began to gleam under the fierceness of his polishing. After a while, the swishing of the brush, like the music, induced in Stella a further drowsiness of the careless kind.

'Do you ever feel,' she asked, 'such total confusion that you don't know where to begin to untangle the various strands? You don't even know what the strands consist of? An amorphous confusion? Do you ever feel that, Joe?'

He glanced at her, saw the beautiful mouth turned down.

'Of course. Often. All the time.'

He held up a huge black shoe, admired its shine, took up a duster. One of the dogs, asleep by the stove, growled in its dream.

'We're the ones who've decided on marriage. Do you think we're right?' Again Joe glanced at her. 'I mean, why are you going to marry Janet?' Even as she asked, Stella realised the silly risk she might have taken.

Joe put down the finished shoe, sat down, picked up his drink. He fought for calm, forced himself to look her in the eye. *Oh God, please give me the strength not to let her see . . .*

'I could ask you the same question. Why are you going to marry Philip?'

Stella gave an embarrassed smile. She shrugged. 'I was in love with an idea – one of my weaknesses. I've been in love with lots of ideas. I thought he was the right person. Perhaps it was the urgency of war . . .'

'You *thought?*'

'I thought.'

'You still think?'

'I don't know. To confess any doubts would be too disloyal.'

'I know those feelings.'

'I've given him my word.'

'I've done the same to Janet. You never said how it was, your weekend in Plymouth.'

'It didn't occur to me you'd be interested.'

'I admit to being intrigued about the sort of man you love.'

Stella hid her face behind a structure of hands and mug. She tried for lightness.

'Philip's a good man. The weekend wasn't . . . entirely perfect.'

Joe nodded, began to chip mud off the second heel. It fell on to the paper in dark curves, like giant nail parings. Stella stood up, took her empty mug to the sink. She was not sure if Joe had heard her last remark. She hoped he had not, for it was a first act of betrayal.

'I must go to bed,' she said.

'We haven't really answered each other's questions.'

'No. Perhaps we will some other time. Call me if you want any help in the night.'

'You need your sleep.'

'Really. Please.'

Joe nodded. He did not watch her leave the room, but continued to work with manic concentration on the shoe. He polished and repolished till no brighter shine could be achieved. A possibility he hardly dared to think about added to the general morass in his mind. Surely it wasn't his imagination: surely, tonight, there was some indication . . .

Joe felt he had seen signs of something so small, so amorphous – in Stella's words – that she herself was perhaps innocent of its existence. But it was there, within her. It had taken root. The question was, should he stamp on it before it flared into consciousness? Or should he abandon all principles and encourage it to life?

Some days later, Ag finished her morning duties earlier than normal, so joined Mrs Lawrence in preparing the lunch. Joe came into the kitchen carrying a couple of dead rabbits. He slung them on the draining board. From the stomach of one of them purple blood oozed through the pale fur on to the dark wood.

'Thanks, Joe. Your father will be pleased.' Mrs Lawrence turned to Ag. 'John's expected home this evening. He'll be wanting his rabbit stew and boiled onions. There's suet left over for a treacle pudding – his favourite, too.'

The news came as no surprise to Ag. She had noticed early that morning that Mrs Lawrence's spirits had risen. Her inner life, always so carefully concealed, emanated in subtle hints of private exuberance. She moved faster between table, sink and stove. Her worn hands, sometimes slowed and dull with fatigue, fluttered happily among soapy plates. She buttered slices of newly made bread with extraordinary speed. Her beige lips, released from their usual cautious clench, kept breaking into a smile.

Ag had often thought how she would have liked Mrs

Lawrence for a mother: the idea was renewed this morning. She sensed that this strong woman, in her state of anticipation, exuded a kind of approachability which was rarely apparent. Ag, who loved as well as admired her, yearned to talk to her. She wondered if it would be untoward to try.

Mrs Lawrence darted to the sink holding a lethal knife. She began to skin one of the rabbits. Ag watched her firm hand grasped round the animal's neck: the head flopped over, an obscene bunch of fur, bone, tooth resting on stiff lip, blubbery balls of dead eyes.

'Could you do the other one for me, Ag? It's not difficult. Common sense.'

'I'm afraid I . . . I'm no good with dead things. Birds, fish, animals. For some reason, I can't touch them.' It was the first time Ag had had to refuse Mrs Lawrence any request. 'I'm sorry,' she added, ashamed of her squeamishness.

Mrs Lawrence glanced at her. 'That's all right. I used to feel the same. I had to get used to it. I was sick, I remember, the first time I drew a pheasant. I don't mind any of it, much, now.'

She tugged at the rabbit skin, turning it inside out as she pulled. It came off clean as a glove. Ag regarded the naked pink body beneath, the legs bent as if still running, their flight frozen by death. Feeling sick herself, she chivvied about, laying the table, not wanting to see more of Mrs Lawrence's butchery.

The rabbits were quickly chopped into a jigsaw of pathetic joints and piled into a large bowl. Mrs Lawrence poured in a dash of cider, bay leaves, juniper berries, pepper. Her movements were light, happy. When the bowl of hideous contents was complete, she carried it to the larder as if it weighed no more than an empty plate.

'John'll love that,' she said, on return. 'When we were first married, not a brass farthing between us, we ate a lot of rabbit.'

She sat down at the table, correcting the position of a

fork, a glass. She tweaked at the few sprigs of forsythia, still in bud, that Ag had arranged in a jug. She put one hand over her heart.

'Ridiculous! I ought to be ashamed of myself, at my age. I'm all of a flutter.'

Ag smiled back at her. Here, perhaps, was her chance.

'We'd be lucky,' she said, 'any of us, if we ended up with a marriage like yours and Mr Lawrence's.'

Mrs Lawrence looked surprised. 'Really? I don't know about that. I think if you're happy working together for the same end, it's a help. We've been so lucky in that respect, John and me. I wouldn't have wanted to marry a man who went off on a train every day. Like that, there's so much of your lives unknown to the other . . . Absence can mean a blurring of the rules. I wouldn't want to go away from home myself, either. I suppose I'm terribly old-fashioned. I can see an age, a generation or so ahead, when women will think it quite natural to go out to work. Mere housewives, like me, perfectly happy with their lot, will be scoffed at. Perhaps we are even today. But I'm too busy to dwell on things like that. I'm so out of the real world, I don't know much of what is going on. But what about you, Ag? Have you thought about what you want to do after the war?'

Ag thought for a silent moment, decided to confide.

'I've been thinking: I'd like to study law, go to the Bar. I'll go on being a land girl, or do some other war work, while I'm needed; then I'll try for law school. The ultimate plan – the old plan –' she gave a self-deprecating smile – 'is to marry Desmond.'

'The one who sent the Christmas card?'

Ag nodded. 'I sometimes think my dream of him is a stupid waste of time and energy. But then I remember the certainty I felt. Instantly. Positively. Mysteriously . . . Foolish, I suppose, but I'm relying on that.'

'You must. You should.' Mrs Lawrence sighed. 'I wish Joe felt such certainty.'

'Doesn't he?'

'What do you think?'

'Well, he shows no great outward signs of it. We don't talk of Janet. We talk about books. But he's a dark horse, Joe.'

There was a long silence.

'Perhaps I shouldn't say this, Ag, and I would ask you not to repeat my indiscretions to the others. But I think John and I may have made the greatest mistake of our lives over Janet. And I don't know what we can do.' Mrs Lawrence spoke quietly, unsure she should be saying such things but compelled, after so many months of silence, to tell this sympathetic girl for whom she had particular affection.

'Joe was such a daffy young boy, seducing every girl for miles, breaking hearts all over the place. We found ourselves lecturing him on the wisdom of looking beyond physical attraction, of choosing a good, solid girl for life. He used to scoff at such concepts, say the only *marriageable* woman he'd ever met was me!' She smiled to show she knew this admission of vanity was an indulgence. 'And of course he didn't change his ways. Then – I don't know how it came about, exactly, he never said – but he announced he'd proposed to Janet. *Janet*! Well, we'd known her for years – they used to live in Somerset. We liked her parents. She was a childhood friend of Joe's – plain, gawky, kindest heart in the world. He treated her like another boy; she loved him from the age of twelve. As I say, I don't know what drove him to his decision, but a lot of bad luck came at once – no Cambridge, no fighting. I suppose he felt bitter, a failure, useless, though he never actually complained.

'Anyhow, unofficially engaged, as it were, he stopped chasing girls. He spent most of his free time with Robert, talking, talking: they have a lot in common. Then, out of the blue, this proposal; entirely to please us, we now think. And at the time we were pleased. We felt, here was security.

Not very exciting, perhaps, but security, support, devotion.

'But then, in a way, he seemed to give up. The life went out of him. He said, "I've done what you want, you ought to be pleased." We said, "Joe, you must do what *you* want." Timing was against him, of course. Just as they'd announced their engagement, Janet was posted to Surrey. Joe didn't express any great sadness. I still have to chivvy him to write to her. As you've seen, they hardly ever have a chance to meet.

'Then, you girls arrived. John and I were worried, of course. Especially, when all of you turned out to be so . . . well, it would have been easy for Joe to fall back into his old ways. We trusted him, naturally. He's an honourable man, Joe. Once he's given his word, he sticks by it. What's happened, you coming, as you've probably noticed, is that he's come out of his shell. He's still tense, restless, full of regrets: but happier. Don't you think? I think you must be his first women *friends*, all three of you. I have to admit I had my suspicions Prue would get her pretty little hands on him, and I dare say she tried, but she wouldn't have succeeded. I know he enjoys *your* company so much.' To Ag's deep discomfort, their eyes met. 'Intellectual equivalent. With all the farm work, he's been denied so much of that sort of stimulus, apart from Robert. Prue amuses him – he's amazed by her capacity for hard work, hand in hand with all her silliness. And he seems to like Stella – their mutual interest in music. Really, you've done him the world of good, the three of you, in your different ways.' She paused, began to knead her knuckles.

'You've also shown him . . . But I don't want to be disloyal to Janet. Suffice to say that at Christmas the contrast between her and all of you . . . must have made him think. Besides which, Janet seems to have changed: jumpy, eager, *irritating* in her desire to be of use, to be liked, to be loved. The poor girl. She must see he doesn't love her, she must see he's merely trying to stick to his word.

'We blame ourselves, John and I. We blame ourselves. We taught Joe to stick by his promises and now, in doing that, he may have a lesser life. What can we do?'

Mrs Lawrence gave Ag a look in which desperation was bound with regret. Ag, astonished by the confession of her normally reticent employer, felt unable to advise. She could give no immediate answer. To play for time, she fetched the warm plates from the stove, stirred the pan of carrot soup. Then she returned to her seat.

'By strange irony,' she said at last, 'I think it's a case where maybe the war can *save*. I mean, as it twists and breaks so much anyway, perhaps it could be used as an excuse. Perhaps both Janet and Joe will just drift apart, and blame only the war. The end of their arrangement could come about for the same reasons as it began: *pressures* of war, decisions forced by an unnatural time.'

'You're not accounting for his honour,' said Mrs Lawrence.

'I am. But even honour, distorted by the events of war, can be seen as foolishness. So if a word is broken, it may be forgiven.'

'I hope that's so. Perhaps events will right themselves. Now: not a word of all this, Ag, please.'

'I promise.'

'Take out the potatoes, if you will. I'll call the others – only a few hours.' She was cheerful again. 'John'll be back about five.'

Mrs Lawrence put on a clean pinafore for her husband's return and her rabbit stew was appreciated by all but Ag, who could not bring herself to eat the running legs even though they were half disguised by gravy, having seen them in their naked form.

Mr Lawrence came back with the news he had expected. His brother's illness was in remission. The prognostication was that he might now live months rather than weeks.

Together they had agreed that the Lawrences would move to Yorkshire in the following new year.

He left no pause, after this fact had been announced, going on to explain his plans for Hallows Farm before their departure. He wanted as much as possible to be turned over to arable land before it was put up for sale. The cows – all but Nancy – would have to go within a few weeks. Sly likewise. At Prue's squeal of protest he refrained from mentioning the fate that would befall her litter. But pig feed was scarcer than ever, he patiently explained to the distressed Prue, and their supply was almost finished. He spoke of detailed plans concerning which fields would be best planted with which crops.

'I'm warning you,' he said, 'it'll be the busiest spring of your lives. Harrowing, ploughing, weeding, sowing: good thing you're all so fit. Half-diamonds well deserved, by the way. But I don't want you to underestimate the hard work ahead. Tell me honestly: do you think we can manage, six pairs of hands and Ratty, or should I think about more help?'

'We can manage,' said his wife quickly, for all of them.

Next only to ratting, Ratty loved shepherd's work. Lambing time was his favourite season, the nights away from home, the 'dozens of bloody miracles', as he called the births. Besides which, the night work afforded him the excuse of sleeping a few hours during the day, thus avoiding the increasingly irascible Edith.

The night Mr Lawrence returned home was a busy one for Joe and Ratty. Nine lambs, including twins, were born. It was six in the morning when he walked home – not tired, the adrenalin of wonder kept him going till the last lamb of the season was born – but hungry. There were signs of a fine day to come. Signs spring was not far away.

Ratty looked forward to an hour's peace in the kitchen, frying himself rashers of bacon in the one pan, and a slice of bread. But to his dismay he found Edith already down-stairs. She stood before a large box on the table, rummaging through deep litter of paper cut-up squares, as if searching for something in a bran tub. The squares, he noticed, had become smaller in the last week or so. Their symmetry took hours of her time.

'Out with the girls again,' Edith greeted him, a strange bleak look on her face.

'I've been lambing with Joe. Nine since midnight, including black twins. You know I've been lambing. I could do with some breakfast.'

'Breakfast!' Edith cackled. 'You can get your own rotten breakfast, or get one of those girls to get your breakfast.'

'Now, look here, Edith . . .' The pleasures and achieve-ments of Ratty's night suddenly left him. They were replaced with a cold anger, spurred by hunger and the desire for peaceful sleep. 'You're being unreasonable,' he said.

'*Unreasonable?*' Edith snapped round. Her hands flew out of the box, scattering paper. She clutched its sides, threw its contents at Ratty. 'That's what I think of you, Ratty Tyler.'

The paper showered over Ratty: bright little sparks from old coloured books and postcards, dull flakes from news-papers, soft, clinging fragments of tissue. They chipped his coat, clung to his cap. Edith began to laugh.

'Confetti! That's it, confetti. We never had any on our wedding day, remember? You wouldn't run to confetti. I should've known then . . .'

Ratty began to shake the paper from his clothes. He was suddenly very tired. Empty. Cold.

'We did, didn't we . . . ? Surely?'

'That we didn't.'

Edith stomped over to the dresser and snatched up a small brass frame containing a sepia photograph. She thrust it at him.

'Our wedding day, right?'

Ratty blinked at the faded image of the young foolish hope in his own wooden smile. Had Edith ever really been like that, smiling too?

'No confetti. *No* confetti! See?'

'It wouldn't show, not in an old photograph. I'm sure we had. Pink stuff, petals.' He was confused, dizzy.

'I'm telling you. This is proof.'

Edith's old indignation died down in her triumph. She stepped back, replaced the frame. 'Well, what we didn't have, at least the Government's getting.' Ratty could not see the logic of this argument, but was too weary to contradict. 'I'll just sweep this lot up, get going on some more.'

'Is there a rasher?' Ratty tried to dodge the broom she had picked up.

Edith swept the kaleidoscope of paper pieces with peculiar relish, for some moments, before she answered.

'No,' she said at last. 'There's not so much as a slice of bread, Ratty Tyler, neither.'

Eleven

For as long as he could remember, Ratty's small patch of garden had been home to a dynasty of blackbirds. Close guardians of their territory, year after year different generations would sing from their inherited place in the lilac tree. They left the cherry tree to the chaffinches.

At the end of February, Ratty heard the first evensong from a couple of old males. Their prime over, he knew that all they would afford him was a run-through of melodies from time past, sung only at dusk, and lacking their former vigour. But this was a sign, too, that a member of the new generation would be shortly taking over. Ratty was keen to catch his first sight of the inheritor.

After a lone breakfast – Edith, for the first time in her life, had taken to staying in bed – Ratty pottered into the garden. There on the grass he found the chap he was looking for: a handsome bird, still the dark brown of its mother, its beak also still brown. The ring round its eye was a pale hint of the gold it would become in the next few weeks.

The bird showed no fear of his presence. Ratty stood quite still, studying it for some moments, then pottered off to the end of the garden past the lilac tree. He turned, leaned against the fence, looked back at his cottage. From the branches of the unpruned tree came the first ripples of familiar song: tentative at first, then swelling in confidence, accelerating among scales, showing off. If Ratty had been a man of sentimental disposition he might have thought the bird had followed him, read his thoughts, sung especially for him. As it was, the music which annually renewed optimism that had been frayed by winter merely reminded him spring was here at last: there was much work to be done. And that this time next year life as he knew it at Hallows Farm would be over. He would be finally retired, not semi-retired like the old blackbirds. God knows, then . . .

Ratty retraced his steps along the path that struggled to keep its identity through neglected grass. Every yard or so he paused, let the blackbird's song – riotous, rapturous, now – lock him into a present of nothing but pure sound. The past and the future were both places he had no wish to be.

He contemplated the back of his ramshackle cottage, not a thought in his head. The music of the bird excited the old skin of his arms into roughness beneath his sleeves. Then, it appeared. He saw ahead of him a monster. At first, he thought the horrible creature, standing there at his own back door, must be a hallucination. He had slept little of late, what with the lambing. Several times he had found himself confused, not remembering, seeing things that vanished into air. And yet he knew he was awake. The ground was firm beneath his feet. The blackbird went on singing.

The monster had one large glassy eye, oval-shaped, and the rubbery black snout of a giant pig. It stood on its hind legs, front legs folded, staring back at Ratty, no expression in the terrible eye. Then it took a few steps towards him and Ratty saw its skin – a horrible blue – was a familiar blue skirt, and its forelegs were human arms in the wrinkled sleeves of a brown cardigan.

It was Edith in her gas mask.

'Dear God, Edith!' Ratty cried.

So great was his relief that he had to lean on his stick to save himself from tumbling. He felt coldness gushing through the precarious joints of his knees. Sweat greased his temples. His hands shook.

'You gave me a fright, you did. Whatever are you doing in that thing?'

Edith pulled off the mask. Her face was pale, her eyes unsteady. Sprigs of white hair, normally caught back into a bun, allowed light to pink the skin of her skull.

'There's lambs in the fields, bombs in the sky,' she said quietly.

Ratty glanced up, unsteady. Two clouds moved across a stretch of silent grey-blue.

'There's never,' he said.

'The war's come here, now, you mark my words.'

'I'm going down to the farm.' Ratty shook his head. He didn't like the look of her.

'You take a gas mask, Ratty Tyler, or you'll regret it.'

'I'll never take one of those things.'

Ratty shuffled past her, eyes on the ground, heading for the lane. He was aware that Edith shrugged.

'We'll all be dead as cowpats, soon,' she said.

While Ag did not share Edith's fear of bombs in the local sky, she became increasingly aware of the war in parts of the world far from their own: fighting in Malta, the Philippines, Hitler's renewed attacks on Russia, the sufferings of the Eighth Army in Egypt. So long and busy were the days, now, that there was little time to keep up with the daily bulletins, and she rarely saw a newspaper. But Ag made a point of trying to listen to the nine o'clock news every night, with the Lawrences. The acceleration of war, even from this comparatively safe corner of Dorset, unnerved her more than it did the others. When she wasn't thinking of Desmond she found herself almost obsessively imagining battles, destruction, killing, corpses.

In contrast to – and perhaps because of – these dark reflections, this spring seemed of particular significance. Ag watched its slow beginnings. Mrs Lawrence had long ceased to tend the garden: priorities these days were fruit trees and the vegetable patch. But Ag, knowing her employer's love of flowers, had bought and planted a few dozen bulbs in November. Now they began to appear, much to Mrs Lawrence's surprise. First, snowdrops. Then the 'rathe' primrose (Ag had never been able to discover the meaning of Milton's arcane word, she admitted to Joe one evening) in the orchard, where one of her tasks was thoroughly to spray every tree with lime sulphur – protection against apple scab. In beds that edged the neglected lawn, a dozen narcissi straggled through the unkempt earth. By March a few scarlet tulips randomly glittered, cold as glass among the weeds. Mrs Lawrence's delight was touching.

'So kind of you, Ag,' she said. 'The pity of it is we shan't be here to see how they've spread, next year.'

Rewards for Ag's autumn labours were beginning to be seen in the hedges, too. She and Mr Lawrence observed buds breaking on the carefully woven young hazel shoots. They found a haze of new leaf on the long, neat thorn hedge that protected two sides of Lower Pasture.

'Beautiful laying, I'm bound to say,' Mr Lawrence gently boasted as they inspected the new growth. 'I think we did a good job, Ag. The new owners, whoever they are, will find themselves with a nicely cared-for parcel of land . . .'

They walked through the woods. Ag had the impression that the farmer's eyes were scouring every view with particular vigilance, as if storing sights and sounds for the future. He pointed out a blackcap, high in an ash tree, paused to listen to its wild song. On the far side of the wood they came across a gathering of fieldfares, preparing for their journey overseas. On another occasion, inspecting a newly sown field, they heard the croaking voice of a corn bunting. And one fine afternoon, from out of an almost eerie silence, the intense bubbles of a skylark's song dropped like a waterfall on the ploughed earth.

'You see it, you hear it, you feel it, year after year,' said

Mr Lawrence, 'and it always catches you out, spring, the wonder of it. Makes you think: funny kind of God. On the one hand there's all this; on the other, thousands of armed men out to destroy each other. And now all this talk of an atom bomb, which could be the end. Doesn't make sense. Look: first woodpecker of the year, cocky bastard.' He placed a hand on Ag's arm to stop her moving. He thought how even now, despite the dimming of the tormenting flames, he would not allow himself to touch Stella in the same innocent way. Their eyes followed a brief flash of emerald feathers. 'Tell you one thing: if we get through this bloody war, if I eventually come to retire – know what I'd like to do? I'd like to write a book about migration. Something that's always fascinated me: something no one really understands.'

'I'd like to read it.' Ag smiled at him.

'You shall have a copy inscribed to the best hedging apprentice I ever came across. You've a real talent for hedging, Ag: there's not many have that. You're pretty smart when it comes to birds, too – not just the dry academic I thought you might be. But then, I was wrong about all of you. I admit that. I was against your coming. It was Faith who insisted. She turned out to be right, of course. You can count on Faith, in most things, to be right. To be wiser than anyone else.'

Mr Lawrence's approbation meant much to Ag. It cheered her for a while. But the underlying melancholy she suffered that spring never entirely left her. Hope that the end of the war might not be too far off began to fade. As did the possibility of Desmond.

While Ag struggled with the feeling of doom within her, Stella tried to understand why – with no prospect of seeing Philip for some time, and scant letters – she felt so content. Pieces of an incomprehensible puzzle kept appearing. There was the day when Prue sprained her wrist and could

318

not drive the tractor: Joe tried to teach her, without much success, to plough a straight furrow. They laughed so hard at her attempts Stella felt weak and giddy, earth and sky spinning about as she leaned up against one of the great mudguards. There was the day Noble had to be taken to the blacksmith. Joe drew a map of how to get there, a simple route of some five or six miles. But then he suddenly changed his mind about Stella's ability to find the way despite his directions: declared if she was to return before nightfall he would have to accompany her. She rode the horse bareback, Joe cycled beside her. Somehow, it all took the best part of the day. They had spam sandwiches at the local pub while the shoeing took place, returned by a longer route through high-banked lanes, rhythmic sparky noise of the horse's hoofs making a bass for the breeze. The pieces of the puzzle all contained Joe.

Looking back much later, Stella could never say when it was exactly that the whole picture fell into place. Unlike Joe, she was not struck by blinding revelation. The building of her own certainty formed so quietly, so subtly, that its culmination was no surprise. What she saw before her – when, *when* exactly? she could not say – she knew had been there for ever, waiting for a cover to be drawn back. She calmly accepted its existence, knowing there was nothing to be done. She knew Joe liked her, had no idea if he felt more than that. They were both committed to other people. It was likely their friendship would come to an end when they left the farm. There was nothing that could be done. Stella's love for Joe was fated to die before it could ever live. He would never know about it. All she must do was exercise caution, contain her happiness, give no clue as to the heartbreak of her feelings. It was worthless to reflect upon the cruelty of mistiming. In the short months left to her, Stella decided, all she could do would be to imprint every possible moment in her mind, to feed on, sometimes, in the years to come: for it would surely never be like this again. This was so far removed from the old, frivolous, silly notions she had had in the past of being in love, based on nothing more than wishful thinking, that she laughed herself to scorn, felt suddenly old. This was certain love: the kind that spreads, and grows and, given the chance, can survive. Stella believed – when she allowed herself the luxury of thinking about it – that she had been blessed with a rare feeling, seldom repeated in a single life. To stifle any acknowledgement of this feeling would be the hardest challenge she had ever known. It would be a kind of murder, something she would live to regret always. But there was no alternative.

Stella did her best to contain herself. By the time the bluebells were coming out in the woods, and the cow parsley, she felt herself well under control. She divided her attentions evenly between everyone, was punctilious in her behaviour. No one, she was sure, could have any idea. All the same – and here was the ghost of a new puzzle – her eyes did inadvertently meet Joe's more than usual. Somehow, they often found themselves working together. Somehow, their paths often crossed. And all the while, to Stella in her confused happiness, the trumpetings of spring were no more than an abstract background of birdsong and new leaf and clear sky. Nothing in nature, this spring, was sharp-edged. Only Joe's face was clear. She tried to read in it any sign of something beyond close friendship, but failed. Her position was a solitary one, then: her secret the hardest thing she had ever had to bear.

For Prue, spring was a dizzying experience. It was the first year of her life she had witnessed it outside Manchester, and she found it a revelation.

'No wonder blood rises,' she observed, skipping about, marvelling at lush new grass and emerald leaf. Indeed, she found the whole process even more captivating than shopping. Several weeks running she chose not to go into the local town on her half-day, but to gather primroses or snow-drops, to stand gazing at a field of ewes with their lambs, until Mr Lawrence accused her of 'idling'. Stella and Ag became impatient with her constant wonder. After a while she kept it to herself.

Three things, however, disturbed the magic of the season. First, the Government's ban on embroidered underclothes and nightwear put Prue in a rage: she had been planning to surprise Robert with some Jean Harlow petticoats she'd seen in a magazine. Now, the shop would be banned from selling them. Second, Sly and her piglets were sold to a nearby piggery. Mr Lawrence took the trouble to apologise to Prue, but explained he had had an offer he could not refuse. He had planned for Sly to go anyhow: sooner was less worrying than later. The screaming, as mother and brood were loaded on to the lorry, was terrible – matched only by Prue's wailings. She was quiet, puffy-eyed, mascara-smudged for the rest of the day, but insisted on being the one to do the final clearing of the sty.

While the matter of the underwear was ridiculous and the departure of Sly sad, these two things caused only a few days of rampant gloom. The third matter was a constant flickering of discomfort that only sprang into clear life when Prue gave herself time to reflect: Robert.

Robert, she was fast coming to realise, was no match for her own rising sap. For almost four months she had enjoyed his company, his love-making, his dry little jokes. She had given up trying to induce warmth into his flesh, and had become used to his chilly limbs and lips. But the fact was there was no spur to continuing the affair for the rest of the year until Prue left. They were useful to each other, liked each other, but had nowhere to go. And no destination, in the curious love map that lived in Prue's mind, meant that a relationship could not and would not survive very long. She sometimes faced the fact that, beast that she was, the only real, lasting aphrodisiac for her was *money*: she could only sustain eternal interest if there was money in the lover's bank.

But she made no indication of her waning interest: pointless, when there was no one to replace Robert. They weren't thick in ploughed fields, the kind of men she fancied – or indeed any men at all. So for the time being, wistfully wishing there was a new challenge to be found in the mossy banks in the woods, she stuck to the arrangement of going out with Robert three times a week.

Some days after Sly's departure, and after the kind of low-key night which Prue found hard to forgive in any man, she was feeling more than usually melancholy despite the glorious spring morning. But at lunch, Mrs Lawrence broke some news which, as Prue saw it, was a once-in-a-lifetime remedy for any kind of tragedy. A letter had arrived from Headquarters of the Land Army in London to say that the King and Queen were to give a tea party, in the summer, for a selection of land girls from all over the country. A limited number of invitations was allocated to each county. Mrs Lawrence was required to send one representative. Prue's incredulous wail cut the reading of the letter short.

'*Buckingham Palace?* I don't believe it . . .'

'Obviously the fairest thing would be to draw lots,' said Mrs Lawrence. Prue's moment of dazzling anticipation collapsed.

'Of course,' she said, 'that would be the only fair thing.'

There was a moment's silence. Stella and Ag glanced at each other, looked at Prue's face, twisted by a mixture of feelings.

'I don't know about Stella,' said Ag, 'but I'd be happy not to go. I've been to London often and I don't like it. The outside of Buckingham Palace is good enough for me.'

'Same here,' agreed Stella, a moment later. She had no desire for a single afternoon away from Joe.

'So why doesn't . . . ?' Ag waved a hand towards Prue. 'There doesn't need to be a vote. I think it's a unanimous decision.'

'Are you sure?' Mrs Lawrence looked anxiously from Ag to Stella.

Both girls nodded. Prue let out another, exalted wail. She ran to hug and kiss each one of them in turn, leaving pink lipstick on their cheeks, and showering them with incoherent thanks for being the most generous, kind, and wonderful friends she had ever known.

Prue needed time to herself, of course, to think about the vital matter of what to wear. That afternoon, a half-day, she wandered off to the woods to marvel at the dog violets and cow parsley and stretches of bluebells, and to find inspiration about what colour and material, and who would make it and where . . . But, for once, she found difficulty in concentrating on the subject of clothes. Her excitement at the prospect of the far-off date at Buckingham Palace had made her more jittery than she would ever admit to the others. She sat down under a tree, struggled between thoughts of *pink* or, more original, *yellow*. She jumped up again, began to wander waist-high among the cow parsley, listening to a crowd of birds doing their nut, bursting their lungs. Restlessness increasing, she began to break off stems of cow parsley with the idea of putting a great jug of the stuff on the kitchen table – beating Ag at her own game – to give Mrs Lawrence the surprise of her life. Then, she came upon an intense patch of bluebells: spreading, they were, as far as she could see, a blue that no paint box on earth can contain, a blue that took her breath away. Prue stood still, marvelling. Then it came to her: *artificial silk this very colour.* Surely, somewhere, she could find it, if it meant searching half Dorset. Thrilled by her idea, she knelt on the ground, began to pluck fast at the flowers, amazed to find that some of the long stalks slipped easily from the

ground, a shining purple-green, untouched by the earth
they had come from. She would add these to the jug:
they'd all think she'd gone potty, but she didn't care.
She'd defy any of them to disagree with bluebell artificial
silk . . .

Some time later, Prue walked back down the path,
sheaves of flowers in both arms, their shadows speckling
her shirt. A high afternoon sun needled through the trees:
Prue was conscious of being warm, of being just right.
This spring business, she thought for the hundredth time,
was incredible. What she wouldn't give to have her mum
here to see it: brighten the salon up a lot, a jug of bluebells.

At the end of the path she could see the opening
between two ash trees, where a gate led to the lane. The
opening was a jagged, blazing patch of light. Prue quickened her step, looking forward to sun, unhindered by leaf
and branch, on her bare arms.

Then she saw it. Across the patch of light cycled the
ghost of Barry.

Prue screamed, and ran.

She did not turn back into the woods, but ran *towards*
the apparition. Made for the gate. In her terror, she knew
only that she must reach the lane, get back to the farmhouse. Should the ghost enter the wood, face her there,
among the shadows, she would pass out with fear.

She scrambled over the gate, shaking, dropping bluebells on each side. As she turned towards the farm, she saw
it again. The ghost was now straddling the bike, black boots
firmly on the ground, hands kneading the handlebars, forage cap tilted to one side, just as Barry always wore his. The
sun dazzled Prue's eyes, confusing: but quickly she saw that
this was no spectre. She screamed again, clutching at her
heart and dropping the rest of the flowers.

'Lord, I'm sorry if I gave you a fright,' said the man,
grinning. 'I'm looking for Prudence.'

'Who are you?' Prue felt foolish in her breathlessness. 'I could have sworn it was Barry, come back to haunt me.'

'I'm his friend, Jamie Morton. I came to say thank you for your letters, and I thought it was time we met. Talked about Barry, you know.'

Prue studied Barry's friend with curious eyes. By now used to the light, she could see that the likeness was superficial: this Jamie figure was larger, clumsier, with high-coloured cheeks and brown eyes. Only the short blond hair, scarcely visible under the cap, was the same. He had a friendly grin: rather sweet, she thought.

'Goodness: you didn't half scare me!'

'Sorry. Cigarette?' He took a packet of Players from his pocket. 'Someone down in the farmyard told me I might find you up here. Big man.'

'Joe.'

They both inhaled. Smoke, sharp-edged, trailed into the air. Its smell mingled with the scent of bluebells that were strewn at Prue's feet.

'Quite a ride, I must say.'

Jamie's eyes travelled up and down Prue like a blowlamp, appraising. She dabbed at her bow, the red spots, by chance: always Barry's favourite. She put a hand on one hip, smiled just enough to power the dimples.

'Want to come up to the farmhouse for a cup of tea, or what? Before you go back. I'm sure Mrs Lawrence wouldn't mind. Barry sometimes came in.'

Jamie looked at his watch. 'Thanks, but I mustn't. I'll be late if I don't go now. Took some time finding you.' The grin again: nice, fat teeth. 'We could make another time, if you'd like that. I could come another afternoon. Or we could meet in Blandford: cup of tea or a drink.'

Prue narrowed her eyes, made a great show of deep thinking. 'Personally,' she said, 'I wouldn't want to miss a moment of this fine weather in a tea-shop. It's my first spring in the country: could well be my last. Why don't we meet right here, this time next week? Two o'clock?'

'Fine by me.' Jamie swung a leg over the bike, turned it.

'I'll walk back up the road with you,' said Prue.

'What about all those flowers you dropped?'

Prue shrugged. The surprise jug for Mrs Lawrence had lost some of its importance. 'I'll come back later: don't want to hold you up.' Her heart was still beating fast, but no longer from fear.

With the coming of the fine weather, Ag and Stella, too, chose to spend their half-days quietly at the farm, reading, sleeping, walking. With the increase of work – harrowing, sowing, rolling, couching – they had little energy, in their scant time off, for taking the erratic bus to shops of little attraction. Most half-days, now, they chose to go their own ways, each feeling the need for a few hours of solitude in the busy week.

On the afternoon that Jamie had made his ghostly introduction to Prue, Ag made her way to the orchard with a rug and a book. It was her favourite place. Each tree was by now familiar to her, having spent so many hours picking fruit. She had sprayed almost every branch, laid potash round the roots. Now, they were in full blossom, the part of the cycle she had not seen last year. Ag spread the rug on the ground. She lay down. Her back ached badly. Last week, the automatic potato-planter had broken down. For two days, while it was being repaired, they had had to plant by hand. Bent over the furrows for hours on end, placing the potatoes at regular intervals – the view nothing but earth, earth – was the most physically exhausting task any of them had encountered since their arrival. Ag's back still had not recovered, still felt as if the muscles were pulled taut as Victorian lacing. She lay flat, feeling the relief of solid ground beneath her. The rug smelt musty. Above her was an arcade of blossom, and beyond it the wider arcade of clear blue sky. It would be easy to sleep, she thought, one hand on her books. Perchance to dream. Where was Desmond, now?

Stella, her ears always attuned to Joe's plans these days, had discovered that he was to drive to a farm some miles away to inspect a tractor which Mr Lawrence wanted to buy. To turn the farm over to arable land fast and as efficiently as possible, more machinery was essential. Stella calculated that Joe would be returning from his inspection at about three o'clock. She would therefore take a short walk – she, too, was suffering from a strained back – ending at Lower Pasture, where the cows were spending their last few days. She would sit on the gate, enjoying the sun. Joe would drive along the lane, see her. Stop, perhaps, for a few inconsequential words about the tractor or the cows. Oh, how devious is love, she thought.

Her wait turned out to be a long one, but Stella did not mind. She sat listening to birds, busy in the thorn hedge. A drowsy bee flew back and forth, indeterminate, as if waiting for some outer force to decide on its next action. The cows, gathered in the far corner of the field not far from the only rick of last year's hay, were lying down. Unsympathetic creatures, really, thought Stella. She enjoyed milking them, but felt no affection for them. Their sameness was dull. Cows, she thought, could never compare with horses (she was very fond of the surly Noble) or even pigs: Sly's eccentricity had great charm. No: she wouldn't miss the cows – only the sight of them, the personification of peace in a green field.

Stella looked at her watch. A Red Admiral flew past her, further confusing the bee. She did not care how long she waited in the warm silence of the afternoon.

Then, from nowhere, came a horrendous scream of machinery: the silence, suddenly split, seemed itself to scream in agony as a hideous black plane scorched across the sky. As Stella fell from the gate, holding her ears, she saw a cluster of small silver incendiary bombs dropping from the plane's belly. By the time they had hit the ground, the plane was out of sight. Its terrible noise lingered, reverberated in its wake. The grass flattened, cowered.

Stella listened to the blistering noise as the bombs landed. Magnesium flames immediately spurted up, a terrible beauty in their many colours. The rick was on fire. She saw the sleepy cows leap wildly to their feet with one mass shudder, like the shaking out of a black and white rug. Their bellows joined the fading sound of the plane. Tails lifted stiffly in the air, they began to gallop about, panicking.

In the split second that all this happened, only one thought persisted in the numbness of Stella's mind: she must get the cows out of the field fast. They kept charging back to the rick, higher flames lapping at its base, now, and where one of their number lay, struggling on her side, stiff-legged, bleeding, roaring. There was no time to run for help. Stella had to act now.

As she was about to race across to the gate that led to the next-door clover field, she heard a squeal of wheels, saw the Wolseley rocking from side to side like a mad thing, and pull up with a great jerk. Joe was beside her, assessing the scene in a moment.

'I'll ring for the fire engine, be right back,' he said. 'Try to get them into the clover. Careful: they're hysterical.'

He was gone.

Stella, even in the panic of the moment, was pleased to think her idea was the same as Joe's.

She contemplated running round the edge of the field: in the shadow of the hedge she would be less conspicuous. But no: that would take too long. She set off straight across the field.

Immediately, two of the cows swerved towards her, heads down, ridiculous tails in the air. They followed her, screaming. Stella took a chance: she spun round, facing them, flapping wildly with white-shirted arms, shouting at them. Surprise penetrated their maddened state. They arced away, tipping sideways like clumsy boats in a wind. Stella registered a flash of wide black nostrils, four surprised eyes, before they careered off to join the rest of the herd, still bucking perilously close to the rick.

No cows followed Stella for the rest of her run to the gate. She struggled with it, back muscles an agony of protest, pushed it open: she had no idea whether all this had taken seconds or minutes. By chance, within feet of the gate, she saw a long stick, the kind Joe always broke off for himself when walking the land. She picked it up, turned.

By now she could see the rick was one dense mass of high flame. From it a shimmer of heat radiated among the jumping animals. They appeared to be a mirage of shattered glass, black and white skins flashing with sun and flames. Somewhere very near the flames Stella could see the figure of Ag, stick in hand, calling the cows' names in a calm voice.

As Stella ran across to join Ag, she saw that Prue had appeared from somewhere, too. And Ratty, hunched and excited, was shouting inaudible instructions from the gate by the lane.

When they reached the cows from their different directions, Stella and Prue slowed to a walk. They could feel on their faces the intense heat from the flames. They could smell the sour smell of the alarmed cows' excrement: shit-scared, Stella said to herself. They shimmered in each other's vision.

'Let's try to get behind them,' Ag called. She was scarlet in the face, but firm of voice.

The three girls, backs to the rick, waving their sticks and shouting encouragement, began to urge the cows towards the gate Stella had opened into the clover. They moved behind the animals towards the centre of the field, trying to avert their eyes from the bespattered corpse, black and white pieces fallen apart and gushing blood: Nancy, the old cow who was to have stayed.

Glad of any form of direction, the cows allowed themselves to be herded towards the opening. Every few moments one of them, in renewed panic, would spurt from the crowd, veer back towards the flames, and had to be chased by whoever was nearest.

The process of persuading the frightened but tiring cows towards the gate seemed endless. Ratty, shaking his stick from his safe distance, shouted more feebly. The girls were drenched in sweat, their faces red, hair sticky and flecked with ash. The cows, too, were dark with sweat. Slime ran from their nostrils. Their breath was hot, damp. Their wailing was a pitiful sound that echoed round the field.

At last they were all through the gate. They charged away through the long grass: relief in their antics, now. Their bellows petered out. Quiet returned over the landscape, but for the dull roar of the flaming rick.

'Christ,' said Prue, 'nothing but a bomb could've stopped my thoughts in their tracks.'

Ag and Stella were too exhausted, and concerned about the raging fire, to ask what she meant. They walked back slowly towards the rick – useless to hurry. A slight breeze cooled their faces.

Joe reappeared. He and Ratty swung open wide the gate on to the lane, ready for the fire engine. Then Joe hurried towards them.

'They'll be too late,' he said.

The rick was by now a fragile skeleton, pale among the crackling flames breaking off in large lumps that then burned on the ground. The heat was so great they could not stand too near. Ag thought of the autumn bonfire at the end of her first day's hedging: the crowd of them at ease around the small flames in a cool evening. This fire was so different in its savagery. Stella observed Joe's impenetrable face. She felt better now he was with them. Prue, now danger to the cows had passed, allowed herself the thought that *flame* red might be a possible alternative to bluebell blue . . . Scorning herself for such frivolity, it occurred to her this was the most dreadful, but most exciting, event she had ever witnessed. It would jolt them all out of any complacency about the war not touching their rural lives. Mr Lawrence, his wife not far behind him, was hurrying across to join the fire's spectators. Each carried pitchforks and rakes.

Joe was right. By the time they heard the pathetic little bell of the fire engine rattling along the lane, the rick was no more than a black smouldering mound. Ratty, still in his position at the gate to the lane, waved in the fire engine with a gesture of great impatience, dignified in its superfluity. The scarlet machine lumbered across the field, bell still ringing. It reminded Stella of fire engines in children's stories.

There was little the four firemen could do but hose down the scorched black earth with their limited supply of water. Wisps of smoke rose up from the bald patch and there was an acrid, powdery smell.

'Bastards,' said Mr Lawrence. 'Probably returning from bombing somewhere in the west, dropping their stuff on the way home for the hell of it.'

'Could have been worse,' said his wife. 'Could have been the house.'

'Your mother and I'll help rake this over: I'd like you to check the cows, Joe.' Mr Lawrence turned towards the lane. Ratty was still at the gate, still waving his stick. 'And I'd be grateful if two of you girls would escort Ratty back home. By the looks of things, he needs calming down.'

Ag and Prue immediately hurried towards Ratty. Stella offered to help Joe.

They crossed the field swiftly, in silence, climbed the gate into the clover. Hidden from sight by the thickness of the thorn hedge, Joe grabbed Stella's hand. With one accord they fell into each other's arms. Joe's chin rested on the top of Stella's head. Her hair smelt of smoke.

'You all right?'

'Fine.'

'I was so terrified that you . . . all I cared about was your safety . . .'

Joe pushed Stella slightly back from him so he could see her face. It was as black-streaked as he imagined was his own. They stared at each other with the kind of wonder that comes from acknowledgement, at last, of something long concealed.

'You must surely have known,' said Joe. 'You must surely have had your suspicions . . . I've tried so hard not to let you see. But you seem not to mind?'

Stella shook her head. Away from the heat, the sweat dried, she was suddenly, gloriously cold.

'That's good, because I'm going to kiss you, very briefly, very quickly, to show you that I love you, that I've been loving you to madness ever since Boxing Night.'

Their kiss was as brief as he promised. From the other side of the hedge they could hear miniature voices, the fire engine roaring its motor.

'We must check the animals.'

'Yes.'

'No time to talk. Don't let's try to talk – there's the whole summer to talk . . .'

'. . . the whole summer to talk.'

Stella heard, from a long way off, her own delirious echo. They parted to walk through the clover grass, sweet-smelling and full of bees. The cows were calm now, but wary-eyed.

'I see this as a beginning,' Joe said.

Edith was waiting for Ratty at her garden gate. Once again she had taken the precaution of putting on her own gas mask, and had brought Ratty's with her so that he might benefit from its protection on the journey up the garden path.

When she saw he was escorted by two land girls she sniffed, inconveniently steaming up the window of her mask. But it was not the occasion for the full force of her indignation. Rather, here was a good chance to show how right she had been. She took off the mask.

'What did I tell you, Ratty Tyler? War's all about us now. Thought the bombs might have got you.'

In truth she had thought no such thing. Terrified by the screech of the plane and the shaking walls of the cottage, she had hurried upstairs and lain under the bed, choked by dust and fluff that had accumulated untouched for years.

'That they didn't,' said Ratty.

He hadn't enjoyed an afternoon so much for ages. Once the bloody noise of the enemy plane had died down . . . all the excitement of the fire, the cows leaping about as if the devil himself had got into them, lovely sight of the girls running about waving sticks, then showing the fire engine where to go . . . No wonder his old ticker was pitter-pattering a bit. But then the holy one and the floozie, bless their hearts, had come and given him an arm up the lane. He had privately leaned harder on the holy one than he had on the floozie, was able to smell her sweet sweat among the smoky smell. And here he was, able to pay back Edith's horrible fright with a trick of his own: stop her in her tracks, it would, to see him on the arms of two pretty girls. Though, of course, he'd pay for it later. Last pan out of the window again, no doubt, but worth it.

'Well, we must be going,' said the holy one, so gentle, all smiles.

'Take care, Ratty.' The floozie gave him a kiss on the cheek, bless her heart, must have been reading his thoughts. Ratty had the pleasure of watching his wife's face contort with disbelief.

333

'None of that now,' was all she managed. 'Come along, Ratty . . . your tea's on.'

A lie, of course, showing off to the girls. His tea was never on. Edith handed him a gas mask.

'I'm not putting that thing on, not for anyone,' he chuckled. He winked at the girls, not unnoticed by Edith.

They turned away, waved. Ratty, leaning on his stick, watched till they were out of sight, impervious to his wife's calling. He chuckled to himself. Best afternoon for as long as he could remember, that's what he thought.

When they had left Ratty, Prue and Ag felt in need of a walk before returning to the farmhouse. They took a long way round through fields far from the burnt-out rick, and met Stella coming up the lane. Ag felt a slight shakiness in her limbs – the memory of Nancy's stiff corpse with its burst tongue would not leave her mind. Prue twittered on about having seen a ghost of Barry that turned out to be his friend. Ag was not fully concentrating on the story. But Stella, striding towards them, Ag noticed, was calm as ever: the only one who looked as if the events of the afternoon had cast no traumas.

Stella herself, a yard or so from the others, saw intuition in Ag's eye. Ag never missed a thing.

'Cows all right?' Ag asked.

'They seemed to have settled down. No injuries.'

'Poor old Nancy,' said Prue.

The girls linked arms, marched towards the farm in step. It was something they had never done before, something it would not normally have occurred to them to do. They laughed at their own silliness. They sang. Their relief flowed tangibly between them. Their fierce closeness was apparent to all three, comforting, binding: it had been growing over the months, and the evening of the bomb it was silently acknowledged.

*

Joe and his father took several hours to bury the dead cow. Joe dug the deep grave – the ground was hard and dry – with the energy of three men. It was twilight by the time they finished. Walking back up the lane, spades in hand, they heard the first nightingale of the year.

'Don't know what he's celebrating,' said Mr Lawrence, whose gaunt face was grey with fatigue.

Supper was waiting for them in the oven. They quickly ate it in the kitchen, then joined the others to listen to the nine o'clock news. There had been an unusual daytime raid on Exeter: about fifty bombers.

'Lawks,' said Prue, 'they're coming closer.'

She was right. A few days later there were attacks on Bath two nights running. The Nazi destruction of Baedeker towns had begun. A new feeling of unease, which even the hardest physical work could not quite obscure, affected everyone at Hallows Farm.

With one accord, and with great difficulty, Stella and Joe continued to act in public as they always had. They avoided glances, they avoided working together more than usual. Joe continued to share his time in the fields equally with all three girls. The day the cows were taken away in two lorries, he allowed Prue to cry on his shoulder. Ag and he would still spend an occasional evening in his room for 'tutorials'. But the thing that he found hardest to conceal was the extraordinary energy that had come upon him. He worked harder, for longer hours, than he could ever remember. Strangely, he suffered no attacks of asthma, usual in early summer, and never felt tired.

But a profound charge between two people is impossible to conceal completely from a beady eye. To the keen observer, a couple attempting to disguise their state surrender many clues. There's the over-careless tone of voice when addressing the loved one, glances slanting away just not fast enough to escape notice, dozens of small coincidences that result in proximity. Ag was aware of all these things. In one of their rare private moments Stella and Joe agreed Ag must know something, though her own suspicions were also carefully disguised; and they did not care. Indeed, it was a rewarding thought that someone else shared their secret: though they themselves, beyond their certainty, knew little of what that secret constituted.

So few and brief were their moments alone that there was no time to talk, to analyse, to make declarations, to try to explain to each other the mystery of what had happened. All they could do was acknowledge the crystallising of their feelings in broken, inadequate words, marvel at the existence of one another each day – 'waking alert with wonder every morning', as Joe said. They kissed, sometimes, very gently, for fear of conflagration. Strangely, they found themselves possessed of a great calm when it came to physical embrace: as if they knew there was time.

One day in early June, Mr Lawrence set Stella the task of rolling a field of young wheat. It would be a long day, he said, but if she kept at it she might finish by the evening. Mrs Lawrence suggested that, to save time, she would send someone down with a basket of food and a thermos for lunch. Stella, who had become almost as expert at ploughing as Prue, looked forward to the day – hours in the field alone with her thoughts.

Despite the departure of the cows, and no milking, the girls continued to get up at five every morning. It had become a habit, and as the weather grew hotter they were glad to start work in the cool of the early morning. Stella and Prue were usually assigned to some job on the tractors. Mr Lawrence had bought a fine second-hand machine, an International. Ag discovered the knack of harrowing with Noble: she enjoyed her days tramping up and down, hands firmly guiding the ungainly machinery behind the patient horse.

It was still misty when Stella skilfully swung the tractor, trailing the roller, through the gate of the wheat field. The sky was a dull silver, gravid with more light than the human eye could discern, but proving its existence by making the emerald spokes of the young wheat shine. Stella looked up, warily. She no longer trusted clear, silent skies. She turned off the engine to plan her route. The cry of an early peewit came from the adjacent clover field. There was a powerful smell of clover (a single flower would, for the rest of her life, bring back that afternoon of the bombs, she knew), and hawthorn, and dew. Then, as she restarted the engine, these scents were joined by a strong whiff of paraffin.

The job of rolling was easy in comparison to that of ploughing a straight furrow. All the same, it required a certain concentration to make sure not a single green shoot went unpressed. The hours sped, as random thoughts of Joe danced in the landscape: the sky paled to a colourless sheen, and by mid-morning a brilliant sun was warming Stella's bare arms.

Just as she was beginning to feel hungry – love, she had found, had increased rather than diminished her appetite – she saw Joe climbing over the gate, carrying a basket. She was surprised. She had expected one of the girls, or Mrs Lawrence herself, who, trapped in the house for so many hours, had a particular fondness for picnics. With the coming of the warm weather, she often made an excuse to take sandwiches to the girls in the fields, where she would join them for an hour on a rug under a hedge.

Joe waved, began to walk round the edge of the crop to the part of the hedge where Stella aimed to stop.

He helped her down from the tractor. She was stiff, sweating: dungarees were not much less hot than breeches. They sat under a single may tree, in the shadow of its pale crust of flowers. Joe unpacked the basket, spread out egg sandwiches, radishes, young lettuce and strawberries from the kitchen garden, a thermos of strong sweet tea.

337

'Mother, in all her innocence, said as I was the least busy I should be the one to come. She even apologised!'

Stella laughed. 'What are the others doing?'

'Prue's discovered a natural affinity for the mechanical potato planter. She's roaring up and down West Field, planting at the rate of knots. Any luck, there'll be no more sowing by hand. Your back better?' He put a hand on her shoulder blade for no more than a second. Stella nodded. 'Ag's got a hard job harrowing: lot of stone. But she seems to enjoy it, all the walking. Dad's gone off to fetch a load of clover seed. That's got to be planted among the young corn –'

'– to come up later,' said Stella.

'You're learning. You're not doing a bad job, either, by the looks of it.' He glanced round the field. 'A third done, I should say. You could be finished by seven.'

'What I can't understand,' said Stella, lying back in the long grass, head on her arm, 'is the whole *point* of rolling. Why aren't the shoots damaged?'

'Rolling firms up the earth, giving them more support to grow from. They're so feeble, so malleable, at this stage, they just rise up again soon after the roller's passed.'

'I've noticed that.' Stella yawned, longing to sleep. 'I think I'd rather enjoy learning more about farming.' She screwed up her eyes against the pinpoints of sun that crinkled through the may.

'I never intended to follow the family footsteps. I suppose I shall have to, now. Still, it's not without its interests. I won't mind that much.'

'Yorkshire?'

'Yorkshire.'

'With Janet?'

'*No.*'

'What?' Stella sat up, faced him.

He sucked at a long stem of wiry grass.

'I'm not going to marry Janet. How could I, now? It

338

would be a travesty. How could I marry Janet now there's you, there's us? *He is no wise man who will quit a certainty for an uncertainty.* Dr Johnson.'

Stella smiled, her mind a turmoil. They were silent for a while. Then Joe took her hand.

'Are you going to marry Philip?'

Deliberately, Stella gave herself no time to think. 'No,' she said. 'Of course not. For the same reasons as you're not going to marry Janet.'

The fluttering shadows, the brilliant haze of the young wheat behind them, the cloudless sky – all trembled, mirage-like, in Stella's eyes. Joe pulled her to him, kissed her, then lowered her head to the security of his chest, arms about her.

'*I know that love is begun by time,*' he said. 'See? I know my *Hamlet* as well as my *Johnson*.'

Stella laughed, pushing back the tears. 'Ag must be a good teacher.'

'Ag's a very good teacher. An original brain behind all that awkwardness.'

'I love Ag and Prue. And your parents.'

'I do, too.' Joe looked at her, half solemn. '*I love you*: that's the hardest line to say. Must be. For everyone, mustn't it?'

'I only said it politely to Philip – unconvincingly.'

'I hope this isn't unconvincing.' He kissed her hair. 'Stella? Did you hear? I said it to you. I shall go on saying it from this day forth, for the rest of our lives.'

'*Joe*. I must get back – I love you too – on the tractor.'

'Hear that? A peewit. I love you, I love you, I love you: three times. How about that?'

'I heard it this morning. God, I love you too. I keep saying thank you to God. He must be absolutely sure, by now, of my gratitude. How did it happen, Joe? How did it creep up on us?'

'Time. From the safety of mere friendship, just observing. Being near. Liking. Liking more and more. Then, one day, the transformation scene. The magic.'

'You saw first. I just kept on being puzzled by things: not understanding why I was put out if I hadn't seen you for half a day.'

Joe laughed. 'The intimations were all too easy to see. No: they're subtle as the traces of a rat's tail, to use Ratty language. Can so easily be missed by the untuned eye. When, I want to know, my Stella, was the precise moment, for you, that you realised . . . ?'

'I think . . .' Stella hesitated. 'It must have been when you held up the dead lamb, and skinned it.'

'Fastest skinning I've ever done.' Joe laughed again. 'I was showing off, of course.'

'Of course. And when, for you?'

'I was teetering on the edge during *They Can't Black Out the Moon*. When it came to *Falling in Love Again* – well, there was no further hope. Wings irreparably burned. It was like no experience I'd ever known. A kind of rebirth. I'm surprised you didn't notice my peculiar state on the way home. I was terrified of touching so much as the sleeve of your coat. And the funny thing was, of course, what you never knew, was that *you* were falling in love again, too. Only differently from all those false alarms before. *Properly.*'

Again they laughed.

'I only wish,' said Stella, 'we had more time to ourselves, more time to talk. I want to talk to you all day long.'

'We'll just have to wait for lucky chances, like this. Store everything.'

Stella, used by now to the warm smell of Joe's wind-dried cotton shirt, again longed to sleep.

'There's one thing we'll have to talk about, though.'

'I know.'

'What will we do . . . about them?'

'We have a valid reason for changing our minds. A real

reason. The war. If it hadn't been for the war, none of this would have happened.'

'No. True.'

'But there'll be time to talk further, to make our plans.' Joe clasped Stella more tightly. 'I'm terrified of touching you.'

'Me too. There'll be a time for all that.'

'God knows, I . . . But not here, at Hallows. Not the barn, or my bed, or Robert's cottage, or even the woods. Not with you.'

'No.'

'So we'll both wait – magnanimously.' Smiling, they stood up. 'I must go. A man's coming to see about buying all the stuff in the dairy. Christ, to think: if it hadn't been for the bombs we both might have kept our silence.'

'I wonder if that would have been possible? Heavens, I miss the cows. I didn't think I would, but I do already.'

'We'll have a new herd, one day,' said Joe. 'But Jerseys, not Friesians. I've never really liked Friesians.' He picked up the basket, rubbed the back of one hand over her cheek, strode away.

Stella returned to her seat on the tractor. The sun was almost too hot by now. She calculated the vast amount of unrolled field left to finish by evening, started the engine with wild heart, and dreaming eyes, and no doubts that she would have it done by the evening.

Harrowing the stony ground of the hill meadow was a tough job, and Ag liked it. It was a great deal more interesting, working with a horse, than was the endless couching which had been her lot of late. And she knew that soon after she had finished this field it would not be long before she must start thinking about the fruit on the plum trees, a job she looked forward to. If potato planting by hand was the most physically exhausting thing she had ever done, harrowing came a close second. The back was spared, but

341

arms and legs were battered. To keep straight, and to keep continually encouraging Noble – who was inclined to slow to a very slack pace – required intense concentration. This concentration was a merciful antidote to the melancholy cast of her mind. Lately, the odd sense of her lack of obvious attraction, appeal, whatever, had returned to haunt her. While the constant flaunting of Prue's conquests caused Ag little more than an envious smile, the more serious state of Joe and Stella (so plain to a sharp eye, Ag could not believe the Lawrences had not observed it) accentuated her own bereft state.

While Stella rolled the wheat field in a state of high ecstasy, half a mile away Ag plodded behind Noble's bay buttocks, lashed rhythmically by his black tail as flies settled, fled, settled again. Half-way up the hill, the horse suddenly stopped. Ag called encouragement. He did not move. Ag went impatiently to his head. What could she do, stranded in a field a long way from the farm, with a horse that refused to move? She took hold of his bridle, tried to urge him forward. Noble yawned, baring grass-stained teeth. Flies flew from round his eyes. Ag tugged again. Noble tossed his head, but still would not budge.

Despairing, Ag looked at the ground ahead. Perhaps there was something that the horse wanted to avoid. She saw that there was.

Just two yards away, right in their path, was a plover's nest with a sitting hen bird. Ag gave Noble an apologetic pat, kept quite still. The bird shuffled slightly, its feathers glinting, its eye jolted by indecision about whether to flee or stay. Ag took the bridle again, guided the horse away from the nest, which they skirted round in a wide sweep. Pushed into this sensible solution, Noble moved eagerly.

Often, during the rest of the day, Ag glanced back at the plover and saw it still there, sometimes visited by its mate. While ruminating on the wisdom of letting broody birds lie undisturbed, some strange transference of thought wove into words what she saw as a signal: something to do with taking initiative, not letting a lifeless situation decay any further. *Doing something.*

Ag could never be quite sure at what point of that long, hot afternoon of the plover that she made her decision: the decision to take matters into her own hands, write to Desmond. There could be nothing untoward in a friendly letter. If there was no response – well, at least she would know where she was, and could give up the agony of hoping. It must be easier to accept nothing, she thought, than to toy with the endless possibility of something.

That evening, Ag began her letter. She wrote seventeen pages, carried away with her own descriptions of life at Hallows Farm. *Dear Desmond*, it began. *Yours, Agatha*, it ended. She posted it to his college in Cambridge.

Twelve

The fine weather continued. Haymaking began. Mrs Lawrence had little time to join the others in the fields. With just six months before the move, every spare moment was spent with accounts books, calculations, lists.

One afternoon in late June, she carried the basket of washed sheets out to the line. It had been hot and sunny in the morning. Now, the sky was overcast and a strong breeze was blowing.

She began the job – which she seemed to have been doing weekly for as long as she could remember – and which, in fact, she found not without its pleasure. There was peculiar satisfaction in the whiteness of the coarse cotton, the wholesome smell of the soap which would be blown away by the wind and replaced with a scent of sun and earth. How many sheets, she wondered, should she take to Yorkshire? Should she reduce her linen cupboard, sell as much of everything as possible? Lately, a dozen such questions had besieged her mind each day.

There were six sheets on the line, now. In the increasing breeze they billowed like low sails. Their flapping noise, softer than canvas above waves, was more like the wings of a flock of large birds. One of the sheets wrapped itself round Mrs Lawrence. She felt its wetness through her apron, her dress. It enveloped her like a ghostly cloak. She stood there, a moment of sudden and unusual fatigue, letting it do with her as it liked. Each side of her, companion sheets were now swollen huge with air, tugging at their pegs. Mrs Lawrence dreaded their falling to the ground. She had no energy to rehang them. While they cooed at her, the free sheet still twisted round her, making her suddenly cold. The solid mass of grey sky, she saw, had been blown into a feathering of small cloud, like the breast of a guinea fowl. The dogs were barking in the yard. Mrs Lawrence's misery was so acute that the familiar patch of garden in which she was imprisoned was contorted into a place she no longer recognised. She was aware only of a turmoil of blowing white all round her, agitated cloud above, the nagging of the breeze on her skin. She felt close to drowning.

Mr Lawrence, by chance returning to the farm for a new scythe, came round the corner to see his wife trapped in a sheet, the others blowing angrily on the line. He ran to her. Reaching her, he felt as if he was entering a surreal picture. Her misery reached out to him. He was alarmed by her face.

Quickly, he unwound her, took her icy hands. She leaned against him with so deep a sigh he could feel a shudder right through her thin body.

'I don't want to go, John,' she said.

'I know,' he said. 'None of us wants to go.'

For the first time Mr Lawrence could remember, his wife sobbed – briefly and quietly. He held her for a long time. They stood clasped together, waiting for her to recover, listening to the soughing of the sheets.

With the increased amount of physical labour, even Prue found herself more tired than before, and was forced to cut down her visits to Robert to two evenings a week. This caused her no great sorrow. Her earlier doubts had hardened into a definite *impasse* with Robert – the kind of *impasse* she often came to with a man of scant means.

Although her respect for him remained intact – there was something mysterious about him which continued to intrigue her – the affair had withered into an unexciting routine which Prue recognised as a signal to its end. Meantime, Jamie Morton was limbering up as a possible successor – though, as Prue explained to the others, it was only lack of choice that forced her to consider him at all.

Jamie dutifully cycled over to the farm several weeks running to meet Prue in the woods on her afternoon off. On closer acquaintance, Prue discovered that similarities with Barry were few. In fact, the only two things they had in common were the RAF, and heavy smoking. Unlike Barry, he did not like Woodbines: Players were what he preferred. He talked about cigarettes at some length. Sometimes Prue – an accommodating girl in some respects, she had switched to Players to please him – felt she could not bear another conversation about the relative merits of various brands, and stories about how many packets Jamie had smoked on various occasions.

Jamie's alternative line of conversation was hardly more endearing. He would describe to her the nature of his fantasies – such coarse dreams, it turned out, that even Prue was shocked. He did not, however, lay a hand upon her. Although she might have conceded, if the moment had come, Prue felt no great desire to be pummelled by the hefty red hands with their swollen fingers and bitten nails. There was a certain simple charm in his face – Prue still admired his teeth – and she had always fancied the blue of the RAF uniform. But to be quite honest, as she told the others, the weekly appointment to smoke in the woods with Jamie Morton was not the sort of thing that would keep her interest alive for long.

For once in her life, there were two things that preoccupied Prue's thoughts, that early summer, more than men. One was the departure of the sheep and lambs, the other was the invitation to Buckingham Palace.

346

When she was able to get a word in edgeways, she tried to tell Jamie about the day she had to spend helping Mr Lawrence go through the ewes' wool looking for maggots – he wanted to sell a clean flock. She had found some. The bugs had made red patches of sour raw flesh at the roots of the wool, which had to be treated. The little buggers, Mr Lawrence had said, could get right down into a sheep's bones, drive it mad. Prue had to give two bloody great tablets to each ewe. Persuading it to open its yellow teeth, and swallow the things, was one of the worst jobs she could remember, she said. All the same, she was fond of the sheep, and loved the lambs. When they were finally hustled aboard a convoy of vans, she sobbed her eyes out, she didn't mind admitting. She'd never heard such a noise in her life. The baaing and bleating would haunt her for years.

Jamie conveyed little interest in Prue's stories of the sheep. The invitation to meet their Majesties, though – that was another matter. While Prue described the difficulty she was having in finding bluebell artificial silk, and the picture in her mind of the King and Queen in their crowns on a golden throne, jewel-studded, Jamie puffed faster at his cigarette, inhaled deeply, blew beautiful smoke rings that flew high into the trees before they broke – a man full of wonder and awe.

'Good heavens, Prue,' he said, when her imagination finally ran out one afternoon in the woods, 'that'll be quite something. Not believable, really.' He stubbed the butt of his seventh Players into a patch of virgin moss. 'I've never shagged with a girl who's been to Buckingham Palace. Know that? Don't suppose any of my mates have, either.'

'Don't suppose they have,' said Prue.

Distracted by her thoughts of the Palace, more real to her than the present scene, Prue noticed Jamie had clamped one of his terracotta hands on her knee. She allowed it to stay there, just for a moment, before encouraging him to engage in the whole studied business of lighting the next cigarette.

The weeks of high summer passed with astonishing speed. There were long days of hay-making in hot sun. There was the cultivating, and spreading the sheep and cow dung left in the fields so that it should not sour small patches. To ensure the successful transformation of Hallows Farm into a good arable holding that would attract buyers in the autumn, the jobs seemed never-ending. Prue, to show her gratitude for the privilege of being the chosen one to go to the tea party, worked with extraordinary energy by day – by night, too, there was so much to be done in preparation. A week before the great event, she refused Robert any favours, saying she had to get her beauty sleep, do her finger nails, her toe nails, try out hair styles, choose her hat, generally pull out all stops so as not to let down the honour of the Women's Land Army at her meeting with their Majesties. Robert was understanding about everything except the toe nails.

And suddenly there she was on the platform of the station, a July morning, Mrs Poodle rounding up a herd of other land girls from the district. In their brightly coloured silks and crêpes, with rouged cheeks and waved hair, they jittered about, all shy smiles and nervous giggles.

Joe had paid Prue no compliments on the journey to the station: his silence was unnerving. But when he whispered to her, on the platform, before leaving, that she looked the best by far, Prue's confidence returned.

Glancing about, she could not but immodestly agree with him. But then, she had taken so much trouble: *weeks* of effort and consultation to achieve the final picture. Her dress, though not quite the bluebell she had in mind, was at least a dazzling blue, with a sweetheart neckline copied from her winter red, and a flirty skirt, though, God forbid, nothing that could possibly cause a frown from the King.

Her mum had dyed some old shoes an almost matching blue, and to cover her hay-scratched hands she wore a pair of white cotton gloves which Mrs Lawrence had kindly embroidered with small patches of forget-me-nots.

But the real inspiration was the hair. Having made a hat with a piece of the dress material, Prue had abandoned it at the dress rehearsal the night before and had replaced it with real cornflowers. She had run out into the warm night, frantically gathered cornflowers from tangled beds and long grass, preserved them in water by her bed. At dawn this morning she had, with Ag's help, pinned them randomly among her blonde curls, and prayed very hard that they would not wilt before five o'clock. And indeed the cornflowers were causing something of a stir. The other girls in their stiff and elderly hats admired Prue's great style. While they bobbed up and down practising their curtsies, at Mrs Poodle's insistence, while waiting for the train, they paid Prue many a generous compliment. All the way to London in the train, warm bristly stuff of the seat prickling her thighs through the artificial silk, Prue basked modestly in their admiration. She could not remember a happier day.

Mrs Poodle had had the idea of taking the girls to the Albert Memorial for their picnic lunch. She thought they would enjoy sitting on the steps in the sun, beneath the gaze of the marble sages as well as Prince Albert, and then stroll in Kensington Gardens before returning to the coach that was to take them to the Palace.

Prue, who had not been to London before, was enchanted by the drive from the station. She had not expected to see so many trees, the lushness of Hyde Park, people lying on the grass impervious to the war or the possibility of a raid. She saw only one devastated building: blackened stone, piles of still uncleared rubble, shreds of once private wallpaper exposed to the world. But nothing could detract from her excitement.

349

At the Albert Memorial, she sat on a step a little apart from the others. She wanted to be alone, to take it all in: if only Stella and Ag had been here – but still, she thought she would try to be a good reporter. She opened her paper bag of lunch, unwrapped the sandwiches from their greaseproof paper, then threw them to the sparrows. No chance of eating till she was *there*. Their Majesties would hardly be impressed by smudged lipstick.

The sun shone warmly down on Prue. The cornflowers, she checked, were still perky in her hair. She stood up, impatient – half an hour before they had to reboard the coach. She smoothed the creases from her skirt, wandered round the side of the Memorial. There, the ground had been turned into allotments. Amazed, Prue stood looking down upon a man who was bent over a row of peas supported by twigs. The sight of such country labour in the middle of London reminded her that Stella and Ag, at this very moment, would be working in the fields. She shut her eyes, imagining the afternoon at Hallows Farm, a place by now light years away, a dream . . . But no! This, surely, was the dream: Prue Lumley, land girl, in artificial silk on the steps of the Albert Memorial, about to be presented to the King and Queen.

Prue's imaginings of activities at the farm were not quite accurate. Stella and Joe were supposed to be cutting the clover field: Joe on the new International, Stella on the Fordson, with which she was now familiar. But the old machine, increasingly cantankerous, refused to start. Stella fiddled with the choke, topped it up with paraffin, finally banged the bonnet in exasperation, but to no avail. Eventually, not wishing to waste more time, she was forced to interrupt Joe, needing his help.

He solved the problem at once: dirty plugs. He removed them one by one, held them up, cleaned them on a piece of rag. The simple solution made Stella feel foolish.

'I didn't know about the plugs,' she said. 'I'm not sure I'd have known where to find them.'

'I haven't fallen in love with a mechanic, thank God,' said Joe.

It was hot in the barn. No breeze stirred the broody shadows. There was a smell of chaff and sacking. In the rafters, drowsy pigeons barely cooed. Outside, sun blazed down on the yard. Stella was glad of a time in the shade before facing the heat of the field.

'I've been thinking,' said Joe. 'I'm not going to say a word to Janet until you girls have left, just before we move to Yorkshire. Weighing up everything – it's a difficult decision to make – that would be the kindest thing. Postponing her anguish, perhaps: but I must tell her to her face.'

Stella, leaning up against the warm metal of a mudguard, watched him carefully.

'I think I should do the same. With Philip. Face him, too. Do you think they'll accept our reasons? Vicissitudes of the war?'

'They'll have to. It's the truth. Can't say I look forward to the announcement, though I don't suppose Janet will be altogether surprised. She must have some idea our so-called engagement is a ghastly mistake. Poor girl: she doesn't have much in her life. Sparking plug tester –' he held up the last clean plug – 'little hope of promotion. I presume she's calculated that marrying the wrong person is better than not marrying at all. I'll have to persuade her she's mistaken.'

'Philip, I think,' said Stella, 'will be very shocked. Devastated. He's no idea of my change of heart. He won't believe it. His pride . . .'

'Christ! We're going to be making a bit of a bloody mess,' said Joe, wiping the sweat from his face, 'but I think our plan is the best one. We'll only be postponing the evil day – for them – by a few months. As for us . . . I've been thinking. It wouldn't be easy, your coming with us to

Yorkshire as a land girl, my having broken off with Janet. My parents . . .'

'I realise that. I thought I could join my mother driving ambulances in London. In my spare time, go back to the piano. But at the end of the war, there's no reason why I shouldn't come to Yorkshire.'

'There's a small cottage belonging to the farm, up in the dales. Needs complete renovation. I've often imagined . . .' He climbed up into the driving seat, pushed the starter button. The engine growled into life. 'You'd like it there.' He climbed down again, gave Stella a hand. 'Tractor awaits you, my love.'

'Thank you! I'll know next time.'

'Any luck, this time next year, we'll be harvesting Yorkshire fields, and bloody Hitler'll be dead.'

Ag and Mrs Lawrence, at adjacent trees in the orchard, were thinning the near-ripe plums. There were several filled baskets on the ground. Ag enjoyed the job, as she did most jobs involving hedges, trees, fruit. She enjoyed the warmth of the sun on her bare arms. She enjoyed thinking, for the thousandth time, of Desmond reading her letter. It was – she could privately admit to herself – a work of such vivid description that it could hardly fail to give pleasure. And there were still two weeks in which she would carry on hoping for a reply. Beyond that, to presume the worst would be the only sensible thing. At that moment she would have to banish dreams, brace herself for a solitary future. But there were fourteen days before she might have to face that trauma, still a modicum of hope in the summer air. Her optimism among the branches, heavy with warm plums, was not in doubt.

'It was *in*credible. I still can't believe it. The red carpet. Honestly. A deep ruby red. *Acres* of it, all up these great wide stairs, all over this grand entrance hall. I mean, you could've carpeted Lower Pasture, easy, with all that red . . .'

Prue had the full attention of her audience. It was past ten at night, the darkness just light enough to see by, so the windows of the sitting-room were still open, the blackout had not been drawn. Scent from a few surviving tobacco plants came into the room, at odds with the heavy scent of Prue's *Nuits de Paris*, which she had been applying extravagantly to her wrists and neck all day. She was slumped on the sofa, artificial silk crumpled, cornflowers wilting in the curls, blue shoes slung off, dreamy-eyed.

'*So*. We go in, up these stairs, like walking on velvet. There's a huge crowd of us by now, from all over. More than three hundred. Mostly in reds and florals – no blues like this, I'm glad to say.' She patted the weary skirt. 'There's a bit of trouble, you can imagine, getting the counties into alphabetical order. Very smart men in tail coats bossing about, very politely. *Ooh*, and the footmen, just like in *Cinderella* . . . Anyway, at last we're in this great room, the Bow Room, overlooking the gardens. Pillars and so on. There's a band playing. My legs were aching to dance. Then the word sort of went round, despite the music, and suddenly there they were, coming in, *the Royal Family*. Me near them – *me*! King and Queen, two princesses. A path cleared for them. They walked down, smiling this way and that. The whole crowd of us went down in a wobbly curtsy, we were that nervous. Actually, I didn't wobble as much as some. And it was the first of about twenty-nine curtsies I did, I tell you. Every time I saw one of *them* nearby, down I went, just in case. Once, I found myself curtsying to a girl from Derbyshire – she got in my line of vision, didn't half laugh, vulgar bit. Anyway, you could see these gentlemen in charge taking up quite a few of the WLA bigwigs to meet the King and Queen. And some land girls. Not me, actually, though I gave them the nod, several times. *Equerries*, I think they're called. Still, I got very near. Especially to the princesses. They were walk-

353

ing about, almost ordinary. I couldn't believe it. Me, myself, within two feet of Princess Elizabeth in a lovely flowered dress.

'We were urged to help ourselves to tea. Tea! Bloody banquet, more like. These huge great long tables covered in white damask cloths so bright they dazzled your eyes. A thousand cups and saucers, plates and plates of tiny sandwiches. And lashings of chocolate cake: you couldn't taste the powdered egg at all. Perhaps they'd used real. I asked one of the footmen if they had a private supply of hens at the Palace, but he didn't answer, just smiled, too discreet to say. Anyway, best of all were the teapots: enormous great silver things with little silver strainers hanging to their spouts – such a sensible idea, I thought. Truth to tell, I drank my tea – I'll remember every sip of that royal tea – but had no appetite for the sandwiches. Just one bit of the chocolate cake, well, two bits – I thought: can't pass up an opportunity like that. I wanted to bring some back but couldn't think how . . . I took my plate over to the windows – tall as this house – to look out at the garden. Well, blow me down if it wasn't all made over to vegetables, neat beds of vegetables between little paths without a weed. I turned round to say something to anyone who happened to be near, mouth full of chocolate cake, when Princess Margaret, in glorious pink, passed not one foot from me. Her eyes! I tell you, I've never seen such eyes. She smiled at me. At least, I think she did. Course, mouth full of chocolate cake it was a bit awkward – just my luck. By the time I'd cleared my teeth, she was gone. Still, I curtsied, just for safety. Hoped she didn't think me unfriendly, but she caught me on the hop.

'I still can't quite believe it. I tell you, it was a dream. I only know it's true because I got chocolate cake on my gloves. I shall never wash them. Never, ever. For the rest of my life the royal chocolate will stay on my white gloves, proof it happened, proof I, Prue, once went to the Palace . . .'

Stopped only by overwhelming tiredness, further details of Prue's excursion came temporarily to an end that night. But next afternoon, at an assignation in the woods with Jamie Morton, she found no difficulty in retelling the story, refining here and there, guessing at the height of the magnificent ceilings, the yardage of silk curtain, the probable value of Her Majesty's diamond brooch, and her pearls the size of goose eggs.

Jamie was impressed. Prue could see that by the way his cigarette went unusually slowly to his mouth. The inhaling was shallow, the smoke rings careless. He had probably never listened to anyone so long, so quietly, so completely enrapt, reckoned Prue. When she at last finished her story he put one of his wedge-like hands on her shoulder, fixed her with an intensity of eye.

'By golly, Pruey,' he said, 'what a thing. Like I told you, I've never had a girl who's been to Buckingham Palace. Could be my only chance. What do you think?'

In the slipstream of her exhilarated state, generosity of spirit further warmed by her unique experience, Prue was happy to concede. While Flight-Lieutenant Morton prepared to ravish the first girl in his life who had brushed with royalty, Prue lay back on the mossy ground and thought of Buckingham Palace.

The morning came when the threshing machine was stripped of its tarpaulin and introduced to the girls. At first they were bemused by the complicated-looking monster, felt they would never understand the intricacies of so many belts, shaking trays and cunningly placed holes all designed to divide each sheaf into separate pieces. But Mr Lawrence was diligent in his explanations, and managed to leave them with a feeling of admiration for the ingenuities of the machine.

Two middle-aged men from the village came to help with the threshing. The machine took a whole morning to

355

set up on an area of flat ground between two ricks. Work began early one hot afternoon. It turned out to be a job the girls unanimously hated.

The rattling and noisy throbbing of the machine quickly gave them all headaches, exacerbated by the uncomfortable goggles they had to wear to protect their eyes. High on the rick, pitching sheaves required more skill than they had imagined. Frustrated by their own clumsiness, hot, itching all over from chaff and dust that penetrated everything, the few days of hard threshing were an endurance test. But none of them gave up or complained.

Looking back, years later, on those hard days, Ag remembered only a single afternoon with any clarity. She was, as usual, on top of the rick – more skilled by now at cutting the string from sheaves and tossing them on to the man who would drop them into the drum. It was a particularly hot afternoon: the shirts of all three girls were dark with sweat, their bare arms a deep brown. The landscape shimmered in a heat haze, doubly blurred behind the goggles. At some moment, watching her own hands mechanically repeat their mind-dulling actions, Ag remembered that Desmond's time was up. No letter. No reply. Too many weeks for any possible excuse. Only thing to be done. *Forget.* Face a new kind of life.

Tears further confused her vision behind the goggles. But she smiled encouragement at Stella, who was clutching her ribs. She remembered allowing herself the sentimental thought that all hopes of Desmond were being shoved into the thresher, along with the sheaves, and, if she looked down the side of the machine, she would see them pouring out of the hole with the chaff: ground to dust, useless, gone.

By harvest-time, the customary peace at Hallows Farm was disturbed more frequently by passing planes: sometimes a Spitfire, sometimes the dreaded shape of the Luftwaffe monsters. Since the occasion of the incendiary bombs, the old, foolish sense of security in remote country was never quite recaptured. Living in anticipation of the next disaster became part of daily life.

But nothing stopped work on the harvest. It was safely gathered in, for the last time, by the Lawrences.

'There's something very satisfactory,' Ag observed to Prue, 'about seeing the barn filled again. Something very comforting, the annual storing of stocks for the winter.'

Prue giggled at Ag's solemnity. 'What I like the thought of,' she said, 'is all these new beds in here.' She looked round the stacks. 'Hope the new farmer's son and his girl-friend will have a good time.'

The harvest supper took place one warm evening, in the corner of the field where they had lit the bonfire last autumn. Rugs and tablecloths were spread over the stubble. A few sheaves of corn were left standing, leaning against each other in wigwam shapes – they were to be taken to church for the Harvest Festival service next day. Noble was employed to pull the cart that once was used to deliver the churns. It was filled with bowls of food, bottles of cider and beer, hunks of cheese and baskets of plums. Mrs Lawrence had been preparing the feast all day: the harvest supper was the occasion she most enjoyed during the year.

The harvesters gathered at seven – three Lawrences, the two helpers from the village, Robert, Ratty and the girls. It was a warm evening of long shadows. There had been no planes to disturb the peace that day: the quietness felt settled. There were smells of warm earth, and Mrs Lawrence's newly baked bread, unwrapped from its cloth. Poppies wavered in the hedgerow. A few survived in the stubble. The ravenous girls, chewing legs of cold roast chicken in their fingers, could not remember a happier occasion.

Each one had her particular reason. Ag had adapted to

her new life of no hope in Desmond. She had filled her mind with other concerns, made plans for the future, read herself to sleep each night, managing almost completely to obliterate the old yearnings. She had returned to enjoying the present – occasions like this supper – rather than leading a double life with an imaginary future forever there shadowing the actual moment. Her efforts had brought their rewards.

Stella, sitting as far as possible from Joe, cocooned in her ever-increasing certainty of their mutual love, wondered if the others could see the indivisible bond between them. Avoiding his eyes, she drank a whole beaker of cold cider, felt a gold rush through her limbs, and doubted if any girl on earth could be so fortunate.

Prue, corn dolly in her hair in honour of the harvest celebrations, took the opportunity to furnish the assembled audience with more details of her afternoon at the Palace, until they laughingly shouted her down. She didn't care: she didn't mind being teased. She felt lithe, fit, strong, and ravenous. Cutting herself a huge wedge of home-made pie, she longed to shock them all with the secret that made the adrenalin charge through her blood. What would they say if they knew she was servicing two men, concurrently? Robert two nights a week, Jamie Morton two afternoons? And there was no let-up in her work and energy, either. If anything, they seemed to have increased. With secret pride she stroked her bare brown legs – since the 'bare legs for patriotism' campaign in May, Prue had refused to wear stockings. She saw Ratty's eyes on her, and laughed.

'So where's Edith?' she asked him.

Ratty took a long time to finish a mouthful of bread and cheese. 'Coming later,' he said. 'With the tea. Usual custom.'

They sat eating, drinking, laughing for a couple of hours, watching the blue of the sky turn to the indigo of

the shadows covering the stubble. Stella began to sing. Her
Vera Lynn repertoire, songs that were on the wireless most
nights.

> *We'll meet again*
> *Don't know where, don't know when . . .*

Ratty thought he had never heard so sweet a voice. Spurred
by a mixture of beer and cider, he ventured to join in. The
others did likewise. The chorus roamed from war song to
war song, the pure voice leading them, till it was almost
dark.

It was Stella – by chance she stood up to relieve a stiff
leg – who first saw a figure standing dimly by the cart.

Ratty, facing Stella, stood up too, back to the figure. It
was his turn, he reckoned.

'Let's have a hymn now, everyone. What d'you say to
"Abide with me" to close the proceedings?' He spoke in his
church voice, the one he used to guide rare visiting wor-
shippers to their seats.

Ratty began to conduct with his hands, croaking voice
leading them in the familiar words. Stella, watching the
figure coming up behind him, saw that it was Edith. She
wore a headscarf and a long skirt, an old woman from
another age carrying a tin churn by its handle. Ah, thought
Stella, she's bringing the tea.

In the speckled darkness, she saw a trembling hand
unscrew the lid of the churn, let the lid fall to the ground.

> *When other helpers fail, and comforts flee,*
> *Help of the helpless, O abide with me!*

As the chorus gathered strength, Stella knew in an instinctive flash what was going to happen. In the second that
Edith swung back the churn to gain the greatest possible
thrust, Stella took a leap towards Ratty. She flung her arms

round his knees so that his body was forced to flop over her shoulder. Carrying him in this fireman's hold, she jumped through picnic things and stretched legs, and ran as fast as she could. The confused Ratty's plea to his Lord to abide with him rose in throttled voice from somewhere near Stella's waist.

Thus Ratty was just saved from the gush of scalding tea that Edith flung at her husband. Thrown by the sudden departure of her target, Edith's aim went mercifully awry. The full blast of the liquid fell on to what remained of the food. Prue's bare legs were splashed. She gave a quick squeal of protest, then leapt up to join the general chaos.

In the muddle of semi-darkness, Ag, Mrs Lawrence and Joe found themselves trying to calm an hysterical Edith, who kicked and screamed on the ground. Her feet clanked against the empty churn as she arched her back, pushing off hands. A cluster of cuckoo spit whitened the corners of her mouth. Mr Lawrence shouted that he would telephone for the doctor, and ran off. The others, between them, managed finally to get Edith to her feet, and dragged her to the back of the cart. She sat writhing on the tailboard, a pathetic old figure, legs swinging loosely, stockings wrinkled round the ankles. Between her screams she muttered incoherently: some daft notion about Ratty and the land girls, Prue thought it was. But Edith's accusations were too confused to make sense of her trouble. Prue and Mrs Lawrence climbed into the cart beside her, clinging to her eel body. Ag walked, trying to make sure the old woman would not slip to the ground. Robert led Noble towards the farmhouse. The two men from the village followed, arms full of the picnic stuff. The procession made its way across the stubble lit by a white harvest moon. Edith never stopped screaming, attempting to escape. She was answered by the screech of a passing owl.

360

A harvest she'd never forget, thought Prue. She wondered if the story would make Jamie pause in his smoking.

Stella had landed Ratty back on his feet some fifty yards from the scene of chaos.

'What was all that about, then?' he asked, beer and cider still making merry in his brain. It was the first time he'd been alone with one of the land girls – with a moon and all, too. Not the sort of thing that happened every harvest.

'Edith's been taken ill. Don't worry. The others are looking after her.'

'Is that right?' Ratty sounded unconcerned. He looked up as Joe appeared out of the darkness. 'The wife?' he asked.

'Doctor's coming. Bit over-excited, she is, that's all. She's riding back to the house in the cart.'

'Is that so?' Ratty shook his head, gave a deep sigh. ' 'Course, there've been signs, haven't there? You could tell she was boiling up for something. These past months. Matter of waiting.'

'Stella and I will walk you home,' said Joe, taking the old man's arm.

'Very well.'

Ratty allowed himself to lean on the two of them just hard enough to be polite. But, considering the drama, he moved with sprightly step and head held high.

Much later that night, a heavily sedated Edith was driven away by the doctor and the district nurse. Ratty, asked if he would like to accompany them, said no he bloody wouldn't.

On the October day that the Eighth Army under Montgomery began a big offensive along the coast of El Alamein, at Hallows Farm there was a small celebration to mark the first anniversary of the girls' arrival. Mr Lawrence brought out the ginger wine, and said a few words of appreciation before proposing a toast. He wished them well, however their time might be spent when they left the farm. In particular, he said, he knew the others would want to join him in wishing Stella all the best in her marriage to Philip. In the general flurry of raised glasses and echoed hopes, he saw a look pass between his son and the blushing girl who had caused him some unnerving moments, in the past year, in his own heart. Not allowing himself time to reflect on what he had seen, he knew that, for Joe's sake, it was perhaps a good thing the girls' days were numbered. As for his own feelings: well, the internal unease had run its course, a shameful secret that would go with him to the grave. He could look easily on Stella now, knowing she was firmly committed to another. She had acted as a warning to him – a warning that the most stable of middle-aged men could be taunted by lascivious desire – and he had taken heed. Now, his energies must be concentrated on his wife, so courageous about the move she dreaded. He would support her to the best of his abilities, show his love and gratitude. He raised his glass, last of all, to her.

'And can we drink to Faith, my wife?' he said. 'Because had it not been for her, for her extraordinary insistence, no land girls would have come to Hallows Farm. We would not all be here today.'

It was Faith's turn to blush: a deep, muddy colour suffused her skin. She held up her pink glass, which flashed at her husband's dear face.

Prue, sensing but not understanding the public reaffirmation, was the first to break the tension of the moment. She stood up, jabbing as usual at her bow.

'Well, I'm going to take this opportunity to kiss *everyone*,' she said, 'before I cry. I trust you'll all do the same.'

Thus Prue, in her innocence, afforded Joe and Stella a

bonus chance, in public, to kiss each other quickly on the cheek.

Edith did not return, and Ratty could never remember so enjoyable an autumn. Within days of her departure he had restocked the kitchen with saucepans, and burned a dozen boxes of cut-up paper. For so many years he had longed to live alone. His solitude, won so late, he was now determined to relish to the full. For some weeks, padding about the house, he found it hard to believe Edith was not going to jump out at him in her gas mask or torture him in one of her sadistic, cunning ways. Not till the official letter arrived, confirming her insanity, did he finally realise that the new peace would be permanent. He could listen to Mr Churchill and *ITMA*, undisturbed: take his tea in by the wireless, spill crumbs on the floor, do as he wished in all respects – even smoke his pipe in bed – and never again be chided. As he said to the holy one in the orchard one afternoon – surrounded by baskets of plums, she was, all smiles – never had the autumn days gone by so fast.

It was a feeling shared by all three girls. Their time seemed to be running out with uncanny speed. It was now, more than in the summer when they were so busy in the fields, that they missed the cows, the sheep, Sly. They looked back with nostalgia to their bewildering start as land girls, just over a year ago. They remembered the mysteries of their early days, and laughed, thinking of the mistakes they made: how strange they had found the life which by now was so familiar. The weather they remembered on their arrival returned. The second time round of experiencing farmhouse and land in misted mornings, yellowing afternoons, frosted nights, was no less beguiling than it had been at first.

Once again, with the change of seasons, the pattern of life shifted in the house in the evenings. Instead of going their own ways, everyone gathered by the fire for an hour or so before going to bed. Mr Lawrence forced himself to make lists of farm implements that might be sold in the auction – the farm was to be put up for sale early in the New Year – while he listened to the wireless. Mrs Lawrence continued with her perennial darning, her needle only pausing at news of Montgomery breaking through Rommel's front, or the hideous rumours that the Nazis had been systematically rounding up Jews throughout Europe.

She was never able to quell her anxiety when the telephone rang, particularly after dark. When she heard it ringing in the hall, late one evening in early December, she put down her work with a beating heart and ran into the darkness. A minute later she reappeared.

'It's for you, Stella.'

Stella left the room. Philip, she knew, was in London for two nights – the much postponed trip with his friend. It was his intention to buy the ring. He had rung only a week ago, insistent that he was off to Bond Street in search of an aquamarine. Stella, who thought a Dear John letter was the coward's way out, had decided to stick to her intention of breaking off her engagement face to face. But there had been no opportunity. Guiltily, she hoped he was not telephoning with news of his find.

When Stella had not reappeared after ten minutes, Joe gave up his game of patience, rubbed his face, anxious. His own unease, he observed, was reflected by all those in the room. A long telephone conversation, at Hallows Farm, was far from a normal occurrence.

Stella came back at last. Pale-faced, her eyes swept dryly over each of them. She tossed back her head, spoke with the efficiency of one only just in control.

'That was Philip's mother,' she said. 'She was ringing to tell me Philip's in hospital. He's lost a leg: seems there's little hope of saving his second foot.'

'*Stella*!' said Joe.

Ag jumped up, put an arm round her friend.

'He was on leave in London, staying with his friend in Bermondsey. They had a day in the West End, apparently . . . Bond Street. They were on their way home. There was an air-raid warning: they were on a bus. It seems they couldn't get to a shelter in time.' She paused. 'Would you mind if I took the day off tomorrow, Mr Lawrence? I must go to London. The hospital. See him.'

'I'll take you to the early train, of course,' said Mr Lawrence.

'Sit down, Stella,' said his wife, leaving her own chair. Joe quietly left the room.

The others did their best: Bournevita, an arm to guide Stella up the stairs, quiet listening faces in the attic, waiting for her to cry, to speak.

Stella thanked them, but said nothing. Before she got into bed she picked up the photograph of Philip that she had kissed with such passion every night, this time last year – and looked at it for a long time. Then she replaced it.

'He expected to be wounded in battle,' she said eventually. 'But to be made useless by a bomb in the street: how will he ever cope with that?'

'Poor, poor Philip,' said Prue, rummaging in her drawer for a black bow which she would wear tomorrow, just as she had for Barry.

The following day was interminable for Joe. Heavy rain, mud, cold. He busied himself sorting out farm machinery in the barn, but flinging heavily rusted iron into various piles was no antidote to his thoughts. Eventually, by late afternoon, dirty light out in the yard, he slumped on to a pile of new straw, tried to slow the thumpings of his heart and think clearly.

Mr Lawrence appeared. He quickly assessed the state of Joe's dejection.

'We're all worried for the poor girl,' he said, 'but Stella's got guts if anyone has. She'll stand by him, legs or no legs.' Joe met his father's eye. 'Look, son, I've got a mass of paperwork still this evening. Would you go to the station, fetch her?'

Joe looked at his watch. 'Tell you what,' he said. 'She might not be up to facing everyone at supper. Might be better if I suggested a sandwich and a stiff whisky at The Bells.'

'Good idea,' said Mr Lawrence.

Stella's train from London was half an hour late. Joe waited in the cold dark of the platform. When finally it steamed in, she was the only passenger to get off. They hugged each other silently, then walked hand in hand to the car park. They sat in the bucket seats of the Wolseley, rich with its smells of old leather and wet dog. There was no moon, dense darkness.

It was Joe who broke the silence. 'I know what you've had to decide,' he said.

He sensed her nod in the dark. 'Joe,' she said, 'you should have seen him.'

'I can imagine. I know what you must do, what *we* must do.'

'I don't know what else . . . I mean, ordinary life has finished for him. Pain, dependency. All the things he hoped for ripped away in a moment. Except me. He was very drugged, of course, but he said the only thing worth living for, now, was me. Us. Marriage. Then he said he'd be the first to understand if I couldn't go through with it, if I wanted my release.' She sighed. 'He was in so many bandages, mummy-like. I looked at his face and I thought: how could I have said to this man, who I don't know at all, or love, that I would marry him? A complete stranger. Just as I was leaving – I was only with him for half an hour, the nurse said he couldn't take any more – he said he'd bought the ring. He said he wouldn't give it to me then, though: that would be tempting fate. But what was I going to do, he said? Somehow he needed to know the answer then. It would be his lifeline, or his death.'

'So?'

'So I said I'd stand by him.'

Joe, one arm round her taut body, moved to kiss away her silent tears. Then he cleared his throat, managed to find a vibrant voice.

'Listen, my love, you must be exhausted. I've said you won't want supper at home, I might take you for a drink at The Bells. Would you like that?'

'I'd rather stay here. Oh, my darling Joe,' she said.

'I love you,' he said. 'There's no new way to say it. I don't know if I can make you believe me, but I shall love you for ever, no matter whom we marry. Remember the certainty of my love. Always.'

'And mine,' she said.

They talked till the cold of dawn. On the journey back to the farm, the wheels of the car split frozen puddles, and early mists rose up from the land.

In their last two weeks at Hallows Farm, jobs began to run out. The girls spent the short dark days helping Mrs Lawrence sort out and pack up things in the house, and Mr Lawrence to do the same outside. Only Prue was grateful for an easing off of physical labour. Busy accommodating and consoling her two men as often as she could before leaving, she was exhausted but radiant. Ag's energies were spent in trying to keep up Mrs Lawrence's spirits. She produced many a reason to persuade her employer that life in Yorkshire could be as rewarding as in Dorset, and was pleased to see the occasional spark of anticipation breaking through the melancholy. Stella's low spirits were understood by everyone: none but Ag saw they were matched, beneath a normal surface, in Joe's heart. To the last, Joe and Stella managed to continue their normal behaviour. To the last, they liked to believe, no one had guessed their secret with its bitter ending.

Mr Lawrence had contemplated for some time how best to manage a swift departure. He was not one for drawn-out, emotional farewells, and to that end he made a plan. He would load the girls' luggage into the boot of the Wolseley while they ate their last breakfast, then make sure they were away fast.

It was a dreary morning, the day of their going: frosty cobwebs the only sparkle in the whitish gloom. The girls wore their coloured travelling suits, the ones that had so alarmed Mr Lawrence on their arrival, he remembered with a smile. Due to the cold, they pulled their WLA great-coats over their shoulders – Prue's had arrived just a week ago. Half-diamonds were sewn on their lapels.

Mr Lawrence hurried them out as soon as they had fin-ished eating, no nonsense. Each girl hugged Mrs Lawrence quickly in the hall. Outside, they stood in a line waiting to see how Joe planned to conduct his farewells. He went up to each in turn, gripped her by the shoulders, kissed her lightly on each cheek. Stella was last. In this, the final part of the act, his behaviour to her could be no different.

Stella sat next to Mr Lawrence in the front of the car. Her natural place, somehow, he thought, after all he had gone through. His private triumph was to be at ease beside her.

Joe stood at the door, his arm round his mother's shoul-der. She flapped a hand at some nearby bantams.

'Remember them, Ag?' asked Prue. She giggled. 'You were so bloody snooty just because I didn't know a bantam from a hen.'

'Sorry,' said Ag.

The Wolseley lurched away. Everyone waved.

Mr Lawrence slowed down as they reached Ratty's

cottage. He could see, in the mist, the old man standing at the gate. As they passed Ratty raised his cap, shook his fist in the air, thumb up. He'd meant to come down to the farm last night and say goodbye officially. But he hadn't much fancied a formal parting from the holy one – or the others, for that matter. Besides, with all the things there were to attend to in the cottage, in his new state of freedom, he liked to spend the evenings at home, marvelling at his solitude.

Epilogue

Stella's bed had been drawn up to the window. Propped up on her pillows, she had a good view of the dales outside, a distant farmhouse half-hidden by trees, the church tower. On the day she was supposed to be lunching with Prue and Ag in London, Janice brought her a little poached fish and purée of carrot on a tray. She tried to eat it – the doctor had said she must try to eat to keep up her strength – but she had no appetite. Instead, she watched the cows. Friesians.

Stella had had every intention of joining the others for the annual lunch. Her recent bad attack was over. For the last week she had been feeling better, getting up, pottering round the garden on warm days. The pain had faded. But last night the wretched business had returned, exhausting her. She had taken as many pills as she dared, thought she would be fine by morning. But she wasn't. When she put her legs on the floor, weakness and dizziness overcame her. Back under the sheets, bent in a certain way she had found eased the pain, she tried to will herself to be all right. They would be so disappointed. She was furious with herself. It was such a nuisance, this persistent bad health, this fading of energy and capacity. She hated being old.

An hour later, Stella knew there was no hope of making the journey. She rang the hotel, asked for a message to be taken to the others when they arrived in the restaurant. She hoped they would telephone her before they left.

At about the time Prue would doubtless be ordering a frivolous chocolate pudding, while Ag demanded English brie (she had become so fierce about all things British, in her old age), Stella laid aside her tray. Outside, the cows were halfway up the hill. Lying down, chewing the cud. She could never get used to them, these alien cows. They were very different from the old herd. She didn't know their names, of course. Didn't want to: they were nothing to do with her. Sometimes, in the gloaming, when one of them was lying stretched on its side, she would confuse it with Nancy's corpse after the incendiary bombs. Then it would jump up, but not be Nancy come to life, and Stella would turn her mind to something else.

She lay back, thought she might doze for a while. These days, there was little time to give much thought to the past. She had to conserve her energies for all that had to be organised now: Joe's moving in, the deciding which room should be his, which shed should be converted to a kennel for his dogs – quite a palaver, it would be, establishing everything to his liking.

But on the day of the annual reunion, so annoyingly missed, Stella fell to thinking about the whole spectrum of their lunches in the past: the charting of their lives over the last fifty years. She closed her eyes.

The first lunch was in 1946. Terrible food, but none of them minded, because there was so much news. Prue, in bright emerald, still wearing a matching bow, had hardly been able to contain herself. Even before the arrival of the tinned soup, she had told them about the second Barry she had recently met – Barry Two, as he became known ever after. According to Prue, a rare and wonderful man. Barry Two, at that time, owned a chain of bicycle shops, but had sights on bigger things. He was negotiating to buy a picture house on the outskirts of Leeds. Prue was convinced of his ambition, his potential, his drive. She believed one day he would own a whole chain of cinemas, and she was right. Ten years after the war, Barry Two could claim to be one of the richest men in the north. Today, he was a multimillionaire, and the gold taps, servants and cocktails Prue had dreamed of, as she ploughed, and had described to Stella from the dung heap, had been achieved long ago. Her only disappointment was no children. Still, Barry Two, a 'real ball of fire', but childlike in many ways, took up all Prue's time. She had adjusted to a childless household, bred spoilt poodles, and been happy for years.

Stella's own news, that year, was fascinating to Prue, who had never guessed a thing at the time. Less surprising to Ag, who admitted she had known all along.

She told them that she and Joe had written to each other every week since the departure from Hallows Farm, though they rarely met. When the war was over, they had taken the Wolseley, by now in the last stages of general corrosion, and had driven round the battered French countryside. They had found sun in the Pyrenees, small cafés that still managed to serve delicious coffee, home-made croissants and apricot jam.

Soon after their return, her marriage to Philip took place. She spent her honeymoon in Torquay.

Ag, that first lunch, told them she was at law school. Enjoying it. No, she was still without a boyfriend. The one who kept most in touch with the Lawrences, she and Mrs Lawrence maintained a regular correspondence. She had gone up to Yorkshire to help out for three months. Nothing like Dorset, she said.

They'd all met, of course, at Prue's wedding to Barry Two. Manchester. What Stella remembered best were the silver bells in Prue's hair. Reminded her of reindeer, which was just what Prue had intended, she said, being a winter wedding. Joe and Janet weren't there: Joe had written to Stella to say he couldn't face such a meeting – her and Philip, him and Janet. She agreed, naturally. It would have been difficult.

It was at Prue's wedding Mrs Lawrence made the suggestion that the girls should address her and Mr Lawrence by their Christian names. No such thing had ever happened at the farm, of course. Young girls did not then behave to their employers as they did today, assuming an unrequested intimacy Stella herself deplored. But by 1947, the wedding of Prue and Barry Two, Stella and Philip already married, the girls were grown up. It was appropriate they should now address the Lawrences as the friends they were, always would be. But Stella found it difficult. Faith and John: she had to remind herself, every time she wrote to them. Sometimes, on the rare occasions they met, she slipped back into the Mr and Mrs by mistake.

Stella shifted herself, uncomfortable. There was still an hour to go before she was allowed the next pill. Why hadn't Prue and Ag rung? How long did they intend to linger over their coffee? They must surely be wondering what was the matter, curious to know how she was. Stella shut her eyes again, restless.

Ratty . . . what had happened to Ratty? Oh, yes. Mrs Lawrence – Faith – had written to them soon after VE Day. Stella still had the letter somewhere. Ratty had had a heart attack bell-ringing for victory. He'd rushed to the church soon as he heard the news on the wireless, insisted on ringing, hours on end. They'd had quite a job, Mrs Lawrence said, freeing the rope from his hands. None of them could think of a better way for Ratty to go, she added. Indeed.

Edith? She never came out of the asylum, poor soul. Outlived Ratty by a decade.

The year of the first avocado – 1948? 1949? – she couldn't be quite sure – was a year she would never forget. Ag's turn for good news. She had re-met Desmond. One of those occasions of such chance that Ag found it hard not to believe in fate. She had gone to the wedding of a fellow law student at St Martin-in-the-Fields. Fearful of being late, she arrived much too early. It was raining. She slipped into the

National Portrait Gallery for shelter. Desmond was standing in front of Branwell Brontë's portrait of his sisters. They went for a cup of coffee. He had never received her seventeen-page letter. No wonder. Called up, he was fighting in France. But they made up for lost time, didn't they? Started seeing each other most days. Over the avocado, Ag talked of *certainty*. A few months later came invitations to Ag and Desmond's wedding. Not long after that, Ag began her long and successful career at the Bar.

The telephone rang at last.

'Hello? Ag?'

'It's Prue. I say, what's the matter, old thing?' The northern accent was still there.

'Awfully stupid, I'm so sorry. Can't get out of bed.'

'Rotten luck. Not at all the same without you. We're squashed into a little wooden room – you know, where they put telephones these days. No air. We can hardly breathe. Ag's fanning herself.' Prue giggled. 'Complaining about my *Nuits de Paris*, as usual.'

'Oh dear.'

'We're waiting for Joshua to come and pick up Ag, take her to the station. She says he drives much too fast, a real tearaway. I'm going to slip into Harvey Nichols myself, see if there's anything to wear. Then take the five fifteen back. I'll come and see you soon.'

'Lovely. Was it a good lunch?'

'Usual sort of thing. Chocolate mousse. We missed you. We missed you, Stella. Here, Ag wants to talk to you. Goodbye, darling.'

' 'Bye, Prue. Is that Ag? I'm so sorry – I . . . this wretched business.'

'Rotten luck, Stella. When you're feeling better, why not come and spend a few days with us? You know I can never get Desmond past the front gate, we've got a few farming troubles, the Friesians may have to go, but we'd love to have you. Devon air'd do you a power.'

'Probably.'

'Well, take care of yourself. I'll ring you from home.'

'Can't tell you how I wanted to be there.'

'Next year.'

'Next year. Definitely.'

' 'Bye, Stella.'

' 'Bye, Ag.'

Next year. Next year she would be the one with the best news. Joe would have moved in. They might even have legalised their arrangement. Stella smiled to herself, rubbed the finger on which she had worn a wedding ring until Philip died. Once she was free, she had thought it would be impolite to Joe to go on wearing it. Even though he was still unavailable. Ten years ago, was it, Philip's thrombosis? No: eleven in November. Expected, of course. How long after that was it that she sold the Surrey house, came here to Yorkshire? It was such a jumble, thinking back. She must have been here all of seven years. Just seventeen miles from Janet and Joe. Made meetings easier. Mrs Lawrence was put into the old people's home in 1968. For some reason, Stella remembered that very clearly. She died very soon after, before Stella managed to visit her. Ag was with her often, despite the long journeys from Devon. Prue sent boxes of expensive chocolates Mrs Lawrence could not eat. Mr Lawrence? About two years later, he died. In his sleep. Without his wife, he found no reason to live, he kept telling Joe.

Stella stretched for a digestive biscuit on a plate beside her bed. She broke off a small corner, crumbled it, put it to her mouth. Her lips were always dry, such a nuisance. Most of the lunches after the avocado one were taken up with domestic news. Children. Ag had four, two girls, two boys, all very clever. Only to be expected with Ag and Desmond as parents. Stella managed only two: James, very soon after she was married, and darling Euphemia – Effie. Prue was godmother to Effie and Ag's Henry. She was wonderful about not seeming to mind about no children for herself. Always took such an interest.

Then came the grandchildren. Ag had beaten her to it – she had seven. She herself had only four, so far. Must be getting on for tea-time. Dog barking downstairs. Racer barked regularly as clockwork when it was time to be fed. Stella hoped Janice wouldn't keep him waiting too long. She swivelled her eyes to the cluster of photographs above the fireplace. Philip: the photograph she used to keep by her bed in the attic room, hardly faded, considering the years. In his uniform. Another, not long after they were married. Just head and shoulders – laughing. Such a brave man, Philip. Never complained. The children, very young, on their rocking-horse. Effie a beauty, she had to admit, from the start. James, with such a strong look of Joe it was incredible no one had ever noticed, not even Ag and Prue. James's own son, too: little William, the first grandchild. Extraordinary. Even Joe could see it.

No picture of Joe. Well, for the children's sake, really.

Still, Joe always, always near. There when needed. Waiting. Both of them waiting.

Janet, actually, was brave, too, like Philip. She was brave to marry a man whom she knew did not love her. But they made an agreement, and stuck to it. Joe was a conscientious husband: Janet a good wife and mother to the three tall sons. She provided an idyllic childhood for them in the Yorkshire farmhouse. Looked after Mr Lawrence, diligently, in the cottage, once his wife had died.

At forty, Stella remembered, Janet had lost some of her shyness. Stella went and listened to her speaking one day at a Conservative gathering. She was better looking than she used to be, too. Not exactly attractive, but less plain. The *surprise*, though, when she went off, overnight, just after her sixtieth birthday. Stella would never forget Joe's telephone call. '*You're not going to believe this* . . .' And of course she could not, for a time. But it was true. It seemed Janet had been waiting for the children to be married, settled, whatever, before she and this rich butcher, who had loved her for ten years, finally went off to spend their old age together. They'd been conducting a long affair. Joe had never suspected a thing. Just as Janet had never suspected . . . Or had she?

They would never know. They'd been so careful. Tried never to reveal . . . but could not be sure.

Of course, since Janet's departure, it had all been so easy. Wonderful. Joe sold the farm, moved into the cottage in the dales – vacant since Mr Lawrence's death – he had once mentioned at Hallows Farm. They visited each other constantly. God knows why it had taken them so long to realise how much easier it would be if they lived under the same roof.

Stella sighed. Perhaps they shouldn't have wasted so much time. Still, Joe was on his way at last. Nearly here. Cottage almost sold: contract to be signed next week. He should be in by the end of the month. That would be good, good. Stella dozed.

When she woke, it was dusk. Couldn't see the cows. A cup of tea would be coming soon: she always told Janice if she was asleep to leave her, come back later. She pushed herself up on the pillows, pulled her shawl round her shoulders. The evenings were cooler.

At six o'clock precisely, Joe would ring. He rang her every evening, even if he had been visiting her earlier in the day. She wanted to be alert for his call. She wanted to be particularly on the ball in order to try to urge him to get the whole business of the sale of the cottage tied up as soon as possible. Last night he had said he'd do his best, solicitors were always so damn slow with contracts, and surely a few more days made no difference. He didn't want to move his stuff out of the cottage and then find the sale had fallen through: much harder to sell an empty place.

Stella had agreed. She'd said quite right, a few more days made no difference. Essential to get it all finalised before moving in. She didn't want to press him. And so she lied to him, saying of course there was no hurry. Well, not exactly *lied*: just retained part of the truth. First time in her life she had not been completely honest with Joe. She hoped, when he discovered, he would understand. Hoped he would understand she had not wanted to burden him with the probable truth. She had always made light of her illness, been able to quell his worries. Surely that was the best thing.

The final part of their waiting would not be too long, with any luck. God willing, she would be on her feet again by the time he came, full of energy to settle him in. She must remember to get the piano tuned. Married to Philip, there had been little time to play. When he died she had, at last, taught privately for a while. But it was too late. She was out of practice. So she had ceased to give lessons when she came north. Nowadays, she just played to herself, in the evenings. She would say to him when he rang – it was two minutes to six – *Joe, don't worry about the sale* – dealing with solicitors had never been his *forte. Why don't you come as soon as you can?* she would say. On the dot of six, the telephone rang. Firm of purpose, Stella gathered her strength. She must be careful to choose the right words to encourage him to hurry just a little, and yet give no hint of alarm.

'Darling Joe,' she began.

Wives of the Fishermen

For Prue Penn

What is a woman that you forsake her,
And the hearth fire and the home-acre,
To go with the old grey widow-maker?

Rudyard Kipling

Part I

It is the habit of fishermen's wives to glance at the horizon many times a day, but only one of their own kind will recognise the furtive looks, the tightening of anxiety behind eyes that have grown prematurely old from checking distant sea.

A moment too late Myrtle Duns flicks her eyes back from the window. Annie, looking up from her cards, has seen.

'Ach, stop worrying,' she says.

She watches Myrtle lift the black kettle from the range, pour boiling water into a brown pot. Unbroken cloud, divided into squares by the panes of a small window, is powered by enough brightness to light the sides of the old teapot with colours of petrol flung upon water: threads of gold and incandescent mauve. Annie knows that Myrtle will now take two mugs from hooks, two tin spoons from a drawer, pour milk into a souvenir jug from Dundee. She will lift the pot with both hands, testing its weight, judging the amount of water to be correct before transporting it to the table with a listing movement that bends and splays the pleats of her long woollen skirts. The rhythm of tea-making is familiar from hundreds of such afternoons spent together.

All the time Annie watches her friend the cards flicker in her hands. Sometimes they rise in fans. Then, disapproving of such petty skill, quick fingers snap them back into a neat pack. The silky sound of their activity is the single noise in the room, for now the kettle has stopped its spluttering. Myrtle stands motionless by the range, waiting for the tea to brew.

She is a large woman, hands rough as salt cod, tall. The kitchen ceiling clears her head by only a few inches. She moves with practised skill among the narrow spaces, managing her wide hips with dignity. Archie says she sometimes put him in mind of an opera singer, the way she glides. It's as if there are wheels under her skirts, he says. For Lord's sake stop scoffing at your wife, Archie, she answers, pleased by his observation, for she recognises the admiration beneath the teasing.

3

But in response she would clench her hands and punch him gently behind his ear till he caught her big wrist and forced it to a halt, the muscles in his arms rising like waves of bone.

'Archie,' says Annie, slapping down the cards, 'is the best skipper any boat could have. You know that.'

'Aye.' Myrtle sits. She arranges the tea things protectively in front of her. The apparent passivity of her face hardens. Blank eyes. Neither mouth nor nose twitch. She no longer has consciously to remind herself that any remark Annie makes about Archie should be greeted with an impassive expression.

'How's Janice?' Myrtle asks after a while.

'She's bonnie. High marks at school again.'

'That's grand.'

Annie finds it hard to resist informing Myrtle of her daughter's high marks several times a week.

'I think they're beginning to see her worth,' she says.

'That's good, too.'

Annie shuffles the cards.

'Mrs Singer said to me not two days ago: "Mrs Mcleoud," she says, "your Janice is on her way to being a great beauty as well as a scholar."' She pauses, looks down. Modesty, or the nearest she can get to it, webs her eyes. 'I couldn't say that to anyone but you, Myrtle. But I believe there's some truth in it.'

'Oh there is, that's for sure,' says Myrtle warmly. She accepts a pile of cards slimy with age. It's not yet time to pour the tea. Her look slides from Annie's small, busy hands to her face: the tiny nose with its nostrils the shape of horizontal petals, the opal eyes, the mouth whose dividing line in repose is the subtlest of shallow curves – a mouth that can jump from solemnity to laughter with astounding speed. In the rubble of dark curls, Myrtle observes that Annie has a few grey hairs. But her friend has changed very little over the years. She was the prettiest child in the school, the village, for miles along the coast. Her looks had tempted admirers from Fife to Dundee. It is no wonder her only child, Janice, is set to follow her mother's reputation. Myrtle sometimes wonders if Janice will cause as much chaos, as much agony of spirit, in her friends. She wonders if she has inherited the same powers of persuasion of her innocence, so that she will always be forgiven. Everyone had always forgiven Annie, Myrtle most of all.

As children, Myrtle and Annie walked to school together holding hands. On cold mornings, Myrtle wore mittens of scratchy wool. Annie wore gloves. The bare ends of Myrtle's cold fingers would burrow into the warmth of Annie's angora hand. She longed for gloves herself. But in her mother's cautious mind they were an extravagance not even to be considered. Very quickly Myrtle gave up hoping her mother would relent. Dot Stewart was not a woman accustomed to changing her mind for the benefit of others. Locked into the narrow disciplines of a hard life, her beliefs in everything – from the rewards of the afterlife to the number of blankets a healthy person should be allowed on the bed – were unchangeable. The firmness of her convictions was a matter of pride. To be caught changing them, no matter how persuasive an argument, would be despicable weakness. Myrtle and her father, understanding these things, learnt it was easier to agree with Dot, do her bidding. Any opposition caused scenes so fraught, so emotionally exhausting, that they suffered the cold of dreaded winter nights rather than try to persuade Dot of their need for more blankets.

In the classroom Myrtle and Annie shared a desk. Myrtle's half was sparsely furnished: pen, text book, exercise books. Annie's was chaotic: school books a despised territory over which things of more interest were strewn. There were skeins of wool, electric colours, that Annie liked to weave into a long tube that grew into a hideous worm from nails punched into a cotton reel. There were plastic hairslides, boiled sweets whose horrible colours were scarcely dimmed by their twists of transparent paper, and cuttings from magazines – shampoo advertisements, lion cubs, travel brochure sunsets. For several months, at the age of ten, Annie was a compulsive cutter-outer. The pictures she chose gave no clue to her interests. She snipped randomly, attracted by bright colours that hurt Myrtle's eyes.

Often the clutter on Annie's side of the desk would drift over its boundaries. Myrtle would gently push the stuff back. She was patient, unreprimanding when it came to Annie's untidiness. And when Mrs Williams began pacing the aisles between the desks, weak eyes straining to detect any hint of something Not in the Rules, in loyalty to her friend Myrtle would hide things under her own books. Sometimes she was rewarded. There was a day when Mrs Williams was particularly disinclined to believe Annie's excuses for the mess on her desk, and Myrtle found herself declaring with extraordinary conviction that most of the offending objects were hers. Punishment was just avoided though there were warnings, as always, that Mrs Williams' patience was running out.

On that occasion, when the bell went for the end of the lesson, Annie turned to Myrtle and hugged her.

'You're my friend, Myrtle,' she whispered. 'I can always count on you.'

In the heat of gratitude and pride Myrtle did not ponder the truth of this statement. When Annie was at her best, and her best was irresistibly endearing, it was easy to forget the other times. Myrtle stood by the desk rubbing her still icy hands. The bell rang out the joy of her secret feelings. Her loyalty to Annie was often rewarded by a suggestion of doing something together in the playground: she hoped this would happen today. Myrtle held on to the back of the chair, its wood still smeared with a shadowy warmth from her own back. She waited, hoping. Watched Annie's eyes flick round the others. When Ross Wyatt passed them he handed Annie an emerald rubber.

'Yours,' he said.

'Thanks,' said Annie. She gave him one of her half-smiles that, despite the braces on her teeth, boys found irresistible.

'Coming outside?' Ross sniffed and wiped his nose on the back of his hand.

'Right.' She turned to the boy standing behind Ross. 'You coming too, Archie Duns?'

The boy nodded, not looking at her. She moved into position behind Ross, in front of Archie. Thus flanked by the two best-looking boys in the school, Annie moved with the queue to the door. In a moment she was across the room, and had forgotten to invite Myrtle.

When all the children had left the classroom Myrtle sat down again. She looked up at the beams that spanned the vaulted ceiling, a roof-scape where she often found ideas. The cobwebs that dulled the skylight, she noticed, seemed to have thickened in the past year. But as Mrs Williams often joked, on the occasions her glance rose from the blackboard, how long is a broom? Never long enough to reach the skylight . . . It was during that lunch break, in early winter, alone in the classroom, voices outside rising and falling like small garments hung out to dry in a wind, that an uneasy thought struck the ten-year-old Myrtle: Annie, her best friend, sometimes preferred to be with boys than to be with her.

Several more games of rummy have been played, several more cups of tea have been drunk. Myrtle wants Annie to go. She wants to get on with the evening – peel the carrots, take the folded clothes from the airing cupboard and put them in their place in Archie's drawers. But Annie shows no keenness to leave. For all that her own kitchen is a smarter place than Myrtle's – white tiles, the occasional one stamped with a sea horse, and formica tops, speckled and shiny as eggshells – she seems to prefer the shabbier kitchen in the Duns' house. Sometimes she does suggest that Myrtle should come over to her place. But then, just as Myrtle is setting out, by chance Annie is passing by. She has come to 'fetch' Myrtle, she says. But as Myrtle has not yet put on her shawl, and Annie is already taking off her coat, it seems pointless to walk up the hill, wind swiping their faces, to the council estate. So they stay. Friendship, as Myrtle points out when guilt spurs Annie to bring the occasional gift of a bannock or oat biscuits, is not about whose house is the meeting place.

'Won't Janice be back?' asks Myrtle. 'Are we forgetting the time, all this card-playing?'

Annie smiles, reassuring. Perhaps she is unaware of Myrtle's impatience. It is more likely she is not.

'She's going over to Joey Brick for her tea. I'll pick her up later.'

'The red-haired one? Does a paper round?'

'That's the lad, aye. She likes a boy with freckles, Janice does.'

Myrtle waits a moment, weighing caution. She has learnt it's all too easy for Annie to detect some note of criticism in anything she might say about Janice.

'Starting young,' she says at last.

'They're grown up at twelve these days. Know just what they want long before that. There's no stopping them.'

Myrtle thinks that if she had a daughter, there would certainly be some stopping her.

'Pity,' is what she says.

They hear footsteps outside, Archie's lopsided tread on the steps. The door opens. A smell of sea comes in on the wind. Archie's dark jersey twinkles with raindrops. Some are perfect sequins. Others are smeared like the trail of an off-course snail across the coarse wool. His face is haggard, exhausted. He smells of cod, rope, pipe smoke. His eyes go straight to Myrtle. Annie stands up.

'Ken's home,' he says to her. The sharpness in his voice has its effect on both women. The defiance in Annie's eyes, that had automatically flared when Archie came in, quavers.

'His supper'll not take a moment in the microwave,' she says. She and Ken bought the microwave, special offer, a couple of months ago. Myrtle and Archie are familiar with the accounts of the magical way in which it changed their lives. 'But I'll be going.'

When Archie has shut the door behind her he moves to the range, leans his hands against the chipped enamel of its side. Then he raises his warmed hands to hold his wife's face. He looks at her silently, re-assessing the rock firmness of the floor, with the eyes of one who has been tossed by a fairground swing, or a stormy sea. He will kiss her later. For the moment he lets the sensation of being home flow through him. The warmth of his own kitchen is what he remembers, if there's a moment to think, at sea. When the boat rocks crazily in giant waves and rain hard as sheet glass crashes into his eyes, there's a lightning flash in his mind: the old stove, his wife beside it, alert to his need of no questions, ready to pour the tea.

*

The kitchen was always the warmest room in the house. Until 1953, just before Myrtle was born, it was the place where Dot Stewart baited the lines. She used to throw a length of tarpaulin over the flagstones and Sandy, who delivered the lines in his cart, would drag in a load so huge that sometimes, Dot said, just the sight of it brought tears of despair to her eyes. The lines, with their lethal hooks, were alive with pernicious intent – snagging, pricking, drawing blood. Dot's hands had bled so many times that the scar tissue criss-crossed the ruddy skin in abstract, knitters' patterns. When her hands were in repose, slumped together on her lap, from Myrtle's side of the table they looked like bundles of silvery twigs. She remembered thinking that from a very young age. She felt very sorry for them, wanting to kiss them. But she did not dare approach her mother's lap. Dot Stewart was not one who took kindly to physical gestures of comfort or sympathy.

Once the lines were stacked on the floor, Sandy would haul in the sacks of mussels. They made a crunching, screeching noise as they scraped the flagstones on landing – a noise, Dot said, that hurt her ears: a noise that she could no more forget than her own cries when Myrtle was born. Often she was left to face the task alone, though on occasions, with no warning, old Cecily, Dot's mother, would drop in to help. Even in her eighties Cecily could work faster on a length of line than women half her age – scoffing all the while at the slowness of the modern young girls. Dot preferred it when Veronica gave a hand – one-eyed Veronica who had lost an eye in a fish-hook accident as a young child. Veronica baited with a recklessness that unnerved every woman in the village, lacerating herself without complaint, bloodying the mussels as she attached them to the hooks, and leaving red smears round her mouth when she licked a flowing thread of blood from a finger. Veronica, in her brief pauses, made Dot laugh with her lively surmises about the fishermen. With no evidence to back up her stories, she recounted such scurrilous tales that to Dot invention became more powerful than reality, and she found it hard to look many of the staid men in the eye. Veronica's slanderous tongue lightened the long mornings.

The women sat on low wooden chairs to do their baiting, thick-stockinged legs slung wide apart to make a copious lap for a clump of line which, once mussel-loaded, would slip on to the floor. They were skilful with their knives. Years of experience had driven them to finding the weakness in the shell before it was visible. A flick of the wrist (no indication that there was any restraint in the shell) and it was jarred open. Two liquid wings lay for a moment in the palm of a hand. Then pitilessly the silvery glistening meat would be gouged out with another flick of the knife, slipped over the next hook. The empty shell was cast to the floor by a movement of the knee, to be swept up later. The women's fingers worked automatically, swift as machinery, their rhythm only broken by the drawing of blood, the quick suck of a damaged finger. They rarely spoke: Veronica's outbursts came only at occasional moments. The small thuds of shell on tarpaulin, and the scrape of line as it was tugged along to the next hook were the only interruptions in the fish-stinking silence. The smell was always there: in the women's hair, clothes, skin. Even on Fridays, baking day, bread in the oven, the black smell of sea depths from which the raw shell-fish had come out-reached the warm brown smell of baking bread. They did not think of listening to the wireless while they worked. Music did not occur to them. Besides, the wireless, with its elaborate Bakelite façade sculpted like a miniature Odeon, was in place of honour on the dresser in the front room. The wireless was for weather forecasts and news: an evening thing. But when the window was open and there was a strong breeze, they could hear the water break against the harbour wall. That was music enough.

Myrtle had listened to her mother's descriptions of all this many times – Dot enjoyed recounting to her daughter all the small details, conjuring the smells and sensations vividly in Myrtle's mind. Dot never read her stories, was never much of a reader. But she was an observer with a beady eye whose visual accounts were her legacy to her daughter. And now that she was grown up, alone in her kitchen, Archie away at sea, Myrtle often felt that time had intertwined itself and she had actually been with Dot and Veronica, baiting the lines. She knew what it was like to watch chapped fingers making the same movement a hundred times an hour; she could feel the same pain those women had felt in their shoulders as they crouched hour after hour over their work. Sometimes, sweeping the floor, she would come across a minute glint of mussel shell, a speck of diamond ground into the cement between the flagstones, and she felt awed at the ease of knowing how it had been in those hard days. Compared with then, present life was much less physically exhausting, though never without worry. There was the same fear through the years – no fish, no money. Many was the time – weather too bad to go out – Myrtle and Archie had been down to their last few pounds. And the shadow that could never be erased was the anxiety. Inherited from generation to generation of women whose men make a living at sea, anxiety was a moth trapped in their insides that flutters, batters, can never escape, is rarely still. When one spell at sea is over, and the fisherman home for a few days, these wings of fear are stilled for so short a time that the places they have damaged cannot hope to heal. As clean clothes are stuffed into a bag ready for another week at sea, the whole inner turmoil began again, the effort to conceal it tightening the skin of pale faces so that the very scalps of the fishermen's wives seemed to be pulled back, exposing the worry in their eyes.

Archie, at the table, is asleep. His head is couched in his arms. A mug of tea cools beside him. Myrtle touches his hair. It's divided by the wind into stiff points, salt-crusted. She strokes his cheek. He hasn't much time for shaving on the boat, though does his best on the day of homecoming. The stubble is thick on his jaws. His top lip, clean-shaven, reveals cracked lips: small shavings of dry white skin that will scratch Myrtle when he kisses her. Archie has been away for five days and four nights.

When he wakes, what shall she tell him? Myrtle wonders. There has been no news, here, apart from the day the washing machine went mad. It was clogged up with a million fish scales from a load of sea-soaked clothes. Water had gushed out on to the floor of the cold little room where the machine is housed. But it was not plain soapy water. Myrtle, in her panic, had seen it as a surreal cascade, full of living eyes horribly twinkling at her among the bubbles. As it soaked her feet, her ankles, thousands of the tiny scales stuck to the hem of her skirt. The dead fish smell was sickening as the water sloshed ruthlessly about, proud of its glitter. Myrtle had run from the house, wet wool skirts hampering her legs, to find Alan, one-eyed Veronica's son and the nearest thing to a plumber in the village. He had swiftly and kindly dealt with the crisis, and helped her mop up the mess. Once she had re-washed the jerseys, and dried them, it had taken her many hours to pick the scales from the wool. Now the garments lay folded in the airing cupboard, neatly as always, as if the drama had never occurred. There was no reason to trouble Archie with a disaster that was over, no point in telling him. Myrtle liked to protect her husband from such trivialities: with so little time together, it was the important things that should consume the hours – plans for the summer holiday, re-acknowledgement of love and wellbeing.

Again Myrtle touches Archie's hair with her big, gentle hand. Grains of salt scratch her fingers. She loves these moments – Archie here and yet not here; exhausted, yet soon to wake, to eat the supper she has made him, to re-settle. Many of the fishermen go straight from the boat to the pub, arrive home drunk and useless with no apologies. Not Archie, thank God. His priority is his wife. Soon as he's ashore, he hurries home. He's best pleased when he finds Myrtle alone. Annie's constant presence annoys him. About this evening, Myrtle will apologise, explain why she was unable to get rid of Annie in time, today – the cards, the chatter. With a silent nod of his head Archie will signal he understands: he, of all people, knows how difficult it is to dislodge Annie. He dislikes her, but does his best to contain that dislike. He understands Myrtle needs a friend when he's away, and Annie is a good friend in many ways, so he lets the matter be. All he asks is that Annie should not hang around when he is home. Myrtle is thus left to the delicate job of keeping her husband and her friend apart. Neither of them can know how difficult this is, what tact and skill it involves. But she has grown used to it and mistimings, like today, when Archie made no effort to conceal his annoyance, are rare.

Every time Archie returns Myrtle thanks God: she imagines the wives of pilots and soldiers and war correspondents – men in dangerous jobs – must all do the same. But the thought is never far off that one day there will be reason to curse God, just as her mother did when Jock Stewart died. The day that Archie does not come back has festered in her mind for so long that the picture is sharp and polished. She described it once – a week of foul weather – to Annie, who said such thoughts were morbid and wicked. Since then she has kept them to herself, tried to extinguish them, but has not succeeded.

Her father died at sea, though not on the fishing boat. He was only half a mile from the shore, a Saturday afternoon, in his rowing boat. Smoking his pipe, most likely, which Dot would not allow in the house. Dot and Myrtle were used to his disappearances when he came home. He did not like many hours to pass not on or near the sea. And when he was 'playing about', as Dot thought of it, in the rowing boat, she was not afraid. A man who had spent his life at sea, respected it, knew its ways, he would not be likely to take it out if he had reason to suspect bad weather was brewing. The afternoon he died there was a strong April sun, sea flat as tin, scarcely a breeze.

When he didn't appear for tea, and darkness gathered, Dot reluctantly put out the alert, worried such foolishness would annoy him. His boat was found quickly, empty. Oars askew. A black-head gull was pecking at a packet of half-eaten sandwiches. It was Archie's father, Ben, who towed the small boat of chipped green paint, *The Happy Wanderer*, back to the harbour where Dot stood waiting, scarf fiercely tied under her aching jaw. He came without a body. Every boat in the harbour had been searching miles of empty water. No body, no drifting clothes – nothing.

Two weeks later Jock Stewart's body was washed up on a beach a mile along the coast. Ben Duns told Archie (who years later, at Myrtle's insistence, passed on the description word for word) that it was a swollen mass of blubber, horrible. The eyes were still open. They seemed to have spilt over their rims, cloudy as jellyfish: though in the quick glance, before he had to turn away to vomit, he could not be quite sure that was really so, he said. But it was the sight of Jock's feet that made him cry: toes the colour of shale, skin blown up so taut – as if the wind itself had been playing balloons – that you could see the passage of every vein. The indignity of seeing a good fisherman, his skipper, stripped of his boots was the thing, Archie confessed, that broke his father, and he had seen many a drowned man.

A post-mortem showed Jock had died of a heart attack. But how had he fallen overboard? Dot liked to think that, knowing he was dying, Jock had decided to speed the process by heaving himself into the waters he loved. She looked at her husband, lying in the morgue, too full of disbelief to shed any tears. The black bruise colour of his skin glowered through the pinkish matt make-up that the mortician had employed to disguise the actuality, and had only succeeded in making it worse. Myrtle, eleven at the time, remembered clearly the bitterness of the rain at the funeral. Cheeks were confused with rain and tears: Dot's brave face was blurred by so much water. Best of all Myrtle remembered Annie, who had pushed her way close to the open grave. Annie took a peppermint from a soggy paper bag of sweets, held it up to Myrtle and said, 'Shall I drop it in?' That was the moment that Myrtle herself felt the warmth of tears collide with rain on her own cheeks. Later, Annie tried to apologise, said she only did it to make Myrtle smile.

Archie is awake, eating. He crams wodges of butter into a huge baked potato, splits his sausages and fills them with English mustard. Between mouthfuls he leans his forearms heavily on the wooden table. Myrtle can tell by the hunch of his shoulders that he is pleased to be home, beginning to relax. Half a day before returning to sea he grows more upright, tenser. He frowns. First evening home, the short nap over, the sea-going frown unclenches.

'How was it?' Myrtle can expect only the barest information.

'Not too bad. We had to go a long way for a fair catch. Mighty small fish again. Always the small fish, now. I don't know . . .'

Archie is so weary of the politics of fishing these days he is reluctant to discuss them. There are old fishermen in the village who talk about the time when fishing was one of our proudest industries, when a man went out knowing there were limitless fish to catch and no one to fight. It was always a hard life, but you could make a decent living. They say the cod war, in the early eighties, was the beginning of the end of the good times. And now it is the fight with the Spaniards with their too-fine nets; the scientists advising about quotas; the rows about TACs; pontificating politicians who don't know a haddock from a herring . . . and all the time over-fishing causing such a disastrous lack of fish that early into the next century there could well be no industry left. What then? Archie does not like to think about it. There is an unspoken rule among the men on his boat that no one should speculate. In the past, speculating on the future had caused too much gloom. Archie did not want to skipper a bunch of downhearted men – they needed to function with all the fire they could muster, these days, to go further, fish longer and, despite the pathetic size of the fish, bring home a decent catch. Archie smiles at his wife.

'Have you been hearing much news of the microwave, then?'

'Aye.' Myrtle smiles in return. 'You can have no idea of the brilliance of that machine. It's brought a whole new dimension to their lives.'

Archie studies his wife's face.

'You can always have one if you're wanting one: you know that, don't you? If it would make a difference to you.'

'Not on your life.'

'We can still afford a microwave.'

'I don't want one, Archie. What would I be doing with it? I don't mind waiting for things to unfreeze slowly, do I? I don't feel the urge to cook things in a moment. Besides, it's not the same. You'd not have a crispy baked potato like that out of a microwave . . .' She laughs.

'Just wanted to make sure I'm not depriving you.'

'Never.' Myrtle rises to take a bread pudding from the oven, and two warmed bowls. 'I'm sorry about Annie. God, how she stays.' Guilt at Archie's homecoming is still within her.

'She's not strong, Annie, on knowing when she's not wanted.'

'No: but she's a good heart.'

'I was never interested, you remember, in her heart, or any of the rest of her.' They both laugh. 'Poor Ken. Does he have any idea what goes on in the wifey's mind? Any idea what she gets up to? Does she say anything to you?'

'No: but it's not hard to guess,' says Myrtle after a while.

Annie has learned, very slowly, that when the men are home she and Myrtle should see less of each other. She keeps up the pretence that this arrangement does not exist, but at the same time she is careful not to drop in on Myrtle if there's a chance Archie might be in the house. What she has not yet done – and pride might never let her go that far – is to caution her daughter, Janice. The child, she feels, should remain ignorant of past events that have led to the present situation, and if this means Myrtle must suffer awkward moments – well, that's something that, as Annie's oldest friend, she must put up with.

It's the morning after Archie's return. He's in the small bathroom, shaving. The first shave, after days at sea, always takes a long time – half an hour, perhaps, among carbolic soap and sweet clean towels. Archie also takes a shower. The water – in the shower he installed himself a couple of years ago – never quite achieves the strong gush he hopes for, but it is very hot, and soon the small room is packed with dense steam. Archie shampoos his hair, washing out the stiff salt, and brushes his teeth more vigorously than he does at sea, with the toothbrush he always keeps at home. All this is a ritual of the first morning back, before breakfast of porridge and bacon and the thick grainy bread that Myrtle has left to rise overnight, and has put in the oven to bake at dawn.

Myrtle stands by the stove stirring the porridge. She listens for Archie's step. She waits, aware of an internal warmth that is never there on mornings when he is away. Through the window there is a bright, colourless sky. On days like this the sea, too, will have cast off its plumage of blues and greens and purples and chosen austerity to match the sky. Later, Myrtle will go with Archie down to the harbour.

The door, rarely locked, opens. Tentatively. Myrtle shifts her position, at once alert, protective of her husband's time. Who has come to disturb him?

Janice stands there. Janice Mcleoud. She has her mother's enquiring eyes, slanting under heavy brows. She holds the bottom half of a biscuit tin filled with hay, or dried grass.

'Mrs Duns? My mother said . . .'

She moves towards the table. Puts down the tin. Lifts from it a brown hamster which she keeps in her hands.

'There's something the matter with him. He's not eaten for two days. My mum said –'

'I don't know what makes your mother think I'm any better than she is with animals. I know nothing of hamsters.' Myrtle moves quickly from stove to table. 'Here, let me have a look.'

Myrtle raises Janice's hands so that the animal is almost on a level with her own eyes. It does not move, its nostrils twitch very slowly. Its eyes are dull.

'The poor wee thing,' says Myrtle. 'He looks quite poorly.' She sees Janice is close to tears. 'I'm afraid I can't say what's the matter. What's he been eating?'

'Just the usual,' says Janice. 'What can I do?'

'Go to the vet, would be my advice.'

'Mum says she's not spending money on the vet just for a hamster.'

'Then do your best for him. Keep him warm. Try a little tepid milk.' Myrtle is sorry for the child, but she wants her to go. Archie will be here in a moment. Janice returns the animal to the tin.

'Can't *you* do anything, Mrs Duns?'

'I'm sorry, but I really can't, Janice. Now if you don't mind, I must be –' She returns to the stove, picks up her wooden spoon, begins to stir, aware the earlier calm has gone. Bother the child. Her own father home, why isn't she calling on *him* for help if Annie is no use?

'Surely you can do *something*?' Thwarted, Janice is cross now, as well as upset.

'No. Nothing. I'm not an expert on hamsters. Now please, Janice –'

'But Mum said that once she remembered when you were children that you found a gull with a broken leg and you made a kind of splint and looked after it till it was mended. If you could do that for a gull, Mrs Duns –'

'That wasn't hard.' He is on his way now. Archie's tread in the passage is heavy with anticipation. Myrtle's voice rises. 'Now Archie's here wanting his breakfast. Go back to your house, Janice. Your mother'll be wondering –'

'She won't! She knows where I am.' Janice turns to see Archie standing in the doorway. His look unnerves her. She picks up the tin, smiles her best smile straight at him. The extraordinary prettiness of her devious little face, so like her mother's at the same age, makes Myrtle's own expression harden. 'I'm sorry, Mr Duns, if it was too early to call, but my hamster is very ill and I thought Mrs Duns –'

'Bugger your hamster when I'm just home,' says Archie, very quietly, and the child, pressing the tin to her chest, runs from the room.

Myrtle spins round.

'What d'you want to go and say that for? She's upset enough.'

'Little minx. Thick-skinned as her mother.'

'There's nothing wrong with Janice except that she doesn't know when she's not wanted.' Archie sits at the table. Myrtle brings him his bowl of porridge.

'I'm sorry about that,' she says more gently, 'but I couldn't be too hard on the child. The creature will be dead before the day's out, and if I know Annie there'll not be too much sympathy. It's not the sort of thing she minds about.'

'Right as usual,' says Archie.

In all the years of Myrtle and Annie's friendship there have been many rows, but only a few they can remember. The first one, that became so violent that Dot had to pull them apart, was when they were five or six years old. That occasion, never forgotten, they laugh about now, but neither speaks of the crystallising of the differences between them that became apparent that day, though at the time both girls were too young to understand why they were struck by uncomfortable feelings which later they realised were jealousy, resentment, partial longing for each other's way of life.

Dot had taken the girls for a picnic on the beach – the very beach where her husband's body was to be washed up some years later. Annie's mother Mag had agreed to come too. But, as Dot had expected, at the last moment she had changed her mind. She sent a message with Annie saying she wasn't well. Of a nervous disposition, Mag was rarely well enough to do anything that did not suit her. Reading romantic fiction occupied most of her day. The fantasies played out in her head had given her over the years a vague, distracted look. It was hard ever to feel you had her full attention: Annie gave up trying from a very young age and her father, an Irishman who had come to Scotland looking for work, returned to his native country weeks after Annie's birth. (He still sent what money he could every month.) In Dot's private opinion Mag suffered from agoraphobia, though in those days the condition was less well recognised and no one knew how to help her. She lived on tranquillisers – the doctor's only solution – and the practical help of kind neighbours. It was always Dot who dropped Annie home from school: she and others 'picked up a few things' for Mag whenever they went shopping. Life at home for Annie – mother's greasy head forever in a book, scant food, no interest in the outside world – was both bleak and boring. It was no wonder that much of her childhood was spent in the Stewart household.

For some reason, that particular day, Annie had believed her mother really would come on the picnic, and was excited by the prospect. So when, once again, at the last minute Mag changed her mind, Annie felt the familiar pebble of disappointment shift round her insides, a physical pain that made her cry, though she could not explain her tears to Myrtle and Dot. But it was a fine day on the beach, which they had to themselves, for the breeze was as stinging cold as the edges of the sea they paddled in – and once Annie had hungrily eaten Dot's banana sandwiches and drunk a bottle of home-made lemonade, she found herself more cheerful. She and Myrtle wandered down the beach to look for shells. Dot perched herself against a small rock, took her knitting from a cavernous bag of ancient patchwork. Lulled by the movements of her own fingers that needed no eyes to guide them, her glance went back and forth between the empty grey sea and the two small girls, bending and shouting, some twenty yards away. She had no idea how much time had passed before she heard the screams – thin scraps of sound muted by the breeze and the brush of breaking waves. But their urgency made Dot leap up from her reflections with no further thought. She flung her knitting down on the sand. The children were hitting each other – kicking, scratching, pulling each other's hair. Dot ran.

The shell Annie had found Myrtle did not particularly want: it was not a special shell, for all its size. But Annie had been nasty, annoying, all day: and now Myrtle wanted her *not* to have the shell more than anything in the whole world.

'I want this one! You've got more than me.'

'*No!* Can't have it! It's mine –'

Myrtle snatched at the shell in Annie's hand. Annie flung a small claw at Myrtle's cheek. Her nails, sharper than shells, tore down the skin. Myrtle grabbed a clump of Annie's curly hair, chaotic in the breeze, and pushed her to the ground. Annie scratched, kicked – any part of Myrtle she could. She bit her arm, tasted salt. Seared by the pain, Myrtle pushed a thumb into a wet red eye. Annie screamed louder. Myrtle felt the slippery flesh of the eyeball, wondered if she pushed hard enough it would fall right back into Annie's head. Annie spat. The glob of slime, cracked by the breeze, splattered across Myrtle's bleeding cheek. Then two large firm hands were pulling the bodies apart, Dot's angry voice telling them to stop at once: disgraceful little fools, they were.

The girls sat one on either side of a panting Dot. She wiped faces, eyes, hands with a hopelessly inadequate paper handkerchief: screwed up the mess of blood and sand and tears and stuffed it in her pocket. Then she lifted the hem of her long skirt and applied it more vigorously to the sniffling children.

'It was her fault,' Annie was the first to say.

'*Her* fault,' said Myrtle.

'I'm not interested in whose fault it was: just remember you've both spoilt a good day.'

'She's bigger than me: it's not fair,' said Annie.

'She's prettier than me,' said Myrtle. 'Her curls.'

'Life isn't fair and I'll not be listening to any more of this stupid talk,' said Dot.

Fight over, they were cold. But they stayed where they were, huddled next to Dot, who did not put her arms around them: physical gestures of comfort or affection she deemed to be unnecessary. They might have remained where they were for some time while Dot gathered the energy to take two unhappy and exhausted children home. But then a divine intervention, as she later described it to Jock, came to the rescue. The knitting! All three of them saw it at once – powered by the wind, the long scarf of intricate colour and design, into which Dot had knitted many hours of her life, was racing towards the sea. The needles, still attached, made funny stiff-legged walking movements that made them all laugh. When the needles fell over, they laughed harder. Then with one accord they all leapt up and began to run towards the water. The children reached the edge first. By now the scarf was curling about on the white spume several yards out. Ignoring Dot's cries, they both high-stepped towards it, lifting their skirts over their bottoms. They each grabbed an end, and tugged it back to the shore with an air of triumphant partnership. Dot, in her wet shoes, was still laughing, praising. The girls, shivering, helped her wring the water from the sodden wool. One needle was missing, but Dot said that was not important. On the walk back to the bus stop the wind dried their clothes. Once on the bus itself they chose to sit together, bare legs splayed wearily across the bristly seat, touching. The warm and smelly air – petrol, sea, discarded food – sent them to sleep in moments. Dot, on a seat beside them, felt the heaviness of her own eyes.

The days that the fishermen spend at home are always edged with the knowledge that time is short – too short to be wasted with disagreements about how they should be spent: and yet, because these breaks are so regular, a part of normal life, they cannot be thought of as holidays, times for treats or unnecessary extravagance.

Myrtle tries to assume an exterior that gives no hint of her feelings. It would be no help to Archie to know the depth of her anguish every time he was away, and she had no wish to risk hindering him with desire of his constant presence when he is home. The luxurious times are when he is working on something in the house. As she goes about her own household jobs, the tap of his hammer or the sawing of wood, signifying his presence in the next room, is the kind of joy that gives lightness to her step and speed to her fingers.

Between chores, Archie takes trouble with his wife. They would go for long walks, often along the beach beneath the church of St Monan's, where they were married. They would have a drink in a pub out of their own village: Archie has no wish, he says, to have to talk shop with his crew – he hears enough of their opinions at sea. Myrtle's private view is that he has even less wish to run into Ken and Annie, who spend much of every shore leave in pubs. Sometimes, on a fine day, Archie would spontaneously suggest a real excursion: the bus to Edinburgh for a day, where Myrtle would filter slowly round the large bookshops, Archie at her side encouraging her to buy. It was high time he made some more bookshelves, he said: he is proud to think she's read every book that was on the shelves he had already made. Sometimes, summer, they would get out the old bikes, pedal in uniform solemnity out to fields of long grass starry with buttercups. Archie would beat down the grass to make a sheltered hollow where they ate their sandwiches, drank their cider.

There was a particular place they loved, where the flat lands behind the village gave way to a gentle rise, scarcely high enough to be called a hill. But at the summit of this rise was a church from which life – apart from a rare service attended by a scant congregation – had fallen away. It was surrounded by graves long since attended to, housing dead too long forgotten to be saluted with flowers. Archie and Myrtle loved this place best in May, when the cow parsley was breast high and the dense shade of the dark trees was scattered by a warm breeze. From the grave-yard where, they decided, to eat their lunch was not a profane act, they could look down on to fields of wheat silvered by the spring sun. In the distance these rippling fields merged into the darker flank of the sea. Bass Rock, from here, was no larger than a human tooth sticking up from the water – for all its distance, a menacing shape. On a clear day, the Lammemuirs beyond the sea were a switchback line against a huge sky. This place, Archie often said, reminded him of north Norfolk, where his parents once took him on holiday as a child after they had been fishing at Lowestoft. The gentle incline of land behind Brancaster, the expanses of sky and sea were very similar to the East Neuk of Fife: this part of the coast was untypical of much of Scotland.

Once, pushing their bikes back down to the main road, Myrtle and Archie passed the open gate of an old stone house, the former manse. It was simple in its architecture as a child's drawing: four large windows and a handsome front door dividing its friendly façade. While Archie admired the thickness of the hawthorn hedges that divided the garden from the lane, Myrtle was excited by the glimpses of lustrous curtains at the windows: even their linings, she reckoned, were made of quality stuff. She imagined herself looking out of one of these windows, waking to see the small herd of enormous white cows that grazed in the field beyond the garden. She could see herself growing familiar with their habits, their movements about the field at various times of day. How easy it would be to grow fond of them, to watch with a drugged, lazy pleasure their heavy stride as they lolled about in their small patch of earth, tails heavy as bell ropes sloshing from side to side to reveal pink-skinned glimpses of fatly upholstered thigh . . . How easy it would be to let time pass standing at an upstairs window, arched by curtains of frosted damask, and to stare down upon these dignified creatures, and the world denied to them beyond, where wind-bent trees became smaller and smaller in their progress towards the sea. Myrtle wondered who were the people – the person – whose good fortune it was to live in such a place: and did they love it as much as she would, given the chance?

'Imagine living here,' was all she said to Archie.

'I canna,' he said, mounting his bike with a suddenness that disturbed Myrtle's reverie.

'Well, I can live with my dreams.'

'You can, too.'

Myrtle, heaving on to her own bike, gave a small, deprecating smile that Archie did not see. He was already some way ahead of her, pedalling fast, as he used to as a child. His mind was on other things. He whistled. Myrtle could just hear the sound of the plangent tune which was carried up to her on the breeze.

*

She stands outside the front door, pot of paint in hand. Archie has gone again. Five more days.

The paint is the Christmas green of holly leaves. There was nothing close to the colour Myrtle had in mind in the chandler's store. She had gone by bus to St Andrews and found exactly the right thing there – a whole afternoon, the expedition had taken her. She liked it when whole mornings or afternoons were taken up by a single project: such demolitions of time hurried the days to Archie's return. Myrtle's sense of perfectionism sometimes unnerved Archie, though it also made him proud. It was a wonder, the way she paid such acute attention to detail that others would regard of no importance. But then, with no bairns to keep her busy, time had to be skilfully marshalled. He could not criticise her way. It was best for her and, for all his gentle teasing, affected him in some funny, pleasurable way, too.

The days with Archie here, as always, have gone so fast. When time is precious, pottering about, getting on with normal chores, does nothing to slow the hours. Archie spent the best part of one day preparing the front door for the new paint: sanding, filling in, smoothing. From her place in the kitchen, Myrtle was lulled by the scrape of sandpaper, the occasional bang and thud of implement on thick wood, indications of sweet proximity. Archie had brought home several pounds of red fish (even in the depths of her subconscious Myrtle, superstitious as all fishing people, never thought of it by its real name: to say the word *salmon* is to dice with fate. They must avoid it as actors avoid *Macbeth*). They had the fish for three meals – grilled, kedgeree and fishcakes. Myrtle, huge in her kitchen, floury hands swiping down her apron only to be re-floured again, listened to the scraping and the sanding which became confused with the distant rasp of the sea, and felt the familiar churn of security which alighted when Archie was home, all the more vital for its transience.

One afternoon she went with him down to the boat – a thing she did not much like doing, for it was all too easy to imagine such a small vessel at the mercy of tumultuous waves. Archie always assured her it would take a storm the like of which he had never seen to capsize *Skyline II*, but Myrtle could not be convinced. Not long ago

Archie had confessed that his father's boat, the old *Skyline* (which Ben Duns had bought from Dot after Jock's death), had once rolled right over, but righted herself. If it came to it, he said, *Skyline II*, an even finer boat, bought in the days when fishing was profitable, would do the same.

Myrtle, standing on the harbour wall, had tried to push such thoughts from her mind. She did not share Archie's affection for the boat, or his faith in her. *Skyline II* was far from the youngest, or most handsome, boat in the harbour: snub-nosed, wide-girthed, her black paint worn away and scratched like an old table. Her decks were an incomprehensible clutter of wires and winches and nets: Myrtle watched in awe as Archie scrabbled among the mess looking for something. He was better acquainted with *Skyline's* decks than he was with his own sock drawer, she often thought. Somehow, before returning to sea, he and the crew always managed to have her ship-shape. To Myrtle she was a boat that looked tired, spent: foolishly, she had once said this to Archie, and angered him. She was an ignorant woman when it came to boats, he said, and should keep such opinions to herself. *Skyline II* had years of buoyant life in her yet. So Myrtle contained such thoughts, but could not rid herself of them. When Archie disappeared into the cabin, she could feel her eyes lock with concern. The boat scarcely moved as the brown harbour water flopped against her sides, a languid low tide. She had the look of an old carcass, awaiting the vulture gulls, shrieking low overhead, to rip her to pieces. Archie, all smiles as he ran up the ladder carrying a cardboard box, caught her stricken face. He put an arm about her. They walked with huge fast strides back along the harbour wall, Archie deflecting her thoughts with some story about Ken's eagerness always to be first to help with the worst jobs. He was the one who most frequently volunteered to clean up the galley or unblock the sink. In a moment Archie had recharged his wife's spirits, and they both silently anticipated the long, quiet evening ahead. And on the last night of this shore leave he put his hand round the back of Myrtle's neck even before they had gone upstairs. He gathered her to him with all the constant love that he found difficult to declare, but

25

Myrtle had come to recognise in the complicated maze of his natural diffidence.

By noon, the undercoat is finished. Myrtle stands back, contemplates her work. With any luck the paint will have dried hard enough for her to begin the top coat this afternoon. Archie advised her to leave it for twenty-four hours, but an impatience for its completion spurs her to ignore such advice. Archie will never find out – and if he does it would not be the kind of infidelity that would concern him. Then, if the topcoat is really hard by tomorrow morning, Myrtle goes on to think, she can spend a good many hours polishing up the black crust of the old brass knocker. That should take care of most of Tuesday.

Until two years ago, when Dot died, the days when Archie was away were charged with duties that did much to speed their length. Dot, who eventually required more expert nursing care than Myrtle could give, went without protest to the Evergreen Home just outside the village. Myrtle and Archie felt all the ubiquitous guilt at organising this move, but as far as they could judge it caused Dot no traumas.

'I shall no longer be a bother to you,' she said with one of her toothless smiles. 'I'll be able to sit and sit and sit, no trouble to anyone.'

At the home, within a very short time, Dot had established that her sedentary life should not be in the company of others. On their first visit, Myrtle and Archie arrived to find she had persuaded the nurses to move her armchair to the bay window overlooking the sea, as far as possible from the rigid circle of other fishermen's wives who dozed round a television set from morning to night. Dot's small body, dwarfed by the rose-blown cushions of the armchair, seemed to have closed in on itself in this new place – its edges reaching hopelessly towards each other like a shell prised half open. Her tiny head, lowered on to her chest, strained upwards so that her eyes could meet the horizon. She was watching, she said, for *The Skyline* to return for her: that was occupation enough till she died. She convinced the nurses this was truthfully all she desired to do, and they soon gave up trying to persuade her to join the others' undignified activities. The 'exercise' class, she told Myrtle – old arms struggling to rise in time to 'Pack up your Troubles' – was worse than any sight she had come across in eighty years on land or sea. It was *indecent*, she declared, and she wanted no part of it. But then Dot had never been one inclined to join a crowd, and in the last two years of her life in the home she rallied gestures of independence with the energy she had left. From her solitary position at the window, she scorned the woollen garments of pale pinks and blues that drizzled from the shoulders of her peers. Dot insisted, despite the stuffy central heating, in wrapping herself in her mother's old Shetland shawl, a woollen garment dyed in natural dyes – 'hedgerow juices', she called them – that she declared must be her shroud. Gloomy, the nurses called it. Why do you want to wear this old thing, dear? Your daughter could bring you a nice bright cardigan. But Dot wanted neither nice bright cardigan nor carpet slippers. She insisted on wearing the lace-up boots, their brown leather polished to a silvery bronze, that she had preserved for thirty years. These were the clothes she had worn when she waved Jock off from the harbour, or went to greet him: and these were the clothes she wished to be in when he came for her again.

'She's what we call our wee Bohemian, your mother,' a nurse once said to Myrtle. They could never understand.

In the two years that Dot was in the home, Myrtle visited her every day. Archie came with her any Sunday he was not at sea. The visits imposed a pattern which Myrtle found soothing, though each one brought evidence of further decline, and each one was heightened by the knowledge that time was running out. Myrtle would sit on the floor beside her mother's chair – thus, their eyes were on a level, though rarely met. Dot's patient gaze was on the sea. Her hands lay side by side on her lap, unmoving, like two small dead fish about to be cast back into the water. Sometimes the fingers would make involuntary movements, as if trying to pluck at an invisible line, or fix bait to a hook. At such moments Myrtle believed her mother to be remembering, but she was often wrong.

'What are you thinking, Mother?' Silence. 'Are you remembering baiting the lines?'

'No,' Dot said, after a long while, and still not moving her eyes. 'Why should I be?'

They would not talk much, mother and daughter. Myrtle found little to say. She knew the only news to interest Dot – before she ceased to take in anything at all – was of tides and winds, so that she could calculate the progress of her dead husband. She had no interest in the present politics of fishing, or how scant were the catches. News of Annie, whose shocking behaviour had once caused her a certain glee, held no interest either. Only the death of one of the old widows stirred her into brief liveliness.

'She fell forward in her chair, Clarrie McFair she was, her Andrew on Jock's crew for a year or two, spit coming out of her mouth in great bubbles like our goldfish Sammy used to blow. You remember Sammy? She upsets her tea all over the place, face a nasty colour. Blow me if she isn't gone, the nurse says. And she'd walked back from the dining room, no help, not an hour before.'

'How did you see all this, Mother, your back always turned on the circle, your eyes out to sea?'

'If you hear a commotion, you turn round, don't you? It was a sight. Some of the old ones, they just kept their eyes shut. One or two of them cried, a horrible noise, and tried to get up to help. But the nurses pushed them back in their chairs. There was nothing they could do – nothing anyone can do when a heart pegs out like that. I turned back to the sea. Poor old Clarrie, I thought, though I'd not seen her for years. I'll be the next one to go, I thought. I'll be the next one to go, though not before your father's come for me.'

When Dot died, Archie had been at sea for two days and was not due to return for another three. Myrtle, who arrived at her usual time at the home in the morning, was told her mother had had a restless night but now appeared more settled. Dot was in her usual position, staring out over the white-chipped sea to the horizon. Her hands were clasped restlessly together as if holding some secret excitement. When Myrtle lowered herself on to the floor beside her, Dot raised one of her hands – the silvery scars so faded they were almost invisible – but did not move her eyes.

28

'He's here at last,' she said. 'Look: there's *The Skyline*! On the horizon.'

Myrtle looked out to sea. There was indeed a ship on the horizon, though it looked a hundred times the size of her father's fishing boat. More like a tanker.

'That's good,' she said.

'He'll no' be long now.' Dot's hands unwrapped themselves, fell back on to her lap. She did not speak again. When Myrtle left her, an hour later, it was clear Dot had more important things to concentrate on than the farewell. Myrtle made her way past Clarrie's empty chair – still not filled, though it was three months since she had died – thinking that although her mother's reason had now completely gone, at least she seemed happy. She did not fret, or complain, or shift about in her chair. Consumed by her long, irrational watch for her husband, her extraordinary firmness of purpose gave her calm, resolve, a kind of peace.

Myrtle had not been back home an hour when the telephone rang. Dot had died moments after she left. Kind timing – to spare me the commotion, Myrtle thought. She sat at the kitchen table, busied herself making a list of things that must be done. She wished that Archie was home, and that she could weep away the diffuse sensations that gather when a much-loved mother dies. But for the moment no tears came, and eventually she telephoned the minister of the kirk to arrange the funeral for the day after Archie's return. Dot's wish was to be buried beside her husband, in a corner of the graveyard that overlooked the sea.

By mid afternoon the front door was finished. Myrtle stood back to consider her work. It would be hard for Archie to find fault, she thought, even if he did not appreciate the subtlety of the green. It was well painted, handsome, lustrous. It distinguished the small stone house, whose roof was now in perfect order, and Archie had done a grand job on the window sills and frames only a year ago. Myrtle was pleased. Impatient for Archie's approval. Four, maybe five days . . .

*

Number five Arbroath Street had been the McGregor family house for many generations. It was a traditional East Neuk village house of thick stone walls, crow-stepped gables, slate roof and well-spaced windows of more aristocratic proportions than are usually found in small village houses. Two flights of stone steps, joined at the top by a stone landing place, led to the first-floor front door. Two hundred years ago the ground floor, a single large room the length of the building, was rented out to a firm of sailmakers. When steam drifters came into general use at the beginning of this century, and sailmakers were made redundant, Myrtle's grandfather had plans to turn the space into part of the house, linking the two floors with an inside staircase. These plans never materialised: Hamish McGregor spent most of his life at sea, and when he was home the last thing he felt inclined to do was building. As there was no possibility of paying anyone else to do the work, the room fell into disrepair. It became a general store for neighbours, and was soon full of ancient nets, rusting machinery and all manner of useless objects.

When Dot and Jock were married they lived, at first, with Dot's parents upstairs. The lack of space meant this was an uneasy arrangement of which they soon tired. Apart from the kitchen, where all daytime life was conducted, there were only two small bedrooms. The first one, hastily converted from the original parlour, was occupied by the elder couple. Dot and Jock were left, albeit gratefully, with a slip of a room into which only a single bed would fit. After a year of discomfort, Jock took a couple of weeks' holiday and put the old storeroom downstairs to rights. It was cold, sunless, damp, in no way luxurious: but it was private. When Jock was home he and Dot kept to themselves in their quarters, the heavy thud of parental feet overhead spurring them to restrict family visits as much as possible. Myrtle was born in that room, five minutes before the midwife arrived. Jock was at sea. It was a stormy day, but according to a much-repeated story of Dot's, no sooner than the baby was born the clouds disappeared and a bar of sunlight made its way into the room, lighting the darkness.

Myrtle was two years old when her grandparents moved to a small modern flat. For the last decade of their life they enjoyed an electric stove, central heating, a bath and inside lavatory (for years they had had to climb down the outside steps, torch in hand on dark nights, to a shed in the scrap of earth they called the garden). Dot and Jock and their young daughter moved upstairs: it was warmer, cosier, lighter, and they could see the sea from the kitchen window. Once again the downstairs room was neglected. Mould grappled the walls, evil-looking fungi sprouted up through the floorboards. By the time Archie and Myrtle married it was in a state of such sad neglect they did not even contemplate making it their first home, poor though they were. They started married life in a council flat of the meanest possible proportions, and hated all that their grandparents had so enjoyed: air stiff with central heating, cheap windows, lack of shelves or space, a bleak and tacky kitchen whose geometrically patterned formica, orange and brown, caused Myrtle daily anguish. So when Dot became ill and needed constant help, to convert the downstairs room in Arbroath Street, and make it into a small flat, was a quick and happy decision.

In the last two years, since Dot had died, Myrtle and Archie had gradually been putting the house further to rights. They moved upstairs to sleep in order to wake up to the view: the two small bedrooms were knocked into one, the old fireplace was unblocked. Sometimes, on cold winter nights, they lit a wood fire in the bedroom. Pale ash in the grate, the occasional red eye of a still-living ember, was their first sight on waking. For them it was a shared pleasure to rise from the warmth of the bed into the bitter air, their breath spectral bulbs of air floating in the semi-dark of dawn. But it was always warm in the kitchen: the ancient range, a temperamental old object that suffered various crises and needed constant pampering, gave out a good heat. In the tradition of Myrtle's forebears, she and Archie spent most of their time there: Archie's old armchair was by the stove, Myrtle's books were thrust between china and jars on Archie's fine shelves. It was the place they felt most at ease, the room where greetings and farewells took place: its window was the vantage point from which Myrtle would daily read the sea. Neither of them could ever imagine spending more time elsewhere.

In the landing between the kitchen and bedroom they had put a spiral staircase to the downstairs room – thereby achieving at last Grandfather McGregor's plan. Their old room was now changed once more: a door led on to the 'garden', now a paved courtyard where Myrtle grew herbs and geraniums in discarded baker's trays. The small bathroom they had put in when they came to live there was furnished with a more amiable bath, and a corner of the room was partitioned off to house the washing machine. They painted the walls white, bought a huge old sofa, and a desk for Archie's accounts. Thus it became the living room, referred to by the jealous Annie as a 'bloody great ballroom'. But rarely did they use it. Sometimes, summer evenings, they would sit by the open door looking out at Myrtle's flowering pots, but they felt oppressed by the high walls of the courtyard. All they could see, from down there, was a few yards of sky: no sea.

Arbroath Street, once only known for the poverty within its thick-stoned houses, was by now a generally smarter place. Neighbours had preceded the Duns with their improvements: roofs were patched, window frames gloss-painted, the wood of old front doors turned yellow and red and blue. Strangers with cameras, in clothes to match the front doors, were often to be found wandering down the street these days – their eyes more dulled than amazed by the sight of what one of them explained to Myrtle was surely 'living history'. And tourists were not the only problem: men with profit in mind had also discovered the east coast of Scotland.

One day Myrtle opened the door to a man who wore a tartan tie and the sort of expression that indicated he was confident of a welcome. He said he hoped it would not be untoward if he were to compliment her on her house.

'A very desirable residence, if I may say so,' he ventured more cautiously, in response to Myrtle's face. 'Now would you ever have it in mind, I wonder, to rent out your quite exceptional – if I may be so bold – home?'

Myrtle stepped back into the kitchen. So preposterous a thought deprived her of an immediate answer. The estate agent, as Myrtle imagined him to be, took the liberty of moving inside as well, where his expert eye took in the decorative order of the place in a moment. As Myrtle was still locked into her speechless state, the man was able to grant her the benefit of his advice.

'You could pick up a nice little rent, place like this, summers,' he said. 'Of course, a modicum of investment, dare I suggest, might be required – nothing to alarm the coffers.' He gave a narrow smile of encouragement, exposing teeth the colour of young bark. Myrtle, lulled by his Morningside accent, sinuous as the cooing of a distant wood pigeon, folded her arms and stared down at his head of mannered hair. 'There are others in this very street in the process of *considering*, aye. Indeed, there are some that have more or less made up their minds: I'd put my money on that, Mrs – eh?'

'Never,' said Myrtle.

'I think you would be wise to reflect on how much you could gain from so little trouble –'

'I said never –'

'The mere changing from the, eh, delightfully *historic*' – here a dark smile was flashed towards the stove – 'in some cases, to the more contemporary aids of modern life that weekenders, bless their hearts, seem more greatly to favour . . .' At this point a small sniff was quickly extinguished by the genteel dab of a tartan handkerchief. He somehow managed to convey that while he himself was not one to approve the vulgarity of modern convenience, he was naturally obliged to consider the taste of his clients. 'What I'm saying is, with a nice little modern stove in here you could command a very fair rent indeed.'

'You're wasting your time,' said Myrtle. She wished desperately that Archie could have been there. He would so have enjoyed Mr Morningside.

'I can assure you that our agency is a very old establishment of highest reputation,' he persisted. 'Your interests are our business. We let all manner of properties on the east coast of Scotland, and, indeed, even further afield . . .' He trailed off. Glanced at the chipped paint of the window frame, the only one still awaiting Archie's attention.

Braced himself for one last attempt. 'You cannot imagine, Mrs eh? just how many satisfied customers we have on our books . . .'

'I'm sorry I can't help you by joining them, but no amount of money in the world would ever tempt my husband and I to let out our house to strangers. Now if you wouldn't mind, I have things to be getting on with . . .'

Myrtle sets about polishing the brass lion's head door knocker. She is impatient to finish the job, has no wish to be interrupted.

'Myrtle? I say, your door looks grand.' Myrtle, when she sees Annie, smiles. Annie, whose presence has the power so often to dissipate Myrtle's agitation or annoyance, has reached the top of the steps by now. She stands beside Myrtle on the stone landing, peering at the door. Eventually she reaches out a finger, touches the hard gloss paint. 'I want to talk to you.'

Myrtle sighs. She feels the sudden chill of evening on her shoulders. The sky is feathered with purple and grey clouds.

'We'll go in,' she says.

In the kitchen Myrtle automatically puts on the kettle, reaches for the tea caddy. Annie doesn't sit in her usual chair. She remains standing. Myrtle sees a tightness in her face that spells trouble. She knows at once when there is something up with Annie. She wonders if she can deflect whatever it is her friend has come to expound: she's in no mood for a confrontation.

'Did you and Ken get to Edinburgh?' she asks.

'We didn't. Ken had to be away a lot with the van. Business.'

'I don't want to talk about that.' Archie has been aware of Ken's 'business' for some time: as skipper of the boat he cannot approve, for it means that days ashore are far from a rest for Ken, who returns to the boat exhausted, unable to pull his weight, though his helpfulness – perhaps fired by guilt – continues. Archie has warned Ken several times he cannot put up with Ken's double life much longer. There have been arguments, rows. At some point, both wives know, there will have to be a showdown. Archie is increasingly suspicious as to the nature of Ken's 'deliveries'. He does not think they are all furniture removals. He has reason to believe that crates of black fish – fish surplus to the legal quota that should be returned to the sea – are stowed among the furniture and delivered to someone in a chain of traders flouting the law. Archie has confessed his suspicion only to Myrtle. When he is angry, he threatens to 'catch Ken out'. Myrtle keeps hoping that he will never do this.

'You asked,' says Annie. 'But I want to know what you meant by Saturday morning. What you did.'

'Saturday morning?' Myrtle's mind spins back, confused.

'You upset Janice, you upset the bairn. She came back in tears.'

A muffled snorting noise comes from Myrtle's nose. Annie takes this to be derision. She pulls back a chair – not her usual chair – with an angry scrape. Sits down.

'There was nothing I could suggest to cure the hamster,' Myrtle says.

'It wasn't that, so much. It was the general feeling you gave Janice of not being wanted. Not welcome.'

'Well she was right, there. She wasn't welcome.' Myrtle slams down two mugs. 'What do you imagine? Archie just home, wanting a bit of peace and quiet for his breakfast, and your daughter comes running round with an ailing hamster. That's not what I'd call good timing.' She pours tea. Annie, silent, has deep pink cheeks, the same marks stretching from eye to jaw that used to appear when she was an angry child.

'The hamster died,' she says at last.

'I'm sorry.'

'I thought you loved Janice as if she was your own daughter.'

'I've never quite said that.' Myrtle sits down heavily, the far end of the table from Annie. 'But it's true I'm very fond of Janice.'

'Sometimes, you wouldn't know it. You're often sharp with her – too sharp, to my mind.'

'There are moments when a child must know the truth. She's too cocky, young Janice. Too pleased with herself. It's not up to me to tell her how to behave in general. But as she seems to be in this house almost as much as she is at home, I've every right to tell her how to behave here. She should learn when she's not wanted. When Archie has just come home – that's one of the times she's not wanted. Doesn't seem unreasonable to me. But I don't blame the child entirely. *You* should tell her, Annie, not to come round here when Archie's –'

'So that's it.' Annie pushes away her empty mug. 'You know what your problem is, don't you? You're just jealous: jealous of Ken and me and Janice. Jealous of any couple with a child.' She takes in the scorn that travels across Myrtle's face. 'That's always been the case. That accounts for your behaviour – everyone says so. Of course, it's not that you don't have our sympathy. You know that. There can't be anything much worse than wanting a bairn and not being able to have one. But who was always at your side, tea and sympathy, when you were going through all those dreadful tests? Me, you remember. And how do you think I felt, having a bonnie wee daughter when you were unable –'

'Stop this, Annie –'

'How do you think I felt? How do you think I still feel? I remember saying to you soon after Janice was born: Myrtle, I said, you can have as much share in her as you want.'

'Stop it! There's no point in all this.' Myrtle is very pale. Her big hands grasp her mug of hot tea. After a while she says: 'I've told you before: if we're not going to quarrel then we should avoid this subject. Besides, you've no idea how I feel about not having –'

'You can't tell me you're not jealous of Janice's existence. You don't like the fact that I have a daughter and you don't.'

'I don't like it, no – not the fact that you have something I don't – I'm pleased about that, you know perfectly well. But the fact that *I* can't, ever, for Archie. I can't have Archie's child. Don't you see? That doesn't make for jealousy of you or anyone else who has children. It makes for something far more deadly: the persistent sense of failure. Of course, there many advantages in having no children, no ties. We can do all sorts of things that you and Ken can't – just go off for the day on a whim. For all I know, you and Ken are jealous of our freedom. And then we're better off than some, with no children's things to pay for. But nothing can compensate . . . Failing to have a child smoulders away . . . You accuse yourself, all your life. There, I've said my bit. That's it, please. End of subject.'

Annie folds her arms, looks up at Myrtle.

'I'm sorry,' she says. 'I don't often fly off the handle like that, do I? We've been having a time, Ken and me. Up and down, all over the place – him out so much with the bloody van we never have time to settle. What do I do once he's gone again? Take it all out on you.'

Myrtle, webbed with thoughts which for the most part she manages to keep at bay, gives her a distracted smile.

'That's no matter,' she says. There's a long silence between the women. While both want to regain the old equilibrium between them, both are still too encumbered with their own preoccupations to come up with a declaration of good intent. 'If I was jealous of you, Annie, there'd be all sorts of good reasons, nothing to do with a bairn. You were always the pretty one, the lively one, the one the boys fought for. But I didn't mind any of that when we were children, when we were young, because you were always such a loyal friend, sticking up for me, insisting I share everything except for the boys – well, they didn't want me, so that wasn't your fault.' She gives a small laugh. 'You did everything to make sure I couldn't feel jealous and I was very proud that you, the most popular girl in the school, were my friend.'

The anger in Annie's cheeks, long since vanished pink, now returns, diffused, in the guise of a blush.

'Well I couldn't have done without you,' she says. 'You were my rock. Still are. Besides, you're remembering all wrong. I'd make you cross as anything. Still do.' Both women laugh. Annie moves towards the door. 'Will I come for cards usual time tomorrow?'

'Aye.'

'I must be gone. Janice'll wonder where I am.' Myrtle takes a bar of chocolate from a shelf.

'Give her that from me,' she says.

When Annie has left Myrtle remains quiescent in the semi-darkness. She feels such desolation that to remain sitting is all she can do. Her hands lie unmoving on the table. She wonders if one of them will shift of its own accord, and break the spell. She senses that rocks have been moved within her, and shale is pouring down between newly made crevices. Her devices for keeping untroubled the friendship with Annie usually work. They can go for months at a time with no arguments, no increase of tension. The sort of flare-up that took place this evening is both rare and, to Myrtle, disturbing. Annie, more volatile than Myrtle, has probably not given another thought to the disagreeable scene, and is heating up Janice's supper in the microwave as if nothing out of the ordinary had happened. Lucky her, thinks Myrtle: Annie's ability to take things lightly – *that* is the area where some fragment of envy lodges. Myrtle watches as her hands – no feeling within them, disconnected things – quiver up to grasp her temples. The emptiness of the room is so acute she knows she must leave it for a while. She picks up her shawl, shuts the window. For some weeks she has not visited her mother's grave. She will go there now for the certainty of quiet and the hope of peace.

Annie's acts of kindness to Myrtle, as a child, sometimes caused her trouble. There was the day when Ross Wyatt, who had been pestering Annie for months, made a final stand for her, and was rejected in favour of Myrtle.

'Come on out in the playground with me, Annie. I've something to show you.'

'I'd rather not, thanks, Ross Wyatt.'

The boy, Myrtle remembers, was desperate. He could not decide how best to appeal to the snooty girl who stood before him. His hands were in the pockets of his shorts. Myrtle could see the fingers whirling round. There were smears of high colour on his cheeks.

'I didn't mean the playground. I meant . . . let's go down to the harbour. Get us some chips.' His voice was breathless, odd. He suddenly turned away from them, flung his head back. Myrtle was alarmed. Was he ill? Should she get someone? But Annie didn't seem to think anything was amiss. She was used to boys having to turn from her, weak with love.

'No thank you,' Annie shouted. 'I don't want to go anywhere with you, ever. So don't bother to keep asking. Do I, Myrtle?'

There was sudden confusion in Myrtle's mind. Not three weeks ago Annie had told her just how much she fancied Ross Wyatt. She couldn't think why he was taking so long to do anything about it, she said. It was clear as anything he fancied her, too. So this peculiar change of mind, now Ross was actually making some move, took Myrtle by surprise. What should she do? Annie nudged Myrtle.

'No she doesn't,' said Myrtle, quietly. 'Annie doesn't want anything to do with you, Ross.'

'There! What did I tell you, Ross?' Annie was thrilled by her friend's quick thinking, her loyalty. 'Myrtle knows. Myrtle's my friend. Come on, Myrtle. We're going.'

Ross spun round to face them, deeply flushed. He looked healthier, despite his high colour, Myrtle thought. The fit, or spasm, or whatever it had been that struck him, had definitely passed. He fixed Myrtle with a look of total scorn.

'You! Friend? You're nothing more than an ugly great parcel, guarding Annie for dear life for you know *you'll* no' ever get a man wanting to get into your pants –'

'You foul-mouthed bugger! Don't you dare speak to my friend like that,' screamed Annie, and threw herself towards him. Myrtle tried to pull her back, but it was too late. Annie kicked Ross very hard in the balls. He went white, moaned, bent double. Myrtle dragged Annie back.

'Leave him, Annie,' she shouted above Ross's moaning, 'the scumbag –'

'I'll kill him!'

'You'll pay for this, bitch.' Ross unfurled himself painfully. Upright, one hand still clutched his groin. 'You stick around with your friend Myrtle, and I'll tell my friend Hamish if he wants you then he'll have to have your ugly friend too!' He laughed.

'Don't you dare!' There was a quiver in Annie's voice. Myrtle knew at once that Ross's threat meant something to Annie. Hamish? Perhaps there had been no chance for Annie to tell her whatever it was about Hamish.

'I'll say to Hamish not to bother with you – you're more concerned

39

with this great parcel, Myrtle Stewart, who no boy would touch if she was the last girl on earth –'

'Get out,' Annie screamed again, 'before I fetch Mrs Williams.'

Ross turned and left the classroom with the air of one who had no intention of wasting any further insults on such despicable girls. His back view conveyed tedium with the whole scene. He slammed the door behind him.

Annie turned to Myrtle with tears in her eyes. Myrtle put an arm round her.

'You shouldn't have stuck up for me so hard like that,' she said.

'Course I should. I won't have anyone saying such beastly untrue things about you. It's wicked.' She sniffed. 'I'll kill him if he goes and messes up everything with Hamish.'

'I don't know what's up, you and Hamish, do I?' asked Myrtle, passing Annie her handkerchief. 'You go so quickly from one to another.' Annie suddenly giggled.

'I liked Ross for a bit before he looked at me. Then when he started up with all his pestering and soppy notes I thought he was revolting. Then just this morning in assembly Hamish winked at me – well, sort of winked at me – and I thought he was nice. I mean, I like curly hair.' She giggled again. Myrtle smiled, conspiratorial. She always enjoyed the turbulent progress of Annie's love life. 'Sorry, I didn't have a moment to tell you.'

'But how,' asked Myrtle, 'if Hamish winked at you only this morning could Ross know already that you –?'

'Och, he just guessed.' She gave a wry smile. 'Suppose you could say that sod Ross Wyatt is a good guesser. And next time he insults you I'll kick him so hard he'll never get up again.' She was punching the air with a clenched fist, pretty eyes flashing. 'No one's rude to my friend.'

It was one of Myrtle's proud moments. Annie's fierce declarations of loyalty filled her with more happiness than anything, surely, that any stupid boy could provide. She knew she had no chance with boys, anyhow. They either ignored her or were rude to her. But none of that mattered so long as Annie loved her and stuck up for her. And she couldn't imagine, even when she was grown up, that she could love any man half as much as she had always loved Annie. The two girls hugged each other, aware of the faint honey smell of each other's tears; then were parted by the clanging of the bell for games. They were twelve years old at the time.

Myrtle stands beside her mother's grave. It is dark by now: the flaked clouds of early evening have given way to a smooth darkness that becomes faded rags round the moon. Its light makes a highway across the sea. There are no ships, no waves. The meeting of sky and sea is lost in velutinous black. How, Myrtle wonders, do people think of the dead?

She herself finds it hard to picture her mother as a whole figure. The images in her mind are scattered miniatures. There are the scarred hands, the deep-lidded eyes, the wary smile, some small questioning gesture of head, the shoulders bent in old age. It's hard to remember her upright. Sometimes, frighteningly, it's hard to remember her face at all, and Myrtle has quickly to turn to a photograph to remind. The scent of her comes back more frequently: fish – the powerful whippy smell of brine – and the milder scent of lavender water. Dot, on Sundays, would dab homemade lavender water on her neck to disguise the fish. Myrtle, as a child, was allowed to give her mother the briefest goodnight kiss: it was enough to catch the familiar combination of fish and lavender on her skin. The smell was there even in the home: the fish marinated into skin over the years, the lavender now daily applied. A terrible extravagance, this, Dot once told Myrtle. But she feared the fish smell still clung, and she had no wish to give offence.

The voice was the part that lived most clearly. Dot's was a sweet, melodious voice, the Scots accent brittle as glass, the intonations choppy as small waves on a windblown sea.

'Myrtle: will ye come here?'

'Myrtle: you've grown into such a fine big lass – your faither's bones.'

'Myrtle, look: there's *The Skyline* on the horizon. He'll no' be long now.'

Dot's voice chimes ceaselessly through Myrtle, all times of night and day. Its persistence is what makes her think the dividing line between life and death is narrower than we might suppose. Perhaps the voices of those we love will never die, she thinks, and that is of some comfort.

'Myrtle, is that you?'

This is not a voice from the grave, but a man's voice. Canadian. Myrtle turns.

Martin Ford stands nearby, one hand at rest on a granite cross almost his own height. His hair is blonded by the moon, his face is in deep shadow.

'Och, Martin.'

'Hope I've not given you a fright.'

'Never.'

'I was caught up on a job, back late. Just wanted to see where I have to start digging in the morning. Rusty Burns. Ninety-three, I believe.'

'I heard. Poor Nancy's in a terrible way.'

'Last of the great bakers, these parts, I'd say.'

Martin is a stonemason. He came over from Canada with his parents when he was seventeen, and served his apprenticeship in the south. But he returned to Scotland to be near his parents – they share with him a divided house just beyond the village. Lack of work has always been his problem. He has established a reputation for being the most skilled stonemason on the east coast, besides the most reasonable – many is the time he has charged merely for the price of the stone. He is kept fairly busy with headstones, the odd monument, or memorial tablet for a church, but each job is long and painstaking and his profits do not reflect the value of his craftsmanship. To supplement his paltry income he digs graves. Martin is a strong and fast digger, and reliable. Indeed his reliability is renowned – always ready to help others, he has never been known to let anyone down. He is generally liked in the village, thought a good man considering he's from overseas. But no one, so far as Myrtle knows, is close to him or is privy to much of his life.

Martin shifts his position.

'Your mother – how long is it, now?'

'Two years almost exactly.'

'She was a rare woman.'

'Aye, she was.'

'And you?'

'I'm doing fine.'

'Archie away so much. Must be hard for you wives.'

'You get used to it.' The lie reverberates down Myrtle's spine. She pulls at her shawl.

'I must be on my way. Would you like me to walk you home?'

Myrtle shakes her head.

'Thanks all the same,' she says. She lets the fingers of one hand alight on the headstone of her mother's grave, then quickly fly away. Dot's name and dates, along with those of her husband, were beautifully carved by Martin. There is no epitaph. Myrtle has still not been able to think of one that she considers perfect.

'You've not come up with something for me to add?' Martin asks.

'Not yet. But I'm thinking.'

'Poor old Rusty. Nancy says RIP is all she can afford. I said don't be silly, I'll do him a line for nothing.'

'That was good of you,' says Myrtle.

'He deserves an epitaph, a baker like that.'

Somehow they are walking side by side down the narrow path between the graves, their feet making a shushing noise in the stone chippings. Martin shuts the cemetery gate behind them. Myrtle stops while he does this. It is the smallest indication that she does not mind his company. She has said she does not want him to walk her home, but when he continues by her side down the road she does not think of objecting.

No one is about in the village. The houses, so friendly-looking by day, have shuttered themselves behind a haughty, defensive look, which is their custom by night. Curtains are drawn. Lights, suffused through unlined fabrics, trick the eye with their three-dimensional quality: the windows appear to be luminous bricks suspended in the dark.

Myrtle and Martin walk in silence. Number five Arbroath Street is soon reached. Myrtle, who has been wondering whether to spend the rest of the evening with a concert on the radio or her book, stumbles on the bottom step.

'Careful.' Martin whips a torch from his coat pocket. A bright beam carves the stone staircase into wodges of light and shadow. The wool embroidery on the hem of Myrtle's skirt becomes ruby-red flowers.

'Whatever am I doing?' she asks. She can feel Martin's hand under her elbow as she remounts the bottom step, easily this time. She pauses there, one hand on the iron rail. Turns to him.

'Cup of tea? Something to eat?'

Martin thinks for a moment. Releases her elbow from his hand.

'Better be getting back,' he says at last. 'Thanks all the same. But I'll have to be up at four if I want to finish Rusty's grave before I go off to see about some marble.'

Myrtle pictures him alone in the churchyard, spade plunging into trim dewy grass, dawn sky lighting the dark earth as he digs fast and deep. She wonders about his life these days. It's not something she has thought about for a long time.

'Very well,' she says. 'It was good of you to walk me home.'

She flies up the steps now, keen to be inside. Martin keeps his torch shining for her. He waits till she has turned the key in the newly painted door before he puts it out. Then he waves: but it's too late. Myrtle has shut the door. Martin is as alone outside as she is within.

It is almost midnight. Myrtle shifts about, unable to sleep. As always, she envisages Archie far out to sea – an image she hates, but one which recurs every night. Then, the endless black water in her mind turns to sea dancing with sunlight, a calm day in the harbour. Martin, newly arrived in the village, strolling along the harbour wall, hands in pockets. He had a modest air as if he wished to be invisible. That was hardly possible, for he is well over six foot tall and wore his blond hair in a wild mess. Already he had become the object of desire of all the local girls: rare sightings increase speculation as to his availability and character in general. Annie, who at the time was going out with one Roddy Fairburn, found that her affection for a good but dull Scots boy did nothing to impede exciting possibilities provided by the Canadian.

'He's a smasher,' she whispered to Myrtle. 'I could do with a bit of him.' Myrtle could not deny the desirability of Martin, but kept this to herself. The idea of his even noticing *her* was laughable.

From a distance they watched him move slowly along the harbour wall, stopping to contemplate each anchored fishing boat.

'Here's our chance,' said Annie. 'Why don't we just go over and be friendly?'

'Not me,' said Myrtle, who learnt long ago the disadvantages of acting as chaperone to Annie. 'You can go alone. But he's too old for you, seventeen.'

'I'm nigh on sixteen,' said Annie, whose fifteenth birthday was not a week past, 'and anyhow everybody takes me for seventeen.' She fluttered her eyelashes, stiff with purple mascara. 'You're just a rotten sport, Myrtle. Never one for taking a chance.'

'There's Roddy,' said Myrtle. 'I thought you were going out with him.'

Annie laughs with a scorn too sophisticated for her years.

'Roddy? What good's he?'

Myrtle guessed Roddy's days were numbered. She had heard that laugh before. Martin had moved to the far end of the harbour wall, back to them. His concentration was now on the horizon.

'Thoughtful type, Martin, if you ask me,' Annie said. She shrugged, then laughed more agreeably. 'Course, the one he'd be really good for is you.' She smiled at the thought of any such impossibility. 'The height, I mean. He's about the only boy around taller than you, isn't he?'

'Don't be daft, Annie.' Now that Annie seemed to have forgotten about approaching Martin, none of her silly suggestions could alarm Myrtle.

'I'm not so daft, you'll see. Just a matter of waiting.' Annie took Myrtle's arm. 'All I ask is a chance to have first go. I don't half fancy him.'

45

'You do what you like,' said Myrtle. 'I don't *want* Martin.' But they were running fast now, late for school. Annie didn't hear.

The unexpected meeting with Martin has brought back this long-past scene very clearly to the sleepless Myrtle. She goes on to remember Annie's next move, and smiles to herself. Then at last she sleeps.

Annie, shuffling cards at Myrtle's kitchen table, is unusually quiet. She has brought a small pot of crocus bulbs which, she says, will be out for Christmas. This, too, is unusual. Annie is not by way of making such gestures very often. She does not describe the bulbs as a peace offering: but this is what they are, Myrtle well knows, and makes much of her pleasure and thanks.

Although the women play in silence for a while Myrtle is aware that something is on Annie's mind. She knows her friend so thoroughly. She knows exactly the cheeky tilt of head that precedes some overture to a man. She knows the look of hopeless caution that means she is doing her best to keep a secret. She knows the fingers that jump faster through the cards when she is harbouring some thought or knowledge she finds hard to contain. Myrtle watches her patiently, amused. Sometimes she feels most fond of Annie when Annie is struggling. Her inability to conceal, her candour, are among the things Myrtle loves her for. Annie knows she is being watched. She enjoys keeping Myrtle waiting. She pretends to concentrate very hard on her hand of cards. But eventually she says:

'So you caused a scandal last night.'

Myrtle meets Annie's mischievous eyes, gives a deprecating smile.

'I don't know what you mean.'

Annie flings out a look that says of course you know what I mean.

'Arm in arm with Martin, all through the village.' Myrtle is already laughing. 'Under cover of darkness. He sees you in, right in. Door apparently *bangs*! What happens then, Myrtle?' In Annie's playfulness there is an edge of suspicion. Myrtle's laughter increases, the warm, bubbling, cooing noise that Archie calls audible hot chocolate.

'There was no one about,' she says. 'Who were the spies?'

'There are always spies behind the curtains.'

Myrtle lays down her cards, folds her big hands. She cuts off the laughter, takes a deep breath.

'This village! I've never heard anything so ridiculous in all my life. The day Myrtle Duns causes a scandal . . .' The laughter breaks again.

'The truth, then. Tell me the truth.'

'It's not in the least interesting. After you left I went down to the churchyard for a while. Martin was there, looking at some plot where he had to dig a grave this morning. Aye, we walked home together – not arm in arm, as you can imagine. He shone the torch for me to get up the steps. I asked him in for a cup of tea – we haven't seen him for some weeks. He said no. I shut the door. Big scandal, that, I suppose.'

'Big scandal. I believe you.'

Myrtle, too, aims for playfulness.

'I should hope so.'

'He's a mystery, that Martin. There's not one of us knows about his life.'

'You got the closest.' It's Myrtle's turn to tease though she thinks, too late, that the subject of Martin and Annie is still, probably, no joking matter.

'Didn't get very close, as far as I can remember. He was always on about this other woman he loved.'

'I do believe you were really taken by Martin, all that time ago.'

'I was. You know that. Well, you know me. Not being able to *get* spurs the attraction. But it was more than that, what I felt for Martin. He represented something good, honest, strong: things I aspired to beneath all the flirting, whatever you may have thought. Last time I saw him he'd put on a fair bit of weight. He looked quite sad, I thought. I'd have liked to have ruffled his hair and said: come on, Martin, I'm still your friend. But I didn't dare. I'm not sure he'll ever like me again.'

'Nonsense.'

'If my carefree days were still here, I could still fancy him. There! Now I've said it. It's brought on your disapproving look.'

Myrtle laughs.

'You'll be fancying people – and they'll be fancying you – till the day you die,' she says. 'I can just see it, when the time comes you have to go into the home: the old boys'll no' stand a chance against you. You'll be chasing them down the passages on your Zimmer. You'll be pulling your armchair across the telly room to make sure you get beside whoever –'

'Now you're being daft. Besides, Ken'll be in there with me. There's no way we're going to be parted in our dotage. At least, that was a plan we once made.'

'How is Ken?' asks Myrtle. They don't normally enquire much about each other's husbands. Myrtle asks in a thoughtless way, perhaps to fill an uneasy silence. Annie shuffles her cards, eyes down, the extraordinarily long lashes making jagged shadows on her cheeks.

'It's not a good time,' is all she says.

Ken, at school, was for some years proud to be the joker in the class. He was always the one to come up with the cheeky answer, to make the others laugh at the teacher's expense; the one to be punished most often. The standard punishment was to be made to stay in after school and learn a hundred lines by heart, either from the Bible or Robert Burns. Thanks to this form of reprimand Ken discovered he had an astonishing memory. It took him moments to learn what would take others an hour or so. Not ten minutes after he had been shut into the empty classroom with a passage of St Paul's letters to the Corinthians, he would hail the teacher with the news that he had 'got it'. To the teacher's amazement, this was true. He would gabble the whole thing off, heedless of punctuation or intonation, but word perfect. Then, just to keep up the sharp edge of his renowned cheekiness, he would offer to learn a couple more passages if that was what was wanted. But no: he was always let off, accused of having a photographic memory, and warned this was nothing to be proud of. With great glee he would recount all this to his class mates who, already admiring of his cheekiness, doubled their respect. In order to be given more passages to learn by heart, Ken had to continue in his irreverent ways to gain punishment. Soon he began to ask if he could branch out from both Burns and the Bible. He was given the *Oxford Book of Verse* and told to learn whatever he liked so long as it added up to a hundred lines. Thus he was introduced to the poets, and came to love them. For two happy years he kept to the busy routine of punishment and learning, punishment and learning. He was kept so busy that he had no time, unlike the majority of the other boys, for thoughts of girls. They did not come into his scheme of things. He spent any free moment dreaming of becoming an actor. This he confessed one day to Myrtle and begged her to keep the secret to herself. If he mentioned the idea to his family, he said, who had been in the fishing business for generations, they would assume he was suffering from some weakness in the head and send him to the doctor.

In those days Ken held no interest for Annie. She was so dizzied by the compliments and desires of almost every other boy in the class that to make a play for one of the few boys who showed no interest in her was pointless. Had Ken been a generally acknowledged good-looker, like Archie, she might have made some effort. But as his sparse charm was more cerebral than physical, she saw no point in wasting her time. She merely joined in the laughter when Ken asked one of his funny but impossible questions, and equally joined the general respect for so singular a boy. Ken, for his part, could not help noticing that Annie was the prettiest girl in the class by about a million leagues, and that his peers – with the exception of his shy friend Archie Duns – made daily fools of themselves trying to please her.

The summer term that Ken turned sixteen there was a post-exam expedition to St Andrews organised by the school. There was to be a picnic by the beach, swimming, games. Not at all the sort of thing that appealed to Ken, but he knew there was no getting out of it. He arrived at the meeting place late to find there were just two seats left, at the front of the bus. He sat by himself, took out his copy of *Hamlet*, which he had disguised in the cover of a thriller for fear of ridicule. The engines started up, the coach was about to go, when there was a cry from Myrtle: Annie! Where was Annie?

Five minutes later, delayed not wholly by chance, Annie made her entrance up the steps. It was clear she had made a stupendous effort, was taking this outing more seriously than most. She wore tight black jeans and a scarlet elastic top, so thin and tight it might have been skin. The nipples of her small breasts played hide-and-seek between the chunks of stone, beads and leather thongs of her ethnic necklaces. It must have taken her at least an hour, Myrtle thought, to perfect her face: eyelids a translucent violet sheen, lips a creamy gloss, cheeks burnished a coppery pink, and long earrings of silver filigree jittered among her dark curls. The sight of her caused a general intake of breath, followed by a whooping and caterwauling which spurred Annie to smile benevolently up and down the bus at her less colourful friends. There was not a girl or boy there who did not recognise that she was in a different class, somehow . . .

Who was it that day Annie had set her heart on sitting next to? Myrtle could not remember. But whoever it was already had someone beside them. The only free seat, Annie saw from a racing glance up and down the bus, was next to Ken. She frowned. Then, not wanting to be unfriendly, she smiled. Both expressions were lost upon Ken, who moved as close as he could to the window, and opened his book.

He need not have feared that he would be interrupted. Annie swivelled round, back to him, and started chattering to those in the seats behind her. The journey, luckily short, passed in a cacophony of voices that Ken, concentrating on his book, tried to shut out. The thing he could not ignore was the smell of Annie: he tried to work out what it was – some kind of warm, honeyed flowers, perhaps. It was the only thing about her that did not intimidate. Rather, it gave him a strange new feeling. Confidence, was it? Whatever – it drew him from his book. He looked up to see the bus was entering the town. At that moment Annie gave one of her flashing turns – this time, towards him. For an infinitesimal moment she dropped a hand on his knee. The second was also an eternity, for in it Ken had time to observe in the minutest detail the shape, weight and contours of that small hand, nails the size of ladybirds blazing with scarlet polish, luminous skin of the fingers scarcely rippled at the knuckles . . . It was a hand that carried some strange venom which punctured his own skin with a thrilling sensation that sped up his thigh and reverberated through his body. The hand had flown, disinterested. But its touch continued to quicksilver through Ken, confusing.

'Ken!' He heard her voice from a long way off. 'You old bookworm, you. You should get together with Myrtle.' There was laughter from somewhere, and Annie had turned her back to him again and carried on her entertaining. As he climbed down the steps of the bus a few moments later, Ken felt curiously weak and tired, as if he had just accomplished some mammoth physical feat.

That day, Myrtle remembered thinking, was not perfect for a picnic. There was an unbroken grey sky and a cool wind which whipped the sea into petulant waves. But free from their exams at last, the pupils made the most of it. They set up a ball game to keep themselves warm, they played silly childish games of hopscotch and leapfrog. They patterned the clean beach with graffiti – the teachers decided to turn a blind eye – and ran random races, pulling each other on to the ground for a skirmish in the sand before they would right themselves and be off after another friend. After a short game of rounders Myrtle detached herself from the crowd and went to sit next to the solitary spectator, Ken. His melancholy air enclosed him like a shadow, but Myrtle was the only one to observe it. He sat hugging his bare, goosepimpled knees, pale of face as if struck down by a sudden illness. A book was stuffed into his back pocket. His eyes were on Annie. As she raced about, followed by some dozen boys, his look never left her. There was a moment when Sandy Strachan, who had caught her in one of the races, flung her to the ground. There were cheers as he rolled quickly over her, mashing her breast with his hand and plunging his mouth into her hair. Ken winced.

'You all right?' Myrtle asked.

'Fine, thanks.'

He was concentrating on Annie's escape. She fled down the beach, soon no more than a small red dot, classmates stringing out behind her. Suddenly she swerved towards the sea. From where they sat Myrtle and Ken could see the splashing and chasing of the faraway crowd. Spume, tossed into the air, made brief arcs that freckled the sky, and the squeals of laughter came to them tiny as the sounds of distant sea birds. Myrtle waited for Ken to make some joke, but he kept his agonised silence. Oh Lord, Myrtle thought: another one.

Later, when the others returned for the picnic lunch, Ken continued to keep his distance. Annie invited Myrtle to come and sit next to her, thus dashing the hopes of at least four boys who had been hoping to be granted this privilege. Pupils and teachers sat on the rounded grey stones that jutted through the sand, gritty hands clamped to thick sandwiches, hair blasted across their eyes by the breeze, the taste of salt on their lips. Overhead, puppet seagulls dipped and rose on invisible strings. Ken, with the air of one to whom noise and collective conviviality are unbearable, got up and wandered down the beach.

'What's the matter with him?' asked Annie, uninterested. Hamish was playing with her shoelaces in what she took to be an erotic manner. Myrtle shook her head, didn't answer.

On the way home, Annie contrived to sit next to Hamish while Myrtle took the place next to Ken. He looked terrible, she thought. Grey, shaken. As soon as the engines started up she enquired at once if anything was the matter. After a long silence he answered so quietly Myrtle could hardly hear him.

'I feel as if I've been in an *accident*,' he said.

'Anything to do with Annie, could it be?'

Ken nodded miserably.

'Your friend,' he said. 'Is she a witch, or what?'

'She's a beguiler,' said Myrtle. 'But she's good, too. She wouldn't want to hurt anyone intentionally. It's just that no boy can resist her – well, you can see why. But then if she doesn't fancy a boy back – there's the suffering.'

'I never gave her a second thought. Never really looked at her, even. Until today. Then she has to go and sit next to me and next thing I know . . .' Ken sighed. Myrtle suspected his discovered tragedy was not altogether disagreeable. 'There's a Keats ode,' he said, 'one of my punishments. "When a melancholy fit shall fall, sudden from heaven like a shower of rain, then glut thy sorrow on a morning rose . . ." Bloody stupid suggestion. Unlike Keats.'

'Quite,' said Myrtle. 'You need more than a morning rose.' She looked at his miserable face. 'I'll tell you something about Annie: for all that she's flattered, she gets a bit overwhelmed by all the adulation. The thing that really intrigues her is a boy who doesn't seem to notice her. So maybe if you go on lying low for a while, give no indication she's made you feel so . . . sick, when she's older and wiser it might come into her head that Ken Mcleoud is the one to interest her.'

Ken gave a pessimistic shrug, but half a smile.

'Thanks for the tip,' he said. And then, a while later he asked: 'Do you know that melancholy ode?'

'Lord, yes: aye, I do. It was after I first read it I thought to myself I'd like to be a teacher.' Ken seemed to be listening intently. His interest encouraged Myrtle to confide further. 'I was in the library one day and I pulled down this book of Keats' poems – I'd never heard of the man. I began reading – I couldn't stop. I took the book home – I couldn't learn so much by heart, like you, but I know it all, it goes all through me. And I thought, why don't we do this stuff at school? Why do they think it's too difficult, we wouldn't like it? And then I thought, if I can get so much out of it there must be others who can too, if only they had the chance . . . That's why it came to me maybe I should be a teacher, explain poetry to children, help them to love books.' By now Myrtle's cheeks were crimson. She knew she had gone too far and would regret this silly outburst to a boy she had scarcely exchanged a word with before today. But he was listening sympathetically as he dug rims of sand from under his nails with the point of a pencil.

'You'n me've got quite a lot in common,' he said.

Myrtle felt the heat of relief. He wasn't scoffing, as Annie would have done had Myrtle confessed such things to her. He seemed to understand. But then she silently laughed herself to scorn – quite a lot in common was of very little worth if you were big and clumsy and generally known to be the plainest girl in the class. Quite a lot in common with Ken would get her nowhere, and the pity of it would remain one more secret in her heart, for she warmed to his sympathy and liked the good nature in his brown eyes.

After this exchange on the bus Ken did not mention Annie again.

But the day at the sea marked some profound turning point in his life. The cheekiness, the spirit went out of him. He no longer entertained the class, he no longer committed deeds fit for punishment. He became one of those whom Annie described as 'no one in particular'. Myrtle watched his confusion and pain with concern. But his aloofness was not easy to broach. As he did not seem to require friends, she felt diffident about the offering of comfort. She liked to think, though, that he trusted her, and one day they would talk to each other again. Myrtle waited patiently, but Ken did not approach her. It was as if their talk on the bus had never taken place. That caused Myrtle herself a certain chafing of regret. But she never allowed herself the indulgence of much hope where boys were concerned, and the feeling faded within a few months. She was able to continue waiting for him to confide in her again with a steady heart.

For once, Myrtle is in Annie's house. Here, they don't play cards. They stand edgily in the box of a kitchen. The microwave has been placed in a position that catches the eye as soon as you're through the door. It has displaced familiar objects, Myrtle notices. A wooden salad bowl filled with wax fruits, and a china jug from Portugal, both things that once were Annie's pride, have now been relegated to distant shelves. A clear space has been left round the microwave, the better to appreciate the symbol of high technology and even easier living.

A bright sun polishes the lime green of the formica tops and the plastic cupboards, and reflects on to Annie's face and bare arms. She boils the kettle with the air of one who is reluctantly using an inferior machine. Had Myrtle wanted a cup of coffee, Annie would have boiled the milk in the microwave, just to prove how brilliant it was at boiling milk. Myrtle smiles to herself. She finds Annie's delight in a machine, undimmed in the six months since she has bought it, touching. Their various simple pleasures are, and have always been, so different, she thinks. Annie regards nature, landscape, walks, as utterly boring. For her the pleasure of an afternoon alone is to lie on her leatherette sofa studying a high-class mail-order catalogue, microwaved pie to hand, feet warmed by the heat of a gas fire that she likes to think looks like the real thing. Gregarious by nature, she avoids aloneness as much as possible. She has never been able to understand Myrtle's odd way of striding off for an afternoon by herself: for her, the vicarious experience is enough. 'You've been five miles in this weather?' she would say. 'Wonderful! I can imagine just how you feel.'

This morning the lime-tinged Annie has something on her mind that cannot wait until they are settled.

'I'm the one to be causing a scandal now,' she says.

Myrtle assumes a look of particular interest. Nothing puts Annie out so much as a blank face in response to an important fact or opinion.

'Martin,' she says, and hands Myrtle pale tea that sways in a cup stamped with an orange flower of no known variety. 'Ran into him not an hour ago. We walked a good hundred yards down the street together, seen by everybody. He was on his way to Creele to buy some crabs for his tea, he said. He said he'd seen you up at the cemetery, and that was nice.' She smiles.

'Big scandal,' says Myrtle, smiling back. In joining in the joke she knows that Annie will be further assured that their recent squabble is forgotten.

Annie gives a beguiling toss of her pretty head so that the green light scatters into a translucent mosaic over her skin.

'To think how I fancied that man, once.' She sighs. 'So, anyway, to make conversation I tell him the news.'

'The news?'

'I would've told you first, but he happened to be *there*.' Annie is amusing herself tantalising Myrtle by drawing out the suspense. Myrtle can tell by the set of her mouth there is still some way to go before the eventual climax of the story is revealed. 'Let's go next door and sit down,' says Annie.

She leads the way. Each of them has one hand beneath their saucer, the other controlling the cup that is in danger of skittering on its bone-china base. Myrtle finds all this cup-and-saucer business tiresome. It's one of Annie's small snobberies. Some years ago, when fishermen were better off, Annie spent a fortune on useless knick-knacks, expensive china and cutlery and crystal glass, all destined for an unused life behind the glass doors of a reproduction cupboard. For *showing off*, Myrtle had once teasingly observed, and Annie had agreed. While clothes held no interest for Annie, status symbols of a household kind she found irresistible. It was her persistent desire to spend that drove Ken to his nefarious ways.

In the living room, as Annie now calls it (upgraded from the front room) the carpet is a frozen sea of blue and green whirls. A sofa and matching armchair are covered in expensive imitation leather the colour of cement. They are at an angle to the complicated fireplace, a patchwork of overdefined brick and filigree wrought iron that both surrounds and overwhelms the small gas fire. The wall above all this frantic brick and iron work is hung with a collection of horse brasses, though as far as Myrtle knows neither Annie nor Ken has ever had any interest in horses. The only indication of Ken's life is the single ornament on the mantelpiece – a miniscule sailing ship made from matchsticks, sailing on a fragment of blue cloth, the whole tiny seascape preserved in a bottle.

Myrtle sits down. The armchair squeaks. Annie, cup and saucer now held high, lowers herself on to the sofa. It greets her light weight with a different set of groans from the chair. Sitting down at Annie and Ken's, Archie once said, put him in mind of an orchestra tuning up. Myrtle smiles at the thought. It must be some years, now, since he made the observation. These days, the men rarely visit each other's houses.

Annie is twitching her spiky little ankle. Northern sky full of slow, drugged clouds, is bright through the panoramic window, illuminating her uncontainable smile. She can hold out no longer.

'I'll tell you what then,' she says, 'I've taken a job.' She shifts excitedly. A pale wave of tea flips over the aristocratic cup into the saucer. The sofa quietly moans.

'Oh Lord, Annie girl,' Myrtle replies at last, trying to suppress a sigh. 'Whatever is it this time?'

Annie, in her time, has tried so many jobs. Up and down the coast she has worked, for grocers, hairdressers, butchers, bakers and newsagents. She had a short spell – some three days – in the baked potato shop, a brief attraction designed for the tourists one summer. But the locals scoffed at the idea of paying someone else ridiculous money to bake a potato, and the enterprise did not survive its first winter. From there, after one of her longer pauses for reflection on the desirability of working at all, Annie graduated to the Breeks a' Serks shop, but soon left on account of its musty air that caused her hay fever. The last job that she 'held down' (as she referred to it if she had remained in place for more than a week) was in Ladies' Fashions, an elderly establishment in a staunch old building inappropriately close to the harbour. When the wind came off the sea, customers were in danger of their purchases being snatched from their hands as they left the shop. On occasions, floral skirts and cobweb scarves had been whisked away and furled irretrievably into the waters of the harbour. Annie, from her place behind the counter in Ladies' Fashions, enjoyed her view of the boats, the feeling that she was at the centre of some small but important part of life. Selling clothes, in her estimation, was a superior business to selling bread or meat. But she could not reconcile herself to the fashions themselves. Her boss, a Mrs Helen Grundy, had a distinct vision of what high fashion on the east coast of Scotland should constitute: that her opinions were not a little out of keeping with current fashion in the wider world, no one but Annie dared suggest. Annie took the liberty of pointing out, one customer-less morning, that here was evidence of her opinion: if things were a little more up to date, customers might more eagerly come running. Mrs Grundy was so affronted by such criticism that all she could do for several silent, raging moments was to stroke the stoat-paw brooch (mounted on a swirl of silver) on her lapel. She would, Annie later told Myrtle, have sacked her on the spot – but there was the matter of two dozen boxes of easy-iron blouses to be unpacked, and Mrs Grundy's elevated position in the fashion world precluded her from unpacking anything. Tension between boss and employee remained high, and furnished Annie with many a lively tale to entertain Myrtle. The end came in early summer, when Mrs Grundy asked Annie to cover the windows with thick sheets of transparent yellow paper that would, she said, prevent the merchandise from fading. Annie pointed out that, displayed behind the yellow glare of protective paper, the slumped dresses and lifeless cardigans would look even less alluring. Mrs Grundy could take no more of such impudence and asked Annie to leave within the hour.

It was always the employers' fault that caused Annie to leave her various jobs: they could never come to terms with the irregular hours she was able to work. Although compromises were sometimes aimed for, they were seldom reached. In the end, for all her charm and winning ways with customers, employers became impatient with Annie's singular attitude to work – she was doing them a favour, not the other way round – and dismissed her with mixed feelings. By now Annie was impervious to dismissal. It meant nothing to her, was certainly not a sign of failure, but the evidence of how unreasonable employers are. She could always get another job, she said, if and when she felt like it. And despite the lack of work locally, and her reputation for unreliability, she always did. Myrtle was familiar with the whole recurring pattern of Annie's working life. First, the enthusiasm.

'Come on,' says Myrtle. 'I've waited long enough.'

Almost imperceptibly, Annie shivers.

'The new café up at the museum,' she says. 'I'm to be a part-time waitress.'

'Waitress?' Myrtle is surprised. Annie serving others is a role hard to imagine. 'Making pots of tea, carrying plates of sandwiches . . . surely that's not the sort of thing you enjoy?'

Annie, choosing to ignore her friend's observation, puts down her cup and saucer with an exaggerated gesture of care, clumsiness banished at will.

'It's so nice up there,' she says, 'what they've done. Fresh tablecloths, homemade scones and cakes. The place always full. You feel life is *going on* up there.' She gives Myrtle a look. 'You're not being too hasty with your congratulations.'

'Congratulations,' says Myrtle. 'I'm pleased for you. I really am. Though I don't understand. You don't need the money.'

'That we certainly do. Ken is going to have to lay off his . . . business or he and Archie will come to blows –'

'I can imagine,' says Myrtle quickly.

'Besides, I want to see the wider world. It would be a way of meeting new people.'

Myrtle laughs.

'The wider world? It's just tourists you'll get up there. Not much time to chat between orders, I don't suppose. You could be disappointed by the bit of the wider world that makes its way to the museum.'

'Think what you like, I'm looking forward to it.' Annie's faint huffiness shows in her risen shoulders, the ankle that suddenly stops swinging. 'It's not often we get the chance to see new faces. The claustrophobia of this place could drive you mad sometimes.' She gazes longingly out of the panoramic window at some convivial imagined scene that Myrtle cannot envisage. Suddenly, she gets up. 'Come on, let's go out. I start Monday. No more free afternoons after that.'

'Where?' asks Myrtle, who has but an hour before she must return to her part-time job at the home.

Annie shrugs.

'The harbour, why not? Who knows: we might run into Martin.'

Sometimes, unplanned, Myrtle and Annie find themselves behaving like girls again. In the harbour lies the brown silk water of a low tide, exactly matching the mud beneath. They can see the bones of the harbour wall, steel girders fixed into the stone. On the wet stone steps they can see the sparkle of barnacles and the slimy curl of seaweed. There are no boats. The emptiness lends a misleading grandeur to the place. When the boats are in it becomes small, crowded, protective.

They walk closely side by side, the large woman and the small one, alert to the possibility of something to laugh at: the scene is too familiar for serious comment. A man in a municipal plastic overall of livid orange, a few yards ahead of them, switches on his machine. He begins to power-hose the empty fish boxes. The jet of water makes a savage hiss, air-renting as a dentist's high-powered drill. Steam rises, chasing low-flying gulls. They scream in protest. Annie clutches Myrtle's arm.

'Do you see who I see?' she asks.

Myrtle, following Annie's glance, sees Mrs Grundy slink out of Ladies' Fashions. Mrs Grundy looks about to make sure no one will notice her nefarious mid-morning break. She does not look seawards or notice Myrtle and Annie, but hurries off towards the newsagent, hand in hand with the stoat paw on her lapel.

'Stupid bitch,' says Annie. 'You go and hide yourself round the corner, make sure she doesn't see you on the way back. I'm going to fix her.'

It's one of those moments when there's no time to question Annie's demand: Myrtle simply obeys. She finds herself running, skirts heavily flapping. What has Annie in mind? Myrtle takes her position, panting, in a doorway. She will not be seen by Mrs Grundy on her return to the shop, but she has a clear view of Annie's territory.

Annie is whispering something to the man with the hose. Myrtle can tell from the way her friend tilts her head, and smiles, she's using her coquettish act to persuade him of something against his better judgement. Then she sees them both laugh. Annie briefly touches the orange plastic arm, then darts away to a hiding place of her own. As soon as she is out of reach, the man points his hose to the sky and draws an arc of water over the gulls, who leap higher in screaming indignation, and a million curved sparks of water are silvered by the pale sun before they fall. Myrtle knows that Annie will take the hoser's gesture, the making of such a beautiful aquatic archway, as a compliment.

Mrs Grundy comes out of the newsagent. A magazine is under one arm of her emerald jacket. Her free hand still clutches the stoat paw. She totters uncomfortably across the uneven ground, eyes down. Daft shoes for such a place, Myrtle thinks. Serve the snooty woman right if she comes a cropper.

The hosing man has his back to Mrs Grundy, apparently concentrating his water jet on stacked boxes that face the sea. How he hears her unsure step Myrtle will never know. But without turning his body, his hosing arm swerves to the left – an involuntary movement, it seems – then speeds back to its old position. An arc of sparkling water catches Mrs Grundy's high-fashion jacket with its full force, at once darkening the terrible emerald stuff and disarranging the neat package of her hair. Her plum mouth opens, but her scream is killed by the noise of the jet. The damp magazine falls open-winged to the ground. She hobbles, bent double with unheard curses, to the safety of her shop.

Annie and Myrtle run from their hiding places, meet in a laughing embrace. Tears are falling from Annie's eyes, mascara zig-zags down her cheeks. She gives a little skip, just as she did as a child when she was pleased, so that for a moment her eyes are almost on a level with Myrtle's. Myrtle sways in her mirth, joy at the silly prank scattering inside her, making her weak, keeping her closely locked to the small Annie in her arms. It all comes back, the fun of their childhood. For several hours the aching, the anxiety, the longing for Archie, have been curtained off, unable to disturb.

'It's good to know we can still be so daft, sometimes,' says Myrtle, the words all cracked up in the laughter.

'Magic,' says Annie.

A moment later they are on their separate ways. Myrtle reaches the corner where she must branch off up the hill. Still buoyant from the happy encounter, she turns to give Annie a final wave. But Annie, back to her, is waving to someone else, and does not see. Myrtle screws up her eyes, inexplicably put out. She focuses on the distant figure of a man carrying a heavy box. It is Martin. Myrtle thinks he nods his head in Annie's direction, but from this distance she cannot be sure.

When Archie is away Myrtle wakes every morning at four thirty. This is the time, she knows, that his first shift begins and she likes to feel he is in her thoughts as he wakes. For a while she lies imagining him brutally disentangling himself from his duvet – that does little to disguise the discomfort of the bunk – and taking a single step to the vile little sink whose tap provides a thread of water to splash on his face. She thinks of him pulling on his trousers and salt-stiffened jersey before pushing an egg round the frying pan that none of them ever considers cleaning. She sees him eating fast, efficiently, mopping up a yolk with a piece of sliced bread favoured by the mates, stomach lurching in time with the rise and fall of the boat. Myrtle imagines it all so hard that sometimes she feels she has become bodyless, weight-less. She is transported out to sea, she's an invisible passenger. It's only when she slides a foot to Archie's side of the bed and finds the sheet, smooth and chill, that she knows she is not there, miles out at sea with Archie, but here, alone The powerful feeling has tricked her again. It is these tricks of the mind, so mysteriously strong and com-forting while the illusion lasts, that Myrtle considers her kind of magic. (She can hear the way Annie says *ma-gic*: it chinks in her head like small beads. Annie's kind of magic, though, is quite different from her own.)

A small breeze through the open window makes the curtains pucker: their gathers are puffed up with air. Soon she must pull them back, begin the day, try to shuffle small tasks into the kind of order that will best speed the hours. Her hand moves from her own lonely pillow to the plumped-up hillock of Archie's. Denied his presence, her body is morose. There is no vigour in her blood. Without him, she moves less keenly by day, lies more heavily by night.

It's five o'clock. Myrtle shuts her eyes but knows that she will not sleep again. Archie is at the galley sink now, rinsing his greasy plate. Or perhaps he is already on deck, zipped into oilskins, assessing sea, sky, fish . . . She never likes to question the exact order of his day for fear he should guess her reasons. With a great effort of will Myrtle puts Archie from her mind, and thinks of Annie.

Magic: the word resounds again – the magic of Annie. There are few days when her extraordinary powers are not reflected upon by Myrtle. For years she has tried to analyse them, for years she has failed. But then perhaps the gift of enchantment, which is bestowed upon very few, is not meant to be analysed, but accepted as a gift that should exist without question. All the same, Myrtle is permanently intrigued. She watches constantly for clues, but the clues give no real answer. What is it about Annie that draws people of both sexes and all ages to her, wanting to please her, wanting to be in her presence? The extraordinarily pretty face is obviously the first signal, but it is far from the whole solution. The solution – and by now, after so many years of trying, Myrtle suspects she is beginning to understand – is to do with the feeling Annie unconsciously conveys that she is the centre of an important part of the universe, and whoever is with her shares that place. Myrtle remembers so well that (then amorphous, inexplicable) feeling as a child: with Annie at her side, she was certain she was at the centre of life, in some kind of mainstream place, even though reality, a small Scottish fishing village, said this logically was not so. In Annie's company, she felt important, courageous. Without her, time was flatter, duller. Annie brought a gladness to bear wherever she was, and it brushed off on others like gold dust. The fact that she was petulant, spoilt, sometimes ill-mannered, frequently thoughtless and constantly selfish made no difference. Annie's mysterious quality of life-enhancement was so strong that her faults were forgiven. Boys, snubbed by her, ridiculed and generally spurned, never gave up hope that at some future time they would be forgiven. To this day there were married fishermen in the village who would confide that Annie, in their youth, was the love of their life: Ken was regarded as the luckiest man on earth. While teachers and other grown-ups – in particular Dot Stewart, who feared Annie's influence over Myrtle – declared they could 'see right through her', they were no less enchanted than Annie's contemporaries when Annie chose to concentrate upon them. Nowadays, no matter how Myrtle disapproved of her friend's behaviour, or was irritated by her self-centredness, she still felt a sense of infinite loss without her. So whatever rows or disagreements they had, Myrtle found she could never go for more than a few days before returning to Annie – who bore no grudges when Myrtle berated her, and was always pleased to see her back. They would resume their old pattern as if there had never been a disruption: games of cards, cups of tea, occasional spontaneous events such as the hosing of Mrs Grundy. Annie would forever scoff at Myrtle's superior intellect, provoking her admonition with too much talk of material matters – the marvel of the microwave or the price of Janice's new boots. But even when Annie's trivial chatter most annoyed Myrtle she felt the warmth of her presence which had been essential to her since early childhood, and she could not imagine life without such nourishment. Myrtle liked to think – though she could not know for certain – that Annie would feel equally deprived were she to lose her own devotion, which she could count on at all times.

Myrtle's own experience with boys had been almost entirely vicarious. In the last couple of years at school, still too lacking in attraction for any girl to think of her as competition, she found herself in the role of confidante, adviser. (This last role amused her. On what experience could she base her advice?) But her peers were grateful for her careful listening, her considered opinion. For such services rendered she won a measure of popularity, and in her turn was grateful for that.

Of all the vicissitudes of young love that Myrtle so attentively listened to, there was none half so interesting, so amazing, as Annie's. There was not a boy in the class who had not at some time been beguiled by her, tried his luck, been rejected but still lived in hope. Since the age of seven Annie had been receiving notes from boys throughout the school. She used to gather them together, a day's takings, small, crumpled bits of paper torn from exercise books inscribed with passionate and ill-spelt declarations. After school she and Myrtle would go to their hiding place behind a bush in the Stewarts' garden, and read through them. *You are the cristal in my heart; I shall love you till the world stops and you and me are left alone on a sea of eternitty; Please come to the moon and back with me, I will buy you roller skates when I am a rich man; When I look at you in maths or some lesson my heart begins to pound and my legs go weak and I feel ill as if I had a fever, I love you so.* At first, Annie enjoyed the notes: they made her squeal with laughter. But over the years, as there was no decrease in their delivery, she grew blasé. They began to bore her. Often she would screw up a whole collection without reading them. 'Same old thing,' she told Myrtle. 'Nothing very original. There's no real romance to be found in this place.'

It was real romance, she confessed to Myrtle a thousand times, that she was after. Her disappointment was to find that her suitors were not of like mind. All they wanted, as quickly as possible, was sex – no hanging about. Annie, who had made flirting into her highest art, let them have a little of their way. (By the time she was sixteen, she once confessed to Myrtle, she had kissed twenty-three boys in the school. But only kissed.) Their impatience was their undoing. No sooner had they made their carefully plotted pass, clutched her with sweaty hands, clashed brace-bound teeth with hers, ground their restless hips against her and whimpered oh, so soppily, Annie's interest died. She would push them away, regard their silly look of frustrated desire with undisguised scorn. Several boys, realising their impetuousness had lost her for good, were reduced to tears. Annie had no pity. Rather, her contempt was increased. She would run away, laughing, to tell Myrtle details of the latest pathetic attempt at seduction.

There were two boys in the class who never attempted to kiss Annie: Archie Duns and Ken Mcleod. Archie, alone of all the boys in the school, did not fancy Annie. When asked why – a question he was often asked – he declared her too small, too spoilt and too flirtatious. He admitted her looks were exceptional, but looks were not what interested him as much as kindness and calm. For such sentiments he was considered by his friends to be a fool. Annie, aged twelve, lured by Archie's resistance, did once offer her mouth behind the coal shed. But it was her turn to be rejected. Archie, who had no intention of becoming another number on her list of snubbed suitors, told her very firmly to go away. It was three days before Annie, more amused than humiliated, was able to bring herself to pass on this information to Myrtle. She'd never really *fancied* Archie, she said – too dour. She was just annoyed he ignored her so blatantly. All she was after was a quick snog to prove to herself she could get anyone she wanted.

As for Ken, since the day out at St Andrews, he had been so tortured by love for Annie it was impossible for him to speak to her. If by chance he found himself close to her, he would move quickly away. Surrounded as always by her admirers, it took Annie some time to notice Ken's avoiding tactics. When she did, she found herself, at last, faintly intrigued. Why was he so unforthcoming? His lack of response to her most coquettish appeals became something of a challenge – only a *wee* challenge, she told Myrtle. Ken was nothing particular, she said. But for the fun of it she made a few overtures. They were always met with silent blushes. Eventually she gave up, left him alone, puzzled. Myrtle advised her there was no point in fretting over one shy boy when she could have her choice among so many who were eager. Even as she produced that small homily, which Annie accepted with a winning smile, Myrtle suspected her own motives. She was aware that, deeply embedded beneath her altruistic good sense, some small hope had risen from the brief closeness of confession on the bus. She also knew that for self-preservation she must do everything she could to ensure this hope did not flower.

By now it is seven o'clock. Myrtle is in the kitchen alone at the table. Archie will have been at work for three hours. He may be in the galley for a ten-minute cup of tea. He may well be sitting next to Ken. How do they get on, at sea? Myrtle often wonders. It's funny to think that the only two men in her life end up on the same boat. Not that Ken was ever exactly *in* her life. Indeed, to this day she cannot be sure that he was aware of the turmoil he caused. Her love for him was a secret she kept from Annie, from everyone. She knew the humiliation that could come from confessing hopeless love: those who confided in her had described it so vividly, pathetic in their despair. She was sometimes amazed that Annie did not guess what was going on in her heart, but then Annie, so consumed by her own preoccupations, was not a keen observer of other people's plights. Besides, it would never occur to Annie that Myrtle, so plainly unappreciated by boys, might fancy anyone. 'You'll find yourself a good solid husband one day,' Annie once told her. 'Older men aren't so worried about looks. What they want is a faithful wife who'll cook their dinners and mend their shirts and be happy with a quiet life.' Myrtle knew this was Annie's idea of consolation – she could not remember what event, or inadvertent hint of weakness in her own armour, brought it about. Naturally, she kept to herself what pain this 'comfort', this patronage caused.

Myrtle goes to the window, waits for the kettle to boil, waits for the familiar sound of its chugging steam to break the silence in the room.

Outside the sky is that naive grey peculiar to early mornings in October. Very high overhead (Dot always said it was worth checking the top of the sky if you wanted to judge the day), there is a lemony thinning of cloud, suggesting that later the sun might break through. Myrtle can smell the sea, but not hear it. The calm, usually some comfort, is disturbed by her thoughts of Ken. For the truth is that of late she has come to despise him. She despises his treachery, his betrayal of Archie. When Ken first became a mate on *Skyline II*, his loyalty was total. Now, since he has taken up his second job of 'removals and deliveries', that loyalty has become divided. He returns to the boat a weak link in a strong and devoted crew. Myrtle knows all this is taking its toll on Archie, though he never speaks about it in detail. Myrtle also senses the rows between the two men are increasing – though never at home – and dreads the moment control is lost, and in temper some violent act is committed. She also finds it hard to accept that the once quiet and morose boy Ken has turned into a weak and dishonest man. The nature of the 'deliveries' has never been specified, but Myrtle has her suspicions, though she cannot guess which law-breaking friend Ken might be helping. He is taking risks merely in order to pay for the silly status symbols his wife demands. He is a fool. He should condemn Annie for her greed, not pander to it. He should know by now that Annie responds well when she is thwarted in her desires for material things, if only for a time. Then Myrtle remembers that before Ken fell for Annie, in his early teens, he was daring in his lack of respect for authority. He was bold and imaginative in his nefarious acts. He enjoyed his punishments, he enjoyed his era as a hero among his peers. Now, there were no punishments – yet. And Annie was the only one to benefit from the profits of his foolishness. When Myrtle had loved him it had been during his quiet phase. Withdrawn, melancholic, his sad dark eyes had wrenched her heart, though shortly after the day at St Andrews she had given up all hope he would ever confide in her again, and her small, foolish spurt of hope had subsided into calm compassion, unspoken sympathy.

But she had always remained on the alert, lest one day there should be a hint of things changing. For a long time she had felt guilt about her advice to Annie to give up trying with Ken, although Annie's interest in him was so half-hearted it petered out very quickly. Even his embarrassed refusals to respond to her overtures could not spur her to keep trying. *Had* Annie, just for the fun of the challenge, won him over – well, that was a situation, in those days when Ken was Myrtle's only hope, she could never let herself contemplate. And when Annie finally declared herself not interested in pursuing Ken further, a warm rush of safety filled Myrtle's being. She herself could never hope for Ken to pay her the attention she craved, but at least there was consolation in knowing that Annie (who still had no notion of his tortured feelings, Myrtle having kept this secret) would leave him alone. This comfortable, if unfulfilling, state of affairs lasted three years. Then came the day of the gala.

Even as she remembers it, Myrtle pulls her shawl tighter and her large body tips forward a little. One hand spreads, and lingers over her ribs. There is still the echo of the pain at that time, a spectre of hurt that she buried long ago, for the sake of her friendship with Annie. But from time to time it rises again to haunt, to mystify – to make Myrtle think there is reason never quite to trust even the closest of friends.

That time: that summer's day. And later, the darkness of the days that followed Annie's innocent, gleeful confession: the past can be so cruel in its clarity, its tangibility. Myrtle, knowing her own foolishness, puts out a hand. She can feel the warmth of Ken's sinewy young arm beneath his rolled-up sleeve, where her finger dared to go. She can see – she will see for ever – the mixture of horror and guilt in his eyes as he bent towards her. For her, that was the end of the night. For him, it was the beginning.

There were galas, then, every year. As children Myrtle and Annie would go down to the harbour, watch as the boats, dressed up for the day in flags and bunting and flowers, sailed out of the harbour in their fancy dress. They made such a pretty flotilla, their normally chipped and battered hulls hidden under skirts of looped flowers, greenery and ribbons that fluttered with every bounce of the waves. Each boat had its chosen Fisher Lass, a beautiful young girl in some extravagant dress that was the result of weeks of indecision and excitement in its creation (and happily paid for by the skipper and crew). The Fisher Lass would sit at the head of the boat, refulgent face tipped up towards the horizon, unmoving as a masthead, self-importance fighting with queasiness if the sea was rocking. Behind her, family and friends would drink and sing. Soon entangled in the ribbons and flags, they would lean merrily over the ship's sides and let the spray cool their faces. All this Myrtle and Annie learned from Dot, who had herself once been a Fisher Lass, and went out every year on *The Skyline* until her husband died. When the children were older, she assured them, someone would invite them on to their boat. The young Myrtle and Annie, eyes never leaving the small, fluttering trail of boats until it vanished into the distance, longed for that time.

It came the summer that they were both seventeen – Annie only days after Myrtle. Archie Duns' father, Ben, had been an old friend of Jock Stewart. Ben's wife, who had broken her leg that year, suggested Dot took her place on the boat, and help with the food. She was invited to bring the two girls, whose intense excitement – they had been waiting for this occasion for so long – was increased to breaking point when they learned that Annie had been chosen to be the Fisher Lass. There followed several weeks of flurried plans concerning her dress, hair, make-up, shoes . . . She would make no decision without Myrtle. The supreme importance of these plans, which seemed to occupy every moment of Annie's thoughts, Myrtle found a little tiring. The excessive talk about scarlet or green or blue, about silk or satin or muslin, began to pall. But she managed to maintain at least a semblance of interest, and was as helpful as she could be. Her greatest contribution to Annie's happiness was in persuading Dot, a natural seamstress, to make the dress. Annie had long since despaired of finding the perfect thing, so clear in her mind, in a shop: Myrtle's suggestion that Dot should make something saved her from a nervous crisis. But when it came to describing the imagined dress to Dot, Annie was surprisingly inarticulate. The picture was clear but hazy, she said – by which time Myrtle, suffering from plan-fatigue, was too exhausted to point out the incongruity of this statement. Annie explained she would recognise the stuff she was looking for when she saw it, which meant dozens of visits to drapers up and down the coast, Myrtle her weary companion. Eventually she lighted on a bale of pale mint lace, and declared all the trouble had been worth it to find the right thing – did not Myrtle agree?

Dot, by now in a panic that there was so little time left, moved the furniture to the edges of the room, cut out the lace on the floor. As the dress progressed, an incredulous Annie came more and more often to try it on, querying every seam, every tuck, requesting that the neck should be a pinch higher, an inch lower, taxing Dot's patience to the limit. While Myrtle slouched in a chair looking, looking at Annie in new wonder, Annie jiggled in front of the small speckled mirror, frustrated at being able to see only her face and neck reflected through its tarnished surface. Impatiently, one day, she snatched it off the wall, then held it facing different bits of her body. As she could never, *never* see the whole, she wailed, it was bound to be a disaster. Myrtle looked on in sympathy, unreasonably cross with her mother because there was no long looking-glass in the house. Dot, tried to the limit by Annie's ungracious striving for perfection, let fly. 'Och, stop your complaining, girl, or I'll no' put in another stitch. And I'll have you put back that mirror on my wall this very minute or I'll –'

Annie's quick smile of contrition, her apology for her nervous state, quelled Dot's fury. She put back the mirror, not looking at her face. She stopped jiggling her hips. The skirts – pink imitation silk beneath the mint lace – froze round her knees, stilled. The room was strangely quiet without their rustling. But it was sour with the scent of Annie's sweat. Myrtle thought how lucky she was, being Annie's friend, to be part of all this excitement. She wondered if Annie had any idea of the extent of her beauty – in the dull evening light, at that final fitting, Myrtle realised with awe that Annie's prettiness, which she had become so used to she scarcely noticed any more – had given way to looks of wondrous and extraordinary beauty which would procure privilege for life. She looked down at her own hands – wistful, but she felt no envy. Then she looked at her mother crouched on the floor fussing with the hem of Annie's dress. She watched as Dot tried to put on her silver thimble. But her fingers had swollen in the many years since she had last used it. It kept falling off. Dot's own moment of shadowy regret was ended by Annie suddenly sliding impatiently out of the dress, standing in childish vest and pants, thin parted legs, bare feet hidden in a rock pool of green lace through which the pink silk petticoat sparkled like sunlight.

On the morning of the gala, Annie and her mother came round to the Stewarts' house soon after seven. While Dot cut sandwiches and Annie's mother inefficiently made a pot of tea, Annie herself jittered about unable to sit down for more than a moment at a time. Myrtle had never seen her in such a state of excitement. She refused to eat anything, saying food would make her sick. She kept touching the dress, which hung on the door: she'd never seen anything so beautiful in her life, she said. Every few moments she hugged Dot, which interfered with the speed of Dot's sandwich-making, and thanked her a dozen times. By eight o'clock she could wait no longer. She slithered into the dress and spun about, making its skirts flash and dance. Everybody laughed at her happiness. Suddenly, facing Myrtle, she stopped: held out her arms.

'What about you, Myrtle? What are you going to wear?'

In all the flurry of organising the Fisher Lass's clothes, Myrtle had given no thought to her own appearance. In answer to Annie's unexpected question, her immediate thought was what does it matter what I wear? I'm only to be part of your audience.

'I'll think of something,' she said. 'It's early yet.'

'You'll wear your jacket,' snapped Dot. 'There's a stiff breeze.'

'In that case, Annie'll be frozen.'

'The Fisher Lass,' said Dot, with some authority, 'will no' feel the cold. There'll be too much on her mind.'

There was already too much on Annie's mind further to concentrate on anyone else: silver shoes to be taken from their tissue paper, earrings to be secured, hair brushed to a shine that would defy the wind – so much trouble all for so few hours of glory, Myrtle thought, as she ate her own large breakfast. But perhaps that was the whole point of glory – the anticipation, the preparation. When the event was actually taking place there might be a sense of anticlimax. She would be watching Annie very carefully.

For all her early start, in the end Annie had no time to put on the carefully planned and purchased make-up. Besides, her hands were shaking too much to apply unsmudged shadow and knife-edged lipstick. The small plastic bag, a cornucopia spilling out its hoard of coloured pots and wands of mascara, was left on the table. But Annie was in no need of artificial aids to her beauty, thought Myrtle, as the two mothers and two daughters walked to the harbour. With silent awe she looked as if for the first time at every inch of her friend's face. She marvelled at the incandescence of Annie's skin, and the black-lashed eyes whose every restless movement sparked a chip of diamond in the blue irises. She wondered at the simplicity of beauty – the undulations of a mouth that by a fraction of a millimetre made it unique, the smile that pushed dimples into cheeks. This was the first day, Myrtle thought, that her friend was really grown up: excited but confident, cool, but generous in her appreciation of others' approbation, she exuded more potently than ever her mysterious sense of centre-life which warmed those in her wake. From today, Myrtle realised, things might happen to Annie that had never happened before. And she, Myrtle, would be left far behind. Perhaps she would no longer even be granted the vicarious experiences. Perhaps, now they were grown up, a new shyness would mean some privacy, and their close ways would diverge. When they reached the harbour wall, they stood looking down at the waiting boat. Annie was laughing at its fancy dress – the crew had done a grand job with flags and bunting. At the point of the bows a chair had been transformed into a magnificent throne of greenery dotted with flowers. Annie's place. Myrtle saw the goosepimples on her friend's upper arms, and was glad of her own clumsy jacket, and was suddenly afraid though she could not define the fear. She moved closer to Annie, in attendance, before the Fisher Lass was urged towards her seat.

Myrtle's own forebodings were further strengthened by the sight of so many passengers on board: a crowd of Archie's friends – Ross Wyatt, Sandy, Roddy, Ken, Hamish. Annie was waving to them, calling their names, acknowledging their catcalls of praise with a series of small bows. A gust of wind flattened her lace skirts against her legs and scrambled her hair into a thousand curls. The boys, looking up, hollered more loudly. Then Archie's father, Ben, made his way through the small noisy crowd, leapt over the side of the boat and ran up the steps of the harbour wall. In a quick, swooping movement, like a predatory bird pouncing on its prey, he lifted Annie up in both arms and carried her down into the boat. There was more laugher and cheering. Myrtle's own mouth felt rigid. She had to make an effort to prise it into a smile.

While Annie was seated on her throne, with much elated help from the boys, Myrtle and the two mothers, clutching boxes and baskets, made their way unaided down the slippery steps. Archie, the only boy who seemed to have no interest in Annie's enthronement, received them: first helping the two women with their loads, then putting a firm elbow under Myrtle's arm as she stepped on to the cluttered deck. Events were now beginning to spin in her head, but beneath them a heavy thought persisted. She knew that Annie, despite all the clamour around her, would not be too preoccupied to notice that Archie was paying her no attention. Only recently Annie had observed that the god Archie had *never* paid her any attention since the 'silly incident' when they were children, and she found this insulting. At some point his stand-offish behaviour would have to be challenged.

Myrtle also realised that there was no point in trying to sit near Annie in the bows. Annie was surrounded by admirers who had no intention of moving. There was no place for Myrtle there. She made her way to the back of the boat where Dot, legs slung wide to make a table of her lap, was already sorting food. Beside her sat Ken, pale face well back into the hood of his plastic windcheater. He nodded to Myrtle. She sat next to him – the only empty seat. This undreamt-of proximity to Ken stirred Myrtle in some vaguely pleasurable way. She would enjoy sitting beside him, would not mind his silence.

The boats set off at last, a line of seven of them, their loops of flags all twittering in the breeze, their Fisher Lasses upright in the bows, heads high, stiffly smiling. They wore dresses of bright primary colours that flashed in the clear light, though none of them had managed the subtlety, the style, of Annie, Myrtle thought with pride. Once the boats had left the harbour they veered off, a rougher line, though all in the same direction.

Distance quickly grew between them. Details of the other boats became indistinct, though the Fisher Lasses remained bright specks. Small clouds of gulls hovered above each mast, puzzled by the flags. Their screeching, above Ben Duns' boat, added to the cacophony of noise from Annie's admirers.

Myrtle had never liked the sea. As a young child, the first time Jock and Dot took her for a treat on *The Skyline*, she had been secretly terrified. She had stared down at the moving surface of water, trembling at the thought of what might lie beneath it, convinced that any moment a demon wave would rise, snatch her up in its curled fist of giant foam and drag her to black depths too horrible to imagine. But later, older, watching with Annie as the gala boats sailed away, she had longed to join them. That would be different, she thought. That would be safe.

That gala day, with the revellers at last, Myrtle's fear of the water had faded to a thin, untroublesome vein that caused nothing more than a feeling of tension which was confused with the excitement. There was a swell, and small coxcomb waves broke randomly over bigger ones, but they were playful rather than threatening. The boat rose and dipped with a rhythm that sometimes broke, and surprised. Then the boat would tip at an unexpected angle, jostling the passengers. On several occasions Myrtle found herself pushed into Ken's side. She apologised each time. He did not seem to mind.

But he kept his silence, so Myrtle concentrated on the distant Lammemuirs, and the way Bass Rock was becoming gigantic as they approached it. By mid morning there was a high sun, though the breeze was still cold. The sea, so far out, was a dense navy – so different from the dead brown water in the harbour. (Why, Myrtle wondered, did such blue not feed into the brown?) The light on the water had a strange thinness, as if it had been dragged over by a feather to enliven the blue, but not to change it. This light made a wide path across the waves which the boats seemed to be following.

Myrtle had not thought of sharing her observations, but suddenly she was aware of herself murmuring to Ken:

'Don't suppose the fishermen, out all the time, are surprised by all this sort of thing.' She nodded in the direction of the path of light. 'Probably don't even notice.'

Ken gave a reluctant movement of his closely packed lips, which Myrtle took as a comprehending smile. Before he could muster a reply, Dot pointed out that they were turning for home now. And indeed Myrtle saw that all seven boats were curving round, their backs now to the Rock and the mist of hills, and were facing the home coast.

Although her fear on the outward journey had been only slight, Myrtle felt a sense of relief now that they were going home. She helped Dot unpack sandwiches and pour out plastic cups of lemonade.

'Take something up to Annie,' said Dot. 'She'll be famished, behaving all this time like a regular masthead.'

Myrtle made her way along the deck, the wind keener now she was upright. The boys, still crowded round Annie on her throne of greenery, its leaves now splashed and sparkling, made way for her.

'She's gone all silent, silent as a bloody statue,' said Hamish.

'We canna get a word out of her,' said Ross.

'She's the dumbest Fisher Lass, that's for sure,' said Hamish, 'and it's very boring.'

Myrtle reached Annie's chair. She saw at once what Hamish meant about a statue. Annie sat upright, rigid, her head thrown back, staring at the horizon, apparently unconscious of her surroundings, impervious to the boys' provocative jibes which by now had replaced the compliments. For a moment Myrtle was alarmed by the look in her friend's eyes. They seemed to be fixed on some invisible place, another world. Her cheeks shimmered with a thousand tears of spray and the front of her green lace dress was darkened with water. Myrtle put out a hand, touched Annie's arm. It was icy cold, rough with goosepimples.

'Here, Annie, I've brought you something to eat,' she said. Annie did not respond. Myrtle touched her again. 'You're so cold. Shall I get you a jacket?' Still no word. 'Come on, Annie. What's the matter? Would you like an egg sandwich?' After a long moment Annie very slightly shook her head. The boys behind them cheered. Still with her eyes locked into some distant place, Annie murmured that she would like Myrtle to go away, leave her. The boys did not hear this request and Myrtle, defeated, moved away. One of the boys snatched the sandwiches and drink from her hands. They jeered at her for having no effect on the sleeping beauty. Fed up, now, with Annie's very long silence, they began to move back towards the boat's stern and help themselves to Dot's food and drink. Myrtle did not join them but stood by the cabin watching Ben at the wheel. Archie stood behind his father, smoking. Archie's eyes sometimes passed over Annie's upright little back view, but without curiosity or interest. Archie was some two inches taller than his father: broad and strong and stern, his blond hair jagged about his forehead. He smiled briefly at Myrtle, shrugged: a message, through the glass of the window, that Annie was a hopeless case, the least entertaining Fisher Lass he had ever seen. The thought flashed through Myrtle's mind that Archie was the most desirable boy along the coast, and had she been a different sort of girl then she might have allowed herself to fancy him. As it was, there was not the slightest possibility that one as exceptional as Archie Duns would ever have reason to be interested in her. He was beyond the scope of her own aspirations, though she did not doubt that Annie's eventual seduction would be successful. Ken, on the other hand – Ken with his nice eyes but sullen ways, his lack of friends . . . if she waited patiently, made no move that would alarm, then perhaps one day Ken would turn to her.

Myrtle saw the hump of a large wave, which had sneaked up on them from nowhere, now only yards away. As it tipped the boat in its hurried way, she could not help a small scream as she was flung to one side and fell on to a pile of coiled rope. In the next instant she saw one of Annie's thin white arms, pearled with water, shoot into the sky as the boat righted itself. Then she felt a strong hand under her own arm, and the nasty blue of Ken's waterproof filled her vision as clumsily he dragged her to her feet. She turned to thank him, but he was gone. And Annie's arm had returned to her side. Still rigid as before, her head was tipped further back. Myrtle had the impression that Annie could feel the clouds on her skin; she had become part of the blue of the sky.

Months later, on one of the many occasions they talked about the gala day, Annie explained she had wanted the journey on the boat just for herself, holding the brief hours to her so that they would be imprinted in her mind for ever, and she could call them up again whenever she needed them: sun, sea spray, cloud; the movement of the boat, the noise of gulls and boys. She went into a kind of trance, she said, which she could not allow anyone to break. The boys might have thought of her as stand-offish, silly, but that was the truth of the matter. Those hours of being locked into herself were the beginning of one of the best days of her life, and not for anything would she have spoiled them by larking about with the boys. That was to come later.

Early afternoon the boats reached a harbour some miles up the coast, the home of a few small craft that went out for lobsters and crabs. Behind the harbour white-painted houses clustered on a small hill. Some had scarlet geraniums at their windows, and front doors of yellow and green. It was a prettier place than Dot and Myrtle's village, and discovered by tourists who came to buy the fresh crabs, sold from a small hut, for bargain prices.

A makeshift dais had been put up a few yards from where the passengers alighted from the boats. It stood in a tangle of torn nets, lobster pots and coils of tarred rope: a precarious-looking little structure to which a skirt of salmon-pink crêpe paper had been inadequately pinned. Quite a crowd had gathered to watch the proceedings – tourists and locals. Dot, an old hand at every moment of the Fisher Lasses' progress, secured herself a place on a lobster pot near the dais. Myrtle stood beside her.

She could see that Annie, tripping up the wobbly steps with the other six Lasses, was showing some sign of nerves. She clutched at the damp skirts of her dress – the pink silk now shone through the lace more dully – and looked vaguely about with an unnatural smile. In bright sun, close at hand, the choices of the other girls' dresses were painfully clear – bundles of spangled netting, glossy red satin cobbled together with clumsy seams, wilted muslin fit for a milkmaid. Diamanté necklaces glinted above deep cleavages: one girl also wore a tiara. Annie was the only one with no jewellery and no make-up. All the girls' cheeks were buffed to a deep red-brown by the journey through the wind, and their carefully organised hair blew free from its various combs and ribbons. They were happy, bonny faces, as Dot observed: but only one was beautiful.

They stood for what seemed an age, shifting from uncomfortable foot to foot – stilettoes of pearly leather seemed to be the ubiquitous order of the day – casting expectant smiles at whoever they knew in the crowd, and giving shudders of exaggerated fear. Briefly Annie's eyes met Myrtle's. Her statue pose a thing of the past, she now allowed herself the odd anticipatory jiggle of the hips further to encourage the compliments of her admirers, proud of her now, which flew up from the crowd.

'This part always takes far too long,' said Dot. 'It's terrible up there, the waiting.'

'Do you reckon Annie's going to win?' Myrtle's own heart was beating very fast. She could imagine just how it was for Annie, up there on the stage, so many calculating eyes upon her.

'You can never account for the judges' taste. They might think Annie too wee for a good Lass. I've seen certain winners disappointed.'

There was a movement in the crowd. The harbour master, another man and two women who, with undisguised looks of self-importance had been conferring near the crab stall, now moved with self-conscious steps, as if they felt they were famous, towards the dais. The harbour master alone mounted the steps – the added weight of his fellow judges would have meant disaster. Revelling in the attention, he slowly shuffled a few scraps of paper on which, it was plain, nothing was written. He took his time, the harbour master: milking his brief moment of eminence, enjoying the sudden hush, palpitating with the importance of his imminent announcement. Get on with it, you old sod, Myrtle thought, and others began to express the same sentiment. But the master of ceremonies – and as there were few ceremonies in his small harbour to be performed he was naturally keen to make the most of it – started with some hesitant little speech about tradition, the necessity of maintaining old-world customs in this lacklustre age, and so forth. Myrtle, her ears pounding with impatience for the climax of his declaration, missed the sonorous words that led up to the announcement of the winner. But she saw the harbour master bend to take the banner from someone in the crowd, and approach Annie with a lascivious smile on his face. There was a roar of approbation that drowned the squealing of the gulls. Dot jumped up from the lobster pot, jumping higher than she had for years, shouting Annie's name like a wild thing. Myrtle, silent but clapping her hands, saw the harbour master fumbling to put the banner over Annie's head, and Annie impatiently pull it into position herself. Fisher Lass 197– was now loud across her bosom. The harbour master then handed her a shield which would later have her name engraved on its silver face. For a second Annie held this away from her, smiling at her own reflection. Then she moved quickly to the very edge of the dais, shut her eyes and stretched both thin arms above her in a gesture of ecstasy.

She opened her mouth to scream with joy, but the scream went unheard in the general noise and excitement. Then she leapt, impossibly high, into the sky, eyes still shut. A dozen arms shot up to catch her. But somehow, mid air, her body twisted, avoiding them all. Annie fell on to a bare patch of cobbles at the side of the dais. Instantly a chaos of admirers were there to retrieve her. Myrtle caught sight of her shocked face and a badly grazed arm. Her own help was unnecessary for the moment. She moved her eyes from the writhings of the crowd and saw that Archie was walking beside his father towards the harbour's edge. And that Ken, still in the safety of his plastic hood, was talking to a fisherman by the crab stall, plainly not interested in Annie's triumph or her fall.

That evening there was the traditional gala dance at The Seafarers' Hotel. The place was crowded with the friends and relations of the Fisher Lasses who had been on the boats, and many others besides. It was evident that most of the Lasses had spent the afternoon celebrating. One of them, who had to be supported to the supper room, dissolved on to a chair and fell asleep at once. Unconscious of the merriments of the evening, her presence served as a reminder of what could happen to an overexcited Fisher Lass. One look at the slumped figure in the corner, in her slippery pink dress – which by cruel coincidence exactly matched the spikes of gladioli that rose in a giant halo behind her drooping head – and they sipped more slowly at their beer or wine.

Annie herself had had nothing but tea all afternoon, and a rest on the Stewart's sofa (her own mother by now was bored with the whole event and had gone home to read her new magazine) where she relived every detail to an attentive Myrtle. So by the evening her energies were restored. Absolutely sober, she was fired by an internal adrenalin. Her object tonight, she told Myrtle, was to win over the elusive Archie. And when she entered the supper room – entrance nicely timed, everyone else was seated – and made her way to the place of honour at the top table, there was a general gasp of admiration. Applause. Before she sat Annie cast her eyes up and down the tables, assessing her audience, it seemed. Myrtle knew better. She knew who Annie was looking for. Her eyes paused at last on Archie's back view – he had deliberately turned away from her, it seemed to Myrtle. But she had no doubt of Annie's power tonight. She would end the evening with Archie. Myrtle would have staked her life on that.

After supper the reels began. By now Annie's stand-offish demeanour had disappeared. She was revelling in the race among her admirers to be her partner. With good humour she tried to distribute her favours fairly. As she twirled up and down the lines, she bestowed smiles on Ross, or Harry, or whoever was the current partner, making each one feel he was in with a serious chance again, no matter how many times he had been spurned in the past. But Myrtle saw that Annie's eyes were also conducting secret hunts that were invisible to anyone else. At safe moments they darted quicker than a lizard's tongue towards Archie. Whenever a reel came to an end, Annie led her partner towards the place Archie stood or sat. Her proximity signalled many times her desire to dance with him, but Archie refused to recognise her invitations.

Myrtle herself watched the progression of Annie's evening from a chair at the side of the room. She knew that her place on such occasions was to be a spectator and she accepted this role with no bitterness. Rather, she was deeply curious. How would the evening end? Above all, she did not want Annie to be hurt by Archie's very obvious rejection. She had complete faith in her friend's powers, but by eleven thirty it was plain she was far from achieving her goal.

Dot came to sit next to Myrtle. She had reached the time in her life when a party is a place for keen observation from the sidelines, rather than an occasion to participate in the dancing. All the same, she found it hard to stifle memories.

'You should take to your feet, dear,' she said. 'When I was your age you couldn't keep me off the floor.'

'I don't like dancing,' said Myrtle, sullen.

'Nonsense! All young girls like a reel. Why don't you go over to the bar? There's a crowd of your friends. One of them's sure to ask you for a dance.'

Myrtle blushed, furious. She resented both her mother's concern at her lack of partners, and her well-meaning help. She had a headache from the bagpipes that sawed through her. She felt large and uncomfortable and longed to go home. But she knew she could not leave until Annie's predicament was resolved.

Ben, Archie's father, came up.

'I can't get Myrtle here on to the floor,' Dot said. In her chair she swayed from side to side, feet tapping on the floor, longing to get there herself.

'Perhaps she doesn't care for reeling any more than Archie,' Ben said. He turned to Myrtle, smiling. Sympathetic. 'Is that it?' Myrtle nodded, aware of the hot red of her face. 'How about you and me have a go at this eightsome? They're looking for a couple, over there . . .'

He was a kind man. Myrtle could not refuse him. Besides, she wanted to get away as far as possible from Dot. She stood, realising she was taller than Ben. He made her feel like an awkward giant, dingy in her beige skirt and white blouse. She wished she had made more effort, but had reckoned that not to be desired when you have made no effort is less humiliating than not to be desired when you have done your best to look alluring.

Myrtle and Ben joined six couples. One of them was Annie and Sandy. Annie raised her eyebrows at Myrtle. But before the flash of a friendly smile could disguise it, Myrtle saw her friend's look of pity. Myrtle, forced to dance with Archie's father . . . such a crying shame. The words were written all over Annie's face.

Never had Myrtle hated an experience so much in her seventeen years. While Annie's delicate little feet twittered skilfully through the steps, and Annie's lean back and arms bent like saplings as the boys twirled her keenly round, Myrtle's huge clay feet struggled to keep in time and place. The boys, who whooped when it was their turn to hold Annie, were silent when it came to Myrtle. She felt them struggle to get their arms round her waist. She felt them pushing her as if she was some piece of large and awkward furniture. Only Ben, old man Ben, gave her an encouraging smile when once again she turned in the wrong direction. Myrtle felt tears burn her eyes. She thought the misery would never end.

When it did, when the bagpipes stopped their dreadful wailing at last and the group broke up, Myrtle thanked Ben and left his side as soon as it was politely possible. She made her way to the crowd by the bar. If she helped herself to a glass of wine, she thought, and just stood, not moving, perhaps no one would notice her. And the wine would blur the pain. She drank fast, took up a position. A moment later Archie passed by.

'Saw you give my old man an enjoyable time,' he said. As far as Myrtle could tell he was neither scoffing nor laughing at her. 'That was kind of you.'

'It was kind of him,' said Myrtle. They both laughed.

'I've had enough of all this,' Archie said then, finishing his drink. 'Not my scene. I'm off. Like me to walk you home?'

For an immeasurable time Myrtle was unable to answer this question. It was the kind of surprise that was too great to be digested instantaneously. Archie, the most elusive and desirable boy in the school, the village, for miles along the coast, asking her, Myrtle . . . While disbelief within her almost snapped, and her cheeks burned outrageously, Myrtle thought very fast. Two very obvious things came to her at once: Archie was only asking her out of kindness. Escorting her home – he had to pass her house on the way to his – would be no trouble. And were she to accept his extraordinary invitation, Annie would never speak to her again. Even as all this was balancing in her mind – shuffling into position for a firm refusal, to be precise – she felt the heat of distant eyes upon her. Perhaps Archie felt them too, for he and Myrtle turned at the same moment and caught the full blast of Annie's look.

Annie was at the other side of the room, furious, puzzled eyes perched on the rim of a glass of lemonade. The knowledge of her misery was a physical blow to Myrtle. To have walked home with Archie would have been the kind of small shaft of excitement she could never have hoped for. She would have read nothing into it, known it was nothing but kindness on his part. But Myrtle would sacrifice anything to avoid Annie's unhappiness. She looked straight at Archie. A terse voice disguised her real feelings.

'I think I'll stay on a while, thanks.' She forced a smile. 'My first Fisher Lass dance – better make the best of it.'

Archie shrugged. He did not care one way or another whether Myrtle came with him. He just wanted to leave as soon as possible.

'Very well, then. I'll be off.'

Myrtle saw Annie's eyes follow his exit. She saw the tears. But in her own misery she had not the heart to go over to her friend and try to comfort, to explain. Suddenly she was exhausted by the whole day – pleasure or unhappiness, experienced vicariously, are more tiring than the real thing. She, like Archie, wanted nothing more than to be home.

As soon as she knew Archie would be well on his way, she slipped unnoticed from the room – there was another reel in progress. Annie, dancing with Sandy, again an uneasy smile on her face, did not notice Myrtle's departure.

Myrtle hurried through the arched passages, their patterned carpet moving like shoals of red and blue fish beneath her feet. Although she had drunk nothing but a single glass of wine all evening, she felt unsteady. Sharp lines trembled; wall lamps had the hazy, perilous look of jellies. In the reception area yet more gladioli were menacing as daggers. She ran towards the revolving door. Captured within two spread glass wings, she found herself going round so dizzily that she missed the moment of escape. Forced to go round again, streamers of light and dark fluttered through the glass, entwining her like maypole ribbons. And suddenly, trapped in two opposite wings of glass, was a figure, the face cut into jagged reflections. In irrational panic, this time Myrtle managed to slip out on to the pavement as the doors spun by. She was aware of a full moon, her own beating heart, the smell of sea in a black wind. Then, the other figure escaped too.

It was Ken. He was smiling.

'More fun than the reels, going round and round,' he said. 'Not my sort of evening.'

Myrtle smiled back. Gradually, the spinning of her head was slowing down.

'I've had enough, myself,' she said.

They began to walk. In silence, at first. The amorphous warmth Myrtle had felt in Ken's presence on the boat was still there, but it seemed to have slid to a deeper place. Above it, like a foolish frill, were more ruffled feelings concerning Archie.

'It was certainly Annie's day,' said Ken at last. Shyly, he took Myrtle's arm, but she could tell from his loose touch it was not her he was thinking about.

'It was.' Myrtle sighed. She slid Ken a sideways look. He was biting his lip. 'Do you still love her?' The unplanned question came out with a harshness that Myrtle instantly regretted. 'I'm sorry: I shouldn't have asked. It's none of my business.' But Ken was not perturbed.

'You don't stop loving someone just because there's no visible hope, do you? You keep thinking something might be possible, one day. The thought keeps you going.'

By now they had reached the house in Arbroath Street. They

stopped at the foot of the steps. In the light from the bright moon Myrtle could clearly see the fatigue of long, hopeless love in Ken's eyes.

'As I told you, that day . . . Annie's intrigued by what she can't easily capture. If you're patient enough . . .'

'But she's so many after her. The whole world's in love with Annie. Do you think she's ever actually . . .?'

Loyalty to Annie rose at once in Myrtle's throat: she could not discuss such private matters with Ken. On the other hand, he had suffered too long. He deserved some crumb of comfort. The devious serpent that thrives on the convolutions of all friendship stirred uncomfortably within Myrtle. If she could be the one to put his mind at rest, then his gratitude to her might even flower into some . . . closer friendship.

'If you're asking what I think you're asking,' she said, 'the answer is no. No.'

Ken's relief was visible. He straightened himself, grew taller. His face was now on a level with Myrtle's.

'Thanks,' he said. 'You've a good heart, Myrtle. Annie's lucky to have such a friend.' He put a hand over Myrtle's. She could feel it was strong with resolve, and felt pleased with herself. This was some compensation for the yearnings of the day. Then, so suddenly she was forced to totter backwards, Ken moved his head towards her and kissed both cheeks. She believed the edges of their mouths just touched. Emboldened, Myrtle ran a cautious finger up his bare arm, under the rolled-back sleeve: warm muscle under hard skin. Dear God, how thrilling it was. Ken pulled swiftly back. Her prying hand was left at a loss.

This was the first time Myrtle had been kissed since she was eleven years old, when Ross Wyatt's lips had brushed her forehead to win a bet with Jake Mackingtosh. The speed and unexpectedness of Ken's kiss left Myrtle with a feeling of ecstatic disbelief. Even as she began to climb the steps to the front door, Ken's departing footsteps merry chinks on the road, she wondered if it had actually happened . . . Only an hour ago Archie's invitation had stirred some hopeless new possibility. Now, that was dead. Ken's kiss may have been merely out of kindness, but the secret warmth for him, contained so long, rushed back. More than warmth, even. Some strange, effervescent feeling that made her catch her breath.

Wholly preoccupied with the sensations of her body, and panting audibly as she turned the key in the door, Myrtle did not look at Ken again. It occurred to her, for some silly, superstitious reason that she was in no condition to analyse, that it was important not to look on him again tonight. So she did not see in which direction he had gone.

Sometimes fragments of that day and night return: today, one of the three days a week Myrtle helps out at the Evergreen Home, it is with Myrtle in its entirety. The pictures push into her vision as she stuffs vein-laced old arms into cardigan sleeves of clotted wool, or spoons melted ice cream into flabby mouths. All day at work she suffers double vision. The kaleidoscope of the gala is superimposed on the reality of her duties. The white scars on a fragile leg are flecks of sunlight on the gala sea. The pink of a shawl is the pink of the gladioli that accosted her before Ken appeared in the revolving door. With her vision playing such tricks, Myrtle thinks perhaps she is sickening for something. She goes to the small room where tea and coffee are made – beverages, the matron insists on calling them. She sits on the only chair waiting for the kettle to boil. There is a strong smell of disinfectant. Someone has hung six blue cloths on a line of string to dry. Boat flags. Myrtle's hand is trembling. One of the helpers, a nervous young girl with a sheen of sweat on her top lip, rushes in. Mrs Bruce has been taken poorly, she says. Collapsed. Would Myrtle come quickly?

Clarrie Bruce is the last of Dot's old friends. As Myrtle feels for her pulse she remembers the toffee apples for which she was famous. She would bring them round to the house, one for Dot, one for her. Sometimes, even better, she would bring homemade doughnuts, warm and bursting with jam. She had bright green eyes, Clarrie: she and Dot were always laughing. As Myrtle pulls her up more comfortably on the pillows, she feels the regret of another imminent death. Mixed with it is the sickness of horror that ended the gala day. But that must be resisted for the moment, for the ambulance has arrived and Clarrie Bruce must be hurried away.

At the end of the long, lost day, Myrtle decides not to go home at once. Despite the low metallic sky she takes the road out of the village to the fields that slope upwards to the hidden church and the old manse. The gorse, so glaringly bright in June, is reduced to random specks of dying yellow on a few bushes. In the distance there is a slash of rapeseed cutting through the duller greens of the earth.

Myrtle walks fast. Speed might submerge the pictures, she thinks. But it's too late. They have gripped the day. Their blight will not cease until the story has rerun to its end. She walks with lowered head, the unclear grass running past her eyes.

What she did not see, or guess at, was the ending of that gala day. She observed that Annie was unwilling to talk about it, which was puzzling. Myrtle had expected her to relive each important moment a thousand times. All she said about Archie's premature exit from the dance was that she was briefly put out. Really, it hadn't mattered to her, she assured Myrtle. There would be plenty more chances. She had enjoyed the dance, she said. She was flattered by all the squabbling between her partners – who wouldn't be? But that was all. Perhaps Myrtle had misjudged the significance of the event in her friend's mind, she thought, and questioned her no more.

Three months went by in which nothing more about the gala was said. Myrtle was working hard, the penultimate year at school, for her exams. She spent less time with Annie, whose attitude to work was frivolous. When they did meet, Myrtle found Annie to be curiously withdrawn, edgy. At school she almost gave up her brazen flirting. All at once she was grown up, Myrtle reflected. Calmer, less thoughtless of people's feelings – though sometimes, when she caught a sly look between Annie and one of the boys, she wondered if something was going on that Annie had decided, in a new phase of life, to keep to herself.

But Annie's habit of telling all to Myrtle, demanding her opinion, was strong. At the beginning of the summer holidays they took a picnic lunch up into the fields – the gorse, then, flamed across the landscape – and Annie (whether by design or by mistake, Myrtle never knew) confessed.

'I've done it,' she said.

'Done what?'

'Don't be silly. You know.' She was plaiting three pieces of grass. Concentrating hard.

'Who with? Sandy? Ross? Harry?' Certainly she'd been much in conversation with Harry, of late, come to think of it –

'Ken.'

'*Ken?*' Myrtle held a sandwich half way to her mouth. She dropped it. Her fingers stung. She was made of glass, ready to break any moment. Annie shrugged, careless.

'It seemed like a good idea at the time.'

'When was that?'

'After the gala dance.'

'*After* –?' Myrtle could not repeat the words. Needles of sun pierced her eyes. Annie sat in so bright a halo that her edges were all shirred.

'I was getting fed up, towards the end of the evening, Archie behaving so rottenly and everything. I saw Ken leave – just after you, I think it was. But then he came back.'

'He came back.' It wasn't a question, but a dumbfounded echo. Annie had no idea what she was saying . . . what she was doing to her friend.

'All the others were arguing about who'd take me home, so I put an end to it all by saying I was going home with Ken as he was the only one who hadn't asked. He looked pretty surprised, I have to say. Blushed deeply.' Annie laughed. 'Well, the others ribbed him a lot, as you can imagine. But they eventually got fed up and left us alone. We started to walk towards home. It was quite awkward, actually, Ken being so silent. I began to think I would have done better to have taken up one of the other offers, though of course the only one I really wanted to be with was Archie. And he'd buggered off, the bastard. Anyhow, Ken was rather sweet. He put his jacket round me. Talked about some seagull he'd found in his garden with a broken leg. He'd been trying to mend it with a splint made from a pencil.' Annie laughed again. 'Not at all the usual sort of conversation you get with boys. Anyway, on and on about this seagull he went, once he'd got going, and somehow we were still walking – towards St Monan's. Ken said: let's go down on to the beach, such a fine night. From him, it didn't sound at all like a filthy suggestion. I really believed he just wanted to walk on the sand. So we climbed down. My feet were hurting like hell by now – all day in silver shoes, imagine. So I kicked them off and we walked by the water's edge. It was lovely, the cold sand under my squished toes. I couldn't be bothered carrying the shoes. I threw them into the waves. Don't know why I did that, I really don't. It was a spontaneous thing, just came to me. Throwing away such expensive shoes. Anyhow, it made Ken laugh. He laughed and laughed. Quite bent double, he was.'

While Annie smiled at the remembrance, Myrtle pulled up her knees in an effort to blanket the audible beating of her heart. She said a small prayer for strength. Please God, don't let me break down until I'm alone. Don't let Annie see what this means to me.

'We went back up to the stones – you know, those big flat stones – and sat down. The moon was so bright it was almost like daylight. If it'd been with someone I'd really fancied, it would have been pretty good. Ken was still laughing about my shoes. Or maybe he was pretending it was that and really it was something else. Hard to tell what's going on in Ken's mind. So there am I, end of the best day of my life, thinking here's the moon and the sea and all that stuff – what a waste. Can't end it just sitting . . . Next thing I know I'm asking Ken to kiss me. And he does.'

Annie paused, scrutinised Myrtle's face. Myrtle prayed she would think the watering of her eyes was caused by the hurting sun.

'And we do it.'

Myrtle could think of no response. She could not speak.

'It wasn't up to much, really. Bit of a disappointment. Ken hadn't a clue . . . Not at all what I'd imagined.' She paused again. High above them a skylark's sudden song cascaded down into the silence. Myrtle moved her eyes but could not see the bird.

'Then, well, it was over. No big deal. But at least I knew I could trust Ken not to slag me off to the others. I knew he wouldn't say a word. We got up, brushed ourselves down. Then an awful thing happened.' Annie bit her lip. 'He began to cry. Really sob. I said come on, Ken – what's the matter? It was horrible, the noise he made. I was glad no one was near. Just us and the sea. Took him ages to calm down. Then he said something about not wanting me to think it was just any old occasion – it meant more to him than he would ever be able to tell me. Well, I reckon he was overcome – his first time, too. And boys are sometimes more sentimental than girls. I said brace up, Ken, you don't have to say anything. I'm glad the first time was with you, I said, lying through my teeth. But don't let it give you any ideas, I said. It was just the end of my Fisher Lass day. We're not going out, or anything. He said that was fine by him, sorry about the crying, and we walked home. Sun coming up.'

Annie lay back on the grass, shut her eyes and covered them with one arm. Myrtle, convinced God had answered her prayer and given her strength, gathered herself. Caution tightened her words.

'Why didn't you tell me before?'

'I couldn't. I tried, but I just couldn't bring myself. I had to work out how you'd take it. You always used to warn me, so sternly, when we were younger. Remember?'

'We're seventeen, now.' Myrtle's lightness of tone was edged with laughter.

'Exactly. So you're not shocked?'

'Of course not.'

Annie sat up again, brushing dry grass from her hair. Their eyes met.

'And since then?' Myrtle could not resist. The agony of not knowing would be unbearable. 'You and Ken?'

Annie shrugged.

'Next day I asked him about his seagull. He said it had died in the night. End of story, really. I wouldn't go with Ken again. He was just the end of the Fisher Lass thing, like I said. He doesn't pester me, I'll say that for him. Seems to have gone back into his shell. Poor old Ken.'

'He's someone you can trust,' Myrtle said.

'More than you can say for the others. Most of them can't keep their bloody mouths shut, can they?'

'What about?'

Annie lowered her eyes to concentrate on plaiting more blades of grass again. Her demeanour suggested a closeness to shame Myrtle had never seen before. Annie answered quietly.

'After Ken . . . I found myself saying I don't mind. Ross – poor old Ross, he'd waited so long; Harry, Sandy . . . Don't know why really. They were all so impatient.'

The skylark had moved away. Myrtle's shock beat like wings in the silence.

'Archie?' she asked, at last.

'Not Archie. Yet. I've been too occupied to have a go at him. One day.'

'They must have been rather surprised, the other boys. You turned them all down so often.' If she kept talking about anything except Ken, Myrtle thought, she would manage to sound quite normal.

'I think they were, rather. Maybe they just thought the right time had come. Sandy said I was showing a green light. News to me.'

'Well,' said Myrtle.

'You're not shocked?'

'Perhaps a bit concerned. I wouldn't want you getting . . . I wouldn't want you to be thought of as some sort of –'

'Easy lay,' interrupted Annie, who knew Myrtle was uneasy with such jargon. 'That's a risk you have to take if you want a bit of fun. Just hope they're not laughing too much behind my back, comparing notes. As for the other – don't worry. I make sure they all take precautions.'

'Good. Though it's not *that* that really worried me.' A feeling of great weariness had begun to overwhelm Myrtle. She was eager to go, now. Be by herself. Reflect on all the things Annie had so innocently confessed. She wanted to be free to cry without restraint, as Ken had, to Annie's scorn, that night on the beach just an hour or so after he had kissed *her* . . . A kiss that had left an indelible imprint. Whereas to Annie his lovemaking had meant nothing more than the proper end of an extraordinary day. The unfairness –

'Sandy's top of my list at the moment,' Annie broke in. 'He's a sweet lad, funny. And a quick learner.' She giggled. 'We came up here one evening –'

Myrtle did not want to know. Quickly she stood up. Unable to bear any more, she hurried off, leaving Annie to the unaccustomed job of packing up the picnic bag. When she had gone some way, running, she heard a shout.

'Have I said something?' Annie cried.

Myrtle did not answer or look back, but ran faster into the lacerating sun.

The impact of Annie's confession and the thought of Ken's innocent betrayal consumed Myrtle for the first few weeks of that summer holiday. She and Annie continued their normal life together when Annie wasn't off with one of the boys. Myrtle managed to conceal her own disturbed feelings. The last thing she wanted Annie to know was that she had ever entertained the most fragile hope of serious friendship with Ken, the boy Annie had used merely for her own gratification to round off a memorable day, and then cast aside careless of his response. It was the first time in their lives Myrtle had ever kept anything concerning her own most private feelings from her friend. Until now there had never been any crossing of interest. Myrtle had kept her docile place as Annie's friend and confidante, never supposing that one day some boy might come between them. Ever since Ken had revealed his secret to Myrtle on the bus, she had kept it securely – securely as her own inclination towards him. As he had never spoken to her about Annie again, she had come to assume that his obsession – love, could it be called? – for her had waned. The friendliness he had shown Myrtle after the dance, followed by the kiss, had briefly fanned these hopes. It had not occurred to her a boy would kiss (albeit chastely) one girl and make love to another within a matter of hours. (Ah, such innocence, she thinks.) Then Annie's news, that Ken plainly still loved her, added to the shock. She felt deeply for Ken, she felt for herself. So much suffering, and it had to be kept secret. She could only sob at night when Dot was asleep. For a while, she was exhausted.

Then, perhaps because she was determined to be rid of the discomfort, her own feelings for Ken slid invisibly away. She awoke one morning to find they had evaporated. Her affection for him, and her sympathy, were still there. But the idea of having some deeper relationship with him made her laugh. She laughed out loud at breakfast, surprising Dot. Ken, with his lack of romantic impulse and his underdeveloped biceps, would never be enough of a man, for her, any more than he would be for Annie. There were visible fissures of weakness in his character she would have come to despise. Ken! However could she have contemplated . . .? How could she have maintained the slightly excited feeling ever since she was fourteen? She supposed the answer was that youthful fantasy has to have flesh and blood to feed on and Ken, being there, flattering with his confessions, had understandably become her object of possibility. She laughed again. Dot observed she hadn't seen her so happy for weeks.

In the void left by thoughts of Ken, Myrtle tried to sort out the sensations Annie's promiscuous life caused: alarm, worry, some diffuse thing that could be jealousy. Not that Myrtle would want or approve such behaviour herself, but she would like occasionally to experience the luxury of being desired. She would like the chance to say no. The boys who were now Annie's lovers were her own friends: they had given up their banter years ago, and treated her kindly – still seeking her advice, though not about Annie. But it never occurred to any of them to think of Myrtle as a girl: not one of them had ever given the smallest indication he fancied her, and this was a denial Myrtle had to endure. As for her friendship with Annie – it was a difficult time. In her daily exuberance, charged with hormones, part of the excitement was to relate every detail to Myrtle. But Myrtle had no wish to hear the sexual skills or failings of the boys she had known most of her life. She begged Annie to keep them to herself.

'Very well,' Annie eventually agreed. 'I won't tell you a thing except the really dreadful bits, or the really funny bits . . .'

They laughed over this arrangement. They still laughed, often. But it was the beginning of the parting of their old ways. There was now careful choice in the exchange of secrets, conscious restraint. At that time, too, Myrtle began to wonder whether there was an element of treachery somewhere in her friend. She despised herself for such misgivings but, unlike the unhappiness caused by Ken, she could not quite extinguish them.

Even today she cannot quite extinguish them, though often they taunt more wildly when Annie is not there than when they are together.

Myrtle walks back through the village weakened and ashamed by her day in the past. She sees Annie come out of the museum door, pause for a moment to glance at the harbour empty of boats. Myrtle curses herself. Had she been less preoccupied with her own pointless thoughts she would have remembered it was Annie's first day at her new job, and dropped in to see how she was getting on. She shouts. Annie turns. They run towards each other.

'It was marvellous!' Annie is all smiles.

'You didn't drop a thing, gave the right change?'

'It was all fine, fine. Wonderful. I'm going to be happy there.' She looks at her watch. 'Like I told you, the whole world is drawn to the museum café . . .'

'Really?' Myrtle knows well enough that Annie's whole world most probably has a single name.

'There was this chappie, Bruce, from the north. Gave me a huge tip, all for one cup of unspilt tea.' She laughs again, so happily. 'Well, we get talking. He asks me would I like a drink this evening. He has to be on his way tomorrow.'

'What about Janice?'

'She'll think something's held me up, first day.' Annie looks at her watch again.

'I'll go round, tell her. Tell her you're held up a while, I mean. Stay with her till you get home.'

'That would be kind.' Annie's mouth puckers. So often Myrtle has seen her like this, torn between right and wrong. To urge in the right direction is always counter productive. 'Only a drink,' Annie repeats, suddenly impatient. 'There's no need for that face.'

In Annie's house Myrtle finds Janice in the kitchen. She sits on a stool at the table, exercise books unopened before her, watching television. Her school shirt has one button too many undone. The sleeves have been rolled up to show the tiny wrists and forearms. Conscious or unconscious, such loosening of clothes? Myrtle can't be sure. But she recognises the signs. Janice's eyes flick from the television screen to Myrtle and back without interest. Since the death of the hamster her usual warmth to Myrtle has been noticeably absent.

'Mum's late,' she says.

'I caught sight of her. She said to tell you she'll not be long.' She paused, contemplating the untruth she was about to tell on Annie's behalf. 'First day in a new job – you know how it is. Sorting things out.'

'Aye.'

'Will I get you something to eat?'

Janice shakes her head.

'Not hungry,' she says.

'Or to drink?'

'I been home ages,' she says, 'but I'll wait till Mum gets back.'

The promise of considerable beauty in Janice, so apparent in babyhood, has receded. Now, at eleven, Janice is nothing like as pretty as Annie was at the same age, but she has the same wide-apart eyes fuzzy with thick lashes, and a languid smile, rarely given, that could lead to success when she is older. What she lacks is Annie's spirit, animation. She suffers from lethargy, or boredom. A dull acceptance of her lot Myrtle finds alarming. No childish ambition seems to goad her: her hamsters and her cat are the central interest in her life. She tolerates the attentions of boys but her natural disinterest means they keep their distance.

Myrtle recognises much of Ken's character in Janice. But, of late, there have been signs of her mother, too. Janice automatically strikes provocative poses. Even alone in the kitchen, expecting no one but her mother, there is an elegance in the slouch across the table. This, too, fills Myrtle with misgiving.

'Very well, then. I'll go next door. Don't want to disturb your homework.'

Her lack of admonition is greeted with a cheeky grin.

'OK. I'll start soon as this is over.' Janice hitches herself up – a
childlike gesture that dispels the disagreeably grown-up pose.

In the front room Myrtle lowers herself on to the sofa. The imitation leather gives its usual squeak. She contemplates the pile of
women's magazines on the table but does not pick one up. She wonders how long Janice will be, and who is this Bruce it's so important
to have a drink with – and what are they doing? She wonders what it
would be like to have a child of her own doing homework at the
kitchen table. She wonders if she would have been a good mother –
better than Annie, most probably, though at moments, at times convenient to herself, Annie takes great trouble with Janice, and even
encourages the child's slow, low-key laugh. Through the panoramic
window she can see the sky is darkening – the sullen dark of a gathering storm rather than the darkness of nightfall.

The distant scrape of voices stops. Janice must have kept her word,
turned off the television. Myrtle wonders what fragment of history or
literature or biology now taxes the child's mind. She is inclined to go
and find out. It would be good to discuss Janice's school work with
her. But she does not want to disturb. Myrtle continues to sit, unmoving, on the hostile sofa in the ever huskier brown light of the room.
Then there is a tap at the glass of the panoramic window. Myrtle
turns her head. She does not see a bird, but imagines it must be one
who has not understood the glass. But no: it's a small clutch of raindrops, the pebble-hard, vicious kind. They begin to tadpole down
the long stretch of glass. Their long, smeary tails, reflecting some
grain of light outside, glint like strands of tinsel. They are jolted into
sudden speed by a loud crack of thunder. The terrifying noise is
sharp, clean as gunshot. It is followed by a second of absolute silence.
This is broken by a livid crashing and growling (clouds head-butting
and breaking, Myrtle imagines) and rain squalls across the sheet glass
so hard Myrtle fears it will break. She jumps up to run to the kitchen:
Janice is clearly alarmed. At that moment lightning flares through

the room, flooding the dreary colours with its silver-milk liquid. In her dash from sofa to kitchen Myrtle feels she is drowning in this surf of strange light. Then there is darkness again, leaving her confused and afraid as she stumbles along the passage. More thunder overhead. There has been no warning of this storm – is it raging at sea? Janice's cries chime like small disjointed bells in the greater clamour of more thunder. Myrtle takes the child in her arms.

By now she is almost hysterical. She clings to Myrtle, hot-limbed. Her tears darken the wool of Myrtle's jersey. With each new bark of thunder Janice tightens her grip. When the lightening comes she shouts that it is blinding her.

Myrtle concentrates on soothing Janice: stroking her head, murmuring that it will be over soon. Janice is curled into a babyish position, legs askew, cheeks blotched with tears. A child who so often appears mature, now seems younger than her years. Myrtle thanks God she decided to come. What if Janice, so afraid of storms, had been alone here while Annie was out with this new Bruce? And what was Annie, at this very moment, thinking?

Half an hour goes by. As Myrtle and Janice cling to each other, it seems much longer. Anger with Annie, and pity for her child, clash within Myrtle. She rocks back and forth, willing Annie to return. Gradually outrage drains from the thunder. Its fury almost spent, the growling after each clap gives way to quieter murmurings. The lightning ceases its erratic flashing, leaving unlit rain to run down the window.

'I hate thunder,' says Janice, for the third or fourth time. 'I think it's coming to get me.'

'It was a nasty old storm but it's on its way out now. Listen, no more thunder.' They listen to the rain. Myrtle dabs the child's face with a handkerchief.

'Do you think they'll be all right in the boat?' Janice repositions her head on the comfortable expanse of Myrtle's breast.

'They'll be fine. They've been out in weather much worse than this.' Myrtle tries to sound convincing.

'I hope so.' Janice sniffs. 'I'm hungry now.'

'I'll get you something.'

'You're very kind, Myrtle.'

'Nonsense.'

'Were you sad to hear my hamster died?'

'I was. Of course I was.'

'I cried a lot. Mum said stop blubbing, Janice, it's only a hamster, we'll get another one. She couldn't understand it wouldn't be the same.' For a moment Janice puts her arms round Myrtle's neck. Myrtle is touched. Janice is a child who, like her father, makes little show of her affection. To disguise her feelings, to stop thinking of the child she and Archie will never have, Myrtle knows she must be brusque.

'Now run upstairs and wash your face. I'll butter you a scone.'

Janice obediently slithers off Myrtle's knee.

'We've no butter,' she says, dully. 'We're always out of butter.'

'We'll manage with jam, then.'

'Don't suppose there's any jam either. Mum's not so good at remembering things like that when Dad's away.'

Ten minutes later Janice is eating hot butterless toast, and Myrtle is drinking a cup of tea, when Annie returns. She is dark with rain, clothes dripping, sodden curls flat against her cheeks, exposing the fine bones. Her eyes skitter with guilt – well they might, thinks Myrtle. Were Janice not there she might have risked telling Annie what she thought of her as a mother, the anger is so fierce. But she says nothing.

'I'm sorry,' Annie shakes her head. Water patters on to the floor.

'Where were you?' Janice gets down from the table.

'First day in a new job – I was kept, didn't like to hurry away –'

Janice is out of the room. They hear her running upstairs. A door bangs. Annie picks up a dishcloth and begins to rub her hair.

'She wasn't alone. You were with her,' she says.

'I might not have been.'

'You said you would be. I would have come straight away, otherwise. Always ready to jump down my throat about Janice, you are, Myrtle Duns. Always accusing. What do you know about children?'

'I know that if you're lucky enough to have them, then they should be your priority. How was he, this important Bruce?'

Annie picks up a bunch of spoons and forks from the draining board, throws them into the sink to make an infuriating clatter.

'That's no business of yours, is it? But if you must know, he didn't turn up. Stupid bastard. Men. I waited. Gave him half an hour then ran back here fast as I could.'

Myrtle stands up.

'If I hadn't been here,' she says, 'God knows what Janice would have gone through on her own. She's terrified of storms, or perhaps you didn't know that –'

'Fuck it, Myrtle,' Annie shouts. 'I've had enough of your preaching! Your *goodness*, your *thought* for others, your *priorities* – they make me sick. You may be more saintly than me, I grant you that. But there's one thing you know nothing about: that's *motherhood*.' She is scarlet-cheeked, furious, panting. The damp cotton of her shirt is stuck to her lively breast.

Response flares up within Myrtle, but she fights against it. She hates such quarrels. They are rare, but unsettling. Telling Annie what she thinks of her as a mother will do no good. References to Janice, except in the most superficial way, are rightly taboo. She curses herself for her lack of restraint. This row will mean several days of unhappy tension, each waiting for the other to apologise, forgive.

'I'll go now, leave you to Janice,' Myrtle says.

Home, the telephone is ringing. Archie, on his ship-to-shore telephone, says the storm has hardly touched them: all is well. Myrtle sits heavily on an upright chair. The good news is clouded by the scene with Annie. Fury with those you love best, she thinks, is unlike any other fury in its destruction. She has not felt more weary, more drained, for months. She sits listening to the rain, gentler now, longing for the day to end. The telephone rings again, startling. It will be Annie – Annie to apologise. Charged with unexpected relief, she hurries to answer it. For a moment she does not understand, or recognise the voice, a man's. Martin? Yes, Martin, he says. Happens he's been given a fine lobster. Would she like it if he brought it round to share?

'That would be grand,' says Myrtle, not giving herself time to think. She is still confused, heavy. Stupid to have supposed Annie would make amends so soon. She fills a huge pan with water, puts it on the stove. It will be good not to have to spend the evening alone, but she doesn't much relish the thought of having to make polite conversation with Martin. As she waits for the water to boil, and for him to arrive, she becomes aware of a lack of sound rather than clean silence. The rain has stopped. Through the window Myrtle can see a scattering of stars in a sky suddenly cleared of cloud. Moments later there is a knock on the door.

Martin comes in carrying the lobster wrapped in newspaper. He is embarrassed to find Archie not at home. Had he been down to the harbour, seen no boats, he would not have come, he says. Myrtle tells him they'll be back tomorrow night. She smiles to see him clutching at his parcel, not sure, as Archie is not here, that sharing his supper with a married woman is in order.

'Perhaps I'd better go,' he says. 'I'll come another time, when Archie's back.'

'Put your lobster down,' says Myrtle. 'Archie'd never forgive me if I turned you both away. Besides, I'm in need of company tonight. I've had a day. Shall I beat up some batter for pancakes while the lobster's boiling? I seem to think you like a pancake with treacle.' How did she remember that? He must have mentioned it, the Lord only knows how long ago.

'Can't think of anything better, if it's not too much trouble.' Martin sits at the table, avoiding what he knows to be Archie's chair. As Myrtle prepares the food they talk about matters they both under-stand: the shortage of fish, problems with the delivery of marble. When they have finished eating, Martin congratulates Myrtle on her cooking.

'I could do with a wife like you,' he says, laughing. 'You should see the stuff I eat. Takeaway, takeaway, the occasional grilled herring. I dream sometimes of coming home and finding a supper like this on the table, a good wife to spend the evening with.'

Myrtle likes the Canadian drawl of his voice, less distinct now than when he first arrived, but far from lost. He has adopted a few Scots words which sound so peculiar in his Canadian accent that people smile when he uses them. She grins, trying to imagine him as a husband. Signs were he'd be a good one: faithful, gentle, sensitive to his wife's desires. Had Archie not existed, Martin was the sort of man Myrtle would have aspired to, though not with much hope. He was a rare figure in this small community: a target for many in search of a husband.

'You could do with a wife, aye,' she says. 'But you've not got one for the lack of offers, have you? Every girl along the coast was after you. Two dozen girls, you could have married, if you'd wanted . . .'

Martin looks down, reddens. Myrtle sees him as he was: blond hair, bronze skin – some had thought he must have Norwegian blood – diffident, shy, awkward among all the sea-going young men of his age. She remembers the excitement, as an unexpected stranger suddenly in their midst, he caused among the girls. She remembers Annie's unusual reticence. 'He's all right,' she said to Myrtle at the time, 'but not really my type. If he knelt at my feet and begged me to marry him, I'd not be interested. You'd not catch me emigrating to Canada.' She was utterly convincing. Myrtle remembers this declaration very clearly as she pours cream over the treacle on Martin's pancakes. She herself has eaten an unusual amount, and feels happier. The day has fallen away.

'None of them was right,' says Martin. 'I had a picture in my mind of just what a wife should be. None of them came anywhere near it. I could never bring myself to go for second best. And now it's something I don't think about very often. Happy in my work. Preoccupied. I've given up looking, I suppose. Given up trying.'

'That's ridiculous,' says Myrtle, sounding fiercer than she means to. 'There are good women about. One of them'll cross your path one day when you're least expecting it.'

'Perhaps,' says Martin, not meeting her look.

Later, when the dishes are cleared and the lamps are lit, they move to the wooden chairs (Myrtle takes her mother's old rocking chair) either side of the stove. Martin declines Myrtle's offer of a dram of

Archie's whisky, but accepts a bottle of lager. Myrtle herself makes do with a mug of tea. The conversation turns to Annie.

'I see your friend, Annie, darting about,' Martin says. 'A real will o' the wisp, she seems to be. Marriage hasn't much changed her, I'd say. How is she?'

'She's fine.'

There's a long, easy silence between them. Myrtle is in half a mind to tell Martin about today's row, but loyalty wins. She says nothing. Martin, the dark skin of his cheeks deepening again, nods his head. It occurs to Myrtle that he looks more weathered than many of the fishermen, which is strange considering most of his working life is spent in a shed. Martin wipes his mouth with the back of his hand.

'I suppose I could have married her,' he says.

'Married Annie?'

'Well, don't think me boasting if I say this, but there was a time when – if I read the signals right – she seemed keen.'

'I didn't know that,' says Myrtle, after a while. Her heart begins to beat as wildly as it did some hours ago, when Annie shouted at her. Irrational feelings of possessiveness consume her. Martin has always been *her* friend – hers and Archie's. She has never understood Annie's lack of enthusiasm – hostility, almost – towards him, though has never questioned it very far.

'Don't suppose she wanted to say too much . . . it was all very awkward at the time. I was younger, inexperienced.' He smiles briefly. 'Couldn't think how to begin to cope. Didn't have any friends, in those days, whose advice I could ask.'

'Annie is very . . . well, there's no one else quite like her.' Questions roar through Myrtle's head that she is determined not to ask. Somehow, she must keep her astonishment to herself.

'That's for sure.' Martin meets her eye now. 'I imagine you did know . . . about Archie. I mean, it was when she was all out for Archie, trying to add him to her list.'

'I knew about that – Lord, I did. Was she a pest, forever telling me about her pursuit of the elusive Archie?' Myrtle laughs so Martin will see all that – events so long ago – means nothing to her, now.

'The way she put it to me was that Archie was a kind of challenge. She didn't really fancy him, didn't love him – nothing like that. No pretence of any great feeling there: she said he was too solemn for her, she couldn't have stood his lack of smiling for long. But, Jesus, did she want to . . . just for the prestige, just to prove to herself she could get any man she wanted, I suppose. Then, I don't know why, she seemed to give up on Archie. Turned her attention to me, instead. Heaven knows why. I didn't do a thing to encourage her. Rather, I kept my distance.'

'That's always been the great encouragement, in Annie's case,' says Myrtle. She has to make a great effort to keep her response low and calm. She can see that Martin has no idea the impact his news is causing.

'Funnily enough, the impression I got was that she was a little . . . afraid of me. Nervous. There was no flirting. None of that come-hither stuff I'd see her exercising on others. Then the letters began to come. Strange, wild, beautiful letters. It seemed she thought she'd fallen in, eh, love with me. Deeply, hopelessly, she said. For all the boys she had accommodated – I remember thinking what an unlikely word for her to use – she'd felt nothing. Nothing. But for me – for some goddamn reason she couldn't explain, and I certainly couldn't – she was eating her wretched little heart out for me. She said nothing of this to you?'

Myrtle shakes her head. Her mind spins back to that time: Annie daft and laughing as ever, looking vaguely for a new job, having been sacked from the post office for unpunctuality. Annie drinking with all her short-time lovers in the pub. Drinking a bit too much sometimes, perhaps. But not unhappy. Certainly never mentioning Martin. As for writing good letters – the idea is beyond comprehension. Myrtle scours her memory for any clue, any incident of no significance at the time but which would in retrospect indicate the truth. But she can remember nothing. Only that Annie had always said that she, Myrtle, was the one privy to her secrets: her secrets then concerned the hope-lessness of inexperienced boys at sex, and if she couldn't win over Archie then she'd have to be off to find an older man. It had all been lightly said. Not a hint of hidden love. Not a clue that for the first time in her life her own feelings were unrequited.

'So what did you do?' Myrtle, desperately curious to hear the rest of Martin's story, feels this question is permissible.

'I have to say I was touched by those letters. Anyone would have been. Beautiful writing, poetic sort of stuff straight from the heart.'

Annie writing beautiful letters? It's hard to believe! Annie who never put pen to paper if she could help it: Annie consistently bottom in English, scoffing at Myrtle's love of Keats . . . Myrtle feels all understanding has been wrenched from her. She shifts abruptly in her chair.

'Does that surprise you?' Martin asks.

'It does, a little.' Myrtle's incredulity is so overwhelming she wonders that Martin cannot see it.

'She became what I can only call obsessive. Following me, jumping out at me at unexpected moments to declare this great love. Needless to say I never laid a finger on her – it wasn't that she seemed to want – or gave her one iota of encouragement. Quite the opposite. I tried to explain she was caught up in some fantasy. Wanting affection, I said, she'd fixed upon me as a figure to provide it, though she didn't know me at all. She wouldn't listen to a word of that.' Martin pauses, smiles. 'I'm no analyst, but I think I had a point. Father gone long ago, little love or attention from her mother – certainly no guidance. Then this great flurry of boys – quick fancies, disillusioning sex. What she was after was something more solid, real, though perhaps that was something she hadn't worked out for herself. So happened she picked on me, almost the only one she hadn't been to school with, hadn't known all her life. I got the impression she was fed up with boys just fancying her, just wanting her for sex. She's a romantic at heart, Annie. What she wanted was love. But I couldn't give it to her.'

'You didn't feel anything for her at all?'

'Only pity. Sorrow that I couldn't help. Of course I saw she was an exceptionally attractive girl, beautiful. She's still an attractive woman. But not for me.' He pauses for so long that Myrtle fears he is not going to continue. She fetches him another bottle of lager from the fridge. Presses him a little.

'So how did you . . . resolve it?'

Martin sighs. He opens the bottle, fills the glass then puts it on the floor without drinking.

'It had to stop. I was worried about her state of mind. Inevitably the end was untidy. She taxed my patience once too often . . . She came round to my place in the middle of the night, woke me up throwing stones at the window. She was sobbing, desolate. I had to let her in – didn't want my parents to be woken. She'd come to tell me of her new resolution, which was to wait for me, no matter how long. God forbid, I said, it's not a matter of waiting, Annie. Don't you understand? I don't love you, I never will love you, and all this nonsense must stop. I'm fed up with it, bored. I rather lost my cool I guess. I wasn't as gentle as I might have been. All I wanted was to get rid of her, stop her preying on me. As usual, my words had no effect. So I decided I'd have one last try at jolting her irrationality. I told her I loved quite a different sort of woman – a quiet, gentle soul who'd never flirted in her life. You mean *dull*? she said. Not dull at all, I said. Unattainable, sadly, but so entrenched in my heart I've no hope of ridding myself . . .' He petered out, embarrassed to have gone so far.

'I didn't know that,' says Myrtle.

Martin reaches down for his glass, drinks.

'No: well, I keep things to myself.'

'And how did she take the news?'

'She said I was making it up to try to put her off. She said it wouldn't make a jot of difference to what she felt – ever. Poor Annie. She was so white. I remember she was leaning against the wall, fists clenched, her head tilted up at me awkwardly. Then – well, this bit is rather shaming. Shall I go on?' Myrtle nods. 'I regret it – but I regret the whole thing. She said I'll strike a bargain with you, Martin Ford. Give me one kindly kiss on the cheek, and I'll leave you alone. I'll not bother you any more, she said. I can see it's useless, now. But one day you'll see how foolish you were to let me go – and I'll still be there. She sounded so . . . pathetic. I said I was sorry I had shouted at her, but I didn't know how to get the truth through to her. Then I did what she wanted. I kissed her gently on the cheek. But as soon as my mouth touched her skin, she fell away from me as if I'd struck her. She was suddenly a heap on the floor – fainted just like a character in a romantic novel. I gave her some whisky, brought her round. She apologised for being a nuisance. I couldn't help seeing how real her fantasy had become – girls don't faint away when they're kissed on the cheek, these days, and I felt for her profoundly. After all, I knew all about unrequited love myself, though I didn't tell her that. Anyway, true to her word, she stopped her pursuing after that. Left me alone, thank God. Avoided me for a while, then just acted normally as if nothing had ever happened. Though she did once ask me to burn her letters.'

'And did you?' Martin has stopped again.

'I did. With some reluctance, I have to say. They were so strange – not about her and me, so much, as about the tricks love plays on daily life . . . I doubt I'll ever have such letters again.' For the third time in the evening he reddens deeply. The magenta skin of his high forehead shines brightly against the blond hair. 'But that was all a long time ago,' he goes on. 'I can't say we're close friends, but she's not unfriendly. Her irrational behaviour, for those few months, was no more than an illness in the form of an illusion. Kind of thing that often strikes confused, unhappy people, I daresay. But it seemed to pass as quickly as it came. I doubt Annie ever gives me a thought, these days. Or if she does, it would only be to laugh at her youthful folly. She seems to be happily married to Ken, doesn't she?'

'Aye. Ken's a good husband to her.'

Martin looks at his watch, stands up.

'My, how I've been going on,' he says, 'tongue running away with me. I'm sorry. It's late.'

Myrtle goes with him to the door.

'And your own . . . unrequited?' she says, not meaning to say anything and not wanting to mention Annie again. 'I'm sorry about –'

'Yes, well, you get used to the insurmountable. You learn how to readjust. Even if the shade – is that the right word? – never quite goes. Anyway . . . thank you for . . . listening, whatever. I've never told that story before. Thought you knew it all, being Annie's friend.' He puts a hand on Myrtle's arm for a moment. His touch ignites a flare of sympathy – is it sympathy, exactly? – through her body. The sensation is faintly unnerving.

'Thank you for coming round,' says Myrtle. 'I like your visits. Thanks for the lobster.'

'My pleasure.' Martin inclines his head.

Myrtle smiles at his old-fashioned courtesy. She sees that once more his face is blazing. Funny how she has never noticed his easy blushing before. But then in all the years they have known one another they have never had anything like tonight's conversation. It is past midnight when Myrtle closes the door.

And sleep is not possible. Myrtle returns to her chair. In her confusion the words *betrayal, disillusion, disaster* swarm through her head. It's not the first time Myrtle has reflected on the treachery of friendship: that happened when Annie confessed about her night on the beach with Ken, and the news was devastating. But even in her youth Myrtle had forced herself to understand, and to forgive. Since then – foolishly, naively, she now sees – it has never occurred to her that Annie, the person she has loved so much for so long, has carried on keeping important parts of her life to herself: vital parts which Myrtle could never have guessed at. The fact that Annie, obviously so unhappy at the time, did not require Myrtle's help, or advice, or sympathetic ear, is a blow of such magnitude that she is consumed by a physical wrenching that leaves her no strength to work out reasons. She shuts her eyes and listens to questions that whimper across her mind. How many other events, loves, losses, has Annie not told her about? How was it that she failed Annie so badly? How could she have been so unobservant, seeing Annie daily, and yet not even suspecting that there were secret traumas in her life? They had sworn, at a very young age, to be best friends and tell each other everything, always. A childish pact, perhaps. But one they had believed in. For so long Myrtle had reason to trust that Annie was keeping her part of the arrangement. Annie confided so many thoughts (mostly about the nature of boys, though some about her wayward mother) that it had never occurred to Myrtle there could possibly be much besides which she was keeping to herself. For Myrtle's own part, she kept scrupulously to the agreement, though inevitably she had fewer secrets to contribute than Annie. Myrtle's life was duller. But – with the single exception of her feelings for Ken – she tried to supply Annie with private information. Sometimes, with a feeling of disloyalty, she would confess that her mother's eccentricities – the stringency over blankets, for instance – depressed her. Or that she was disappointed she had not a higher mark for an essay. Most private of all her secrets was to do with the shame of her large hands and feet. But she had felt bound to confess something of even this most delicate subject to Annie, confident she would receive sympathy. She had told Annie that while she knew she would never be the kind of woman who would attract men, and she had come to accept that, she wondered if physically she might improve? Annie had said yes, of course; everyone gets better once they've lost their puppy fat. Carelessly she said it. Annie was never much of a comforter with words – small, unexpected gestures was more her way. And in truth, Myrtle was aware from a very young age, Annie was not much interested in Myrtle's confessions. They were neither surprising nor exciting. So the pact soon became mostly a one-way thing. The whirligigs of Annie's existence, delivered in exhausting detail, far outweighed Myrtle's own diligent contributions. But she had no intention of ever breaking her youthful promise to her friend, so continued to supply some secrets, no matter how dull Annie found them.

Myrtle remains in her shocked, unmoving state for a long while in the chair. She hears that it has begun to rain again, a gentler rain than earlier, shimmying down the window panes. And she remembers – the memory gathers unfocused as smoke – but there it is, a day of light rain. She and Annie were standing looking in the newsagent's window. Annie had red, puffy eyes. She said she had some infection: already they had been to the chemist for ointment. Outside the newsagent Annie was acting strangely. She was whispering out loud all the names of the magazines. Her face was very pale. Myrtle asked what was the matter? Nothing, said Annie. Nothing now. *Now* is the word that in these nocturnal reflections hurtles weightily as a cannon ball. *Now* meant nothing, then: or not more than some reference to the future healing of her eyes now that the ointment had been acquired. *Now*, in the middle of Myrtle's night of agonising, is so obvious in its significance that Myrtle wants to roar her regret out loud. *Now* meant *now that something has happened. Now that something important is over. Now that I've given up all hope of Martin's love.* How could . . . how *could* Myrtle have been standing so close to Annie and had not the smallest inkling of what her friend was going through?

Shocked by her own insensitivity that day, that time, Myrtle curses herself years too late. And one further memory returns. It is in the street, possibly later that day. Definitely outside, for Annie's swollen cheeks and eyes glistened wetly – tears, rain? Myrtle did not know which. Annie tugged at her sleeve. She told Myrtle, with a pathetic attempt at light-heartedness, that her plan is to have one more attempt at seducing the elusive Archie. Myrtle thought nothing of this declaration at the time: a mere passing guess that Annie's determination would achieve her desire in the end. Certainly there was no reason to think that was a courageous or defiant remark. But now, almost two decades after the moment has passed, Myrtle sees the bravado of it, and the fury against Annie, that has been uncoiling itself since Martin's story, begins to ebb. She remembers instead all Annie has been to her since they were children: the exuberant leader, the encourager, the one so generous in her small acts of unpremeditated kindness – the joker. Their friendship has often astonished others – no one can understand its fine balance. But the point is they understand it – Myrtle the rock, Annie the spark. The pattern is rarely upset, it suits them both. And perhaps, Myrtle thinks, deceit of a certain kind among friends is a form of self-preservation. Small betrayals must be forgiven. She is calmed by the thought. She knows that an act that would break them for ever is unimaginable, and that in the end her love for Annie will overcome everything.

When Archie returns the following evening Myrtle can tell at once that he is in good spirits. The signs are in his movements rather than in his expression. A slow, ponderous tread is his normal gait – it becomes even slower if he is anxious. But happiness, or relief, spur him a little faster. The indications, this evening, are clear: he slaps down two hunks of fish on the table rather than bothering to find the usual tin plate that raw fish is kept upon. He throws his damp jersey at Myrtle rather than hanging it over the back of his chair.

'What's all this, Archie?'

Archie smiles. The taut solemnity of his face is broken up into unaccustomed lines and dips and puckerings round eyes and mouth.

'Here, wifey,' he says. She goes to him.

'I thought of you through your storm yesterday afternoon. Wish to God I'd been here.' Archie laughs and Myrtle privately rejoices: she never likes to ask Archie whether he thinks of her at sea. She can taste salt on his lips. His rough jowls scratch her cheeks. His hands are on her breasts, covering them. Myrtle feels strong. The traumatic journeys of the night may have acted like depth charges upon her soul, but her body is impatient. Eager.

'Let's not eat for a while,' Archie says.

They go to the bedroom, lie on the bed in their clothes. Archie, as always on returning, smells powerfully of sweat and fish and cold salt water. Myrtle smiles to herself: storms have always been an aphrodisiac to Archie. She can remember a jumble of nights with thunder crashing overhead while the two of them have risen and fallen like wind-lashed waves in this bed. Archie puts out her smile by clamping his mouth to hers. Sometimes he is not gentle, and on those occasions Myrtle is glad of her size. She takes one of his hands, guides it to her neck. His salt-stiff fingers pull at the small buttons. Clumsy in his impatience, it takes a long time to undo them. Myrtle, engaged in other overtures, does not help him. She likes his urgency, the way that the heavy solidity of his body seems to lighten in its quivering. She likes the way he begins tunelessly to hum, or moan. The noise reminds her of wind in sails, the calls of dolphins and the depths of the sea.

But it is not in bed that Archie will tell Myrtle what has caused him gladness beneath the storm-induced desire. Myrtle knows she must not ask. He will tell her in his own good time. Or will he? For a moment, pulling on her skirt again, pushing back her enlivened hair,

Myrtle wonders whether Archie, too, keeps things from her . . . She knows she must dismiss such absurd thoughts, but since last night it will not be easy.

After supper Archie says he is going down to the boat to fetch his large torch. He wants to inspect the roof of the house, fearing the storm may have dislodged some weak slates. Myrtle says she will go with him.

She takes his arm. His smell, now, is of carbolic soap and the clean cotton of his shirt. Myrtle feels that curious combination of melting weakness and newly lighted strength that comes from perfect love-making. This, perhaps, she thinks, is the meaning of being at one with someone: a transitory feeling, but so long as it keeps recurring, then there is little to worry about. They make their way, in step, down to the harbour. There are lights in some windows, but it's still not quite dark.

'How's Annie?' Archie asks out of habitual politeness every time he comes home.

'She's fine.' Myrtle's response is automatic. She knows Archie's feelings about Annie, has no intention of boring him with her news. This is a calculated reason for keeping the matter of Annie private, she quickly thinks in her newly alert-to-secrets way. It is simply to protect him from things that he would find of no interest.

'She's not going to be so pleased with Ken, this evening. He made me a promise. We thrashed it all out – went over it all for hours one night. Finished up shaking hands on it. No more of his bloody stupid "deliveries". He's going to sell his van. Live on his fishing wages like the rest of us.'

'That's all good,' says Myrtle.

'I've told him. If he's off again, driving himself to the useless mate he's become – that's it. He's out of the boat. None of that'll please Annie, I reckon. It'll mean less microwaves, less expensive rubbish.'

'She's got a new job,' says Myrtle. 'Waitress up at the museum café. That should make up a little –'

'That won't last long if the others are anything to go by.' Archie cannot resist a trace of scorn in his laugh.

'Who knows? Maybe she's found the right thing this time. She thinks she's going to meet a lot of dynamic folk up there.'

'Another of her illusions.'

A feeble moon struggles for recognition among passing clouds. The clouds are reflected smearily in the dark, high water of the harbour, crowded with sea-battered boats of coarse and thickset build. Myrtle and Archie stand looking down at the scarcely visible deck of *Skyline II*. The particular set of its funnel and bulge of its bows are so familiar that even Myrtle feels she could instantly recognise it in a crowd of a hundred similar boats. She feels the kind of affection for it that is inspired by inanimate objects whose function is to provide and to protect.

Archie lowers himself down the iron ladder cut into the harbour wall, jumps on to the deck. Myrtle can hardly see him. She can hear thuds as he tramps about (sated, his movements have slowed down again) pushing coils of rope, and boxes, out of his way. Then suddenly there is a whiplash of light scouring the boat. For infinitesimal moments Myrtle catches sight of a dozen objects that are part of Archie's life – line, nets, empty crates – and seeing him among them, trapped in the picture made by the torchlight, she feels as close to him as she did just an hour ago in bed.

It is cold by now. Myrtle folds her arms under her breasts and draws her mother's old shawl more tightly round her. Patiently she waits. At last the skipper's face appears over the wall, and she cries out with wordless delight, as if he had been away for a long time. She takes his arm again. With his free hand Archie drags the light of the torch across the harbour water. The tricks of shadows, finely edged in the foreground, fade in the distance. There is no dividing line between the boats' sides and the water they rest on: solid black sea-shadow indicates depths that always make Myrtle shiver, and thank God she is on dry land. She has always been apprehensive of empty boats – *that* was something she once confessed to Annie, who had not been interested. There is a ghostliness about them that perturbs her. Tonight, their stillness on the flat water, their creaks in the silence, their cargoes of machinery and nets etiolated by moonlight and torchlight, make them a spectral fleet which Myrtle would not have had the courage to stand close to on her own. But with Archie beside her she feels courageous, safe. She can smile at her own foolishness.

'How about going for a drink?' Archie asks. 'Would you like that?'

The invitation is so unusual that Myrtle has to pause before answering that she would love a small whisky. She is cold by now. The thought of the warmth and noise of the pub is appealing, though normally she has no desire ever to join a crowd in a public place.

'Very well, then. A wee drink it shall be. Tomorrow we must up to the cemetery, you remember.'

'The cemetery?'

'Dad.'

'Och, aye. Ben . . .' She hopes she does not sound as if she has forgotten the anniversary of Ben's death. How many years is it? Myrtle cannot remember and does not like to ask. A long time. But a long time gone so fast.

Ben Duns died of cancer in a hospital in St Andrews. It was the same hospital in which his wife had died of the same illness ten years before. Her fortune was that the end had been swift – a matter of weeks after the tumours were found. Ben's own death had been a slow and appalling process observed by Archie, in his early twenties, with increasing horror and desolation. For as long as possible Ben stayed at home, looked after by Archie and the district nurse. His bed was dragged to the window so that he could see the harbour, watch the boats come and go. His loyal crew, who had all been together many years, visited his bedside each time they came ashore and reported on catches, weather, problems. Their fading skipper gave his orders as if he was still on board. 'Clear up that bundle of nets, Billy,' he would say, and his look defied any of them to observe they were sitting in his bedroom. They assured him that all on board was shipshape.

Ben was transferred to hospital for the last month of his life. Archie, who scarcely left his side, watched the encrustations gather over his father's face, chest, arms – the rest were hidden by the sheet – and tried to answer the constant question: 'Why can't this dying business be hurried along?' Then one October morning, sun bright on the hospital sheet and hideous skin, Ben pulled himself up on the pillows with a rare show of strength and declared it would be a good day at sea. He'd be down at the harbour in a moment, he said. He patted Archie's hand, told him to be a good skipper, then closed his eyes and died.

To outward appearances the only sign of Archie's devastation was a harder setting of the solemn expression, a feeling of greater distance, detachment. Only to a very few did he reveal the profound sense of loss and despair he was determined to conceal. At first, he occupied himself with reorganising the boat, replacing old members of the crew who wished to retire, now Ben was gone, with younger ones. He arranged longer trips than usual to sea – the new young crew, all unmarried and keen to make money – did not seem to mind. On his return home he would find bunches of flowers and kindly notes from girls he had briefly fancied at school. Whereas their teenage offers had been flirtatious, they were now of a more practical nature. How can I help? Let me do your washing. I'll send you over a pie, just needs warming up.

Archie was touched by such kindness, and accepted food pressed upon him, but never requested help. And after some months, instead of passing most of his shore leave in his house – where Ben's things lay untouched – he began to pass the days in the Stewarts' house. Dot and Ben, after the deaths of their respective spouses, had become great friends. Ben had been almost a father replacement to Myrtle, just as Dot had mothered Archie after Sarah Duns had died. So it was in Dot's kitchen he felt most comfortable, eating her copious meals, listening to her familiar stories of disasters at sea. He was used to Myrtle's silent ways, her diffident smile, her care not to intrude. Archie had been one of the few boys at school who had not joined in the teasing. Armed with gratitude for this long after they left school, Myrtle regarded him with the affection of a sister. She often wondered where he would find a girl fit to be his wife. Safe in the knowledge there was no possibility of Archie ever regarding her as anything other than a loyal friend, she was able to act towards him with an openness, a lack of awkwardness, that eluded her in the company of other young men. In the period after Ben's death when Archie frequently began to come round, while her mother did the chattering, Myrtle's assuaging of Archie's grief came in the unconscious form of a warm and sensitive presence, always ready to fall in with his wish for a game of cards or a walk in the fields behind the village.

One day, some three months after Ben's death, Dot gave the command that Archie should go through his father's things – throw out the rubbish, take the clothes to a charity shop, generally reorganise a new life in the small house. Archie indicated his reluctance to such a job, but there was no disobeying Dot. 'Go on with you,' she said, 'it's got to be done sometime. Myrtle here will help you.'

The house, untouched by a woman's hand for the last decade, was a sad shambles. In the stuffy air there was a smell of dust and salt, and damp clothes that had dried to an alien crispness over a string line in the kitchen. Archie's efforts at domesticity were not impressive. Myrtle found a surge of unwashed cutlery and pans; opened tins, half full of mildewed beans and soup, crowded the table. It was no wonder he spent so much time under the Stewart roof, was her sympathetic thought.

'It's not usually this bad,' he apologised. 'Just lately it's all got rather out of hand, being at sea so much . . . Let's get the worst over first.'

He led her up the short flight of steep, narrow stairs – carpet worn to its strings – to Ben's bedroom. This had plainly not been visited since the day Ben was taken by ambulance to hospital: sweat-stained sheets pulled back into a violent twist of coarse cotton; thick dressing gown abandoned like a shot-down body on the floor; a hairbrush in which a bramble of grey hairs was woven through the greasy, greenish bristles. And over everything a mildewed look of dust.

'Oh, God,' said Archie, hand to his nose.

A smell of impending death had been trapped and horribly preserved in the airless room.

'Open the window,' said Myrtle.

Archie struggled with the small casement. Fresh sea air gushed in, cutting through the stale-death stench within, but not extinguishing it. Myrtle made her way to the small cupboard, pulled open the thin little door. The short rail was by no means fully occupied by Archie's parents' clothes. There was Ben's Sunday suit, a brown pinstripe. The stripes were worn and smudged round the back of the collar, where two grey hairs clung and moved like ghostly tendrils. Two pairs of stiff, sea-stained heavy jeans, and a light jacket, also badly marked. Pushed to one side, its sense of isolation almost alive, was a dress of drooping crushed velvet, the blue-pink of old gums. Circles a deeper pink of long-dead sweat were dotted like beading under the arms. A moth wavered out from its skirt and flew towards the window. Archie turned, saw the clothes.

'Oh God,' he said again, 'Mother's wedding dress. Da would never throw it away.'

He took a step backwards, sat heavily on the bed. He held out his hands, one on top of the other, fingers pressed together as if he was about to receive a communion wafer. Then slowly his head descended into the shaking receptacle of his own hands, and he began to sob. At first it was quite silent as his body swayed back and forth. Tears thick as blood fanned out from his closed eyes and fell over his fingers on to his knees. Then he began to moan, a deep, pitiful noise that reminded Myrtle of a sea cave she had once dared enter as a child, where strange echoes lobbed between the rocky walls.

She had never seen a man cry before, and was alarmed. It occurred to her she should run and fetch Dot, who would know what to do. Then she saw that she should not leave Archie in his wretchedness. Bereft of comforting words, at least she should just be there.

She sat on the bed beside him. After a while she put a hand on Archie's heaving shoulder. The strong, acrid smell of his sweat added to the other pungent smells in the room. Sometimes a puff of wind through the open wind would shift them a little, then they would congregate again, claustrophobic.

Myrtle had no idea for how long the two of them sat there. A couple of hours, perhaps. Eventually, the sobbing lost its strength.

Finally drained of tears, Archie took up a clump of the dirty sheet and wiped his face, fiercely scrubbing at his eyes. Myrtle removed her hand. He threw back the bit of mangled sheet, stood up.

'Sorry,' he said. 'That hasn't happened before. Won't happen again. Thanks for being here.' He picked up a plastic rubbish bag, shook it open. 'I'll hold it. You shove in the clothes.'

'No,' said Myrtle, rising too and taking the bag from him, 'we'll not do that. It's a job best done by Ma and me. We'll do the whole house for you next week when you're at sea. We've plenty of time. We're good at that sort of thing.'

Archie shrugged, attempted a smile with his bloodshot eyes. He had no energy to protest. Myrtle smiled strongly back.

'You'll come back to find everything sparkling,' she said. 'Ma and I will enjoy that. Let's go now. There's a stew for dinner. You must be hungry.'

Archie followed her downstairs. A pink envelope lay on the door-mat. Myrtle picked it up: Annie's ill-formed writing. Whatever? She handed it to Archie.

Archie evidently did not recognise the writing. Exhausted, he opened it without interest. He read the single page quickly to himself, then handed it to Myrtle.

Dear Archie, she read, *I'm sorry I'm such a long time in writing but I thought you must have so many letters all at once. Just to say how sorry I am about your dad. He was a good man with not an enemy in the world, wasn't he? I will never forget when he chose me to be Fisher Lass on his boat and told me that as skipper it was his duty to pay for my dress. I asked him how much that should be, and he said you go ahead lass and spend whatever is necessary. I thought that was very nice of him, very generous. Do hope by now you are not still too much down in the dumps. Love for now, Annie.*

'Good of your friend,' said Archie.

What was Annie up to? wondered Myrtle. What was her idea? She had threatened one last assault on Archie some time ago, but the plan had to be postponed because of Ben's death. Myrtle chided herself for such uncharitable thoughts: Annie was merely showing her sympathy, like everyone else in the village. It was a friendly letter, unlikely to be part of some grand scheme. It meant nothing to Archie. Myrtle imagined his horror and amazement should he have any idea that Annie still had intentions towards him. As teenagers he had rejected her overtures so many times, distanced himself. Only in the last few years had he become a little more unbending, talking to her occasionally, innocently thinking that her youthful fancy was over. These brief encounters, Annie reported to Myrtle, had given her hope. Myrtle had tried to tell her it would be better to forget any such hope, but Annie was stubborn in her anticipation and could not believe otherwise.

Archie threw away the letter. He and Myrtle returned to the Stewart house for Dot's long-simmered stew. Myrtle was aware of a disturbing unease. She knew it was nothing to do with having been witness to Archie's exploding grief: that was an occasion she would keep to herself for ever. As they sat at the table, Dot busying about with hot bread from the oven and homemade barley water, she was also aware of the warmth of the thought of rescuing Archie's house from its present depressing state. She was not, like her mother, a natural lover of cleaning and polishing. But to have Archie's house all ready for him when he next got back from fishing . . . to surprise him with fresh air and tidiness and order, Ben's old clothes magically all gone – now there was a secret, strangely exciting thought. She was aware of the calmness of her surface: *Come along, Myrtle lass, eat up. I will, Ma, I will. I'm just not very hungry.* Beneath the non-reflecting glass of her normal appearance, a curious excitement simmered, a new feeling she could not put a name to at the time.

She and Dot worked hard on Archie's house. He returned from the next fishing trip to find it transformed into a welcoming place, clean and shining and full of fresh air. Myrtle had put a jug of cornflowers on the kitchen table and bought a new linen dishcloth (which he did not notice) illustrated with pictures of fishing boats, some similar to Archie's *Skyline II*, the boat with which Archie had replaced *The Skyline* some years after Jock's death. Archie's delight, though apparent, did not inspire him to unusual rhetoric. He merely said the place hadn't looked or smelt so good since his mother was alive, and he thanked them. His pleasure was evident in his absence, after that, from the Stewart house. He still paid visits, was asked to meals, did small jobs for Dot round the house, but he spent far more time at home now that the place was no longer alien. Alone, Myrtle imagined.

She found herself more carefully observing Annie than usual. Annie's moods fluctuated, as they always had: she seemed restless, more prone to melancholy which she could not explain. She was irritated by Myrtle's part-time job (coaching children to read for several hours a week, payment a tin of shortbread or sometimes a pound) while she herself was unemployed. Seeing her friend's plight, Myrtle suggested they should take a short holiday together – neither of them had ever been far from home. They spent a few days in the Shetland Isles, one fine spring. Myrtle persuaded Annie to walk with her over the treeless hills for the best part of most days. Once they took a boat to one of the smaller islands and spent the day listening to the clatter of a million birds which soared in huge arches over their heads, darkened the sky for a moment, then broke up like a million pieces of tumbling masonry. Annie, despite herself, seemed to be enjoying the enforced dose of nature. She visibly cheered. They talked idly of mutual friends, though Archie was not mentioned except when Annie, with unusual generosity, praised Myrtle and Dot for all their good work on his house. She did mention, on the only afternoon heavy rain blighted their walk through the heather, that she thought her best plan would be to marry soon. *Though God knows where I'll find a good man in our neighbourhood, Myrtle.* Myrtle replied with feeling that there were plenty of good men: Annie would do better to put her mind to some form of employment. She said this so sharply that it had effect: on the long train journey Annie made no further reference to her matrimonial hopes, but did say she would apply for the job in the post office as soon as they got back.

Annie took the job, and bided her time. For a while she went out with a fisherman from Aberdeen. But his erratic visits and the closeness of his eyes did not suit her. He was given his marching orders after six weeks, an event which Annie recounted with much glee.

Once this luckless character had been made to understand he was no longer required in her life (a bucket of water over his head had been Annie's final desperate gesture to underline the seriousness of her meaning) she was manless and restless again. Her past boyfriends – Ross, Sandy, Hamish – were marrying girls from their old class. Archie, on the few occasions she saw him, in the street or in the post office, looked more cheerful. Time, Annie told Myrtle, to have one last lighthearted attempt. Nothing serious, she assured her. *You know I'd never think of marrying a serious man like Archie, don't you? Archie will end up marrying some serious woman just like him, and they'll be happy ever after*. She laughed her scoffing laugh, and Myrtle felt so sick she put her hand to her mouth and turned away. It was just four months after Ben died, and a winter of particularly vicious cold.

A week or so after Annie's announcement Myrtle went to the post office early one morning for stamps. Annie was behind the counter. She wore angora mittens. The sight of them brought vividly to Myrtle's mind those cold mornings of their childhood walking to school, the soft furriness of Annie's small hand in Myrtle's large one. The thought made her smile. But she received a freezing look in return.

'Didn't work, did it?' she said. 'Silly bugger. Doesn't know what he's missed. We could have had some fun, but he's too bloody serious.'

'It was a bit soon after Ben's dying,' ventured Myrtle. There was such a leaping of relief, such a gladness of heart within her that she had to control her words very carefully.

'You can't mourn for ever. Life's got to go on. I'll tell you all about it one day. It was quite funny, quite amusing, I'll say that.'

Later that day Archie came round for tea before returning to the boat for a long trip. He was his usual quiet self: hung a picture for Dot, asked Myrtle if she would keep an eye on the flowers on his parents' grave. He liked it always to have fresh flowers. No mention of Annie. From his behaviour, it would have been impossible to guess anything untoward had taken place. The only unusual thing was that he asked Myrtle if she would like to walk down to the boat with him: she could carry the tin with Dot's cake while he managed other supplies.

It was an icy, black night, frost already fuzzing the edges of stone walls. Archie was to sleep on board: departure was at dawn next morning. A punctilious skipper, he always arrived first at the boat and took the stuff on board. Then he climbed back on to the harbour wall to tell Myrtle to hurry home. He didn't want her to catch cold, he said, and patted her arm with a distracted little frown. Myrtle obeyed him, much though she wanted to linger for a few moments. On her fast walk back through the streets she wondered if her imagination was playing cruel tricks, but did not allow herself to think too far in that direction.

For some time after Annie delivered her letter to Archie, Myrtle could not help wondering if she then took any further steps to carry out her plan of seduction. There was no evidence of any progress, and Myrtle asked no questions. She did not want to risk anything to do with Archie coming between them, and after a while she put the whole matter from her mind.

It was not till some years after she and Archie were married that she learnt the full story. Archie had been up in the woods collecting kindling for the fire. The place reminded him, he said, of the whole silly incident with Annie which had completely gone from his mind until his return, by chance, to a particular bit of the wood. Myrtle believed him. By now Myrtle felt secure enough to hear whatever had taken place. As Archie recounted the tale her overwhelming feeling was one of puzzlement, sadness, that Annie had chosen not to tell Myrtle the story herself.

Archie had had a feeling, he said, that for some time after she had written the pink letter, Annie had been following him, spying on him in a mild way. Several times she turned up at the same place as him, too often to believe it was coincidence. On the first occasion, at the baker, he had thanked her for her letter and they exchanged a few words. On subsequent occasions they didn't speak, merely nodded agreeably. Then came the winter evening Archie had gone for a walk in the fields with his gun, thinking he might pot a rabbit for supper. Or to give it to Dot to deal with, he said. In fact the fading light made shooting impossible. But Archie, needing to stretch his legs after a week at sea, wandered on, further than he meant, into the woods. He liked to listen to the roosting pigeons.

He had not gone far along the path when he heard a crackling of twigs and someone calling his name – Annie, it was. Her voice friendly. Archie turned. Annie stood some yards behind him, an innocent-looking Red Riding Hood figure if ever there was one, he told Myrtle, in some sort of knitted cape with a hood. Black with flecks of white in it so it looked as if she had been walking in snow. In fact the only thought in Archie's mind at that moment – nothing had alerted his suspicions, although in Annie's presence he was always on his guard – was that perhaps it had started to snow, but they were protected here in the woods. It was cold enough.

Annie carried a bundle of hastily gathered twigs under one arm. Having observed that it was funny to run into Archie here, of all places, she explained that she was gathering firewood for their neighbour, an old man with arthritis unable to get out. The explanation was rather too long and elaborate. There were details about the neighbour's recent fall and general misfortune. (Archie felt a warning buzz down his spine. There was something odd here, he thought: the firewood story was very unlikely. Annie was not a known walker. From harbour to pub to home was as far as she ever went. Had anyone in the village heard she was off on a winter's evening to gather kindling in a wood half a mile away, they would have been very surprised.

Annie chattered on, impervious to his silence: the sudden cold, the pity he hadn't got a rabbit, her slight fear of woods, her relief when she had seen a familiar figure ahead of her. When her bright little remarks ran out, she suddenly pushed past Archie on the path, and made her way ahead of him, calling out that she was going back to the road through the other side of the wood, and it had been nice seeing him. In a moment she was out of sight round a bend of the path. The light was very poor by now.

Archie remained where he was, wondering what to do. He could not help feeling that the enjoyment of the evening had been spoiled by Annie's unexpected presence. There was also the uneasy thought that the meeting had been arranged by devious means. The idea of Annie spying on him, tracking him down, was disagreeable. On the other hand – Archie's foremost thought – it was not safe for a young girl to be alone in these woods on a dark evening. He had better make sure she was all right.

Gun hitched over his shoulder, eyes on the murky distance, Archie carried on down the path. He walked quickly, expecting to see Annie after a hundred yards or so. But no sign. He stopped, listened. From behind a tangle of bushes on his right, he heard laughter. His name was called again. Annie urged him to join her in a little clearing she had found. Had he got a match? she shouted. She rather fancied putting a light to her bundle of sticks. Having a bonfire.

Annoyed, Archie made his way round the clump of brambles into the clearing. It was divided by the trunk of a fallen tree, long dead, its roots a giant scraggy fist raised in the air at one end. Annie was sitting on her cape which she had laid across the trunk. She was swinging her legs against it, banging the sodden bark with her heels, childlike. Her wood was scattered on the ground: it had never been a very serious bundle. Annie grinned up at Archie, laughed at what she called his solemn face.

At this moment in his story Archie paused to try to impress upon Myrtle the sudden strangeness of light – or, rather, the dusk – which confused him. On the path it had been a normal winter gloaming, brownish among the bushes and trees. But there in the small clearing, the density was a surprising blue-white, like sea mist. The close trunks of the trees had turned the dull navy of gaberdine. It was these dreamlike, dull-grained blues, he tried hard to explain to Myrtle, that unnerved him, made him unsure what to do. Most disorienting of all was the fact that Annie had thrown off her cape. Beneath it she wore a cardigan the exact blue of her eyes. It was made of soft, fuzzy wool, done up to the neck with a line of small pearl buttons.

They stood looking at each other through all the dark blue. The wood pigeons had begun to purr. The occasional flutter in high branches was the only sound. Eventually, as if to make some gesture to free himself, Archie put down his gun. He asked Annie if she wasn't cold. She replied she never felt the cold. The only thing she felt was romantic.

Even as she said this, head tilted, eyes fluttering as they had a thousand times at a dozen boys, one hand ran up the line of buttons, pulling them apart. The two sides of the garment were thrown open – the efficiency of the gesture added shock to the confusion of other feelings rampaging through Archie – and was flung to the ground. Archie's eyes followed the progress of its silent wings till it landed. He then looked slowly, reluctantly, up to Annie's feet. She was still banging her heels against the tree. Finally, inexorably, his reluctant eyes climbed further, rested on the bare breasts. *There*, said Annie.

At twenty-three, this was Archie's first view of naked breasts. He had not had much experience, physically, with girls. To date his knowledge of their bodies had been confined to their curious, soft rises and slopes explored under cover of darkness. He had never encountered a girl so bold as to sit before him, naked. Trust Annie to have no such inhibitions . . . In the indigo gloom the outlines of her breasts were hazy, but clear enough to make Archie feel a shortness of breath. There was a noise like loud water in his ears. He sensed his hands stirring – desperate, for an appalling second, to cover the skin which must surely be icy cold. In the nightmare of the moment, he told Myrtle (anxious to furnish her with the most trivial details of the story), the phrase *marble breasts* came to him from some dimly remembered text at school. He had never known what it meant. Now, he did: these were marble breasts, all right: not a vein in sight, the nipples no more than the faintest smudge on skin the blue-white of skimmed milk. He clenched his fists and kept them firmly at his sides, smiling at the thoughts. Foolish, that. Annie took his smile for encouragement. She wriggled her shoulders. The milky, ethereal shape of her, which every second was becoming harder to focus upon, moved gently in invitation. *I'm here for you, Archie*, she cooed – yes, *cooed*, he snarled, at this bit of the story. Took it into her stupid head to imitate the wood pigeons – as if that would make any difference.

It was her voice, the pathetic little phrase attached to her offering, that broke the spell. Archie's previous turmoil of feelings, which he was too ashamed to name, was replaced with embarrassment, anger. He shouted at her to put on her clothes, come to her senses. He didn't want her – he never had wanted her and never would want her. Surely she had understood that when they were teenagers? And now, he ranted on, if she didn't make herself scarce for ever, she'd be sorry. She was nothing more than the village slag – used by everybody, loved by no one, and serve her right for her years of revolting behaviour. Yes, she was beautiful, but she was an unfeeling bitch not worthy of a good man, so if she had any plans for future happiness she had better change her ways. Yes, he went too far. He put things more fiercely than he meant to – spurred by guilt, perhaps, for having briefly con-templated an ignoble act.

By now it was completely dark. Annie was no more than a pale smear, her vague shape suggesting she had moved into a hunched position, head on raised knees. Archie could hear her sobbing and was unmoved. He knew that the smallest word or gesture of compassion would be misconstrued. He left her to her misery in the cold night, stumbled clumsily back through the thicket to regain the path. When he reached the edge of the wood, still far from calm, he fired his gun into the air. He had no care for the alarm this would cause the wretched Annie. He wanted only that she should know that the gun-shot was the end of the matter, an evening for both of them that should be forgotten with all speed. After that, Annie avoided Archie cunningly as she had previously stalked him. They did not speak again for many months.

It's the last afternoon of this shore leave. Though neither has found it necessary to mention the fact, both Archie and Myrtle have had a par-ticularly good time. Some shore leaves are too cluttered with jobs in the house or meetings with the bank manager or the FMA – general administration – for any real peace or pleasure. This time, unexpect-edly, there has been little to do but enjoy themselves. The four days have flown.

Archie is down at the boat. Myrtle is not expecting him back for a couple of hours. She is aware that the pleasure of the last few days has softened her edges. She feels sleepy, although she is not tired. She drifts about the kitchen, moves pieces of china on the shelves that don't need moving but there is nothing of real importance to do while she waits for the bread in the oven she has baked for Archie's tea. Once he has gone she will return to her normal, faster pace. Resume her usual efficiency. But for the moment she is enjoying her dreamlike state, the infusion of pleasure that makes the solid things of every day to dance.

There is a knock on the door. A visitor will break the spell Myrtle wants to last, a warm, protective covering, till Archie leaves. Her shout to come in is reluctant. She guesses it's Annie – they haven't spoken since the storm – and composes her face.

Ken comes into the room. He is agitated, she can see at once. He keeps rubbing a hand over his mouth and jaws as if with an invisible towel. Myrtle tells him to sit. Unknowingly, he sits in Archie's chair at the table. Automatically Myrtle puts the kettle on to boil.

'Annie wants a car,' he says.

'What?'

'A *car* – can you believe? She's off her head. How can we afford a car?'

'She's not mentioned it to me.'

'It just came to her last night, late. We were arguing about something quite different. Then all of a sudden, this ranting about a car. Says she's stuck here, a prisoner. Can't get out. She's at the mercy of public transport, she says. Buses out of the village are hopeless. What she wants is to get in a car and drive about when she feels like it. Drive about where? I took the liberty of asking. Besides, I said, you only drove for a few months after your test. You're not an experienced driver, Annie, I said. I'd not like to think of you alone on the roads.'

Ken sighs, pushes his thin, highly strung fingers through his hair.

'Perhaps the novelty's worn off the microwave and she has to have something new to aim for. You know our Annie.' Myrtle hands him a mug of tea.

'I do,' says Ken. He sounds rueful. 'I expect Archie's told you,' he goes on, 'of our agreement. We shook hands on it Friday night. It's a relief, I can tell you. I mean, I'm not a man to enter willingly into the black economy. Apart from anything else the lack of sleep, working nights when I come home, is taking its toll. But Annie . . . I only did it for Annie. She wanted so many things I couldn't afford to buy otherwise – things for the bairn and herself. I like to please her. I like to keep her happy. I mean, it's a rough life for you wives, us away so much, the worry, the small bits of time together that are never enough.'

'But Annie must be pleased you and Archie have sorted things out, put it behind you. She can't have been happy in her bones, knowing her husband was heading for a breakdown, putting in all those hours. She must have seen you couldn't keep it up much longer, something bad would happen.'

Ken shrugs.

'To be honest, I'm not sure she was all that bothered.'

'Oh, I'm sure she was.'

'You're a good friend to Annie, Myrtle. Don't know what she'd do without you. She relies on you for so many reasons. But I sometimes wonder what the hell you get from her in return. I used to wonder that even when we were at school. You'd follow her around – very quiet, you were – supporting her at every turn, helping her with her homework, giving her good advice about how to handle all the boys – and what did you get out of it? Bugger me if I could see.'

'I got a lot,' says Myrtle, a defensive look hardening her eyes. 'I loved Annie when I was a very small child, and I've loved her ever since, no matter what. Beneath all the nonsense there's a good heart, and a special way with her that's hard to describe. She's impatient with people, dismissive. She sometimes judges too quickly. But, my good-ness, when she's concentrating on you she makes you feel on top of the world. She gives you a kind of hope . . . I'm not putting this well, but there's nothing I'd not do for Annie.'

'I know what you mean,' says Ken. 'It's that mostly unseen bit I fell in love with when she was a girl.' He pauses. 'You remember the very day . . . Well, you were there. I told you. I had to tell someone. Couldn't keep it to myself. You were very understanding, far as I remember.'

While he speaks Myrtle remembers his face on the beach at St Andrews: soft with youth but contorted by his sudden confusion, the dark eyes almost black with yearning. The image melts into one a few years later, the night of the Fisher Lass ball, when some dull old hope had settled into his longer, harder, thinner face. She looks at him with the complete dispassion of one whose feelings have once been engaged, but are now totally severed. She is filled with the kind of wonder that comes in such situations. How *could* she ever have been so drawn, even for a short time, to the difficult, clever but bloodless Ken? How could she ever have thought that it was some form of love? She remembers the agony of humiliation, the feeling of having been betrayed by Ken when Annie had told her, on that sunny picnic, how the night of the Fisher Lass had ended. She smiles to herself at the thoughts of youthful innocence, and senses the gush of strength that comes from feeling *nothing*, now, for the man opposite her who had once caused her so much anguish.

There is a silence. Myrtle assumes Ken is remembering the day itself: his triumph and rejection, the one following cruelly after the other on the cold beach. Did he ever know, Myrtle wonders, the despair similar to his own that he caused her that night?

'How can I help you?' she asks at last.

'I thought you might persuade her, if she says anything to you, that it's a bloody silly thing to want, a car. Make her see sense. She knows we can't afford it. She knows I don't want any more hire purchase payments hanging over me . . . It's one of her madder ideas.' He finishes his tea, stands up: a thin, hunched figure with arm muscles lean as leather straps. Archie says he's stronger than you'd expect. And not clumsy, like some of the mates. He can untangle nets faster than any man on board and works fast and well at whatever job is at hand. It's only since he's been doing his deliveries that he's become inefficient, made mistakes in his tiredness. Not two weeks ago Archie reported Ken had misread the radar system and taken them miles out of their way. Archie had blasted him: such miscalculations cost precious time and money. Ken had apologised, admitted he'd not been concentrating. Myrtle sensed such tensions between Ken and Archie were increasing. All the same, she knew Archie would hate ever to lose Ken from his crew.

'I'll do what I can if she mentions any car nonsense to me,' says Myrtle. 'Try to avert her mind to something cheaper.'

They both smile: recognition of their mutual love for Annie, and understanding of her singular ways. Then Ken makes his way to the door.

'Have you seen anything of Janice, of late?' he asks. His back is to her, so Myrtle cannot see his face.

'I was with her during the storm. She doesn't like storms. But she was fine. She's a bonnie lass, growing up fast –'

'Where was Annie?'

'Her first day at the museum. She was held up.'

Ken nods.

'Well, thanks. Nice talking to you. Keep an eye on both mother and daughter, if you would.'

Myrtle, standing by him at the open door, sees a quick, grateful smile, but the anxiety still there.

'Of course. I'll do what I can. Maybe now all this . . . business is over we can all four of us get together again. We haven't done that for a long time.'

'Maybe,' says Ken.

When he has gone Myrtle takes the bread out of the oven. It is a little burnt on top. She curses herself for leaving it too long, holds it like a brick between her hands, feeling its heat through the oven gloves. The smell of new bread Ken would never find in his own kitchen, she reflects, but that is not something he would mind about. She continues to think of him. His anxiety has rubbed off on her. It's evident all is not well between him and Annie, as Annie recently hinted. For Ken himself to come to Myrtle signifies a possible seriousness Myrtle has not previously guessed at. She catches her breath, saddened. Fearing to imagine what might happen, her mind takes refuge in the past. She remembers a cold afternoon, here in the kitchen, a week or so after Annie had announced – but given no details – that her assault on Archie had gone wrong. They were eating a plate of Dot's scones, Myrtle remembers. Annie piled hers high with home-made raspberry jam.

'You'll never guess what I'm doing tonight, Myrt,' she said.

'No,' agreed Myrtle. Her friend could scarcely keep still in her chair. She was wriggling about, good-humoured, licking up jam from the plate with her finger. Her pleasure seemed to be more childlike than the grown-up anticipation of some romantic assignation.

'I'm going for a drink with Ken.'

'*Ken?*'

'Well, he asked me, didn't he? Why not? I thought. There's not that many that ask me out these days. Ken's an old friend, isn't he? He's kept his word, not bothered me since . . .' She looked down but did not blush. 'How long ago was it, the Fisher Lass dance? So anyway, I said all right, Ken. But no funny business, mind. Well, no one could *fancy* Ken, could they? He didn't seem to mind. Understood. Can I have the last scone?'

'Go ahead,' Myrtle said. The warmth of her own feelings for Archie guarded her against any retrospective jealousy. But having become used to the fact that Annie had no interest whatsoever in Ken, she was not unshaken by an irrational irritation: here was Annie *messing* with a kind and innocent man who remained Myrtle's friend.

'Don't you go causing him any harm,' said Myrtle, lightly.

'Course not.'

'Not that you would on purpose. It's just that Ken's held a candle for you for so long. Suddenly taking his hospitality might make him think there's some hope. Besides, it's hard for a man never to be allowed to lay a finger, especially as there was one occasion in the past.'

Annie sighed, impatient.

'Trust you to take it all so seriously. One drink is all that's on the cards. We may never go out again, according to how he behaves. So you don't need to worry.'

Myrtle remembers their conversation went something like that. The next day Annie reported Ken had borrowed his father's old car and they'd driven to a pub several miles inland. Had a good time, Ken the perfect gentleman, no suggestion of anything else. Hadn't even held hands, hadn't even brushed hands lighting their cigarettes. Top marks, he got, first evening, Annie said. As a reward, she accepted another invitation. From then on, although she still went out with one or two others, who she swore were nothing more than platonic friends, her chaste relationship with Ken continued. There was no hope of that ever changing, she said. But Myrtle, observing Ken, remembers she could not agree.

The men have returned to sea. They went at five this morning. It's late afternoon, almost dark. Myrtle is back from a hard day at the home, too tired to iron Archie's shirts. She plans to sit down with a cup of tea and ring Annie. It's been six days, now, since the storm. Six days since they last spoke. Too long. Out of touch with Annie, albeit due to some silly squabble, makes Myrtle uneasy.

The door opens. Myrtle spins round from the stove, kettle in hand. Annie, who never knocks, stands there smiling.

'Janice is over with a friend for the night,' she says. 'Thought I'd come round. It's a long time since we had a game.'

She takes a box from a paper bag she is holding, puts it down on the table. A new pack of cards. Their backs are decorated with a this-tle head set against tartan.

'That's great,' says Myrtle. 'We needed some new ones.'

'I got them from the museum. The gift shop. Staff discount. If there was more I wanted in the gift shop I could save a lot of money.'

'You're enjoying it, then, still?'

'Oh, aye. It's not a bad job. Better than some. I'll stay a while.'

They sit at their usual places at the table, pot of tea between them. Annie pushes the cards over to Myrtle. Their hard new edges warn they could cut her fingers. Their stiffness will take some getting used to – to be honest, Myrtle prefers the soft slappiness of the old cards. But she shifts them about, shuffles them, her big hands cold from the walk home, inaccurate.

'Do you know what happened?' asks Annie. 'I asked Ken for a car.'

'Why ever do you need a car?'

'Freedom. Just to be able to go off at will, when I want to. Not to have to be forever at the mercy of the bloody awful buses.'

'Like a lot of us.' Myrtle pushes the cards towards Annie, watches her delicate fingers deal with them more skilfully.

'I daresay. That doesn't stop me wanting . . .' She pauses. 'Did Archie tell you he and Ken have come to an agreement?'

'He did.'

'They shook hands on it.'

'I'm glad.'

'Me too. Though, mind, all Ken was doing was *deliveries*. Removals and that.' She gives Myrtle a look. 'Seems reasonable to me. The mates are having such a thin time –'

'The skippers have no' done much better –'

'– that it's hard to blame them. The price of children's shoes – not that you'd know about that.'

Myrtle quickly decides to let this pass, despite the anger in her throat.

'Archie knows your reasons, Annie. But the whole business is over, now. Let's not talk about it again.'

'Aye, you're right.' Annie begins to shuffle the cards. Myrtle refills Annie's cup. There is nothing to lose, she decides, in just one attempt to make Annie see reason.

'Do you really want a car?' she asks. 'It's not just the buying price, it's the upkeep that's so expensive. I mean, isn't that pushing Ken a bit far? He gives up the source of income that's paid for the microwave and all your gadgets, and you immediately ask for something way beyond his means. Is that fair?'

Annie sighs.

'Perhaps not. He went away worried, I'll say.' She gives a small laugh. 'I said Ken, we can sell the van now, get a car with the money. He says we'll not get more than a hundred pounds for it if we're lucky. Perhaps I'll shut up about the car for the moment. Suggest a better telly. He could run to that, I daresay . . .'

They begin their game, play in silence for a while. Both rub their fingers round the edges of the cards, unconsciously to speed familiarity with their strange feel.

'Janice is very fond of you,' Annie says after a while. 'You were very good to her the other night.'

'That's all right. You know I love the child.'

'I don't think I said thank you for that. I felt badly when you'd gone.'

'I would have rung you tonight to say –'

'We always get over these silly skirmishes, though, don't we? We can't always agree. You can't expect even the oldest friends not to drive each other potty now and then. It was my fault the other night, Myrt. I know that. You're very patient, very forgiving. I never forget that. Me, I've not been myself lately and you still put up with me.'

'I wouldn't say you've been that much different.' They smile at one another, lay down their cards in fans on the table. 'Shall we have a glass of whisky?'

Annie nods. Myrtle fetches bottle and glasses.

'Nerves about the new job – I mean, nobody could call me a *quali-fied* waitress, Myrt, could they? And Ken being so on edge . . .' They chink their glasses together. 'Archie'd never believe this, would he? The wifey drinking behind his back?' She laughs again, more easily. Her cheeks are pink after the first sip of her drink. 'I've a favour to ask you . . . concerning Janice. She's not doing too brilliantly at school. Well, you know how it is: they don't have the sort of teachers we had. No one to inspire. She's bored out of her mind, doesn't try, gets rotten marks. I was wondering, might you have time to fit her in with a little coaching? I'd pay you . . .'

'Don't be silly. I'd love to help Janice.' The idea instantly appeals. 'But only on condition there's no further stupid talk of money. I'd not take a penny to help young Janice.'

'What would I do without you? You're a brick.' Annie giggles. 'You've been a brick, the best brick ever, all my life, though I could only say that after three sips of this. Come on, your turn to deal. God, we haven't played for too long.'

Warm and flushed on their small but unaccustomed amount of whisky, the two women return to their silent game. For once, thoughts of their men at sea are put aside. They concentrate wholly on the cards, by now more familiar in their hands. The hours, secure, pass magically fast as always. Annie does not stir, and pull on her thick coat, till past midnight. Myrtle, too, puts on her shawl so that she can see Annie down the stone steps.

It's a dark night, moonless. No lights in other houses in the street. Myrtle takes Annie's arm. Annie's hand jerks down the iron rail. They feel their way cautiously down the steps, hunched figures, dark against dark. At the bottom, they hug.

'Fool I am! I forgot, I've brought my torch.' Annie pulls it from her pocket. She swoops its narrow blade of light over sleeping façades.

'Will you be all right, walking back alone?'

'What do you think I am? A helpless woman?' They both laugh, happy. 'You know what? Ken says there'll be snow before Christmas.'

Annie moves away. In a moment she is consumed by darkness. The slanting light of her torch appears to be a ghostly walking stick travelling on its own. With a small shiver Myrtle returns up the steps. There's a hard, dark scent in the black air that often comes before snow – could be Ken is right. Its purity warns that the gravid sky is ready to burst: a smell Myrtle will associate with a particular Christmas for the rest of her life.

That Christmas, almost twenty years ago, the traditions of the Stewart household were the same as always. But there was a reason for the sharpened edges of familiarity: Archie was coming for lunch. The kitchen was fugged up with steam, the smells of warm bread and fresh pastry were almost tangible. At the table Dot was preparing mince pies and chopping up chestnuts – enough food for half a dozen hungry eaters, though Archie was to be the only guest. Myrtle opened the window to clear the air, clear her head. It was then she sniffed the bright crispness of impending snow, and Dot said the clouds would break tomorrow, Christmas Day.

She was right. Archie turned up at one thirty, flakes on his shoulders. It was so dark outside that they lit candles as well as the lamps, and afternoon felt like evening. After they had eaten they exchanged small presents – Archie had bought Myrtle an ivory comb which to this day sits unused on the bedroom chest of drawers – and drank his bottle of red wine, and watched the thickening snow slam silently against the window and pile high on the ledge. Intrigued by the snow, no one wanted to draw the curtains. The tree, with its tiny coloured lights, stood on the window ledge speckling the high ridge of white with dots of red and blue and green. In the warm clutter of the room Dot and Myrtle and Archie played three-handed whist until it was time for the Christmas cake bound in scarlet ribbon, and Myrtle wanted the day never to end. It had been ages since Archie had spent so long a spell in the house, and she dreaded his going.

But he would not stay for supper, left soon after seven. Myrtle stood watching him hunch his way up the street in the densely falling flakes, white figure soon invisible in the greater white that swirled through the darkness. His footsteps were covered in seconds. No traces, Myrtle thought, with a heaviness of heart. He had not said when he would be round again. She wondered how long it would be before they next saw him. That Christmas evening she could not quite hide her sudden melancholy, and was aware of Dot's enquiring looks. After a light supper of vegetable soup, she apologised to Dot and went early to her room. There, she looked at her reflection in the mirror, but from some distance. She combed her hair with the ivory comb for a long time, deep in thought, before she drew the curtains over the window against which a bank of snow now almost reached the top.

She woke next day feeling the hollow rattle of Boxing Day – the emptiness of a day that follows celebrations. She wondered how she would pass the time, and how she would keep from Dot the agitated feelings that made her so restless she could not concentrate on any task for more than a few moments. After a small breakfast she looked out of the window.

'What are you after, I wonder?' Dot could never contain pressing questions.

'I was wondering, the weather . . .'

'Snow's melting.'

It was, too. Melting fast under a bright sun. Shrinking from the edges of the street, edging away from window panes. Myrtle longed to go out, walk. Walk anywhere, very fast. Be far away from Dot, whose silent perception made her uneasy. But she could not leave for fear of questions, surmises. Dot gave her some chore at the table – carrots: scraping, chopping. The morning loomed up like the side of a vast mountain Myrtle had no energy to climb. She picked up a knife, listless. Then there was a bang on the door.

Archie. Such a fine morning, he said. Pity to waste it. Would Myrtle like to stretch her legs? He planned to walk a few miles.

'I'll do the carrots,' said Dot, with the voice of one who had had every intention of doing them all along. 'Don't you bother, child. Put on your warm boots, won't you?'

Myrtle, exasperated by her mother's keenly approving eyes, could not stop herself blushing. She dragged on boots, thick coat, was at once too hot. She and Archie hurried down the steps. The village was deserted, silent except for the wail of a lone gull. They made their way up the wynd that led to the main road. The thaw had destroyed the untrammelled whiteness of yesterday. Roofs were slatted with thinning snow: gutters ran with melting water.

'How many days do you have off?' Myrtle asked. She hoped Archie would not observe the new unease within her.

'We've given ourselves a week or more, depending on the weather.' He took her arm to cross the road, something he had never done before.

They walked along a path beaten hard as rock beside a ploughed field. Dark earth showed through its chipped icing of snow. Sometimes one was ahead of the other, sometimes they were abreast. A thorn hedge protected them from a south-easterly wind and the sky, flax blue, was stripped of cloud.

'The postcards never get it right,' said Myrtle.

'What?'

'The blue.' Myrtle lifted her head, eyes scanning the heavens. She instantly regretted so foolish a remark, but was relieved when Archie laughed.

'You do say the oddest things. Who but you would go on about the precise blue of the sky? You're a very precise woman.'

136

Myrtle smiled. She still thought of herself as a girl. It would take a moment to become accustomed to *woman*.

'I would have thought fishermen were acutely aware of every shift in the sky, the slightest change in colour,' she said.

'No. It's just fair weather or foul. We're not poets.' Archie had stopped just ahead of her. Turned to look at her. 'What are we doing, talking about the sky?'

Myrtle felt the chill of her own foolishness. Beneath the hugeness of the heavens she would not mention again, she regretted her silly observations. There was an iridescent sliver of sea behind Archie that merged into the distant outline of the Lammemuirs, indeterminate as horizontal smoke. (Another fanciful notion Myrtle would keep to herself.) This was the view that was part of her vision most days of her life, but now its familiarity was blighted by the foreground figure of Archie with his accusing eyes. Backlit as he was, she could not see the humour, and so failed to find comfort.

'Wouldn't it be better if we talked about getting married?' he said.

Myrtle stumbled backwards off the path. She could feel thorns snarling into her coat, tearing at her hands (in her hasty confusion she had forgotten gloves) as she stretched them to support herself.

'Am I to drag you out of the hedge before I get an answer?'

Archie took both her hands, impatiently pulled her back on to the path. Myrtle's immediate thoughts were for the snagged wool at the back of her coat. Whatever would Dot think? Archie was dragging her towards him, smudging the stupid thoughts as he put his arms round her shoulders. Their heads were on a level. He kissed her on both cheeks with an ironic formality that seemed to please him, for there was a smile on his lips. The stubble on his jowls scraped Myrtle's cold skin. So this is a proposal, she thought, looking at herself from a long way off.

'So is it to be aye?'

'Of course, Archie. Aye a thousand times. Yes, yes, yes.'

'I've not proposed before, as you may have guessed. It's not worked out too delicately.'

'Oh, I don't know. I'm not experienced in proposals, either. But I'd say you've managed it beautifully.' Both laughed, newly shy.

'I'd been working up to it. Christmas Day, I'd planned. But some-how there was never a chance.'

'No.' She dared very gently to put a hand on his arm.

'So it's late, but at least spontaneous. It suddenly came to me. Ploughed field, I thought: good as anywhere.'

A long silence then quivered between them.

'Why do you want to marry me?' Myrtle asked at last.

'Always known you'd be the best wife in East Neuk, in the world I daresay. Always loved you.'

'*Always loved me?*'

'Well, years and years. Since school.'

'Since *school*? You never gave the slightest clue.'

'Course not. Had to be sure. Takes a long time to be sure, when a man is choosing a wife.'

'But . . . all those other girls after you. I always knew you were quite out of my range – just a distant hero. Then you became a friend, and I couldn't believe my luck.'

'And then?'

'And then, quite lately, friendship turned into something else. I didn't dare admit it, even to myself. I thought I should go to my grave loving Archie Duns, and no one would ever know.'

Archie turned suddenly away from her with the stiff, dignified movement of a man who turns away from a lowered coffin, wishing to hide his powerful feeling.

'Thank God it's turned out like this,' he said.

'I love you,' said Myrtle.

'That's all I wanted to hear. Hoped it might be the case. I'm a lucky man, but I'll have to warn you: I'm not a man of many fine words. Well, you must have gathered that by now.' He patted Myrtle's hand, still on his arm. 'This could be the only time we say all these sort of things to each other. But you'll know it's there, my love for you, for ever, God willing. I'll be a faithful, loving husband, though I can't promise many frills.'

'We're grown up,' said Myrtle. 'I don't need roses. Just assurance.'

'That's fine, then.' Archie was a little brusque, looking at his watch.

'I'd planned a good long walk but we've been a while, all this standing about. Maybe we should be getting back to Dot, have a cup of tea, tell her.'

'She won't be surprised,' said Myrtle.

'That she won't,' said Archie. 'There's nothing she misses, your mother.'

They walked back the way they came, pushed together by the narrowness of the path. The pale sun defrosted their faces and soon, walking briskly, even their bare hands began to feel warm.

They spent a chaste week making their plans. Dot, in her total delight, offered them the ground floor of her house so that they could sell Archie's house and have money to invest. Archie was pleased by the plan. He had never liked his parents' house, and since his father's death it was too full of unhappy associations, despite Dot and Myrtle's efforts to clean and cheer the place. Now, he wanted to distance himself from the memories, start somewhere new with his wife. Archie put the house on the market and returned to sea early in the New Year. He said that he would break the news to Ken when they were some miles from the shore, and ask him to be best man.

Not until he had been gone for some days did Myrtle tell Annie: harbouring the secret had provided a peculiar pleasure. Until now she had had so little excitement to share with Annie. Now the time had come she wanted to keep it to herself, unbroken, for a while. She feared that once Annie knew the whole precious matter would be splintered and swept up like broken glass – Annie with her opinions and enthusiasm and overwhelming surprise. When she did break the news at last, Annie went so pale that Myrtle thought she was close to fainting. But in her state of shock, and annoyance at not having been told sooner, Annie did manage suitable congratulations. Her show of pleasure, though, was less – immediately – than Myrtle had anticipated. Then Annie took a hold of herself and behaved in character. Even her friend's important news could not deflect Annie's natural references to herself.

'Oh Myrtle, it's wonderful! I never thought you'd make it up the aisle before me.'

'You probably never thought I'd make it up the aisle at all.'

Annie laughed, ignoring, or not noticing, the slight waspishness of Myrtle's tone. Then they hugged, glittery-eyed.

'Nonsense. You'll be the best wife. I'll never make as good a wife as you.'

'Course you will.'

'Never. I know it in my bones.'

'To be honest, I never imagined I could end up so lucky. I still can't believe it. Archie Duns! . . . *Me*.'

Annie moved away, not much concentrating on her friend's incredulity.

'I hope you won't think too badly of all that silly business when we were at school,' she said. 'Me threatening to go after Archie. Dreadful mistake. We'd never have been right for each other. But you know me: always spurred on by a challenge. I always knew I'd never get any-where. It was nothing at all serious. I'm sorry.'

'I'll never give it a thought. It's forgotten for ever.'

'Do you think Archie forgives me?'

'I doubt it ever enters his mind. Besides, he knows you're my friend and nothing will ever alter that.'

'Marriage will, a bit.' For a moment Annie was downcast.

'Not really.'

'I'll have to find myself a husband too. God forbid: where to start? So what will the wedding dress be? Big and white?'

Myrtle laughed.

'Big and white'll have to be for your turn. My size, I'd look like a fridge.'

'You'll look beautiful – honest.'

They laughed and hugged again. At twenty years old they were on the brink of the new era in their friendship that Myrtle's marital status would cause. Anticipating the reality was not easy. Best to smother the anticipation by envisaging less serious matters.

'So what do you have in mind? Oh Myrt, I'm so excited for you! So jealous.'

'Ma's got out the yards of velvet she's had stored away for years. She bought it for curtains in a sale when she was just married, then never had time to make them.'

'Old curtains won't make you a very fashionable bride.' Annie looked appalled.

'I'm not after being a fashionable bride, am I? That would scare Archie to death, wouldn't it?'

'I wouldn't have thought so, but then I don't know Archie, do I?' Annie sighed at the hopelessness of her friend's lack of romantic vision. 'But I expect you'll get away with it. Long as you expect me over first thing, morning of the wedding day, Carmens to the ready. Promise? By the time I've finished with you, you won't know yourself.'

'I wouldn't want to surprise Archie too much,' said Myrtle. 'He seems to love me as I am, amazing though that is.'

Annie put out a hand and held up a clump of Myrtle's heavy, straight hair.

'Trust me,' she said.

Dot spent a week cutting out and sewing yards of musty-smelling velvet the colour of loganberries. The fittings, in contrast to those of Annie for her Fisher Lass dress, were silent, serious occasions: Dot pinning and tweaking with slow and loving care, Myrtle impatient and uninterested, urging her to hurry. She was agitated by Archie's absence – the beginning of feelings that were to grow and torment for many years to come, the first taste of the chronic anxiety that becomes the norm for fishermen's wives. There had been storms. There was scarcely a moment of the day she did not imagine the man she loved exposed to a wild sea. One afternoon, her impatience for his return almost unbearable, a wearying fitting was interrupted by a knock on the door.

Martin came in. He carried a small box.

Myrtle turned so swiftly – for a foolish moment thinking it might be Archie home early – that Dot, on the ground, hands working on the hem, was swung round on her knees in a slipstream of velvet. Martin was silenced by the sight of the bride swathed in the gloomy stuff, its shadows melancholy in the thin violet light that came through the window. They stared at each other: Myrtle in friendliness, Martin still too surprised to speak. He had not imagined he would be intruding on such a scene.

'I'm sorry,' he said at last. 'It seems to be an inconvenient time. My goodness, Myrtle: you're looking grand.'

'No it's not,' said Dot, through the pins in her mouth which kept their balance on her lips. 'Come and sit down and tell us what's going on.'

'You're the ones with the news,' Martin said.

Myrtle felt a tug on her tacked skirt. Her mother was lumbering up from the floor. She moved automatically to the kettle.

'I heard,' said Martin, turning to Myrtle. 'You and Archie. That's good.' He held out the box. 'Small wedding present.'

'Martin! There was no need. Thank you. Our first wedding present.' (So strange, so thrilling to say *our*.)

'I was wondering if I might appoint myself . . . official photographer?' Martin gave a hesitant smile. He was not a man experienced in the art of selling himself. 'I've just bought myself a new . . .' He took a small instamatic from his pocket. 'I thought – just outside the church. I wouldn't be any bother.'

'I'm sure Archie wouldn't mind,' said Myrtle. (Oh, the luxury of having to consider and imagine the opinion of the man she loved.) 'Though we hadn't planned any photographs. There'll be nothing much to – I mean, it'll be a very small affair.'

'All the same, it should be recorded.' Though his voice was light, Myrtle found herself touched by his clouded look – a mixture of joy and regret.

'Course it should,' said Dot, glancing at a faded record of her own wedding to Jock, the sepia print diminished by a brass frame polished till it blazed with light.

'Very well, then; of course.' Myrtle found it hard to concentrate on Martin's plan, and Dot was chivvying the folds of the skirt again. She did not open the box until Martin had left. It was a lump of rock crystal, its tiny milky peaks glittering with a faint voltage on so dark an afternoon. But Myrtle could imagine how it would be on a bright day, and bent to show it to Dot, who complained that never had she known so fidgety a bride.

The very small affair took place on a bitter February afternoon in St Monan's church. It was so cold Myrtle was forced to wear her grandmother's old cape, thick as a horse rug, over the velvet dress. But unassailed by vanity, even on her wedding day, it did not occur to her to be put out by such an ungainly addition to her wedding clothes. Her concern was not to be distracted by the cold.

She and Dot and Annie were driven to the church by a taxi that heaved over the lumpen roads like an old boat. An onlooker might have thought that Annie was the bride, her dress being more appropriate wedding material than Myrtle's. Also, she carried a small bunch of snowdrops. She remembered to give these to Myrtle just as they were alighting from the taxi into the heavy rain. They found Archie and Ken waiting in the porch, shifting uneasily in their unaccustomed suits. Archie wore a tie covered with small anchors. His shirt, to Dot's dismay, was missing a button.

The small group went into the church where the priest was lighting the altar candles. This job done, the gloom was only slightly dispelled by two murky halos of light. The place smelt of the ineradicable damp that comes from centuries of sea spray bashing against stone. As Myrtle's eyes travelled round the whitewashed walls she saw that patches where the wet had seeped through were the colour of old men's sweat.

Bride and wedding guests stood beneath the fine model of a sailing ship that hung from the ceiling. Each one looked about, eyes not meeting. They were unsure how to proceed. The priest eventually turned from finding a page in the Bible and invited them, being so few, to walk down the aisle together. The red carpet – a touch of modernity incongruous in so ancient a place – was only wide enough to accommodate three. Ken and Archie flanked the bride. Dot and Annie followed them. There was no music, the organist being indisposed with flu, but rain was hard on the windows.

As they progressed up the aisle Myrtle found herself remembering the stories her father told her, as a child, about this church. Built in the time of King David I of Scotland it was, at the end of the eleventh century – a time too far past for Myrtle to imagine. Had other brides, nine hundred years ago, walked down this very aisle feeling the same mixture of strength and peace and nervous anticipation that assailed her now? Had brides through the centuries felt their minds escaping like a cloud of butterflies, settling on irrelevant thoughts, even as they neared the moment they were to take their vows? The cold little stems of the snowdrops had become warm, she realised, in her hot fingers: was that a timeless thing, a common experience through the years? Her father had always dealt so easily with past and present, finding events hundreds of years before his birth no harder to envisage than events of last week at which he had been present. He often spoke of Scottish kings as if they were friends, contemporaries.

'He was a good man, the first King David,' he would say. 'The legend goes that he suffered a terrible arrow wound, and the monks of St Monan's saved him. As thanks, the King had this church built for them.' Myrtle remembered her father lifting up her hand to run it over the rough carving of one of the twelve consecration crosses carved into the walls. She hated the feel of the chill, bristly stone, but had said nothing for fear of offending him.

So slowly, they walked up the aisle, passing the carvings. Her fingers, grinding the snowdrops, remembered the feel of the stone noses just as fingers remember scales on a piano taught long ago. David II, her father told her so many times, was the next king to take more than an interest in the church. He, poor man, was caught in a fierce storm when sailing from Leith to Ardross, just a mile from St Monan's. He swore that if he landed safely he would rebuild the church. This promise was carried out between 1362 and 1369 at a cost of £750. Why should she remember that on her wedding day? And the carpenter was paid just £1 13s 4d for his labours. Whenever Myrtle's father told her that – and he was inclined to repeat his favourite stories – he whistled through his teeth at the paucity, even in those days, of the sum. Myrtle could hear that off-key whistle, full of spittle, against the pebbling of the rain against the windows. She wished he was here, escorting her up the aisle in conventional fashion. She wished he could see her, know of the happiness he had always wanted for her but had doubted she might achieve. 'You're such a big girl,' he used to say, sadly, as if that was an impediment to happiness. And indeed, for many years it had been, although Myrtle's way of coping with it was to take her father's advice: *don't hope for anything, lass, and then you might find yourself surprised.* Surprised! Surprised scarcely described it, here at the altar at last, struggling through the flock of butterfly thoughts to the present, trying to persuade herself this was not a ridiculous dream, but the elusive present which would only become solid in her mind once it was over. Here he was, Archie the unobtainable, smelling of mothballs and toothpaste, about to become her husband, 'with no frills', in the eyes of God.

When the simple ceremony was over, bride and groom, priest and congregation, stood at the church door looking out at the rain that bulleted down on the sea. The sky was so low and heavy it was hard to know where light came from to illuminate Bass Rock, a distant spectral monument in this weather. They were all standing there, the small crowd, wondering when to make a dash for the taxis, when a sodden figure suddenly appeared from behind a gravestone – Martin. He approached them, camera in hand. First he photographed them huddled in the porch, then he persuaded them out on to the squelchy slopes of the graveyard, backs to the sea, for more pictures. One of these, blown up and framed, has stood on the chest of drawers in the bedroom for the Duns' entire married life. The enlargement enfeebled the original colours, but the spirit of the moment was caught: black rock covered with the slime of weed; thrashing waves, lifesize granite crosses above gravestones and the startled, disbelieving faces of the wedding group – Annie the only one bearing a proper wedding smile. Curiously, the light that shone so mysteriously on Bass Rock does not show in the photograph. Sometimes Myrtle wonders whether it had been a figment of her heightened state.

Later, after food and drink in a pub, Myrtle and Archie made their way on buses and trains to Mull. There they spent a week in a small guesthouse overlooking the island of Iona. Myrtle was fascinated by the provision of flannels in the pristine bathroom – a whole pile of them, of unimaginable fluffiness, in different colours. Archie was more intrigued by the size and quality of the breakfasts.

The honeymoon was a time of relentless bad weather, landscape all but obscured by dense mists. They ventured out only briefly each day. Mostly they kept to their room. Archie confessed that, desirable though he may have been to local girls (a modest blush accompanied this admission), he had never slept with anyone. Myrtle laughed at the solemnity of this announcement, deeply relieved. She liked to think of their starting out to discover this unknown territory of physical passion together. It gave her confidence. On the first night she walked naked across the room to the bed, where Archie awaited her, huge shoulders looming above the sheet. He murmured about the wonder of her.

It was in Mull that he fell in love with his wife, and she with him. The exhilaration of those early days of lovemaking, perhaps fuelled by Archie's absences at sea, never seemed to flag. Myrtle had observed in Dot the destructive effect of chronic anxiety when the men were at sea. Married to Archie, a stern and wise skipper who would never contemplate any risk to his men's lives, it was her turn to live the regular days of unease. But she understood that it was this threat to life itself that heightened the value of the times she and Archie had together. Each homecoming was a celebration, a reason to be thankful. At each departure they both secretly prayed for *Skyline II* to be spared. Even after years of surviving storms, they resisted any measure of complacency. For their entire married life Myrtle and Archie remained alert to the shadow of mortality, which endows all love and pleasure with its cutting edge.

In the eighteenth, and even the nineteenth century, Myrtle explains to Janice, fishing boats were still remarkably similar in design to their Viking forebears. She shows her a picture of a *sixern*, or six-oar boat, found rotting in the Shetland Isles quite recently. She does not mention the feeling of distaste the picture holds for her. Myrtle's dislike of rotting boats is even greater than her dislike of empty working boats:

wrecks, rust and softened wood, old boats that are leaking but just afloat, fill her with peculiar fear. She has always kept her distance from ship skeletons, disturbed by their lack of life, though that same lack of life in deserted buildings holds no menace. Once, as a child, she came across a rotting rowing boat, its bows split and gaping, its paint raised in dozens of blistering sores, tipped up on a stretch of shingle. Unaccountably, she burst into tears, would not go near it. Annie had wanted to creep into its shade to play houses, but Myrtle refused. Loony, Annie had thought her. 'Loony loon,' she had shouted over the crack of pebbles as Myrtle ran away. Well, yes, she was: a fisherman's wife, and still a bit odd about boats.

But now, indicating nothing of her own feelings, she points a firm finger at the picture: the faded sepia of the dead *sixern* at Vemmenty in Shetland. Janice, close to her, is intrigued.

'I'd like to see it,' she says.

'Doubt it'd still be there. It would have broken up long ago.'

'I'd like to go to the Shetland Isles.'

'Your mother and I went, once. Long before you were born.'

'I'd like to go.'

'The birds! Millions of them. The noise!'

'Maybe one day you'll take me.'

They are at the kitchen table. Janice sits in the place Annie usually occupies when she comes to play cards. Several books are spread open between them. Janice is at work on a project on the local fishing industry. Myrtle has agreed to coach her in several subjects. This project, it turns out, is Janice's favourite. Originally, she had hated the whole idea of such a boring old project. Who wanted to know about boats? she asked. The harbour was stuffed with them. Her father talked of nothing but fish. She'd had it up to here with everything to do with stinking fish. She wasn't going to try. Nothing could make her interested.

But somehow, with Myrtle, fishing did become interesting – fascinating. Myrtle put things quite differently from her boring old teacher Miss Simmons, who droned on in a voice that sounded as if she was talking through a mouthful of scones. Myrtle tells stories, asks Janice the sort of questions it's actually good fun to answer. Then, Myrtle *listens*: she listens to Janice as if she is really interested, which makes Janice want to go on and on with her ideas to please her. Myrtle has persuaded Janice what fun it is to go to the library at the museum and look through old documents and records, find photographs which can be copied for her book. Janice has done this and triumphantly produced the fruits of her excavations. She received high praise and homemade cinnamon biscuits from Myrtle. She is beginning to feel she is not as stupid as they say she is at school. Her marks are rapidly improving. The lessons with Myrtle go too fast. She looks forward to them, she loves them. In just a few weeks, as Annie observed to Myrtle, the child has *blossomed*. She loves the poetry Myrtle is now introducing her to – comes home talking about people called Sorab and Rustum. Only yesterday Janice refused to go home until they had finished reading *The Ancient Mariner*.

'You ought to be an all-the-time teacher,' Janice says, 'so that lots of children can have all this fun, not just me.'

'Maybe: one day. I've often thought of it. But I've no training.'

'Surely that doesn't matter. You'd be brilliant.'

Myrtle is gathering up photocopies of pictures of ancient fishing boats. In preparation for these lessons she herself has spent hours in the museum. Mornings, thus engaged, have flown by. Sometimes she has broken off to go down to the café to see Annie, by now the accomplished waitress. Annie brings coffee with all speed, 'on the house'. 'You the tutor, me the waitress,' she says, laughing. There is both admiration and jealousy in her comment. She would like to inspire her daughter herself, ignite her enthusiasm for learning in a way that Myrtle has so quickly managed. But she knows that is beyond her. And she is pleased that at least her childless friend is able to play an important part in Janice's life. To Myrtle, Annie likes to think, Janice is surely second-best to a daughter of her own.

'On to the herring industry, tomorrow,' says Myrtle. 'I've found pictures for you of clinker-built ships knee deep in herrings. I'll be telling you all about the disaster in 1848 when a hundred boats and a hundred fishermen died.'

'Good.'

'But it's time to go, now.'

Janice does not move. She concentrates on writing HERRINGS in elaborate capital letters. Eyes down, her lashes, thick and curly as Annie's, make spiked shadows on her cheeks. Her hair, of late, has become curlier, more abundant. There are red lights in the brown. It falls over her eyes. She makes no attempt to push it back. Annie was just the same, at that age: stubborn about her rebellious hair. 'Tie it back, Annie, or you'll earn yourself a black mark,' the teachers used to threaten. Annie earned herself dozens of black marks and didn't care. Past and present interweave confusingly. For a moment Janice is the child Annie. She looks up, smiles the same smile. Dimples press into her cheeks, plumper than Annie's ever were, and she's herself again. Eleven years old and full of spirit. Her father's heavy jaw means her own looks will never quite equal her mother's. But there is an unruly appeal, a wicked eye, that will be both invaluable and dangerous when it comes to grown-up life.

'I'd better be off, then,' says Janice. 'Though I don't want to go.' She stands, gathers up her things. She looks round the kitchen, memorising its geography to take home with her. Myrtle notices her nails are bitten to the quick. 'There's a boy at school called Arthur Dilk. He writes me such silly notes.' Myrtle smiles. Again, history repeating. 'I haven't told Mum – don't say anything.'

'Of course not.' There were dozens of boys writing silly notes to Annie, too, when she was eleven, Myrtle remembers.

Janice moves round to Myrtle and kisses her quickly on the cheek. This is something she has not done since she was a very small child.

'I'm looking forward to hearing about the disaster,' she says. 'I wish my dad and Archie and all of them didn't have to keep going to sea. I'm never going to marry a fisherman. I hate men being fishermen.'

'Not much choice for a man, here,' says Myrtle.

'Then I'll move. I quite fancy the thought of the south. Stratford-on-Avon, or Weston super Mare – I've read about that. Perhaps you'd tell me about lots of nice places in the south next geography lesson?'

'Perhaps.' Myrtle goes with Janice to the door, big hand lightly on small shoulder. 'See you tomorrow at five.'

'Twenty-three hours till then.'

'Aye.'

'Hope they go quickly.'

Myrtle watches Janice's slow progress down the steps, one side of her slight body weighed down by her satchel. She fears for the child. She loves her.

The time when Archie and Myrtle were trying for a child of their own is a time that both of them have closed away. They never reflect on the weariness and disappointments of those days: there is too much else to be glad of in their lives. But regret can be perennial and to deny that it did not assail them – Myrtle in particular – from time to time would be an untruth. News of friends giving birth, the constant sight of babies in prams, the well-meaning invitations to be a godparent – such things could not but remind of their own 'failure', as Myrtle saw it. Long ago both she and Archie had come to accept this 'failure'. But accepting is different from growing accustomed. It was growing used to the idea of impossibility, short of a miracle, that savagely eluded them. Sometimes, they wondered if this anguish would be with them for the rest of their lives.

Myrtle's attempts to conceive went on for almost five years. First, came the natural hopes. Myrtle pictured herself running down to meet the boat with news of her confirmed pregnancy, too excited to await Archie's return home. But as there was no reason for any such event to take place, Myrtle began to suspect something was wrong. She was the first to be subjected to tests, questions of a loathsomely intimate nature, examinations. While Archie was at sea she would spend many hours waiting in hospital corridors, hope writhing like some wretched, dying bird within her. Sometimes the pregnant Annie would come with her.

'Well, if nothing happens, you can share this bairn – Jesus, how it kicks! Feel it kicking, Myrtle.' Innocent of Myrtle's reaction to this offer, she would tap her stomach with long silver fingernails. To

Myrtle they represented an alarming sign of Annie's less than instinctive maternal feelings. 'How'll I ever manage looking after one myself?
Oh, it's not fair. Though you mustn't give up for a long while yet.
Then just when you're least expecting . . .' Annie did her best, in those
sleazy hospital waiting rooms, to raise her friend's hopes and spirits,
always innocent of her own blundering.

When months of ignominious examinations finally came to an
end, the answer was that nothing seemed amiss. And so it was Archie's
turn to be confronted. Perhaps he was the 'culprit', as the gynaecolo-
gist put it. Archie's misgivings at subjecting himself to tests, that made
him feel sick to think about, he kept to himself. But for the sake of a
child, for the love of his wife, he would go through anything. And so,
refusing Myrtle's company, one shore leave he braced himself for the
bus journey to the hospital. He faced the appalling indignity, at nine
in the morning, of being shown into a sterile cubicle armed with a
plastic jar and a couple of very old magazines. How many other hopeless, desperate hands had trembled unwilling through the crumpled
pages of obscene buttocks and breasts? 'Just do your stuff,' com-
manded a stiff little nurse, her own breasts buttoned tightly into a
lust-defying uniform. Superior, pitying, mocking she managed to be,
in the few dreadful moments of their acquaintance. Archie hated her.
She shut the door behind her with a smug, all-knowing look.
Imprisoned in the silent white cube, it was only the thought of
Myrtle's last hope that gave him the strength to carry out the disagreeable command.

But there were no problems concerning Archie's sperm count, it
turned out: nothing amiss with him, either. All a great mystery, as the
consultant put it in their last interview. How about trying the fertility
drug? With one accord Myrtle and Archie dismissed the idea. Then it
was in God's hands, the man went on, attempting to be helpful but too
busy to spend a long time trying to persuade so adamant a couple.
Obviously there were sometimes pyschological barriers to pregnancy
that could be excavated through long sessions with a therapist . . .
This parting shot met with equal distaste. No thank you, said Myrtle
and Archie again. In that case it's up to God, the consultant repeated

wearily, closing the Duns' file before him. He glanced at his watch, indicated that in his opinion even a barren couple should not be allowed to overrun their time too long. Yes, God was probably the best – the only – hope, he went on, standing up. Indeed his own father was a minister of the kirk and had taught him the power of faith. He looked down on his patients with an encouraging little turn of his mouth that was a poor substitute for a smile. Archie and Myrtle stood. Now they could look down on him, the man they could not help despising because he could do nothing further for them. The consultant's final advice was not to give up hope – and, who knows, the good Lord might provide them with a surprise in his own time. Remember, His ways were mysterious, He could not be hurried . . . With that, the consultant's own rising hurry could no longer be contained, and he showed the Duns to the door.

Not greatly encouraged by his little homily, to await God's surprise was all Myrtle and Archie could do. But His mysterious ways did not include, for them, the provision of a baby. Meantime Annie gave birth to Janice, a healthy girl. Myrtle, for the first two years of the child's life, helped greatly with her upbringing. She grew to love the child – not like her own, no use pretending that – but without reserve. Archie observed his wife. He understood how she felt, and was grateful that there was at least a baby upon whom Myrtle could bestow her naturally maternal feelings. But he himself harboured an amorphous kind of antipathy that he could not bring himself to fathom. Something to do with resentment? Why should the undeserving Annie be blessed with a child while his own, far superior wife, was denied this gift? Janice was a beguiling and pretty child: no denying that, though by three years old she was already showing the dangerous precocity and petulant ways of her mother. On the occasions that Archie was accosted by the child (often he would return home to find her on Myrtle's knee) he behaved as well as might be expected – dandled, swung, told stories of mermaids and fishes, made her laugh. But in truth he could never feel much affection for the child. By the time she was eleven his indifference had turned to keen animosity. He requested that she should visit the house as little as possible while he was home. His intention to avoid her did not go unheeded by Annie. Myrtle was saddened by the confusion of Archie's strong feelings, though she could not fault his behaviour.

'I'll never understand why you've got it in for her so, Archie.'

'Something about her.'

'She's an innocent wee thing, for heaven's sake.'

'Not so innocent.'

'What do you mean? What rubbish you talk! She's not twelve years old.'

'She's manipulative as her mother.'

'That's unfair. Pure prejudice.'

'Let's not discuss her. You'll see I'm right, one day.'

'Nonsense.'

Janice was the only source of disagreement between them, though the discomfort she caused them for the most part lay fallow. When arguments did erupt, they were quickly extinguished, but left both parties resentful, angry, unreasonable. The air was clouded for a day – 'wasting precious, happy time', Myrtle said. But Archie, back from an hour's work on the boat, would return with his normal, equable mood reinstated and rest his head on his wife's shoulder, like a contrite child, seeking forgiveness for his outburst. In comforting him, Myrtle herself was eased. The strength of love for her husband ran eagerly through her as she stroked his coarse and sea-bleached hair, and they stood locked together in their kitchen chiding themselves for their stupidity. How could they be so foolish as ever to let Annie's daughter come between them?

The day after Myrtle and Archie came back from their honeymoon Archie went to sea. Within moments of his departure, Annie dashed round to the house. Her state of excitement was unconnected with Myrtle's return. She hurried through some perfunctory questions about whether Myrtle had had a good time, then her own uncontainable news burst forth.

'I'm engaged!' she shrieked, and held up her left hand. A minute speck of red stone perched like a firefly on her fourth finger.

'*Engaged?* Who to?'

Annie tossed her head, dismissing the importance of that part of the question. She twisted the almost invisible ring, assuring herself of its significance.

'Ruby,' she said. 'Or maybe garnet. I don't remember which. I just wanted something red. Great, isn't it?' She waved the finger under Myrtle's nose.

'But Annie – you're engaged who *to?*'

Annie fluttered her eyelashes, blushed, put on her most mischievous look. She liked to surprise.

'Ken,' she said at last.

'Ken?' Myrtle sat down, heavy with astonishment.

'Ken himself.' She looked down, rubbed the firefly again. Myrtle's incredulity was embarrassing.

'How on earth did that come about?'

'Well, he's loved me for ages, hasn't he? I made up my mind following you down the aisle. I thought to myself – why not marry Ken? He's a good man. I'm fond enough of him. Not everyone has to be passionately in love, you know, to have a happy marriage.' There was a sneer in her voice so faint that Myrtle might have imagined it. She looked away. She could not face her friend's eye.

'Are you so surprised?' Now, she mocked.

'Yes, in truth.'

'I thought you'd be *pleased*.' Myrtle's less than enthusiastic response to her news was not at all what Annie had envisaged. She pouted, petulant. 'It may not be the love match of the century like you and Archie Duns, but he loves me all right, you know that perfectly well. You're the person he confessed to. He'll be good to me, and I'll try to be a good wife.' She gave a wisp of a smile. 'We'll get on, see if we don't.'

Myrtle sighed. She made a quick decision to ask just one question, and then to brace herself for loyal support.

'But you've avoided Ken for so long,' she said. 'Scoffed at him, even. The idea of *marrying him* . . . you would have laughed at the very suggestion a few weeks ago. You've never loved him. You don't love him. As far as I know you don't even fancy him. Is it fair to marry him?'

Myrtle's tone was less harsh than her words. Annie shrugged.

'You have to be a bit practical when it comes to marriage, in my reckoning,' she said. 'There's not much choice left, locally, is there? I don't want to move away. I want to stay here. I've never had anything positive against Ken, except embarrassment that I flung myself on him in that silly way. But he's been a regular gentleman about all that – never mentioned it again. I think I could grow to love him. If he wasn't a good man he'd no' be Archie's friend, or yours. I respect him, and that's important in marriage, respect. So if one half loves, and the other respects – well, that's more than can be said for a lot of marriages. I think we'll be fine.'

'I hope so.'

'We both want a lot of bairns. We both want lots of the same things – we made a list the other night. Really. Don't look so worried. There's lots going on for us, I promise.' She giggled. 'Having waited for me for so long . . . I'll tell you something: he's a grand lover, Ken. I can hardly walk.' Annie moved round in a small circle, legs bowed, limping like a wounded bird. She laughed at herself, encouraging Myrtle to laugh too.

But Myrtle looked away, a confusion of feelings contorting her face. She controlled them, rose and went to her friend, kissed her on the forehead. Briefly they clutched each other's hands.

'That's all good, then, Annie,' she said. 'I'm pleased for you. I hope you'll be very happy.'

'We will be.' Annie laughed again. 'It gave him quite a shock, I can tell you, when I proposed. You should have seen his face!'

'When *you* proposed?' The calm Myrtle had fought for so hard now erupted again into shock.

'Not an hour after you and Archie had left on the train for Mull. Ken was walking me home. I mean, there weren't many wedding guests to choose from to walk home with, were there? I said how about you and me getting married, too, Ken? He said I'd had too much to drink. I said no, I'm serious. He said if you're serious, and I doubt it, I'm on. Of course I'll marry you, he said. I've loved you for years. Never in my wildest dreams, he said. Then he grabbed me. God almighty, how he grabbed me. We raced down to the beach, didn't stop till next morning . . . Came back wet through from the rain, and icy cold, but *engaged* . . .'

Myrtle's determination to disguise her horror failed her at this point. Annie was quick to try to quell her friend's misgivings.

'The wise thing Ken said was – and he's a wise man, believe me – he said all marriages involve risks, and we've got a lot more going for us than some. Provided, he said, I make it my business to be a faithful wife, there shouldn't be any problems.' She fluttered her eyelashes, suddenly red-cheeked.

'And when will you be getting married?' Myrtle asked primly, for there was no point in speculating on the likelihood of Annie's future fidelity.

'Oh, that. Sometime soon, I expect. Haven't had time to discuss it all really, have we? The important thing is, we're *engaged*, Ken and me.' She went back to rubbing the firefly stone on her finger. Like real fireflies, in daylight its glow was scarcely visible. Myrtle's disapprobation, she felt, was so plain she must distance herself from Annie's gaze. She moved to the stove, put on the kettle.

'Then there's cause for celebration,' she said. 'I'll make us a cup of tea.'

It's an hour or so after Janice has gone home. Myrtle notices a darkening in the room. She goes over to the window. Outside, a haar, thick as custard, obliterates everything in its greyness. There are no gulls' cries to splinter the silence. Myrtle wonders whether the haar has spread twenty miles north over the sea, where Archie should be casting his nets. It is time for supper. She contemplates taking the baked potato from the oven, but does not feel like eating it. A sense of isolation has wrapped itself round her like a caul. 'Archie,' she says out loud.

Then the dense quietness that has drifted over the village is split by a shriek – the shriek everyone most dreads: the rockets. The alarm scorches through the walls of the house, attacking the silence like a wild animal, pounding against Myrtle's entrails, making them hot and fluid. She trembles. It can't be Archie, she thinks – she hopes, she prays. He would have rung her on the ship-to-shore had anything been wrong. But some boat is in trouble.

Myrtle grabs the big torch, runs without her cloak from the house. It is dark, now, as well as foggy. There's confused shouting in the street. The rockets continue to savage the air, terrifying invisible gulls who have set up their own alarm system of petrified screams.

Myrtle follows other blobs of light. Down at the harbour, the lights are gathered at different heights, like the lanterns held by a group of carol singers. Their beams are useless little swords in the impenetrable air. Lustreless. Myrtle, looking down, cannot see her own feet, let alone the water in the harbour.

There's a boat in trouble on the rocks, someone says. *The Swallow*, says another. Myrtle's heart contracts with relief. The fear still grips, but when a disaster does not include your own loved ones, the fear is different. Relief breeds acute sympathy. Other faces nearby reflect the same feelings. Thank the Lord there's no' a rough sea, says one: that's one blessing. The lifeboat went off ten minutes ago. Someone's gone for brandy. Mary Tunnit, shouts a voice, is coming over queer. Mary Tunnit, wife of *The Swallow*'s skipper, is calling to the wives of her husband's mates to be calm. Her face is thick with creamy sweat, her hair wet and black. There's a catch in her voice. Myrtle remembers that catch. At school, always uncertain, called upon for an answer Mary could only produce one in a broken voice. She was never a leader. Now, in an emergency, she has to be the good influence, the calm and sensible one, or her skipper husband Duncan Tunnit would want to know about it.

'They're going to be all right,' she shouts, 'so stop panicking, for God's sake.' Firm of voice, now: shyness forgotten. She wipes the sweat from her face. In a flash from a lamp Myrtle sees Mary's skin is pale as oatmeal, unshining. Faceless voices chime, swinging this way and that. Myrtle feels a cold hand in hers: Annie.

'I was looking for you,' she says.

157

'I was looking for you.'

'Bloody rockets break up your heart.' Annie is trembling too. There's not a woman in the crowd unshaken. In the darkness the general quivering can be seen in the stirring of the lamps. Then the screech of the rockets stops.

The silence is dense as a cushion. The wives fall back on it, faces still alert but no longer clenched. Footsteps crump on the invisible ground. A man's voice shouts the good news: boat located, crew all safely on their way back in the lifeboat. Not much damage done: a line will get it off the rocks soon as the haar has risen. In the morning, most probably. Not much anyone can do in this murk. Footsteps retreat.

In the collective sigh of relief the lamps bob about faster, almost gaily. Mary Tunnit lets forth a wail of joy. The wives of *The Swallow*'s mates lumber about to hug each other, clasping at others on their way. Annie, still close to Myrtle, takes her arm. She must go home, she says: Janice is on her own.

The two women push their way out of the crowd. Relief, almost tangible, runs like a lighted fuse through the figures who are bloated by mist and thick clothing.

'Thank God,' says Annie, crossing herself – although not a believer, she likes the fancy gestures of the Roman Catholic Church. 'It could have been . . .'

'This has happened so often, hasn't it?' says Myrtle. 'There's good weather, you're conscious that the general worry has faded a bit, then something like this comes to shock you . . . You know you should never trust the bloody sea for a single day, but sometimes you're ground down, worn out by not trusting. I suppose we can only ever have limited moments of peace, when our men come ashore.'

'And I wouldn't say *they* were all peace and light and happiness,' Annie says sourly. 'Hell: who'd be married to a fisherman?'

Arms still tightly linked, they follow the guiding beams from their torches – inadequate little sticks of light in the dark and swirling gloom.

*

Once, when they were children – eleven or twelve – Myrtle and Annie were lost in a mist. Dot was walking them home from school. She stopped to go into the baker, urged them to wait for her outside without moving. But some devil, as Annie later told Myrtle, snuck up and twisted her guts. She was overcome with the desire to see what it was like running into dense mist. She imagined it would feel like running through clouds, she said. Or perhaps it would feel like being blind. She spun round and ran, without a word.

In the moment Myrtle realised she had gone, her instinct was to follow. She did not think to tell Dot, but plunged into the mist calling Annie's name. No response; no answering call. Myrtle panicked. She had lost all sense of direction. She had no idea where she was going, but kept running. The comforting smear of shop lights had disappeared. She sensed she was no longer in a narrow street, but had reached some sort of clearing. She stopped, listening. The density of the mist bound her like a dank shroud. But suddenly there were voices: boys' voices, calling Annie's name. There was laughter, too. How could they laugh? This was no ordinary game of hide-and-seek. This was frightening. This was horrible. Myrtle recognised Ross's voice, Ken's, Sandy's stupid giggle. She could not see them and the voices moved about, sometimes far away, sometimes a little closer.

Then her own name was called, and it was Annie calling. Annie ignoring all the boys: Annie calling her. Myrtle felt a great sob of strange happiness jerk through her. She called back. Somehow their voices led them blindly to each other. Their cold hands stretched out. Smudgily they touched. Annie was crying, too, more loudly than Myrtle – saying what a fool she was, how frightened she'd been. What would Dot say? What would her mother do when she heard? Myrtle mumbled words of reassurance. They held hands, stumbled along guessing the way. The boys' ragged laughter grew fainter. Some immeasurable time later they found an anxious Dot in the baker's shop. In her relief at their return, she handed them doughnuts instead of a scolding. Their fright had been punishment enough, she reckoned.

The incident had not lasted more than ten minutes, endless though it had seemed to the girls. On their way home, one firmly each side of Dot, Myrtle looked at Annie, saw the mixture of sugar and tears round her mouth, and felt an odd satisfaction. Although too young to work it out at the time, she was aware that, in a crisis, it was she, Myrtle, who Annie needed. She was consumed by thoughts of boys in ordinary life, but when something horrible happened it was Myrtle Annie could rely on. Myrtle would be the one to come and rescue her from the mist. It was Myrtle she called for, Myrtle she counted on.

That small event of many years ago – probably long forgotten by Annie – Myrtle regarded as a significant confirmation of her friend's dependency. In moments of carelessness, waywardness or unkindness on Annie's part, Myrtle often looked back on that frightening afternoon, and the memory reassured her. On the night of *The Swallow*'s grounding, she is reminded. The memory is so powerful she licks her lips, half expecting to taste sugar among the salt of tears. Always, when the haar comes down, the sharp and the sweet come back to her. She is glad to be with Annie.

It is with particular grateful joy that fishermen's wives welcome their husbands home after there has been a drama at sea. When Archie returns, two days after *The Swallow* has been dragged off the rocks, Myrtle leaps from her chair when she hears his footsteps outside, and runs out to greet him.

He looks surprised. He takes her in his arms, kisses her briefly on the cheek, but without attention. His mind is elsewhere. Even as Myrtle follows him up the steps she is aware of his distraction.

'They got *The Swallow* off,' she says. 'She's not too badly damaged.'

'So I hear.' He conveys no interest. Normally, if one of the harbour boats has been in trouble, Archie is the first to go down and offer help, consolation. Myrtle is puzzled. Anxiety, which usually fades when he comes through the door, spirals through her. What has happened? She waits.

Archie takes his place at the table, eats hungrily, preoccupied. Myrtle keeps her silence. She knows he will not welcome questions. It's the belief of fishermen that wives should be spared from incidents at sea. Myrtle's father waited ten years to confess to Dot that once *The Skyline* had rolled right over, and it was a miracle they had not drowned. Archie had taken even longer to pass on this information to Myrtle. The world of the men at sea is a shut-off place, its realities unimaginable to anyone who has not spent several days imprisoned in a fish-stinking bark bashing lonely over the waves; a place where off-duty hours must be spent in cramped and foul quarters never free from the smell of old frying, never free from the close proximity of unwashed fellow members of the crew. When they come home, the men want to forget all that. They want to put out of their minds the savagery of storms that try to kill the boat, tossing it without mercy from one cliff of wave to another, drenching decks and men over and over again, leaving them frozen, exhausted, numb, but still hanging on. They have no wish to recollect the rows, the flaring of tempers miles from home under an alien sky, the sickening disappointment of a poor catch. Fishermen want their lives to be divided, even from their wives.

So Myrtle allows this unusual silence to lumber on. It is so heavy she thinks a crack of explanation must come soon. Whatever the rules, Archie cannot leave her in this sort of suspense. She polishes the stove, going over and over bits that have no further need of polishing. Her back is to Archie.

At last she hears him put down his empty glass, push back his chair.

'It's Ken,' he says. 'He'll no' be much longer on the boat if he carries on.'

Myrtle turns. At some point when her back was to him Archie must have run his hands roughly through his hair. It stands up in stiff, clownish points. He looks a little crazed. Saddened.

'What do you mean? I thought it was all agreed. What's Ken done now?'

Archie shrugs. Myrtle can see he is still undecided whether to tell her. At last he says:

'Same old thing again. For a week or so he was back to his old self. But this trip he wasn't pulling his weight, hell he wasn't. Driving the lot of us mad with his moaning. Complaints of chronic tiredness. Of course you're tired, I say. Shore leave's for a mite of rest, not working yourself to the bone delivering stuff in that old van all over Scotland – of course you're knackered, I say. Besides, we agreed he'd give it up. We shook on it, didn't we? But he's not been keeping his word. And I'm afraid a lot of it is Annie's fault – nag nag nag as usual. He says she's given up asking for a car, but she despises him for not getting one. And now it's a lot of other stuff she's demanding – new shoes for the bairn, a tumble dryer, whatever. Daresay he's being driven beyond the bounds of rational behaviour . . . but he's going to have to make up his mind finally. Is he a fisherman or a removal man? And what exactly is he fitting in with his removals? So far I haven't asked him, straight out. But he knows I've a pretty good idea. If he's delivering black fish for Charlie Roberts . . . I tell you, his days are numbered. My patience is running out.'

Archie gets up from his chair, moves over to the window. He is flushed. He stands, looking out, back to Myrtle. His big shoulders block the light. The room is evening-dark and it's still early afternoon. Unnerved by the strange atmosphere, Myrtle keeps her place by the stove, leaning against it.

'Annie's dropped small hints,' she says carefully, 'but I'd no idea of so much . . . bad feeling still between you and Ken. She told me not long ago Ken was planning to sell the van and they'd spend the money on a holiday.'

'Well he's obviously made some effort, but has changed his mind. I warned him before we came off the boat this morning. I said Ken, this is your last chance. You sell that bloody van or get off the boat. God, how I hate all this. Until Ken went to pieces we were as good a crew as you could find along the coast. I say that myself. And now there's an atmosphere. I want it cleared. I want to trust Ken'll come to his senses, not be so bloody daft. But I don't want to bother you with all this. I only mentioned it because a crisis is looming. I'm surprised Annie hasn't been on at you about it all. She must know something's still up, be aware of the tensions. She's no fool, your friend Annie. Just ruthless when she's after something.'

'Sometimes,' says Myrtle, allowing a moment to register all Archie has said, 'even after all these years, I get the impression I don't know anything that's going on in Annie's head. She likes to make me think she's telling me everything, but I doubt that's the truth.' In her loyalty, she chose the word *doubt* rather than the phrase *know that's not*.

'If Annie betrayed you one day, I wouldn't be surprised.'

'She'd never do anything calculated to hurt. She's a good heart.'

'I'm not so sure.'

'Of course she has! You've never liked her, long before the stupid business in the woods.' Myrtle hears her voice rising. 'You've never tried hard enough to understand her.'

'Oh, I have. But seeing her through different eyes from you, it didn't seem worth the effort.'

Myrtle shifts her position. She wishes Archie would turn to face her. But he remains mesmerised by the view he knows so well beyond their small window.

'Well, anyway,' she says, attempting a lighter voice, 'whatever you say or think about Annie will make no difference to my feelings for her. You know that. I'm familiar with all her faults, all her cunning ways, and it doesn't make any difference. I love her. She's my friend.'

Archie gives an almost inaudible laugh. Myrtle can just hear the note of scorn within it.

'Aye: she is, too,' he says. 'More's the pity, sometimes.'

Silence flops between them again. Myrtle is conscious of the alarmed beating of her heart. She wants this uneasy exchange to come to a quick end, things to return to normal. However did they drift into talking about Annie? She was the one subject that they had both learnt to avoid with such skill . . . A single gull flies past the window with a long and dreary moan. Myrtle watches Archie's head move a little, following its flight.

Then the quiet is blasted by a battering of footsteps outside. There's angry banging on the door. Before Myrtle can urge the caller to come in, it's flung open. Annie runs in, scarlet-faced, ugly smears of red running down her neck and on to her chest. She does not look at Myrtle, but pummels the table – the place where she usually fans out her cards – and screams.

'Archie Duns! You've a lot to answer for! What is all this? What the hell have you been saying to Ken?'

Archie turns round very slowly. He looks down on the furious woman battering his kitchen table. Myrtle steps quickly forward, puts a hand on Annie's leaping shoulder.

'Get off, Myrtle! Leave me alone. I'm here to speak to your husband.'

'What seems to be the matter?' The languid voice of Archie's question infuriates Annie further.

'What's the matter? What d'you think's the matter? You've no idea why I'm here, I suppose?' A small pellet of spit flies out of her mouth and lands on her own flailing fist. 'I'm here because Ken, my husband Ken, comes home a broken man. You've been getting at him again, not a month since your agreement, and he can't take it any more. And nor can I. I don't want a broken husband. Beneath your – your *boring* exterior, Archie Duns, you're nothing but a sodding great bully, and I hate you for it. What has Ken ever done to deserve such a bashing from you?'

'Calm down, Annie –'

'Shut up, Myrtle. This is between Archie and me.' Annie moves quickly to the window. With small fists still whitely clenched, she reaches up and punches Archie on the chest. 'I want an explanation!' she shrieks.

'Stop it, Annie!' Myrtle cries. In a lightning shift of time Annie's angry hands become her childhood hands, the nails tearing at Myrtle's own face, the screams of fury ripping through the wind on the beach. 'Stop it, please. For heaven's sake . . .'

She sees Archie looking down on Annie with a disparaging smile, an expression she has never seen on his kindly face in all the years she has known him. He touches the place Annie has just punched on his chest. Her small fists have made no more impression on his bone-hard muscles than two alighting butterflies. Her pathetic gesture seems to amuse him.

'You shouldn't go hitting people,' he says, 'especially those a lot larger than yourself.'

'I'd willingly kill you for what you've done to Ken.' Annie no longer shouts. Her rabid fury is abating.

'What have you done, Archie?' Myrtle asks. 'I'm at a loss here.'

Archie's eyes pass thinly over his wife, and return to Annie.

'If you want an explanation, a proper explanation, you shall have one. Ken's been a dead loss on the boat for months, now. All his old energy gone, his enthusiasm. You of all people know very well the reason for this. Ken can't be relied on any more. What I said to him this morning was that he could have one last chance – sell the van and give up his deliveries, as we agreed a month ago, and get back to being his old self. The old Ken. As it is, we can't afford to carry a man like him on the crew. He's useless.'

'That's your story,' says Annie. 'You've always had it in for Ken. Always been looking for a chance to get at him. He was fine till you started to put the boot in.' She moves backwards, away from Archie, so that now she is equidistant between husband and wife.

'I've been warning him for months,' says Archie. 'He keeps promising things will be different. But they aren't. We made what I took to be a final agreement. He broke it.'

'Ken's done nothing wrong.' Annie is sullen now.

'I'm sorry to say, Annie, he has. I don't like reporting tales from sea, but the time's come for you to face the fact that Ken's going off the rails. Last week he couldn't even cope with the job he's best at, the nets. When Ross came to help him, he got nothing but abuse. Then a punch on the chin. Ross flung him on a bunk where he slept for three hours. Woke up saying he wasn't used to brandy and he'd had a slug or two to give himself energy. Meantime, two hands short, we were up against it. This can't go on. You must see. He's taken too many liberties, affected the general well-being of the boat.' Archie is quiet, forlorn. Annie shrugs.

'Well, I don't know. You must sort it out for yourselves.'

'Can't have a man on board who not only doesn't pull his weight, but could be a risk –'

Annie cuts him off with a laugh.

'Don't be pathetic, Archie! So dramatic. It doesn't suit you. How could Ken be a risk? If you'd stop nagging him, he'd be all right. You're the one who gets his wick. I'm telling you, if you ever put Ken off the boat, there's no accounting for how the score will be repaid.'

'Please, both of you . . .' says Myrtle. She feels an outcast, kneads her skirt.

'I'll not put Ken off the boat if I can help it,' says Archie. 'Last thing I want. But you better warn him. You better stop pestering him for things he can't afford. *You're* a lot to blame for all this, as you must know.' His eyes are hard on her.

'*Me*? I do nothing but support him.'

'You goad him. You want this that and the other, a lot of material rubbish you can't afford. You do your best to make him feel a wimp, not being able to afford the things you want that you have some daft idea will bring you happiness. So what does Ken do? Because he loves you, stupid bastard, he spends his shore leave running round in the van trying to earn a few quid to buy the junk you want. The more you get, the more you want. The last straw was your idea of a car. How the hell can Ken afford a car? You know perfectly well what the fish have been like lately. We're all having to cut back –'

'I don't want to hear any more such rubbish!' Annie cups her hands over her ears. She used to do that as a child: block her ears should a teacher scold her. Anger flares in her eyes again. She shakes her head – so pretty in her fury – and folds her hands firmly under her breasts, as if to support herself. 'I ask Ken for a few mod cons, yes, all right. What wife doesn't, husband away most of the bloody time? And yes, money's tight. Some of us haven't had the luck of a father's house to sell – money in the bank.' Her eyes lash from Myrtle to Archie. 'But to say I goad him . . . That's just the vicious side of you, Archie Duns. That's the side Ken and I know about.' She looks at Myrtle.

'Vicious?' says Myrtle, appalled. 'There's not a kinder man in the world. Archie says nothing without good reason.'

Annie gives a small laugh.

'The supportive wife! The perfect couple, so brave about no children –'

'Shut up.' Archie goes white. Annie tosses her head at him, defiant.

'Well, I will say you were right about the car. But you're out of date, so happens – we don't pass *all* our latest disagreements on to you two, so happens. I did want one, I don't deny that. But I've changed my mind. I've come round to thinking a better telly would be more within Ken's means.' She gives a contemptuous laugh. 'But here's one thing you know-alls don't know – Ken *likes* his moonlighting, earning a bit to get me things . . . That's why he broke the agreement, hasn't sold the van yet. And anyway, unlike some people, we're not the sort of couple who want to spend four days' shore leave sitting by the fire holding hands. We've got better things to do with our time – and what we do is bloody well nothing to do with *you*, skipper Duns –'

'It is if it affects Ken's job as one of my crew.'

'You're nothing more than a bully. Everyone says so. Ken would be better off without you. There's plenty who'd like him.'

'Then he can go.'

A trace of alarm flickers over Annie.

'I'm not saying he wants to go.' She moves to stand beside Myrtle, back momentarily to the door.

'What's that?' Ken's voice startles them all. He stands in the doorway. None of them has heard him coming up the steps. Myrtle, close to Annie, feels her shock.

'I told you not to come here, Annie.' says Ken. He is pale, unshaven – same look as all men when they come back from a stint at sea. But there is no immediate evidence of the broken man Annie declared had returned to her.

'I couldn't take any more,' Annie says. 'If you won't stick up for yourself, Archie's bullying, then I'll have to do it for you.'

'I can stick up for myself, thanks. Sorry about this, Myrtle. Archie and I can work it out between us. It's a private matter. It's nothing to do with the wives.' He turns to Archie. 'Shouldn't have blurted it out to her: sorry.'

Archie nods briefly: apology accepted for that. But he looks no less grim. Myrtle puts on the kettle. Ken's young face, blanched by moon-light, fills her mind: his quick, tantalising kiss, while all the time he was thinking only of getting back to Annie the Fisher Lass. The betrayal between friends is as punishing as loss, as death, she thinks. Myrtle sighs, misery coming at her from all directions. She wonders how this horrible scene is going to end.

'Tea, everyone?' she asks, and registers a general nodding.

Annie slumps, all energy spent, into the chair that is always hers for the card games. Now Ken has arrived, interrupting her confrontation, the fight is leaving her. Ken dithers beside her. She tells him to sit, too. But Ken remains standing, eyes warily on Archie. Myrtle pours tea.

Then Archie moves towards Ken, hand outstretched.

'Look here, Ken,' he says, 'this has all gone too far. Things shouldn't have got to this.' Ken looks at the hand with suspicion. 'Besides: what are we doing to our wives, involving them in all this? Can't we call it a day? You know what I'm asking. I don't want to lose you from the boat. I'll give you one more chance.'

'Go on, Ken,' says Annie, subdued.

The men shake hands. Ken turns his head aside so that he does not meet Archie's eye. Myrtle, in a warm rush of pride at her husband's magnanimity, puts mugs on the table. Ken gives a wan smile, sits beside Annie, who sniffs. She is scornful of a second deal sealed with a handshake.

'Do my best by both of you,' Ken says. 'But I'm a torn man.' This, Myrtle realises, is supposed to be a small joke. Ken is the only one to smile. Archie takes the huge pot from Myrtle and sits beside Ken. Myrtle sees how tired Archie looks. She also sees, beneath the chari-table front he has fought for, that he remains determined to carry out his threat should Ken fail him again. That this really is Ken's last chance is in no doubt. Myrtle prays that Ken will not be so foolish as to break his word a second time. Though if what Annie said is true about his *liking* the moonlighting, the firmness of his purpose could easily be shaken again. And then . . . but Myrtle will not let herself think of the consequences.

It's a long time since the two couples have sat down together round a table, and this unplanned gathering is not the easiest of occasions. But united in their disturbed feelings – each one different from the other – they make an effort to cover the awkwardness. The easiest way, having all known each other so long, is to resort to talk of the shared past. Archie tells the story of some childish escapade on his uncle's boat, and they manage to laugh. But a void remains beneath the paper-thin politeness. Not one of them is free of concern that the smallest mistake could cause a further explosion. They drink their tea swiftly.

Then Archie gets up and says he is taking Ken to the pub: they deserve a drink. The gesture is so out of character that Myrtle is unable to suppress a look of astonishment. Unlike most of his peers, Archie is not a man who frequents pubs often, and when he does it is for the sake of others.

It is for the sake of Ken, now, Myrtle realises: the last piece of his extraordinarily charitable behaviour in the past hour. Alone with Ken, he obviously thinks, the final agreement about Ken's future can be decided. And then, please God, may the matter be put away for ever.

As the four of them scrape back chairs in the dimly feathered light of the kitchen, in Myrtle's eyes Archie shines with benevolence. Although she is still innocent of much detail, she knows that Ken has caused Archie serious trouble for the last few months, and forgiveness can't be easy. But Archie has put aside his own anger about Annie's insults and accusations. For his wife's sake he has offered forgiveness, peace, a last chance. Never has Myrtle been so moved by his goodness. Tears approach her eyes. Through a blurring of vision she sees that Ken, following Archie out of the door, wears a feeble, guilty smile.

The two women are left alone. Myrtle turns away from Annie to dab her eyes with a dishcloth. Now is her chance to berate Annie for all the loathsome and untrue things she said about Archie. Now is her chance to ask what exactly has been going on, all these months, that everyone has known about but her.

She takes a deep breath, for control. Then, as she knew they would, sympathy and forgiveness surge over her. Annie, in a rage, had surely been saying things she did not mean. There had been deep trouble between her and Ken that Myrtle could only guess at – and the slight hurt of Annie's keeping these matters from her, Myrtle feels, is not worth dwelling upon. In a word, she deems it wise to carry on as if the storm had never happened. Annie would be expecting her support.

Myrtle turns round. Annie is sitting down again, pushing away things on the table in front of her, clearing a space as if for a game of cards.

'Glad that's over,' she says, airily, as if the whole incident had been nothing to do with her.

'Aye. No one can have enjoyed it.' Myrtle sits, too.

'Archie was the pourer of oil, I'll say that. Ken should never have come round.' She sniffs, searches for something in her pocket.

'Perhaps it was best it's all come to the boil. God willing, every-thing'll be back to normal now.'

Annie gives Myrtle a look in which a hint of defiance is still just visible.

'Maybe. Hope so. Bad things were said.' This, Myrtle realises, is the nearest Annie will ever come to an apology. Annie pulls an old packet of cards from her pocket. 'Shall we?' she says.

Myrtle nods. The cards are slapped down, the friends bow their heads in concentration. They are safely back in a place they know. This kitchen and the familiar game fortress them against the discom-forts of the world outside. For a while, as calm returns, they play in silence. Then Myrtle looks at the clock.

'Gone two hours,' she says. 'They must have a lot to talk about.'

'Ken's got to be off at nine. A delivery first thing in the morning. He'll have to drive through the night.'

Myrtle puts down her cards. 'But I thought . . .?'

'Just one final job, worth a bomb,' Annie says quickly. 'Maybe Archie'll persuade him against it, but I doubt it. Maybe they'll agree it's the *very* last job he does.'

'For God's sake, Annie! After all this. I can't believe it. We have all this discussion here not an hour ago, and Ken fails to mention he's another job lined up for tonight. Archie'll . . . I don't like to think what Archie'll do.'

Annie looks impatient.

'What none of you understands, as I said to Archie, is that Ken *likes* the extra work. It gives him a real buzz, coming home from some delivery – an easy drive up to Aberdeen and back. It gives him a real buzz to hand me over a wodge of notes and tell me to go and spend them.'

'Well I don't know, but it sounds to me pretty daft, and anyhow the arrangement is . . .' Myrtle fights hard to sound uncondemning. She is determined to say nothing that will resurrect the row. But fear for a troubled future returns. If Ken, encouraged by Annie, is unable to honour his promise to Archie, then God knows what will happen. Annie shrugs.

'Don't worry, Myrt,' she says. 'It'll all work out all right.'

Myrtle has little faith in this declaration. Unsettled, she concentrates hard on the cards again. They play in silence until they hear the sound of footsteps. The women's eyes meet in mutual relief. But the man who enters is neither Archie nor Ken, but Martin.

He carries, as he often does when he drops in on the Duns, a newspaper parcel. It's usually either a lobster or a crab, given to him by his parents. In return, he gets an hour or so sitting with Myrtle and Archie, who realise that beneath the cheerful exterior lodges a lonely man.

Tonight, Martin has miscalculated. He thought he would find the Duns on their own, enjoying one of their quiet evenings together. He has never run into Annie in their house. Knowing her visits are in the afternoon, to play cards with Myrtle when the men are at sea, he is careful to avoid those times. Seeing her at the table, he is confused, put out.

His feelings are transparently clear to Myrtle, who makes a quiet but firm show of welcoming him. While she fetches beer from the fridge, he hesitates over which chair to take at the table. Eventually he seats himself beside Annie.

His choice delights her. In a trice her various black moods of the past hours are gone, and a rosy blush spreads over her face and neck. She taps Martin's forearm with mock severity. His horror at the sight of her long silver nails comes upon him too fast to conceal.

'So! You bringing a lobster to my friend! You've been caught out, Martin. You never bring a lobster to me.' Annie pouts, childlike. Martin smiles, shrugs, lifts his arm to take a bottle from Myrtle, so that Annie has to remove her hand.

'I wanted Archie's advice,' he says to Myrtle. 'I've been offered a job part-time filleting. I've got the time. I could do with the money.'

'*There!*' Annie bangs her hand on the table, triumphant. She swerves round to Myrtle. 'How about that? Another one who isn't afraid of two jobs! I'd say it was fairly normal practice, these days, wouldn't you, Martin? If you're offered the work, you'd be a bloody fool not to take it.'

Martin and Myrtle exchange a look. On an evening not long ago they had touched upon Ken and Annie's problems, and the trouble they were causing Archie, though Myrtle could only tell Martin the little she herself knew. Martin plainly has no wish to be involved in an argument whose traces still linger in the air.

'Part-time grave digger, part-time filleter, part-time stonemason – and I'd still be far from a wholly employed man,' he says.

'Well,' says Annie, deflated by his unhelpful response, 'I daresay . . .' She tries another tack. 'So what have you been *up* to? Why haven't I seen you for so long?' The questions are accompanied by her most flirtatious look, a beguiling widening of the eyes. The expression is deeply familiar to Myrtle, who turns away. But not before she notices Annie's bottom lip quiver like a child's about to cry. Perhaps she still loves Martin, or imagines she still loves him, Myrtle thinks. Perhaps, in the blindness of this love, Annie will fail to see how pathetic are her small efforts still to attract him and – there being few other excitements in her life – she will go on making a fool of herself for years to come. Even as such harsh thoughts run through Myrtle's mind, sympathy overtakes them. For all her extraordinary appeal, Annie has had nothing but empty disasters with boys, with men. Ken is a compromise husband, not the man she loves, or even pretends to love, with the kind of energy that seals a marriage. Perhaps her real love – or the love most potent in the crowd of her fantasies – is Martin. But Martin has little respect for Annie – no interest. However she behaves, it's unlikely his feelings for her will change. So even if, in some future calamity, Ken and Annie part, Martin would not be the man to come to her rescue.

Myrtle is so entangled in her own thoughts that she has not been concentrating on Annie and Martin's last few exchanges. Now she notices that again Annie's approach has changed. She is talking in a more ordinary way, and Martin is paying more attention. She is talking about Janice, and how she is enjoying her private lessons. Martin is definitely interested. Myrtle busies herself unwrapping the lobster. As she moves back from the fridge she sees that Annie has pulled up her skirt over her crossed knees. The top leg swings gently while she spins her tiny ankle. It moves like a well-oiled mechanism whose works never fail. Martin's eyes trail the turning foot for a moment: then, conscious of a look flashed from Myrtle, he quickly shifts his look. Myrtle has no intention of joining their conversation even though much of what Annie is telling Martin is wrong: it's plain Janice has not bothered to tell her mother precisely what Myrtle is teaching her. Martin's interest appears to be increasing. He smiles at Annie, something he has not done for a long time. She blushes, and the ankle twirls faster.

Myrtle feels the necessity of occupying her hands. The events of the evening have made them shake. She takes a place at the far end of the table from the other two and begins to fold the sheets of newspaper in which the lobster had been wrapped. They are damp and limp at the edges, and smell of salt water. Myrtle folds them into small squares very carefully, as if they were to be preserved. Martin's eyes are still on Annie – more polite than interested, now, Myrtle thinks. She wonders how the encounter will end. She longs to know, though realises that is perverse. A new kind of unease, to which she cannot put a name, begins to possess her. She fears something worse than the previous row is going to take place. But then she tells herself that it's merely the trauma of the whole evening that fills her with such irrational thoughts. With hot, swollen, clumsy fingers she finishes her pointless task of folding the newspaper, and Martin, with surprising suddenness, rises and leaves with a perfunctory excuse about not wanting to be late.

'Well, that was a nice surprise,' says Annie, when he has gone. Her ankle no longer twirls. 'You're lucky in your visitors, I'll say that.' Myrtle is saved from answering by Archie and Ken's return. Archie, it's plain to see, is upright and sober as when he left, while Ken sags by his side, a benign but stupid grin on his face. Archie turns to Annie.

'As you can see, Ken here has to postpone his job. He's in no condition to drive the van tonight. But he'll be off in the morning, and that'll be his last job.' He says this with good humour, but casts a forbidding look at Annie. 'That's our final arrangement and I have every reason to suppose Ken will keep to it.'

Various reactions shift across Annie's face. There is an annoyed frown for Archie, a scornful glance for Ken. But what Myrtle sees rising most powerfully in her friend is the hopelessness of a woman married to a weak husband. Annie opens her mouth to say something, but thinks better of it. Ken moves his grinning face very slowly, like a mechanical toy whose battery is running down.

'That's our arrangement,' he says, slurrily, and puts out a hand roughly in Annie's direction. 'Home.'

He needs support. But Annie, dizzy with so many charged feelings, chooses not to indulge him. She sweeps past both Archie and Ken and out through the door without a word. By the time Ken has yanked round his eyes to follow her progress, she is gone. Archie takes pity on his helplessness, puts a hand on his arm and guides him to the door.

Archie and Myrtle, with the place to themselves at last, silently acknowledge the need to extinguish the traumas of the evening.

'Let's hope that's final,' Archie says. Then he laughs. 'What did you think of my way of stopping Ken's delivery until the morning? He just downed the whiskies, happy enough. No thought!'

'Grand,' says Myrtle.

They move to the window. Myrtle opens it. Frosty air gushes past them eager to devour the warm pad of the room. It's a clear night, full of stars. Archie's eyes rise automatically across the skyscape with the kind of humility that is natural to fishermen who put their trust in the sky – a look of his familiar to Myrtle. She never ceases to wonder at his knowledge of the stars, how he can use them to chart his path on the sea, or warn him of the weather. To her they are a confusion of twinkling specks, to Archie they are a well-worn map.

'See if you can find me the Bear,' he says.

This is an old tease. For years Archie has been trying to teach his wife the way round the night sky, but she remains at a loss. He never scoffs at her – just explains it's a knack, like the knack she has of observing curious things about people that he would never see for himself.

'I can't.' Myrtle's eyes are frantic among the millions of sparkling tracks, searching. She wants to please him. She wants to surprise him, as she sometimes can, and wave triumphantly to the Bear. But tonight the sky is smeared too densely with scintillating lights, and the air is very cold on her bare arms.

'The Plough, then. The Plough's so clear.'

'Really, Archie. I'm trying, but I can't. It's cold.'

Archie puts an arm round his wife's shoulder, and laughs.

'One day you will,' he says. 'One night you'll suddenly see it clear as anything, your way round the stars, and you'll wonder however you couldn't see it before.'

Myrtle feels the weight of Archie's arm on her shoulders, and bends her head against him. She wonders how it's possible to be so close, and yet so far apart in different kinds of knowledge. Archie is a man who knows about winds and currents, preying storms almost as soon as they have left their distant lair. He can read signs in the waves and remember where hidden rocks lie, across hundreds of miles at sea, without having to consult his radar screen. Better than any skipper along the coast he knows where the fish are gathered: some instinct draws him to them like a magnet, though each time he finds them he confesses surprise – Ken told Myrtle this years ago. Archie's knowledge has always been a mystery to her, a mystery that fills her with excitement, awe, respect. She loves learning from him, though there will never be time to gather more than a fraction of what he knows. But the very thought of things she must still glean from him spurs her love as keenly as his quiet ways and his stubborn resistance to romantic declaration.

After a while, too cold to remain standing against the night air – which Archie does not seem to feel – Myrtle shuts the window. She senses the kitchen is cleansed, but keeps this thought to herself. In their long marriage she has learnt which inconsequential thoughts to harbour, and which to pass on to Archie. One of the skills needed for a happy marriage, she has always believed, is to spare your spouse the general grain of thought that daily fills your head: choose, instead, only the particles that have some hope of interesting, enlightening or informing.

'You *are* cold, too,' Archie is saying. He is rubbing her arms, her shoulders, her cheeks – gently, with his thumbs. He is urging her to leave things till the morning. Myrtle sees the fan of cards on the table, where Annie left them: single reminder of an earlier part of the evening whose discomfort has been quelled by Archie. Relieved, but longing for further comfort, Myrtle follows her husband out of the room to bed.

'Is Ken happier, do you think, now everything's resolved?' Myrtle asks Annie. It is three weeks since the row, which has never been mentioned. Myrtle knows her enquiry is a risk.

Annie looks up from her cards.

'I'm not sure it's all been resolved in his mind.' She suddenly giggles. 'You know what? He never made that last job. Archie saw to that, getting him so drunk. He had a head on him next morning . . . didn't get out of bed till three in the afternoon. I said to him you've lost yourself a hundred pounds, Ken. There goes our last chance of a few savings. He didn't seem to care – his head was throbbing that badly. Savings! he said. You'd have spent it in an afternoon. I don't know what he thinks I am.'

Myrtle smiles kindly, as she always does at Annie's moments of most profound self-illusion.

'Anyway, I've persuaded him that all I really want is this big plaid coat I saw in a catalogue. A hundred and fifty-nine pounds. It would last me for ever, Ken, I said. He said that shouldn't be too far beyond our resources if I can hold out for a week or two . . .'

Now Myrtle sighs, and in her anxiety not to be trapped into a conversation about Annie's material desires, which could lead back into the dangerous territory, she finds herself taking an unwise path to deflection.

'Archie's been contemplating buying a bit of land,' she says. 'There's a small field going: Farmer Ricks is selling off his horses. It's nothing much, just over an acre, but protected.'

Annie eyes her with plain contempt.

'You're to be *landowners*? What would you want that old field for?'

Myrtle pauses, regretting her mistake. She should never have mentioned the matter at this time. Annie, in this mood, is bound to be unreceptive to the idea that she and Archie have so enjoyed for the past few weeks. It came to Archie the morning after the row: its planning has taken up the shore leaves ever since.

'Archie has it in mind to plant this coppice, this small wood.'

'What on earth for?' In her amazement, Annie puts down her cards.

'He's always liked trees. He thinks it would be a challenge, finding trees to withstand the weather up here . . .' Aware she is losing Annie's comprehension, and having plunged recklessly in so far, Myrtle decides to go one dangerous step further. 'Besides,' she says, quietly, 'Archie and I have nothing to leave behind. You've got Janice. We've nothing. No one. We just have this feeling we'd like to plant something.'

'Well.' Annie's astonishment is enfeebling. 'I don't know what to make of that. Seems to me to be a funny way to spend money.'

Myrtle, desperately wanting Annie to understand, tries further to convince.

'Just imagine: in twenty years or so there'd be this wood – for birds, wildlife, people to walk in, bluebells . . . Don't you see?'

'Not really.' In silence she wrestles for a long time with thoughts that Myrtle cannot guess at. 'It must be nice to be rich,' she says at last. 'Able just to go and buy a field if you want one.'

'We're not rich,' says Myrtle, quickly. This is another conversation she would prefer to avoid.

'Oh no? You got a fair price for your father-in-law's house, didn't you?'

'Most of that was sunk into the new boat, you know that.'

'You got this place for nothing from your ma. You don't know what it's like, paying rent.' Annie's mouth is twisted, resentful. She reflects in silence again. 'The funny thing about you and me,' she says at last, 'is that you're rich and you don't care about money. We're poor and I mind very much.'

'We're not rich, I tell you: we're far from rich. A few thousand in the bank. If we buy this field and trees there'll not be much left.'

'A few thousand in the bank! We're up to the limit of our overdraft, I'll have you know. You in your cushy position can't understand the worry of that.'

'Of course I can, Annie. And I know what it must be like, all the expense of a growing daughter –'

'You've no idea what it's like, the feeling of having nothing to fall back on. Don't try to pretend you can understand that.'

'Let's not talk about money –'

'Aye: it's always the thing that's come between us. In my book, the rich and the poor can never be true friends.'

'That's nonsense! Besides, you know we're not rich, Annie, though I'm not denying we've a bit more than you, and we don't spend much –'

'You're rich in my eyes.'

'What can I say? Except that money's not the most important –'

'It's bloody important if it's not there.'

'And, besides' – Myrtle feels herself flustered – 'you know that you can call upon Archie and me whenever –'

'Thanks. But never. You know we'd never do that.'

Both women are flushed. Myrtle feels provoked, defensive about her modest savings. Annie, consumed by the resentment of the Duns' wealth, is unreasonably angry. She would like Myrtle, for once, to shout at her, respond in equal anger. But that is never Myrtle's way. Myrtle's way is to hand out patient advice.

'Perhaps,' she says, 'if you could sometimes resist the extravagant things you always seem to crave . . . that might ease the strain.'

'I'll take no such criticism from you,' Annie explodes. 'Who are you

to criticise my innocent longings for a microwave, a coat, whatever?'
Her voice is breaking. 'You're always criticising, Myrtle. When you
keep back the words I can see them in your eyes. I get fed up with
your disapproval.'

Suddenly she is sobbing. She lowers her head on to her folded
arms: hair tumbles, speckled with lights. Myrtle is unnerved, shocked.

'Whatever's the matter, Annie? You can't expect us to agree on
everything. That would be very dull. We've never done that, have
we? And ever since we were children we've spoken our minds to each
other, haven't we? That's part of friendship, isn't it? Come on: sit up.
Tell me what's really the matter.' She pushes back the auburn hair.
Annie looks up, her stricken face streaked with mascara.

'Hell: it's nothing to do with you and me, with money, with criticism.' Annie sniffs, dabs at her eyes with her sleeve. 'Put it all down to
a difficult time at home. Ever since that night here, the new agreement
between him and Archie, Ken's been . . . well, not the man I know.' She
sits up, swats her face with a piece of kitchen paper but makes no
improvement on the dark state of her cheeks. 'He's become *obsessed*
with earning more money. Obsessed with providing me with things he
thinks I might want, things he thinks will make our marriage . . .
better.'

'Oh Lord, Annie. I thought everything was well, now. Archie's not
said a thing, except that all's back on track now.'

'Archie wouldn't know. Ken's keeping his word. No more deliveries. The van's up for sale, though God knows who'll take an old load
of junk like that off our hands. But he just keeps on and on . . . how's
he going to afford this and that for me? I suppose it was my own fault
in the first place, asking for things. Pressing him too hard. But now
he thinks he'll never keep me unless there's a constant stream of
things. I keep saying he's got it all wrong. I've got everything I want –
except just the one coat.' She manages a half-smile. 'And the kind of
husband I once imagined. But he's so convinced by his own idea it's
become a sort of madness. He starts up soon as he's through the
door, goes on and on. I find myself longing for him to go back to sea.
Few days' peace. Even Janice is pleased when he's gone. Home

tomorrow, aren't they? It'll all start up again. I don't know what to do.'

'I'm so sorry. I'd no idea anything was – well, seeing Ken so little, there was no chance for me to guess.' Myrtle's sympathy and concern rise automatically: she also feels both helpless and tired. A picture of Ken, all those years ago on the bus, comes to mind: Ken eaten with a sudden obsession. She had listened. Perhaps her attention had helped. 'Tell him to come and see me,' she says. 'Perhaps I could –'

'He never would,' says Annie. 'He's not that sort, a confessor. He keeps things to himself – always has. You remember him at school? Still, I'll say something. Thanks.' She looks at her watch. 'I must be going, Janice needs more bloody shoes.' She stands, her smeary face calmer. 'Sorry I flared up, said stupid things.'

'That's all right.'

The two women briefly hug, a less exuberant version of their old childhood embrace, but a signal that misunderstandings, differences, have been wiped from the slate again for a while.

'You'll never know how much Janice loves her lessons with you,' she says suddenly, gaily. 'If she does well, it'll be all because of you.'

'Janice is a good girl,' says Myrtle. 'I'm proud of her.'

Sometimes, for all that she loves Annie, Myrtle wants to be rid of her. She wants not to have to think of her troubles, provide sympathy, listen, comfort, assure. She wants a month's rest from the card games: she wants to be relieved of Annie's presence for a long time. Such irrational feelings induce guilt, but nonetheless, on sudden, unsignalled occasions, they assault Myrtle with a strength that confuses and saddens. This is one of those times. She is glad when Annie is gone.

The few weeks since the row have been particularly happy for Myrtle and Archie. Each time he has been home they have been involved in the negotiations for their field. (What Myrtle kept from Annie was the fact that the contract is ready for signing. This will be done tomorrow, when Archie gets home.) Myrtle has been engaging herself in the study of trees. Catalogues arrive. She goes through them slowly, marking the possibilities she can point out to Archie. She selects reference books in the library, makes notes. For the first time since her mother died, what with Janice's lessons and the planning of the copse, her days are fully occupied. She revels in the feeling of busyness, and the joy of working towards something again with Archie. Not since the renovation of the house, after Dot died, have they shared anything so closely and with such anticipation.

On the day before Archie's return, Myrtle is kept busy going through papers with the solicitor. Her walk is much later than usual. The evenings are getting lighter, but by the time she arrives at the field twilight is pressing down, causing her to think of their wood at the end of the day – longer, denser shadows, branches smudged into an indistinct mass of purplish brown. She feels intense excitement, and equal impatience for the few hours till Archie's return to pass. He expects to be back at seven a.m. Soon as the catch is unloaded they will be off to sign the contract, and then home to study the latest suggestions for planting on Myrtle's list. As Myrtle walks among the trees in her mind, watching the real sky close down into the kind of lively darkness that is a familiar harbinger of spring, her mind is so entirely free of Annie and her problems that she feels no guilt. She thinks only how fortunate it is, in the kind of uneventful life that she and Archie lead, that the occasional excitements that flare in the quietness are all the more precious for their rarity. The evening passes in greater than usual anticipation of Archie's return. Restless, Myrtle paces the room, studies the stars, knows she will not sleep at her normal hour.

It's three a.m. when Myrtle last looks at her clock. She then dozes for a while, dreams of branches, many of them fallen and rotted on the paths. There is birdsong but, more loudly, the harsh crack of a pheasant's cry. The dream is faintly disturbing. But when she wakes it goes quickly from her, overridden by the thought of the day to come.

At 6.30 Myrtle is sitting at her table drinking a cup of tea. She does not put on the lamp, watches light slowly unfurl across the small bit of sky framed by the window. In ten minutes she will put on her cloak, for it's a chilly morning, and go down to the harbour. She enjoys the moment when *Skyline II*, snub-nosed and a little battered now, pushes its way through the harbour's entrance. She likes to watch the way Archie skilfully manoeuvres the vessel into its place beside others tied to the wall. She knows that if she witnessed the homecomings regularly, they would become commonplace events of no great significance or wonder. As it is, Myrtle goes to greet Archie's arrival so rarely that her pride and pleasure never fade.

She picks up her mug, puts it by the sink. Her hand, she notices, is shaking. Her excitement is laced with nervousness – she can't think why, except that she's unaccustomed to important events: and the buying of their piece of land, and the planning of their coppice for posterity, is an event quite out of the ordinary. No wonder she is shaky. Archie will laugh, she thinks, when she tells him of her child-like sensations this morning. He may even confess he was in a particular hurry to get back. *The next time I'm standing by the stove* she thinks, *the contract will have been signed. We may be too excited to eat much breakfast.* All the same, so that Archie will not guess at the extent of her ungrounding, she takes two plates from the shelf and sets them on the table.

As Myrtle goes to swipe her cloak from the peg behind the door, the telephone rings. She curses it. On her way, now, she does not want to be held up for a moment.

The crackling, as she picks it up, tells her at once it's a ship-to-shore phone. The voice she can't immediately distinguish. Ross, perhaps. Shouting.

'Get an ambulance down to the harbour. At once! Quickly.'

'What?'

'There's been an accident.'

'Who?' The line is indistinct. Her immediate thought is Ken. One of his mistakes . . .

'Myrtle –?'

But she has slammed down the receiver, fled down the outside steps, left open the door. As she runs, she remembers an accident not long after they were married. Archie cut his thumb badly at sea. He arrived back with his hand a balloon of blood-soaked bandages. Went straight to hospital. No ambulance needed then. Whoever it is must have cut something more seriously this time.

Myrtle has run so fast that when she arrives at the harbour icy knives of pain are shooting up through her chest. Several boats are already in, unloading their catch. Not *Skyline II*. No sign of her. A group of fishermen some yards away are talking. One of them turns to Myrtle, shakes his head. What do they know? What have they heard? Should she ask? And Christ! She has forgotten to ring the ambulance! In her thoughtless panic she has failed to carry out the vital order. Myrtle turns to run to the telephone box outside the chandler's. At that moment she sees the ambulance tottering down the hill, an aged, cream-coloured vehicle with no sense of urgency. Ross, or whoever, must have rung someone else as well. Thank God. And the ambulance's blue light isn't flashing. Its siren isn't screaming. It parks unhurriedly on the harbour wall. It must know this mission is no great emergency.

Others have gathered. Some of the wives. Word has flown round. It always does, when something out of the ordinary happens. Weddings, funerals, accidents: there they suddenly are, the villagers, a mixture of loyal support and curiosity. Witnesses to an event that can be talked about, exaggerated, diminished, until it's superseded by the next happening.

A largish crowd has gathered by now. Myrtle moves along the harbour wall. She does not want to catch anyone's eye. She looks out to sea. There is a low, light mist. If Archie has to deal with an injured member of his crew, she realises, the signing of the contract may have to be postponed. Well, never mind. What is a few days? She sees that there's no horizon. It's one of those moments when the sky – a deep storm blue – is an arc that curves right into the water, no demarcation line, making one vast bowl of the elements. It's a miracle, she thinks, that on such occasions every fishing boat at sea isn't consumed by this void. Then she thinks how silly she is: for it's all an illusion to one standing on the land, a trick of the eye.

Jutting through the low mist, which lazes round its bows, comes *Skyline II* at last. Her meridian-blue paint is bright against the flat grey water. She moves very slowly, like something filmed in slow motion, moving and yet seemingly at a standstill. Myrtle runs back to the place where she will berth. Others are there before her, gathered round the ambulance. A stretcher, and its scarlet folded blanket, are waiting on the ground.

Myrtle clasps her hands. Their rough skin is very cold. Someone offers her a jacket. She wonders at this, but she shakes her head. Someone else shouts the *Skyline*'s nearly here . . . Head down, Myrtle swerves only her eyes to see the familiar shape of the boat nosing very close to the harbour wall.

Two ambulancemen, in livid orange coats, move to the edge of the wall. Myrtle moves to stand beside them. She looks down at the sullen brown water slapping at the slime-covered wall. She looks at the iron ladder cut into the wall – the ladder that Archie and his mates hurry up and down as if it is no more difficult to negotiate than a domestic staircase.

'Are you going down first, Jock, then? Or am I?'

'You go. You're nippier on your feet.' The two men laugh. Somewhere in the tightness of her own terror, Myrtle understands their lesser anxiety.

Skyline II is below them now, perfectly in place. A blast of smells rises up: fish, salt winds, iodine. The engine stutters quietly, then cuts out. The crowd is curiously quiet. Ross is running up the ladder, rope in hand, to tie up. His flesh is green-white under his stubble. As his face appears over the wall, Myrtle enquires with her eyes. But he doesn't see her. He doesn't see anyone.

'Hurry,' he whispers to the ambulancemen. One of them lowers himself, dithers a foot among the top rungs of the ladder. The other picks up the stretcher. Myrtle forces herself to look down.

Among the clutter of the deck a body lies covered in blood-soaked rugs. It looks too big to be Ken, and Annie is nowhere to be seen. Only a sprout of hair is visible, and a hand. The fingers are splayed: it could be a bleached starfish. Squiggles of blood pattern the small clearings of deck. Dozens of dead fish lie beside the body, tipped from a box that was meant for the hold. Their silver scales are streaked with blood. They lie among bloody footprints. Chains and nets are splattered with blood . . . The man must have erupted like a volcano of blood. It's everywhere.

Myrtle hears an echoing moan within her, like the call of dolphins in the sea's depths. She thinks she may faint, but clasps her own hands tighter and her vision clears. Someone has an arm round her and is saying things that make no sense. Both ambulancemen are on board now, making a space for the stretcher.

The crew all seem to be there, too: helpless, alert. As the body is lifted gently on to the stretcher, the blanket falls from one arm. Myrtle sees it is Archie's jersey, but for a moment the fact means nothing to her. Once the fisherman is in place, the two ambulancemen stand rigid with concern. How will the stretcher come up the wall? Myrtle can feel the whole crowd wonder, too.

In the end, she does not see how it is done. Once the mates have leapt forward to take charge of this particular part of the procedure, she turns away, unable to watch, for by now the connection between Archie's jersey and the wounded man has made insane sense. When she next looks – seconds, minutes, hours later, time is so contorted she has no idea – the bloody red parcel of her husband is rising above the ground of the harbour wall. It swings perilously for a moment, then is secured firmly at each end by Ross – sweat pouring down his face, and another member of the crew. The ambulancemen appear over the wall, hurry after the stretcher, their gratitude to the mates visible on their faces. Myrtle finds herself pushed towards the open doors of the ambulance. Ross takes her elbow, helps her up the steps.

She sits opposite the bunk where Archie is lying. His hand hangs down under the sodden rug: the great white starfish hand, the only thing not smirched with blood. She leans over and touches it. It's icy cold. She's pushed gently back into her place by the ambulanceman who is doing something to Archie she does not want to see.

The doors are slammed shut, cutting off the numerous faces of the now large crowd of fishermen and their wives who have come to see what has befallen Archie Duns. Myrtle is aware that Ross is by her side. She wonders vaguely, where is Ken? Surely Ken ought to be here with Archie? And where is Annie? Why isn't Annie here?

The ambulance moves forward, its siren shrieking. Myrtle looks through the clouded window. In the watery view beyond it – everything streaming, shredded, no shape or line unbroken – Myrtle sees Ken vomiting over the harbour wall. Annie stands beside him. Something in her stricken figure makes her seem on a different planet from her husband, for all her physical closeness to him. As the ambulance gathers speed Annie's shocked white face is a thin frame round the great black hole of her open mouth. The image dances in the blackened window all the way to the hospital: ugly, ugly.

Myrtle sits on a plastic chair in a small hospital waiting room that once might have been part of a corridor. There are shiny tiles halfway up the wall, the colour of beetroot. The detached part of her mind asks who on earth could have chosen such a colour for such a room, where people await bad news. She longs for the balm of blue or green on which to rest her eyes. She shuts them. The beetroot makes her feel sick. Cold sweat is guttering down her back. Ross, sitting beside her, keeps patting her knee. She has no energy to ask him to stop. Where is Annie? Still not here.

A long time has passed since the bloody mound of Archie was rushed past her through rubber doors which swung shut in her face. She managed to ask a doctor in a white coat, gashed with Archie's blood, what hope there was.

'Your husband's suffered a terrible injury, Mrs Duns,' was all he said, and ran from her.

A nurse had shown Ross and Myrtle into this beetroot cell. Tea was offered. Tea! Myrtle shook her head. Her throat was closed, so she was unable to ask Ross a single question, or utter a word. Her query to the doctor had used up her entire store of energy. So she and Ross sit in silence in the airless, stuffy place – the silence occasionally jabbed by the cry of a seagull beyond the shut window. Myrtle studies the pile of old magazines on the low table, their paper crumpled to a repellent softness. The cover of the top magazine is a photograph of a symbolically perfect wife. She has blonde hair that ripples like frogskin. She smiles a smile of china teeth. She wears an apron covered in orange roses. *Make your man an old-fashioned meal* is the headline that flies across her neat little hips. How can you make your man an old-fashioned meal if your man is no longer there? The question throbs through Myrtle sharp as frostbite.

Suddenly the door opens. The nurse – a tinge of anxiety just visible on her impassive face – ushers in Annie, and Ross's wife, Jean. Jean is very pale, her face glassed with sweat. Annie is red in the face, eyes bruised with tears. She is making a lot of noise, sobbing. She dashes over to Myrtle, flings her arms round her neck. Myrtle, rock hard in her upright position on the plastic chair, doesn't yield. She seems scarcely to notice Annie is there.

'Stop that noise, Annie,' says Ross. 'Doesn't help any of us.' His arm is round his wife's shoulder.

Annie, jarred by the note in his voice, stops crying at once. She disentangles herself from Myrtle and sits on the empty chair beside her.

'Is there any news?' she asks.

Myrtle turns to her. Despite Annie's distress, her smeared face and swollen eyes, Annie is pretty again. Myrtle shakes her head.

'We're waiting,' she says. 'Waiting, waiting.' Then she asks: 'Where's Ken?'

'Ken?' The question is flat, so empty, it is as if Annie has never heard of Ken. 'I don't know.'

There are footsteps. The door opens again, cautiously. A doctor Myrtle hasn't seen before comes in. Thick glasses make his eyes look as if they are set inches back into his head. There are two wings of sweat on his top lip, like a transparent moustache. He looks at Myrtle.

Ross and his wife stand up. 'Jean and I will wait for you outside,' he says, and they leave the room.

Annie puts a shaking hand over Myrtle's. The doctor swallows. He takes a biro from his top pocket and looks at his clipboard as if expecting to find good news there.

'I'm afraid I have to tell you, Mrs Duns, that your husband has passed away. We did everything we could.'

Passed away? For a moment the phrase is confused in Myrtle's mind with *passed by*. 'He's just passed by,' someone once said when she was looking for him. *Passed by* it couldn't be: though perhaps it was.

'You mean he's dead?' she asks at last.

'I'm afraid so. He stood no chance, really.'

Annie's fingers are cold spiders all over the clump of Myrtle's hands. She tries to shake them off. Annie is whimpering.

'I'm so sorry,' the doctor adds.

'Horrible for you, having to break this sort of news,' Myrtle hears herself saying in a voice that is bright, controlled.

'We never get used to it. There's no best way of doing it. Now, if there's any way we can help . . . When you feel ready, we can make arrangements.'

'Thank you. I can manage. Annie here will come home with me.' There is a feeling of alcohol in Myrtle's veins. She is so in control it is uncanny. The doctor coughs.

'I don't know if you'd like to see your husband –'

'No thank you –'

'– pay your last respects?'

'No.'

'Go on,' says Annie. 'You must say goodbye to Archie.'

'I want to remember him alive, not dead,' snaps Myrtle. She glares at Annie, then at the doctor. Her eyes are hard and dry as glass, not a tear in them. No tears behind them ready to soften.

'Very well,' says the doctor. 'Whatever you wish, of course. People feel differently. But if you change your mind, just let us know. Mr Duns will be tidied up within the hour.'

The doctor looks as if he's aware of his own clumsiness. He backs out of the room, inclining his head a little in Myrtle's direction, muttering further words of regret.

When he has gone Annie says:

'I'll go and see him if you like.'

'No.'

'Someone ought to see him.'

'Why?'

Annie shrugs.

'Last respects,' she says. 'Though I suppose that doesn't mean much.'

'No.'

'Oh Myrtle, how could this happen?'

'How did it? That's the question.' Myrtle stands up very fast. Her hands hang at her sides, heavy as buckets. Annie shakes her head.

'I don't believe any of this,' she says.

'It's happening,' says Myrtle, 'and I want to go home now.'

Annie goes to fetch Ross and Jean. Ross screws the balls of his thumbs fiercely into his eyes to scotch the tears. The three of them walk with Myrtle back to the house. The few people about lower their eyes as the small troop passes, and murmur words of sympathy. The news, it seems, has reached every corner of the village. Myrtle keeps herself very upright, silent. She remembers what Dot said when Jock died: you have to keep going till everyone's gone away.

At the house Myrtle runs up the steps. The front door is open. For a second she can't remember why. She goes in and the comfortable sight that has met her on a million ordinary entrances into the kitchen is there as always. The only difference is that the contract for the buying of the field lies on the table awaiting their signature – hers and Archie's.

Myrtle is surrounded by kindness, sympathy, friends, company, offers of help, offerings of flowers. She is brought soup and pies and shortbread biscuits, in the pathetic belief that at some point she will feel hungry. For the rest of the day people come and go – Archie's schoolfriends, his mates, their wives. They try to find words, try to hide their tears, marvel at Myrtle's apparent calm. 'When she takes it in,' she hears one of them whisper as soon as she is outside the door, 'she'll crack.'

But Myrtle has no intention of cracking. All she wants is to be left alone. Annie is a constant presence, making endless mugs of tea and finding her way among the biscuit boxes with an efficiency she has never before shown. She offers to stay the night, but Myrtle insists she wants to be alone. Annie accedes to this wish at last, cries again, and hugs her friend.

'You're so strong,' she says. 'No one can believe it.'

'Where's Ken?' Myrtle asks.

'I don't know. When he comes home shall I send him over?'

'Aye. Tell him I want to know, from him, how it was.'

'I will.'

'I don't want to know from anyone else.'

'I'll make sure of that. Promise me you'll ring if you want me in the night.'

'Promise.'

'And I'll be round in the morning first thing. Oh God, Myrtle. What did Archie ever do –?'

Myrtle cannot contain her impatience, though she tries to be gentle.

'There's no accounting for the Lord's decisions, I've always known that. Now, thank you for being here . . .'

When Annie has gone Myrtle moves brusquely about in the emptiness, drying mugs that the many visitors have left to drain by the sink. She watches her actions from some distant place outside herself. She watches herself move towards Archie's old jacket hanging on the door. She watches herself, for a moment she can't help despising, bury her head in its coarse wool stuff that is alive with the smell of him. She sniffs hungrily at his sweat mixed with the salt winds and sea spray that are embedded in its texture. Then she moves quickly to the table, picks up Archie's pen. On the back of the unsigned contract she begins to make a list of arrangements that must be made for the funeral. She stays up till midnight, but Ken does not appear.

Five days later, an hour before the hearse is due, Annie comes round. She wears a black velvet beret – plainly bought especially for the occasion – which balances precariously on her curls. A sprig of heather is pinned to her dark coat. She carries a bunch of bright flowers wrapped in a cone of cellophane.

'Didn't think he'd want anything too gloomy, knowing Archie,' she says, dumping them on the table.

Knowing Archie. Annie didn't know Archie at all. Her claim is annoying, but Myrtle manages a faint smile.

'Thanks,' she says. 'Lovely. Do you want to come in the hearse with me? There's room.'

Annie nods, pleased by the offer. To be involved in the local importance of a death is no less gratifying than being singled out in any other important event. She sits, undoes her coat.

'Ken came home last night,' she says.

'Did he say where he'd been?'

'No. But then I didn't really ask. It's not as if I cared.'

'It was worrying,' says Myrtle.

'Aye, on top of everything else. I'm sorry for the extra –'

'That's all right. I'm just glad he's back. It must have hit him badly, his old friend . . . for all their differences. I'm glad they'd made it up, the quarrels. Is he coming to the funeral?'

'He didn't say. But I imagine so. He wouldn't miss Archie's funeral.' She glances at the clock. 'Half an hour. Shall we have a game?'

Annie takes a pack of cards from the pocket of her old navy coat and begins to shuffle them. Myrtle pulls the bunch of flowers towards her so that she can read the message. Annie's writing is fat and unruly, just as it was when she was ten years old. *Dear dear Archie*, it says, *missing you already and always will. Much much love, Annie.*

Much much love? Annie had no such thing for Archie, nor he for her. As for missing him: Annie's could only be a thin, polite sort of missing. Again Myrtle has to quell a stab of annoyance. She knows this is no time to be ungrateful for the small hypocrisies of death.

'All right, is it? Took me ages to think what to put.'

'Fine, fine,' says Myrtle.

'Ken'll bring his own bunch, I daresay.'

They concentrate on their game of cards till the hearse arrives. Annie sits one side of the coffin, which is covered in spring flowers, Myrtle the other. Tears pour down Annie's cheeks, drip from her jaw on to her coat. Myrtle's own eyes remain hard and cold, solidified in their sockets, so that on the journey to the church she sees nothing but the transparent salmon skin of the driver's ears that stand to attention under the brim of his official black hat.

Late that night, when it's all over – the ceremony, time, reality, all an incomprehensible flotsam in her mind – Myrtle goes automatically to the kitchen window to close it. Her exhaustion, a weariness unlike any she has ever known, seems to walk beside her: she longs only to lie down, now, beside it, and sleep it away. But she takes a moment to look up at the clear night sky, full of stars as it was that last time she and Archie contemplated it, Archie so full of his teasing.

In a single glance Myrtle sees the Bear. It shines out at her more clearly than any of the other gatherings of stars, impossible to miss, to confuse. The sadness of not being able to please Archie by her discovery is what causes her finally to weep, and she knows that widowhood has begun.

Part II

It's early morning, two years after Archie's death, at the fish market. In the large shed, where neon bulbs fizzle sourly against sunlight, the floor is covered with plastic crates of fish. Through the spiky coverings of crushed ice, their heads all face the same way. Myrtle, shawl over her head, wanders about the wet floor looking at them. She sees how in death every one is different. Some look resigned. Some are still open-mouthed in indignation. Some have a chinless, weary look as if the catastrophe of being caught in a net was of no consequence. All their eyes are open. They have in common huge black pupils almost filled with highlights. Their irises are uniformly the colour of moonstones. Within hours each one of these thousands of creatures will be reduced to separate flesh and bone by a few lethal flicks of a knife. Tomorrow they will be replaced by a shoal just as large, their fate just the same.

The place is crowded. Men in grubby white coats and yellow rubber boots stomp about among the crates making notes, shouting prices. There is a sense of customary speed, urgency. Many of the fishermen, having dumped their fish, want to go straight back to sea for a further twenty-four hours before taking a couple of days off. Political problems in the fishing industry are taking their toll. They must go much further, these days, to find their fish, come back with a much reduced catch. The good days of plenty, and rich takings, are over. The fight for survival, now, by those who have not abandoned it all and gone off to the rigs, is harder by the week. What would Archie have made of it all? He would have shared in his mates' dejection. He might even have turned in the *Skyline II* for a smaller boat, as many of the men along the coast had done, and gone fishing up in the northern waters.

Myrtle leaves the shed for the harbour's edge and looks down at the fat, grubby boats, each one scabby with rust. From one of them fish are still being unloaded. The boxes are hauled up on primitive cranes, dumped on the ground with a stinging crash of ice, loaded on to a trolley and wheeled into the shed to be sold. On the decks of the boats are large piles of green net, tidily rolled up, plastic floats bunched over them like giant necklaces. They are a favourite look out place for gulls. A few are perched on the floats now: enormous birds standing on stilt legs, birds of voracious eye and savage beak. As a load of boxes swings on the crane from the boat to the land, a single flat-fish falls to the ground. The gull whose anxious watch happened to be in the right direction is the one who swoops and catches it. The fish is bolted down, too big for the beak but tossed back with much jerking of the head: then the neck is swollen to a puff of goitre feathers. The gulls who missed their chance keep up their moaning. There is no sharing among birds who must fight for survival.

'They're starving,' says a voice behind Myrtle. She turns to see Alastair Brown, the harbour master. He, too, is watching the desperate little scene. 'The Lord knows what'll happen to them.'

Alastair Brown is a newcomer to the village since Archie died, a Cornishman by birth, who likes to give the impression that he has inherited Mediterranean blood. Perhaps it is to underline this fiction he wears dark glasses, no matter how overcast the sky, or dim the lights in the shed. These perch importantly on a nose shaped like a parrot's beak. No one has ever seen his eyes. His excessive black hair is disciplined by quantities of Brylcreem, a trick he has learnt from watching videos of forties films, the passion in his life only second to fish and the sea. Beneath his impeccable navy Guernsey, he always wears a clean white shirt and the kind of sunset-streaked tie that is laughed at, behind his back, for being poncy. In all, he is a singular character, standing out in a community of unflamboyant men, but agreeable and efficient at his job. His small vanities give rise to friendly amusement, but he is generally liked.

Alastair Brown is a bachelor. On his arrival in the village he was treated to the scrutiny of every unmarried woman of approximate age. Some fancied his harbour-side house, much in need of a woman's touch; some saw themselves as the first to rip off the dark glasses, stare deeply into the long-hidden eyes, and get on with things. Polite though he was to all these ladies eager to win his favours, no definite relationship seemed forthcoming. An occasional drink in the pub was all they secured, not a hint of anything more promising, for all their competitive declarations to each other of his serious intent. Sometimes he is seen leaving his house with a small tartan suitcase on a Friday night. There is a rumour that Dundee is his destination. Further rumour suggests there must be a Dundee woman who has something the locals lack. There would be no surprise if Alastair Brown came home one day with a bride on his arm. Should this ever happen, the wife would receive a restrained greeting.

Annie, unsurprisingly, was one of the many who cast both eyes and hopes on the suave harbour master. Bolder than many of the others, she wooed him first with free cups of coffee in the café, which he accepted with grace and pleasure. But he made no suggestions of returning her hospitality. Annie grew impatient. She had never met a man remotely like Alastair Brown before. Although she admitted to Myrtle her attraction to him was set more on his originality than his body, she saw him as a challenge that could not go untried. She laid her plans and was rewarded in part.

The reward was to be granted entry into Alastair's house. This was something none of his other pursuers had achieved. Annie's way was to knock on his door one night, and his politeness prevailed. Without asking why she had come, he invited her in to join him watching the end of *They Were Sisters*, one of his favourite forties films. He ushered her to an upright chair, gave her a glass of milk and whisky, and returned to his own armchair for the rest of the film. It was soon apparent to Annie he was so engrossed in Margaret Lockwood that she was able to look about, taking in his habitat, as she later told Myrtle, quite freely.

She saw a sparsely furnished, bachelor sort of room, though there were shelves of books and a glass case full of antique nautical instruments. Also, the curtains were plainly interlined, and might even have been a silk mixture. From such clues Annie was able to guess that Alastair Brown, harbour master extraordinary, was a man of some means. As the credits of the film came up at last, her enthusiasm to get to know him better increased.

She handed him a small paper bag that had been resting on her knee, explaining this was the reason for her unannounced visit. She hoped he would not think her . . . Annie could not immediately find the right word, but Alastair Brown did not notice as he pulled a multi-coloured tie from the bag. As he looked at it in some surprise – she could not tell for the life of her, she said to Myrtle, whether he liked it or not, as the black glasses concealed most of his expression – Annie explained she had come across it at a car boot sale and thought it just the thing for his collection. He responded to this piece of infor-mation with silence. Annie, by now unnerved, went on to explain that as it had only cost ten pence she felt it could not be considered as a gift with a message. To this Alastair Brown was bound to agree. A defi-nite smile indicated his approval was gathering. He thanked her, put it back in the bag, and said it would indeed be a valuable addition to his collection. Then there was more silence.

But Annie, encouraged by his signs of feeling honoured by her attention, felt she should go one step further in her mission – having got this far, having got *into* the house, unlike any of the others – before she left. She asked him if he ever took off his glasses: it was the question the whole village was asking, she added, lest he should think the impertinence was solely hers. Alastair Brown answered by re-arranging the angle of his spectacles across his beak nose. Finally, he said *no* was the answer to that question. Except, of course, in bed.

When it came to tactics, Annie told Myrtle in her recounting of this whole story, never had she been so stretched. She decided to pause for a moment, then take the plunge. Take the bait – she was convinced it was bait – he had offered her. She wondered if he would pay her the compliment, she said, sweeping her own lashes about in the way that could be relied on for effect, of allowing her to be the first one to see his eyes. Alastair Brown remained unmoving, in astounded silence. But there was something that did not suggest he was insulted, just amazed. To counteract any alarm she may have caused him, Annie gave a small laugh, and quickly explained that, of course, it had never entered her mind that bed was the only place in which he could be seen with naked eyes. No such cheeky thought, she tried to convince him, had entered her head. But how about a compromise? How about snatching off his glasses just for a moment, and in return she would give him a kiss? Annie laughed again, suddenly feeling the power of her own ingenuity. She felt things were going well. But she laughed alone.

Suddenly Alastair Brown stood up very fast. He put his hand to his mouth. In his smart navy jersey, he reminded Annie of a station master about to blow his whistle, keen for the train to leave his station. The dark glasses, in which she could see a miniature portrait of her own confused face, were turned hard on her. *That would be most improper*, he said. *That would not be the done thing at all: and now if you don't mind, Mrs Mcleoud, I'll show you to the door.* His dismissal bit deeply into Annie as he led her to the door, shook hands, and bid her a polite goodnight. Alastair Brown was her only failure since the day in the woods with Archie.

Myrtle, entertained by the story, had managed to make Annie promise not to repeat it to anyone else, both for her own sake and Alastair Brown's. Annie had kept her word. She remained the only one to have entered his house, but even that small triumph she managed to keep to herself. Alastair Brown continued to be approached in various ways by women from villages all up the coast – the news of an available bachelor of means, a harbour master to boot, had travelled fast. There was nothing to suggest any of them had been any more successful in their overtures than Annie, although speculation that something was afoot was renewed when there were fewer sightings of Alastair Brown and his tartan suitcase bound for weekends in Dundee.

While subtle competition for his favours continued, the story began to go around that the woman he was actually waiting for was the widow Myrtle Duns. She was one of the few women who, with no inclination ever to set up with a man again (though this fact was known only by Annie) had never shown the slightest interest in, or even warmth towards, Alastair Brown. They were mere acquaintances. Their communication extended to no more than a few polite words on the rare occasions they ran into each other. Annie was not slow to pass on the rumour to Myrtle. The absurdity of the whole idea made Myrtle smile. She could not imagine what fuelled it, but put it down to the foolishness of empty minds. She hopes Alastair Brown has not heard the gossip too. It would be embarrassing, make their brief encounters awkward.

The morning at the fish market, when the harbour master observes the seagull's plight, is only the fifth or sixth time he has offered a polite comment to Myrtle in the year that he has been in the job.

Myrtle, scornful of those who see her slightest exchanges with Alastair as evidence of anything other than common decency to a neighbour, is ready to go along with his friendliness.

'You're right,' she says. 'Archie was always concerned about the gulls.'

Alastair Brown is standing beside her now. He rests a bare hand on a stack of full fish boxes. One of his fingers is only an inch from an open mouth frilled with spike teeth. He picks up a handful of crushed ice, watches it melt and run down his thumb. The hand is not that of a fisherman. The skin is wind-burnt but unblemished. Myrtle looks at it with interest. 'Going to be another fine day,' he says at last.

'I think it is, aye.'

'And hot,' he says. 'Almost like Cornwall.'

As Myrtle does not respond to this, Alastair Brown turns and moves towards the ice house. She follows for a few paces, then stops. Ice is being pumped from the machine, through the baggy overhead tube and straight into the hold of one of the boats. The process makes a loud scrunching noise, like hundreds of feet on gravel. Ken must be at work, she thinks, and stops, not wanting to go any further. She does not want to run into Ken. After Archie's death he never went to sea again. Two months later the one-man job came up at the ice house and he took it. His knowledge of what's going on at sea is now vicarious, his life duller. But Annie likes the regularity of the wages. And Ken, Annie says, likes the fact he has more time for reading. He spends many of his free hours up at the library. He doesn't tell Annie what he reads, but she suspects it's 'poetry and stuff'. He has become very quiet in the last two years: reverted to the taciturnity of his boyhood. But none of this is any concern to Myrtle. Her wish is simply to see him, even in the distance, as little as possible.

Alastair Brown is at the door of the ice house. He turns and waves to her. She waves back. He goes in. She stands just where, as a small child, she used to stand holding Dot's hand, watching the men unload sacks of ice from a van that came from Edinburgh. She remembers the excitement when the ice machine was first installed. Most of the villagers came down to watch it work the first time, marvelling at the speed with which the stream of ice tumbled down into the hold of the first boat in the queue. Now, of course, the modern device no longer holds any awe. Like all improvements, it soon became the norm. Even the old men who used to hunch the heavy bags from vans to boats are no longer impressed. The marvel of progress is a short-lived thing, Myrtle thinks.

She turns her eyes to the harbour mouth, half expecting, as always, to see *Skyline II*. But the boat has been sold. She works from Aberdeen. She'll not be coming back here again. Ross and two of Archie's crew have a small boat now. They fish up on the west coast, near Inverness, away for several weeks at a time. Myrtle averts her eyes from the place where *Skyline II* used to berth. She does not want to see the strange red boat that has taken her place. She looks at her watch. Eight o'clock. A quarter of an hour before she must be at school. Time to fill in. She has managed to structure her life pretty well – part-time job at the school now, the planting of the coppice, one day a week at the Evergreen Home, Janice's lessons a few hours a week: yes, she is busy. But unexpected moments fall upon her, still, jagged as broken glass, cutting, empty. Just as she thinks both her mind and body are employed, the scorch of singleness assaults her, reminding her that whenever the small occupation that engages her comes to an end, she must return to an empty house, an empty bed, an emptiness that reaches far back beyond the horizon.

Myrtle becomes impatient at such moments. She turns quickly now to leave the harbour and walk up the hill to the shed where Martin does his filleting in the mornings.

Martin is hard at work on his first load of fish – several crates must be ready for collection by midday. He stands behind the slab, intent on the fish he is preparing. The thin blade of his knife makes the barest sound of splitting silk as it runs through the raw flesh. The only other noise in this bleak little work place is a dripping tap over the sink. Martin spends six hours a day here. Myrtle wonders at his constant cheerfulness. She chooses a place to stand on one of the few dry patches on the stone floor, looks down at his hands, so skilful, so fast – trained to chip stone, not to slice fish.

'Myrtle! Tea?'

'No thanks.' There is a single mug by the sink. On the ceiling, in the bulbs of the special lights, there are small coils of such intense blue that they hurt Myrtle's eyes. She cannot imagine how he can work in such alien conditions.

'So what are you doing? Here so early?'

'I don't seem to be able to stay in bed much after five-thirty. I wake up so alert. I went down to the harbour.'

'What's going on down there?'

'Nothing much. I ran into Alastair Brown.'

They smile at each other. Martin is aware of the rumour. He throws the carcass of a small haddock into a crate on the floor. It's already half full of slobbery skins and milky spines. Stripped of their flesh, they are bent like the fronds of delicate plants. He lays the fillets beside a row of others, iridescent little silvery strips of matching neatness.

'Any progress in his courting?'

'Don't be silly! We've scarcely exchanged a word since he's been here.'

'Maybe he's a slow mover. Though I have to say I don't see him as quite the ideal man for you, should you ever want to marry again.'

'I'll never want to do that.'

'No. Well. That's understandable.' Swish, swish goes his knife. Off comes a head. Its gold eyes, not long enough dead to have dulled, look at Myrtle. 'Have you thought any more about the headstone? It's been, what? Almost two years now. I'm keeping aside that fine bit of marble I showed you. You only have to give me the word.'

'I have thought, yes. Thought and thought. "Archie Duns, husband and fisherman", I thought. How about that? And the dates, of course.'

Martin's thumbs fumble swiftly through the fish while his eyes look up to meet hers.

'That sounds fine to me,' he says. 'That sounds good. I'm sure God prefers understatements. I mean, wandering around as many cemeteries as I do, you'd think the dead *en masse* were saints – such tributes. So you're not thinking about adding something from the Bible, too?'

'I'm still trying to find something. I'm being a little slow, I know. I want to get it absolutely right.' Martin nods. 'I must be on my way. Assembly's in three minutes.'

'You're liking it, the job at school?'

'Oh aye, it's grand. It's what I've always wanted, teaching. Nine- and ten-year-olds are my lot. Wonderful, that age.'

'Shall I bring you up a piece of haddock on my way home?'

'You're always bringing me fish.'

'And why not?'

'Well, that would be nice.'

'See you later, then.'

Myrtle pushes through the doors of thick transparent plastic, breathes fishless air, sees a ribbon of pale sun on the sea. She looks forward to the warmth of her classroom – a much more cheerful and painted place since she herself was there. She looks forward to the recitations, one by one, of *When fishes flew and forests walked* . . . They are good learners, her class. She is proud of them. The school bell echoes down the wynd: she hurries. She's been up so long almost a whole day seems to have passed. This evening there's Martin's piece of haddock to look forward to, and in the afternoon Annie is coming round for a game of cards. That is what she looks forward to most of all, for they have not had the chance to see each other for a while.

The evening after Archie died, Martin went round to see Myrtle. He found her alone at the table surrounded by a small chaos of paper, lists. There were signs of last night's weeping in her eyes, but she seemed calm, and glad to see him.

'I'll be the one to dig Archie's grave,' he said. 'It's all arranged.'

'Thank you. That would be best.'

'And . . . as for the headstone, when it comes to the time to think about it, you can rely on me to find the finest bit of marble.'

Myrtle, grateful for a visitor who did not offer well-meaning platitudes, made an attempt to smile. The softness of his Canadian drawl was comforting as wool on skin.

'You're a good man, Martin,' she said, and turned her eyes to the window. She gave a small, self-deprecating laugh. 'Why, I haven't even found the right epitaph for Mother, yet. Years late. And now there's Archie. I'll do my best, try to concentrate when things have –'

'There's plenty of time. You've enough to think about at the moment, arranging the funeral. Is there anything I can do?'

'I think it's all done. I've been making arrangements all day.'

'If there's anything, anything at all . . . you know you only have to call on me.'

'I know.' Myrtle nodded. 'Thanks.'

They fell into silence for a while. Several times Myrtle cocked her head as if she heard footsteps outside. Once she put up her hand, as if expecting to find Archie's reaching over her shoulder. But when all she grabbed was air she gave an impatient sigh, annoyed with herself for such foolishness. Eventually she said:

'I don't know how it happened. I don't know what sort of accident it was. Nobody has told me. I don't want to ask. I expect one of them will come and explain when they can find the words. Ken was meant to come. Annie asked him. I've been expecting him. But no sign of him yet.'

'I'm sure he will.' Martin moved uneasily in his chair. He had heard bloody rumours.

'Also, I don't know when he died. Was it in the boat, in the ambulance, in the hospital? I don't know. No one told me. I didn't ask. I couldn't ask. I held his hand, but did he know I held it? Did he know I was there? I'll never know. How will I live without knowing?'

'All these things . . . You must try not to let them torment you in the next few days. You must keep your strength for yourself and others.'

Myrtle looked at him with interest. She was suddenly more alert.

'That's an unusual thing to say to someone whose husband's just died . . . Others. But you're right, of course. My mother told me that when my father died she needed all her energy to comfort those around her. I've had to do a fair bit of calming down. Annie's wept herself to a standstill crying for Archie, crying for me, crying for herself. I don't feel much like tears, myself. One burst of weeping last night, when they'd all gone, and I saw the Bear, and there was no Archie to congratulate me. But now I feel quite dry – bone dry, parched, scraped, arid. The machinery that should be making my widow's tears is too feeble to start them. There's no power, there. There's nothing, nothing, nothing. No Archie. Nothing.'

'I can understand.' Martin had to turn his head away lest she should see the tears that had sprung to his own eyes.

'But how can it have happened, Martin? The accident, whatever it was? Archie was the most conscientious man you could ever find when it came to safety. If one of the crew was ever careless, endangering others, Archie'd come down on him like a ton of bricks. What could have happened? Dear God, what could have happened? My Uncle John knew a man who was decapitated when the winch broke – cables snapped. That can't have been . . .'

'There's no use asking yourself these questions when the answers aren't ready.' Martin stood up, aware of his clumsy sympathy, sharing her emptiness. 'I'm sure Ken will be the one to tell you. He was Archie's oldest friend, despite their differences of late. He was the one there, he saw the horror, he knows he has to be the one to tell you when you're ready, and he's ready. Imagine how he must feel. He'll need to give himself a little time to gather his strength to come to you. After the funeral, perhaps.'

'Aye: you're right again. I'll wait.' Myrtle shrugged, and stood too. 'It's not *how* I really want to know – I'm a coward, there. It's not *when*, really, either. All I want to know is *why*? Why did Archie die? Why?'

Martin shook his head, unable to speak. He wanted to stretch out a hand to her, touch her hair, her cheek, her bruised eyes – make some small physical gesture to show he understood the magnitude of her sorrow. But he felt that to do so would be inappropriate.

Restrained acts of friendship are often of more value than those whose show is innocently mistimed. Martin merely shook his head as he went to the door, sensing it was time for Myrtle to be alone again. He knew she was a woman to whom solitude is consolation, and he had no wish to intrude a mite too far into her aloneness. With promises of returning next day, he left with a swiftness that was much appreciated by Myrtle, who went back to her lists of things that must be done to ensure Archie's funeral was the sort of occasion due to such a man.

Myrtle and Annie sit at their usual places playing cards. It's a bright afternoon. The kitchen is filled with light. The aged wall clock ticks – relentless, hollow, nagging the concentration. One of Archie's old navy jerseys still hangs on the back of the door. The wool on a sleeve is snagged in a couple of places, making small holes that Myrtle means one day to darn.

Annie arrived a little late for the game, and flustered. Soon after Archie died she left the job in the museum café to be a receptionist in a hairdresser. Within a week she grew tired of making scant appointments, and left for a series of other equally unsatisfactory jobs. Eventually she returned to the café where she was welcomed back and offered a promotion. Now, she is in charge of three waitresses and the punctual delivery of the homemade cakes is her responsibility. She works longer hours than she needs, lingers over a cup of coffee with whoever else is on duty long after the last customer has gone. Anything, as Myrtle observes, to put off the moment of going home.

Myrtle is used to reading Annie's hands. Today she sees that they are a little shaky as they arrange the cards. Indication of some sort of confrontation: a thin blade of dread stabs at Myrtle's innards. There have been too many confrontations with Annie since Archie's death. Too many arguments, disagreements, promises not to be so stupid again, apologies . . . Peace, then, for a week or so – untroubled friendship almost like the old days, before Annie – always Annie – provokes some new unease between them.

Today Myrtle knows she is not going to get away with a peaceful, silent game of cards. Some accusation, that she cannot guess at, is boiling within Annie, whose eyes glitter dangerously. Annie slams down her cards.

'Myrt: I can't not say this any longer. I think you should see someone. Everybody thinks so.'

'Everybody?' The thought of people discussing what might be best for her makes Myrtle feel sick, cold. 'See someone?' she says lightly. 'What sort of person?'

'You know: one of those people who help. A counsellor.'

'Why should I want to see one of them? Why do you suppose I need help? What sort of help do you think a counsellor could be?' Despite herself, she knows there is scorn in her voice.

Annie sighs. There is suffering in her face. Afflicted by so much do-gooding earnestness, Myrtle thinks.

'The fact is, it's almost two years since Archie died, and as far as I know, you've never broken down, never given in to hysteria, never acted like any normal woman whose husband has been killed in a ghastly accident. You didn't even cry at the funeral. Just watched all the rest of us snivelling, a superior expression on your face.'

'Is that how you saw it?' Myrtle tries for patience. 'I appreciate your concern,' she says, aware of her own formality, 'but I've no intention of seeing anyone. I don't believe in that sort of help. I don't want it, I don't need it. The fact that I'm not a weeper shouldn't be any cause for you to worry that I'm not behaving "normally" as you call it. It's just how I am. We're all made differently, so naturally we all react differently. There's nothing very odd about that.'

'You're impossible sometimes,' says Annie. 'So stand-offish, even to me. So sure of your own strength, your own independence. So unwilling, since Archie's been gone, to let anyone get near you.' She begins to fiddle with a line of cards, not meeting Myrtle's eye. 'The fact is, you've been acting strangely. Shutting yourself away, almost hermit-like. I know you enjoy your teaching, and you love your pupils, and Janice. And I know a lot of your time is taken up planting your wood – none of us ever invited to see it, mind. And I'm not saying you're not just the same to me, in a way. Here I am: cards as usual. Chit-chat, cups of tea. But the thing is, you can't deny it, you've gone away from us. You've left me, your friends, for somewhere of your own where no human company seems to be needed.'

'I'm sorry,' says Myrtle, 'if it feels like that.'

'All I'm trying to say is, it's time for you to try to return to a less secret, solitary life. For God's sake, Archie wouldn't have wanted you to become a sort of nun just because he had died. He'd want you to carry on as normally as possible.'

'I do,' says Myrtle. 'At least, I'm trying.'

'And quite apart from that, you don't tell me much now, about how you're feeling – it's as if you don't trust me any more, don't need me as a friend any longer, don't want me to know what's going on in your – well, your soul.'

'I don't,' says Myrtle, firmly. 'I'm sorry if this distresses you, but I don't. In the first place I could never describe it. And if I could, I wouldn't want to. Not even to you.'

'I see.' Annie's wounded look now meets Myrtle's. 'It didn't used to be like that.'

'Perhaps you don't quite remember. You were the one who always confessed everything – well, not everything, but a good deal. I was the one who said less.'

Annie's head snaps back.

'What didn't I tell you? Far as I remember, I told you everything.'

Confronted by this untruth, Myrtle feels reckless. She answers before she can stop herself.

'You never said a thing about your love for Martin. That is, you admitted you fancied him. But you never said anything about the seriousness of your love for him.'

'For Martin?' The blood blows across Annie's face, reddening it from forehead to chin. Then quickly as it has come it drains away, leaving her a ghastly white. 'Who told you about Martin?'

'I'll never tell you that.'

'The bastard. It must have been him. No one else knew.'

'It was a long time ago. You can trust me.'

There's a long silence. Then Annie says:

'Well, since you know, I don't mind telling you it's true. I loved

Martin. I mean I really loved him. I would have married him in five minutes, had he asked. But he didn't love me. Funny, really. I've had so many men, never a shortage. I suppose I didn't want to admit to you of all people my *failure*. I'd always been so good at getting every man I wanted. Although all *they* ever wanted was the same thing, and it was never love – except Ken.' She gives a small, self-deprecating laugh. 'Whereas you, big, solid, plain Myrtle – you've only ever looked at one man, and that man turned and saw you and loved you completely. He may have died too soon, but you've been so lucky. You don't know how lucky.'

'Aye, I do,' says Myrtle. 'There's not a day I don't remember that. But you shouldn't underrate Ken's love for you. You've a devoted husband there . . .'

'Ah! Ken. The loving husband. We scarcely speak these days.'

'There you are! That's another thing you haven't told me.'

'Not something I want to talk about, think about.' Annie sounds weary now. 'I keep myself busy as I can so I don't have to think. I'll find it hard ever to forgive that man.'

'But you should,' says Myrtle. 'I mean, I have. And if it wasn't for Ken, Archie would be here today.'

'You're a bloody saint, then. A bloody *stupid* saint.' The harsh words are forlorn. 'How can I forgive a man who caused *your* husband to die, Myrt? And he hasn't laid a finger on me since Archie . . .'

'I'm sorry,' says Myrtle. 'Perhaps, time –'

'Time? What's time got to do with anything? You of all people must know that. Time makes no difference, does it?'

'Not to . . . no,' agrees Myrtle. Annie pulls on her coat.

'I don't know where we've got to. Nowhere, I think. I came here to try tactfully to suggest you need help, and you snap my head off. You take the chance to tell me you no longer want to tell me things, but can't resist letting on that you know about my pathetic love for Martin in the past. You also scoff at me for not forgiving Ken for killing your husband – something you, the saintly Myrtle, apparently have done. I don't know where that leads us. I feel totally . . . and then I go and tell you about Ken not wanting me any more – or maybe it's just impotence brought on by guilt. I don't know. I'm not sure I care.' Tears begin to run down her cheeks. 'Maybe I'm the one who needs the help, you're the strong one. Well, you've always been the strong one, really. I've always relied on you. Taken you for granted, perhaps. I hate your new distance.' She holds out her arms. 'Please come back.'

Myrtle holds out her arms, with some reluctance, and allows Annie to shift her sad head on her shoulder. She murmurs vaguely comforting words, assures Annie she hasn't gone, she'll always be there, but since Archie died there are great tracts of life she wants to deal with entirely on her own. Annie nods, wipes away her tears. Myrtle has no idea whether or not her friend understands, or has taken comfort. And in a strange, hard way that puzzles her, she doesn't care very much. A selfish longing to be alone consumes her. She disentangles Annie from her arms and goes to open the door. But Annie does not move. Myrtle can tell from her face that a sudden thought has come to her to lighten the sombre air between them.

'Shall I tell you something, Myrt?' she asks. Her red eyes are mischievous now. 'Seeing as you know about Martin, all past history . . . I have to confess I wrote him smashing letters. Know how? I went up to the library – yes, I did – studied a few books of love letters between famous people. Well, I took a bit from one, a bit from another, nothing too high-faluting, joined them up with a word or two of my own. I was proud of them, I can tell you. It was good fun.' She is laughing now; so is Myrtle. 'Martin must have been that surprised. Don't suppose he ever imagined I was a talented writer.' She stands. 'But I tell you something else – he's the only one I'd ever have gone to all that bother for. If he ever says anything about those letters, you won't let on, will you?'

'Of course not. Never.' The laughter, which has lifted them, dies. 'But please, Annie, never say again that Ken killed Archie. He didn't. It was an accident. You know that.'

'Ken's fault. You know *that*.'

'And please don't come round suggesting any more counsellors.' Myrtle manages to say this lightly. 'You should know I'm the last person in the world who'd welcome some stranger's prurient questions, some futile attempt at understanding. How on earth could that be a comfort? It'd be the greatest intrusion . . . If I've inherited anything from my mother, it's how to deal with things on my own.' She manages a smile as Annie goes down the steps.

'I'll remember that,' says Annie. But she can't return the smile.

When Annie has gone the picture of Ken's confession returns to Myrtle, as it has done many times since Archie's death. She fights it, but it will not go away because it is never absolutely clear. No matter how carefully she scours Ken's explanation, it is always misted. She is still unable to see, to understand, how exactly those terrible moments were. She accepts that full realisation may always elude her, but knows she will never be able to give up the search.

Ken came to the funeral, silent, pale, unweeping. He stood far away from Annie and made no attempt to speak to Myrtle. As she stood throwing a handful of earth into the grave, she was aware of his slipping away down the path. His mysterious exit merely added another puzzle to the dreadful mysteries of the day: why had Archie died? Who among the mourners knew? Was it only Ken who was party to the whole truth? Such questions, that day, merely dappled Myrtle's more profound reflections and were put aside. She would find the answers eventually, but while his coffin lay exposed in the jaws of newly cut black earth, they seemed irrelevant.

Two weeks later Ken paid his visit to Myrtle. He confessed he could find no adequate words to express his sympathy and sorrow – this news was greeted with an impatient, dismissive wave of Myrtle's hand. All he could do, he said, was to explain what happened.

'This is difficult for me to say, Myrtle,' he began, 'but if I don't tell you the truth I'll never be able to live with myself.'

'I daresay it will be just as difficult for me to hear the truth as it is for you to explain it. But I'd be obliged if you'd just get on with it.' Myrtle had never heard herself speak like that, so roughly.

Ken kneaded his hands, lowered his eyes, further unnerved.

'There was this argument. Archie and me.'

'Argument?'

'I'm afraid we'd got round to squabbling again. At sea.'

'I thought you'd sorted out all your differences.'

'We had. I was about to sell the van, as you know. No more deliveries. I kept my word. But I just couldn't get it out of my mind that we
on *Skyline II* were being a bit foolish . . . the only honest ones.
Christ . . . I wasn't doing *much*. Just selling a few fish that the bloody
stupid law says should be thrown back. Not the *Skyline*'s, of course.
I'd never have done that. I was just helping a friend, delivering a
crate or two for him. All I said to Archie was that if others were doing
it, why not us? By that I didn't mean I had any intention of carrying
on – I'd given my word. I just wanted to know why we should be in
a minority, these hard times . . .'

'You were stuffing crates between the furniture?' Ken nodded.
'You're a fool, Ken.' Myrtle's voice was a knife-slash. 'Besides, you
knew nothing in the world would persuade Archie to contemplate
anything dishonest.'

'Of course I knew that. But this wasn't exactly dishonesty on a
large scale. Just the occasional crate or two, if I happened to be going
in the right direction. Didn't think there was much harm in that.'

'What friend?'

'You can't expect me to tell you that. But once again there was a
shortage of money. Annie always wanting more than we had. This was
to have been my last try at persuading him. Then I would have given
up – hell, I'm not a crook, just worn down by disappointing my wife.
Anyhow, that day I made my suggestion – fully expecting him to say
no, fully expecting to sell the van when we came ashore, the job on
the boat being more important to me than anything . . . and Archie
lost his temper. I've never seen a man so angry, bawling me out. Only
thing concerns him is his rage with me. Just for that moment he lost
his concentration. Then the chance in the million happens: winch
snaps. Cable snaps back at the speed of light, gets him in the
throat . . .' Here Ken's voice was so thickened by a rising sob that it
was hard to distinguish his words. But Myrtle, hearing the facts at last,
felt no mercy. Now she desired to know the full horror. Better to live
with the reality than ghastly imaginings.

'And then?'

'One minute he was punching the air, screeching blue murder at me. The next – a cracking noise when the wire broke. Archie stopped shouting and was slewed over on the deck.' Ken's sobs were articulate by now. 'Blood gushed out. Never seen so much blood. Jugular sliced. He didn't make a sound. No cry, nothing. To be honest, Myrtle, it happened all so quickly, and it was all so terrible, the most terrible thing I've ever seen, that it's still confused in my mind.'

'Yes, yes.'

'In the daytime, that is. Asleep – nightmares – clear as anything. Then when I wake the confusion starts again . . .' He broke off to blow his nose, tried to stop the sobbing.

Myrtle's hands were folded in her lap. She sat very upright, eyes on something out of the window.

'One of the many things Archie always believed in was that a fisherman should keep his concentration. Let it lapse for a moment, he used to say, and disaster can strike.' She spoke in the high, thin voice of her younger self. Ken looked up, half expecting to see Myrtle the child. 'If you hadn't been having a row, and God knows how you must have put your crazy idea to provoke him to that sort of anger, Archie wouldn't be dead. He'd be here now.'

'Possibly,' said Ken. His sobs were ebbing. 'He could still have had his back to the winch, might not have got out of the way in time . . .'

Myrtle turned on him, rigid in her contempt.

'You know that's not true, Ken Mcleoud, so don't go trying to soothe your conscience with any such delusions. Archie's reactions to danger were quicker than a wild animal's. He could sense disaster a mile off. There's no possible chance he would have been caught by that wire if he hadn't been concentrating on your loathsome suggestions instead of the job in hand –' Her normal voice had returned now, deep and scarred. Ken stood up, shoulders hunched as if against rain.

'Myrtle, please. I know how it is for you – it's bad for me, too. How am I going to live with myself?'

'I don't know.'

'I don't suppose there's anything I can say by way of –'

'No, nothing. Don't try.'

'You'll never forgive me – how can I cope with that?'

'Oh, that. No need to worry there.' Myrtle gave a small laugh. 'Forgiveness – if that's what you want. I forgive you. You didn't set out to murder Archie, just to goad him. Your foolishness, trying to persuade an honest man to agree to a dishonest arrangement – was beyond belief. But that's not the point. Forgiveness isn't going to bring him back. The thing you should worry about is keeping out of my way. As you can imagine, I don't want our paths to cross any more, Ken. I don't want any more to do with the man who . . . I'm warning you, keep out of the way. Not easy in a place this size, but possible. Nothing's changed between me and Annie, of course. She's my friend, whatever. Not her fault, your –'

'Annie's not all innocence in this. Her pushing me –'

'I'll not hear a word against Annie, and besides, I'd like you to go now.'

'Very well.' Ken shrugged, wiping his eyes with the weight of a man who has run out of words. He left the room in silence.

When he had gone Myrtle remained in her chair, in the quiet of her empty kitchen. Visions of the accident crowded her vision, worse than anything she had imagined. Archie's bloody head, almost severed from his body, rose before her, no matter how she shifted her eyes. She heard herself moaning, the quiet cooings of a strangled dove. Archie's voice was in her head, smatterings of things he had said over the years. His presence was so strong she was convinced his absence was some madness within *her*, and soon he would be back to comfort. In her stillness she realised she was waiting for him: she also knew the uselessness of that wait. It was the first time the absurdity of her position struck her with a feeling of utter helplessness. It was to strike again and again in the months to come.

Ken, for his part, kept to his word. He avoided Myrtle: there was no occasion for them to speak. Until the afternoon of Annie's outburst, the two friends never mentioned Ken's name. He became a ghost between them.

*

In the five minutes before Martin arrives, Myrtle wonders if she has been too hard on Annie. Annie meant well. Others, concerned for her, mean well too. But their presumptions annoy her. Their anxiety is an intrusion into her dearly held privacy. It provokes unreasonable anger. She wants to be left to deal in her own way with her aloneness. She wants to be the sole witness to her own foolishness, eccentricity, small spasms of irrational behaviour. These things will pass, she believes. The chasm that surrounds her will never be filled, but the footholds will become stronger. In time the rawness of skin and soul will lessen, and she will be less wary of the proximity of others. The figure of her own mother, widowed, is bright in her mind. Dot was dignified, strong, at ease with her husband's death: her way was to carry on abiding by his rules – their rules – and to regard his absence as a temporary matter of not much more significance than a long trip to foreign waters. Dot's belief in the reunion with her husband was buoyant – her cheerfulness, by day, made the loss easy for others. (There were a few occasions on which Myrtle had heard her weeping in the night – occasions when she knew any offer of comfort would be abhorred, and so left her mother to battle undisturbed.) Dot was more approachable in widowhood, Myrtle realises, than she is herself. She vows to try to be less distant, less defensive. She is aware her need to grieve privately causes some people concern, even offence. She wishes she could make them understand she is not lonely, just alone. And aloneness, if accommodated in the right spirit, has as many riches as a peopled world.

Myrtle gets up from the table and moves round the room. Under her long skirts her feet shuffle in shy dance steps. Her body sways. Her big hands sprawl on her hips, clutching at the material gathered round her waist. She moves cautiously as a ship coming into berth: from table, to stove, to chair. As she passes the door she slows down even further. The smell of Archie's jersey is still there. Like his voice in her head, it has not faded a jot. *Stop moving about, Myrtle wife. Sit down, won't you?*

Perhaps this is madness, she thinks. But she has found this criss-crossing the room, weaving in and out like the wool of a darn, is comforting. It furnishes a miniscule part of the emptiness, in the same way that nets interrupt the depths of the sea. And no one has caught her at her dancing: no one has proof of her occasionally eccentric behaviour. So why do they think she is in need of help? I'm as fine and strong as any woman can be whose husband has been dead for nearly two years, she tells herself – though perhaps I'm becoming stuck in too rigid a groove of self-discipline. Perhaps the time has come to shift a little . . .

When Martin arrives with his parcel of fish, he finds Myrtle still moving about, humming to herself, her eyes unfocused. He sees it takes her a moment or two to disentangle herself from her reflections. Then she looks at him gladly, unembarrassed that he has caught her in this private act, and suggests they should walk out and see how the trees are doing.

This is the first time Myrtle has invited anyone to the coppice. As they walk up the road she feels an irrational guilt. The wood was Archie's idea: he should be the first one to check its progress. But Martin is talking about other things – how he had cut his hand quite badly, yesterday, still not highly skilled at filleting. He is trying to describe how hands deal so differently with different materials. There could hardly be a greater contrast between the rubbery flesh of fish and the unyielding hardness of marble, he says: and yet his own hands felt it much easier to chip the stone than to knife through the flesh. Odd. It would be a luxury to cut through silk with sharp scissors, he adds. Or even fine tweed. Perhaps he should have been a tailor – a bespoke tailor. And what is a bespoke tailor, incidentally? He once looked it up in a dictionary but couldn't find it. Did Myrtle know what the word *bespoke* means? She shakes her head, eyes dazzled by the poppies flaring along the hedgerows. Martin's voice is soothing, no matter what he says. It's a fine warm evening. In the distance a tractor stutters up and down the seam of rich dark soil, The Golden Fringe, as it's known locally, near the sea. The tractor is very old, topples to one side, caught in a net of gulls. For a moment the daft idea comes to Myrtle that if it wasn't for the gulls it would keel over completely. The guilt she felt at the beginning of the walk has disappeared.

And when it comes to showing Martin round the wood, she begins to enjoy herself. The enjoyment runs up the veins of her arms, tingling, an active thing. They walk up and down the paths that Myrtle has spent months designing between the trees – young saplings, each one strapped into a protective covering, just a few thin branches and tiny leaves sprouting out at the top.

'Imagine all this in ten years' time,' says Myrtle. 'Ground ivy, moss, bluebells, primroses, birds nesting in the branches.'

Martin is impressed. He strokes his chin, nods his head.

'You organised all this yourself? Choosing the trees, planning the planting? It's quite something.'

'We'd decided on a good many things together, it wasn't all me. At one moment, soon after Archie died, I thought I should abandon the whole project. But then I thought, no: the whole idea had given him so much pleasure. He was so looking forward to getting it under way. I thought the least I can do is to go ahead, do the best I can alone. And I have to say it's taken up a lot of time, which has been a good thing.'

They reach the centre of the wood, the place where all the paths end.

'This,' says Myrtle, 'I'm going to keep as a clearing. I might put a bench here. Somewhere to ruminate in my old age.'

'I could make you a bench,' says Martin. 'I haven't worked with wood for years, but I enjoy a bit of carpentry.'

He's not sure Myrtle has heard his suggestion, for she does not answer, but moves to the place she judges to be the very centre of the clearing. She turns to him.

'Here,' she says, 'I want a rock. Do you think that would be possible? I want a rock to be a memorial stone to Archie.'

'I think that would be possible.'

'Could you find me one? Could you help me to arrange the transport? It'll be quite difficult, I know.'

'I'll see what I can do.'

'It would need some sort of . . .'

'. . . simple carving. Name and dates. On the rockface, or perhaps a separate piece of stone. I'd like to do that for Archie.'

'If you could, I'd be so pleased – though you've already done the headstone. You've done a lot for Archie. Do you like it here? Can you see how it will all be eventually?'

Martin nods again. He knows he is the first person to be invited to the wood, and is touched by her pleasure and excitement. She moves, smiling, towards him, pointing to the only path they have not tried. Then she trips over a hidden stone, and falls. It's not a bad fall, though she whimpers briefly and clutches an ankle. In a moment Martin is by her side. He kneels, briskly examines the ankle like a doctor.

'It's nothing but a slight twist,' says Myrtle. 'Give me a hand.'

Martin grips the hand she offers, puts the other one beneath her elbow, heaves her to her feet. For a moment they stand as close as is necessary for Martin to provide support while Myrtle tries putting weight on her foot. There is a stab of pain, but nothing unbearable.

'It's fine,' she says. 'Thanks.' She frees her hand and arm from Martin and moves awkwardly away from him, turning her head so that he shall not see the scarlet flush that has spread over her. This is the first time since Archie died she has had any physical contact with a man. She hates having let him touch her, albeit innocently, helpfully. The guilt rushes back. First she brings a man to see Archie's wood before any one else, and then in the memorial place itself she lets him hold her hand. Grip it quite hard. An enjoyable sensation. This is betrayal indeed.

'Let's go back this way,' she says, and hobbles down the new path.

'Sure you're all right?'

'Sure. It's only a very slight twist.'

Walking ahead of Martin gives her the chance to rethink her opinion of herself as her face cools down. With surprising speed she changes her mind. Archie, she tells herself, would have been delighted that their old mutual friend Martin was the first visitor to the wood. He would also have thought it the natural and right thing to do, to help Myrtle up when she stumbled. So why on earth had she been so put out? Why had such an innocent event caused her such anguish? Could it be because that moment of being in Martin's grasp was an unbidden comfort? Leaning on him, she had felt strong, hopeful – hopeful of what she could not say: something to do with the kindness of a good man still having the power to touch her.

She and Martin walk slowly back along the road to the village. The poppies' heads are bowed now, their petals closing. The tractor has gone, the net of gulls dispersed. One or two are left floating across the sky, aimless in the arc of fine silver webbing formed by evening clouds. When they reach the house Myrtle, her calm restored now, invites Martin in for a glass of beer. But he declines.

'I promised Annie I'd deliver a bit of fish for her supper. She's not too happy, I reckon. Having a difficult time, I guess.'

'She is, too,' says Myrtle quickly. Martin waves.

'Take care of that ankle,' he says. 'And thank you for taking me to your wood. It's a grand place. Archie would have been proud of what you've done.'

Myrtle begins to climb the steps to the front door.

'Would you mind . . .?' she says.

'. . . not saying anything to anyone? You can rely on me. I shan't say a word.'

As Myrtle fries the slivers of fresh haddock Martin has given her, she wonders whether Annie has invited him to join her and Janice for supper. The thought ruffles her very slightly. To deflect it she takes out her old copy of *Sorab and Rustum* to prepare herself for Janice's lesson tomorrow. As always, she looks forward to Janice's visit. The child loves the poems Myrtle has chosen to study – she has a particular liking for narrative poetry. Tomorrow will be the introduction to Matthew Arnold. Myrtle reads as she eats – a habit she has acquired of late, although often she becomes so engrossed in the book that the food grows cold. Tonight, most of Martin's haddock is left to become unappetising on the plate, and has to be thrown away.

Unlike many who are widowed, Myrtle does not suffer from nightmares. Deep and dreamless sleep returned to her not long after Archie was buried. Instead, it is the day-pictures that assault her – jagged little sections that sometimes lock together easily, but sometimes a piece is missing from her memory, and she panics. Recently she has been unable to recall, after the wedding, their arrival in Mull. She remembers the dour house, the friendly landlady, the Swiss sort of bedroom, the delicious breakfasts . . . But their actual arrival at this house has gone from her. Unnerved, Myrtle wonders how important this vanishing is. Does it mean rebellion by a mind overtaxed by remembering? Should she try to stop indulging in memory of things past, and fix her mind instead on the nebulous stretches of the future? This is difficult. She does try, sometimes. But there are no peaks in the mist. Nothing clear to aim for, no apparent path. No conscious desires.

And of late a new and strange phenomenon has come to trouble her: the sky. In her rational mind Myrtle knows this inconvenient phobia must have sprung from the trauma of Archie's death. But in the moments before she has time to reason with herself, scoff at her absurdity, fear clammies her skin and jolts her heart.

The menace of the sky began one evening when, on impulse, she walked down to the harbour. This was something she often made herself do, to try to overcome her loathing of the place from which *Skyline II* was gone, but where Archie's friends still berthed. Used to absence, they were, perhaps, by now. On this particular evening there was a fine sunset: ruddy cloud densely reflected in the harbour waters, staining their brown to rust. It was a sky much like the one on the morning that Archie, mortally wounded, came ashore for the last time. Then, Myrtle remembered, as she waited for the boat to appear, she looked up and thought someone had shot the sky. Blood oozed from the clouds, streaked across gashes of peacock blue. On the recent evening she had forced herself to visit the harbour – almost two years since Archie's death, for heaven's sake – a similarly murderous sky had returned with all its old menace: she was overcome by a cold and enfeebling fear. Hurrying home, she stumbled several times, like a woman much older than herself. Safely in the kitchen, a sense of her own absurdity came quickly to her rescue. She laughed out loud in the silence, made herself a cup of tea. There was nothing for it but to deal with the undesirable surprises of widowhood with as much patience and reason as she could muster.

But from that evening it seemed that it was not just the sunset that unnerved her. A dun sky, next morning, was just as alarming. On the way to school she felt it hunched over her, ready to pounce, flatten, destroy. Safe indoors, the clamour of her class put flight to such silly fears, but she dreaded the journey home when the bell rang at three, and found herself small needless tasks to postpone her departure. She took a hold on herself – *always take a hold on yourself when the going gets rough*, Dot used to say – and left by four. The afternoon sky was lighter, more cheerful, cloudless. But still it oppressed, weighed heavily, filled her with unease. Subsequently, every outing required a summoning of strength. She could not give in, she knew, to some peculiar form of agoraphobia; she could rely on herself to beat this irrational fear. Out of doors, she kept her eyes down, unable to look up, dreading the whiteness of cloud shapes in her vision. She could no longer remember how she had ever taken pleasure in the massive skyscapes that arched over this part of the Scottish coast. She could only pray that her strange new fear was nothing more than a passing inconvenience bred of widowhood. Determination to overcome the distortion of her widow's senses was the task she now set herself, convinced that in time it would surely evaporate as mysteriously as it had descended.

Janice arrives a little early for her lesson. Her clumpy shoes clatter on the stone floor as she spins about disturbing the peace. She is pink-cheeked and bright-eyed as she empties her satchel of books on to the scrubbed table. Myrtle senses a time-spin moment. She knows this restless mood so well: Janice is Annie at thirteen, inflamed with anticipation, almost visible sparks flying off her. Janice is a more serious pupil than Annie ever was. But Myrtle doubts she will be wholly able to concentrate on the poem today.

They sit. Myrtle eyes Janice fiercely. She wants to make quite sure the girl is aware of her priorities. She is here to study Arnold. She must put aside whatever the event is that has caused this obviously excited state.

Myrtle picks up her open book. She begins to read.

> *For very young, he seemed, tenderly reared;*
> *Like some young cypress, tall and dark and straight,*
> *Which in a queen's secluded garden throws*
> *Its slight dark shadow on the turf,*
> *By midnight, to a bubbling fountain's sound –*

'Oh, Myrtle, I'm sorry. I can't concentrate on the words today. It's a great poem and that, but I'm all of a dither.'

'So I can see.' Myrtle fixes Janice with a look in which interest is underlined with impatience. 'What's the matter? What's clogging your mind?'

'Clogging?' Janice laughs. Her hands fidget about, moving pencils, rubbers. Myrtle frowns at the iridescent green nail polish. She also notices the girl's eyelashes – long, but not half the length of her mother's – bunched clumsily together by mascara which looks as if it was put on a long time ago. Myrtle feels a swell of unease which spoils the morning. She allows a beat or two of silence. Janice breaks it with her announcement.

'I'm in love,' she says.

'In love?' Myrtle feels her face being scanned: Janice is eager for a reaction. Myrtle tries to remember the boys in Janice's class: indeterminate youths as disparate as were the boys of her own generation. There must be Rosses and Kens and similar others there. Not an Archie, of course. There could never be another Archie.

'Don't ask me who,' says Janice.

'Right, I won't. It's nothing to do with me. Would you like a cup of tea?'

'Couldn't touch a thing, thanks. Shit: it gets you in the guts, doesn't it?'

'That's horrible language,' says Myrtle.

'Sorry. Slipped out.' Janice giggles. 'Those kind of words are ordinary among my friends.'

'Pity. They're not necessary.'

'No: but everyone uses them. I'd be different if I didn't, wouldn't I?'

'You should be brave enough to do and say what you think is

right. Following the others just for the sake of it is pretty feeble, I'd say. Not admirable.' The unease is making Myrtle fiercer than she intended. She doesn't know why Janice's sudden crude language has hit her so hard. Annie has always sworn: it is hardly surprising Janice takes after her. But until this morning, at this table, Janice has always been careful with her language. Annie has probably warned her that Myrtle is a prude in that way. And perhaps I am, Myrtle finds herself thinking. Why else should the child's sudden lapse be so oddly shocking?

Janice's hands come to rest at last on the open book in which the poem awaits. She is taken aback by Myrtle's admonition – a rare thing. But still she is unable to drag herself back to the story of *Sorab and Rustum* which only a week ago she had found so compelling.

'As I was saying, it gets you – it messes everything up, this love business.' A pout mushes the words. She puts a hand on her stomach. 'Can't eat, can't sleep, can't think of nothing else.'

'Anything else.'

'Well, you know what I mean. Spend all my time looking out for him. Anything just to catch a glimpse.'

Myrtle's glance, despite herself, is sympathetic. She decides to risk a single question.

'Is this love requited?' she asks.

'Req – what?'

'Does he love you back?' Myrtle is anxious the lesson should not altogether disappear. She does not want the short hour to give way to discussions of teenage fancy, for all that she understands Janice's heightened need to explore.

'Love me back? Fancy me, you mean? Don't suppose he even knows I exist.'

'Then you shouldn't waste too much time on him.'

'How can I help it? How can I stop what I feel? I only have to see him and my legs turn to jelly and my knees wobble out of joint and my heart batters like I'm going to die – don't you remember ever feeling like that?'

Myrtle smiles.

'I think most people have gone through that sort of experience at some time or other.'

'Bloody awful.'

'Janice, please.'

'Sorry.'

'Does your mother know?'

'Course not. Couldn't talk to her about that sort of thing. Please don't tell her. Promise not to tell her.'

'Promise.'

'What shall I do?'

'Such feelings wear off. Such turbulence fades. It can't last at such fever pitch for long.'

'Hope not. And yet –'

'Besides, at your age there's nothing much you can hope for, is there? I mean, except for friendship. Teenage crushes rarely develop into anything more lasting, more mature.'

'I know all that.' Janice is petulant. 'But I still can't do anything about it. It's, like, *gripped* me. It's all over me. It's much more than just a teenage crush, as you call it.'

'Janice, you're not yet thirteen and a half. You are a teenager. This is just part of the growing-up process which seems to have hit you rather hard, rather early. If I were you I should try to concentrate on the other bits of your life that give you most enjoyment. Our lessons, for instance.'

'Sorry. I'm trying.'

'Like a biscuit?'

'Please. I'm starving, though I feel sick when I eat.' She looks very young.

Myrtle gets up and goes to the tin. When her back is to Janice she asks:

'Didn't you manage the nice piece of haddock last night?'

'What haddock?'

'I thought Martin brought round a bit –'

'Oh he did, aye.'

Myrtle has a quick struggle with herself, and loses.

224

'And did your mother ask him to stay and share it for his pains?' she asks, despising herself.

Janice drags her eyes back from some remote place, blushing, as if she knows Myrtle has a picture in mind of the boy she loves. But Myrtle has no such thing, nor is she trying to envisage him.

'She did, I think,' says Janice, 'but he said he had to be on his way.' There is a sadness about her now, thoughts far from Martin and his fish. 'I couldn't eat the stuff. I've always hated fish, except fish fingers. My dad says I'm a living shame.'

The smallest reference to Ken causes Myrtle to wince, but she is determined the child shall have no clue as to what she feels.

'Try this,' she says, and hands Janice a slice of recently made ginger-bread. Amorphous relief at the news about Martin – a sensation she would not like to scrutinise for fear of what it might reveal – flows through her. In this deliquescent state she thinks she has been too hard on the child, and berates herself. She returns to her seat, watches Janice hungrily eat the food, her eyes with their pathetically clotted lashes never still, confused, grateful.

'Oh Myrtle, thanks,' she says.

'It's something most people go through,' says Myrtle. 'When it's over – and you might be surprised how soon that is – you'll look back at yourself and laugh.'

'No I won't,' says Janice, very serious, licking crumbs from her fingers. 'I'll never laugh about this.'

'Well, whatever. But you won't do anything foolish, will you?'

'What d'you take me for?' She giggles but looks scornful. 'Can you remember when it happened to you? Fancying a guy – *really* fancying a guy for the first time?'

The warmth Myrtle felt for Janice's father comes back to her: the uncomfortable knowledge that hers had been unrequited love, and then the blasting of her hopes, all the same, when Ken betrayed her.

'I do believe I can,' she says, 'but that's not a story for today. There's not much time left and we've hardly read a thing.' She picks up the book, and Janice sighs.

Later, when Janice leaves, Myrtle feels she has failed to divert the child's thoughts. It was impossible to regain her interest, concentration, enthusiasm. She remembers Ken's keenness for poetry as a boy: then how it fizzled out, once he fell in love with Annie, and he read no more. She hates to think of Janice going the same way as her father, and hopes this childish state is but a temporary phase.

It's a Saturday morning. The exercise books Myrtle was intending to mark she finished late last night. They sit in a neat pile on the table. She wishes she had left them for this morning, as she had planned.

There is nothing to do. With no one to cook for, no plans to meet Annie, the hours stretch emptily ahead. It's one of the few times since Archie has died, Myrtle realises, that she has been at a loss as to know what to do. She is grateful for the rarity of such occasions. But, in the meantime, how best to fill the hours? Saturday mornings used to be such busy times, speeding along in their happiness . . .

What Myrtle would like to do is to walk to the coppice, see how the trees have progressed over the last few days – their new growth never fails to astound her. She would like to reflect further on the placing of the rock and the bench. But her enemy the sky bars her from leaving the safety of the house. Through the window she can see it's a hard, unbroken blue: a bright glare she cannot face flooding directly down upon her. Perhaps it will be less menacing this afternoon, she thinks: perhaps she will try to confront it then.

She sits at the table, big hands slabbed on its familiar wooden surface, cogitating on the feebleness of one who is supposedly so strong. A long silence is interrupted by a knock on the door. By now Myrtle has acclimatised herself to the thought of a solitary day devoid of tasks, and small anticipated pleasures are beginning to stir. Not ten minutes ago she would have been delighted by a visitor. Now, she is not so sure.

Alastair Brown, it is. The shaky smile on his face indicates he has been practising its uneasy stretch for some time. His navy blazer looks suspiciously new. He holds a bunch of yellow roses secured in a cone of transparent, spotted paper. Its edge is painted to look like a lace frill. Whatever will florists think up next? Myrtle finds herself pondering.

'Mr Brown?'

'Mrs Duns?'

'Might I step over your threshold for just a moment? Might I come in?'

'Of course. Please do.'

Myrtle shuts the door behind him. She can't see his eyes, hidden as always behind dark glasses. But his head is bowed. He seems to be concentrating very intently on the roses. Then with a small shrug of impeccably blazered shoulders, he puts them quickly down on the table – a gesture almost of distaste. The scrunched paper that he has been holding glints with tiny flecks of his sweat. Myrtle sees his hands are shaking. He slips them into his pockets, aware of her eyes. The rigidity of the blazer is now destroyed by bulges. Myrtle offers him coffee.

'That would be a kindness,' says Alastair Brown.

While the kettle boils he filters back and forth round the kitchen. His innocent movements cause Myrtle a feeling of betrayal. The presence of any man in this kitchen, Archie's place, seems like infidelity. She watches Alastair Brown's dark glasses come to rest on various objects, and they swoop across the view out of the window. What can he be thinking? Why has he come? Plainly he's ill at ease. The sophisticated man from sophisticated southern parts, so apparent in his strutting down at the harbour, has left him here. His whole being suggests he has misjudged the wisdom of calling on Myrtle. He should never have embarked on this visit, he is cowed by regret. He's made a mistake, but it's too late to escape without some explanation.

Myrtle hands him a mug of coffee. He thanks her too profusely. She sits in her usual place at the table, indicating he should sit opposite – she doesn't want him to take Archie's seat. Sitting, he stares at his strong coffee. Then he makes so bold – Myrtle can see his struggle – to ask if she could oblige him with a touch more milk. He's quite unusual in his fondness for milky coffee, these health-conscious days, he says, with a thin little laugh.

Milk is added. Silence hangs between them again. Myrtle, growing more curious about the reason for the visit, finds it welcome despite the unease. Whatever Alastair Brown's mission, it will break the morning, the pleasures she had begun to anticipate would probably not have been so interesting as this strange call. He stirs his coffee, so that the small chipping sound of spoon against china will temper his words, perhaps.

'Not having been here at the time of your husband's death,' he begins at last, 'I offered no condolences. But I imagine that when a spouse dies the time for sympathy does not run out.'

'No,' says Myrtle.

'I've taken my time in coming here to offer my . . . but, as you can imagine, I could not be sure it would be appropriate.'

'It's very kind of you to . . . thank you.'

Alastair Brown allows another silence while he forms his next words.

'I hear – I mean, in a small place like this one hears everything, doesn't one? – that you are a very brave and gallant widow, crying on nobody's shoulder, as happy as can be expected in yourself. I hope that is the case.' Myrtle senses that behind the dark glasses Alastair Brown's eyes shut with relief now the worst part of his little speech is over. His taut shoulders rise, and he continues. 'I can see that after many years of happy marriage to have one's companion snatched away *untimely*, as it were, would put quite a different light on the rewards of solitude. It must make it less desirable. Strange.'

Myrtle nods. She sees her visitor's confidence rising. She sees his careful balancing of words is giving him a certain pleasure, now he is under way. She smiles, not consciously to encourage him further. But Mr Brown takes the small movement of her lips as the green light.

'I also hear,' he says, 'as I daresay you do, that my rejection of all the kind offers of help and friendship from local ladies – and, indeed, it has to be said, from others further afield – is because there is a rumour that the woman I am in fact awaiting is the Duns widow, the elusive Myrtle. You, Mrs Duns.'

Myrtle raises her eyebrows. She senses she is blushing, can think of no reply.

'But worry not. This is not the case. This is merely a silly rumour that has got out of hand. My reason for coming here this morning is to assure you absolutely, Mrs Duns, that there's not a jot of truth in the foolish story. The thought had never crossed my mind. I mean, we've scarcely met. But I didn't want you to suffer any embarrassment. I thought it best to come here and, well, put my cards on the table.'

Myrtle allows herself a long moment in which to think how best to answer.

'That's very kind,' she says again. 'Thoughtful. I had of course heard something of the silly rumours, but I naturally dismissed them. Still, it's good to hear from you yourself that the whole idea seems as absurd to you as it does to me.'

The muscles round Alastair Brown's mouth relax. Myrtle warms towards this awkward man: she's concerned to vanquish his fears for her discomfort. She would like to put him completely at his ease, and wonders how to guide a conversation into a new direction, deflect him from his concern – which may have caused him weeks of worry – over this visit. But before she can come to any decision Alastair Brown braves his next difficult point.

'But there is something I should like to put to you, Mrs Duns, now we have cleared up the matter of the rumours, cleared the air. I hope you won't take this as speaking out of turn. But – I hope you will understand this – there is something I am after, something very precious, very innocent, but proving very elusive to a bachelor of middle years.' He turns his head towards the window. Miniature curtains flap in the black discs of his glasses. 'What I am after is companionship.'

Myrtle, intrigued and amused by his formal use of language couched oddly in his Cornish brogue, is scarcely taking in the thrust of the words themselves. Alastair Brown pauses only for a moment to register a blurred query in her eyes, then hurries to enlighten.

'As you must know yourself, Mrs Duns, to be a single figure in a society crowded with couples has its drawbacks. It's assumed one is looking for a partner, and to that end all sorts of kind people offer up enthusiastic suggestions – but not, unfortunately, for companionship alone. You must have experienced this. Even in your two years of widowhood you must have turned down numerous suitors anxious to enter your life.'

'You flatter me,' says Myrtle, feeling herself redden again, 'but that really isn't the case.'

'Whatever. For my own part – and forgive me if this sounds like vanity – a good many ladies have pressed their suits upon me' (the visual image forces Myrtle to control a smile) 'and I've had to discourage them because their own aims have not exactly coincided with mine. What they are after is fun, romance, a sexual relationship, but all pointing towards the big commitment on the horizon – marriage. Well, I don't want that, ever. I've no wish to be a married man, though I have every wish to be a companionable man. I can offer plain food by my fireside, a drop of double malt, old films on the telly – as you may have heard from your friend Mrs Mcleoud' – here he allows himself a wry smile. 'I can offer excursions up the coast in summer in my little boat – but nothing more, really. Nothing of significance. My old mother lives in a home in Dundee. I feel obliged to visit her regularly. She's pleased to be back in these parts – born and bred in Dundee. Never liked Cornwall.' He breaks off to sigh. 'What a dull life, you must be thinking. But it's all I have to offer. In return I would enjoy an occasional agreeable female presence, someone who's looking for nothing beyond my meagre –'

'I'm not thinking it's a dull life,' Myrtle interrupts.

'Then you're a woman in a million.'

'Just one of simple tastes, like you. I've little ambition beyond getting through each day to the best of my ability.'

'Funny, I'm of that school, too.' Alastair Brown now smiles more openly. Myrtle's few words encourage him to reveal further thoughts pertaining to himself.

'It's also funny, you know, that any woman should ever consider pursuing me. I mean, not only do I lead a very quiet life and have little money and no car or other attractions, but I'm scarred . . . Of course, they don't know that. Dark glasses signal mystery, don't they? Stupid idea.' He taps a lens with his finger. 'They're also considered an affectation. I've heard the scoffing, believe me. But dark glasses that never come off are a challenge, I suppose. Well, mine don't come off for a very good reason.'

With no warning, the harbour master suddenly snatches off his glasses. They fall on to the table. He turns to face Myrtle.

'This, Mrs Duns. Take a good look and you'll see the reason I can never hope to offer any woman –'

He stops. Myrtle is too surprised to contain a gasp. One eye has a permanently lowered lid. The rim of white that shows beneath it is a cloudy brown, the iris invisible. The unsteady iris of the other eye is of no recognisable colour; the eyeball is surrounded by a mess of scarred and puckered skin. The result of some botched operation, perhaps, Myrtle thinks, but nothing very shocking. She stares back at the eyes thrust defiantly towards her. Ashamed of her initial reaction, she now attempts an impassive face.

'Accident,' says Alastair Brown.

'I'm sorry,' says Myrtle.

'So you understand.'

'I don't think you should be quite so sure that a scarred face will put people off.'

'But I do think that. I'm sure of it. I've had experience. I've seen people backing away, aghast. That's why I never take off . . . I can see all right. Sight's luckily not impaired. But you have to admit, I look pretty monstrous.'

Myrtle shakes her head. She can understand his wounded eyes might inspire distaste in some people, but to her the scarred face remains curiously fine, with its strong parrot nose and engaging smile. Reflecting on all this, she fails to come up with quick words of comfort. Alastair Brown, again with the air of a man who has made a mistake but knows it is too late to retract, puts the dark glasses back on. The metamorphosis, Myrtle is forced to admit to herself, is instant. His strange attraction once more positively confronts her. In the backwater of her mind, unformed, the thought occurs that progressive friendship with this man could be beneficial to both parties. But for the moment she intends to be cautious. Show her reserve.

'You've seen enough,' he says. 'I'm sorry. I didn't mean to . . . I'd be grateful if you would keep this to yourself.'

'Of course.'

By now it is time for more coffee, the right amount of milk. Myrtle's composure has returned. She feels pity for the man. She's intrigued by his mixture of vanity and lack of confidence. Perhaps they often go together, she thinks.

The morning is slipping by curiously fast. When will Alastair Brown leave? Will he further expand on his wish for a companion? As if sensing her thoughts, he pushes the cone of roses across the table towards her.

'I'll be off in a minute,' he says. 'These are for you.'

'Thank you.'

'But just to return for a moment to my request for a companion. I came to you with the thought that perhaps, as a widow, you might be looking for something of that nature yourself. Nothing more.'

'I haven't consciously thought in those terms,' says Myrtle, anxious in her delicacy, 'but I like to see friends. I'm no hermit.'

'Then from time to time we could get together? Share a herring?'

'Why not?' Myrtle smiles. Alastair Brown smiles back.

'Do you like old films?'

'I've not seen many.' The thought of even an occasional evening with the harbour master in front of his television causes Myrtle a lack of enthusiasm she has to conceal. She does this by shifting herself into a very upright position, back straight, signifying formality, a hint of unapproachability.

'I could try to convert you. Stewart Grainger, Margaret Lockwood . . . another world.'

His eagerness touches Myrtle. She thinks her defensive position might look too severe, and the last thing she wants to do is to offend so gentle a man. She slumps a little in her chair, and allows him a glimpse of her natural sympathy.

'I do enjoy a game of cards,' she says.

'Why, so do I!' His eagerness is almost pathetic. 'Though I haven't played anything but patience for a good many years now.'

Myrtle notices his second cup of coffee is untouched. She plans a small lie merely to ensure the visit will have a definite cut-off time, for she feels that given the slightest measure of encouragement Alastair Brown could still be sitting at her table at noon.

'I have an engagement at twelve,' she says, 'but we could play a game now, if you like.'

The effect of this offer upon Alastair Brown is out of all proportion to the invitation: he beams at the prospect, though even in his keen anticipation of further time in Myrtle's company, he does not abandon his well-mannered hesitation.

'I would not want to prevail upon your kindness,' he says.

'You're not prevailing on anything.' Myrtle, a little impatient, slaps down the cards.

'Now you're making a mockery of my language.'

'Well, it is quite distinctive,' Myrtle answers in a teasing voice. 'You can tell you watch a lot of old films.'

'I don't assume such language down at the harbour, with the men, as you can imagine.'

'I can. They'd have no idea what you were on about. You're plainly not a man of your time.'

'Nor do I want to be,' says Alastair Brown, cutting the pack with an elegant flick of his wrist which indicates a suddenly frivolous and easy heart. Myrtle observes that he has decided that his visit is not a mistake after all, and he's beginning to enjoy himself.

Two hours pass. Myrtle and the harbour master are still silently at their cards. Myrtle seems to have forgotten her engagement: her visitor has not reminded her. A plate of buttered scones is on the table beside them, but both are concentrating too hard to bother with food. Alastair Brown is taxing Myrtle. He is a good card player, much better than Annie.

The door opens – no knock – and Annie hurries in. She regards the two bowed heads. Myrtle looks up, dragging her concentration from her fine hand of cards to her friend's incredulous face.

'Oh, Annie,' she says, 'Mr Brown, here, has just dropped by –'

'I'm so sorry.' Alastair Brown, rigid with confusion, leaps up at once. The legs of his chair make a horrible squawk on the floor. His cards fall from his hands to splatter over the table. 'I just dropped in for a moment –'

'So I see,' says Annie. 'And why not?' Her eyes are on the roses, still in their cone of paper but thrust into a jug. 'Well, don't mind me. I was just dropping in, too, to see if Myrtle was all right, to see if she fancied a game of cards. But I see I've been beaten to it.'

'Sit down,' says Myrtle, her fluster receding. This is ridiculous, she thinks: why should she and Alastair Brown be so put out by Annie's appearance? 'Have a scone.'

'Not on your life.' The words are quiet and furious.

'I for one am on my way,' offers Alastair Brown. He pulls at his parrot-beak nose, fingers working fast. 'Thank you for your hospitality, Mrs Duns. I enjoyed our game. Perhaps we can have a return match, one day.' This is said with a small defiant toss of his head in Annie's direction. 'Mrs Mcleoud, good to see you again, too –'

He is gone. Annie looks down on Myrtle, who is calmly gathering up the cards. Then she sits in her usual place.

'So? What was all that about?' she asks.

'Annie!' Myrtle gives a small laugh. Her friend's entrance may have made her uneasy for a moment (though why this was so she cannot imagine), but it has done nothing to affect her good humour. 'Mr Brown –' she begins.

'Alastair, to me –'

'– maybe, to you. Mr Brown, to me, dropped by unexpectedly. He had one cup of coffee, left the other untouched, refused a scone and played several games of two-handed rummy. He's a good man at cards.' She smiles. Annie sniffs.

'So they're true, then, the rumours? Harbour master pants after the widow Duns.'

'Don't be ridiculous. He strikes me as a lonely man. Short of friends up here.'

'Not for the lack of opportunity. There's several keen to befriend him.' Annie is mellowing. She drags her look to the roses – a slow, vacant trawling of the intensely blue eyes that Myrtle knows so well. It means a thought has occurred to her.

'Well, he's all yours. Not my type, anyway. Leaves others free.'

'What do you mean?'

'Och, never mind.' Annie smiles. 'How do you fancy the roses?'

'There's not much choice, locally, is there?'

'Did you ask him why he always keeps his glasses on?'

'No.'

'Pretentious.'

'He might have something the matter with his eyes.'

'Doubt it. But you always go for the kindest explanation, don't you?' Annie begins to shuffle the cards. 'Actually, I came over to tell you something funny. I came to tell you Janice is in love.'

Myrtle dislikes the triumphant way in which Annie produces the news that Myrtle already knows. She barely raises her eyebrows.

'Thirteen,' goes on Annie, 'imagine. Well, I suppose I was a good deal younger than that, wasn't I? Had every boy in the class lined up for his turn, didn't I?'

'You did,' says Myrtle. 'Who's the boy?'

Annie shrugs.

'She's a dark horse, Janice. Won't tell me. She'll only say I'd be surprised. A lot of boys walk her home after school. Some of them stop off for a bite of tea, or go off for a walk. God knows what they do. She comes back very pink in the cheeks, sometimes.'

'They start so young these days – the pity of it. Perhaps you should make it your business to find out what she's up to.'

'No younger than some of us, thank you very much.' Annie laughs. 'Find out what she's up to? She'd never tell us. I have my suspicions about a certain Gus Gowering – I'm keeping my ear to the ground.'

'What's been your advice to her?'

'Advice?' Again Annie laughs. 'What advice can a mother give a daughter that she's going to listen to these days? Course I said don't do anything silly, but go for it, I said. Have fun.'

'Hope the whole business won't detract from her work,' says Myrtle, shoulders rising prissily. 'She's doing so well.'

'Heavens above, Myrtle, you have to keep up with the times. You're too nervous, over cautious. Of course a crush on some spotty boy isn't going to put Janice off her work.'

'It put you off yours, if you remember,' says Myrtle, giving her a sharp look. But she's in no mood to quarrel with Annie today.

'Feel like a quick game?' Annie is dealing out the cards. '*If* you remember, I didn't have half Janice's brains.' Then, after she has reflected on this for a while in silence, she goes on: 'You'll find me pretty boring to play with after Mr Romantic Hero Harbour Master, I daresay. But at least you're familiar with my game.'

'Don't be silly, Annie.'

'You know you can nearly always beat me, unless by some fluke . . .' She cuts the cards.

Half an hour later a white envelope is slipped through the door. Myrtle, her back to the door, does not hear it drop on to the mat. Annie, vicariously expectant, puts down her cards and hurries to pick it up.

'From Martin,' she says.

'How do you know?'

'He left me a note once. Sort of writing you'd always recognise.' She looks at Myrtle with such powerful curiosity that Myrtle, despite herself, slits open the envelope and takes out a single sheet of paper. She reads quickly to herself.

Bench settled. All in place. Hope you won't take this as a liberty. I'll be up at the coppice at 5.30 for your approval if that is convenient. If it isn't ring me and I'll remove it at once and apologise for acting with such haste. I was spurred by what I thought was a good idea. Yours, Martin.

'Something urgent?' There's an edge in Annie's voice.

Myrtle feels herself blushing as deeply as she did some hours ago in front of the harbour master, and is annoyed with herself for such irrationality.

'Nothing at all urgent,' she says. 'Martin's arranging some sort of memorial thing for Archie. This is news that he's found the very thing.'

'Oh? And where's that going to be?'

Later, Myrtle realised she could have avoided the truth with another truth – explained about the headstone for the grave without an inscription. As it is, in her silly confusion, she blurts out the thing she has been keeping from Annie.

'Up in the wood,' she says.

'Up in the *wood*?' Annie's eyes flare indignantly. 'The wood where none of your friends are allowed? Only Martin taken up there? Martin the privileged?'

'What's the matter?' Myrtle is astonished by the resentment she seems to have caused. 'You know perfectly well the reason. I've told you a thousand times. I want you to see it when it's a *wood*, when the trees have grown. At the moment there's nothing much to see . . .'

'As your oldest friend, I wouldn't have minded being shown the nothing, the bare ground, before the bloody trees were even planted. I wouldn't have minded being in at the beginning of things. But oh no – only Martin –'

'I'm sorry.' Their eyes lock. Annie's are hostile, hurt. Her mouth droops, petulant. 'I wouldn't have thought it was the kind of thing to interest you much, a wood,' says Myrtle.

'Don't know me very well, then, do you?' Annie is huffy as a child. 'How come Martin's the lucky one?'

'I wanted him to find me a bench to put there. Something I can sit on and think about Archie.' She sighs patiently, aware that such a concept is beyond Annie's understanding.

'I'd say that's a morbid plan, isn't it?'

'Not to my mind.'

'Archie would have wanted you to get on with your life a bit, wouldn't he? Even get married again. Give the harbour master a chance.' Annie can't resist a smile. As always, her good humour returns as quickly as it has disappeared.

'Don't be silly,' says Myrtle, smiling too. It's too often it happens this way, between her and Annie. One moment they are at loggerheads, then one of them breaks away, teasing, giving in to sudden mirth which the other immediately employs too. 'You do go on.'

'He's a kind man, Martin,' says Annie. 'Everyone knows that. I mean, he showed no resentment over my silly behaviour. He never mentions it. Real gentleman!' She pauses. 'He's bringing me a dressed crab tonight. If I'm patient enough, who knows? One day he might have more to offer than fish.'

'He might, too,' agrees Myrtle, keeping her eyes firmly on the cards.

When she arrives at the coppice, 5.30 precisely, Martin is already there. He sits at one end of the bench, eyes on a wheeling swallow.

The bench is a firm and ancient thing of dark wood: not at all what Myrtle had in mind. But quickly she sees it is better than her imagining. She appreciates its air of permanency, as if beneath its thick legs roots descend far into the earth to join with the young roots of the trees. Already it looks as if it has been here for years. Martin jumps up. He seems nervous.

'You didn't object to my plan, then?'

'Of course not.' Myrtle's happy smile is partially due to the fact that in her haste to arrive on time she had given no thought to the sky, and it had not troubled her.

'What do you think?'

'I like it. It's good, solid.'

'Funny thing is, it's been outside my workshop for as long as I can remember. It was there when my parents bought the place, but I've never sat on it before. I suddenly thought, on my way home last night – why, it's just the thing. A seasoned bench. You wouldn't want something too new-looking in a place like this, would you? Here, try it.'

Myrtle sits at the other end. She puts an arm on its wide wooden arm. She shuffles herself, feeling the safety of the thick planks beneath her skirts.

'Oh Martin,' she says, enthusiasm rising, 'it's lovely. Thank you very much.'

'Needs a bit of sanding down. A coat of protective stuff.' He looks pleased, relieved. 'I'll come up at the weekend. It's a much better bench than anything I could make. I'm not much of a carpenter, really.'

'I must pay you for it.'

'You'll do no such thing. I'm just happy it's found a good resting place. Reckon it'll see us all out.'

Myrtle smiles up at him.

'Thank you,' she says again. And then: 'Would you mind if I sit here alone for a while?'

'You do that.' Martin turns away at once and walks down a path edged with waist-high saplings. Myrtle watches him till he is out of sight. She is grateful for his instant understanding. Annie would have chided her for planning to indulge in morbid thoughts.

But once she is alone Myrtle does not think of Archie. She looks up at the broad evening sky, lavender blue unbroken by cloud, and is aware that the fear has gone. Yes: her new, strange fear is no longer there. The vastness above her is no longer intimidating, nor does it threaten. The irrational alarm seems to be conquered, its disappearance as mysterious as its coming, just as she had believed it would be. That, surely, must be one small step in some new direction.

Myrtle's eyes follow the tiny arrow of the swallow. What strange rites people go through on their own, she thinks. What subtle junctions they make for themselves between one era of their lives and another . . . She stands, stretches, yawns, looks round at her wood of healthy young trees, then sets off for home knowing that there has been some change of the tides within her, and Archie would be glad.

On the road just outside the village Myrtle sees Janice running towards her. The child is wearing a light-coloured dress with a fidgety hem that rises and falls in small waves as she moves. She reaches Myrtle: pink cheeks, high spirits.

'What's up with you, Janice?'

'I'm just so *happy*.'

'That's good. Done your homework?'

'Oh, Myrtle . . . I'm going to. I was on my way.'

'This is hardly your way home.' Myrtle hears herself sounding severe. Janice shrugs, gives a small skip.

'You know what? I told my mum. I told her I was in love, there was someone I really fancied.'

'Did you, now?'

'She laughed. She said: have fun. She said: don't do anything I wouldn't do. That gives me a pretty free rein, doesn't it?'

'I don't think you should speak of your mother like that,' says Myrtle.

'But it's the truth. I know it's the truth – my mum was up to all sorts. I've heard things. Well, I'm proud of her. She's so pretty. When she was young she must have been . . . *ace*, wasn't she?' Janice scans Myrtle's face. Finding no response, she changes tack. 'I just ran into Martin,' she says. 'He said he'd just been doing some business in your wood.'

'He delivered a very good bench,' says Myrtle. 'We were trying it out.'

'You mean,' says Janice, incredulously, 'you and Martin were just sitting on a bench talking? Is that how you try out a bench? God, grown-ups do the most boring things in the world. Just *sitting on a bench* – fun? I don't believe it.'

At last Myrtle is laughing and they reach the village.

'Run along, no more skiving,' says Myrtle, ruffling the child's hair. 'I want the whole of the second stanza off by heart, remember?'

'No hassle,' says Janice, turning away. As she runs off, Janice is Annie, one evening in early summer. She was twelve years old and wearing a similar dress with a flippety hem. She and Myrtle were walking back towards the village when Annie suddenly burst into tears. She confessed to Myrtle she could not live unless some boy paid attention to her. Myrtle cannot remember which of the many it was – Hamish, perhaps. But she remembers Annie's despair, her claim never to have fancied any boy so much in her life. She then admitted she'd gone round to his house the evening before, knowing his father was at sea and his mother was on late shift at the pub. She'd just boldly walked up to the front door, knocked, heart battering fast. Hamish had let her in, none too pleased to be interrupted from some puzzle he was doing. She followed him into the front room where he carried on with the puzzle – a picture of an old steam train, Annie said. When he asked her what she wanted Annie could think of nothing to say. So she took up a pose by the fireplace and began to undo the buttons of her shirt, just as she had seen some actress do on television. When Hamish glanced at her, she lifted her skirt above her knee. He went white, she said. A ghastly white. Then he started shouting at her. Annie couldn't remember the words precisely, but they were all insults: she was a slag, a slut, she'd end up as the village tart, get into rare trouble if she didn't mind out. Just as Annie was about to run from the room, tears streaming down her face, the hostile Hamish came over and rammed his face down on to hers. He kissed her, bit her, so rough. He squeezed her breast till she cried out in pain, and pinched the top of her bare arm. Then he dragged her to the front door and pushed her out into the night, shouting that perhaps now she had learnt her lesson. Annie's mouth was bleeding: she had to wipe the blood with the hem of her skirt, and creep upstairs at home without her mother hearing – well, that wasn't difficult, her mother was deep in some romantic novel as usual. She had cried herself to sleep and at school next day explained away her swollen lip convincingly: a neighbour's dog had bitten her, she said.

Myrtle remembers Annie shaking in her arms as she told her this story. She remembers when cars went by the passengers gave them funny looks. So they went into a field, sat out of sight behind a hedge. There Annie showed Myrtle the bruises on her arms and breast, and Myrtle, in her horror, could find no words. They clung to each other for immeasurable time. Eventually Myrtle begged Annie never to do anything so silly again. She promised she wouldn't: she had learnt her lesson, she said. But within a few weeks she was fluttering her beautiful lashes at some other boy, and impatiently brushed aside Myrtle's warnings. Now, as Myrtle watches Annie's daughter skipping into the dusk, bent on some foolish action, she feels a profound sense of misgiving – a feeling horribly familiar from her childhood, when she had helplessly watched Annie's compulsive behaviour.

'Janice,' she calls. She wants to say something – warn her, stop her, though exactly how she can put it she has no idea. But Janice is out of sight. She does not hear. Myrtle sighs. She knows she must do something before it is too late. But what? Perhaps Martin will have an idea, she thinks. Martin, so full of good sense, will know what to do, and he can be trusted to keep the matter to himself. Comforted by this thought, Myrtle makes her way home, tipping back her head fearlessly to confront the sky which by now is mottled with darkening cloud. For the first time since Archie died she feels hunger, and looks forward to the vegetable soup that has been simmering on the stove.

Life, Myrtle senses, is beginning to speed up. She is aware of a feeling of pace, activity, which is hard to analyse. But her door seems to open more often. People seem to come and go more frequently, as they used to when Archie was alive. Annie comes again to play cards several afternoons a week, other fishermen's wives invite her to drop by, Martin arrives regularly with a piece of fish, and the harbour master, in his quest for companionship, makes formal applications to come round once a week for a game and something to eat. He has invited her several times to an evening of herrings cooked in oatmeal, and old films, but Myrtle has always managed to switch the invitation. By now she feels a certain affection for Alastair Brown, but the desire to enter his territory still eludes her. She promises she will come, one day, but not just yet. The harbour master waits patiently, fearful that if he presses too hard he may risk impairing their delicate friendship.

One Tuesday evening there is a particular feeling of bustle. Myrtle is marking books at the kitchen table when Martin comes in – these days, although he knocks, he also takes the liberty of pushing open the door at the same time. The confidence of this action indicates a deepening of their friendship, thinks Myrtle, though she realises that Martin himself has probably not given the matter any conscious thought. Now, Myrtle is surprised. She was not expecting Martin this evening. He never comes on a Tuesday, the day he collects marble from a yard near Edinburgh. She sees that, for once, he does not carry a newspaper parcel of fish.

'Bench finished,' he says. 'Sanded, sealed, looks terrific. I've been up there most of the afternoon.'

'That's wonderful. I'll go and see it tomorrow. I don't know how to thank you.'

'For heaven's sake. I don't want any thanks from you. I loved doing it. Now all we have to settle is the inscription for the headstone on Archie's grave.'

'I know.' They both smile. Ever since Archie died Myrtle has been searching the Bible for a suitable sentence, and has failed to come up with the perfect thing. 'I'm making my final choice,' she says

Martin is pacing about, uncalm. He has the air of one who has just achieved something and can't quite contain the delight that has given him.

'Look here,' he says, 'I have to go north next week, collect a consignment of marble. Somewhere up near Perth. I was just wondering . . . if you might like to come with me. I mean, it would only be a very minor outing, but I was thinking it's about time you went somewhere. Got out a little. You've scarcely left the village since Archie died, have you?'

Myrtle puts her hand on to the thick black handle of the kettle, its enamel worn into the shape of her palm. She leans against the stove, needing support. The implications of this innocent invitation have ungrounded her. Martin watches her carefully. He sees the force of her hesitation.

'It wouldn't be *much* of an invitation,' he says. 'Not exactly a historic day out. But the van's quite comfortable, and it's fine country up there in the hills. I have to pick up the stuff by five. Then we could find ourselves somewhere for an early supper – be back here soon after nine.' Myrtle has turned very pale. The internal argument with herself, the weighing-up of her various feelings, is almost visible. 'Earlier, if you like,' says Martin, gently. 'Or we could skip supper altogether.'

The ancient growl of the kettle is the only sound in the room for a while.

'That's a very kind thought, Martin,' Myrtle says at last. 'A lovely invitation, and I'm tempted.' She pauses. 'But I think I'm not quite ready for it yet . . .'

'Ready for what?'

'Ready for . . . sitting beside a man, being driven by someone who isn't Archie . . .' She gives a small laugh. 'It sounds silly, I know.'

'I'm sorry,' says Martin. He suppresses a sigh. 'I was trying to find the right moment. I misjudged.'

'I find it hard to judge, myself. At the moment, anything beyond these walls, within the village, the wood – and you're the only one who comes there – it would seem like infidelity.'

Martin smiles. Wry, disappointed.

'It's been two years, Myrtle.'

'I know. And things are beginning to change. I'm beginning to feel a little . . . speeded up. Less unsafe. But there's still a way to go.'

Martin moves closer to her. She can see he considers putting an arm round her shoulder, but resists, and she is grateful for that.

'I understand,' he says. 'I'll try to be patient. Then one fine day I'll suggest we go off for a drink to some far-off place – at least two miles away – and you'll say yes. You might even enjoy yourself and think it was just what Archie would have wanted. So I hope I'll persuade you in the end.'

They are both smiling at this light rendering of his hopes. And shortly after that, having refused a cup of tea, he leaves.

For all his cheerful countenance, Myrtle knows he is a disappointed man. She reruns the short scene between them in her mind, wondering whether she has hurt him as well as disappointed him. Her refusal of his agreeable invitation, she knows, was irrational, foolish. It would have been an enjoyable day and – Martin was right – she needed to get out of the village, see a broader landscape. She trusted him absolutely: he had become the best male friend she had. He had never given any indication of what Janice would call 'fancying' her: indeed, the only time they had had any physical contact was when she had fallen in the coppice. She had no fears that his attitude would suddenly change, and he would take the liberty of making some untoward physical gesture. So why had she been overwhelmed by reluctance to accept his offer? Myrtle could not answer her own query. She could only be sure of an amorphous apprehension that had stopped her. And now she was faced with the worrying question: had her decision endangered the depth of their friendship? Would Martin, once rejected, keep to his word and wait patiently for a more opportune time? Or might he feel it was not worth bothering again . . .? The thought was a painful one. Myrtle had it in mind to run after him, say how silly she had been, she'd love to come to Perthshire with him after all. But so quick a change of mind and action was not in Myrtle's nature. It would be undignified, the act of a torn young girl rather than an almost middle-aged woman who should know her own mind, stick to the firmness of her purpose. Having taken down her jacket from the hook, Myrtle puts it back.

There is another knock at the door. Webbed by her quandary, Myrtle moves with restless heart to open it. She hopes it might be Martin returning: this time she would not be so foolish. Yes, she would say. Yes, I would love to come. And there would be the outing to Perth to look forward to, a bright star in her mind.

It is Ken. They stand looking at each other. Myrtle makes no attempt to hurry her thoughts from the new possibility of Perth to the disagreeable reality of Ken's presence. He wrings his hands.

'What are you doing here?' Myrtle asks at last. 'You know I've no wish to see you. I told you not to come here any more. It's not as if we have anything further to say to one another . . .'

'Please: let me in for a moment. It's important.'

Myrtle stands aside to let him enter. She doesn't know why she has done this. Still preoccupied by Martin's visit, perhaps. Or touched by Ken's look of desperation. Ken hurries over to the window.

'Thanks,' he says. 'I won't keep you long – I've done my best to keep out of your way.'

'That's true,' agrees Myrtle. Since his visit soon after Archie's funeral they have scarcely exchanged a word. 'Is all well at the ice house?'

'Hardly stimulating, but fine,' says Ken. 'But that's not what I've come to talk to you about. I need your help. Annie! Your friend Annie's off her rocker. She says she's going. Leaving.'

Myrtle, to hide her surprise, takes mugs down from the dresser. She has been aware of Annie's discontent for the last few years – a feeling which doubled in strength after the tragedy of Archie. But there has been no recent mention of the marriage being in serious trouble.

'Has she said anything to you?'

'Not a thing.'

'That's curious. I mean, with your being such friends.'

'Even the best of friends cordon off certain areas,' says Myrtle. 'What's the problem?'

Ken irritates Myrtle by a long, noisy sigh.

'Hard to say. I've done my best. Earn the money, try to keep out of her way. She's on about Archie all the time. Won't listen to a word I say. There seems to be no such thing in her nature as forgiveness. She doesn't know the meaning of redemption. I don't know how to per-suade her there's nothing further I can do about something in the past – no way on earth I can bring Archie back, God that there were. Regret doesn't get you bloody anywhere, nor does the confessing of sins, far as I can see . . . And now even Janice seems to have turned against me. Suddenly she's very cold. God knows what Annie's been saying to her.'

'I'm sorry,' says Myrtle. Despite herself, she has pity for the man. 'I know nothing of all this. And why does Annie suddenly want to go?'

'Just says she can't stand being under the same roof as me any longer. If you ask me, there's probably someone else. Leopards don't change their spots, do they? And I still haven't been allowed to lay hands on her since the day Archie died. She must be getting it from somewhere –'

'Ken –'

'Well, you know Annie. If there is someone, though, beats me who it is. Martin's the only one who comes round, bringing his do-gooding pieces of fish – I hear he hands it round half the village, wants to be in everyone's good books. It couldn't be St Martin she fancies, boring man. No: I think there's someone visits her up at the café, someone from St Andrews. I've seen her talking in the street to some fellow in a kilt, some smarmhead with a big car. I may be wrong, but all I do know is Annie wouldn't go off to be on her own. No chance of that. She wouldn't last a minute without a man. As for me, I wouldn't last long without her, I can tell you that. She may be a right bitch, Annie, but I love her. Do you mind if I sit down?'

Before Myrtle can answer, Ken sits, rubs his eyes so fiercely Myrtle finds it a wonder he doesn't look up at her with crushed eyeballs.

'What do you want me to do?' she asks.

'I don't know. Find out what's going on. Suggest it'd be best for her to stay – that is, if you believe that yourself.'

'Of course I do, provided you can work things out somehow.'

'You'd best not tell her I've been round, said anything. She's forbidden me ever to come here. She'd go mad.'

'We'll have to risk that,' says Myrtle. 'I'm not prepared to enter into some devious arrangement. I'll do what I can, but she'll have to know you've been here. Otherwise what reason would I have for suddenly enquiring about her private life? We don't go in for those sort of conversations, so much, these days. Annie fights shy of my disapproval, and she knows there's a lot in her life I can't agree with.'

'Very well. You know what's best. I leave it to you.' Ken stands, a trace of relief on his face. Myrtle sees the blades of his shoulders stick sharply through the thin, worn wool of his jersey. He is a bad colour: dry skin flakes through a dense stubble on his chin. 'Thanks, Myrtle. You can imagine how grateful . . . letting me in like this. It's taken me weeks, making up my mind whether or not to come. It was only her outburst last night decided me. You're a good – well, I suppose not a friend any more.' He scratches his head. The dry hair stands up in silly points.

'It'd be difficult ever to forget the part you played, that's for sure. But you know in my heart I can't bear you any hatred. Anger runs its course. I just needed a bit of time. But all the avoiding – I'd say there's no point, any more. It might help with Annie, if she sees my forgiveness as well as knowing it exists. Come round whenever you want.'

Ken rubs his eyes again, incredulous. He goes to the door.

'You're a woman in a million, Myrtle,' he says. 'No wonder Archie . . . And if you don't mind my asking, how are you doing after all this time?'

'I'm doing fine.'

'I miss the man every day of my life. I miss life on the boat, the sea, I could do with a week's wind on my face. But that's nothing as to how . . . well, we were friends, till the end, all those years. Matter of fact, despite our quarrels, we were still friends.' Ken speaks with the soft urgency of one who hasn't been listened to for a long time. Myrtle gives him a sympathetic nod. 'This room brings it all back, Christ it does.' Ken opens the door. 'I never knew you could miss a man so much.'

'Oh, you can, too,' says Myrtle. 'Aye, you can.'

When Ken has gone, Archie – whose presence has occasionally been less vivid of late – comes roaring back, so close to flesh and blood it is only the rational part of Myrtle's mind that stops her from putting out a hand to touch him. This is natural, she supposes. There are so many memories of Archie and Ken together – playing as children, working on the *Skyline II* as grown-ups – it's no wonder that seeing Ken again brings the pictures back with such terrible clarity.

Archie's jersey, she notices, still hangs on the back of the door. Its blue wool is muted with dust. It wasn't his favourite jersey. That had been the green, the one that Dot had knitted for him years ago, which he had been wearing when he died. Myrtle takes the jersey down, slaps at it with one hand. Sprays of dust fly out, their minute particles fired by a shaft of sun through the window. For a split second the dust is thus turned to sparks, as if blown from some fire of life that still exists within the jersey: Myrtle smiles to herself for entertaining such fanciful thoughts. All the same, unnerved, she rolls it up – its old smell of salt and sea and sweat faintly haunt the air – and stuffs it into the bin. Should have done this long ago, she thinks, pleased with herself. But her eyes are filled with unusual tears. Archie's voice is so loud in her head – nothing profound, just a jumble of ordinary greetings and farewells. *Good to be back, Myrtle wife* . . . It was always good to be back, sad to go. Myrtle realises that all his homecomings and departures through the years are now rolled into just two acts so familiar that they cause a burning sensation along her skin: Archie, clean-shaven, clean-clothed, bag in hand, brief kiss, fading footsteps, the empty week ahead whose thud never dimmed. Then, the returning Archie: tired, unshaven, dirty, wet, fish-smelling, salt lips – Archie *back*, his presence causing a magic change in the room that makes it tip and sway so that Myrtle herself, until she has grown accustomed to it, knows the feeling of what it is like to be on a boat tossed by the sea.

'But Archie, you're gone for ever, now,' she says out loud, brusquely. (Of late she has caught herself talking out loud sometimes, and puts it down to the tricks of the solitary life.) 'And I must . . .' What she must do is to employ her old standby, deflection. This evening she is lucky enough to have some positive action to hand. Annie must be confronted as soon as possible. Och, quite a day, she thinks, pulling on her coat, and averting her eyes from the bareness of the door now that Archie's jersey no longer hangs there.

Myrtle has not been to Annie's house for some time. As she hurries up the path she sees through the window that Annie is lying on the sofa watching television. From Janice's open window upstairs comes the persistent thump of rock music. Myrtle lets herself in. There is dread in her heart. She loathes confrontations, but her blood is up.

Annie furrily turns on the cushions, a lazy-cat movement that makes a backwash of dark streaks in the dralon fabric, as Myrtle comes in. Her bare feet nuzzle each other, twirling in a sensuous way that Myrtle finds repellent. The minute toenails are skilfully painted dots of scarlet. The sight of them further – unreasonably – enrages her. Annie smiles up at her friend's censorious face, enjoying the disapproval.

'Here's a surprise,' she says. 'I was just watching a quiz show. If I'm actually watching something Ken doesn't dare switch to his blasted football.' She flicks the remote control, drags herself into a sitting position, pulling her legs under her skirt. 'So what brings you here –?'

'Ken's just been round,' says Myrtle. She sits, back to the window.

'He's obviously said something to put you in a rare old mood. I told him not to come round to your place, ever.'

'I'm glad he did.'

Annie sniffs, indelicately. Strokes her throat, languorous.

'What was he on about, then?'

'He's says you're threatening to leave. If that's so, I felt we ought to talk about it.'

Annie begins to laugh. It's her usual beguiling laugh, but behind the cooing Myrtle detects a note of scorn.

'Could this be called interfering, Myrtle, by any chance? Poking you nose into matters between Ken and me that have nothing to do with you?' She is doubled up with laughter, now. Hands are running through her hair. When she raises her head her pretty teeth glint whitely as they did when she was a girl. Myrtle stares at her, unsure what move to make next.

'You could call it that, I suppose,' she says, when at last Annie stops laughing. 'But when it's something this important, surely –'

'You know me,' butts in Annie, 'always threatening to leave Ken. He should be used to it now. We had a particularly noisy row the other night. I shouted a few home truths, suppose that alarmed him.'

'You mean you're not about to go?'

'Course not. It might come to that one day. But not yet. Where would I go? What would I do? What about Janice? There's her to think of.'

Myrtle feels herself falling more deeply into the chair. Relief makes her heavy, calm.

'I'm glad to hear it,' she says.

'He shouldn't have come running to you. Our troubles aren't your business.'

'Don't be stupid, Annie. Ken's in a bad way. He needed my help – not that there's much I can do. One can't hope to sort out other people's marriages. All I said was I'd try to talk to you, make you see sense.'

'No need for your good advice, thanks very much. We've always had different ideas about right and wrong, haven't we? All our life your good advice has started off by condemning me for something or other. Well I'm sick of your disapproval, if you want to know. I'm quite able to make my own judgements, thank you. If it'll give you any satisfaction I don't mind telling you I'll stick around with Ken till

I can't bear it a moment longer, and that'll probably be some time yet. But you might as well know it's a high price to pay for a roof over my head. I can barely stand the sight of him, those soulful eyes begging for forgiveness that I'll never hand out – never in my life will I grant him that satisfaction, so don't waste your breath trying to persuade me.'

There is a long silence.

'I told him I'd be glad if he comes round when he wants to,' says Myrtle at last. 'No point in carrying on with all this silly avoidance. You know I forgave him right from the start. It's time to show I mean it. Two years of never meeting is enough. It's unnatural. He was Archie's friend. I'd like to see him from time to time: Archie would have wanted that.'

'That's up to you then.' Their eyes meet.

'For God's sake, Annie, remember it was an accident. Ken's had punishment enough.'

'There speaks St Myrtle. Well at least he's got *your* forgiveness.'

'That's not enough.'

'That's all he's getting.'

'I wish you weren't so adamant.'

'You've always wished me to be things or do things that wild horses wouldn't make me . . .' She swings one leg on to the floor. Curls the toes through the pile of the swirling carpet. 'And I suppose Ken took it upon himself to mention a certain gentleman with a large car?'

'He did say something.'

Annie laughs, merrily this time.

'Silly bugger! Jealousy's his problem, always has been. Can't bear anyone to look at me, yet can hardly meet my eye himself. The chap he's referring to gave me a lift home one night from the café – raining cats and dogs. Ken happened to be coming down the path just as we arrived. Went berserk. Banged on the windscreen, shouted bloody murder, hauled me up the path by the scruff of my neck. What's all this about, Ken? I said, when we got indoors. He's a boring old businessman from St Andrews, owns a chain of stationery shops, drops in when he's passing this way and gives me a nice big tip, I said, but he's never stepped an inch out of line, never laid a finger on me, and can you imagine me lowering myself so far as *him*? I said . . . But of course Ken didn't believe me. Then I showed him the marks *he'd* made on my arm. He takes one look and breaks down sobbing. He's a jealous *wimp* if you want the truth. Trouble is, I never loved him in the right way to begin with, did I? I should never have married him.'

'Be that as it may, I'm pleased to hear there isn't anyone else,' says Myrtle.

'No: the Jaguar man hasn't been back since, as you can imagine. He was my best customer, too. I miss the tips. She smiles, casts a wan look out of the window. 'There's no one I've met recently I fancy in the slightest, so you needn't worry. I'm beginning to think there may never be anyone else again. The sterile life from here to the grave.'

It's Myrtle's turn for a small smile. When Annie subsides into self-pity it's time to change tack.

'Do you remember,' she asks, 'how when we were first married we so hated it when the men went off? Leaving us to empty days? All the worry on our own?'

'You took all that harder than me,' says Annie. 'I'd do anything, now, for Ken to be off to sea for a week . . . have an evening to myself. The husband back every night wanting his meal on the table, complaining about his day in the ice house – fishermen's wives don't know how lucky they are having time to themselves . . .' She happens to glance back at Myrtle, sees the tight mouth and big clenched fists on the arms of the chair. Remorse comes too late. 'Oh God, Myrtle,' she cries, 'what am I saying? I don't mean that! Really I don't. How could I be saying that to you of all people, you with no choice but being alone for the rest . . .' She leaps up, rushes to put an arm round Myrtle. 'Please believe – what was I doing?'

'Just carrying on in your usual blundering way,' says Myrtle. She stands up, pushing Annie from her. 'Blurting things out with no thought for others.'

'I'm sorry.'

'Easy enough to say you're sorry.'

'But I really am. No excuses. And I should have told you about things here. I often thought about it, then I thought no, it's too complicated. I didn't want to involve you. Besides, you don't tell me much these days. It's not like it used to be. Your disapproval makes it difficult to decide where to begin . . . No, don't go. Stay a bit. Have a cup of tea.'

But Myrtle is sweeping out of the door.

'I'm away,' she says. 'Another time.'

In her brisk walk home Myrtle allows herself to wonder what it would be like were she and Annie no longer friends. Such a situation is unimaginable. But in the safety of her own kitchen her friend's voice rings out. *You with no choice but being alone* . . . It's odd that Annie, in her cruel moments of truth, can be so accurate. It occurs to Myrtle she should have reacted to this statement with indignation, although she secretly acknowledged its accuracy. But the fact was she could not be bothered. Let Annie think what she likes. She had wished for no further argument at the end of a long day. All the same, Myrtle wishes she could prove her wrong. But that is a possibility not worth a moment's thought. Drained by her day, Myrtle sits at the table and listens for Archie's voice. But at moments when she most needs it, it fails her. The dead can be as elusive as the living. They go from you, they return in their own unheeded time. Myrtle stretches out her hands on the table, trying to make sense of all this. It is an occasion for the interminable passing of widowed hours. Then a full moon slides into the window, interrupting.

Five days have passed since Myrtle turned down Martin's invitation to Perth. She has not seen him since then. But they have been busy days – the new feeling of bustle continues – and she has not thought much about his absence. It has lain gently as hoar frost on her mind, untroubling. But now, on the sixth day of no sign of him, anxiety begins to glitter. She fears she may have caused him offence, though doubts this can be so – a man of his sensitivity and understanding. She wonders what she should do, hesitates to be the one to get in touch.

On the afternoon of the sixth day a strong wind from the sea attacks the coast. Myrtle walks home from school clutching at collar, scarf, flapping books in her basket. It occurs to her she has very good reason to get in touch with Martin: she has found at last an epitaph for Archie's headstone. Martin has been awaiting her decision for ages. He will be pleased.

The wind scrapes across her eyeballs causing streamers of tears. She has no free hand to wipe them away, so feels them tickling and irritating across her cheeks until they dry. Her vision is blurred. But in the distance, on the other side of the street, she sees Martin. At least, she cannot be quite sure . . . She blinks rapidly. In the few seconds that her eyes are clear she sees it is him. A woman walks beside him. They are arm in arm.

Too fast for any logical thought, Myrtle moves into the porch of a newsagent – thus she can watch their progress but can't be seen by them. For a second she contemplates going into the shop, hiding. But curiosity overcomes her. She decides to stay where she is for a few moments, to recover her composure, then be on her way. They will be sure to see her. What happens then will be up to Martin.

Myrtle watches Martin and his companion walk slowly up the street. Like everyone else abroad today, they concentrate on fending off the wind. Neither of them speaks, though Martin is smiling. The woman's hair, a reddish colour, stands straight up from her head making her look like an aggressive character in a children's book. She is much shorter than Martin, obviously thin beneath the ballooning stuff of her windcheater. She carries a plastic bag from a tourist shop, indicating she is not a local. She and Martin are now but ten yards away. Myrtle judges it time to move from her hiding place.

She is aware of the battering of her heart, and is puzzled. Why should she be so shocked, amazed, at the sight of Martin with a woman? It had never occurred to her that he might have a girlfriend, but it had also never occurred to her there was no one in his life – simply, she did not think of Martin in those terms. He was her dearest friend and for the most part they skirted one another's private feelings by mutual, though unspoken, consent. He had once told her that there was someone he loved: but that was long ago. Myrtle assumed that he had resigned himself to a bachelor life, and was quite happy. Sometimes it occurs to her her lack of curiosity about the part of his life hidden from her is due to a fear of discovering some unwanted truth. At other times she tells herself the depths of Martin are not her business, and do not bother her. She appreciates the ease of their friendship and is satisfied with its present form.

As she moves back on to the pavement the wind renews its attack, once more pulling strings of tears from her eyes. So it is as if through watered silk she sees Martin wave, smile, begin to cross the street. At once she summons a generous smile in return, and tastes the salt tears gathering in the corners of her mouth. She is determined to welcome whoever this woman may be: how good, how very good that Martin has found someone, perhaps, with whom to share his life.

They face each other, a yard apart. Martin greets Myrtle, shouting through the wind. He puts his arm round the woman's shoulders. She is dabbing at her upright bunch of hair but to no avail: it remains erect, silly. But she's smiling. She has a friendly face, no denying. Freckles running into each other.

'My sister, Myrtle,' Martin is shouting. 'Gwen. Suddenly over from Canada – no warning. Sorry I haven't been in touch. We took a small trip up to Perth . . . Wanted to show her the scenery.' Gwen is nodding and bobbing and slamming her hand at her hair. She and Myrtle are smiling at each other, trying to concentrate against the annoyance of the elements. Myrtle's heart is thumping still, but benignly, now.

'Why don't you both come and have a cup of tea?' she shouts. Martin moves nearer to her. 'We're on the way up to the cemetery. Want to show the sister some of my work. Could we drop by later?'

'Supper?' shouts Myrtle. Then she remembers something that would undoubtedly change the tone of the evening. 'Alastair Brown is coming round, but . . .'

'We'd like that. We'll be there.' More nodding and smiling, clutching and waving. Then they go their separate ways.

Myrtle turns into the wind. She sails home as if carried by a buoyant sea, dipping and tossing like a small boat, the familiar streets running like smudged watercolours through the tears in her wind-blown eyes.

Home, the practical part of her nature takes over. Her mind whips through the almost empty fridge. She will have to add vegetables to the venison stew which was meant to last her for several days. She will have to make a quick treacle tart (the harbour master's favourite), iron rough cotton napkins unused since Archie died, and unlock the special cupboard where his whisky is kept along with a couple of bottles of wine.

It has been so long since Myrtle has entertained more than one guest that she finds herself in an unusual dither. Her hands shake as she rolls the pastry. She has to run to the shop for a pot of cream, then go back again for forgotten candles. The wind clamours through the cracks in the frame of the small window, making the curtains restless. Time goes so fast there is no moment for Myrtle to change her old skirt or brush the salt-stiff chunks of her hair. She knows, as she opens the door, she is unattractively flushed, all awry, far from the picture of a calm hostess.

But the evening – she feels from the start – works. Alastair Brown, new yellow satin tie poised like a tulip beneath his chin, is plainly surprised but gratified to find himself one of a *party*, as he calls the evening. He and Martin know each other slightly and seem keen to refurbish the acquaintance. There is an enjoyable moment when each takes it upon himself to open the bottle of wine – a slight race, indeed, to be first with the corkscrew. (This Martin wins, knowing its place in the drawer. The harbour master wastes precious seconds looking for it on a shelf near the stove.) But having had his small triumph, Martin is adamant the harbour master should be the one to open the bottle. Alastair Brown does not take much persuading. He even admits that once in his youth he worked as a wine waiter in Paris, so he's not unacquainted with dealing with even the most obstinate of bottles. All this is explained with a lightness of touch, amid laughter. But Myrtle is conscious that an almost invisible sense of competition has been established – perhaps the men are not even aware of it themselves – as to whose proprietorial rights are strongest in this kitchen. Myrtle knows it's not her favours they are sparring for – they merely want to make quite sure the other one is familiar with the home of china and glass, the right hooks for the coats, and the whereabouts of the box of matches. (There is another slight race to light the candles.) All this Myrtle secretly enjoys.

As the men fall into conversation about fishing matters, she is able to study Martin's sister. Gwen, she judges, must be a few years her junior: a good-looking woman now that her hair has fallen back into place – sharp-jawed, like Martin, and they share the same cautious, beguiling smile. She answers Myrtle's questions about her life in Canada: divorced, no children, she teaches physical education in the village school, and in her spare time writes plays which are from time to time put on by the local drama club. She misses Martin and her parents. But the school and her pupils have become her life, and she could not envisage changing it again now. Myrtle listens eagerly as Gwen describes the Canadian system of education, and the venison simmers on the stove till almost nine o'clock.

Myrtle's cooking is much appreciated. There is more general conversation over supper, and Myrtle reflects she has never seen the harbour master in better spirits (he is often very silent, melancholy, during their card games) and she is pleased to see him enjoying himself with abandon. He tells an almost disproportionate amount of anecdotes, encouraging laughter in stories against himself. Myrtle can see that Martin, initially prejudiced by blazer and important tie, is warming to this strange man – and here Myrtle feels a sense of small achievement. Two lonely men: if they could become friends that would be to their mutual advantage. For the third or fourth time during the evening she feels a warm rush of both surprise at her own ability to have organised this spontaneous evening, and pleasure at seeing it work so well.

It's past midnight when Gwen and Martin leave. Gwen is to return to Canada at the weekend. Martin says he will come round when she has gone. It is plain, in the out-of-character profusion of his thanks, he has much enjoyed the evening.

The harbour master, still sitting at the table, does not have the look of a man much inclined to make his immediate departure. He has poured himself yet another of his strange drinks – whisky with a touch of milk. Myrtle has lost count of how many of these he has consumed since he arrived. He looks up at her. It's disconcerting, on such an occasion, not to be able to see the expression in his eyes: all Myrtle can see is her own head reflected down to a couple of pinpoints. Alastair Brown stands up, begins to unbutton his blazer.

'Let me help with the washing-up,' he says.

'No, please. I can do it in a moment in the morning.' There is urgency in her voice. Myrtle is suddenly very anxious that the blazer should remain in its buttoned-up state: she has no desire to see the harbour master in shirt sleeves, let alone taking Archie's place beside the sink, dishcloth in hand.

'Very well. Whatever you wish.' His quick agreement with her suggestion fills Myrtle with relief. 'But the night is young. Should we have just one game of cards while I finish my nightcap?'

'It's not that young,' says Myrtle, lightly. 'Getting on for one o' clock.' She has no wish to offend, merely to speed him on his way. At the back of her mind she is beginning to feel the pressure of what might be in her visitor's mind, and must be avoided. 'So I think it's too late for me. I'm past concentrating.'

Alastair Brown leaps to his feet as if a bomb has gone off beneath him – one hand rebuttoning the blazer, the other clinging to the dazzling yellow knot of his tie. He is a man mortified by his own impropriety, ashamed by his untoward act. He should have seen how late it was, how tired Myrtle must be. These musings are clearly visible to Myrtle who, shocked by his incredible leap from the chair, tries to contain a smile. She realises that although the glasses of whisky were small, the number consumed has fired the harbour master's sense of companionship beyond its normal calm. He stands looking down at her, a little unsteady, bending gently from side to side like a young tree in its first breeze.

'Oh, what came over me, for heaven's sake? Forgive such an inconsiderate thought. Of course it's too late for anything but bed –' Here he gives a hare-leap towards the door, realising that once more he has said the wrong thing. 'I'm on my way, you see, on my way, on my . . .'

Myrtle swiftly follows him to the door. He is having trouble with the handle.

'Calm down, Alastair.' She does not often use his Christian name. It has effect. It also gives the harbour master courage to make a final gesture. He takes both Myrtle's hands in his – backing away from her as he does so to indicate this is the total extent of his intention – and rubs them gently, as a woman judges the texture of cloth between her fingers.

'This was a wonderful evening,' he says. Her hands are still in his. 'I've not enjoyed myself so much for a long time.'

'Good.'

'I think that went for all of us, Gwen and your friend Martin.'

Alastair bows his head and squeezes Myrtle's hands more seriously.

'You're a fine-looking woman, Myrtle,' he says, dark glasses pointed towards her skirts.

To humour him, Myrtle thinks quickly, is the best way. If she tries to release her hands there will be a tussle. She does not want that. Perhaps the mention of Archie will caution him.

'Archie used to say he loved my smile,' she says, 'and my height and my weight. But in all his love for me he never tried to pretend he saw me as any kind of beauty. That would have been foolish. Luckily for me, looks weren't a priority in Archie's mind.' She laughs lightly. Her plan has worked. Alastair releases her hands. But his train of thought is not deflected.

'God knows, Myrtle,' he says, 'you underrate yourself. You do something to a man. I know I asked only for companionship, but I find myself wanting more: your calm, your strength.' He pauses. 'Your love, even.'

Myrtle is unnerved by the seriousness of his declaration but also, despite herself, intrigued.

'You're like a distant mountain in my life,' Alastair goes on, 'which more than anything in the world I want to –'

'Climb?' suggests Myrtle. She is still trying to make a joke of it all.

Alastair smiles reluctantly. Then his mouth is on hers, the glasses cold against her cheeks. He is kissing her. There is no taste of salt on his nibbling lips. No suggestion of sea, fish. Nothing like Archie. Instead, intimations of tea, whisky, milk. As the harbour master's tongue worms gently round her teeth she is both scandalised by her own behaviour, and excited. She shifts her position. Alastair moves back at once, though again he holds her hands.

'Have I offended you?'

'No.' No: he hadn't offended, exactly. Though elements of shame were shooting through the odd desire.

'I had no intention . . . Not for the world would I do anything to frighten you, to lose our friendship. I just wanted so much to touch you.' He lets go of her hands, wipes his mouth with a folded handkerchief. Smooths his hair. Replaces himself as if at the end of some violent lovemaking, rather than a mere kiss.

'That's all right.' By now, curiously, it is all right. Myrtle's heart is still skittering.

'You won't hold it against me?'

'Of course not.'

'Then farewell, dear Myrtle. I'm on my way.'

He goes. Myrtle quickly shuts the door behind him. She does not want to watch his descent down the steps. She wants to return to the table, regard the detritus of the evening, rerun it in her mind. The success of it all, and the unexpected ending, have filled her with spinning energy. As for Alastair Brown . . . her admiration for the dignified and gentle way in which he comported himself, when his feelings overcame him, has added to the warmth of Myrtle's own affection. He is a good man, to be trusted. She is glad he has come to the village: Archie would have wanted her to make new friends. One day, perhaps . . . she can imagine the sympathy she feels for Alastair could change into a kind of love. There could even be some kind of permanent arrangement – though she cannot conceive of either leaving this house, or sharing it with anyone but Archie. Still, they are well matched, she and the harbour master. As if from a distance, Myrtle can see that: a middle-aged widow of determined character, quiet and plain, unlikely to attract the rare outsiders who pass through the village. And a kind, scarred, shy, in some ways pitiful man. Yes, they could be suited. There is a final truth to be faced: the kiss, now, does not seem like a betrayal. Rather, it was a relief – relief to know physical pleasure could still flare. The sensitive Alastair Brown has stirred in Myrtle something she had thought might never exist again. This realisation adds to the sense that her life is in some curious way speeding up, and she is glad.

By two a.m. Myrtle has finished the washing-up. Everything is back to normal. She goes to the window, looks up at the Bear. The wind has died down, but is still just strong enough to carry the smell of the sea into the room. She closes the window: wonders, wonders.

The next afternoon Alastair Brown is waiting for her at the bottom of the steps when she arrives home from school. He offers to take her bags and basket, but she refuses. He had occupied a part of her mind this morning, while she was baking, but had been banished from it this afternoon in class. His unexpected presence was not altogether welcome. She is in a hurry. There is a load of books to mark, then she wants to write down the epitaph for Archie – she felt she could judge it more properly once she has written it – and send it with a note to Martin. Myrtle can see that the harbour master is clearly in some kind of an agitated state. Her previous feelings of warmth are suddenly overcast with annoyance. But she invites him to follow her in, knowing quite well her sense of hospitality will overcome any inconvenience, and once more they will share a pot of tea.

Alastair Brown's cheeks are pale beneath the dark glasses. His inflamed behaviour of the night before has obviously caused him deep remorse and probably a sleepless night. He paces the room, wringing his hands, in an elaborate warm-up to his apology. He does not take off his waterproof jacket, indicating his stay will not be a long one. Myrtle thinks it suits him better than his blazer. He looks stronger in it, hardier. More appealing, endearing . . . attractive – not a word Myrtle is accustomed to using without care, but it comes to her now. By the time they are sitting at the table with their mugs of tea, her previous irritation has fled. It's replaced by sympathy.

'I do hope my inappropriate behaviour last night has not caused you the anguish it has caused me, dear Myrtle,' the harbour master begins. 'I know the boundaries of companionship, and I know they must not be overstepped. My only excuse is that I got quite carried away by the enjoyment of the evening. I do apologise.'

'There's no need,' says Myrtle, smiling. 'So stop tormenting yourself.' She pauses for a moment to calculate, then goes on: 'If you ask me, I'd say the number of drams of whisky you drank may have exaggerated in your mind the exact nature of your behaviour. As far as I was concerned, you were the perfect gentleman.'

'Oh, Mrs Duns, Myrtle . . .' Alastair Brown interrupts the flight of his mug to his mouth, returns it to the table and wraps his hands round its hot china. He bows his head. Once again, in his relief, he is tempted to overstep the boundaries he has just mentioned, and once again he exerts all his strength to resist the temptation he feels. 'You've no idea how good it is to hear you say that,' he murmurs. 'Your understanding means more to me than I can –'

'Yes, well, let's put the whole incident aside now, shall we?' Myrtle is brusque in order to deflect his course. 'And for heaven's sake don't brood any more on something of so little importance. I wouldn't want you to do that.'

When he looks up Alastair Brown struggles with his mouth and produces a tepid smile. It's this grappling with himself, and winning, that inspires Myrtle's admiration.

'Of so little importance?' he says, sadly. Then quickly continues: 'I know that there's no use asking you round to my house one evening – I know you're not ready for that, though I should like to think I will entertain you there one day. But now the weather's improving . . . I couldn't help wondering if I could persuade you for a little jaunt up the coast in my boat? We could take a picnic – just go for an afternoon.' His glasses are on her face. '*The Swift* is nothing very grand, of course, but a friendly little boat. My mother, who hates the sea, used to trust me. I think she rather enjoyed our little excursions.'

Myrtle remembers her recent foolishness in turning down Martin's equally innocent invitation to Perth.

'Of course: I'd love to come one afternoon,' she says. 'When it's warmer. In a few weeks . . .'

The harbour master, like a man who has snatched what he wants and feels he must escape before it's taken back from him, makes one of his sudden leaps towards the door – his physical agility in leaping about is becoming familiar. He has not even finished his tea.

'Then *there's* a plan to look forward to,' he says, and runs excitedly from the room, leaving the door open behind him.

Myrtle goes to shut it a moment later, to find Annie on the doorstep.

'Just collided with your fancy man again,' she says.

'Och, Annie, I was just about to get down to my marking.'

'So you've time for him, but not for me.'

'Don't be so daft. Come on in. I'll make a fresh pot.'

Since the confrontation concerning Ken, Annie has been round more frequently than usual. Their mutual avoiding of the subject of Ken (Myrtle's belief that the best of friendships can only be maintained by the avoidance of matters likely to cause conflict) has caused only the faintest shadow between them: Annie has been in high spirits, full of stories about weird customers at the café – her mimicry can always make Myrtle laugh – and the cantankerous old witch who is her new boss.

Today she is in no less good humour, though her face is serious.

'Come on, what's going on?' she says, taking her usual place. 'You and the harbour master. There must be something. He's always here.'

In the moment that Myrtle has to form her answer, a dozen alternatives spin through her mind. She rejects the thought of lying: decides that while there are so many things she wants to keep from Annie, she deserves to be let into some secrets. And so far the subject of the harbour master, while decidedly intriguing, is not yet of great importance.

'Nothing,' she says. 'Honestly. He's just a friend. He knows that's all I want. I don't think he'd overstep the mark.'

Annie laughs.

'Seems pretty keen to me,' she says. 'All these visits. Are you sure you're not being naive? Anyhow, I've been trying to imagine it: my friend married to the harbour master. Must say I find it difficult. Has the thought never crossed your mind?'

'Never.'

'Suppose I must believe you.'

'Archie's only been dead two years.'

'How long must a widow wait?'

'Depends what she wants.'

'I mean, how long must it be to feel something for a new man when the man she's always loved has died?'

'God knows. It's not something I think about.' Here, Myrtle questions herself silently. Is this quite true?

Annie sighs.

'You know what? I've been trying to imagine what it's like being you.'

Myrtle laughs. She decides to confront Annie with the thought that immediately springs to her.

'You've been overtaxing your imagination then, lately, haven't you? You're not usually by way of thinking how things are for other people.'

'Right as usual,' concedes Annie with a pretty smile. 'But I suddenly find myself curious. I mean, I imagine widowhood must be so empty: you must feel so empty.'

Myrtle dislikes the way this conversation is going, for the impossibility of conveying to anyone precise feelings of loss will make it worthless. How would Annie ever understand, for instance, the continuing strangeness of this very room since Archie no longer lives here? The physical changes in inanimate things only visible to her? But Annie is in a rare mood of sympathy and concern. Myrtle tries to be patient.

'I don't feel empty,' she says. 'I've never felt that. To feel empty is the easiest assumption to make about someone left on their own through death. It may be true for others: not for me.' She pauses, taking in Annie's incredulous eyes – she feels renewed love for her at this moment, the sort of love she felt as a child when Annie listened to Myrtle's stories with wonder and awe.

'That sounds to me like boasting,' says Annie.

Myrtle places her big hand somewhere near her heart. 'Then I've put it badly,' she says. 'It's not meant to sound self-satisfied. What I'm trying to explain – and I don't like even attempting these sort of hope-less explanations – is that I feel over-full of new things. The wreckage within has to be sorted out – a long process, I daresay. But I think that there's a lot that can be rescued. So I wait, quite patiently.' She is heavy with the inadequacy of her explanation.

'Not at all as I imagined, then,' says Annie after a silent reflection. 'You make me feel there's hope for you, no reason for pity. I'm glad about that: I'm not much good at pity.' She shifts, sips her tea. Myrtle has never seen her look so grown-up. 'You know what? I've been thinking about what you said . . . how we hated the men going off to sea and all that, and how lucky I am for all that way of life to be over now, have my man all the time while you've . . .'

'You've been doing a lot of thinking!' Myrtle smiles. She's relieved that Annie's interest in her widowed state is spent.

'Yes, well: twenty years too late I'm beginning to grow up, perhaps. Anyway . . .' She looks directly at her friend. 'I let Ken have it last night. First time for so long.'

Myrtle's answer is the merest lift of an eyebrow. Although she scorns herself for her inability, she has never been able to respond to Annie in Annie's naturally crude language.

'It was nice,' Annie goes on, entertained by Myrtle's prudish blush. 'I don't suppose it'll mean anything amazing like me suddenly falling in love with him, but perhaps it'll make things easier. This morning, on her way out of the door to school, Janice says to me: "Mum, do you realise it's the first morning for months you haven't shouted at Dad at breakfast? What's got into you?" So maybe . . .'

Both are smiling. But Myrtle is drained by the unusual exchange with Annie, the harbour master's apology, the short night. She wants to put everything aside, now: get down to her marking. She sees Annie is still restless, excited.

'Trouble is,' she goes on, 'if you can't stop thinking about another man, then it's difficult to concentrate on a husband you've never really loved.'

Myrtle can bear no more. She takes a pack of cards from the drawer. 'How about a quick game? Just one, before I get down to work.'

Annie nods. She has the unfocused look of one torn by conflicting thoughts: the bittersweetness of a secret though unrequited love, the equal bittersweetness of physical release provided by an unloved husband. Myrtle regards her severely, defying further confidences. She has no wish to know any more about the two men in Annie's ill-ordered life. Annie responds silently to the look of familiar severity that locks her friend's features. With distracted fingers she picks up the pack of cards, begins to shuffle.

The peace when she has gone is not to last. Myrtle tries out the epitaph several times, finds it satisfactory. She writes a brief note to Martin, which she will post – no energy to walk up to his cottage this evening. Then she begins to go through the exercise books, marvelling as always at the singularity of each of her pupils. Some have treated the set essay, *The Storm* – please concentrate, she had said, on the sounds and smells and colours and noises – with great enjoyment, while others have scarcely been able to scrape together a sentence. But her concentration on her pupils' work is interrupted by the telephone. It is the matron of the Evergreen Home, desperate for help: two members of staff are sick. Myrtle has not been to the home of late: she agrees to go as soon as she has finished her books.

It is almost dark by the time she arrives at the Evergreen. As soon as she is through the door the smells of floor polish and reheated stew, urine only half suppressed by disinfectant, and the sickly odour of drying clothes come giddyingly back to her. She is greeted by the grateful, harassed matron, and hurried to the parlour, as it is still called. There, every chair in the semicircle round the television is occupied. Heads are slumped so low on chests it's as if some invisible slayer has just been in and broken every neck. Hands droop from the arms of floral chairs lifeless as old gloves. Sharp planes of kneecap and shin bone give edges to sloppy rugs. Bandaged feet, plump in gaping slippers, are absolutely still on the swirling carpet. Myrtle swings her eyes carefully from one to another of them: her old ability at assessing comes back to her. She concentrates very hard, determined not to look out of the window where the horizon will still be just visible – the horizon worn to nothing by Dot's constant gaze as she searched so long for *The Skyline*, convinced of its return.

'All this lot – bed,' says the matron. 'It's way past time. If you could start moving them, I'll get the Horlicks. Careful of Mrs Jackson, there. She's falling to pieces.'

For the next few hours Myrtle does her best. She spoons drinks, that take an age to cool, into dithering mouths bereft of teeth. She tries to understand confused murmurings – mostly grumbles: helps find words that won't come to etiolated minds. She peels off warm wrinkled stockings: sees her hands are splattered with particles of dry skin that blow off flesh-starved legs beneath. She tucks in narrow beds in narrow rooms, a single photograph or ornament the only reminder of a previous life. She pats the gristle of shoulder bones beneath crocheted shawls, and wishes each old thing a good night, wondering for which one it will be the last. Then, refusing to accept payment, she hurries away.

On the walk home, Myrtle decides never to go to the home again. She admits to herself that due to pressure of conscience this decision could one day be reversed. But for the moment she is angry and depressed: not so much by the sadness of the home's function, as by the thought of being the widow who can always be counted on to help out. She wants passionately to rebel against that role, has absolutely no intention of helping out any more. While her own lack of charity adds to her rage, nothing, for the moment, will change her mind.

She is by now very tired, and longs for bed. But she has forgotten her torch and the darkness of the night means she cannot hurry. She looks up. There is no moon, but a mass of small, hard, dense jet clouds, as if the contents of a coal scuttle had been scattered in the sky. Myrtle is glad when she reaches the houses at the end of the lane that runs down from the home. She scoffs at herself for having felt afraid, but is relieved by the lights.

She turns a corner and sees the figure of a man just ahead of her – he has obviously just come out of the pub. It's Ken. She calls him. He turns, and is at once by her side. She can smell whisky, smoke.

'Why, Myrtle! I'll walk you home.' He takes her arm, so much more firmly than he did all those years ago. It's plain he's in very good humour.

'You been out enjoying yourself?' he asks.

'I've been up at the home, helping out.'

'You're a good woman, Myrtle. A good woman. A woman to be relied on.' His own high spirits preclude interest in further information about her evening.

'I'm not, you know. I've all sorts of uncharitable thoughts.'

'Well,' says Ken, not up to finding a pertinent response to this surprising fact, 'I'll tell you something: I'm a happier man, Myrtle. I'm definitely a happier man.'

'Good. I'm glad.' They have reached Myrtle's house. She takes her arm from his. 'Thank you for walking with me.'

'I'm not swearing on this, mind,' says Ken, 'but I think maybe change is in the air. God knows why, but I think maybe Annie's coming round . . .'

'I hope so,' says Myrtle. She is halfway up the steps. 'Goodnight.'

Ken turns back the way he has come. He hurries off with a bounding step, a lightness of heart, knowing what awaits him at home. Myrtle, visualising their night, is caught unawares by a thrust of something very painful to which she would be ashamed to put a name. Physically, the pain stabs so lividly she doubles up, clings to the iron handrail for support. This *jealousy* (for that is what, undeniably, it is) clashes with the previous anger that has been furthered by Ken's praise of her worthiness. Alone on this alien night outside her own front door, Myrtle wonders how just twenty-four hours can bring such change of feeling. The joy of last night is now far away as the hidden stars. She is cold, and loathes herself for her base feelings. How, just two years since Archie's death, can she possibly be jealous . . . of such a thing as Ken and Annie's renewed physical joy?

The picture of the harbour master presses into her mind. It would be so easy.

Then: the picture of Martin, laughing with his sister last night. That would be less easy . . . It takes Myrtle a long time to pull herself into an upright position, find her keys and let herself into the dark emptiness of the house.

Once Martin's sister has returned to Canada he resumes his old habit, dropping round to see Myrtle every few days. Sometimes they go up to the copse, express surprise at the growth of the trees, and 'test out', as Martin calls it, each one of the paths, now bushy with new rough grass. The day he gets Myrtle's note about her final decision for Archie's epitaph, he hurries round after his morning's filleting, knowing this is the day she does not go to school until two.

'This is a cause for celebration,' he says. 'I'll get working as soon as I can.'

Behind his smile Myrtle sees a look of unusual weariness. A muscle flickers under one eye. The smile faded, his mouth is grim in repose. He sits in his usual place at the table. In the warm air a smell of fish comes powerfully off him. Myrtle fetches a bottle of beer from the fridge, and sits too. She decides to ignore the signs of trouble. Her belief is that if someone wants to talk about what is on their mind, they will do so. There is no need to enquire. Instead, she asks if his sister enjoyed her stay.

'I think she did. She'd never been out of Canada before. She needed a break – running a smallholding on her own, it's a lot for a single woman.' Martin pauses. 'The real reason for her visit was to tell me she'd set up with some man. He wants her to move in with him in Vancouver. She's thinking about it.' He swigs at his beer, tosses back his head, closes his eyes for a moment. 'I've decided to give up the filleting job, end of the month,' he says. 'It's not a way to spend the mornings. Besides, the pay . . .' He opens his eyes. 'I went round to Annie last night. Ken there for once. Quite a surprise.' He flicks another smile, conveying nothing. 'The girl Janice was there, in a foul mood. God knows what had got into her. When I arrived she dashed straight up to her room and stayed there.'

'Teenagers,' says Myrtle. 'She tells me she's in love with some boy. Perhaps that's the trouble.'

'Annie said that was the explanation, too.'

'Aye, I believe it is.' Myrtle is conscious of her disloyalty.

'But you teach Janice, don't you? Private tutoring: lucky her.'

'I enjoy it. She's a clever girl, loves poetry. Ken was just the same at her age. He would have liked to have tried to get into Edinburgh. But his father scoffed at him. He came from a long line of fishermen, could not imagine his son not wanting to follow the family tradition. Ken argued a bit, but his father was a strong man and in the end he gave up, went to sea. He was on my father's boat, then joined Archie. I don't think he ever really enjoyed fishing. He's happier in the ice house. As for the learning, his ambition seemed to slip away. He said there was no time to read any more, though I believe that lately, since Archie . . . I've seen him coming out of the library sometimes. Still, he's proud Janice is so bright. I think he'd like to see her achieve what he himself never managed.'

'He's an awkward man, distant. But I like him. Daresay they're not the ideal parents.'

'They're not indeed,' says Myrtle. 'Janice is spoiled rotten one minute, ignored the next. And Annie's showing signs of wanting to relive her own youth through Janice – urging her to go for it, whatever that means. If Janice manages to escape some terrible trouble, it'll be no thanks to her mother. Though of course she'll never be quite so desirable. There was no one prettier than Annie along this coast when she was younger. Janice isn't blessed in quite the same way – lucky, perhaps. She's pretty enough, though more like her father.'

'She's pretty enough to cause trouble,' says Martin. 'I've seen the look in her eye. She should be warned.'

'I try,' says Myrtle, 'but I doubt I make much impression.'

Martin stands, makes to leave. In the ten minutes with Myrtle his expression has mellowed. She assumes he has been worrying over the decision about the filleting. On his next visit she is determined they will further discuss his work: she will encourage him to seek jobs further afield, advertise his skills as a stonemason.

'You're a wonder, Myrtle,' he says, as he goes. 'So many of us wouldn't know what to do without you.'

When she is alone Myrtle does not think about this remark, but puts it away to reflect on later. She crosses the room with her dipping gait, half dancing, enjoying her imitation of a small boat on a buoyant sea, her silly secret. Outside there is blue sky. It's very warm. She looks forward to walking back to school, sun on her bare arms. Then she remembers: now this good weather has settled in there's no excuse to delay for much longer the excursion on the harbour master's boat. This she has been looking forward to and dreading in equal measure. She cannot work out why both feelings accost her so strongly: and now her strongest desire is to get the whole thing over and done with. She is convinced the picnic will be some sort of turning point, will straighten things in her mind – though, again, the precise nature of her thoughts is not easy to define. I'm floating, she thinks, on a sea of unknown depths: no idea which way I'll drift, what I'll do. But at least I'm not drowning any more: I'm stronger, though the missing is unchanged, will never change. Myrtle picks up her school bags and hurries out. The new shift of pace in her life is tentative but still exciting, which is curious, because until quite recently she thought nothing would ever be exciting, or joyful, again.

With the delicacy and tact that he considers his speciality, Alastair Brown proposes a date for their excursion, and makes arrangements. Myrtle insists only that the whole thing should be secret. She is puzzled by her own insistence on this point, but instinct tells her it should be so. She does not relish the idea of gossip at her expense – and such inaccurate gossip it would be, too.

On the morning of the appointed day she prepares herself – a headscarf, by way of slight disguise, and a jacket in case the weather should change. While tying the scarf in a knot that makes no attempt at elegance, she thinks with amusement how very differently Annie would prepare – does prepare – to go out on a date. Hours of elaborate making-up, half a dozen dresses slipped on and off till the right one is found, sparkling combs flitting in and out of the much-tossed hair. Myrtle wears her oldest summer skirt, nothing on her face, and ties back her hair.

With a certain nefarious enjoyment she slips out of the house and makes her way to the bus stop. She enjoys the journey five miles along the coast to a neighbouring fishing village – though lobster boats are the only ones left there now – where she is to meet Alastair Brown at the harbour. There is hot sun, the sea a tightly stretched blue a shade deeper than the cloudless sky. The gleaming tooth of Bass Rock is unusually clear in the distance. On each side of the road tall daisies glint among the ripened wheat, while further inland a field of violent yellow rapeseed burns between proper green fields. Myrtle remembers she has not been out of the village, except to the copse, for a very long time. The short journey feels like an adventure.

At the harbour – the very place Annie was awarded her Fisher Lass's sash – Alastair Brown sits at a wooden table provided for customers at the stall where lobsters and crabs are sold. Annie, walking down the hill, sees him before he sees her. She is puzzled. Surely he is not breakfasting on shellfish at this time of the morning? No: nearer, now, she sees he is holding a mug of tea, a commodity not usually provided by the owners of the very small business. Myrtle taps him on the shoulder.

'The VIP treatment, I see?' she says, knowing the flippant remark is quite out of character. But what with the breeze coming off the water, and the sun, she feels lighthearted, careless. Alastair Brown jumps to his feet like a man surprised: perhaps this is to disguise the fact that he has been waiting, anticipating, for a long time.

'Case of one HM treating another,' he explains. 'My friend Captain Travers lives up in that cottage, saw me sitting here, brought me some elevenses. Don't worry: he'll keep my unexplained visit to himself. If we hurry on down to the boat he won't even see you.' He pulls his shoulders back, stands very upright, a glimmer of self-importance visible in his stance. Myrtle reads his mind. He is not averse to the fact that he has been treated with propriety by a retired naval captain. Myrtle smiles, to convey her appreciation of this fact. But despite the captain's boosting gesture, Alastair Brown is nervous. He pulls the peak of his waterproof cap further down over the glasses: the sun is small diamonds in the black lenses. His hands jump in and out of the deep pockets several times before one of them dares to land on Myrtle's arm, and they move towards the steps in the harbour wall that lead down to the water.

The Swift, unsurprisingly, is an immaculate little boat. Myrtle can't help wondering just how recently she has been repainted: her scarlet sides are dazzling. It occurs to her the new paint might have been planned to coincide with this outing – but then she hastily puts the vain thought aside. There is no doubt the harbour master has taken great trouble. Everything is swept and polished, nothing is out of place. There is a cushion on one of the wooden seats. A wicker picnic basket is lodged under another. Myrtle finds herself touched, and pleased that someone should go to all this trouble for her . . .

She takes her place on the cushion. Alastair Brown wedges himself into the tiny cabin that houses nothing more than a seat and steering wheel. Slowly *The Swift* putters out of the harbour and gathers a little speed on the open sea. The water's tautness, seen from the bus, Myrtle realises, was an illusion. Here, it dips and sways in a lively way. Sometimes a small wave is driven to break, its peak flurrying for a moment like a white bird before its feathers are dashed back into the darker water.

Myrtle's old fear of the sea has not quite left her. A trace of apprehension still lingers, though less troubling than on the day of the Fisher Lass outing. But she cannot be completely at ease, bouncing about in so small a boat, and is glad Alastair Brown seems content to keep close to the coast rather than heading out for the Lammermuirs. To her surprise she soon realises that he himself shares her unease. She had always supposed him to be a man knowledgeable about all kinds of boats. Perhaps he felt more at home on a larger craft. As captain of *The Swift*, he is far less in command than when safely pacing the harbour. And he does not seem well acquainted with the workings of his boat. Sometimes there is a surprising leap forwards followed by a slackening of speed. To judge from his hands racing on the wheel, and his jerking head, both activities surprise him. He does not have the air of one who actually likes the sea. He might much have preferred a picnic somewhere on a hillside, Myrtle thinks, but has calculated that to go to sea is a more appropriate invitation from a harbour master.

The sun is hot by now, despite a breeze. Three or four gulls fly in convoy behind the boat, mewling softly. Myrtle is lulled by the rocking, and the heat. She is back on her much longer sea voyage, the day Annie was *The Skyline's* Fisher Lass – a much rougher day: that moment she was tipped against Ken, that moment he took her arm and dragged her to her feet. Then he was gone. There was no chance to cling to him. Disappointment snagged at her, but only mildly, for in truth her feelings for Ken were only faintly stirred – or did she remember that wrongly? Looking back now, it seems obvious she was merely searching for someone to love, to fancy, and Ken, not much sought-after or seeking, seemed the best bet. She also remembers the seasick way her stomach lurched when Archie smiled at her that day – nothing more than a friendly smile, confirming he was not the sort of boy she could even contemplate befriending . . . but all the same, the thought of Annie determined to seduce him, and succeeding, increased the sickness. Never in her maddest dreams, that day, could she have foreseen how things were to turn out, what havoc and surprises the whirligig of time can bring forth.

And now, more or less middle-aged, wiser, she sits looking at the waves, trying to read the signals in her stomach, and finding this almost as difficult as when she was young. She recognises a blunt-edged excitement, a feeling of pale anticipation, akin to what she felt about Ken – nothing very specific, nothing either certain or troubling. Just the comfortable sensation that is the nature of good companions. No sooner has she made these calculations then Archie appears – Archie! How he would laugh, the very idea of her off on a sea picnic with the harbour master! His voice is so loud she jerks her head round, expecting to find him beside her. But boat and sea, empty of him, tighten the void within her. She closes her eyes, feels the balm of sun on her lids, knows without doubt that the rest of her life, whatever it may be, will be a double life: on the one hand there will be reality to deal with – on the other, always haunting that real life, will be the spirit of Archie.

Myrtle is jolted from her cogitations by a definite slowing-down of the boat. The harbour master shouts that he thinks it's time to eat. Myrtle agrees. Sun and wind have made her hungry.

They go to within a few yards of the shore. There is no one on the small grey beach, just rocks scarved with blowing seaweed.

'Shall we wade ashore? We'd be sheltered. Make ourselves comfortable.'

Myrtle pictures herself hitching up her long skirts, fighting off possible suggestions from Alastair Brown of carrying her ashore. She sees a picnic in a rocky corner as perhaps he sees it: an opportunity . . . She sees a second kiss. She sees further. Her pity and affection for the harbour master, her new desire for arms around her, could wing beyond set boundaries here under the sun, lulled by the plash of the sea. Is this what she wants? There's no time to calculate.

'I'd rather stay here,' she says.

'Very well. Whatever you wish.' If the harbour master is disappointed, he conceals it nobly. He drops the anchor, moves to sit opposite Myrtle – thus the boat is nicely balanced. He pulls the wicker basket between them, and with hands that visibly tremble, begins to sort out plates and carefully wrapped packages. There are crab and watercress sandwiches, homemade lemon biscuits from the bakery, peaches and grapes. Myrtle is touched by the trouble he has taken. It's a strange feeling to be handed things, waited upon, looked after again. Agreeable. She accepts a glass of dry cider, chilled in a special box. For himself, the harbour master has brought a carton of milk. What a strange man he is. They sit in easy silence for a while, gently rocking.

As Myrtle's guest, playing cards, Alastair Brown is not a keen talker. He produces short sentences from time to time, conveying disparate bits of information which Myrtle has strung together, but still has no coherent picture of his life. But now, on this sea picnic – a time he has perhaps been waiting for with impatience and some trepidation – he takes his opportunity to tell Myrtle the story of his life.

'I've been to most parts of the world,' he says, with the sudden rush of a man who usually has no one to talk to, 'but find there's still nowhere to beat this part of Scotland, or Cornwall.'

He tells her that he was born in the small village of St Germans, near Plymouth, though the family moved to Truro when he was six and lived in a cottage by the sea. At eighteen he found a job with a firm that transported animals to foreign parts, hence his experience of the world. 'Though it was mostly in the company of a mule or an elephant on a leading rein,' he said. 'Up and down ramps in terrible heat, in and out of aeroplanes – not how I'd imagined my life, really.'

The sun and cider have made Myrtle sleepy. She shuts her eyes but keeps up a small smile to show she is listening. In truth his story becomes a little hazy – the many jobs, the death of his parents within a week, his inability to find in any of the kind women who come his way the necessities of a wife; his love of milk stemming from some week on a farm of Jersey cows . . . How was it he decided to leave Cornwall and move up here? Myrtle cannot be sure. Through the mists of her sleepiness it is all very endearing but confusing. Soporific. Almost asleep, she suddenly feels a hand on one of hers. She snaps open her eyes.

'I've been looking forward to today,' the harbour master says.

Myrtle broadens her smile, shifts on her cushion. She hopes that this will show she has felt the same. She leaves her hand beneath his, lest moving it away in under a minute would seem impolite. She notices the skin on her forearm is a ruddy pink. Burnt a little. Annie would have come on such an expedition armed with lotions and creams against the sun.

'Hope I haven't bored you, babbling on.'

'Not at all. What a life you've had. I've hardly been anywhere. The Shetland Isles, Newcastle – my furthest north, my furthest south. Haven't even quite made it to Perth, and I've always wanted to go there. Archie and I had plans for a holiday in Italy one day. But now . . . I can't see myself moving. I love it here.'

'Ah! *La bella Italia!*' The harbour master is suddenly vivacious. 'I once had to fly a crate of mallard out to Rome. Some very rich Florentine prince had this sudden desire for English ducks on his pond – lake. He agreed to pay the company I was working for a fortune to send someone out at once – very impatient, Italian princes. So four hours of driving through the Italian countryside in a hired car, ducks quacking beside me, is my only rather reduced experience of Italy, I'm afraid . . . I have to say I've always had it in mind to return in different circumstances.' Myrtle laughs. Her response triggers a squeeze of her hand, which she now gently removes. The harbour master begins to gather up the picnic things. 'You could take off your scarf, here,' he says, subdued again.

Myrtle has forgotten her scarf. She unties it. Her hair blows about. The wind on her neck is wonderfully cooling. A gust snatches the scarf, drops it in the sea. At once Alastair Brown leaps to Myrtle's side of the boat, leans perilously over, hands outstretched, calling to the floating scrap of cotton as if it was a duck. The boat tips alarmingly. Myrtle, convinced they are about to capsize, pulls at the harbour master's jacket. He falls back into her arms. The boat rights itself. He quickly moves back to his old seat, put out by his failure.

'Sorry, sorry, sorry, so very sorry,' he says. The incident has unnerved him. 'I'll get an oar. I'll easily reach it with an oar.'

'Please: don't bother.' Myrtle cannot bear the thought of another attempt at rescue. 'It's not at all important. I've plenty more scarves.'

'Oh my dear Myrtle: I'm not very competent. As you can see, I'm not a man nimble in my ways.' His melancholy sense of failure, like his crab sandwiches, touches Myrtle. She is now the one to make a gesture. She puts a hand on his arm.

'It's a lovely day,' she says. 'I'm enjoying myself so much. How lucky we were with the weather.' Behind the black glasses, she is convinced, his eyes are incredulous. His mouth falls open, wavers in his search for words.

'Dear, dear Myrtle,' he says, 'I was so worried it might all have gone wrong – well, we might have capsized.' He gives a small laugh. 'I was so anxious to make it a happy day for you.' Here, Myrtle retrieves her hand once more. He pauses, searching for pre-planned words. 'I'm bound to admit – and forgive me in advance if this is untoward – but I'm bound to admit that a not inconsiderable amount of hours a day are spent wondering . . . how best to please you.' He pauses again, glasses two black scanners turned on Myrtle's face. They listen to the tap-tapping of small waves against the bows. 'I find that my desire merely to be a companion, since the other night, has changed immeasurably. I know that any possible alternative to your husband, to Archie, is beyond contemplation, at least for several years. But if ever you so had it in mind to require anything beyond our happy companionship – our card games, further days at sea, perhaps – then you must know that I would be far from averse . . . to changing the solitary nature of my life.'

It sometimes happens that serious moments in one person's life give rise to irrelevant humour in another's. Even as the harbour master labours with his convoluted declaration, Myrtle finds herself editing it down to the kind of simple English she does her best to encourage in her pupils. Disentangling her thoughts from this private précis, she takes some time to answer.

'What you say is a great comfort,' she begins at last. 'Och: I'm lucky to have you as a friend and can only hope that any . . . visions you may have of a change in the future won't disturb our present friendship.' Even as she speaks the inadequacy of her reply – also something which would not earn high marks for her pupils – sears through her. She can see it brings disappointment, dashed hopes. But she has not expected such serious sentiments. There has been no time to prepare a more delicate response. She can only try to reassure her companion-turned-suitor she will take his words seriously, be grateful for them. 'I'll think about what you said. I won't forget it.'

'I'd be grateful for that. Well, now: I've had my say, and I'll not bother you with the matter again. We'll go on just as before.' The harbour master stands, looking at his watch. 'I rather think it's time we were getting back.'

The boat tips rapidly from side to side as he returns, with great dignity, to start up the engine. Myrtle thinks that never has she felt such

admiration for this awkward man. The admiration veers into heightened affection, an affection so lively that, cocooned here in the blues
of sky and sea, under a high sun, she wonders once again if it might
be possible to turn it into something deeper . . . indeed if one day the
harbour master's visions of a future together could be a possibility.

The unexpected thoughts cluster in her mind: she stretches her
bare arms out along the sides of the boat. They move off, heading
back the way they've come, but keeping even nearer to the shore.
Myrtle studies Alastair Brown's parrot profile. He lifts the carton of
milk to his mouth, drinks. And swiftly as the new thoughts of a possible future have come, they evaporate. There is no reasoning, here,
Myrtle tells herself: but the heart can be a wayward thing. She suddenly now knows, beyond any doubt, that the idea of life with the
milk-drinking harbour master is not, and never will be, something she
would want. The sun and sea air must have pressed her to take leave
of her senses, causing momentary imaginings to flutter wildly. But
now they are quite dead – dead for ever, as realised absurdities so
quickly become. The fact that she contemplated even for a
moment . . . is folly beyond her dottiest imaginings. But that is how it
is, she tells herself, when you allow yourself to be misguided by a
vague longing to love again. When you are confused by the sensations
of a single kiss, having had no physical contact with a man for two
years. She is grateful to have come to her senses.

Myrtle reflects on these things so hard that perhaps her thoughts
are transferred to the harbour master on his seat, shoulders grimly
hunched. For back in the harbour – the homeward journey is so
much faster than the outward one – his spirit seems withdrawn. There
is the pretence of a smile, a helping hand as Myrtle climbs out of the
boat, courteous thanks for having given up her day. Myrtle's own
thanks, and her evident delight in the day, seem not to touch him. He
says he will come round for a game of cards one day soon, and Myrtle
leaves to make her way home. On the bus she is convinced he was
aware of the swift turn her thoughts took on the homeward journey.
She hopes that the time would never come when she would have to be
more specific, be forced to spell out to him the reason she must turn

him down . . . Then, tired from so much serious cogitation, her mind darts to an unlikely idea: after all these years without one, she thinks, perhaps the time has come to consider buying a television . . .

Archie had always been a radio man, keen never to miss a shipping forecast. He liked news bulletins three times a day, and the gardening programmes. The thought of owning a television would never have occurred to him. His time at home he had wanted to spend talking to his wife, or doing small jobs around the house. He regarded the idea of people slumped round a screen, night after night, as a waste of life. Better study the stars. Myrtle agreed with him, though sometimes felt a yearning to watch a good play or documentary. On a few occasions, when Archie was at sea, she had joined Annie to watch a particular programme, and had later confessed to Archie. He had laughed, but not minded. But of course he had not suggested that they should get a set, too. Excited by her new idea, Myrtle convinces herself that he would understand that in her life alone a television – sparingly used – might be a companion on the few evenings when neither Martin, Annie nor the harbour master did not come round.

She is so preoccupied with these thoughts – the sea picnic and its implications have gone from her mind – that it takes a moment when she reaches home to register a child sitting at the bottom of the stone steps. Janice. A furious and sulky Janice, by the look on her face. She stands as Myrtle approaches.

'Where've you been? I've been waiting half an hour,' she says.

'I've been out.' Myrtle is confused, put out by the child's hostility.

'What about my Saturday lesson?'

'But I thought . . .? I mean, you haven't been for the past three weeks. You said you didn't want any more Saturday lessons this term, just the Tuesdays.'

'Changed my mind.'

'Well I'm sorry, but you didn't let me know.'

'I told Mum to tell you when she came round yesterday.'

'She must have forgotten.'

'She never remembers *anything* except the time of her hair appointments.'

'I'm sorry you had to wait: come on in.'

The kitchen is cool – the thick stone walls keep it cool on the hottest day – and rubbled with shadows of late afternoon. Myrtle can feel the skin of her face and arms burning. She opens the window, makes tea. She's glad to be home.

Janice slams her books down on the table, sits in her usual gawky position, knees together, calves widely spread, clumpy shoes of hideous green turned to glare at each other. Her grumpiness fills the room. The day on the boat with the harbour master hangs thin as gossamer somewhere in the back of Myrtle's conscience. More strongly burns the idea of the television: she looks forward to thinking more about that when Janice has gone.

'I've written something I thought about *Michael*,' Janice says, 'though I have to tell you, I think Wordsworth's bloody gloomy.' She pushes an open exercise book towards Myrtle.

'Janice, your language,' says Myrtle, despite herself. She scans the offered paragraph, a crude attack on the poet quite unlike anything Janice has ever written before. Janice watches her face.

'You know what? The other day at school I mentioned Wordsworth by mistake, and course none of the others had ever heard of him. Turned out they'd never heard of any of the stuff I do with you – Arnold, Coleridge, Keats, Shelley, anyone like that. Well, why would they? We're not taught that crap at school. Only poetry we get is John Hegley. I like him, mind. They thought I was bananas, wanting to know *more* poetry: I pretended I'd seen some programme about Keats and the others. If they thought I was having extra lessons they'd think like I was a bloody swot, do me over. You'll never, ever tell anyone, will you?' Her eyes are hard, but hold a suggestion of tears.

'Janice, what's happened? Of course I won't tell anyone.'

'What's happened is, I'm not interested any more. I don't want any more lessons, thanks very much. I've gone off of poetry. I've got other things on my mind. That's what I've come round to tell you.'

Myrtle sighs, thinks quickly. Janice is in no mood to be persuaded.

'Well, I'm sorry to hear all that. I've enjoyed our lessons. I thought you had, too.'

'Oh, I have.' Janice shrugs. 'It's just I don't want any more.'

'I would be very sorry,' says Myrtle slowly, 'to see you go the same way as your father. He was a clever boy, very keen on literature. He wanted to go to university. But he went to sea and his interest seemed to dry up. Such a pity.'

'First I've heard of it. Anyways, I don't want to go to university. I want to be an air hostess. Travel. Get out of this dump.'

'I see. But remember, there's a chance you may change your mind. All sorts of things that seem very firm, quite positive, at fourteen, get shifted by events, growing up. That may seem unbelievable now . . .'

'I tell you, I'm right off those old poets.' A single tear glitters down Janice's cheek. She wipes it away with the back of her hand, suddenly childlike. 'I tell you, they'd never leave off if they ever found out at school.'

'I know it's hard,' falters Myrtle, 'to be brave enough to do something different from the crowd. But it's always worth trying to stick to what *you* really want, what *you* really believe in, no matter how much ridicule that may earn you –'

Further tears are running from Janice's eyes now. She pummels at them with scornful fists, gives a choking laugh.

'Have you ever been mocked by a whole class? Jeered? They nearly died laughing when I mentioned bloody Wordsworth –'

Myrtle passes Janice a clean, folded handkerchief from her pocket. She remembers similar occasions. Her classmates were always laughing, scoffing. Until the last two years at school she always had to try to conceal her love of learning.

'Sometimes,' she says, 'if you stick out for your own thing, don't follow the crowd, you get recognised in the end . . . one other person thinks it worth following you, and then they all do the same, sheep-like . . . and you find yourself a leader.' She remembers she had thought this might happen to her, but it never did.

Myrtle knows she is not doing well. Janice laughs more loudly, nastily. She stands.

'Very funny.' she says. 'I can just see my class – a lot of mega-thugs, in case you didn't know – all suddenly thinking Janice Mcleoud and her swotty love of old poets is the hip thing . . . And anyways, I don't want to be lectured by you,' she says. 'One thing I liked here was you never lectured me.'

Myrtle stands too. She forces a smile, attempts lightness.

'I can see I'm getting nowhere. I'll not try further. How's the boyfriend?'

For a second Janice's face crashes, then she sticks up her chin, controlling herself.

'I don't know if you've ever fancied someone so rotten it gets you everywhere like all the time, so you can't stop thinking for a moment of anything else, but it's a bloody nightmare.'

She gives a leap towards Myrtle – childlike, again – flings her arms round her shoulders, leans her head on Myrtle's breast. Myrtle feels the sharp thinness of her. She takes the handkerchief, wipes away the tears, strokes the frenzied head. But she does not clutch the child tightly to her, indicate she wants her to stay, for fear of alienating her further.

'Anyways, thanks, Myrtle,' Janice says, pulling herself away.

'Come round whenever you want. I'm always pleased to see you.'

Janice runs out of the door, dragging her satchel, bangs the door purposefully behind her. She has left her open exercise book on the table. Myrtle picks it up, drags her eyes down to the last sentence.

Wordsworth is a load of crap, she reads, and feels the pleasures of the day seeping from her.

A few days later Alastair Brown returns at his usual time. They settle down to a game of cards.

It's very warm in the kitchen, despite a thread of air that hangs between open window and open door. After many days of sun the thick stone walls have relinquished their cooling influence. A wasp travels from point to point on the ceiling, its voice the faint sizzle of frying fat. The harbour master asks permission to take off his jacket. Beneath it he wears a shirt no other man in the village would contemplate – a fancy garment of blue, yellow and green stripes, expensive cotton, sharp collar. He also wears turquoise cuff links set in gold.

Myrtle smiles.

'Those are very smart,' she says. 'Did you get them abroad?'

'Hong Kong airport. Over there to deliver a panda.' His answer is deadpan. Myrtle sees that his spirits are still withdrawn. He is behaving in his usual companionable way, makes no reference to the day out. But something has gone from him. Myrtle pours glasses of home-made lemonade. They play in silence for a while. Then a small frown dislodges the harbour master's glasses. He has to move them back into place.

'I suppose,' he says, eyes on his fan of cards, 'that for the wife of a fisherman, widowhood is in some respects easier. I mean, you must be so used to absence, to being on your own.' The difficulty he has saying this indicates to Myrtle it's something that has been occupying his mind, a thought he wants confirmed, perhaps to ameliorate a problem concerning his feelings for Myrtle.

She is silenced by his observation. She cannot believe that a man of such keen sensitivity, in some ways, is so lacking in imagination. But she is careful not to seem to snub him in her reply.

'It may appear like that,' she says, nicely. 'I can quite understand that's how it could. But it's not so. This is an absence that will never end, that you carry round with you for the rest of your life, never get used to. You can't avoid its normal presence – it's always there, whatever else happens. And the hardest thing is that you know that sometimes it won't just remain passive: it'll leap out, take you in a stranglehold, causing havoc again with all the things you believed you'd managed to get into some form of order . . .' She is speaking quietly, as if to herself. 'But there! What am I saying? I don't like to try to explain such things: I was just trying to answer your question. Fishermen's wives – I believe we all must feel the same – never quite get used to the constant absences, the anxiety that's always there. But at least there's hope, a very good chance, the men will be back. The occasional disaster puts paid to any feelings of complacency – but the men know their sea, they're not fools, they don't take risks. So anxiety when they're gone is only caused by instinctive lack of trust of the water, the fear of a sudden storm. But in reality, each time they go out there's very high hope they'll come back. Archie's death is the end of that hope for me, but I must go on hoping for the others.'

Alastair Brown lays down his hand of cards, bows his head.

'I'm sorry, Myrtle,' he says, 'I seem to have presumed something very foolish, very thoughtless, and yet I found myself thinking about it so much. I've said the wrong thing again.'

'Oh no. No you haven't.' Myrtle is quick to reassure. She hates his distress. 'Lots of people wonder how it is to be widowed, just as they wonder about all sorts of states of life. They ask. You can't tell them. You can't ever explain the sensations, any more than you can explain the precise feeling of a physical pain to a doctor. Other people can only guess.'

The harbour master now shuffles sadly.

'It was clumsy of me to suggest,' he says. 'But I'm honoured – believe me I'm honoured – that you should have explained so well things which you have no reason to explain to another living soul . . .'

'You're a good friend to me,' Myrtle says. 'You asked. It would have been cowardly not to have tried to answer.' Once again she finds herself drawn to this awkward man, and yet detached. Nothing could induce her to make any physical gesture of reassurance, today, as she had on the boat, lest he misunderstand it and find his hopes revived. Yet the pathos of the man moves her deeply, and she hates her inability to help him. She can only hope he understands.

As they return to their game, in silence again, Myrtle sees in the harbour master a melancholy that is familiar: it was what she herself lived with for years before she met Archie – the aridity of resignation. Alastair Brown looks like a man who has dared to hope, been rebuffed, and now must return to the emptiness that had been his life before the hope beguiled him. Myrtle feels guilt. She knows that with a few words she could change his life. But she cannot say them. The harbour master knows she cannot say them. They are joined in their sadness.

The air of mutual anguish is scattered when Annie comes running in, laughing, restless. She wears a muslin summer dress that mists her limbs, clings to the points of her knee bones, breasts. She fiddles with

285

a long pink silky scarf flung round her neck, tosses her hair. In the low shadows of the kitchen she could be eighteen again, running in to urge Myrtle out: how pleased Myrtle was when Annie seemed genuinely determined to include her in some plan, how she loved her. She loves her again now: it suddenly comes upon her, a vibrant, smothering warmth, a gladness at her presence, her existence. She has felt angry with Annie on many occasions of late, so it's a relief to find the intrinsic feeling, the one that bound them as children, is still there. Also, she is grateful for this visit. Annie's entrance is perfect timing. Now Myrtle will be spared any further explanations when Alastair Brown decides to leave.

Which he does at once. The presence of Annie always causes him unease: he is never able to put from his mind past scenes with women who have been keen to get closer to him than he has to them. Annie, he imagines, has probably put wicked stories round the village concerning his lack of enthusiasm, his inability to take his chance.

'Here, take over my hand,' he suggests, getting up.

'Willingly, Alastair. Myrtle and I've not played in an age. I think it's my turn.' She looks up at him with an enchanting smile that makes him hurry on with his jacket – so fast does he try to slide his arms into the sleeves that he finds himself in a muddle, further exacerbating his general state of confusion. Annie slumps dramatically down in his chair, as if exhausted but elated by some secret event. She pulls the rumpled skirts above her brown knees, turns in her toes – a childhood habit never outgrown. One glance at the scarlet nails twinkling through the peep-toes of pink stiletto slingbacks, and the harbour master gives one of his customary hare-leaps to the door. Myrtle follows him out.

'Thank you for coming,' she says. 'Come again soon.' Then, with no forethought, no intention, she bends forward and kisses him on the cheek. The gesture causes them equal astonishment – Alastair Brown cannot know this, but Myrtle has never kissed a man on the cheek in her life: meaningless social habits are not her way. She is stunned by her own boldness, at this unpremeditated act which is more surprising, in a way, than her yielding to Alastair Brown's kiss the other night. She watches the harbour master skim down the steps, adjusting his glasses, tugging at his tie. At the bottom he turns to give a small, etiolated wave – the wave of a man grateful for kindness shown, but fully aware of the limitations between them that will always exist.

Myrtle turns back into the kitchen. Annie is still shifting on the seat in the fretted shadows. The odd sliver of sunlight spears a part of her arm, makes miniature forks of lighting through the blue of her eyes. Annie is always happiest in summer. The sun is her spur. Her skin, warmed, rubs against hard surfaces, nestles into cushions or rugs. Myrtle sees all the signs: Annie today resembles the Annie of so many youthful summers, when she declared herself inflamed with love for some boy. Myrtle can't help laughing.

'So!' Annie is laughing too. 'Caught you and the harbour master at it again. I think it's bloody marvellous. When's the happy day?'

'Don't be so daft, Annie. He's a good man, a good friend, but that's all.'

'I've heard that one before. You might as well tell me the truth, you know. All these years.'

'I'm telling you the truth.'

'In that case, it's a pity.'

'You're in high spirits.' Myrtle fetches clean glasses, ice. Pours more lemonade. Annie gives her a triumphant grin.

'Ken took the afternoon off. Have to take our chance when Janice is at school.'

'You're happier, then? Things still going better?'

'I'd say they're far from perfect, but a few per cent better. We don't row so much, but we have our time cut out dealing with Janice and her moods. She's all over the place at the moment. Don't know what's got into her. Bloody nightmare to live with, I can tell you.'

'She'll come round. She tells me she doesn't want any more tutoring, but I daresay she'll change her mind.'

'She told me. I'm sorry. She was enjoying your lessons so much. You were an inspiration in her life – everyone needs one of those. Hope she'll come to her senses. All due to hormones, of course, I suppose. But I wasn't ever like this, was I, Myrt? Down in the dumps for weeks because some crass boy wouldn't respond?'

'I don't ever remember a boy who wouldn't respond to you,' says Myrtle, and Annie laughs again, delighted at the truth of this. Then her thoughts return to Janice.

'Still, in some way she's brought us closer. That and . . .' Annie looks away from Myrtle. 'I don't know. I suppose my anger's petered out. You can't go on blaming someone for ever. I've come to see Archie's dying was enough punishment for Ken. Daresay I've been too hard on him, on your behalf, even though I know you forgave him long ago. Then, he's been so patient, I'll say that. I respect patience. And he's tried not to inflict his despair on us – Janice and me. I respect that too. It's made me feel much fonder of him. Not the kind of love I felt, still feel, for Martin – but a nice comfortable sort of old fondness. We're used to each other. And now the sex is back – that's terrific. That's grand.'

'Oh Annie, I can't tell you how relieved I am. How pleased,' says Myrtle quickly. 'It's what I kept hoping for.' She makes no mention of the single piece of information that troubles her: Annie's admission of her continuing love for Martin. But perhaps by now that is just an old habit, remembered more than felt. Whatever the truth, a warning registers in Myrtle's mind: she must never confess to Annie that her own friendship with Martin provides a growing warmth in her life. Annie interrupts her reflections.

'I think you should seriously consider Alastair Brown,' she says. 'Imagine it: of course you couldn't love him like you loved Archie, but he could widen your life. He could urge you into the modern world – I was saying to Ken only the other night, Myrtle must be the only person on the coast who still doesn't have a television, doesn't even want one.'

'All that may be going to change, it so happens.'

'The things you keep from me! That's good news. Wonderful. But also, you've never been anywhere, you don't show any signs of wanting to explore other places, holiday abroad. I said to Ken let's go to Spain next year, Benidorm or somewhere, see the world. He liked the idea. But you! Wild horses wouldn't drag you further south than Edinburgh. Think about it: you've forty years of good life ahead and if you never set foot outside this place you'll never meet anyone. Seems to me the harbour master is a golden opportunity. Could be your last chance.'

Myrtle smiles. She is not in the least offended by Annie's light-hearted criticisms, or worried by her concerns.

'I've no particular wish to meet anyone else,' she says. 'I like it here. I can't imagine moving.'

'You know what? You're really, really old-fashioned – like people in the olden days who never went anywhere. But you've got the opportunities, enough money, and what do you do? You stick around here, quite happy. I bet you Archie would have wanted you to see a bit of the world . . . Are you mad at me, saying all this?'

'Not in the slightest. You must understand, I'm rooted here, happy. I feel safe being where I've been with Archie. Of course, one day, I might venture further afield, see a little. But I'm in no hurry. I'm one of those who finds more than enough in a small world.'

'Wish I could feel the same way. I keep wanting to be off, though God knows where to. What'd I do? You're stumped, really, without some rich bloke behind you. Ken's doing his best, I'll say that. He gets a regular wage, but we'll never be rich. He says one day we might go to Australia. Don't know how I'd feel about that or even if we'll stick together long enough to make any real plans. One thing'd stop me: missing you.'

'You'd get used to that. I'd come and visit you one day.'

'Bet you wouldn't.'

'Well, no, to be honest, probably not.'

'Don't suppose we'll go. It's only an idea.' Annie's previous exuberance has mellowed. She picks up the cards. Myrtle glances out of the window. Annie laughs. 'You still checking on the weather and there's no need now. I like that. Fine calm day. No worry.'

'Habit,' says Myrtle. 'I always glance at the sky first thing in the morning. Sometimes I can't help thinking thank God Archie's not out in that . . . Then I think of the others.'

'You're a rum one, Myrt. Pretty out of place in this modern world. I don't know what goes on in your head sometimes. Here: cut.'

Myrtle takes up half the pack. They play until late. Dusk curtains the room. The glass jug, refilled with lemonade, glows like a low-watt lamp between them. The silken wood of the table supports their forearms, elbows – the feeling of the wood so familiar it's as if this particular evening is a concentration of a thousand games played here through the years. Annie says Ken is getting takeaway for Janice this evening, so she can have a night off. Myrtle says there's cold meat and tomatoes in the fridge. They smile at each other, enjoy the thought of a late supper when the game comes to an end. Fluctuations in the moods of friends, Myrtle thinks, are their life blood. This evening all the love and awe and admiration she has ever felt for Annie are reassembled in the darkening room. In the void left by Archie, this peace with Annie, sometimes so elusive, she knows must not be allowed to escape. Their importance to each other must continue for the rest of their lives.

Their evening is a merry one. They talk about the old days, laugh at old jokes, tread safe ground. There is no mention of the forgiveness of Ken by Annie, but Myrtle is certain that – possibly not consciously – that has been achieved. She knows there will never be a time she does not worry about Annie's firecracker ways, her thoughtlessness, her dubious morality. But since Archie's death, and Janice's troublesome behaviour, a kind of maturity seems to be reaching Annie at last. Also, now that the two frozen years between her and Ken seem to be thawing, her natural high spirits and her energy are returning. But even as she reflects upon these things Myrtle knows she could be wrong. So often in the past Annie has wiped out Myrtle's feelings of love and trust by a single, foolish – often unkind – act. So often she has had to start all over again, rebuilding her affection for her friend. It has been a wearying and depressing business, but never so bad as to think of giving up. Now her parents and Archie are dead, Annie is the most important person in the world to Myrtle, and on an evening like this it is impossible to imagine ever falling out with her again.

When at last Annie leaves it is almost midnight. Myrtle goes out of the door with her, pauses at the top of the steps, just as she had with the harbour master. The women hug each other for longer than usual. The warm boulders of the night press against them. When they draw away each sees the other cloudily – there is an unclear moon: the few stars play *pianissimo* in a sky that is hardly dark.

'Bugger Australia,' says Annie, as she runs down the steps.

A week later, another warm summer's evening, Myrtle prepares to walk to the graveyard. Martin has sent word that he has finished work on the headstone and would like her opinion on a few last details in the carving.

Myrtle walks with lightness of step towards the cemetery. Agreeable evenings seem to have been gathering: this is to be another of them. The matter of the headstone sorted out, Martin is to come back with her for the red fish he brought her that morning, which she will grill with a little butter. They will sit talking in their easy way. Myrtle may ask his opinion about the idea of a television for the autumn. She sees the quiet pattern of her life stretching for years ahead – the unaccountable restlessness, and worse, which struck her recently, seems to have faded. Now it will be cards with Annie, suppers sometimes with Martin, visits – though no more secret excursions – with the harbour master: the pleasure of teaching at the school and the time to read all the books she has always wanted to read. What else could a widow, bound for ever to her husband's spirit, ask?

Myrtle lets herself through the gate, shuts it behind her. She decides to spend a moment in the church before going to meet Martin at Archie's grave. She moves fast along the path of crushed stone whose heat, through her open sandals, she can feel. Inside the church it's almost winter-cold, dank. Plaster on the walls is crumbling, flaking – a small snow-pile has fallen to the floor near the pew into which Myrtle slips to take a seat. She looks round at the bareness. There's a single vase of flowers on the altar, gladioli and daisies, both wilting. The two candles, their ivory wax slumped but rigid, remind Myrtle of rigor mortis. They are coming to the end of their life. She remembers the dozens of candles that the church liberally blazes for weddings, but more particularly for the funerals of fishermen. Myrtle cannot count the number of services round coffins she has been to here: every seat full, every voice imploring God to hear us when we cry to thee for those in peril on the sea. Her father, Archie . . . they sang the hymn for Dot, too. It was her favourite.

Myrtle likes it here, the few moments of 'peace and holy quiet'. She covers her face with her big hands and tries to imagine the unfurnished golden vastness that is her idea of heaven. She tries to pray that her dead family are reunited, but she cannot imagine how, or visualise them. Are there chairs in heaven? She finds it impossible to picture, so instead her prayer turns to thanks for all she has been left with. Then she returns to the porch.

The heat of the evening drenches her again. She puts up a hand, touches the warm stone. She turns towards the sea: the family grave is close to the wall that divides graveyard from shore. She can just see the kneeling figure of Martin – bright blue shirt – working with his chisel, back to her. His figure is backlit by the sun: the illusion is of a halo surrounding him. The halo also frames a second figure, a slight young girl, it seems to be, leaning against the headstone.

Myrtle moves on to the short, neat grass between the graves, approaches warily. She wants to see more before she herself is seen. Ten yards from Archie's grave she stops, conceals herself behind a mausoleum of rotting mossy stone, an edifice about the size of a beach hut. Although both figures are still blazed with sunlight, she can now see them quite clearly. The girl is Janice.

Janice leans against the headstone, one skinny arm drifts along its top. She wears a very short dress of the same muslin stuff that Annie was wearing last week. It clings to hips and small breasts, only knickers underneath it. Her free hand swoops to the buttons at the neck: languorously, like some caricature film star, she undoes two. The gesture, like her stance, is a mature design of provocation. She flutters her eyelashes, as she must have seen her mother do a thousand times: she bunches her mouth into a ridiculous pout.

'*Look*, Martin,' she suddenly screams. 'For shite's sake look at me. Please!'

From the speed with which Martin rises to his feet Myrtle can measure his anger. For a second she registers the two figures – the man with a hand on the girl's shoulder, shaking her, shouting at her, and the girl's open, screaming mouth, both on fire among the sun's rays, burning. She runs towards them. Janice screams louder. Martin turns.

'Janice! Whatever can you be thinking –? You little trollop, you –'

Myrtle is too horrified, too angry to fashion useful words. She pushes past Martin, drags Janice away from the headstone – the idea of the child touching it causes a sour nausea in her chest – and slaps the defiant, upturned face.

The screaming stops. Silence: then a gull protests overhead. Myrtle is aware of Martin's arm on hers, pulling her away.

'How dare you?' Janice's face is still upturned, still defiant, sneering. 'You'll be sacked for this.'

Myrtle is conscious of little beyond her thundering heartbeat. Martin is pulling her further away.

'Leave her alone,' he says.

'You lay another finger on me and you'll be locked up for assault,' says Janice. There are red slashes on her cheek, imprint of Myrtle's hand.

'*Do up your buttons*,' says Myrtle. Her voice is a long way off, nothing to do with her, unable to say the hundred things she wants to say. 'What do you think you were doing?'

Janice smiles, the nastiest smile Myrtle has ever seen on a child: a smile that has never come from Annie or Ken.

'What would you know about anything? What would you know about desperateness that eats into you so you can't do anything night or day? What would you know about passion, desire, months and months seeing Martin being nice to my mum, kind to you, and not even *noticing* me?'

'I think you should run home now, Janice,' says Martin.

'You're *fourteen*, Janice . . .' Myrtle, shaking, ashamed at her violence, tries to imitate Martin's gentleness.

'So? What's that got to do with anything? I wasn't doing anything wrong. Only trying to make Martin *notice* me. Say something to me. Realise I exist.'

'Go on,' says Martin again. 'Home. I think we should forget all this as quickly as possible.'

'Forget?' Janice laughs. She fiddles with the buttons of her dress, doesn't do them up. She picks up a jersey from the ground, slings it round her shoulders. 'Right. I'm off. Leave you two to it. Perhaps – hey! Perhaps that's what got you, Myrtle. Perhaps you fancy Martin yourself! That would be a good laugh! Well, I shouldn't bank on your chances there. You're old and plain and no man in his right mind would give you a second –'

'Get away!' Martin now shouts, all gentleness gone. 'Now. Go on.'

Janice, barefoot, runs through the tombstones towards the gate.

Myrtle sits down on Archie's grave. Martin lowers himself to sit beside her. He hides his head in his hands. Myrtle longs to weep, but she cannot.

'Whatever did I do?' she asks at last. 'Hitting someone else's child . . . Hitting Janice, who I've loved since she was a baby. Janice: three years of lessons we both loved. What happened to me? What's happened to her?'

Martin raises his head. He puts an arm around Myrtle.

'She deserved it. She's out of control, that child. Disturbed. I suppose I should have told you what's been happening. In fact I had made up my mind to tell you . . .' He sighs. 'For months now, she's been tracking me down – nothing physical, like today. But making suggestive remarks, doing all she can to provoke me. As for the letters . . . page after page of how she loves, thinks, dreams, will wait for ever – pathetic, childish stuff. I stopped opening them. I told her I would read no more. Then she started ringing . . . pornographic stuff this time. What she'd like to do – before I slammed down the telephone. I was going to go to Annie and Ken: I didn't want to get the child into trouble. But she needs help. She's in a bad way . . . And now this.'

'Oh, God,' says Myrtle.

'I found her waiting here. I tried to humour her, begged her to stop being silly, go away. But no good. I daren't get angry – she'd have accused me of child abuse in a flash. I could only pray you wouldn't be late.'

294

'And there was I in the church . . . What do we do now? I've hit a child. I've hit Janice. She may have deserved it – that's no excuse. That's goodbye to my job, she's right. And that's the least of it.'

'No,' says Martin. 'It won't come to that. We'll work it out, rationally, with Annie and Ken. They know how peculiar Janice has been of late. They'll understand.'

'I can only hope so,' says Myrtle, 'or things will be very bad. Just when I thought . . . Annie and I were on an even keel again . . .' Her voice breaks, but still she does not cry.

They remain sitting on the grave for a long time, listening to the occasional gull, and the striking of the church clock. The sun is hovering on the horizon, about to disappear: the sea is grazed with gold light. Poppies in a vase that Myrtle arranged on the grave yesterday are a clutch of smaller suns, their petals flakes of sunlight clinging together against the onset of night. Myrtle can smell fish from Martin's hand. She stares at the fine-grained marble of Archie's headstone where Martin has done his careful work. But she has no heart to discuss that now.

'Would you mind, another evening?' she says, and struggles to rise. 'I can't concentrate on the headstone just now. But it's beautiful.'

'Of course.' Martin helps her up.

'And would you mind if . . . I cooked the fish tomorrow? This evening I'd rather . . . Well, I've no doubt Annie will be round. I'd rather face her on my own.'

'Fine. Shall I walk with you to the house?'

'I'll be all right, thanks.'

'You look as if you're in a state of shock . . .'

'You look pretty shocked yourself.' It's only now Martin is standing that Myrtle is aware of the strained lines under his eyes, and the grave sadness of the eyes themselves. They hold each other's hands for a moment, then Myrtle turns to go.

'The poor wee girl,' she says. 'Whatever's happened to her? Whatever's happened to me? What did I do?'

She makes her way through the gravestones and their long shadows. In just an hour, she realises, she has travelled from the highest of spirits (the smuggest of spirits, perhaps) to dejection that is equally low. And there is no voice from Archie to tell her what to do.

Home, Myrtle has scarcely settled to a few moments reflection when Annie comes bursting in, cheeks scarlet, furious-eyed.

'You hit my child,' she says, quietly. And then shouts: 'You hit Janice. How dare you?'

'She deserved it,' says Myrtle.

'It's not up to you to decide what anyone else's child deserves. You know nothing of Janice beyond your superior books. You know nothing, what's been going on. The last thing in the world the child needs is to be attacked by you. I could have you up for assault. Martin the witness. But don't worry. I'm not going to. I'm going to give you a piece of my mind in a way that'll give me far more satisfaction –'

She rushes at Myrtle, swings at her cheek with a hard open hand. She slaps with every ounce of strength in her furious body. The blow, surprising in its force, sends Myrtle tottering backwards to the stove. Her cheek stings, flames. One of Annie's fingers must have caught the corner of an eye, for Myrtle's sight in this eye is unfocused through a tear. Her heart is beating wildly, but she feels no desire to shout back. A heavy, almost slumberous calm seems to have drugged her. She regards Annie, and herself, as if from some far-off place – as if she is watching a fight between two unknown people.

As soon as Annie has struck her blow, she steps back, shocked. She grasps the hand that struck the blow in her other one as if to withhold it from further damage. But her fury is not spent. She is still defiant, chin still tipped high in the air, eyes lashing.

'That's what you deserve, Myrtle Duns, and I'm bloody glad I was the one to do it. Maybe it'll make a chink in your bloody superiority, your high-mindedness, your arrogant ways, your general . . . *smugness*.' She peters out, backing away. 'Often, St Myrtle, you know what I think? Often I think you're nothing less than a cow. A *cow*,' she repeats, and backs to her usual chair at the table, sits. 'And don't you go thinking that in a few days' time we'll make up as usual. Because we won't. You've gone too far this time. There'll be no more of this . . .' She snatches up the pack of cards from the table, raises her hand above her head and throws them with an uncontrolled gesture. Myrtle's eyes follow some of the cards as they drop like heavy leaves in various places all round the room. She listens to the quiet taps, separate sad notes, as they land on floor, wood, iron of stove. When they have all landed, there is a moment of absolute quiet again. Then Annie thrusts her head into her hands and begins to sob. Myrtle fingers her cheek. After a while she says:

'Of course I shouldn't have struck Janice. I'm sorry.'

'You bloody shouldn't.' Annie's shoulders are heaving. She smears her mascara as she wipes her eyes with the clenched backs of her hands.

'Spontaneous fury. I couldn't believe what I was seeing. It was mad, I know. I've no explanation, beyond the shock. For what it's worth, you can imagine how I feel, letting fly like that. You know I love Janice as if she –'

'I don't give a toss how you feel. Serve you right if you're up to your neck in remorse for ever and ever.' Annie's voice is high, childlike. Suddenly she looks up, locks eyes with Myrtle. 'Are you quite sure,' she asks, 'your fury wasn't something to do with the fact that the man Janice was being stupid with was *Martin*?'

Myrtle's mouth opens. Her big hand leaves her cheek, drops heavily to her side.

'Of course not,' she says. 'I don't know what you mean.'

'Then you're not as clever as you claim. Don't tell me Martin doesn't mean something to you – you're always asking Janice if he's been bringing us a piece of fish for supper. Martin the only one allowed up to your stupid wood. I've got eyes.'

Myrtle sighs.

'Martin's a good friend, he's been wonderful since Archie died. So has Alastair Brown, in a way.' Here Annie gives a sneering little laugh. 'I don't know what I'd have done without them,' Myrtle falters on, 'without you.'

'You'd have managed. You're so bloody good at managing, remember?'

'Martin and Alastair Brown are only friends, no matter what you think. This isn't the time for any alternatives in my life.' She lifts the kettle, automatically calculates how much water it holds. Puts it on the stove.

'I don't want any of your tea.' Annie stands, tears over. 'I'm going.'

'Before you go, shouldn't we talk about Janice? I've been worried about her for some time.'

'Janice is none of your business. Spare yourself the worry.'

'For Lord's sake, I've known her all her life: taught her, looked after her, I love the child. I don't know what's got into her lately, but something very disturbing.'

'You don't know the half of it,' says Annie. Her hostility is waning. Myrtle pours two mugs of tea. Annie shakes her head, but takes one. Myrtle sees there is no time to work out moral complications. She knows only where her loyalties lie. For the first time in her life she is going to lie to Annie.

'She's been mentioning this boy she's fallen for, but she wouldn't tell me his name,' says Myrtle.

'Boy!' Annie gives a small laugh. 'It's a wonder you didn't guess: it's Martin. Some boy.'

Myrtle spins round from the stove to face Annie. One eye is still blurred with tears.

'Martin! I didn't guess. He told me just now. Did you know?'

Annie shrugs. There's a long pause.

'Not till an hour ago when Janice comes screaming in,' she says. 'I must admit. And that's not the all of it.' She goes to the window. 'As I told you, I once really loved Martin. None of the others came anywhere near him, in my book. I didn't get anywhere. But I've never stopped loving him.'

Myrtle feels a great desire to say she is sorry about that, but she keeps her silence.

'So you can see what it was like when Janice comes running home in tears to tell me you hit her because she was having a bit of fun with the . . . man she's been doing her nut for these last months, and that man is the man I love most in the world.'

In this icy revelation Myrtle senses a core of toughness. Annie, she has no doubt, will sort out Janice in her own way. The chances are

Annie will win Martin in the end, though God knows what that will do to Janice.

'The pity of it,' are the only words she can find.

Annie drags her eyes from the sea, sighs deeply. She is not completely stricken by the drama, somehow. Now her score is paid – her eyes smile across Myrtle's scarlet cheek – she seems in no hurry to go.

'Janice has certainly been acting crazy, lately,' she says. 'I haven't known what to do. Ken's been sympathetic but useless, says he's not going to interfere. When he heard Janice just now, hysterical, he said the best place for him was down his mum's. Left me to sort it out.'

'Why haven't you said anything of all this?'

Annie shrugs.

'Playing your game,' she says. 'Keeping things that most matter from a best friend. That's always been your way, your superior show of strength. Thought I'd try it.'

'Annie,' says Myrtle.

'Anyhow, she wasn't doing anything wrong. Only having a bit of fun – something you don't know much about. Flirting – just trying to make him look at her, say something nice.'

'That may be what she intended. It didn't look like that. She was acting provocatively. Reminded me of a child prostitute –'

'You prissy old woman!' Annie flares up again. 'That's always been your trouble! How dare you call Janice a –'

'Let's not shout at one another any more,' says Myrtle. 'The point is, whatever the truth of what she was up to this evening, something's got to be done about her.'

'Yes, well, thanks for pointing that out. But I'd be grateful if you'd not interfere. I'll deal with it. She'll get over her silly obsession, I daresay. Martin when he comes up with the fish never gives her a glance. She'll soon learn how hopeless it is, what a waste of time. I'm buggered if I'm going to stop him coming round. She'll soon find some boy of her own age, forget all about this silly crush on Martin.'

Myrtle can see how it will all be: the confusion, the anger, the hurt that will ensue. She looks round the safe harbour of her kitchen, and the ordinary things of everyday life have scattered. Anguished feeling between Annie and herself is subversive as always – it's shifted the walls, scattered the comfort, blasted all that is familiar. She is amazed and disturbed by the effects that both heights and depths of feeling can have on inanimate things.

Annie has finished her tea, bangs down the mug on the table. Her face is a mess of mascara, her hair a stormy tangle of curls. Myrtle tries to replace the sight of her with the picture of their last, happy meeting. Annie laughing, smiling, loving. But she can't. Annie in all her wrath and confusion – and perhaps regret – is too strong to be supplanted by the alternative creature that Myrtle loves.

'I hope we can get over all this,' she hears herself saying.

'We can't. I'm not as good as you at forgiveness, remember? Far as I'm concerned, the end of a friendship can be every bit as savage as the end of a love affair. Pity, but there it is. There's too much against us now to carry on. So best not to have anything more to do with each other, isn't it? Safer. And I don't want you anywhere near Janice any more, that's for sure. I'll deal with her, deal with Ken, deal with the whole crowd . . . Don't look at me like that. I'm not in need of your pitying looks, thanks very much. If you don't like what's happening – well, too bad. Blame yourself. Janice is an innocent child, head over heels about some man, acts stupidly one day, but he hasn't a clue what she's on about, she's never given him so much as a sign before about how she feels . . .' Annie is near Myrtle now, looking closely at her still reddened face. 'That's what she told me: that's what I believe. If she'd been causing Martin any aggravation he'd have told me, wouldn't he?'

'I daresay.' Myrtle turns her head from her friend's glare, glances at the horizon. Even that is unsteady. She is in no doubt that she must keep her knowledge to herself. To reveal what she knows would not help, now.

'So I'm going,' says Annie. 'I'm off. You won't miss the cards. The harbour master's a much better player.'

She hurries to the door. Everything within Myrtle cries out to her to delay Annie – say stop, this is ridiculous, let's not leave it like this. But no voice emerges from the chaos within her. She does not watch Annie go, but stays leaning against the stove, arms folded. After a long silence the telephone rings: Martin. He wants to know how she is, if he would like her to come round. Myrtle explains that Annie has gone, and she would prefer to be on her own. Martin asks no other questions, and Myrtle is grateful for that but assures him she will see him tomorrow.

After a while Myrtle lights the lamps, and the moths, which have been waiting on the window ledge, begin their fluttering, daring themselves to go ever nearer the lights. Myrtle takes no notice of them, but stoops down and begins to pick up the cards.

It has been the bleakest week since Archie died. Myrtle has spent many hours in reflection, cursing her own untoward behaviour in the churchyard that has brought about this crisis – condemning herself for not having enquired further into Janice's obsession, which had been plain to see, and tried to help her. She also blames Annie: a self-obsessed, irresponsible mother, always wanting to win her child's approbation by giving in to her wishes, however unsuitable. But she has learnt that it has never been any good, criticising Annie's abilities at motherhood. Annie has always been deaf to all constructive suggestion concerning Janice. In the past they had many a useless quarrel: Annie's case was always that Myrtle could not know what it was like, being a mother, so was not one to give advice. In her greater rages she would claim Myrtle's criticism was fired by jealousy, the bitterness of the barren state. So, long ago, Myrtle had given up, kept her silence as she watched Janice yearning for the barriers of discipline that are every child's right, and being alarmed by the empty spaces granted by her parents.

Myrtle also goes over the last quarrel, the lacerating words. Despite the wounds they have left, she misses Annie. She misses Janice. She fears for them both. She plays patience, waiting for one of them to come round. But Martin tells her Ken has hired a caravan and the whole family has gone off somewhere. This is so unusual – Myrtle has never known the three of them go away together – that she is further alarmed. The days are very long, listless. She has noticed that when she goes out to shop she causes a disagreeable stir. People who are her friends, acquaintances, give her looks that she cannot quite read, but she feels the tension, the disapproval. She holds her head high and ignores them, with as much dignity as she can manage, until she reaches the safety of her kitchen. There, she slumps at her empty table, fiddles drearily with a pack of cards, wonders at the length and grimness of the hot summer days. Never has she missed Archie so much. The ache, which she had thought so recently was beginning to dull, has now returned more piercingly than before. And the exciting feeling of the new bustle in her life has disappeared as fast as it had come. Perhaps it had all been an illusion, wishful thinking. But now there is no bustle, nothing but the maturing of the trees to look forward to.

The harbour master remains loyal. The day after Annie ran out he appeared with a bunch of poppies and daisies and long grasses. Myrtle was touched by the thought of him pottering along the hedgerows in his blazer, choosing the flowers. He told her he had heard the silly rumours (they had spread so fast?) but she could rest assured he would always stand by her, always be there if needed. Once again Myrtle found herself on the brink of unbending, giving herself up to him to ensure companionship for life. Once again she withheld. Alastair Brown was not the right man for her. Remembering her own moment of weakness, she gives a small scoffing smile and shuffles the cards. She is grateful to this sad, kind man, but knows gratitude is no reason for commitment. She believes he understands the situation but has not given up hope.

Indeed, in the stifling week since Annie's departure the harbour master has been round three times: gentle, his sympathy alive in his quietness. He asks no questions and Myrtle makes no effort to explain. They merely play their card games and drink iced lemonade, glad of each other's company. By now, there is that ease between them which comes to people who recognise their friendship will never converge, but never fade. The small element of tension is fired by their different desires, but it does nothing to trouble their pleasure in each other's company.

Martin, too, comes round most days – brief visits, bringing small slivers of fish, for Myrtle says she has no appetite. He tells her he saw

Annie only for a moment before she went away. She shouted at him, slammed the door in his face. He could hear Janice crying upstairs, and Ken shouting from somewhere. The whole household was in an unhappy state, he said. He left quickly, had no intention of returning.

'They'll have to sort it out for themselves,' he said.

But he and Myrtle did not speak of Annie after that. Instead, Martin – a little wanting in spirits, Myrtle thought – reported progress on the finishing of Archie's epitaph, interrupted that memorable evening. It was coming along well, he said. He hoped it would be completed in a matter of days.

In the long hours between visits from her two loyal friends, Myrtle sits thinking that, if you look around, everywhere you see people frightened of beginnings, frightened of endings. She is not unusual in that, and this present time is both some kind of ending, and some kind of beginning that she cannot envisage. She is a little afraid, but Archie's voice comes to her, strong, firm, wise – encouraging her in some way she cannot exactly comprehend, but comforting.

It's a week to the day that Annie left with her terrible threats, and Martin comes round to say he has finished the engraving. He would like her to come and see it.

They walk together through the plushy warm air of a late summer evening. They stand by the headstone: the epitaph is finely carved. Martin has done a wonderful job. But Myrtle does not want to stay long. The ghost of Janice, leaning against this very stone, in her outrageous pose, is still too new, too raw. So after a few moments, when Myrtle has given her thanks, they decide to walk on up to the copse. They have not been there for some time.

The saplings are strong, and bright with young leaves – noticeably taller since the last visit. The sight of them provides Myrtle with the first dart of real pleasure since Annie left. She cries out loud in delight, tripping fast up and down the paths, ruffled with new grass now, so that Martin has to hurry to keep up with her. They reach the clearing at the heart of the wood. They sit on the fine old bench which is Myrtle's memorial to Archie – to which, Myrtle knows, she will return for many years ahead until she is too old or infirm to walk. In silence she and Martin look about them: at the trees, the brightness of the grass. And they look up to the arc of unclouded blue sky, where swallows swoop in lazy whiplash circles. On the back of a languid breeze the smell of the sea reaches them.

'The rock?' says Myrtle. 'I'd still like to put a rock here. Did you manage to find one?'

'I've been looking,' says Martin. 'And I'm glad to say I think I've found the perfect thing – I was going to tell you. I found it on a small beach, a cove, a couple of miles up the coast. I was looking for driftwood for an artist friend. I suddenly saw this handsome rock, all by itself, looking out to sea. I thought: that's the one for Myrtle. Only trouble will be transporting it. There's no access to the beach for a van. But I'll work that out somehow. I'll have it here soon. It'll have to be soon.'

'That's wonderful news,' says Myrtle. 'It'll go so well, here. I look forward to it.' She pauses. 'It's the thing I most look forward to, now.'

In the silence that follows she hears Martin sigh. He allows a few more moments to pass before speaking.

'I've news for you, Myrtle,' he says at last. 'I fear it's not a good moment, but time is running out. I would have told you last week, but then there was all the . . . disruption. Anyhow, I'm going back to Canada.'

Myrtle turns her head and looks at him.

'I'm off at the end of the month if everything's tied up by then. It was my sister who made up my mind. She came over to tell me she couldn't really cope with the smallholding any more – the house and bit of land where we lived with our parents as children. It had become all too much for her. Besides, she's met this man. He wants her to move in with him, somewhere near Vancouver. It will be good for her. I'm pleased. Her only worry was selling the old place. She didn't like the idea, wondered if I might consider . . .'

As he speaks, Myrtle sees the days, weeks, months, years ahead. No Martin with his fish and his devoted friendship. Perhaps no Annie for a very long time – though surely, in the end, things would be all right between them. She sees the stacks of books to be marked, the possibility of a television set. She sees the harbour master, his black hair turning to grey, beating her at cards for years and years to come. She sees her own funeral: the widow Duns laid to rest beside the good fisherman Archie, who died many years before her.

'So I've been considering,' Martin goes on, his voice striking her again, 'I've been thinking very hard. The decision was very difficult. But I think the right one. After all, there's not a great deal of satisfying life for me here. I scrape around for work, earn very little, feel I'm not doing enough. I'm haunted by a sense of unfulfilment. Besides that, though I've been here a long time, I still feel I don't really fit in – never have, never will. I'm a friend of a lot of the fishermen, but I'm not one of them. I don't have their understanding of the sea, I don't even like it. I hate cutting up their fish to try to earn a bit more. I don't like the doleful atmosphere in the village for days on end when the men are away. I shall miss my parents, though they've said they might join me in the homeland in a few years' time. I shall miss this place, the people, friends . . . But I'm tired of the sense of my own uselessness, here. In Canada, I could be working to some real purpose.'

Myrtle sees herself in the kitchen, through the seasons, listening for Archie's voice, living with the spirit of him but denied the flesh, and wonders if that is how it should be, if that is the proper plan of things. She thinks of Annie's return: surely they will forgive each other. But also she sees years of watching the friendship become more threadbare as ever more wearying quarrels outweigh the love. Perhaps friendships, like love affairs, have their appointed time, and when too much has blasted them it is better they should end . . . Unimaginable though that is.

'Besides,' says Martin, 'there's one other thing.' He pauses. Then speaks so quietly Myrtle has to strain to hear his words. 'I once confessed to you there was just one woman I loved – had loved for years. I never told my love because of the impossibility of a life together. She married another. She was widowed. She became my greatest friend, and I never stopped loving her. I waited for a very long time, wondering how long it takes for widowhood to heal – for the desire for fresh life to become acceptable. I tested the water very gently. I asked her to come for a small trip to Perth with me.' Here, he allowed himself a small, grim smile. 'But no, she said: she wasn't ready to come even as far as Perth. I took that as a final no, for she must have seen where I was leading, and wanted to stop me in my tracks before I did anything that might upset our friendship.'

'Oh, Martin,' says Myrtle, turning to face him, cheeks blazing. 'Believe me. I never for one moment supposed . . .' She sees his eyes are dull with resignation.

'And so I gave up, I suppose,' he says. 'But I never left off loving her, I never will. But when my sister made her suggestion . . . well, I thought, there's nothing to keep me here. Hope runs out. The sensible thing to do is to return home, work hard to make it the thriving farm it once was. It's a remote, lonely place, but I've never minded solitude. Rather like it. And who knows, I may meet someone who'd like to join me there, even become my wife.'

Myrtle thinks of some Canadian wife, without a face, greeting Martin as he comes through an open door into his childhood house. Outside there are mountains, fir trees, sky of a blue unknown in Scotland. No sight of the sea.

'And so, I'm off to Canada. It breaks my heart, but it would be foolish not to go.'

Myrtle remembers the times she's been jealous – yes, jealous – of Martin taking fish to Annie. How puzzled she was by that. Her keen regret over refusing his invitation to Perth – puzzling, too. She remembers the flash of lightning between them the day Martin helped her to her feet just yards from here – a moment recognised but ignored by them both. She remembers how constantly she has relied on him since Archie died. But because of her concern about fidelity to a dead man, she has not allowed herself to accept what her feelings have become for one who is alive.

Myrtle looks away from him, slides her eyes back up to the evening sky. We could write, she thinks. I'd write more than Annie, of course, but still. Maybe she'd come for a visit one day – always wanted to see the world. Myrtle sees a single swallow, spinning so fast it's hard to imagine how the bird will right itself as it tumbles towards the ground. But it does: and the next moment it's soaring very high again in unpremeditated pleasure. She keeps her eyes on its flight.

'I could always come with you,' she says.

Then for a long time she and Martin remain sitting on the memorial bench, looking at each other in astonishment and wonder.

EASY SILENCE

Angela Huth

The Handles, happily married for many years, have reached the point in their lives where easy silence, an acceptance of each other's ways, is the norm. Grace has her painting, and the children's reference book she has long been working on. William has his music, and his string quartet, even if his name isn't quite spelled like the great composer.

Then Grace encounters a young man, Lucien, who adopts her, haunts her, threatens her – and provides her days with a bittersweet frisson. And William becomes so besotted by his new viola player, he decides to murder his wife . . .

'A lovely novel – both witty and menacing . . . Strongly recommended'
Daily Express

'Murder set to music'
Sunday Telegraph

'A wry tale of marital harmony threatened'
Marie Claire

'Delicious black comedy'
Woman's Journal

'Angela Huth is at the top of her form . . . a brilliantly comic social exploration, with overtones arbitrarily and mischievously grotesque'
John Bayley

Abacus
0 349 11136 7

<u>NOWHERE GIRL</u>
Angela Huth

Estranged from her second husband, Jonathon, Clare Lyall
is less sure than ever about the role men should play in her
life. Her first husband, Richard, was much older than her,
and his casual disregard for youth gradually hardened into
indifference. And Jonathon, if anything, was too easy – too
attentive, too concerned and just a little pedantic.

So when she meets Joshua Heron at a party, the offbeat
Clare isn't exactly thirsting for love. But she is mildly
impressed when Joshua stubs her cigarette out on his
thumb, and swayed still further by the advice of her new
friend, the indomitable Mrs Fox. 'Take a lover,' she says,
'it's better to have a lover when young than neurosis when
you're old . . .'

Abacus
0 349 10630 4

SOUTH OF THE LIGHTS

Angela Huth

South of the Lights weaves the story of Evans and Brenda,
lovers in a Midlands village, whose happiest hours are
spent in the hayloft of the chicken farm on which she
works. They have no other roof under which they can be
alone together – until the mysterious, romantic Augusta
comes to their aid. Evans' desire to possess Brenda results
sometimes in passion, sometimes in violence, but Brenda
finds sympathy in the company of the fragile and sweet-
natured Lark with whom she shares a flat in the local town.

Excelling in the illumination of the surprising facets of
people's daily lives, Angela Huth reveals their private
hopes, rages, fantasies and despair, with an original and
moving blend of humour, imagination and pathos.

'In this unexpectedly comical forerunner of the "Aga"
novel, English village life of the late 1970s yields to Huth's
wicked scalpel a gruesome mix of bleak and racy secrets'
Saturday Times

'An excellent exponent of the traditional English
social comedy'
Daily Telegraph

Abacus
0 349 10554 5

WANTING

Angela Huth

Harry Antlers, a once successful theatre director, falls obsessively in love with Viola Windrush when she comes to New York for an audition. He immediately sends her a hundred red roses and convinces himself that her lack of response is purely temporary. Indeed, he is certain that if he makes enough extravagant and expensive gestures, she will be his. There follows a wild pursuit, which takes Harry to Viola's beautiful old Norfolk house, to London, where she is decorating a flat for her uncle, until finally, Harry is driven to desperation . . .

A brilliant study of a blind, bullying passion, with a rich cast of supporting characters, *Wanting* is a sharp, cleverly drawn novel on the curious psychology of the obsessive.

'Angela Huth is always good value and, in this wry black comedy, displays all her charcteristic sense of mischief . . . A gentle satire on the rules of the mating game, it is also a much darker study of male psychology'
Sunday Telegraph

'*Wanting*, for all its surface fun and farce and surrealist tragi-comedy, is about a deep mystery'
Jane Gardam

Abacus
0 349 11415 3

Now you can order superb titles directly from Abacus

☐	Easy Silence	Angela Huth	£6.99
☐	Nowhere Girl	Angela Huth	£6.99
☐	South of the Lights	Angela Huth	£6.99
☐	Wanting	Angela Huth	£6.99

Please allow for postage and packing: **Free UK delivery.**
Europe; add 25% of retail price; Rest of World; 45% of retail price.

To order any of the above or any other Abacus titles, please call our
credit card orderline or fill in this coupon and send/fax it to:

Abacus, 250 Western Avenue, London, W3 6XZ, UK.
Fax 020 8324 5678   Telephone 020 8324 5517

☐ I enclose a UK bank cheque made payable to Abacus for £ ....
☐ Please charge £.............. to my Access, Visa, Delta, Switch Card No.

☐☐☐☐☐☐☐☐☐☐☐☐☐☐☐☐☐☐☐

Expiry Date ☐☐☐☐   Switch Issue No. ☐☐

NAME (Block letters please) ....

ADDRESS ....

....

....

Postcode ....Telephone ....

Signature ....

Please allow 28 days for delivery within the UK. Offer subject to price and availability.

Please do not send any further mailings from companies carefully selected by Abacus ☐